PENGU...

THE PORTA...

Each volume in The Viking Portable Library either presents a representative selection from the works of a single outstanding writer or offers a comprehensive anthology on a special subject. Averaging 700 pages in length and designed for compactness and readability, these books fill a need not met by other compilations. All are edited by distinguished authorities, who have written introductory essays and included much other helpful material.

"The Viking Portables have done more for good reading and good writers than anything that has come along since I can remember."
—Arthur Mizener

Page Stegner teaches English at the University of California at Santa Cruz and is the author of *Escape into Aesthetics: The Art of Vladimir Nabokov*.

The Portable

NABOKOV

Selected, with a critical introduction, by

PAGE STEGNER

PENGUIN BOOKS

Penguin Books Ltd, Harmondsworth,
Middlesex, England
Penguin Books, 625 Madison Avenue,
New York, New York 10022, U.S.A.
Penguin Books Australia Ltd, Ringwood,
Victoria, Australia
Penguin Books Canada Limited, 2801 John Street,
Markham, Ontario, Canada L3R 1B4
Penguin Books (N.Z.) Ltd, 182–190 Wairau Road,
Auckland 10, New Zealand

First published in the United States of America under
the title *Nabokov's Congeries* by
The Viking Press 1968
Viking Portable Edition published 1971
Reprinted 1971, 1973, 1974, 1976
Published in Penguin Books 1977

ISBN 0 14 015.073 0

Printed in the United States of America by
Kingsport Press, Inc., Kingsport, Tennessee
Set in Linotype Times Roman

The preparation of this collection was supported,
in part, by the Ohio State University Development Fund through
its Faculty Fellowship Program.

New Directions Publishing Corporation: "The Government Specter" from *Nikolai Gogol,* Copyright 1944 by New Directions, reprinted by permission.

The New Yorker: "The Refrigerator Awakes," "A Literary Dinner," "A Discovery," "An Evening of Russian Poetry," "Restoration," "Lines Written in Oregon," "Ode to a Model," "On Translating *Eugene Onegin,*" "Rain," and "The Ballad of Longwood Glen," all from the book *Poems,* Copyright 1942, 1943, 1945, 1953, © 1955, 1956, 1957 by Vladimir Nabokov. "Terra Incognita," © 1963 The New Yorker Magazine, Inc., reprinted by permission.

G. P. Putnam's Sons: Selections from *Despair,* Copyright © 1965, 1966 by Vladimir Nabokov; *Invitation to a Beheading,* Copyright © 1959 by Vladimir Nabokov; and *The Gift,* Copyright © 1963 by G. P. Putnam's Sons, Inc. "On a Book Entitled *Lolita,*" appearing as the Afterword to *Lolita* published by G. P. Putnam's Sons, New York, Copyright 1955 by Vladimir Nabokov. Selections from *Speak, Memory* (G. P. Putnam's Sons, New York 1966), Copyright 1948-1951, © 1960, 1966 by Vladimir Nabokov and used by permission of the copyright owner. The story "First Love" originally appeared in *The New Yorker;* it is used here in the revised version that was reprinted in *Speak, Memory.*

Time-Life Books: Introduction to *Bend Sinister,* by Vladimir Nabokov. Reproduced from *Bend Sinister,* a volume in the Time Reading Program, Copyright © 1965 Time, Inc.

Contents

A NOVEL AND THREE EXCERPTS

POEMS

Editor's Introduction

I

When Vasiliy Ivanovich Rukavishnikov died in 1916 he left his seventeen-year-old nephew, Vladimir Nabokov, a country estate of some two thousand acres and a fortune that would amount today to a couple of million dollars. Had the Russian political structure not been altered radically in 1917 that inheritance might have remained intact and its recipient's adult life would have been shaped by another set of values and influences than those of emigration and exile. As it happened, in March 1919 the Nabokov family departed from their Russian homeland to escape the activities of the Bolsheviks and a newly formed police state, and their eldest son's term as a wealthy aristocrat came to an abrupt end. The direct, though delayed, result of this uprooting was that English literature gained one of its most superb voices: a family's loss became art's gain.

Nabokov's father, a gifted jurist and statesman, was fated, it seems, to be always on the wrong side of power. In 1905, as a result of an article he published in *Pravo* denouncing the brutality of the police in promoting the Kishinev pogrom, he was stripped of his court title, and he immediately severed his connections with the Tsar's government. He became one of the leaders of the Constitutionalist Democratic Party, an important liberal faction opposed to despotic rule, and in 1906 was elected to the First Russian Parliament, but in less than a year the Tsar dissolved that body. It continued to meet illegally at

Vyborg, with the result that in 1908 Nabokov and a number of his colleagues were imprisoned for their revolutionary views.

The sentence was short, however, and in three months he was back working with all of his energy for the liberal reforms that he championed. When the revolution began in 1917 he held a position in the initial Provisional Government, and he was elected to the Constituent Assembly in the winter of 1917-1918. But history was quickly altering its course, and the liberals once again found themselves on the weaker side of the political struggle. The November Revolution brought the Bolsheviks into power, and the Nabokovs, along with others like them, fled to the Crimea, where they remained for some months until they went finally into "voluntary" exile in Western Europe.

What the family left behind—a country, a heritage that extended back for generations, wealth, influence, reputation—all are revisited and recalled in Nabokov's *Speak, Memory,* and since thirty thousand words of that book are included in this collection an editorial paraphrase is scarcely necessary. It is a memoir of extraordinary conception and execution, as remarkable for its lack of bitterness and sentimentality as for the lyricism of its nostalgic recollections. One thing it makes quite clear is that Nabokov's investment in the past is in its "unreal estate" and not in its once-upon-a-time riches. "The nostalgia I have been cherishing all these years," he says, "is a hypertrophied sense of lost childhood, not sorrow for lost banknotes."

Since the initial flight in 1919, Nabokov's life has followed a pattern of perpetual moves—from England, where he took a degree in foreign languages at Cambridge, to Berlin, where he met his wife, Věra, and where he began in earnest his career as a writer; then to Paris, where he went in 1937 to escape the Nazis; and then to America in 1940 when the Nazis overran France. He remained in the United States for twenty years, returning to Europe in 1960. He has never owned a house. He has lived always in rented rooms, apartments, hotels. He has been, in short, a man of many countries and many residences. "If I could construct a mosaic of time and space to suit my desires and demands," he once said, "it would include a warm climate, daily baths, an absence of radio music and traffic noise, the honey of ancient Persia, a complete microfilm library and the unique and indescribable rapture of learning more and more about the moon and the planets. In other words, I would like my head to be in the United States of the 1960's, but I would not mind distributing some of my other organs and limbs through various centuries and countries."

Those wanderings would hardly be worth remarking upon were it not that an author's experience is generally impressed on his creations. Almost without exception, Nabokov's heroes are, like himself, homeless wanderers, forced by real or self-imposed exile to replace their terrestrial roots with various forms of distracting obsessions—chess, Russian literature, serial selves, the art of fiction, nymphets (only the last may be omitted from the author's dossier)—obsessions that enable them, through an absorption with the aesthetics of their various infatuations, to escape the difficulties and suffering in part produced by a vagrant existence. In part, one has to say, because homelessness is by no means the single source of his characters' suffering, and rarely can be blamed for their neurotic behavior. It is, however, the experience that almost all of them have in common, and it would seem that something more than coincidence is behind Nabokov's repetition.

Four of the early novels, *Mashenka*, *The Eye*, *The Exploit*, and *The Gift*, are populated exclusively by Russian *émigrés* in Europe, as are a great many of the short stories written between 1924 and 1938. Luzhin, in another early novel, *The Defense*, is not a political exile, but from the time he becomes a chess prodigy until his death he is an inveterate traveler, living in rented rooms and hotels, drifting across the Continent from match to match. He is, to say the least, a social outcast, and his grasp of "reality" is so tenuous that he might, in that respect, be called an exile.

In 1938 Nabokov abandoned the Russian language as his literary voice and began to write in English. Four of the five novels he has since produced have at their centers expatriates. Both V and Sebastian in *The Real Life of Sebastian Knight* were born in Russia and left for an English education, followed by a life of wandering in western Europe. Humbert Humbert in *Lolita* is a European who has emigrated to America, and that is only the beginning of his travels. Pnin is a Russian exile, twice an *émigré*, first to Paris and then to America! "Battered and stunned by thirty-five years of homelessness," he teaches for a few years at Waindell College before departing for places unknown. Charles Kinbote in *Pale Fire* is, or thinks he is, the exiled King of Zembla. The only hero of the English novels who is fixed in one spot (unless you consider John Shade to be the hero of *Pale Fire*) is Adam Krug in *Bend Sinister*, and he is exempt from exile only because he is destroyed before he can escape the murderous goons who have taken political power in his homeland.

In an interview with Alfred Appel several years ago, Nabokov offered some advice to literary critics. He suggested that, along with learning to recognize banality and the fashionable message and their own muddy footprints in the midst of detected symbols, they "by all means place the 'how' above the 'what' but do not let it be confused with the 'so what!'" If the only point one could make about Nabokov's personal exile was that he often created characters of a vaguely similar mold, then the reader might rightly ask, "So what?" But Nabokov's experience as a Russian *émigré* who could not (and would not) go home again not only is reflected in his characters but also underlies the dramatic and thematic content of a great many of his novels and stories—sometimes directly, sometimes indirectly—and that is of greater relevance.

Like most things one says about Nabokov, "the dramatic and thematic content of his novels and stories" needs qualification. Homelessness is seldom of primary importance. He has never written a book dealing specifically with what it is like to be "un-countried." The subject smacks of social problems, and he tends to become abusive when anyone accuses him of trading in them —rightly so, for his books do not have "social significance," and those who mistake parody for social satire are confusing intention. The former, he points out, is a game, the latter a lesson. Even when he does invent a totalitarian state, as in *Invitation to a Beheading* and *Bend Sinister*, his interest is not in the ideology of despotism but in the stifling of the creative consciousness that inevitably ensues. These novels are not about politics; they are about the fate of the imagination in "utopia." Don Marquis once remarked, "There will be no beans in the almost perfect state." There will be no art either.

In an oblique way, however, exile has given birth to a number of the recurrent themes in Nabokov's fiction. There is inherent in the very word a strong element of the past—the condition from which one cannot return, the condition from which one can look back at a place but not forward to it. Nabokov's characters are very often looking back at the past, yearning after it, and often they attempt to recoup their losses by artificially (and artistically) re-creating the ghosts that inhabit their memories.

2

Andrew Field, in his book on Nabokov, tells us that *The Exploit* (one of two still untranslated novels) concerns the illegal return to Soviet Russia of a rootless exile named Martin Edelweis. Edelweis's exploit, the crossing of the forbidden border (which we never actually see because the book ends with his departure), is an attempt to meet a not wholly rational challenge and conquer it. At the same time it is an attempt to return to the past with which he is constantly preoccupied and from which he has been permanently excluded.

Adam Krug, in *Bend Sinister*, lives in the past, and it is his refusal to recognize or acknowledge the political realities of the present that keeps him from escaping his destruction. Only the brutal death of his son can jolt him into an awareness of his real dilemma, and by then it is too late. In the madness that his creator (Nabokov) mercifully inflicts upon him at the end of his ordeal, the present *becomes* the past. Krug loses his sense of time and with it his fear of mortality. When he is led from prison and stands before his persecutors, he confuses the "confrontation ceremony" with boyhood games, the prisonyard with a schoolyard; and he dies leading a bravado charge against his old childhood enemy, Paduk—once a fat schoolboy, but now the dictator of the "new state."

In Nabokov's most celebrated novel, *Lolita*, Humbert Humbert pursues a "fairy child" who is, for him, little more than a metaphoric extension of an attachment he recalls from his own childhood. He says, in regard to his obsession:

> Since the idea of time plays such a magic part in the matter, the student should not be surprised to learn that there must be a gap of several years, never less than ten I should say, generally thirty or forty, and as many as ninety in a few known cases, between maiden and man to enable the latter to come under a nymphet's spell. It is a question of focal adjustment, of a certain distance that the inner eye thrills to surmount, and a certain contrast that the mind perceives with a gasp of perverse delight. *When I was a child and she was a child, my little Annabel* [his first love] *was no nymphet to me: I was her equal, a faunlet in my own right on that same enchanted island of time. . . .* [Italics mine.]

Humbert's attempt to possess his nymphet is an attempt to recapture and possess the past; his lust a lust for the impossible —for the immortal, uncomplicated, never-never land in which preadolescents live unaffected (briefly) by the boundaries of time.

To recognize that Humbert is hopelessly yearning for an intangible element in the private universe of children, an ideal state beyond space and time, is not to excuse his destruction of a young girl or the murder of his "double," Quilty. But the recognition must certainly alter our attitude toward his crimes and toward the degree of his guilt. If he is a monster (and he would be the last to deny it), he is a very lonely and rootless monster; and as he sits in his prison of consciousness sketching the bars of his cage, he evokes our pity if not our sympathy. Humbert is an exile—a self-made exile, to be sure—but nevertheless a man who stands outside life without hope of re-entry. His only redemption, as he so clearly perceives, is through art, and quite consciously in the telling of his tale, in the choice of his language and the selection of his metaphors, he perverts the sordid reality of his relationship with Lolita (just as in an opposite way he once perverted the real creature) and transforms her life and his into art.

Humbert's extraordinary obsession with the irretrievable past is nearly equaled by that of the mad critic who confronts and confounds us in the novel that follows *Lolita*. Charles Kinbote, the magnificently comic and grotesque commentator on John Shade's narrative poem, *Pale Fire*, explicates a text using all the apparatus of literary criticism—foreword, commentary, and index—and at the same time writes an autobiography. Kinbote is under the delusion that a story he told Shade about the mysterious land of Zembla and its exiled king (fully recounted in the Commentary) has provided the inspiration and the substance of the poem. When Shade is accidentally killed, Kinbote filches the manuscript, runs off to apply himself to its explication, and with shaky hand and shaky logic attempts to match up the two apparently unrelated narratives. As he frantically tries to find himself in the poem, we discover that *he* is the exiled king and Zembla is his kingdom—all fantasy, of course, though that does not affect its "reality." We also discover that Kinbote is a pedant, a pederast, and a lunatic; moreover, he has bad breath. He is too ridiculous to elicit the kind of compassion that Humbert does, but the two are not altogether dissimilar. In his obsessive pursuit of John Shade, his inexhaustible clamor for the poet's attention, and his systematic attempt to twist *Pale Fire* to fit his own fantasies, Kinbote, like Humbert, is attempting to re-create through art (in this case not his own) the past from which he has been excluded, the past which exists only in his imagination and his memory.

V, the narrator of *The Real Life of Sebastian Knight,* is a man without friends, without country, without even a name. He is totally obsessed with tracking down and recording the factual circumstances of his dead brother's life as a means, we soon discover, of trying to identify himself. The novel is an excursion into the past, but instead of yielding up a comfortable reality that V can grasp, the past gives off only illusory shimmers that leave him as much confused at the end of his search as when he began, and he eventually fades away into a disembodied voice. V is another of Nabokov's self-conscious narrators (like Humbert, Kinbote, Hermann in *Despair,* Smurov in *The Eye*) who are *writing* their stories, who are attempting to "create" themselves through language, and in the process are hopelessly confusing art with life, illusion with reality. Nearly all Nabokov's heroes, it has been pointed out by numerous critics, are artists concerned with the problems of artistic composition.

Pnin, the hero of the novel included in this collection, is perhaps the one "preterist" who is completely aware of the disparity between art and life and whose escape into the literature and language of his past is a conscious defense against the inhumanity he has both witnessed and suffered. The novel that bears his name is in many ways the most straightforward of Nabokov's works, and it is the one generally admired by those who find most of the others too laden with puzzles and word games and sleights of hand. Admiration of the book is well deserved, though not for that simple reason. *Pnin* is extremely funny and at the same time terribly sad. The farce and anguish of Timofey's situation are magnificently balanced, and he is one of the few characters in Nabokov's novels who evoke a real compassion in the reader. Of all those who live in the past, Pnin is the most engaging.

But Pnin is more than a sweet buffoon stumbling through a world that he doesn't understand and that doesn't understand him. He is more than a pathetic victim of the ambitious, self-centered, self-inflated culture in which he will always be an exile. What is important about Pnin is that he has style; a style that consists not simply of the oddities of his Russian-European mannerisms and inverted patterns of speech, but of a consciously adopted method of existence that protects him from the excessive cruelty invading his life and redeems him from the tediousness of self-pity. It is a style in which the past provides a means of drawing a veil over the present.

For Nabokov the escape from the impossible suffering and vulgarity that prevail in this world is through art, through irony, parody, and the intricacies of composition. As he says in *Speak, Memory*:

> I have to make a rapid inventory of the universe, just as a man in a dream tries to condone the absurdity of his position by making sure he is dreaming. I have to have all space and all time participate in my emotion, in my mortal love so that the edge of its mortality is taken off, thus helping me to fight the utter degradation, ridicule, and horror of having developed an infinity of sensation and thought within a finite existence.

The way Nabokov fights this horror is obviously with language: he transcends his finite existence through art. For Pnin, escape is into a private Eden of Russian literature, into his Gogol and his Pushkin, into his "scriptorium in the stacks" of the college library. In this "paradise of Russian lore" he collects information for a history of Russian culture. He will never write it, but no matter. His uncontrollable delight in the subjects he presents in the classroom, his getting drunk on "private wines as he produced sample after sample of what his listeners politely surmised was Russian humor," and the pear-shaped tears that roll down his puffy cheeks when the fun becomes too much for him, are all symptomatic of his complete involvement and surrender to the art of the past.

Pnin is a great source of amusement to his colleagues. He is their clown, their straight man. But painful as their subtle persecution may be, it is not the real source of Pnin's suffering. We discover when he goes to the country house of his friend Alexander Petrovich Kukolnikov that the past provides certain memories that are as horrible as others are comforting. Evening at The Pines, with the soft illumination of kerosene lamps and people involved in cards, chess, reading, and so on, reminds Pnin of the summers of his youth in a Baltic resort and a girl named Mira whom he had loved before the Bolshevik revolution overturned their lives. The pain of a politically interrupted love and the horror of Mira's eventual extermination in a Nazi concentration camp have affected Pnin's whole response to life. "Only in the detachment of an incurable complaint, in the sanity of near death," Pnin thinks, would it be possible to cope with the image of Mira even for a minute, ". . . because, if one were quite sincere with oneself, no conscience, and hence no consciousness, could be expected to subsist in a world where such things as Mira's death were possible."

Although Pnin is, in a figurative sense, a crucified victim of his environment, he never indulges in self-pity, as do so many of his fellows in contemporary American literature. Nor does he find his dignity through symbolic subjugation to fate or acceptance of a victim's role: his style is not an assertion of being by letting oneself become a passive scapegoat. Self-humiliating bravado is not a Pninian gesture; nor does he attempt to transcend cruelty and violence by committing it himself. Affirmation by negation is a most inartistic, uncreative, and finite method of asserting one's being, and it certainly is not the Nabokovian or Pninian way.

In the community of sufferers to which Pnin belongs, the causes of his suffering matter. Pnin is the victim of a *real* exile, a *complete* loss of home and cultural ties, a *total* absence of love;

and the monsters that must inhabit his dreams are not projections of self, but very real Bolshevik and Nazi torturers. Pnin's hell, the one he strains to avoid, is not private. Being a perpetual wanderer, always ridiculed for his peculiarities, always depending for his very existence on the benevolence of other and generally lesser men, he has something substantial to suffer about. His response is not a self-destructive howl at past horrors, but a legitimate and admirable refuge in the antithesis of nightmare—the beauty of Russian lore and literature, the aesthetics of art. It is, one might simply add, Nabokov's response as well.

3

One of America's more perceptive politicians remarked (in reference to the California redwoods) that when you've seen one tree you've seen 'em all. He would undoubtedly make a similar judgment about Nabokov's *oeuvre*, if he had read any of it, because each part of that literary structure is, in many ways, a mirror image of its predecessor: when you have read one book you have encountered "patterns in the game" that you will find in them all. Perhaps the greatest evidence of Nabokov's genius is that he can make each work unique in the very act of echoing the others; that he can transform through language the same characters and subjects into something always fresh and original.

He has repeatedly insisted that he is the kind of author whose sole purpose in working on a book is "to get rid of that book . . . an adorable but sometimes intolerable burden." The reader soon perceives that there are certain things (to use his words in quite another context) that he is always getting rid of —in fact, annihilating: things like conventional patterns of thought, stock ideas, and stock themes that imply stock responses toward "reality." He gets rid of the conventional most often by parodying it, by taking a traditional "idea" or a fashionable subject and twisting it until it is forced to bite its own tail.

Most of Nabokov's novels parody to some degree standard literary forms and formulas: the mystery story in *The Real Life of Sebastian Knight* and *Despair*; the love triangle in *King, Queen, Knave, Laughter in the Dark,* and "An Affair of Honor"; the Freudian case history in *Lolita*; scholarly exegesis in *Pale Fire*; the utopian novel in *Bend Sinister* and *Invitation to a Beheading.* In nearly all the novels and a great many of the short stories there are parodies of various literary themes: the quest for reality, the tragic suicide, the conquest of the alter-ego, the hero as crucified victim, the endurance of a destructive love.

One finds parody not only of forms and themes but of specific styles as well. Frank Kermode, in his book *Puzzles and Epiphanies,* discusses the reflections of *Tristram Shandy* that he finds in *Bend Sinister.* Andrew Field has remarked on Nabokov's aping of Russian writers—Gogol, Pushkin, etc.—and other commentators have been equally alert to his use of various celebrated styles for comic purposes. In *Lolita,* to take a single example, Humbert borrows a poem from Poe ("Annabel Lee") for the substance and language of the passage in which he "explains" the origin of his nympholepsy, his first love, Annabel Leigh. He borrows the opening paragraphs of "The Fall of the House of Usher" for his description of the journey to Quilty's mansion where the climactic murder of his "double" takes place. He borrows a few facts from Poe's life to flesh out his own (both lost their mothers at the age of three, for instance), and the greatest joke of all is his inversion of Poe's sexual problem in his obsession with Lolita. Poe married a girl to acquire a mother. Humbert marries a mother to acquire a girl. Humbert does not limit himself, however. He mimics a number of famous authors in the course of his narrative, from Shakespeare to Flaubert.

In *The Real Life of Sebastian Knight,* V makes a number of observations about his dead brother's literary habits that are quite obviously observations of Nabokov's habits as well. ("I think of myself today as an American writer who has once been a Russian one," Nabokov says, and it is no accident that the dead hero of his first novel written in English is half Russian and half English and endowed with many of his creator's opinions about art.) V says:

> As often was the way with Sebastian Knight he used parody as a kind of springboard for leaping into the highest region of serious emotion. . . . With something akin to fanatical hate Sebastian Knight was ever hunting out the things which had once been fresh and bright but which were now worn to a thread, dead things among the living ones; dead things shamming life, painted and repainted, continuing to be accepted by lazy minds serenely unaware of the fraud.

Parody serves Nabokov in more than one fashion. It is a constant source of humor in his work. It is a way for him to trip up his readers, and to involve them—once they become aware that they have been deceived by their own complacency—in a search for the "infinite levels" of perception that are buried in his novels and stories. At the same time it is a means by which he can expose the tiresome unoriginality of overworked themes and borrowed patterns of thought.

Psychotherapy is constantly under attack in Nabokov's fiction, and it becomes a kind of outstanding symbol for the clinical, sterile, stereotyping mind that perceives its surroundings in hackneyed and rigid terms. "Oh, I am not up to discussing again that figure of fun," Nabokov said about Freud in the interview with Appel. "He is not worthy of more attention than I have granted him in my novels and in *Speak, Memory*. Let the credulous and the vulgar continue to believe that all mental woes can be cured by a daily application of old Greek myths to their private parts. I really do not care." But this anti-Freudianism, which has often been commented upon and sometimes criticized as an ill-tempered crochet, is closely related to Nabokov's attitudes concerning art. Language is a writer's first love, and the language of depth psychology has become, through popular overuse, an endless series of clichés. With some frequency language, in the hands of social scientists, has been criminally assaulted. But more important, Freud and his followers make a sharp distinction between illusion and reality (the one being simply a distortion of the other), and little or no distinction between the artist and the neurotic. Both assumptions are, of course, repugnant to a writer who insists that the perceptions of the imagination are as "real" as anything else. Nabokov's blending of appearance and reality is a *deliberate* strategy that bears no relationship to the neurotic's *inability* to distinguish the real from the imaginary.

The "psychoasinine" characters and situations that Nabokov invents—Liza and Eric Wind, for example, in *Pnin,* with their "tension-releasing" group; or *Bend Sinister*'s Institute for Abnormal Children, where orphans serve as "release-instruments" for the criminally insane; or the psychiatrists whom Humbert teases with phony "primal scenes" in *Lolita,* or Headmistress Pratt, who is so concerned with Lo's development zones, all enable Nabokov to demonstrate his contempt for second-hand assumptions about human behavior. The clinical thinking that is consistently exhibited by the "Viennese delegation" he holds to be destructive to art, and that is why he takes the trouble to ridicule it. John Ray, the fictitious author of the preface to *Lolita,* and himself an obvious parody, inadvertently makes this threat clear when he acknowledges "that had our demented diarist gone, in the fatal summer of 1947 to a competent psychopathologist, there would have been no disaster; *but then, neither would there have been this book.*" (Italics mine.) If the mind could be permanently balanced—that is to say, imagination and memory silenced—then there would be no such thing as mental disturbance. There would be no such thing as art either. And it is only through art, Humbert reminds us at the end of his narrative, that a man can use that "infinity of sensation and thought within a finite existence" to escape the barriers of time that hold him a prisoner.

"I have no social purpose, no moral message," Nabokov

writes, "I've no general ideas to exploit but I like composing riddles and I like finding elegant solutions to those riddles that I have composed myself." Certainly one of the most character- istic aspects of Nabokov's art is the composition of riddles, word games, sleights of hand, false bottoms that drop out from under a reader like the trap door in a gallows. In *Speak, Memory* he re- marks that when he was a little boy he enjoyed performing sim- ple tricks, "turning water into wine, that kind of thing," and in an often-quoted passage from the same work he discusses the composition of chess problems, which are obviously analogous to problems of literary composition. The contest in chess, he says, is between the composer and his hypothetical solver, just as in fiction the contest is between the author and his reader, and the value of a problem lies in the number of " 'tries'—delu- sive opening moves, false scents, specious lines of play, astutely and lovingly prepared to lead the would-be solver astray." The author establishes certain rules to which he adheres, creates barriers which he tries to hurdle, takes the most devious and difficult route from point A to point B, and invites the reader to follow.

Sometimes the game is an open one, as in *Despair,* where the narrator constantly plays with the possibilities of his art. Chap- ter Three, for instance, begins: "How shall we begin this chap- ter? I offer several variations to choose from. Number one (readily adopted in novels where the narrative is conducted in the first person by the real or substitute author) . . ." Nabokov then goes on to try out different styles and points of view just for the sheer fun of it. Sometimes the puzzle is simply a cryptic al- lusion to some future event—a dangling thread that we cannot fully understand because we have not yet come to the spool from which it was unwound. In the second chapter of *Despair* Hermann describes a place in the woods where he and his wife and Ardalion go for a picnic:

> A lonely spot, quite so! The pines soughed gently, snow lay about, with bald patches of soil showing black. What nonsense!

How could there be snow in June? Ought to be crossed out, were it not wicked to erase; for the real author is not I, but my impatient memory. Understand it just as you please; it is none of *my* business. And the yellow post had a skullcap of snow too. Thus the future shimmers through the past. But enough, let that summer day be in focus again; spotty sunlight; shadows of branches across the blue car; a pine cone upon the footboard, where some day the most unexpected of objects will stand; a shaving brush.

We encounter that yellow post, that snow, that car with a shaving brush on the running board, nearly a hundred and thirty pages later (Chapter Nine, included in this collection) when Hermann takes his "double," Felix, to the same spot in order to murder him. Memory (and the whole book is a memory) ignores chronology and a pattern of composition is established.

The same thing occurs in *Lolita,* where we find Humbert making curious, veiled allusions to *his* "double," Quilty, whom we have never met and whom we don't really meet face to face for some two hundred and fifty pages—when *he* is murdered. (In more ways than one, *Despair* is a precursor of this later work.) It happens again in John Shade's poem, *Pale Fire,* where in oblique ways the poet seems to prophesy his own death. (Also a murder. "It's queer. I seem to remember my future works," says Fyodor in *The Gift,* speaking, it would appear, for Nabokov.) And in *Speak, Memory* Nabokov writes, "The following of . . . thematic designs through one's life should be, I think, the true purpose of autobiography." It is, quite obviously, a game that he plays in his fiction as well.

In *The Real Life of Sebastian Knight* the sleights of hand are perhaps more subtle than in any other work except *Pale Fire.* Ostensibly we are accompanying the narrator on his search for truth—Sebastian's real life—but the farther we go, the more we investigate the acquisitions and associations of the past, the less we know, until eventually we decide that Sebastian is an illusion and we have been following a circular path. The clues that have been dropped, the hints of meaning suggested, the discoveries we are always on the verge of making, are simply "specious lines of play" that lead us to conclusions about the novel that are very different from those we have expected.

Structural puzzles are only a part of the conjurer's art. Most of Nabokov's work is full of word games as well: Sebastian Knight's name, for instance. Innumerable antecedents are hinted at throughout the novel—Saint Sebastian, the Christian martyr; Sebastiano, the Italian colorist who filled in many of Michel-angelo's paintings; King Sebastian, a fourteenth-century Portu-guese ruler and mystic; and the Sebastian of Shakespeare's *Twelfth Night,* who, we recall, is separated from his twin sister, Viola, just as our hero is separated from his half-brother, V. None of these namesakes helps exactly to pin down the "real" Sebastian Knight—and that is the point. In "The Vane Sisters" the last paragraph in an acrostic (unnoticed by the narrator), used, Nabokov says, "by two dead girls to assert their mysteri-ous participation in the story. This particular trick can be tried only once in a thousand years of fiction. Whether it comes off is another question." *Pale Fire* is so full of games that one could write a book as long as the original merely to explain them—a hideous and useless task that some future Kinbote will no doubt undertake. In *Lolita* there are endless word puzzles, ranging from the more obvious cryptograms that Humbert deciphers in his cross-country pursuit of the chimerical Quilty, to the more subtle plays like Quilty's name. *"Qu'il t'y*—what a tongue-twister," Mona puns, and we wonder who indeed is Quilty? "Quine the Swine. Guilty of killing Quilty. Oh, my Lolita, I have only words to play with."

The point I should like to make is that these games are by no means gratuitous. All the fun (and it *is* fun until some critic works it all out for you) is integrally related to an "idea" that Nabokov continually examines; an idea about illusion and real-ity, or more accurately, the illusion *of* reality. What we discover in *The Real Life of Sebastian Knight* is characteristic of our discovery in most of Nabokov's work. It is not a book about "real" life at all. It is a book about art. It is about the subjective appearance of reality and the absolute distinction between art and life. We know a good deal about Knight's literary genius, but nothing about the face behind the mask. And all the word games and "delusive moves" in this (and every other) book simply reinforce the theme of deceptive reality that is central in Nabokov's artistic vision. Moreover, they force our attention to the "how," and not the "what."

A lily, he once said, "is more real to a naturalist than it is to an ordinary person. But it is still more real to a botanist. And a further stage of reality is reached with the botanist who is a specialist in lilies." In short, one gets closer to the truth of an object the more intensely one studies it, but no final or pure state of knowledge can ever be attained about anything. You can get closer and closer to reality, but you never reach an end because "reality is an infinite sucession of levels, levels of perception, or false bottoms, and hence unquenchable, unattainable." Nabokov's remark, as I have been suggesting, is really a metaphor for his own fictional techniques, for his novels and stories that are composed like chess problems and "meant for the delectation of the very expert solver."

4

When Nabokov was a boy he discovered that Hegel's triadic series was simply an expression of the "essential spirality of all things in their relation to time." He does not believe in time, at least not in any ordinary conception of the term. When the spiral unwinds, things warp into new dimensions—space into time, time into thought, thought into a new spatial dimension. His disbelief in time arises, no doubt, from that infinity of sensation that exists in the creative imagination, and when he discusses the subject he generally associates it with imagination and memory. "When we speak of a vivid individual recollection,"

he says, "we are paying a compliment . . . to Mnemosyne's
mysterious foresight in having stored up this or that element
which creative imagination may use when combining it with
later recollections and inventions. In this sense, both memory
and imagination are a negation of time."

The artificial wall between what Fyodor in *The Gift* calls
"the watery abyss of the past and the aerial abyss of the future"
is one of Nabokov's constant preoccupations. Time is central
in the stories "Lance" and "Time and Ebb" and in the poem
Pale Fire; it figures largely in many of the novels, most particularly *Invitation to a Beheading* and *Bend Sinister*; Humbert
Humbert, Fyodor, and John Shade are all disbelievers in time
and comment on the unreality of the concept; *Speak, Memory*
contains many passages that express Nabokov's agreement with
them; and the novel he is working on at the moment, *Ada,* is
framed, he has said, by an essay on the "texture of time."

His belief in the infinite spirality of things in their relation to
time has a number of effects on his fiction. For one thing it seems
to suggest a kind of metaphysical imagery, one that constantly
links the most disparate objects in order to describe experience
in terms of its bizarre echoes or its reflections in a curved mirror. In *Bend Sinister,* for example, there is a passage describing two antiquarians who have given in without a struggle
to their political oppressor, Paduk.

> . . . as the car stopped at last and bulky Beuret crawled out
> in the wake of his beard, the anonymous muser who had been
> sitting beside him was observed to split into two, producing by
> sudden gemination Gleeman, the frail Professor of Medieval
> Poetry, and the equally diminutive Yanovsky, who taught Slavic
> scansion—two newborn homunculi now drying on the paleo-
> lithic pavement.

The splitting apart of these two gentlemen as they emerge from
the car implies their essential grotesqueness by associating them
with an insect. They are like a moth emerging from its cocoon.
"Homunculi" reinforces the already strange image by making

them dwarfs, and the "paleolithic pavement" on which they are drying suggests both the archaic direction of their intellectual preoccupations and the inverted evolution of humanity in the "new state" established by Paduk. The past and present are fused.

Or Pnin, when he returns home after having all his teeth pulled, is struck by how fond he had become of them.

> His tongue, a fat sleek seal, used to flop and slide so happily among the familiar rocks, checking the contours of a battered but still secure kingdom, plunging from cave to cove, climbing this jag, nuzzling that notch, finding a shred of sweet seaweed in the same old cleft. . . .

Nothing is left but a "terra incognita of gums," and when he gets his new plates he thinks of himself as a "fossil skull" which has just been fitted with "the grinning jaws of a perfect stranger." One could fill pages with similar examples, but what is so remarkable about these passages is the free-ranging imagination that created them; an imagination that seeks always to transcend as far as possible the limitations of the consciously perceived world, to recombine and re-create sensory phenomena into a fresh and original vision of existence.

The "spiral unwinding of things" seems also to suggest to Nabokov a basic design of much of his fiction. Many of the novels and stories make a 360-degree turn, ending where they began, or, in effect, not ending at all. We leave Humbert Humbert sitting in the prison where we found him. At the end of *The Real Life of Sebastian Knight* we rush with V to the bedside of his dying brother, but it is too late. In fact, he died before the book began and we are back at the point from which we started. We first meet the narrator of *Pnin* in the last chapter when he comes to Waindell to take Pnin's job. On the last page he watches our hero as he leaves town: "Then the little sedan . . . spurted up the shining road, which one could make out narrowing to a thread of gold in the soft mist where hill after hill made beauty of distance, and where there was simply no saying what miracle might happen." He walks back to the house of his host,

Pninian mimic Jack Cockerell, and we leave him as he is about to hear a story. "And now," Cockerell says, "I am going to tell you the story of Pnin rising to address the Cremona Women's Club and discovering he had brought the wrong lecture." We are back to the event that begins the novel—Pnin's journey on the wrong train to deliver a talk on Russian politics to the Cremona Women's Club. At the end of *Bend Sinister* and *Invitation to a Beheading,* the puppet characters dissolve back into the consciousness that invented them and we are jolted into an awareness that we have been witnessing simply another twirl of the infinitely spiraling imagination. Indeed, in all Nabokov's works we are constantly reminded that we are watching a literary performance and that the only "reality" about which we may feel certain is the reality of a creative mind expressing itself in a highly articulate and playful way.

We find the same "spirality" controlling specific passages as well as the structure of entire novels. In the story "First Love" there is a lyrical recollection of the last encounter with a little girl, a recollection so tightly interwoven and self-contained that it becomes a prose poem in the middle of the narrative.

> She carried a hoop and a short stick to drive it with, and everything about her was extremely proper and stylish in an autumnal, Parisian, *tenue-de-ville pour fillettes* way. She took from her governess and slipped into my brother's hand a farewell present, a box of sugar-coated almonds, meant, I knew, solely for me; and instantly she was off, tap-tapping her glinting hoop through light and shade, around and around a fountain choked with dead leaves, near which I stood. The leaves mingle in my memory with the leather of her shoes and gloves, and there was, I remember, some detail in her attire (perhaps a ribbon on her Scottish cap, or the pattern of her stocking) that reminded me then of the rainbow spiral in a glass marble. I still seem to be holding that wisp of iridescence, not knowing exactly where to fit it, while she runs with her hoop ever faster around me and finally dissolves among the slender shadows cast on the graveled path by the interlaced arches of its low looped fence.

One notices immediately the associative mode of progression in the passage, an impressionistic device for expressing and intensifying a mood. The girl tapping her hoop around a fountain filled with dead leaves suggests the color of the leather shoes and gloves that are flashing around and around the central image. These articles of clothing recall another part of her attire, a ribbon or pattern on a stocking, which, in its turn, suggests the spiraling colors imprisoned in a glass marble. "A colored spiral in a small ball of glass, this is how I see my own life," Nabokov writes in *Speak, Memory*, and while no such statement occurs in the passage from "First Love" the whole notion of "the essential spirality of all things in their relation to time" is implicit in the associative movement in the narrator's mind, in the whirling girl who runs faster and faster around the fountain until she dissolves into shadow. It is equally implicit in the air of reverie with which the narrator surrounds his memory of the past. The hoop, the fountain, the circling girl, the "interlaced arches" of the "low looped fence" combine into a kind of master image around which the narrator's associations revolve, and the passage in its entirety becomes an effectual symbol for that moment of timeless beauty which Nabokov so loves.

For Nabokov all poetry and prose is an attempt to "try to express one's position in regard to the universe embraced by consciousness." The fleeting moment, the fragmented and unregenerate world of the impressionist, becomes for Nabokov a world in which all phenomena are thematically linked in a spiral relation to time, and which he attempts to represent by extending the "arms of consciousness" as far as possible to encompass a single point in time.

> . . . a car (New York license plate) passes along the road, a child bangs the screen door of a neighboring porch, an old man yawns in a misty Turkestan orchard, a granule of cinder-gray sand is rolled by the wind on Venus, a Docteur Jacques Hirsch in Grenoble puts on his reading glasses, and trillions of other such trifles occur—all forming an instantaneous and transparent organism of events, of which the poet (sitting in a lawn chair, at Ithaca. N.Y.) is the nucleus.

The foundation of this "cosmic synchronization" is the poet's ability to observe and register instantly and almost unconsciously the variety of his surroundings, and it is an ability (the artist's unique sense) that enables Nabokov not only to re-create images but to transform them into a completely original vision of the phenomenal world.

5

There is in all Nabokov's writing the stamp of an aristocrat; a man well born and well educated, brought up in surroundings both expensive and cultured; a man who is at once a linguist, a scholar, a natural scientist, and a creative genius. In his subjects, his language, and his wit he exhibits the depth and control of an artist for whom knowledge has always been a generative acquisition. In every line of his prose one listens to a supremely articulate voice re-creating experience in a carefully structured and highly poetic manner. As Clarence Brown remarked in an article in the *Wisconsin Studies in Contemporary Literature* on Nabokov's translation of Pushkin: "Nabokov is a consummate master of style. He is capable of more exquisite modulation, nuance, beauty, and power than is any person who has written of his work." One might reasonably extend that statement to include most of the people who have *written* in this century.

Commentators are fond of talking about an author's "early works"—those experimental preludes to the later masterpiece, but with regard to Nabokov such discussions seem rather artificial. There are better and worse novels, good stories and indifferent stories, but one never has the feeling that the author is groping for his form and style. One never feels that Nabokov, even in those early works, is not completely in command of his fictional world. *Lolita,* which appeared in 1955, may be his first masterpiece, but *Invitation to a Beheading,* 1938, must also be considered a work of great genius. Among the stories, *The Eye* (a *nouvelle,* really) and "Spring in Fialta" are two of the very best; they appeared in 1930 and 1938 respectively.

I do not mean to suggest, as some of Nabokov's admirers do, that one must take communion before opening one of his books. It is even permissible not to like what he does, but because he is an innovator and not an imitator one should, I think, make sure one knows what he does before one dislikes it. A reader should never substitute his own *donnée* for the author's. But whether or not one is enchanted by Nabokov's work, one must recognize that he is not merely a practitioner of an established literary art. He is very much like those authors, Joyce, Proust, Kafka, Gogol, with whom he is often associated; an author who has assaulted the walls of tradition and convention, who has been willing to experiment with form and language, who has refused to adopt an already tested method. Nabokov, like the artists mentioned above, has extended the boundaries of fiction by recombining forms and techniques into something incomparably his own.

The stories, poems, memoirs, critical essays, and novel gathered in this collection will provide the reader with solid evidence of Nabokov's range and depth as a man of letters, but it is my hope that they will also provide an incentive for further reading. Even two hundred thousand words is only a small percentage of this most productive author's *oeuvre*. Although English readers have by no means all Nabokov's work available to them, they have a substantial portion. And there is much to look forward to, not only translations of older material, but new things to come—new departures, new artistic adventures, new bridges (to paraphrase a paraphrast) across the abyss that lies between thought and expression.

—PAGE STEGNER
April 22, 1968
Santa Cruz

A Bibliographical Note

In the more than half century since Nabokov's first volume of poetry was privately printed in St. Petersburg (1914), his literary output has been enormous, and only a part of it is known by his English readers. There was a second volume of sixty-seven poems in 1916, also privately printed, and a third volume in 1918 called *Two Paths,* to which Andrei Balashov contributed eight poems and Nabokov twelve. In 1923, shortly after he graduated from Trinity College, Cambridge, two more collections, *The Empyrean Path* (*Gorniy Put'*) and *The Cluster* (*Grozd'*), were published in Berlin. Together they contain about a hundred and eighty-nine poems, including translations into Russian of Keats's "La Belle Dame sans Merci" and Byron's "Sun of the Sleepless." (Nabokov published numerous verse translations from other poets—Baudelaire, Musset, Shakespeare, Tennyson, Rupert Brooke, etc.—in various *émigré* newspapers and journals during the twenties and thirties.) *The Return of Chorb: Stories and Poems* (*Vozvrashchenie Chorba*) was published in Berlin in 1930 and contained twenty-four poems; *Poems 1929-1951,* published in Paris in 1952, offered fifteen more, and *Poems,* published by Doubleday in 1959, another fourteen. In addition to these there are nearly a hundred uncollected poems which have appeared in various journals from 1919 to 1966. A rough total indicates at least four hundred and ten altogether. Only twenty-eight (twenty-nine, if one counts *Pale Fire*) have been translated into or written in English.

Also relatively unknown in this country are Nabokov's plays. He has written six verse dramas: *Death* (*Smert'*), in 1923; *The Grandfather* (*Dedushka*), also in 1923; *Agaspher* (*Agasfer*), also in 1923; *The Pole* (*Polius*), in 1924; *The Tragedy of Mister Morn* (*Tragediya gospodina Morna*), in 1925. *The Wanderers* (*Skital'tsy*) was begun in 1923 but never finished. And he has written three plays in prose: *The Man from the USSR* (*Chelovek iz SSSR*), in 1927; *The Event* (*Sobytie*), in 1938; *The Waltz Invention* (*Izobretanie Val'sa*), also in 1938. Only *The Waltz Invention* is available in English.

Non-Russian readers are more fortunate when it comes to the short story. Of the fifty-three Nabokov has published, twenty have appeared in English, including two ("The Passenger" and "The Potato Elf") from his first collection, *The Return of Chorb*. *The Eye* (*Soglyadatai*), a *nouvelle,* and eleven stories, appeared in Paris in 1938; *Spring in Fialta and Other Stories* (*Vesna v Fialte i drugie rasskazy*) in New York, 1958; *Nabokov's Dozen,* published by Doubleday in 1958 (an extended version of an earlier New Directions collection, *Nine Stories*); and most recently, *Nabokov's Quartet,* which contains three early works, "Visit to a Museum," "Lik," and "An Affair of Honor," as well as his most recent story, "The Vane Sisters."

Nearly all Nabokov's major scholarly work (*Nikolai Gogol; Three Russian Poets: Translations of Pushkin, Lermontov,* and *Tiutchev*; his translation with commentary of *Eugene Onegin*; his translation and introduction to *The Song of Igor's Campaign*; his introduction to Lermontov's *A Hero of Our Time,* which he translated in collaboration with his son, Dmitri), was done after he had emigrated to America and was published in this country. But in the twenties and thirties he did a number of translations of various poets into Russian and French, translated Lewis Carroll's *Alice in Wonderland* and Romain Rolland's *Colas Breugnon* into Russian, and wrote a great many reviews and articles for *émigré* journals, particularly

The Rudder (*Rul'*), a Russian-language newspaper in Berlin, which his father edited until he was assassinated by two Russian reactionaries in 1922. None of this material has been collected or made available in English.

It is, of course, as a novelist that we know Nabokov best. All of his novels originally written and published in Russian have now been reworked by the author into English: *Mary* (*Mashenka*), 1926; *King, Queen, Knave* (*Korol', dama, valet*), 1928; *The Defense* (*Zashchita Luzhina*), 1930; *Glory* (*Podvig*), 1932; *Laughter in the Dark* (*Camera obscura*), 1932; *Despair* (*Otchayanie*), 1936; *The Gift* (*Dar*), 1937; and *Invitation to a Beheading* (*Priglashenie na Kazn'*), 1938. (Dmitri Nabokov and Michael Scammell have often collaborated in the translations.) *The Real Life of Sebastian Knight*, 1941; *Bend Sinister*, 1947; *Lolita*, 1955; *Pnin*, 1957; *Pale Fire*, 1962; and *Ada*, 1969, were originally composed in English.

There are two extensive bibliographies of Nabokov's work. Dieter E. Zimmer compiled an excellent listing (*Vladimir Nabokov Bibliographie des Gesamtwerks*) that was published in Germany in 1963 by Rowohlt Verlag. Zimmer's bibliography gives all the translations of Nabokov's work as well as their Russian titles. A more complete list is contained in Andrew Field's *Nabokov: His Life in Art*. Containing over three hundred entries, Field's bibliography includes—in addition to the novels—stories, poems, and plays, articles on lepidoptera, reviews, interviews, and other miscellaneous material. Field gives the first lines of poems in the poetry collections and individual titles in the story collections and lists nearly all the uncollected poetry and articles from *The Rudder* and various other *émigré* journals.

As far as secondary sources are concerned, there are three full-length studies of Nabokov's work: my own book, *Escape into Aesthetics: The Art of Vladimir Nabokov* (published by The Dial Press in 1966); Andrew Field's *Nabokov: His Life in Art* (published by Little, Brown in 1967); and Carl Proffer's *Keys to Lolita* (published by Indiana University Press in 1968). There are also chapters or sections on Nabokov in F. W. Dupee's *"King of the Cats" and Other Remarks on Writers and Writing*; Richard Kostelanetz's edition, *On Contemporary Literature*; Howard Nemerov's *Poetry and Fiction*; and Alan Pryce-Jones's *The Creative Present—Notes on Contemporary American Fiction.*

The Wisconsin Studies in Contemporary Literature, Spring 1967 (reissued in a hardbound edition as *Nabokov: The Man and His Work,* edited by L. S. Dembo; University of Wisconsin Press, 1968), is a special issue devoted entirely to Nabokov and contains, in addition to a number of excellent articles on both specific and general aspects of Nabokov's art, a forty-seven-page checklist of secondary sources compiled by Jackson R. Bryer and Thomas J. Bergin, Jr. Nearly two hundred essays in periodicals are noted, and literally hundreds of book reviews—all cited under the primary source to which they refer. It is an orderly and extremely useful list for any student of Nabokov's work.

I have tried in this note to cite all the major primary and secondary materials by and about Nabokov, and I have tried also to indicate the great extent of his productivity. But because the Zimmer, Field, and *Wisconsin Studies* bibliographies are readily available it has not seemed necessary to be more specifically detailed. Anyone needing more specialized information can easily check existing sources.

Vladimir Nabokov:
A Chronology

1899   Born on April 22 in St. Petersburg to Vladimir Dmitrievich and Elena Ivanovna Nabokov.

1900   His brother Sergey born on March 12. In *Speak, Memory* (pp. 256-58) Nabokov discusses his relationship with this brother, and certain parallels with V and Sebastian in *The Real Life of Sebastian Knight* become obvious. Sergey died in January 1945 in a German concentration camp, where he had been interned as a "British spy."

1903   His sister Olga is born on January 5.

1906   His sister Elena is born on March 31.

1906-17   Nabokov's father co-edits one of the few liberal papers in Russia, *Rech*, as well as a jurisprudential review, *Pravo*.

1911   His brother Kirill is born. Kirill is also discussed in *Speak, Memory*. He died of a heart attack in Munich in 1964.

1914   Nabokov composes his first poem. "A miserable concoction," he says, "containing many borrowings besides its pseudo-Pushkinian modulation." During this year a verse brochure containing a single poem is privately printed in St. Petersburg.

1916   His Uncle Ruka (Vasiliy Ivanovich Rukavishnikov) dies and leaves his nephew a two-thousand-acre estate and "what would amount nowadays to a couple of million dollars." All of this was confiscated by the Soviets several years later.

During this year *Poems*, an edition of sixty-seven poems, is privately printed in St. Petersburg.

1917-18　His father is elected to the Constituent Assembly. During the winter the family goes to the Crimea and settles near Yalta.

1918　*Two Paths,* poems by Vladimir Nabokov and Andrei Balashov, is published in Petrograd.

1919　The Nabokovs emigrate from the Crimea and take up residence in London for a few months before settling finally in Berlin. Nabokov begins his studies at Trinity College, Cambridge.

1919-22　Nabokov's father joins Iosif Hessen in editing a Russian *émigré* newspaper, *The Rudder* (*Rul'*), in Berlin.

1922　Vladimir Dmitrievich Nabokov is assassinated by two right-wing extremists named Shabelsky and Taboritsky during a political meeting at the Berlin Philharmonic Hall. He dies defending the intended victim, Pavel Miliukov.

1923　Nabokov graduates with honors from Cambridge and publishes two volumes of poetry, *A Cluster* and *The Empyrean Path.* He takes up residence in Berlin.

1925　He marries Véra Evseevna Slonim.

1926　*Mary*

1928　*King, Queen, Knave*

1930　*The Defense*
The Eye appears in *Contemporary Annals,* No. 44.
The Return of Chorb

1932　*Glory*
Laughter in the Dark

1934　Nabokov's only son, Dmitri, is born.

1936　*Despair*

1937-38　*The Gift* is serialized in *Contemporary Annals* without the fourth chapter of the 1963 Putnam's edition. The Nabokovs move from Berlin to Paris because of the increasing terrorism of the Nazis.

1938   *Invitation to a Beheading*
       The Event and *The Waltz Invention* appear in *Russian Annals (Russkie Zapiski).*

1940   The Nabokovs emigrate to America.

1941   *The Real Life of Sebastian Knight*

1942-48 Nabokov becomes a research fellow in the Museum of Comparative Zoology at Harvard University and at the same time lectures three days a week at Wellesley College.

1943   Awarded a Guggenheim fellowship.

1944   *Nikolai Gogol*

1945   Nabokov becomes an American citizen.

1947   *Bend Sinister*

1948   Becomes Professor of Russian and European Literature at Cornell University.

1951   *Speak, Memory* (originally entitled *Conclusive Evidence*)

1953   Second Guggenheim fellowship. Awarded one thousand dollars by the American Academy of Arts and Letters.

1955   *Lolita* is published by the Olympia Press in Paris. It did not appear in an American edition until 1958.

1956   *Spring in Fialta and Other Stories*

1957   *Pnin*

1958   *Nabokov's Dozen*

1960   Nabokov returns to Europe (Switzerland).

1962   *Pale Fire*

1964   Translation of Pushkin's *Eugene Onegin* is published by the Bollingen Foundation and becomes the source of much controversy (see "Reply to My Critics" in this collection).

1966   *Speak, Memory: An Autobiography Revisited.* An altered and expanded version of the 1951 edition.

1969   *Ada*

The Portable
N A B O K O V

THE ARTIST
HIMSELF

From Speak, Memory:
An Autobiography Revisited

৵৵৵৵৵

৵ৎ *From Chapter One* ৵ৎ

I
___

The cradle rocks above an abyss, and common sense tells us that our existence is but a brief crack of light between two eternities of darkness. Although the two are identical twins, man, as a rule, views the prenatal abyss with more calm than the one he is heading for (at some forty-five hundred heartbeats an hour). I know, however, of a young chronophobiac who experienced something like panic when looking for the first time at home-made movies that had been taken a few weeks before his birth. He saw a world that was practically unchanged—the same house, the same people—and then realized that he did not exist there at all and that nobody mourned his absence. He caught a glimpse of his mother waving from an upstairs window, and that unfamiliar gesture disturbed him, as if it were some mysterious farewell. But what particularly frightened him was the sight of a brand-new baby carriage standing there on the porch, with the smug, encroaching air of a coffin; even that was empty, as if, in the reverse course of events, his very bones had disintegrated.

Such fancies are not foreign to young lives. Or, to put it otherwise, first and last things often tend to have an adolescent note—unless, possibly, they are directed by some venerable and rigid religion. Nature expects a full-grown man to accept the two black voids, fore and aft, as stolidly as he accepts the extraordinary visions in between. Imagination, the supreme delight of the immortal and the immature, should be limited. In order to enjoy life, we should not enjoy it too much.

I rebel against this state of affairs. I feel the urge to take my rebellion outside and picket nature. Over and over again, my mind has made colossal efforts to distinguish the faintest of personal glimmers in the impersonal darkness on both sides of my life. That this darkness is caused merely by the walls of time separating me and my bruised fists from the free world of timelessness is a belief I gladly share with the most gaudily painted savage. I have journeyed back in thought—with thought hopelessly tapering off as I went—to remote regions where I groped for some secret outlet only to discover that the prison of time is spherical and without exits. Short of suicide, I have tried everything. I have doffed my identity in order to pass for a conventional spook and steal into realms that existed before I was conceived. I have mentally endured the degrading company of Victorian lady novelists and retired colonels who remembered having, in former lives, been slave messengers on a Roman road or sages under the willows of Lhasa. I have ransacked my oldest dreams for keys and clues—and let me say at once that I reject completely the vulgar, shabby, fundamentally medieval world of Freud, with its crankish quest for sexual symbols (something like searching for Baconian acrostics in Shakespeare's works) and its bitter little embryos spying, from their natural nooks, upon the love life of their parents.

Initially, I was unaware that time, so boundless at first blush, was a prison. In probing my childhood (which is the next best to probing one's eternity) I see the awakening of consciousness as a series of spaced flashes, with the intervals between them gradually diminishing until bright blocks of perception are formed, affording memory a slippery hold. I had learned numbers and speech more or less simultaneously at a very early date, but the inner knowledge that I was I and that my parents were my parents seems to have been established only later, when it was directly associated with my discovering their age in relation to mine. Judging by the strong sunlight that, when I think of that revelation, immediately invades my memory with lobed sun flecks through overlapping patterns of greenery, the occasion may have been my mother's birthday, in late summer, in the country, and I had asked questions and had assessed the answers I received. All this is as it should be according to the theory of recapitulation; the beginning of reflexive consciousness in the brain of our remotest ancestor must surely have coincided with the dawning of the sense of time.

Thus, when the newly disclosed, fresh and trim formula of my own age, four, was confronted with the parental formulas, thirty-three and twenty-seven, something happened to me. I was given a tremendously invigorating shock. As if subjected to a second baptism, on more divine lines than the Greek Catholic ducking undergone fifty months earlier by a howling, half-drowned half-Victor (my mother, through the half-closed door, behind which an old custom bade parents retreat, managed to correct the bungling archpresbyter, Father Konstantin Vetvenitski), I felt myself plunged abruptly into a radiant and mobile medium that was none other than the pure element of time. One shared it—just as excited bathers share shining seawater—with creatures that were not oneself but that were joined to one by time's common flow, an environment quite different from the spatial world, which not only man but apes and butterflies can perceive. At that instant, I became acutely aware that the twenty-seven-year-old being, in soft white and pink, holding my left hand, was my mother, and that the thirty-three-year-old being, in hard white and gold, holding my right hand, was my father. Between them, as they evenly progressed, I strutted, and trotted, and strutted again, from sun fleck to sun fleck, along the middle of a path, which I easily identify today with an alley of ornamental oaklings in the park of our country estate, Vyra, in the former Province of St. Petersburg, Russia. Indeed, from my present ridge of remote, isolated, almost uninhabited time, I see my diminutive self as celebrating, on that August day 1903, the birth of sentient life. If my left-hand-holder and my right-hand-holder had both been present before in my vague infant world, they had been so under the mask of a tender incognito; but now my father's attire, the resplendent uniform of the Horse Guards, with that smooth golden swell of cuirass burning upon his chest and back, came out like the sun, and for several years afterward I remained keenly interested in the age of my parents and kept myself informed about it, like a nervous passenger asking the time in order to check a new watch.

My father, let it be noted, had served his term of military training long before I was born, so I suppose he had that day put on the trappings of his old regiment as a festive joke. To a joke, then, I owe my first gleam of complete consciousness—which again has recapitulatory implications, since the first creatures on earth to become aware of time were also the first creatures to smile.

2
———

It was the primordial cave (and not what Freudian mystics might suppose) that lay behind the games I played when I was four. A big cretonne-covered divan, white with black trefoils, in one of the drawing rooms at Vyra rises in my mind, like some massive product of a geological upheaval before the beginning of history. History begins (with the promise of fair Greece) not far from one end of this divan, where a large potted hydrangea shrub, with pale blue blossoms and some greenish ones, half conceals, in a corner of the room, the pedestal of a marble bust of Diana. On the wall against which the divan stands, another phase of history is marked by a gray engraving in an ebony frame—one of those Napoleonic-battle pictures in which the episodic and the allegoric are the real adversaries and where one sees, all grouped together on the same plane of vision, a wounded drummer, a dead horse, trophies, one soldier about to bayonet another, and the invulnerable emperor posing with his generals amid the frozen fray.

With the help of some grown-up person, who would use first both hands and then a powerful leg, the divan would be moved several inches away from the wall, so as to form a narrow passage which I would be further helped to roof snugly with the divan's bolsters and close up at the ends with a couple of its cushions. I then had the fantastic pleasure of creeping through that pitch-dark tunnel, where I lingered a little to listen to the singing in my ears—that lonesome vibration so familiar to small boys in dusty hiding places—and then, in a burst of delicious panic, on rapidly thudding hands and knees I would reach the tunnel's far end, push its cushion away, and be welcomed by a mesh of sunshine on the parquet under the canework of a Viennese chair and two gamesome flies settling by turns. A dreamier and more delicate sensation was provided by another cave game, when upon awakening in the early morning I made a tent of my bedclothes and let my imagination play in a thousand dim ways with shadowy snowslides of linen and with the faint light that seemed to penetrate my penumbral covert from some immense distance, where I fancied that strange, pale animals roamed in a landscape of lakes. The recollection of my crib, with its lateral nets of fluffy cotton cords, brings back, too, the pleasure of handling a certain beautiful, delightfully solid, garnet-dark crystal egg left over from some unremembered Easter; I used to chew a corner of the bedsheet until it was thoroughly soaked and then wrap the egg in it tightly, so as to admire and re-lick the warm, ruddy glitter of the snugly enveloped facets that came seeping through with a miraculous completeness of glow and color. But that was not yet the closest I got to feeding upon beauty.

How small the cosmos (a kangaroo's pouch would hold it), how paltry and puny in comparison to human consciousness, to a single individual recollection, and its expression in words! I may be inordinately fond of my earliest impressions, but then I

have reason to be grateful to them. They led the way to a veritable Eden of visual and tactile sensations. One night, during a
trip abroad, in the fall of 1903, I recall kneeling on my (flattish)
pillow at the window of a sleeping car (probably on the long-
extinct Mediterranean Train de Luxe, the one whose six cars
had the lower part of their body painted in umber and the panels in cream) and seeing with an inexplicable pang, a handful
of fabulous lights that beckoned to me from a distant hillside,
and then slipped into a pocket of black velvet: diamonds that I
later gave away to my characters to alleviate the burden of my
wealth. I had probably managed to undo and push up the tight
tooled blind at the head of my berth, and my heels were cold,
but I still kept kneeling and peering. Nothing is sweeter or
stranger than to ponder those first thrills. They belong to the
harmonious world of a perfect childhood and, as such, possess a
naturally plastic form in one's memory, which can be set down
with hardly any effort; it is only starting with the recollections of
one's adolescence that Mnemosyne begins to get choosy and
crabbed. I would moreover submit that, in regard to the power
of hoarding up impressions, Russian children of my generation
passed through a period of genius, as if destiny were loyally
trying what it could for them by giving them more than their
share, in view of the cataclysm that was to remove completely
the world they had known. Genius disappeared when everything had been stored, just as it does with those other, more
specialized child prodigies—pretty, curly-headed youngsters
waving batons or taming enormous pianos, who eventually turn
into second-rate musicians with sad eyes and obscure ailments
and something vaguely misshapen about their eunuchoid hind-
quarters. But even so, the individual mystery remains to tan-
talize the memoirist. Neither in environment nor in heredity
can I find the exact instrument that fashioned me, the anonymous roller that pressed upon my life a certain intricate wa-
termark whose unique design becomes visible when the lamp of
art is made to shine through life's foolscap.

〜 *From Chapter Two* 〜

I

As far back as I remember myself (with interest, with amusement, seldom with admiration or disgust), I have been subject to mild hallucinations. Some are aural, others are optical, and by none have I profited much. The fatidic accents that restrained Socrates or egged on Joaneta Darc have degenerated with me to the level of something one happens to hear between lifting and clapping down the receiver of a busy party-line telephone. Just before falling asleep, I often become aware of a kind of one-sided conversation going on in an adjacent section of my mind, quite independently from the actual trend of my thoughts. It is a neutral, detached, anonymous voice, which I catch saying words of no importance to me whatever—an English or a Russian sentence, not even addressed to me, and so trivial that I hardly dare give samples, lest the flatness I wish to convey be marred by a molehill of sense. This silly phenomenon seems to be the auditory counterpart of certain praedormitary visions, which I also know well. What I mean is not the bright mental image (as, for instance, the face of a beloved parent long dead) conjured up by a wing-stroke of the will; *that* is one of the bravest movements a human spirit can make. Nor am I alluding to the so-called *muscae volitantes*—shadows cast upon the retinal rods by motes in the vitreous humor, which are seen as transparent threads drifting across the visual field. Perhaps nearer to the hypnagogic mirages I am thinking of is the colored spot, the stab of an afterimage, with which the lamp one has just turned off wounds the palpebral night. However, a shock of this sort is not really a necessary starting point for the slow, steady development of the visions that pass before my closed eyes. They come and go, without the drowsy observer's participation, but are essentially different from dream pictures for he is still master of his senses. They are often grotesque. I am pestered by roguish profiles, by some coarse-featured and florid dwarf with a swelling nostril or ear. At times, however, my photisms take on a rather soothing *flou* quality, and then I see— projected, as it were, upon the inside of the eyelid—gray figures walking between beehives, or small black parrots gradually vanishing among mountain snows, or a mauve remoteness melting beyond moving masts.

On top of all this I present a fine case of colored hearing. Perhaps "hearing" is not quite accurate, since the color sensation seems to be produced by the very act of my orally forming a given letter while I imagine its outline. The long *a* of the English alphabet (and it is this alphabet I have in mind farther on unless otherwise stated) has for me the tint of weathered wood, but a French *a* evokes polished ebony. This black group also includes hard *g* (vulcanized rubber) and *r* (a sooty rag being ripped). Oatmeal *n,* noodle-limp *l,* and the ivory-backed hand mirror of *o* take care of the whites. I am puzzled by my French *on,* which I see as the brimming tension-surface of alcohol in a small glass. Passing on to the blue group, there is steely *x,* thundercloud *z,* and huckleberry *k.* Since a subtle interaction exists between sound and shape, I see *q* as browner than *k,* while *s* is not the light blue of *c,* but a curious mixture of azure and mother-of-pearl. Adjacent tints do not merge, and diphthongs do not have special colors of their own, unless represented by a single character in some other language (thus the fluffy-gray, three-stemmed Russian letter that stands for *sh,* a letter as old as the rushes of the Nile, influences its English representation).

I hasten to complete my list before I am interrupted. In the green group, there are alder-leaf *f,* the unripe apple of *p,* and pistachio *t.* Dull green, combined somehow with violet, is the best I can do for *w.* The yellows comprise various *e*'s *and i*'s, creamy *d,* bright-golden *y,* and *u,* whose alphabetical value I can express only by "brassy with an olive sheen." In the brown group, there are the rich rubbery tone of soft *g,* paler *j,* and the drab shoelace of *h*. Finally, among the reds, *b* has the tone called burnt sienna by painters, *m* is a fold of pink flannel, and today I have at last perfectly matched *v* with "Rose Quartz" in Maerz and Paul's *Dictionary of Color*. The word for rainbow, a primary, but decidedly muddy, rainbow, is in my private language the hardly pronounceable: *kzspygv*. The first author to discuss *audition colorée* was, as far as I know, an albino physician in 1812, in Erlangen.

The confessions of a synesthete must sound tedious and pretentious to those who are protected from such leakings and drafts by more solid walls than mine are. To my mother, though, this all seemed quite normal. The matter came up, one day in my seventh year, as I was using a heap of old alphabet blocks to build a tower. I casually remarked to her that their colors were all wrong. We discovered then that some of her letters had the same tint as mine and that, besides, she was optically affected by musical notes. These evoked no chromatisms in me whatsoever. Music, I regret to say, affects me merely as an arbitrary succession of more or less irritating sounds. Under certain emotional circumstances I can stand the spasms of a rich violin, but the concert piano and all wind instruments bore me in small doses and flay me in larger ones. Despite the number of operas I was exposed to every winter (I must have attended *Ruslan* and *Pikovaya Dama* at least a dozen times in the course of half as many years), my weak responsiveness to music was completely overrun by the visual torment of not being able to read over Pimen's shoulder or of trying in vain to imagine the hawkmoths in the dim bloom of Juliet's garden.

My mother did everything to encourage the general sensitiveness I had to visual stimulation. How many were the aquarelles she painted for me; what a revelation it was when she showed me the lilac tree that grows out of mixed blue and red! Sometimes, in our St. Petersburg house, from a secret compartment in the wall of her dressing room (and my birth room), she would produce a mass of jewelry for my bedtime amusement. I was very small then, and those flashing tiaras and chokers and rings seemed to me hardly inferior in mystery and enchantment to the illumination in the city during imperial fêtes, when, in the padded stillness of a frosty night, giant monograms, crowns, and other armorial designs, made of colored electric bulbs—sapphire, emerald, ruby—glowed with a kind of charmed constraint above snow-lined cornices on housefronts along residential streets.

2

My numerous childhood illnesses brought my mother and me still closer together. As a little boy, I showed an abnormal aptitude for mathematics, which I completely lost in my singularly talentless youth. This gift played a horrible part in tussles with quinsy or scarlet fever, when I felt enormous spheres and huge numbers swell relentlessly in my aching brain. A foolish tutor had explained logarithms to me much too early, and I had read (in a British publication, the *Boy's Own Paper,* I believe) about a certain Hindu calculator who in exactly two seconds could find the seventeenth root of, say, 3529471145760275132301897342055866171392 (I am not sure I have got this right; anyway the root was 212). Such were the monsters that thrived on my delirium, and the only way to prevent them from crowding me out of myself was to kill them by extracting their hearts. But they were far too strong, and I would sit up and laboriously form garbled sentences as I tried to explain things to my mother. Beneath my delirium, she recognized sensations she had known herself, and her understanding would bring my expanding universe back to a Newtonian norm.

The future specialist in such dull literary lore as autoplagiarism will like to collate a protagonist's experience in my novel *The Gift* with the original event. One day, after a long illness, as I lay in bed still very weak, I found myself basking in an unusual euphoria of lightness and repose. I knew my mother had gone to buy me the daily present that made those convalescences so delightful. What it would be this time I could not guess, but through the crystal of my strangely translucent state I vividly visualized her driving away down Morskaya Street toward Nevski Avenue. I distinguished the light sleigh drawn by a chestnut courser. I heard his snorting breath, the rhythmic clacking of his scrotum, and the lumps of frozen earth and snow thudding against the front of the sleigh. Before my eyes and before those of my mother loomed the hind part of the coachman, in his heavily padded blue robe, and the leather-encased watch (twenty minutes past two) strapped to the back of his belt, from under which curved the pumpkin-like folds of his huge stuffed rump. I saw my mother's seal furs and, as the icy speed increased, the muff she raised to her face—that graceful, winter-ride gesture of a St. Petersburg lady. Two corners of the voluminous spread of bearskin that covered her up to the waist were attached by loops to the two side knobs of the low back of her seat. And behind her, holding on to these knobs, a footman in a cockaded hat stood on his narrow support above the rear extremities of the runners.

Still watching the sleigh, I saw it stop at Treumann's (writing implements, bronze baubles, playing cards). Presently, my mother came out of this shop followed by the footman. He carried her purchase, which looked to me like a pencil. I was astonished that she did not carry so small an object herself, and this disagreeable question of dimensions caused a faint renewal, fortunately very brief, of the "mind dilation effect" which I hoped had gone with the fever. As she was being tucked up again in the sleigh, I watched the vapor exhaled by all, horse included. I watched, too, the familiar pouting movement she made to distend the network of her close-fitting veil drawn too tight over her face, and as I write this, the touch of reticulated tenderness that my lips used to feel when I kissed her veiled cheek comes back to me—*flies* back to me with a shout of joy out of the snow-blue, blue-windowed (the curtains are not yet drawn) past.

A few minutes later, she entered my room. In her arms she held a big parcel. It had been, in my vision, greatly reduced in size—perhaps, because I subliminally corrected what logic warned me might still be the dreaded remnants of delirium's dilating world. Now the object proved to be a giant polygonal Faber pencil, four feet long and correspondingly thick. It had been hanging as a showpiece in the shop's window, and she presumed I had coveted it, as I coveted all things that were not quite purchasable. The shopman had been obliged to ring up an agent, a "Doctor" Libner (as if the transaction possessed indeed some pathological import). For an awful moment, I wondered whether the point was made of real graphite. It was. And some years later I satisfied myself, by drilling a hole in the side, that the lead went right through the whole length—a perfect case of art for art's sake on the part of Faber and Dr. Libner since the pencil was far too big for use and, indeed, was not meant to be used.

"Oh, yes," she would say as I mentioned this or that unusual sensation. "Yes, I know all that," and with a somewhat eerie ingenuousness she would discuss such things as double sight, and little raps in the woodwork of tripod tables, and premonitions, and the feeling of the *déjà vu*. A streak of sectarianism ran through her direct ancestry. She went to church only at Lent and Easter. The schismatic mood revealed itself in her healthy distaste for the ritual of the Greek Catholic Church and for its priests. She found a deep appeal in the moral and poetical side of the Gospels, but felt no need in the support of any dogma. The appalling insecurity of an afterlife and its lack of privacy did not enter her thoughts. Her intense and pure religiousness took the form of her having equal faith in the existence of another world and in the impossibility of comprehending it in terms of earthly life. All one could do was to glimpse, amid the haze and the chimeras, something real ahead, just as persons endowed with an unusual persistence of diurnal cerebration are able to perceive in their deepest sleep, somewhere beyond the throes of an entangled and inept nightmare, the ordered reality of the waking hour.

3

To love with all one's soul and leave the rest to fate, was the simple rule she heeded. *"Vot zapomni* [now remember]," she would say in conspiratorial tones as she drew my attention to this or that loved thing in Vyra—a lark ascending the curds-and-whey sky of a dull spring day, heat lightning taking pictures of a distant line of trees in the night, the palette of maple leaves on brown sand, a small bird's cuneate footprints on new snow. As if feeling that in a few years the tangible part of her world would perish, she cultivated an extraordinary consciousness of the various time marks distributed throughout our country place. She cherished her own past with the same retrospective fervor that I now do her image and my past. Thus, in a way, I inherited an exquisite simulacrum—the beauty of intangible property, unreal estate—and this proved a splendid training for the endurance of later losses. Her special tags and imprints became as dear and as sacred to me as they were to her. There was the room which in the past had been reserved for her mother's pet hobby, a chemical laboratory; there was the linden tree marking the spot, by the side of the road that sloped up toward the village of Gryazno (accented on the ultima), at the steepest bit where one preferred to take one's "bike by the horns" (*bika za roga*) as my father, a dedicated cyclist, liked to say, and where he had proposed; and there was, in the so-called "old" park, the obsolete tennis court, now a region of moss, mole-heaps, and mushrooms, which had been the scene of gay rallies in the eighties and nineties (even her grim father would shed his coat and give the heaviest racket an appraisive shake) but which, by the time I was ten, nature had effaced with the thoroughness of a felt eraser wiping out a geometrical problem.

By then, an excellent modern court had been built at the end of the "new" part of the park by skilled workmen imported from Poland for that purpose. The wire mesh of an ample enclosure separated it from the flowery meadow that framed its clay. After a damp night the surface acquired a brownish gloss and the white lines would be repainted with liquid chalk from a green pail by Dmitri, the smallest and oldest of our gardeners, a meek, black-booted, red-shirted dwarf slowly retreating, all hunched up, as his paintbrush went down the line. A pea-tree hedge (the "yellow acacia" of northern Russia), with a midway opening, corresponding to the court's screen door, ran parallel to the enclosure and to a path dubbed *tropinka Sfinksov* ("path of the Sphingids") because of the hawkmoths visiting at dusk the fluffy lilacs along the border that faced the hedge and likewise broke in the middle. This path formed the bar of a great T whose vertical was the alley of slender oaks, my mother's coevals, that traversed (as already said) the new park through its entire length. Looking down that avenue from the base of the T near the drive one could make out quite distinctly the bright little gap five hundred yards away—or fifty years away from where I am now. Our current tutor or my father, when he stayed with us in the country, invariably had my brother for partner in our temperamental family doubles. "Play!" my mother would cry in the old manner as she put her little foot forward and bent her white-hatted head to ladle out an assiduous but feeble serve. I got easily cross with her, and she, with the ballboys, two barefooted peasant lads (Dmitri's pug-nosed grandson and the twin brother of pretty Polenka, the head coachman's daughter). The northern summer became tropical around harvest time. Scarlet Sergey would stick his racket between his knees and laboriously wipe his glasses. I see my butterfly net propped against the enclosure—just in case. Wallis Myers' book on lawn tennis lies open on a bench, and after every exchange my father (a first-rate player, with a cannonball service of the Frank Riseley type and a beautiful "lifting drive") pedantically inquires of my brother and me whether the "fol-low-through," that state of grace, has descended upon us. And sometimes a prodigious cloudburst would cause us to huddle un-der a shelter at the corner of the court while old Dmitri would be sent to fetch umbrellas and raincoats from the house. A quar-ter of an hour later he would reappear under a mountain of clothing in the vista of the long avenue which as he advanced would regain its leopard spots with the sun blazing anew and his huge burden unneeded.

She loved all games of skill and gambling. Under her expert hands, the thousand bits of a jigsaw puzzle gradually formed an English hunting scene; what had seemed to be the limb of a horse would turn out to belong to an elm and the hitherto un-placeable piece would snugly fill up a gap in the mottled back-ground, affording one the delicate thrill of an abstract and yet tactile satisfaction. At one time, she was very fond of poker, which had reached St. Petersburg society via diplomatic circles, so that some of the combinations came with pretty French names *brelan* for "three of a kind," *couleur* for "flush," and so on. The game in use was the regular "draw poker," with, occasion-ally, the additional tingle of jackpots and an omnivicarious joker. In town, she often played poker at the houses of friends until three in the morning, a society recreation in the last years before World War One; and later, in exile, she used to imagine (with the same wonder and dismay with which she recalled old Dmitri) the chauffeur Pirogov who still seemed to be waiting for her in the relentless frost of an unending night, although, in his case, rum-laced tea in a hospitable kitchen must have gone a long way to assuage those vigils.

One of her greatest pleasures in summer was the very Rus-sian sport of *hodit' po gribï* (looking for mushrooms). Fried in butter and thickened with sour cream, her delicious finds ap-peared regularly on the dinner table. Not that the gustatory mo-ment mattered much. Her main delight was in the quest, and this quest had its rules. Thus, no agarics were taken; all she picked

were species belonging to the edible section of the genus *Boletus*
(tawny *edulis,* brown *scaber,* red *aurantiacus,* and a few close
allies), called "tube mushrooms" by some and coldly defined
by mycologists as "terrestrial, fleshy, putrescent, centrally
stipitate fungi." Their compact pilei—tight-fitting in infant
plants, robust and appetizingly domed in ripe ones—have a
smooth (not lamellate) undersurface and a neat, strong stem. In
classical simplicity of form, boletes differ considerably from the
"true mushroom," with its preposterous gills and effete stipal
ring. It is, however, to the latter, to the lowly and ugly agarics,
that nations with timorous taste buds limit their knowledge and
appetite, so that to the Anglo-American lay mind the aristocratic
boletes are, at best, reformed toadstools.

Rainy weather would bring out these beautiful plants in profusion under the firs, birches and aspens in our park, especially
in its older part, east of the carriage road that divided the park
in two. Its shady recesses would then harbor that special boletic
reek which makes a Russian's nostrils dilate—a dark, dank,
satisfying blend of damp moss, rich earth, rotting leaves. But
one had to poke and peer for a goodish while among the wet
underwood before something really nice, such as a family of
bonneted baby *edulis* or the marbled variety of *scaber,* could
be discovered and carefully teased out of the soil.

On overcast afternoons, all alone in the drizzle, my mother,
carrying a basket (stained blue on the inside by somebody's
whortleberries), would set out on a long collecting tour. Toward
dinnertime, she could be seen emerging from the nebulous
depths of a park alley, her small figure cloaked and hooded in
greenish-brown wool, on which countless droplets of moisture
made a kind of mist all around her. As she came nearer from
under the dripping trees and caught sight of me, her face would
show an odd, cheerless expression, which might have spelled
poor luck, but which I knew was the tense, jealously contained
beatitude of the successful hunter. Just before reaching me,
with an abrupt, drooping movement of the arm and shoulder

and a "Pouf!" of magnified exhaustion, she would let her basket sag, in order to stress its weight, its fabulous fullness.

Near a white garden bench, on a round garden table of iron, she would lay out her boletes in concentric circles to count and sort them. Old ones, with spongy, dingy flesh, would be eliminated, leaving the young and the crisp. For a moment, before they were bundled away by a servant to a place she knew nothing about, to a doom that did not interest her, she would stand there admiring them, in a glow of quiet contentment. As often happened at the end of a rainy day, the sun might cast a lurid gleam just before setting, and there, on the damp round table, her mushrooms would lie, very colorful, some bearing traces of extraneous vegetation—a grass blade sticking to a viscid fawn cap, or moss still clothing the bulbous base of a dark-stippled stem. And a tiny looper caterpillar would be there, too, measuring, like a child's finger and thumb, the rim of the table, and every now and then stretching upward to grope, in vain, for the shrub from which it had been dislodged.

From Chapter Four

I

The kind of Russian family to which I belonged—a kind now extinct—had, among other virtues, a traditional leaning toward the comfortable products of Anglo-Saxon civilization. Pears' Soap, tar-black when dry, topaz-like when held to the light between wet fingers, took care of one's morning bath. Pleasant was the decreasing weight of the English collapsible tub when it was made to protrude a rubber underlip and disgorge its frothy contents into the slop pail. "We could not improve the cream, so we improved the tube," said the English toothpaste. At breakfast, Golden Syrup imported from London would entwist with its glowing coils the revolving spoon from which enough of it had slithered onto a piece of Russian bread and butter. All sorts of snug, mellow things came in a steady procession from the English Shop on Nevski Avenue: fruitcakes, smelling salts, playing cards, picture puzzles, striped blazers, talcum-white tennis balls.

I learned to read English before I could read Russian. My first English friends were four simple souls in my grammar—Ben, Dan, Sam and Ned. There used to be a great deal of fuss about their identities and whereabouts—"Who is Ben?" "He is Dan," "Sam is in bed," and so on. Although it all remained rather stiff and patchy (the compiler was handicapped by having to employ—for the initial lessons, at least—words of not more than three letters), my imagination somehow managed to obtain the necessary data. Wan-faced, big-limbed, silent nitwits, proud in the possession of certain tools ("Ben has an axe"), they now drift with a slow-motioned slouch across the remotest backdrop of memory; and, akin to the mad alphabet of an optician's chart, the grammar-book lettering looms again before me.

The schoolroom was drenched with sunlight. In a sweating glass jar, several spiny caterpillars were feeding on nettle leaves (and ejecting interesting, barrel-shaped pellets of olive-green frass). The oilcloth that covered the round table smelled of glue. Miss Clayton smelled of Miss Clayton. Fantastically, gloriously, the blood-colored alcohol of the outside thermometer had risen to 24° Réaumur (86° Fahrenheit) in the shade. Through the window one could see kerchiefed peasant girls weeding a garden path on their hands and knees or gently raking the sun-mottled sand. (The happy days when they would be cleaning streets and digging canals for the State were still beyond the horizon.) Golden orioles in the greenery emitted their four brilliant notes: dee-del-dee-O!

Ned lumbered past the window in a fair impersonation of the gardener's mate Ivan (who was to become in 1918 a member of the local Soviet). On later pages longer words appeared;

and at the very end of the brown, inkstained volume, a real, sensible story unfolded its adult sentences ("One day Ted said to Ann: Let us—"), the little reader's ultimate triumph and reward. I was thrilled by the thought that some day I might attain such proficiency. The magic has endured, and whenever a grammar book comes my way, I instantly turn to the last page to enjoy a forbidden glimpse of the laborious student's future, of that promised land where, at last, words are meant to mean what they mean.

2

Summer *soomerki*—the lovely Russian word for dusk. Time: a dim point in the first decade of this unpopular century. Place: latitude 59° north from your equator, longitude 100° east from my writing hand. The day would take hours to fade, and everything—sky, tall flowers, still water—would be kept in a state of infinite vesperal suspense, deepened rather than resolved by the doleful moo of a cow in a distant meadow or by the still more moving cry that came from some bird beyond the lower course of the river, where the vast expanse of a misty-blue sphagnum bog, because of its mystery and remoteness, the Rukavishnikov children had baptized America.

In the drawing room of our country house, before going to bed, I would often be read to in English by my mother. As she came to a particularly dramatic passage, where the hero was about to encounter some strange, perhaps fatal danger, her voice would slow down, her words would be spaced portentously, and before turning the page she would place upon it her hand, with its familiar pigeon-blood ruby and diamond ring (within the limpid facets of which, had I been a better crystal-gazer, I might have seen a room, people, lights, trees in the rain —a whole period of *émigré* life for which that ring was to pay). There were tales about knights whose terrific but wonderfully aseptic wounds were bathed by damsels in grottoes. From a windswept clifftop, a medieval maiden with flying hair and a youth in hose gazed at the round Isles of the Blessed. In "Misunderstood," the fate of Humphrey used to bring a more specialized lump to one's throat than anything in Dickens or Daudet (great devisers of lumps), while a shamelessly allegorical story, "Beyond the Blue Mountains," dealing with two pairs of little travelers—good Clover and Cowslip, bad Buttercup and Daisy—contained enough exciting details to make one forget its "message."

There were also those large, flat, glossy picture books. I particularly liked the blue-coated, red-trousered, coal-black Golliwogg, with underclothes buttons for eyes, and his meager harem of five wooden dolls. By the illegal method of cutting themselves frocks out of the American flag (Peg taking the motherly stripes, Sarah Jane the pretty stars) two of the dolls acquired a certain soft femininity, once their neutral articulations had been clothed. The Twins (Meg and Weg) and the Midget remained stark naked and, consequently, sexless.

We see them in the dead of night stealing out of doors to sling snowballs at one another until the chimes of a remote clock ("But Hark!" comments the rhymed text) send them back to their toybox in the nursery. A rude jack-in-the-box shoots out, frightening my lovely Sarah, and that picture I heartily disliked because it reminded me of children's parties at which this or that graceful little girl, who had bewitched me, happened to pinch her finger or hurt her knee, and would forthwith expand into a purple-faced goblin, all wrinkles and bawling mouth. Another time they went on a bicycle journey and were captured by cannibals; our unsuspecting travelers had been quenching their thirst at a palm-fringed pool when the tom-toms sounded. Over the shoulder of my past I admire again the crucial picture: the Golliwogg, still on his knees by the pool but no longer drinking; his hair stands on end and the normal black of his face has changed to a weird ashen hue. There was also the motorcar book (Sarah Jane, always my favorite, sporting a long green veil), with the usual sequel—crutches and bandaged heads.

And, yes—the airship. Yards and yards of yellow silk went to make it, and an additional tiny balloon was provided for the sole use of the fortunate Midget. At the immense altitude to which the ship reached, the aeronauts huddled together for warmth while the lost little soloist, still the object of my intense envy notwithstanding his plight, drifted into an abyss of frost and stars—alone.

3

I next see my mother leading me bedward through the enormous hall, where a central flight of stairs swept up and up, with nothing but hothouse-like panes of glass between the upper landing and the light green evening sky. One would lag back and shuffle and slide a little on the smooth stone floor of the hall, causing the gentle hand at the small of one's back to propel one's reluctant frame by means of indulgent pushes. Upon reaching the stairway, my custom was to get to the steps by squirming under the handrail between the newel post and the first banister. With every new summer, the process of squeezing through became more difficult; nowadays, even my ghost would get stuck.

Another part of the ritual was to ascend with closed eyes. "Step, step, step," came my mother's voice as she led me up— and sure enough, the surface of the next tread would receive the blind child's confident foot; all one had to do was lift it a little higher than usual, so as to avoid stubbing one's toe against the riser. This slow, somewhat somnambulistic ascension in self-engendered darkness held obvious delights. The keenest of them was not knowing when the last step would come. At the top of the stairs, one's foot would be automatically lifted to the deceptive call of "Step," and then, with a momentary sense of exquisite panic, with a wild contraction of muscles, would sink into the phantasm of a step, padded, as it were, with the infinitely elastic stuff of its own nonexistence.

It is surprising what method there was in my bedtime dawdling. True, the whole going-up-the-stairs business now reveals certain transcendental values. Actually, however, I was merely playing for time by extending every second to its utmost. This would still go on when my mother turned me over, to be undressed, to Miss Clayton or Mademoiselle.

There were five bathrooms in our country house, and a medley of venerable washstands (one of these I would seek out in its dark nook whenever I had been crying, so as to feel on my swollen face which I was ashamed to show, the healing touch of its groping jet while I stepped on the rusty pedal). Regular baths were taken in the evening. For morning ablutions, the round, rubber English tubs were used. Mine was about four feet in diameter, with a knee-high rim. Upon the lathered back of the squatting child, a jugful of water was carefully poured by an aproned servant. Its temperature varied with the hydrotherapeutic notions of successive mentors. There was that bleak period of dawning puberty, when an icy deluge was decreed by our current tutor, who happened to be a medical student. On the other hand, the temperature of one's evening bath remained pleasantly constant at 28° Réaumur (95° Fahrenheit) as measured by a large kindly thermometer whose wooden sheathing (with a bit of damp string in the eye of the handle) allowed it to share in the buoyancy of celluloid goldfishes and little swans.

The toilets were separate from the bathrooms, and the oldest among them was a rather sumptuous but gloomy affair with some fine panelwork and a tasseled rope of red velvet, which, when pulled, produced a beautifully modulated, discreetly muffled gurgle and gulp. From that corner of the house, one could see Hesperus and hear the nightingales, and it was there that, later, I used to compose my youthful verse, dedicated to unembraced beauties, and morosely survey, in a dimly illuminated

mirror, the immediate erection of a strange castle in an unknown Spain. As a small child, however, I was assigned a more
modest arrangement, rather casually situated in a narrow recess
between a wicker hamper and the door leading to the nursery
bathroom. This door I liked to keep ajar; through it I drowsily
looked at the shimmer of steam above the mahogany bath,
at the fantastic flotilla of swans and skiffs, at myself with a harp
in one of the boats, at a furry moth pinging against the reflec-
tor of the kerosene lamp, at the stained-glass window beyond,
at its two halberdiers consisting of colored rectangles. Bending
from my warm seat, I liked to press the middle of my brow, its
ophryon to be precise, against the smooth comfortable edge of
the door and then roll my head a little, so that the door would
move to and fro while its edge remained all the time in soothing
contact with my forehead. A dreamy rhythm would permeate
my being. The recent "Step, step, step," would be taken up by
a dripping faucet. And, fruitfully combining rhythmic pattern
with rhythmic sound, I would unravel the labyrinthian frets on
the linoleum, and find faces where a crack or a shadow afforded
a *point de repère* for the eye. I appeal to parents: never, never
say, "Hurry up," to a child.

The final stage in the course of my vague navigation would
come when I reached the island of my bed. From the veranda
or drawing room, where life was going on without me, my
mother would come up for the warm murmur of her good-night
kiss. Closed inside shutters, a lighted candle, Gentle Jesus,
meek and mild, something-something little child, the child
kneeling on the pillow that presently would engulf his humming head. English prayers and the little icon featuring a sun-
tanned Greek Catholic saint formed an innocent association
upon which I look back with pleasure; and above the icon, high
up on the wall, where the shadow of something (of the bamboo
screen between bed and door?) undulated in the warm can-
dlelight, a framed aquarelle showed a dusky path winding
through one of those eerily dense European beechwoods, where

the only undergrowth is bindweed and the only sound one's thumping heart. In an English fairy tale my mother had once read to me, a small boy stepped out of his bed into a picture and rode his hobbyhorse along a painted path between silent trees. While I knelt on my pillow in a mist of drowsiness and talc-powdered well-being, half sitting on my calves and rapidly going through my prayer, I imagined the motion of climbing into the picture above my bed and plunging into that enchanted beechwood—which I did visit in due time.

🙠 *Chapter Six* 🙠

I

On a summer morning, in the legendary Russia of my boyhood, my first glance upon awakening was for the chink between the white inner shutters. If it disclosed a watery pallor, one had better not open them at all, and so be spared the sight of a sullen day sitting for its picture in a puddle. How resentfully one would deduce, from a line of dull light, the leaden sky, the sodden sand, the gruel-like mess of broken brown blossoms under the lilacs—and that flat, fallow leaf (the first casualty of the season) pasted upon a wet garden bench!

But if the chink was a long glint of dewy brilliancy, then I made haste to have the window yield its treasure. With one blow, the room would be cleft into light and shade. The foliage of birches moving in the sun had the translucent green tone of grapes, and in contrast to this there was the dark velvet of fir trees against a blue of extraordinary intensity, the like of which I rediscovered only many years later, in the montane zone of Colorado.

From the age of seven, everything I felt in connection with a rectangle of framed sunlight was dominated by a single passion. If my first glance of the morning was for the sun, my first thought was for the butterflies it would engender. The original event had been banal enough. On the honeysuckle, overhanging the carved back of a bench just opposite the main entrance, my guiding angel (whose wings, except for the absence of a Florentine limbus, resemble those of Fra Angelico's Gabriel) pointed out to me a rare visitor, a splendid, pale-yellow creature with black blotches, blue crenels, and a cinnabar eyespot above each chrome-rimmed black tail. As it probed the inclined flower from which it hung, its powdery body slightly bent, it kept restlessly jerking its great wings, and my desire for it was one of the most intense I have ever experienced. Agile Ustin, our town-house janitor, who for a comic reason (explained elsewhere) happened to be that summer in the country with us, somehow managed to catch it in my cap, after which it was transferred, cap and all, to a wardrobe, where domestic naphthalene was fondly expected by Mademoiselle to kill it overnight. On the following morning, however, when she unlocked the wardrobe to take something out, my Swallow-tail, with a mighty rustle, flew into her face, then made for the open window, and presently was but a golden fleck dipping and dodging and soaring eastward, over timber and tundra, to Vologda, Viatka and Perm, and beyond the gaunt Ural range to Yakutsk and Verkhne Kolymsk, and from Verkhne Kolymsk, where it lost a tail, to the fair Island of St. Lawrence, and across Alaska to Dawson, and southward along the Rocky Mountains —to be finally overtaken and captured, after a forty-year race, on an immigrant dandelion under an endemic aspen near Boulder. In a letter from Mr. Brune to Mr. Rawlins, June 14, 1735, in the Bodleian collection, he states that one Mr. Vernon followed a butterfly nine miles before he could catch him (*The Recreative Review or Eccentricities of Literature and Life,* Vol. I, p. 144, London, 1821).

Soon after the wardrobe affair I found a spectacular moth, marooned in a corner of a vestibule window, and my mother dispatched it with ether. In later years, I used many killing agents, but the least contact with the initial stuff would always cause the porch of the past to light up and attract that blundering beauty. Once, as a grown man, I was under ether during appendectomy, and with the vividness of a decalcomania picture I saw my own self in a sailor suit mounting a freshly emerged Emperor moth under the guidance of a Chinese lady who I knew was my mother. It was all there, brilliantly reproduced in my dream, while my own vitals were being exposed: the soaking, ice-cold absorbent cotton pressed to the insect's lemurian head; the subsiding spasms of its body; the satisfying crackle produced by the pin penetrating the hard crust of its thorax; the careful insertion of the point of the pin in the cork-bottomed groove of the spreading board; the symmetrical adjustment of the thick, strong-veined wings under neatly affixed strips of semitransparent paper.

2

I must have been eight when, in a storeroom of our country house, among all kinds of dusty objects, I discovered some wonderful books acquired in the days when my mother's mother had been interested in natural science and had had a famous university professor of zoology (Shimkevich) give private lessons to her daughter. Some of these books were mere curios, such as the four huge brown folios of Albertus Seba's work (*Locupletissimi Rerum Naturalium Thesauri Accurata Descriptio . . .*), printed in Amsterdam around 1750. On their coarse-grained pages I found woodcuts of serpents and butterflies and embryos. The fetus of an Ethiopian female child hanging by the neck in a glass jar used to give me a nasty shock every time I came across it; nor did I much care for the stuffed hydra on plate CII, with its seven lion-toothed turtleheads on seven serpentine necks and its strange, bloated body which bore buttonlike tubercules along the sides and ended in a knotted tail.

Other books I found in that attic, among herbariums full of alpine columbines, and blue palemoniums, and Jove's campions, and orange-red lilies, and other Davos flowers, came closer to my subject. I took in my arms and carried downstairs glorious loads of fantastically attractive volumes: Maria Sibylla Merian's (1647-1717) lovely plates of Surinam insects, and Esper's noble *Die Schmetterlinge* (Erlangen, 1777), and Boisduval's *Icones Historiques de Lépidoptères Nouveaux ou Peu Connus* (Paris, begun in 1832). Still more exciting were the products of the latter half of the century—Newman's *Natural History of British Butterflies and Moths*, Hofmann's *Die Gross-Schmetterlinge Europas*, the Grand Duke Nikolay Mihailovich's *Mémoires* on Asiatic lepidoptera (with incomparably beautiful figures painted by Kavrigin, Rybakov, Lang), Scudder's stupendous work on the *Butterflies of New England*.

Retrospectively, the summer of 1905, though quite vivid in many ways, is not animated yet by a single bit of quick flutter or colored fluff around or across the walks with the village schoolmaster: the Swallowtail of June 1906 was still in the larval stage on a roadside umbellifer; but in the course of that month I became acquainted with a score or so of common things, and Mademoiselle was already referring to a certain forest road that culminated in a marshy meadow full of Small Pearl-bordered Fritillaries (thus called in my first unforgettable and unfadingly magical little manual, Richard South's *The Butterflies of the British Isles* which had just come out at the time) as *le chemin des papillons bruns*. The following year I became aware that many of our butterflies and moths did not occur in England or Central Europe, and more complete atlases helped me to determine them. A severe illness (pneumonia, with fever up to 41° centigrade), in the beginning of 1907, mysteriously abolished the rather monstrous gift of numbers that had made of me a child prodigy during a few months (to-day I cannot multiply 13 by 17 without pencil and paper; I can add them up, though, in a trice, the teeth of the three fitting in neatly); but the butterflies survived. My mother accumulated a library and a museum around my bed, and the longing to describe a new species completely replaced that of discovering a new prime number. A trip to Biarritz, in August 1907, added new wonders (though not as lucid and numerous as they were to be in 1909). By 1908, I had gained absolute control over the European lepidoptera as known to Hofmann. By 1910, I had dreamed my way through the first volumes of Seitz's prodigious picture book *Die Gross-Schmetterlinge der Erde*, had purchased a number of rarities recently described, and was voraciously reading entomological periodicals, especially English and Russian ones. Great upheavals were taking place in the development of systematics. Since the middle of the century, Continental lepidopterology had been, on the whole, a simple and stable affair, smoothly run by the Germans. Its high priest, Dr. Staudinger, was also the head of the largest firm of insect dealers. Even now, half a century after his death, German lepidopterists have not quite managed to shake off the hypnotic spell occasioned by his authority. He was still alive when his school began to lose ground as a scientific force in the world. While he and his followers stuck to specific and generic names sanctioned by long usage and were content to classify butterflies by characters visible to the naked eye, English-speaking authors were introducing nomenclatorial changes as a result of a strict application of the law of priority and taxonomic changes based on the microscopic study of organs. The Germans did their best to ignore the new trends and continued to cherish the philately-like side of entomology. Their solicitude for the "average collector who should not be made to dissect" is comparable to the way nervous publishers of popular novels pamper the "average reader"—who should not be made to think.

There was another more general change, which coincided

with my ardent adolescent interest in butterflies and moths. The Victorian and Staudingerian kind of species, hermetic and homogeneous, with sundry (alpine, polar, insular, etc.) "varieties" affixed to it from the outside, as it were, like incidental appendages, was replaced by a new, multiform and fluid kind of species, organically *consisting* of geographical races or subspecies. The evolutional aspects of the case were thus brought out more clearly, by means of more flexible methods of classification, and further links between butterflies and the central problems of nature were provided by biological investigations.

The mysteries of mimicry had a special attraction for me. Its phenomena showed an artistic perfection usually associated with man-wrought things. Consider the imitation of oozing poison by bubblelike macules on a wing (complete with pseudo-refraction) or by glossy yellow knobs on a chrysalis ("Don't eat me—I have already been squashed, sampled and rejected"). Consider the tricks of an acrobatic caterpillar (of the Lobster Moth) which in infancy looks like bird's dung, but after molting develops scrabbly hymenopteroid appendages and baroque characteristics, allowing the extraordinary fellow to play two parts at once (like the actor in Oriental shows who *becomes* a pair of intertwisted wrestlers): that of a writhing larva and that of a big ant seemingly harrowing it. When a certain moth resembles a certain wasp in shape and color, it also walks and moves its antennae in a waspish, unmothlike manner. When a butterfly has to look like a leaf, not only are all the details of a leaf beautifully rendered but markings mimicking grub-bored holes are generously thrown in. "Natural selection," in the Darwinian sense, could not explain the miraculous coincidence of imitative aspect and imitative behavior, nor could one appeal to the theory of "the struggle for life" when a protective device was carried to a point of mimetic subtlety, exuberance, and luxury far in excess of a predator's power of appreciation. I discovered in nature the nonutilitarian delights that I sought in art. Both were a form of magic, both were a game of intricate enchantment and deception.

3

I have hunted butterflies in various climes and disguises:
as a pretty boy in knickerbockers and sailor cap; as a lanky
cosmopolitan expatriate in flannel bags and beret; as a fat
hatless old man in shorts. Most of my cabinets have shared the
fate of our Vyra house. Those in our town house and the small
addendum I left in the Yalta Museum have been destroyed,
no doubt, by carpet beetles and other pests. A collection of
South European stuff that I started in exile vanished in Paris
during World War Two. All my American captures from 1940
to 1960 (several thousands of specimens including great rarities and types) are in the Mus. of Comp. Zoology, the Am.
Nat. Hist. Mus., and the Cornell Univ. Mus. of Entomology,
where they are safer than they would be in Tomsk or Atomsk.
Incredibly happy memories, quite comparable, in fact, to those
of my Russian boyhood, are associated with my research work
at the MCZ, Cambridge, Mass. (1941-1948). No less happy
have been the many collecting trips taken almost every summer,
during twenty years, through most of the states of my adopted
country.

In Jackson Hole and in the Grand Canyon, on the mountain
slopes above Telluride, Colo., and on a celebrated pine barren near Albany, N.Y., dwell, and will dwell, in generations
more numerous than editions, the butterflies I have described
as new. Several of my finds have been dealt with by other work-
ers; some have been named after me. One of these, Nabokov's
Pug (*Eupithecia nabokovi* McDunnough), which I boxed one
night in 1943 on a picture window of James Laughlin's Alta
Lodge in Utah, fits most philosophically into the thematic spiral
that began in a wood on the Oredezh around 1910—or perhaps
even earlier, on that Nova Zemblan river a century and a half
ago.

Few things indeed have I known in the way of emotion or

appetite, ambition or achievement, that could surpass in rich-
ness and strength the excitement of entomological exploration.
From the very first it had a great many intertwinkling facets.
One of them was the acute desire to be alone, since any companion, no matter how quiet, interfered with the concentrated
enjoyment of my mania. Its gratification admitted of no compromise or exception. Already when I was ten, tutors and governesses knew that the morning was mine and cautiously kept
away.

In this connection, I remember the visit of a schoolmate, a
boy of whom I was very fond and with whom I had excellent
fun. He arrived one summer night—in 1913, I think—from a
town some twenty-five miles away. His father had recently perished in an accident, the family was ruined and the stout-
hearted lad, not being able to afford the price of a railway ticket,
had bicycled all those miles to spend a few days with me.

On the morning following his arrival, I did everything I could
to get out of the house for my morning hike without his knowing where I had gone. Breakfastless, with hysterical haste, I
gathered my net, pill boxes, killing jar, and escaped through
the window. Once in the forest, I was safe; but still I walked
on, my calves quaking, my eyes full of scalding tears, the whole
of me twitching with shame and self-disgust, as I visualized my
poor friend, with his long pale face and black tie, moping in the
hot garden—patting the panting dogs for want of something
better to do, and trying hard to justify my absence to himself.

Let me look at my demon objectively. With the exception
of my parents, no one really understood my obsession, and it
was many years before I met a fellow sufferer. One of the first
things I learned was not to depend on others for the growth of
my collection. One summer afternoon, in 1911, Mademoiselle
came into my room, book in hand, started to say she wanted to
show me how wittily Rousseau denounced zoology (in favor of
botany), and by then was too far gone in the gravitational process of lowering her bulk into an armchair to be stopped by my

howl of anguish: on that seat I had happened to leave a glass-lidded cabinet tray with long, lovely series of the Large White. Her first reaction was one of stung vanity: her weight, surely, could not be accused of damaging what in fact it had demolished; her second was to console me: *Allons donc, ce ne sont que des papillons de potager!*—which only made matters worse. A Sicilian pair recently purchased from Staudinger had been crushed and bruised. A huge Biarritz example was utterly mangled. Smashed, too, were some of my choicest local captures. Of these, an aberration resembling the Canarian race of the species might have been mended with a few drops of glue; but a precious gynandromorph, left side male, right side female, whose abdomen could not be traced and whose wings had come off, was lost forever: one might reattach the wings but one could not prove that all four belonged to that headless thorax on its bent pin. Next morning, with an air of great mystery, poor Mademoiselle set off for St. Petersburg and came back in the evening bringing me ("something better than your cabbage butterflies") a banal Urania moth mounted on plaster. "How you hugged me, how you danced with joy!" she exclaimed ten years later in the course of inventing a brand-new past.

Our country doctor, with whom I had left the pupae of a rare moth when I went on a journey abroad, wrote me that everything had hatched finely; but in reality a mouse had got at the precious pupae, and upon my return the deceitful old man produced some common Tortoiseshell butterflies, which, I presume, he had hurriedly caught in his garden and popped into the breeding cage as plausible substitutes (so *he* thought). Better than he was an enthusiastic kitchen boy who would sometimes borrow my equipment and come back two hours later in triumph with a bagful of seething invertebrate life and several additional items. Loosening the mouth of the net which he had tied up with a string, he would pour out his cornucopian spoil—a mass of grasshoppers, some sand, the two parts of a mushroom he had thriftily plucked on the way home, more grasshoppers, more sand, and one battered Small White.

In the works of major Russian poets I can discover only two lepidopteral images of genuinely sensuous quality: Bunin's impeccable evocation of what is certainly a Tortoiseshell:

> And there will fly into the room
> A colored butterfly in silk
> To flutter, rustle and pit-pat
> On the blue ceiling . . .

and Fet's "Butterfly" soliloquizing:

> Whence have I come and whither am I hasting
> Do not inquire;
> Now on a graceful flower I have settled
> And now respire.

In French poetry one is struck by Musset's well-known lines (in *Le Saule*):

> *Le phalène doré dans sa course légère*
> *Traverse les prés embaumés*

which is an absolutely exact description of the crepuscular flight of the male of the geometrid called in England the Orange moth; and there is Fargue's fascinatingly apt phrase (in *Les Quatres Journées*) about a garden which, at nightfall, *se glace de bleu comme l'aile du grand Sylvain* (the Poplar Admirable). And among the very few genuine lepidopterological images in English poetry, my favorite is Browning's

> On our other side is the straight-up rock;
> And a path is kept 'twixt the gorge and it
> By boulder-stones where lichens mock
> The marks on a moth, and small ferns fit
> Their teeth to the polished block
> ("By the Fire-side")

It is astounding how little the ordinary person notices butterflies. "None," calmly replied that sturdy Swiss hiker with Camus in his rucksack when purposely asked by me for the benefit of

my incredulous companion if he had seen any butterflies while
descending the trail where, a moment before, you and I had
been delighting in swarms of them. It is also true that when I
call up the image of a particular path remembered in minute
detail but pertaining to a summer before that of 1906, preceding, that is, the date on my first locality label, and never revisited, I fail to make out one wing, one wingbeat, one azure flash,
one moth-gemmed flower, as if an evil spell had been cast on
the Adriatic coast making all its "leps" (as the slangier among
us say) invisible. Exactly thus an entomologist may feel some
day when plodding beside a jubilant, and already helmetless
botanist amid the hideous flora of a parallel planet, with not a
single insect in sight; and thus (in odd proof of the odd fact
that whenever possible the scenery of our infancy is used by an
economically minded producer as a ready-made setting for our
adult dreams) the seaside hilltop of a certain recurrent nightmare of mine, whereinto I smuggle a collapsible net from my
waking state, is gay with thyme and melilot, but incomprehen-
sibly devoid of all the butterflies that should be there.

I also found out very soon that a "lepist" indulging in his
quiet quest was apt to provoke strange reactions in other creatures. How often, when a picnic had been arranged, and
I would be self-consciously trying to get my humble implements unnoticed into the tar-smelling charabanc (a tar preparation was used to keep flies away from the horses) or the tea-
smelling Opel convertible (benzine forty years ago smelled
that way), some cousin or aunt of mine would remark: "Must
you *really* take that net with you? Can't you enjoy yourself like
a normal boy? Don't you think you are spoiling everybody's
pleasure?" Near a sign NACH BODENLAUBE, at Bad Kissingen,
Bavaria, just as I was about to join for a long walk my father
and majestic old Muromtsev (who, four years before, in 1906,
had been President of the first Russian Parliament), the latter
turned his marble head toward me, a vulnerable boy of
eleven, and said with his famous solemnity: "Come with us by

all means, but do not chase butterflies, child. It spoils the rhythm of the walk." On a path above the Black Sea, in the Crimea, among shrubs in waxy bloom, in March 1918, a bow-legged Bolshevik sentry attempted to arrest me for signaling (with my net, he said) to a British warship. In the summer of 1929, every time I walked through a village in the Eastern Pyrenees, and happened to look back, I would see in my wake the villagers frozen in the various attitudes my passage had caught them in, as if I were Sodom and they Lot's wife. A decade later, in the Maritime Alps, I once noticed the grass undulate in a serpentine way behind me because a fat rural policeman was wriggling after me on his belly to find out if I were not trapping songbirds. America has shown even more of this morbid interest in my retiary activities than other countries have—perhaps because I was in my forties when I came there to live, and the older the man, the queerer he looks with a butterfly net in his hand. Stern farmers have drawn my attention to NO FISHING signs; from cars passing me on the highway have come wild howls of derision; sleepy dogs, though unmindful of the worst bum, have perked up and come at me, snarling; tiny tots have pointed me out to their puzzled mamas; broad-minded vacationists have asked me whether I was catching bugs for bait; and one morning on a wasteland, lit by tall yuccas in bloom, near Santa Fe, a big black mare followed me for more than a mile.

4

—————

When, having shaken off all pursuers, I took the rough, red road that ran from our Vyra house toward field and forest, the animation and luster of the day seemed like a tremor of sympathy around me.

Very fresh, very dark Arran Browns, which emerged only every second year (conveniently, retrospection has fallen here into line), flitted among the firs or revealed their red markings and checkered fringes as they sunned themselves on the roadside bracken. Hopping above the grass, a diminutive Ringlet called Hero dodged my net. Several moths, too, were flying—gaudy sun-lovers that sail from flower to flower like painted flies, or male insomniacs in search of hidden females, such as that rust-colored Oak Eggar hurtling across the shrubbery. I noticed (one of the major mysteries of my childhood) a soft pale green wing caught in a spider's web (by then I knew what it was: part of a Large Emerald). The tremendous larva of the Goat Moth, ostentatiously segmented, flat-headed, flesh-colored and glossily flushed, a strange creature "as naked as a worm" to use a French comparison, crossed my path in frantic search for a place to pupate (the awful pressure of metamorphosis, the aura of a disgraceful fit in a public place). On the bark of that birch tree, the stout one near the park wicket, I had found last spring a dark aberration of Sievers' Carmelite (just another gray moth to the reader). In the ditch, under the bridgelet, a bright-yellow Silvius Skipper hobnobbed with a dragonfly (just a blue libellula to me). From a flower head two male Coppers rose to a tremendous height, fighting all the way up—and then, after a while, came the downward flash of one of them returning to his thistle. These were familiar insects, but at any moment something better might cause me to stop with a quick intake of breath. I remember one day when I warily brought my net closer and closer to an uncommon Hairstreak that had daintily settled on a sprig. I could clearly see the white W on its chocolate-brown underside. Its wings were closed and the inferior ones were rubbing against each other in a curious circular motion—possibly producing some small, blithe crepitation pitched too high for a human ear to catch. I had long wanted that particular species, and, when near enough, I struck. You have heard champion tennis players moan after muffing an easy shot. You may have seen the face of the world-famous grandmaster Wilhelm Edmundson when, during a simultaneous display in a Minsk café, he lost his rook, by an absurd oversight, to the local amateur and pediatrician, Dr. Schach, who eventually won. But that day nobody (except my older self) could see me shake out a piece of twig from an otherwise empty net and stare at a hole in the tarlatan.

5

Near the intersection of two carriage roads (one, well-kept, running north-south in between our "old" and "new" parks, and the other, muddy and rutty, leading, if you turned west, to Batovo) at a spot where aspens crowded on both sides of a dip, I would be sure to find in the third week of June great blue-black nymphalids striped with pure white, gliding and wheeling low above the rich clay which matched the tint of their undersides when they settled and closed their wings. Those were the dung-loving males of what the old Aurelians used to call the Poplar Admirable, or, more exactly, they belonged to its Bucovinan subspecies. As a boy of nine, not knowing that race, I noticed how much our North Russian specimens differed from the Central European form figured in Hofmann, and rashly wrote to Kuznetsov, one of the greatest Russian, or indeed world, lepidopterists of all time, naming my new subspecies *"Limenitis populi rossica."* A long month later he returned my description and aquarelle of *"rossica* Nabokov" with only two words scribbled on the back of my letter: *"bucovinensis* Hormuzaki." How I hated Hormuzaki! And how hurt I was when in one of Kuznetsov's later papers I found a gruff reference to "schoolboys who keep naming minute varieties of the Poplar Nymph!" Undaunted, however, by the *populi* flop, I "discovered" the following year a "new" moth. That summer I had been collecting assiduously on moonless nights, in a glade of the park, by spreading a bedsheet over the grass and its annoyed glowworms, and casting upon it the light of an acyte-

lene lamp (which, six years later, was to shine on Tamara).
Into that arena of radiance, moths would come drifting out of
the solid blackness around me, and it was in that manner, upon
that magic sheet, that I took a beautiful *Plusia* (now *Phytome-*
tra) which, as I saw at once, differed from its closest ally by its
mauve-and-maroon (instead of golden-brown) forewings, and
narrower bractea mark and was not recognizably figured in any
of my books. I sent its description and picture to Richard South,
for publication in *The Entomologist*. He did not know it either,
but with the utmost kindness checked it in the British Museum
collection—and found it had been described long ago as *Plusia*
excelsa by Kretschmar. I received the sad news, which was
most sympathetically worded (". . . should be congratulated
for obtaining . . . very rare Volgan thing . . . admirable
figure . . .") with the utmost stoicism; but many years later, by
a pretty fluke (I know I should not point out these plums to
people), I got even with the first discoverer of *my* moth by giving his own name to a blind man in a novel.

Let me also evoke the hawkmoths, the jets of my boyhood!
Colors would die a long death on June evenings. The lilac
shrubs in full bloom before which I stood, net in hand, displayed clusters of a fluffy gray in the dusk—the ghost of purple. A moist young moon hung above the mist of a neighboring
meadow. In many a garden have I stood thus in later years—in
Athens, Antibes, Atlanta—but never have I waited with such
a keen desire as before those darkening lilacs. And suddenly it
would come, the low buzz passing from flower to flower, the vi-
brational halo around the streamlined body of an olive and pink
Hummingbird moth poised in the air above the corolla into
which it had dipped its long tongue. Its handsome black larva
(resembling a diminutive cobra when it puffed out its ocellated
front segments) could be found on dank willow herb two
months later. Thus every hour and season had its delights.
And, finally, on cold, or even frosty, autumn nights, one could
sugar for moths by painting tree trunks with a mixture of mo-

lasses, beer, and rum. Through the gusty blackness, one's lantern would illumine the stickily glistening furrows of the bark and two or three large moths upon it imbibing the sweets, their nervous wings half open butterfly fashion, the lower ones exhibiting their incredible crimson silk from beneath the lichengray primaries. *"Catocala adultera!"* I would triumphantly shriek in the direction of the lighted windows of the house as I stumbled home to show my captures to my father.

6

The "English" park that separated our house from the hayfields was an extensive and elaborate affair with labyrinthine paths, Turgenevian benches, and imported oaks among the endemic firs and birches. The struggle that had gone on since my grandfather's time to keep the park from reverting to the wild state always fell short of complete success. No gardener could cope with the hillocks of frizzly black earth that the pink hands of moles kept heaping on the tidy sand of the main walk. Weeds and fungi, and ridgelike tree roots crossed and recrossed the sun-flecked trails. Bears had been eliminated in the eighties, but an occasional moose still visited the grounds. On a picturesque boulder, a little mountain ash and a still smaller aspen had climbed, holding hands, like two clumsy, shy children. Other, more elusive trespassers—lost picnickers or merry villagers—would drive our hoary gamekeeper Ivan crazy by scrawling ribald words on the benches and gates. The disintegrating process continues still, in a different sense, for when, nowadays, I attempt to follow in memory the winding paths from one given point to another, I notice with alarm that there are many gaps, due to oblivion or ignorance, akin to the terra-incognita blanks map makers of old used to call "sleeping beauties."

Beyond the park, there were fields, with a continuous shimmer of butterfly wings over a shimmer of flowers—daisies, bluebells, scabious, and others—which now rapidly pass by me in a kind of colored haze like those lovely, lush meadows, never to be explored, that one sees from the diner on a transcontinental journey. At the end of this grassy wonderland, the forest rose like a wall. There I roamed, scanning the tree trunks (the enchanted, the silent part of a tree) for certain tiny moths, called Pugs in England—delicate little creatures that cling in the daytime to speckled surfaces, with which their flat wings and turned-up abdomens blend. There, at the bottom of that sea of sunshot greenery, I slowly spun round the great boles. Nothing in the world would have seemed sweeter to me than to be able to add, by a stroke of luck, some remarkable new species to the long list of Pugs already named by others. And my pied imagination, ostensibly, and almost grotesquely, groveling to my desire (but all the time, in ghostly conspiracies behind the scenes, coolly planning the most distant events of my destiny), kept providing me with hallucinatory samples of small print: ". . . the only specimen so far known . . ." ". . . the only specimen known of *Eupithecia petropolitanata* was taken by a Russian schoolboy . . ." ". . . by a young Russian collector . . ." ". . . by myself in the Government of St. Petersburg, Tsarskoe Selo District, in 1910 . . . 1911 . . . 1912 . . . 1913 . . ." And then, thirty years later, that blessed black night in the Wasatch Range.

At first—when I was, say, eight or nine—I seldom roamed farther than the fields and woods between Vyra and Batovo. Later, when aiming at a particular spot half-a-dozen miles or more distant, I would use a bicycle to get there with my net strapped to the frame; but not many forest paths were passable on wheels; it was possible to ride there on horseback, of course, but, because of our ferocious Russian tabanids, one could not leave a horse haltered in a wood for any length of time: my spirited bay almost climbed up the tree it was tied to one day trying to elude them: big fellows with watered-silk eyes and tiger bodies, and gray little runts with an even more painful proboscis, but much more sluggish: to dispatch two or three of these dingy tipplers with one crush of the gloved hand as they glued themselves to the neck of my mount afforded me a wonderful empathic relief (which a dipterist might not appreciate). Anyway, on my butterfly hunts I always preferred hiking to any other form of locomotion (except, naturally, a flying seat gliding leisurely over the plant mats and rocks of an unexplored mountain, or hovering just above the flowery roof of a rain forest); for when you walk, especially in a region you have studied well, there is an exquisite pleasure in departing from one's itinerary to visit, here and there by the wayside, this glade, that glen, this or that combination of soil and flora—to drop in, as it were, on a familiar butterfly in his particular habitat, in order to see if he has emerged, and if so, how he is doing.

There came a July day—around 1910, I suppose—when I felt the urge to explore the vast marshland beyond the Oredezh. After skirting the river for three or four miles, I found a rickety footbridge. While crossing over, I could see the huts of a hamlet on my left, apple trees, rows of tawny pine logs lying on a green bank, and the bright patches made on the turf by the scattered clothes of peasant girls, who, stark naked in shallow water, romped and yelled, heeding me as little as if I were the discarnate carrier of my present reminiscences. On the other side of the river, a dense crowd of small, bright blue male butterflies that had been tippling on the rich, trampled mud and cow dung through which I trudged rose all together into the spangled air and settled again as soon as I had passed.

After making my way through some pine groves and alder scrub I came to the bog. No sooner had my ear caught the hum of diptera around me, the guttural cry of a snipe overhead, the gulping sound of the morass under my foot, than I knew I would find here quite special arctic butterflies, whose pictures, or, still better, nonillustrated descriptions I had worshiped for several seasons. And the next moment I was among them. Over the small shrubs of bog bilberry with fruit of a dim, dreamy blue, over the brown eye of stagnant water, over moss and mire, over the flower spikes of the fragrant bog orchid (the *nochnaya fialka* of Russian poets), a dusky little Fritillary bearing the name of a Norse goddess passed in low, skimming flight. Pretty Cordigera, a gemlike moth, buzzed all over its uliginose food plant. I pursued rose-margined Sulphurs, gray-marbled Satyrs. Unmindful of the mosquitoes that furred my forearms, I stooped with a grunt of delight to snuff out the life of some silver-studded lepidopteron throbbing in the folds of my net. Through the smells of the bog, I caught the subtle perfume of butterfly wings on my fingers, a perfume which varies with the species—vanilla, or lemon, or musk, or a musty, sweetish odor difficult to define. Still unsated, I pressed forward. At last I saw I had come to the end of the marsh. The rising ground beyond was a paradise of lupines, columbines, and pentstemons. Mariposa lilies bloomed under Ponderosa pines. In the distance, fleeting cloud shadows dappled the dull green of slopes above timber line, and the gray and white of Longs Peak.

I confess I do not believe in time. I like to fold my magic carpet, after use, in such a way as to superimpose one part of the pattern upon another. Let visitors trip. And the highest enjoyment of timelessness—in a landscape selected at random —is when I stand among rare butterflies and their food plants. This is ecstasy, and behind the ecstasy is something else, which is hard to explain. It is like a momentary vacuum into which rushes all that I love. A sense of oneness with sun and stone. A thrill of gratitude to whom it may concern—to the contrapuntal genius of human fate or to tender ghosts humoring a lucky mortal.

〰 *From Chapter Nine* 〰

I

I have before me a large bedraggled scrapbook, bound in black cloth. It contains old documents, including diplomas, drafts, diaries, identity cards, penciled notes, and some printed matter, which had been in my mother's meticulous keeping in Prague until her death there, but then, between 1939 and 1961, went through various vicissitudes. With the aid of those papers and my own recollections, I have composed the following short biography of my father.

Vladimir Dmitrievich Nabokov, jurist, publicist and statesman, son of Dmitri Nikolaevich Nabokov, Minister of Justice, and Baroness Maria von Korff, was born on July 20, 1870, at Tsarskoe Selo near St. Petersburg, and was killed by an assassin's bullet on March 28, 1922, in Berlin. Till the age of thirteen he was educated at home by French and English governesses and by Russian and German tutors; from one of the latter he caught and passed on to me the *passio et morbus aureliani*. In the autumn of 1883, he started to attend the "Gymnasium" (corresponding to a combination of American "high school" and "junior college") on the then Gagarin Street (presumably renamed in the twenties by the short-sighted Soviets). His desire to excel was overwhelming. One winter night, being behind with a set task and preferring pneumonia to ridicule at the blackboard, he exposed himself to the polar frost, with the hope of a timely sickness, by sitting in nothing but his nightshirt at the open window (it gave on the Palace Square and its moon-polished pillar); on the morrow he still enjoyed perfect health, and, undeservedly, it was the dreaded teacher who happened to be laid up. At sixteen, in May 1887, he completed the Gymnasium course, with a gold medal, and studied law at the St. Petersburg University, graduating in January 1891. He continued his studies in Germany (mainly at Halle). Thirty years later, a fellow student of his, with whom he had gone for a bicycle trip in the Black Forest, sent my widowed mother the *Madame Bovary* volume which my father had had with him at the time and on the flyleaf of which he had written "The unsurpassed pearl of French literature"—a judgment that still holds.

On November 14 (a date scrupulously celebrated every subsequent year in our anniversary-conscious family), 1897, he married Elena Ivanovna Rukavishnikov, the twenty-one-year-old daughter of a country neighbor with whom he had six children (the first was a stillborn boy).

In 1895 he had been made Junior Gentleman of the Chamber. From 1896 to 1904 he lectured on criminal law at the Imperial School of Jurisprudence (*Pravovedenie*) in St. Petersburg. Gentlemen of the Chamber were supposed to ask permission of the "Court Minister" before performing a public act. This permission my father did not ask, naturally, when publishing in the review *Pravo* his celebrated article "The Blood Bath of Kishinev" in which he condemned the part played by the police in promoting the Kishinev pogrom of 1903. By imperial decree he was deprived of his court title in January 1905, after which he severed all connection with the Tsar's government and resolutely plunged into antidespotic politics, while continuing his juristic labors. From 1905 to 1915 he was president of the Russian section of the International Criminology Association and at conferences in Holland amused himself and amazed his audience by orally translating, when needed, Russian and English speeches into German and French and vice-versa. He was eloquently against capital punishment. Unswervingly he conformed to his principles in private and public matters. At an official banquet in 1904 he refused to drink the Tsar's health. He is said to have coolly advertised in the papers his court uniform for sale. From 1906 to 1917 he co-edited with I. V. Hessen and A. I. Kaminka one of the few liberal

dailies in Russia, the *Rech* ("Speech") as well as the jurisprudential review *Pravo*. Politically he was a "Kadet," i.e. a member of the KD (*Konstitutsionno-demokraticheskaya partiya*),
later renamed more aptly the party of the People's Freedom
(*partiya Narodnoy Svobodï*). With his keen sense of humor he
would have been tremendously tickled by the helpless though
vicious hash Soviet lexicographers have made of his opinions
and achievements in their rare biographical comments on
him. In 1906 he was elected to the First Russian Parliament
(*Pervaya Duma*), a humane and heroic institution, predomi-
nantly liberal (but which ignorant foreign publicists, infected
by Soviet propaganda, often confuse with the ancient "boyar
dumas"!). There he made several splendid speeches with
nationwide repercussions. When less than a year later the Tsar
dissolved the Duma, a number of members, including my father (who, as a photograph taken at the Finland Station shows,
carried his railway ticket tucked under the band of his hat),
repaired to Vyborg for an illegal session. In May 1908, he began a prison term of three months in somewhat belated punishment for the revolutionary manifesto he and his group had issued at Vyborg. "Did V. get any 'Egerias' [Speckled Woods]
this summer?" he asks in one of his secret notes from prison,
which, through a bribed guard, and a faithful friend (Kaminka), were transmitted to my mother at Vyra. "Tell him
that all I see in the prison yard are Brimstones and Cabbage
Whites." After his release he was forbidden to participate in
public elections, but (one of the paradoxes so common under
the Tsars) could freely work in the bitterly liberal *Rech*, a task
to which he devoted up to nine hours a day. In 1913, he was
fined by the government the token sum of one hundred rubles
(about as many dollars of the present time) for his reportage
from Kiev, where after a stormy trial Beylis was found innocent
of murdering a Christian boy for "ritual" purposes: justice and
public opinion could still prevail occasionally in old Russia;
they had only five years to go. He was mobilized soon after the

beginning of World War One and sent to the front. Eventually he was attached to the General Staff in St. Petersburg. Military ethics prevented him from taking an active part in the first turmoil of the liberal revolution of March 1917. From the very start, History seems to have been anxious of depriving him of a full opportunity to reveal his great gifts of statesmanship in a Russian republic of the Western type. In 1917, during the initial stage of the Provisional Government—that is, while the Kadets still took part in it—he occupied in the Council of Ministers the responsible but inconspicuous position of Executive Secretary. In the winter of 1917-1918, he was elected to the Constituent Assembly, only to be arrested by energetic Bolshevist sailors when it was disbanded. The November Revolution had already entered upon its gory course, its police was already active, but in those days the chaos of orders and counterorders sometimes took our side: my father followed a dim corridor, saw an open door at the end, walked out into a side street and made his way to the Crimea with a knapsack he had ordered his valet Osip to bring him to a secluded corner and a package of caviar sandwiches which good Nikolay Andreevich, our cook, had added of his own accord. From mid-1918 to the beginning of 1919, in an interval between two occupations by the Bolshevists, and in constant friction with trigger-happy elements in Denikin's army, he was Minister of Justice ("of minimal justice" as he used to say wryly) in one of the Regional Governments, the Crimean one. In 1919, he went into voluntary exile, living first in London, then in Berlin where, in collaboration with Hessen, he edited the liberal *émigré* daily *Rul'* ("Rudder") until his assassination in 1922 by a sinister ruffian whom, during World War Two, Hitler made administrator of *émigré* Russian affairs.

He wrote prolifically, mainly on political and criminological subjects. He knew *à fond* the prose and poetry of several countries, knew by heart hundreds of verses (his favorite Russian poets were Pushkin, Tyutchev, and Fet—he published a fine essay on the latter), was an authority on Dickens, and, besides Flaubert, prized highly Stendhal, Balzac and Zola, three de-testable mediocrities from *my* point of view. He used to confess that the creation of a story or poem, *any* story or poem, was to him as incomprehensible a miracle as the construction of an electric machine. On the other hand, he had no trouble at all in writing on juristic and political matters. He had a correct, albeit rather monotonous style, which today, despite all those old-world metaphors of classical education and grandiloquent clichés of Russian journalism has—at least to my jaded ear—an attractive gray dignity of its own, in extraordinary contrast (as if belonging to some older and poorer relative) to his color-ful, quaint, often poetical, and sometimes ribald, everyday ut-terances. The preserved drafts of some of his proclamations (beginning *"Grazhdane!"*, meaning *"Citoyens!"*) and editorials are penned in a copybook-slanted, beautifully sleek, unbeliev-ably regular hand, almost free of corrections, a purity, a cer-tainty, a mind-and-matter cofunction that I find amusing to compare to my own mousy hand and messy drafts, to the mas-sacrous revisions and rewritings, and new revisions, of the very lines in which I am taking two hours now to describe a two-minute run of his flawless handwriting. His drafts were the fair copies of immediate thought. In this manner, he wrote, with phenomenal ease and rapidity (sitting uncomfortably at a child's desk in the classroom of a mournful palace) the text of the abdication of Grand Duke Mihail (next in line of succes-sion after the Tsar had renounced his and his son's throne). No wonder he was also an admirable speaker, an "English style" cool orator, who eschewed the meat-chopping gesture and rhetorical bark of the demagogue, and here, too, the ridiculous cacologist I am, when not having a typed sheet before me, has inherited nothing.

Only recently have I read for the first time his important *Sbornik statey po ugolovnomu pravu* (a collection of articles on criminal law), published in 1904 in St. Petersburg, of which a very rare, possibly unique copy (formerly the property of a "Mihail Evgrafovich Hodunov," as stamped in violet ink on the flyleaf) was given me by a kind traveler, Andrew Field, who bought it in a secondhand bookshop, on his visit to Russia in 1961. It is a volume of 316 pages containing nineteen papers. In one of these ("Carnal Crimes," written in 1902), my father discusses, rather prophetically in a certain odd sense, cases (in London) "of little girls *à l'âge le plus tendre* (*v nezhneyshem vozraste*), i.e. from eight to twelve years, being sacrificed to lechers (*slastolyubtsam*)." In the same essay he reveals a very liberal and "modern" approach to various abnormal practices, incidentally coining a convenient Russian word for "homosexual": *ravnopolïy*.

It would be impossible to list the literally thousands of his articles in various periodicals, such as *Rech* or *Pravo*. In a later chapter I speak of his historically interesting book about a wartime semiofficial visit to England. Some of his memoirs pertaining to the years 1917-1919 have appeared in the *Arhiv russkoy revolyutsii,* published by Hessen in Berlin. On January 16, 1920, he delivered a lecture at King's College, London, on "Soviet Rule and Russia's Future," which was published a week later in the Supplement to *The New Commonwealth*, No. 15 (neatly pasted in my mother's album). In the spring of the same year I learned by heart most of it when preparing to speak against Bolshevism at a Union debate in Cambridge; the (victorious) apologist was a man from *The Manchester Guardian*; I forget his name, but recall drying up utterly after reciting what I had memorized, and that was my first and last political speech. A couple of months before my father's death, the *émigré* review *Teatr i zhizn'* ("Theater and Life") started to serialize his boyhood recollections (he and I are overlapping now—too briefly). I find therein excellently described the terrible tantrums of his pedantic master of Latin at the Third Gymnasium, as well as my father's very early, and lifelong, passion for the opera: he must have heard practically every first-rate European singer between 1880 and 1922, and although unable to play anything (except very majestically the first chords of the "Ruslan" overture) remembered every note of his favorite operas. Along this vibrant string a melodious gene that missed me glides through my father from the sixteenth-century organist Wolfgang Graun to my son.

4

Belonging, as he did by choice, to the great classless intelligentsia of Russia, my father thought it right to have me attend a school that was distinguished by its democratic principles, its policy of nondiscrimination in matters of rank, race and creed, and its up-to-date educational methods. Apart from that, Tenishev School differed in nothing from any other school in time or space. As in all schools, the boys tolerated some teachers and loathed others, and, as in all schools, there was a constant interchange of obscene quips and erotic information. Being good at games, I would not have found the whole business too dismal if only my teachers had been less intent in trying to save my soul.

They accused me of not conforming to my surroundings; of "showing off" (mainly by peppering my Russian papers with English and French terms, which came naturally to me); of refusing to touch the filthy wet towels in the washroom; of fighting with my knuckles instead of using the slaplike swing with the underside of the fist adopted by Russian scrappers. The headmaster who knew little about games, though greatly approving of their consociative virtues, was suspicious of my always keeping goal in soccer "instead of running about with the other players." Another thing that provoked resentment was my driving to and from school in an automobile and not traveling by streetcar or horsecab as the other boys, good little democrats, did. With his face all screwed up in a grimace of disgust, one teacher suggested to me that the least I could do was to have the automobile stop two or three blocks away, so that my schoolmates might be spared the sight of a liveried chauffeur doffing his cap. It was as if the school were allowing me to carry about a dead rat by the tail with the understanding that I would not dangle it under people's noses.

The worst situation, however, arose from the fact that even then I was intensely averse to joining movements or associations of any kind. I enraged the kindest and most well-meaning among my teachers by declining to participate in extracurricular group work—debating societies with the solemn election of officers and the reading of reports on historical questions, and, in the higher grades, more ambitious gatherings for the discussion of current political events. The constant pressure upon me to belong to some group or other never broke my resistance but led to a state of tension that was hardly alleviated by everybody harping upon the example set by my father.

My father was, indeed, a very active man, but as often happens with the children of famous fathers, I viewed his activities through a prism of my own, which split into many enchanting colors the rather austere light my teachers glimpsed. In connection with his varied interests—criminological, legislative, political, editorial, philanthropic—he had to attend many committee meetings, and these were often held at our house. That such a meeting was forthcoming might be always deduced from a peculiar sound in the far end of our large and resonant entrance hall. There, in a recess under the marble staircase, our *shveitsar* (doorman) would be busy sharpening pencils when I came home from school. For that purpose he used a bulky old-fashioned machine, with a whirring wheel, the handle of which he rapidly turned with one hand while holding with the other a pencil inserted into a lateral orifice. For years he had been the tritest type of "faithful retainer" imaginable, full of quaint wit and wisdom, with a dashing way of smoothing out, right and left, his mustache with two fingers, and a slight fried-fish smell always hanging about him: it originated in his mysterious basement quarters, where he had an obese wife and twins—a schoolboy of my age and a haunting, sloppy little aurora with a blue squint and coppery locks; but that pencil chore must have considerably embittered poor old Ustin— for I can readily sympathize with him, I who write my stuff only in very sharp pencil, keep bouquets of B 3's in vaselets around me, and rotate a hundred times a day the handle of the instrument (clamped to the table edge), which so speedily accumulates so much tawny-brown shag in its little drawer. It later turned out that he had long got into touch with the Tsar's secret police—tyros, of course, in comparison to Dzerzhinski's or Yagoda's men, but still fairly bothersome. As early as 1906, for instance, the police, suspecting my father of conducting clandestine meetings at Vyra, had engaged the services of Ustin who thereupon begged my father, under some pretext that I cannot recall, but with the deep purpose of spying on whatever went on, to take him to the country that summer as an extra footman (he had been pantry boy in the Rukavishnikov household); and it was he, omnipresent Ustin, who in the winter of 1917-1918 heroically led representatives of the victorious Soviets up to my father's study on the second floor, and from there, through a music room and my mother's boudoir, to the southeast corner room where I was born, and to the niche in the wall, to the tiaras of colored fire, which formed an adequate recompense for the Swallowtail he had once caught for me.

Around eight in the evening, the hall would house an accumulation of greatcoats and overshoes. In a committee room, next to the library, at a long baize-covered table (where those beautifully pointed pencils had been laid out), my father and his colleagues would gather to discuss some phase of their opposition to the Tsar. Above the hubbub of voices, a tall clock in a dark corner would break into Westminster chimes; and beyond the committee room were mysterious depths—storerooms, a winding staircase, a pantry of sorts—where my cousin

Yuri and I used to pause with drawn pistols on our way to Texas and where one night the police placed a fat, blear-eyed spy who went laboriously down on his knees before our librarian Lyudmila Borisovna Grinberg, when discovered. But how on earth could I discuss all this with schoolteachers?

5

The reactionary press never ceased to attack my father's party, and I had got quite used to the more or less vulgar cartoons which appeared from time to time—my father and Milyukov handing over Saint Russia on a plate to World Jewry and that sort of thing. But one day, in the winter of 1911 I believe, the most powerful of the Rightist newspapers employed a shady journalist to concoct a scurrilous piece containing insinuations that my father could not let pass. Since the well-known rascality of the actual author of the article made him "non-duelable" (*neduelesposobnïy,* as the Russian dueling code had it), my father called out the somewhat less disreputable editor of the paper in which the article had appeared.

A Russian duel was a much more serious affair than the conventional Parisian variety. It took the editor several days to make up his mind whether or not to accept the challenge. On the last of these days, a Monday, I went, as usual, to school. In consequence of my not reading the newspapers, I was absolutely ignorant of the whole thing. Sometime during the day I became aware that a magazine opened at a certain page was passing from hand to hand and causing titters. A well-timed swoop put me in possession of what proved to be the latest copy of a cheap weekly containing a lurid account of my father's challenge, with idiotic comments on the choice of weapons he had offered his foe. Sly digs were taken at his having reverted to a feudal custom that he had criticized in his own writings. There was also a good deal about the number of his servants and the number of his suits. I found out that he had chosen for second his brother-in-law, Admiral Kolomeytsev, a hero of the Japanese war. During the battle of Tsushima, this uncle of mine, then holding the rank of captain, had managed to bring his destroyer alongside the burning flagship and save the naval commander-in-chief.

After classes, I ascertained that the magazine belonged to one of my best friends. I charged him with betrayal and mockery. In the ensuing fight, he crashed backward into a desk, catching his foot in a joint and breaking his ankle. He was laid up for a month, but gallantly concealed from his family and from our teachers my share in the matter.

The pang of seeing him carried downstairs was lost in my general misery. For some reason or other, no car came to fetch me that day, and during the cold, dreary, incredibly slow drive home in a hired sleigh I had ample time to think matters over. Now I understood why, the day before, my mother had been so little with me and had not come down to dinner. I also understood what special coaching Thernant, a still finer *maître d'-armes* than Loustalot, had of late been giving my father. What would his adversary choose, I kept asking myself—the blade or the bullet? Or had the choice already been made? Carefully, I took the beloved, the familiar, the richly alive image of my father at fencing and tried to transfer that image, minus the mask and the padding, to the dueling ground, in some barn or riding school. I visualized him and his adversary, both bare-chested, black-trousered, in furious battle, their energetic movements marked by that strange awkwardness which even the most elegant swordsmen cannot avoid in a real encounter. The picture was so repulsive, so vividly did I feel the ripeness and nakedness of a madly pulsating heart about to be pierced, that I found myself hoping for what seemed momentarily a more abstract weapon. But soon I was in even deeper distress.

As the sleigh crept along Nevski Avenue, where blurry lights swam in the gathering dusk, I thought of the heavy black Browning my father kept in the upper right-hand drawer of his desk. I knew that pistol as well as I knew all the other, more salient, things in his study; the *objets d'art* of crystal or veined stone, fashionable in those days; the glinting family photographs; the huge, mellowly illumined Perugino; the small, honey-bright Dutch oils; and, right over the desk, the rose-and-haze pastel portrait of my mother by Bakst: the artist had drawn her face in three-quarter view, wonderfully bringing out its delicate features—the upward sweep of the ash-colored hair (it had grayed when she was in her twenties), the pure curve of the forehead, the dove-blue eyes, the graceful line of the neck.

When I urged the old, rag-doll-like driver to go faster, he would merely lean to one side with a special half-circular movement of his arm, so as to make his horse believe he was about to produce the short whip he kept in the leg of his right felt boot; and that would be sufficient for the shaggy little hack to make as vague a show of speeding up as the driver had made of getting out his *knutishko*. In the almost hallucinatory state that our snow-muffled ride engendered, I refought all the famous duels a Russian boy knew so well. I saw Pushkin, mortally wounded at the first fire, grimly sit up to discharge his pistol at d'Anthès. I saw Lermontov smile as he faced Martïnov. I saw stout Sobinov in the part of Lenski crash down and send his weapon flying into the orchestra. No Russian writer of any repute had failed to describe *une rencontre*, a hostile meeting, always of course of the classical *duel à volonté* type (not the ludicrous back-to back-march-face-about-bang-bang performance of movie and cartoon fame). Among several prominent families, there had been tragic deaths on the dueling ground in more or less recent years. Slowly my dreamy sleigh drove up Morskaya Street, and slowly dim silhouettes of duelists advanced upon each other and leveled their pistols and fired—at the crack of dawn, in damp glades of old country estates, on bleak military training grounds, or in the driving snow between two rows of fir trees.

And behind it all there was yet a very special emotional abyss that I was desperately trying to skirt, lest I burst into a tempest of tears, and this was the tender friendship underlying my respect for my father; the charm of our perfect accord; the Wimbledon matches we followed in the London papers; the chess problems we solved; the Pushkin iambics that rolled off his tongue so triumphantly whenever I mentioned some minor poet of the day. Our relationship was marked by that habitual exchange of homespun nonsense, comically garbled words, proposed imitations of supposed intonations, and all those private jokes which are the secret code of happy families. With all that he was extremely strict in matters of conduct and given to biting remarks when cross with a child or a servant, but his inherent humanity was too great to allow his rebuke to Osip for laying out the wrong shirt to be really offensive, just as a firsthand knowledge of a boy's pride tempered the harshness of reproval and resulted in sudden forgiveness. Thus I was more puzzled than pleased one day when upon learning that I had deliberately slashed my leg just above the knee with a razor (I still bear the scar) in order to avoid a recitation in class for which I was unprepared, he seemed unable to work up any real wrath; and his subsequent admission of a parallel transgression in his own boyhood rewarded me for not withholding the truth.

I remembered that summer afternoon (which already then seemed long ago although actually only four or five years had passed) when he had burst into my room, grabbed my net, shot down the veranda steps—and presently was strolling back holding between finger and thumb the rare and magnificent female of the Russian Poplar Admirable that he had seen basking on an aspen leaf from the balcony of his study. I remembered our long bicycle rides along the smooth Luga highway and the efficient way in which—mighty-calved, knickerbockered, tweed-coated, checker-capped—he would accomplish the mounting of his high-saddled "Dux," which his valet would bring up to the porch as if it were a palfrey. Surveying the state of its polish, my father would pull on his suede gloves and test under Osip's anxious eye whether the tires were sufficiently tight. Then he would grip the handlebars, place his left foot on a metallic peg jutting at the rear end of the frame, push off with his right foot on the other side of the hind wheel and after three or four such propelments (with the bicycle now set in motion), leisurely translate his right leg into pedal position, move up his left, and settle down on the saddle.

At last I was home, and immediately upon entering the vestibule I became aware of loud, cheerful voices. With the opportuneness of dream arrangements, my uncle the Admiral was coming downstairs. From the red-carpeted landing above, where an armless Greek woman of marble presided over a malachite bowl for visiting cards, my parents were still speaking to him, and as he came down the steps, he looked up with a laugh and slapped the balustrade with the gloves he had in his hand. I knew at once that there would be no duel, that the challenge had been met by an apology, that all was right. I brushed past my uncle and reached the landing. I saw my mother's serene everyday face, but I could not look at my father. And then it happened: my heart welled in me like that wave on which the *Buynïy* rose when her captain brought her alongside the burning *Suvorov*, and I had no handkerchief, and ten years were to pass before a certain night in 1922, at a public lecture in Berlin, when my father shielded the lecturer (his old friend Milyukov) from the bullets of two Russian Fascists and, while vigorously knocking down one of the assassins, was fatally shot by the other. But no shadow was cast by that future event upon the bright stairs of our St. Petersburg house; the large, cool hand resting on my head did not quaver, and several lines of play in a difficult chess composition were not blended yet on the board.

❦ *Chapter Eleven* ❦

I

In order to reconstruct the summer of 1914, when the numb fury of verse-making first came over me, all I really need is to visualize a certain pavilion. There the lank, fifteen-year-old lad I then was, sought shelter during a thunderstorm, of which there was an inordinate number that July. I dream of my pavilion at least twice a year. As a rule, it appears in my dreams quite independently of their subject matter, which, of course, may be anything, from abduction to zoolatry. It hangs around, so to speak, with the unobtrusiveness of an artist's signature. I find it clinging to a corner of the dream canvas or cunningly worked into some ornamental part of the picture. At times, however, it seems to be suspended in the middle distance, a trifle baroque, and yet in tune with the handsome trees, dark fir and bright birch, whose sap once ran through its timber. Wine-red and bottle-green and dark-blue lozenges of stained glass lend a chapel-like touch to the latticework of its casements. It is just as it was in my boyhood, a sturdy old wooden structure above a ferny ravine in the older, riverside part of our Vyra park. Just as it was, or perhaps a little more perfect. In the real thing some of the glass was missing, crumpled leaves had been swept in by the wind. The narrow little bridge that arched across the ghyll at its deepest part, with the pavilion rising midway like a coagulated rainbow, was as slippery after a rainy spell as if it had been coated with some dark and in a sense magic ointment. Etymologically, "pavilion" and "papilio" are closely related. Inside, there was nothing in the way of furniture except a folding table hinged rustily to the wall under the east window, through the two or three glassless or pale-glassed compartments of which, among the bloated blues and drunken reds, one could catch a glimpse of the river. On a floorboard at my feet a dead horsefly lay on its back near the brown remains of a birch ament. And the patches of disintegrating whitewash on the inside of the door had been used by various trespassers for such jottings as: "Dasha, Tamara and Lena have been here" or "Down with Austria!"

The storm passed quickly. The rain, which had been a mass of violently descending water wherein the trees writhed and rolled, was reduced all at once to oblique lines of silent gold breaking into short and long dashes against a background of subsiding vegetable agitation. Gulfs of voluptuous blue were expanding between great clouds—heap upon heap of pure white and purplish gray, *lepota* (Old Russian for "stately beauty"), moving myths, gouache and guano, among the curves of which one could distinguish a mammary allusion or the death mask of a poet.

The tennis court was a region of great lakes.

Beyond the park, above steaming fields, a rainbow slipped into view; the fields ended in the notched dark border of a remote fir wood; part of the rainbow went across it, and that section of the forest edge shimmered most magically through the pale green and pink of the iridescent veil drawn before it: a tenderness and a glory that made poor relatives of the rhomboidal, colored reflections which the return of the sun had brought forth on the pavilion floor.

A moment later my first poem began. What touched it off? I think I know. Without any wind blowing, the sheer weight of a raindrop, shining in parasitic luxury on a cordate leaf, caused its tip to dip, and what looked like a globule of quicksilver performed a sudden glissando down the center vein, and then, having shed its bright load, the relieved leaf unbent. Tip, leaf, dip, relief—the instant it all took to happen seemed to me not so much a fraction of time as a fissure in it, a missed heartbeat, which was refunded at once by a patter of rhymes: I say "patter" intentionally, for when a gust of wind did come, the trees would briskly start to drip all together in as crude an imitation of the recent downpour as the stanza I was already muttering resembled the shock of wonder I had experienced when for a moment heart and leaf had been one.

2

In the avid heat of the early afternoon, benches, bridges and boles (all things, in fact, save the tennis court) were drying with incredible rapidity, and soon little remained of my initial inspiration. Although the bright fissure had closed, I doggedly went on composing. My medium happened to be Russian but could have been just as well Ukrainian, or Basic English, or Volapük. The kind of poem I produced in those days was hardly anything more than a sign I made of being alive, of passing or having passed, or hoping to pass, through certain intense human emotions. It was a phenomenon of orientation rather than of art, thus comparable to stripes of paint on a roadside rock or to a pillared heap of stones marking a mountain trail.

But then, in a sense, all poetry is positional: to try to express one's position in regard to the universe embraced by consciousness, is an immemorial urge. The arms of consciousness reach out and grope, and the longer they are the better. Tentacles, not wings, are Apollo's natural members. Vivian Bloodmark, a philosophical friend of mine, in later years, used to say that while the scientist sees everything that happens in one point of space, the poet feels everything that happens in one point of time. Lost in thought, he taps his knee with his wandlike pencil, and at the same instant a car (New York license plate) passes along the road, a child bangs the screen door of a neighboring porch, an old man yawns in a misty Turkestan orchard, a granule of cinder-gray sand is rolled by the wind on Venus, a Docteur Jacques Hirsch in Grenoble puts on his reading glasses, and trillions of other such trifles occur—all forming an instantaneous and transparent organism of events, of which the poet (sitting in a lawn chair, at Ithaca, N.Y.) is the nucleus.

That summer I was still far too young to evolve any wealth of "cosmic synchronization" (to quote my philosopher again). But I did discover, at least, that a person hoping to become a poet must have the capacity of thinking of several things at a time. In the course of the languid rambles that accompanied the making of my first poem, I ran into the village schoolmaster, an ardent Socialist, a good man, intensely devoted to my father (I welcome this image again), always with a tight posy of wild flowers, always smiling, always perspiring. While politely discussing with him my father's sudden journey to town, I registered simultaneously and with equal clarity not only his wilting flowers, his flowing tie and the blackheads on the fleshy volutes of his nostrils, but also the dull little voice of a cuckoo coming from afar, and the flash of a Queen of Spain settling on the road, and the remembered impression of the pictures (enlarged agricultural pests and bearded Russian writers) in the well-aerated classrooms of the village school which I had once or twice visited; and—to continue a tabulation that hardly does justice to the ethereal simplicity of the whole process— the throb of some utterly irrelevant recollection (a pedometer I had lost) was released from a neighboring brain cell, and the savor of the grass stalk I was chewing mingled with the cuckoo's note and the fritillary's takeoff, and all the while I was richly, serenely aware of my own manifold awareness.

He beamed and he bowed (in the effusive manner of a Russian radical), and took a couple of steps backward, and turned, and jauntily went on his way, and I picked up the thread of my poem. During the short time I had been otherwise engaged, something seemed to have happened to such words as I had already strung together: they did not look quite as lustrous as they had before the interruption. Some suspicion crossed my mind that I might be dealing in dummies. Fortunately, this cold twinkle of critical perception did not last. The fervor I had been trying to render took over again and brought its medium back to an illusory life. The ranks of words I reviewed were again so glowing, with their puffed-out little chests and trim uniforms, that I put down to mere fancy the sagging I had noticed out of the corner of my eye.

3

Apart from credulous inexperience, a young Russian versificator had to cope with a special handicap. In contrast to the rich vocabulary of satirical or narrative verse, the Russian elegy suffered from a bad case of verbal anemia. Only in very expert hands could it be made to transcend its humble origin —the pallid poetry of eighteenth-century France. True, in my day a new school was in the act of ripping up the old rhythms, but it was still to the latter that the conservative beginner turned in search of a neutral instrument—possibly because he did not wish to be diverted from the simple expression of simple emotions by adventures in hazardous form. Form, however, got its revenge. The rather monotonous designs into which early nineteenth-century Russian poets had twisted the pliant elegy resulted in certain words, or types of words (such as the Russian equivalents of *fol amour* or *langoureux et rêvant*) being coupled again and again, and this later lyricists could not shake off for a whole century.

In an especially obsessive arrangement, peculiar to the iambic of four to six feet, a long, wriggly adjective would occupy the first four or five syllables of the last three feet of the line. A good tetrametric example would be *ter-pi hes-chis-len-ni-e mu-ki* (en-dure in-cal-cu-la-ble tor-ments). The young Russian poet was liable to slide with fatal ease into this alluring abyss of syllables, for the illustration of which I have chosen *beschislennïe* only because it translates well; the real favorites were such typical elegiac components as *zadumchivïe* (pensive), *utrachennïe* (lost), *muchitel'nïe* (anguished), and so forth, all accented on the second syllable. Despite its great length, a word of that kind had but a single accent of its own, and, consequently, the penultimate metrical stress of the line encountered a normally unstressed syllable (*nï* in the Russian example, "la" in the English one). This produced a pleasant scud, which, however, was much too familiar an effect to redeem banality of meaning.

An innocent beginner, I fell into all the traps laid by the singing epithet. Not that I did not struggle. In fact, I was working at my elegy very hard, taking endless trouble over every line, choosing and rejecting, rolling the words on my tongue with the glazed-eyed solemnity of a tea-taster, and still it would come, that atrocious betrayal. The frame impelled the picture, the husk shaped the pulp. The hackneyed order of words (short verb or pronoun—long adjective—short noun) engendered the hackneyed disorder of thought, and some such line as *poeta gorestnïe gryozï,* translatable and accented as "the poet's melancholy daydreams," led fatally to a rhyming line ending in *rozï* (roses) or *beryozï* (birches) or *grozï* (thunderstorms), so that certain emotions were connected with certain surroundings not by a free act of one's will but by the faded ribbon of tradition. Nonetheless, the nearer my poem got to its completion, the more certain I became that whatever I saw before me would be seen by others. As I focused my eyes upon a kidney-shaped flower bed (and noted one pink petal lying on the loam and a small ant investigating its decayed edge) or considered the tanned midriff of a birch trunk where some hoodlum had stripped it of its papery, pepper-and-salt bark, I really believed that all this would be perceived by the reader through the magic veil of my words such as *utrachennïe rozï* or *zadumchivoy beryozï.* It did not occur to me then that far from being a veil, those poor words were so opaque that, in fact, they formed a wall in which all one could distinguish were the well-worn bits of the major and minor poets I imitated. Years later, in the squalid suburb of a foreign town, I remember seeing a paling, the boards of which had been brought from some other place where they had been used, apparently, as the inclosure of an itinerant circus. Animals had been painted on it by a versatile barker; but whoever had removed the boards, and then knocked them together again, must have been blind or insane, for now the fence showed only disjointed parts of animals (some of them, moreover, upside down)—a tawny haunch, a zebra's head, the leg of an elephant.

4

On the physical plane, my intense labors were marked by a number of dim actions or postures, such as walking, sitting, lying. Each of these broke again into fragments of no spatial importance: at the walking stage, for instance, I might be wandering one moment in the depths of the park and the next pacing the rooms of the house. Or, to take the sitting stage, I would suddenly become aware that a plate of something I could not even remember having sampled was being removed and that my mother, her left cheek twitching as it did whenever she worried, was narrowly observing from her place at the top of the long table my moodiness and lack of appetite. I would lift my head to explain—but the table had gone, and I was sitting alone on a roadside stump, the stick of my butterfly net, in metronomic motion, drawing arc after arc on the brownish sand; earthen rainbows, with variations in depth of stroke rendering the different colors.

When I was irrevocably committed to finish my poem or die, there came the most trancelike state of all. With hardly a twinge of surprise, I found myself, of all places, on a leathern couch in the cold, musty, little-used room that had been my grandfather's study. On that couch I lay prone, in a kind of reptilian freeze, one arm dangling, so that my knuckles loosely touched the floral figures of the carpet. When next I came out of that trance, the greenish flora was still there, my arm was still dangling, but now I was prostrate on the edge of a rickety wharf, and the water lilies I touched were real, and the undulating plump shadows of alder foliage on the water—apotheosized inkblots, oversized amoebas—were rhythmically palpitating, extending and drawing in dark pseudopods, which, when contracted, would break at their rounded margins into elusive and fluid macules, and these would come together again to reshape the groping terminals. I relapsed into my private mist, and when I emerged again, the support of my extended body had become a low bench in the park, and the live shadows, among which my hand dipped, now moved on the ground, among violet tints instead of aqueous black and green. So little did ordinary measures of existence mean in that state that I would not have been surprised to come out of its tunnel right into the park of

Versailles, or the Tiergarten, or Sequoia National Forest; and, inversely, when the old trance occurs nowadays, I am quite prepared to find myself, when I awaken from it, high up in a certain tree, above the dappled bench of my boyhood, my belly pressed against a thick, comfortable branch and one arm hanging down among the leaves upon which the shadows of other leaves move.

Various sounds reached me in my various situations. It might be the dinner gong, or something less usual, such as the foul music of a barrel organ. Somewhere near the stables the old tramp would grind, and on the strength of more direct impressions imbibed in earlier years, I would see him mentally from my perch. Painted on the front of his instrument were Balkan peasants of sorts dancing among palmoid willows. Every now and then he shifted the crank from one hand to the other. I saw the jersey and skirt of his little bald female monkey, her collar, the raw sore on her neck, the chain which she kept plucking at every time the man pulled it, hurting her badly, and the several servants standing around, gaping, grinning—simple folks terribly tickled by a monkey's "antics." Only the other day, near the place where I am recording these matters, I came across a farmer and his son (the kind of keen healthy kid you see in breakfast food ads), who were similarly diverted by the sight of a young cat torturing a baby chipmunk—letting him run a few inches and then pouncing upon him again. Most of his tail was gone, the stump was bleeding. As he could not escape by running, the game little fellow tried one last measure: he stopped and lay down on his side in order to merge with a bit of light and shade on the ground, but the too violent heaving of his flank gave him away.

The family phonograph, which the advent of the evening set in action, was another musical machine I could hear through my verse. On the veranda where our relatives and friends assembled, it emitted from its brass mouthpiece the so-called *tsïganskie romansï* beloved of my generation. These were more or less anonymous imitations of gypsy songs—or imitations of such imitations. What constituted their gypsiness was a deep monotonous moan broken by a kind of hiccup, the audible cracking of a lovesick heart. At their best, they were responsible for the raucous note vibrating here and there in the works of true poets (I am thinking especially of Alexander Blok). At their worst, they could be likened to the apache stuff composed by mild men of letters and delivered by thickset ladies in Parisian night clubs. Their natural environment was characterized by nightingales in tears, lilacs in bloom and the alleys of whispering trees that graced the parks of the landed gentry. Those nightingales trilled, and in a pine grove the setting sun banded the trunks at different levels with fiery red. A tambourine, still throbbing, seemed to lie on the darkening moss. For a spell, the last notes of the husky contralto pursued me through the dusk. When silence returned, my first poem was ready.

5

It was indeed a miserable concoction, containing many borrowings besides its pseudo-Pushkinian modulations. An echo of Tyutchev's thunder and a refracted sunbeam from Fet were alone excusable. For the rest, I vaguely remember the mention of "memory's sting"—*vospominan'ya zhalo* (which I had really visualized as the ovipositor of an ichneumon fly straddling a cabbage caterpillar, but had not dared say so)—and something about the old-world charm of a distant barrel organ. Worst of all were the shameful gleanings from Apuhtin's and Grand Duke Konstantin's lyrics of the *tsïganski* type. They used to be persistently pressed upon me by a youngish and rather attractive aunt, who could also spout Louis Bouilhet's famous piece (*A Une Femme*), in which a metaphorical violin bow is incongruously used to play on a metaphorical guitar, and lots of stuff by Ella Wheeler Wilcox—a tremendous hit with the empress and her ladies-in-waiting. It seems hardly worthwhile to add that, as themes go, my elegy dealt with the loss of a beloved mistress—Delia, Tamara or Lenore—whom I had never lost, never loved, never met but was all set to meet, love, lose.

In my foolish innocence, I believed that what I had written was a beautiful and wonderful thing. As I carried it homeward, still unwritten, but so complete that even its punctuation marks were impressed on my brain like a pillow crease on a sleeper's flesh, I did not doubt that my mother would greet my achievement with glad tears of pride. The possibility of her being much too engrossed, that particular night, in other events to listen to verse did not enter my mind at all. Never in my life had I craved more for her praise. Never had I been more vulnerable. My nerves were on edge because of the darkness of the earth, which I had not noticed muffling itself up, and the nakedness of the firmament, the disrobing of which I had not noticed either. Overhead, between the formless trees bordering my dissolving path, the night sky was pale with stars. In those years, that marvelous mess of constellations, nebulae, interstellar gaps and all the rest of the awesome show provoked in me an indescribable sense of nausea, of utter panic, as if I were hanging from earth upside down on the brink of infinite space, with terrestrial gravity still holding me by the heels but about to release me any moment.

Except for two corner windows in the upper story (my mother's sitting room), the house was already dark. The night watchman let me in, and slowly, carefully, so as not to disturb the arrangement of words in my aching head, I mounted the stairs. My mother reclined on the sofa with the St. Petersburg *Rech* in her hands and an unopened London *Times* in her lap. A white telephone gleamed on the glass-topped table near her. Late as it was, she still kept expecting my father to call from St. Petersburg where he was being detained by the tension of approaching war. An armchair stood by the sofa, but I always avoided it because of its golden satin, the mere sight of which caused a laciniate shiver to branch from my spine like nocturnal lightning. With a little cough, I sat down on a footstool and started my recitation. While thus engaged, I kept staring at the farther wall upon which I see so clearly in retrospect some small daguerreotypes and silhouettes in oval frames, a Somov aquarelle (young birch trees, the half of a rainbow—everything very melting and moist), a splendid Versailles autumn by Alexandre Benois, and a crayon drawing my mother's mother had made in her girlhood—that park pavilion again with its pretty windows partly screened by linked branches. The Somov and the Benois are now in some Soviet Museum but that pavilion will never be nationalized.

As my memory hesitated for a moment on the threshold of the last stanza, where so many opening words had been tried that the finally selected one was now somewhat camouflaged by an array of false entrances, I heard my mother sniff. Presently I finished reciting and looked up at her. She was smiling ecstatically through the tears that streamed down her face. "How wonderful, how beautiful," she said, and with the tenderness in her smile still growing, she passed me a hand mirror so that I might see the smear of blood on my cheekbone where at some indeterminable time I had crushed a gorged mosquito by the unconscious act of propping my cheek on my fist. But I saw more than that. Looking into my own eyes, I had the shocking sensation of finding the mere dregs of my usual self, odds and ends of an evaporated identity which it took my reason quite an effort to gather again in the glass.

❧ *From Chapter Fifteen* ❧

I

The spiral is a spiritualized circle. In the spiral form, the circle, uncoiled, unwound, has ceased to be vicious; it has been set free. I thought this up when I was a schoolboy, and I also discovered that Hegel's triadic series (so popular in old Russia) expressed merely the essential spirality of all things in their relation to time. Twirl follows twirl, and every synthesis is the thesis of the next series. If we consider the simplest spiral, three stages may be distinguished in it, corresponding to those of the triad: We can call "thetic" the small curve or arc that initiates the convolution centrally; "antithetic" the larger arc that faces the first in the process of continuing it; and "synthetic" the still ampler arc that continues the second while following the first along the outer side. And so on.

A colored spiral in a small ball of glass, this is how I see my own life. The twenty years I spent in my native Russia (1899-1919) take care of the thetic arc. Twenty-one years of voluntary exile in England, Germany and France (1919-1940) supply the obvious antithesis. The period spent in my adopted country (1940-1960) forms a synthesis—and a new thesis. For the moment I am concerned with my antithetic stage, and more particularly with my life in Continental Europe after I had graduated from Cambridge in 1922.

As I look back at those years of exile, I see myself, and thousands of other Russians, leading an odd but by no means unpleasant existence, in material indigence and intellectual luxury, among perfectly unimportant strangers, spectral Germans and Frenchmen in whose more or less illusory cities we, émigrés, happened to dwell. These aborigines were to the mind's eye as flat and transparent as figures cut out of cellophane, and although we used their gadgets, applauded their clowns, picked their roadside plums and apples, no real communication, of the rich human sort so widespread in our own midst, existed between us and them. It seemed at times that we ignored them the way an arrogant or very stupid invader ignores a formless and faceless mass of natives; but occasionally, quite often in fact, the spectral world through which we serenely paraded our sores and our arts would produce a kind of awful convulsion and show us who was the discarnate captive and who the true lord. Our utter physical dependence on this or that nation, which had coldly granted us political refuge, became painfully evident when some trashy "visa," some diabolical "identity card" had to be obtained or prolonged, for then an avid bureaucratic hell would attempt to close upon the petitioner and he might wilt while his dossier waxed fatter and fatter in the desks of rat-whiskered consuls and policemen. *Dokumentï*, it has been said, is a Russian's placenta. The League of Nations equipped *émigrés* who had lost their Russian citizenship with a so-called "Nansen" passport, a very inferior document of a sickly green hue. Its holder was little better than a criminal on parole and had to go through most hideous ordeals every time he wished to travel from one country to another, and the smaller the countries the worse the fuss they made. Somewhere at the back of their glands, the authorities secreted the notion that no matter how bad a state—say, Soviet Russia—might be, any fugitive from it was intrinsically despicable since he existed outside a national administration; and therefore he was viewed with the preposterous disapproval with which certain religious groups regard a child born out of wedlock. Not all of us consented to be bastards and ghosts. Sweet are the recollections some Russian *émigrés* treasure of how they insulted or fooled high officials at various ministries, *Préfectures* and *Polizeipraesidiums*.

In Berlin and Paris, the two capitals of exile, Russians formed compact colonies, with a coefficient of culture that greatly surpassed the cultural mean of the necessarily more diluted foreign communities among which they were placed. Within those colonies they kept to themselves. I have in view, of course, Russian intellectuals, mostly belonging to democratic groups, and not the flashier kind of person who "was, you know, adviser to the Tsar or something" that American clubwomen immediately think of whenever "White Russians" are mentioned. Life in those settlements was so full and intense that these Russian *"intelligentï"* (a word that had more socially idealistic and less highbrow connotations than "intellectuals" as used in America) had neither time nor reason to seek ties beyond their own circle. Today, in a new and beloved world, where I have learned to feel at home as easily as I have ceased barring my sevens, extroverts and cosmopolitans to whom I happen to mention these past matters think I am jesting, or accuse me of snobbery in reverse, when I maintain that in the course of almost one-fifth of a century spent in Western Europe I have not had, among the sprinkling of Germans and Frenchmen I knew (mostly landladies and literary people), more than two good friends all told.

Somehow, during my secluded years in Germany, I never came across those gentle musicians of yore who, in Turgenev's novels, played their rhapsodies far into the summer night; or those happy old hunters with their captures pinned to the crown of their hats, of whom the Age of Reason made such fun: La Bruyère's gentleman who sheds tears over a parasitized caterpillar, Gay's "philosophers more grave than wise" who, if you please, "hunt science down in butterflies," and, less insultingly, Pope's "curious Germans," who "hold so rare" those "insects fair"; or simply the so-called wholesome and kindly folks that during the last war homesick soldiers from the Middle West seem to have preferred so much to the cagey French farmer and to brisk Madelon II. On the contrary, the most vivid figure I find when sorting out in memory the meager stack of my non-Russian and non-Jewish acquaintances in the years between the two wars is the image of a young German university student, well-bred, quiet, bespectacled, whose hobby was capital punishment. At our second meeting he showed me a collection of photographs among which was a purchased series (*"Ein bischen retouchiert,"* he said wrinkling his freckled nose) that depicted the successive stages of a routine execution in China; he commented, very expertly, on the splendor of the lethal sword and on the spirit of perfect cooperation between headsman and victim, which culminated in a veritable geyser of mist-gray blood spouting from the very clearly photographed neck of the decapitated party. Being pretty well off, this young collector could afford to travel, and travel he did, in between the humanities he studied for his Ph.D. He complained, however, of continuous ill luck and added that if he did not see something really good soon, he might not stand the strain. He had attended a few passable hangings in the Balkans and a well-advertised, although rather bleak and mechanical *guillotinade* (he liked to use what he thought was colloquial French) on the Boulevard Arago in Paris; but somehow he never was sufficiently close to observe everything in detail, and the highly expensive teeny-weeny camera in the sleeve of his raincoat did not work as well as he had hoped. Despite a bad cold, he had journeyed to Regensburg where beheading was violently performed with an ax; he had expected great things from that spectacle but, to his intense disappointment, the subject had apparently been drugged and had hardly reacted at all, beyond feebly flopping about on the ground while the masked executioner and his clumsy mate fell all over him. Dietrich (my acquaintance's first name) hoped some day to go to the States so as to witness a couple of electrocutions; from this word, in his innocence, he derived the adjective "cute," which he had learned from a cousin of his who had been to America, and with a little frown of wistful worry Dietrich wondered if it were really true that, during the performance, sensational puffs of smoke issued from the natural orifices of the body. At our third and last encounter (there still remained bits of him I wanted to file for possible use) he related to me, more in sorrow than in anger, that he had once spent a whole night patiently watching a good friend of his who had decided to shoot himself and had agreed to do so, in the roof of the mouth, facing the hobbyist in a good light, but having no ambition or sense of honor, had got hopelessly tight instead. Although I have lost track of Dietrich long ago, I can well imagine the look of calm satisfaction in his fish-blue eyes as he shows, now-adays (perhaps at the very minute I am writing this), a never-expected profusion of treasures to his thigh-clapping, guffaw-ing co-veterans—the absolutely *wunderbar* pictures he took during Hitler's reign.

2

———

I have sufficiently spoken of the gloom and the glory of exile in my Russian novels, and especially in the best of them, *Dar* (recently published in English as *The Gift*); but a quick re-capitulation here may be convenient. With a very few excep-tions, all liberal-minded creative forces—poets, novelists, crit-ics, historians, philosophers and so on—had left Lenin's and Stalin's Russia. Those who had not were either withering away there or adulterating their gifts by complying with the political demands of the state. What the Tsars had never been able to achieve, namely the complete curbing of minds to the govern-ment's will, was achieved by the Bolsheviks in no time after the main contingent of the intellectuals had escaped abroad or had been destroyed. The lucky group of expatriates could now follow their pursuits with such utter impunity that, in fact, they sometimes asked themselves if the sense of enjoying absolute mental freedom was not due to their working in an absolute void. True, there was among *émigrés* a sufficient number of good readers to warrant the publication, in Berlin, Paris, and other towns, of Russian books and periodicals on a compara-tively large scale; but since none of those writings could circulate within the Soviet Union, the whole thing acquired a certain air of fragile unreality. The number of titles was more impressive than the number of copies any given work sold, and the names of the publishing houses—Orion, Cosmos, Logos, and so forth —had the hectic, unstable and slightly illegal appearance that firms issuing astrological or facts-of-life literature have. In serene retrospect, however, and judged by artistic and scholarly standards alone, the books produced *in vacuo* by *émigré* writers seem today, whatever their individual faults, more permanent and more suitable for human consumption than the slavish, singularly provincial and conventional streams of political consciousness that came during those same years from the pens of young Soviet authors whom a fatherly state provided with ink, pipes and pullovers.

The editor of the daily *Rul'* (and the publisher of my first books), Iosif Vladimirovich Hessen, allowed me with great leniency to fill his poetry section with my unripe rhymes. Blue evenings in Berlin, the corner chestnut in flower, light-headedness, poverty, love, the tangerine tinge of premature shoplights, and an animal aching yearn for the still fresh reek of Russia— all this was put into meter, copied out in longhand and carted off to the editor's office, where myopic I. V. would bring the new poem close to his face and after this brief, more or less tactual, act of cognition put it down on his desk. By 1928, my novels were beginning to bring a little money in German translations, and in the spring of 1929, you and I went butterfly hunting in the Pyrenees. But only at the end of the nineteen-thirties did we leave Berlin for good, although long before that I used to take trips to Paris for public readings of my stuff.

Quite a feature of *émigré* life, in keeping with its itinerant and dramatic character, was the abnormal frequency of those literary readings in private houses or hired halls. The various types of performers stand out very distinctly in the puppet show going on in my mind. There was the faded actress, with eyes like precious stones, who having pressed for a moment a clenched handkerchief to a feverish mouth, proceeded to evoke nostalgic echoes of the Moscow Art Theatre by subjecting some famous piece of verse to the action, half dissection and half caress, of her slow limpid voice. There was the hopelessly second-rate author whose voice trudged through a fog of rhythmic prose, and one could watch the nervous trembling of his poor, clumsy but careful fingers every time he tucked the page he had finished under those to come, so that his manuscript retained throughout the reading its appalling and pitiful thickness. There was the young poet in whom his envious brethren could not help seeing a disturbing streak of genius as striking as the stripe of a skunk; erect on the stage, pale and glazed-eyed, with nothing in his hands to anchor him to this world, he would throw back his head and deliver his poem in a highly irritating, rolling chant and stop abruptly at the end, slamming the door of the last line and waiting for applause to fill the hush. And there was the old *cher maître* dropping pearl by pearl an admirable tale he had read innumerable times, and always in the same manner, wearing the expression of fastidious distaste that his nobly furrowed face had in the frontispiece of his collected works.

I suppose it would be easy for a detached observer to poke fun at all those hardly palpable people who imitated in foreign cities a dead civilization, the remote, almost legendary, almost Sumerian mirages of St. Petersburg and Moscow, 1900-1916 (which, even then, in the twenties and thirties, sounded like 1916-1900 B.C.). But at least they were rebels as most major Russian writers had been ever since Russian literature had existed, and true to this insurgent condition which their sense of justice and liberty craved for as strongly as it had done under the oppression of the Tsars, *émigrés* regarded as monstrously un-Russian and subhuman the behavior of pampered authors in the Soviet Union, the servile response on the part of those authors to every shade of every governmental decree; for the art of prostration was growing there in exact ratio to the increasing efficiency of first Lenin's, then Stalin's political police, and the successful Soviet writer was the one whose fine ear caught the soft whisper of an official suggestion long before it had become a blare.

Owing to the limited circulation of their works abroad, even the older generation of *émigré* writers, whose fame had been solidly established in pre-Revolution Russia, could not hope

that their books would make a living for them. Writing a weekly
column for an *émigré* paper was never quite sufficient to keep
body and pen together. Now and then translations into other
languages brought in an unexpected scoop; but, otherwise,
grants from various *émigré* organizations, earnings from public
readings and lavish private charity were responsible for prolonging elderly authors' lives. Younger, less known but more
adaptable writers supplemented chance subsidies by engaging
in various jobs. I remember teaching English and tennis. Patiently I thwarted the persistent knack Berlin businessmen had
of pronouncing "business" so as to rhyme with "dizziness"; and
like a slick automaton, under the slow-moving clouds of a long
summer day, on dusty courts, I ladled ball after ball over the
net to their tanned, bob-haired daughters. I got five dollars
(quite a sum during the inflation in Germany) for my Russian
Alice in Wonderland. I helped compile a Russian grammar
for foreigners in which the first exercise began with the words
Madam, ya doktor, vot banan (Madam, I am the doctor, here
is a banana). Best of all, I used to compose for a daily *émigré*
paper, the Berlin *Rul'*, the first Russian crossword puzzles, which
I baptized *krestoslovitsï*. I find it strange to recall that freak
existence. Deeply beloved of blurbists is the list of more or less
earthy professions that a young author (writing about Life and
Ideas—which are so much more important, of course, than
mere "art") has followed: newspaper boy, soda jerk, monk,
wrestler, foreman in a steel mill, bus driver and so on. Alas,
none of these callings has been mine.

My passion for good writing put me in close contact with various Russian authors abroad. I was young in those days
and much more keenly interested in literature than I am now.
Current prose and poetry, brilliant planets and pale galaxies,
flowed by the casement of my garret night after night. There
were independent authors of diverse age and talent, and there
were groupings and cliques within which a number of young
or youngish writers, some of them very gifted, clustered around

a philosophizing critic. The most important of these mystagogues combined intellectual talent and moral mediocrity, an
uncanny sureness of taste in modern Russian poetry and a
patchy knowledge of Russian classics. His group believed that
neither a mere negation of Bolshevism nor the routine ideals
of Western democracies were sufficient to build a philosophy
upon which *émigré* literature could lean. They thirsted for a
creed as a jailed drug addict thirsts for his pet heaven. Rather
pathetically, they envied Parisian Catholic groups for the sea-
soned subtleties that Russian mysticism so obviously lacked.
Dostoevskian drisk could not compete with neo-Thomist
thought; but were there not other ways? The longing for a
system of faith, a constant teetering on the brink of some accepted religion was found to provide a special satisfaction of
its own. Only much later, in the forties, did some of those writers finally discover a definite slope down which to slide in a
more or less genuflectory attitude. This slope was the enthusiastic nationalism that could call a state (Stalin's Russia, in this
case) good and lovable for no other reason than because its
army had won a war. In the early thirties, however, the nation-
alistic precipice was only faintly perceived and the mystagogues
were still enjoying the thrills of slippery suspension. In their
attitude toward literature they were curiously conservative;
with them soul-saving came first, logrolling next, and art last.
A retrospective glance nowadays notes the surprising fact of
these free belles-lettrists abroad aping fettered thought at home
by decreeing that to be a representative of a group or an epoch
was more important than to be an individual writer.

Vladislav Hodasevich used to complain, in the twenties and
thirties, that young *émigré* poets had borrowed their art from
from him while following the leading cliques in modish *angoisse*
and soul-reshaping. I developed a great liking for this bitter
man, wrought of irony and metallic-like genius, whose poetry
was as complex a marvel as that of Tyutchev or Blok. He was,
physically, of a sickly aspect, with contemptuous nostrils and

beetling brows, and when I conjure him up in my mind he never rises from the hard chair on which he sits, his thin legs crossed, his eyes glittering with malevolence and wit, his long fingers screwing into a holder the half of a *Caporal Vert* cigarette. There are few things in modern world poetry comparable to the poems of his *Heavy Lyre,* but unfortunately for his fame the perfect frankness he indulged in when voicing his dislikes made him some terrible enemies among the most powerful critical coteries. Not all the mystagogues were Dostoevskian Alyoshas; there were also a few Smerdyakovs in the group, and Hodasevich's poetry was played down with the thoroughness of a revengeful racket.

Another independent writer was Ivan Bunin. I had always preferred his little-known verse to his celebrated prose (their interrelation, within the frame of his work, recalls Hardy's case). At the time I found him tremendously perturbed by the personal problem of aging. The first thing he said to me was to remark with satisfaction that his posture was better than mine, despite his being some thirty years older than I. He was basking in the Nobel prize he had just received and invited me to some kind of expensive and fashionable eating place in Paris for a heart-to-heart talk. Unfortunately I happen to have a morbid dislike for restaurants and cafés, especially Parisian ones—I detest crowds, harried waiters, Bohemians, vermouth concoctions, coffee, *zakuski,* floor shows and so forth. I like to eat and drink in a recumbent position (preferably on a couch) and in silence. Heart-to-heart talks, confessions in the Dostoevskian manner, are also not in my line. Bunin, a spry old gentleman, with a rich and unchaste vocabulary, was puzzled by my irresponsiveness to the hazel grouse of which I had had enough in my childhood and exasperated by my refusal to discuss eschatological matters. Toward the end of the meal we were utterly bored with each other. "You will die in dreadful pain and complete isolation," remarked Bunin bitterly as we went toward the cloakroom. An attractive, frail-looking girl took the check for our heavy overcoats and presently fell with them in her embrace upon the low counter. I wanted to help Bunin into his raglan but he stopped me with a proud gesture of his open hand. Still struggling perfunctorily—*he* was now trying to help *me* —we emerged into the pallid bleakness of a Paris winter day. My companion was about to button his collar when a look of surprise and distress twisted his handsome features. Gingerly opening his overcoat, he began tugging at something under his armpit. I came to his assistance and together we finally dragged out of his sleeve my long woolen scarf which the girl had stuffed into the wrong coat. The thing came out inch by inch; it was like unwrapping a mummy and we kept slowly revolving around each other in the process, to the ribald amusement of three sidewalk whores. Then, when the operation was over, we walked on without a word to a street corner where we shook hands and separated. Subsequently we used to meet quite often, but always in the midst of other people, generally in the house of I. I. Fondaminski (a saintly and heroic soul who did more for Russian *émigré* literature than any other man and who died in a German prison). Somehow Bunin and I adopted a bantering and rather depressing mode of conversation, a Russian variety of American "kidding," and this precluded any real commerce between us.

I met many other *émigré* Russian authors. I did not meet Poplavski who died young, a far violin among near balalaikas.

Go to sleep, O Morella, how awful are aquiline lives

His plangent tonalities I shall never forget, nor shall I ever forgive myself the ill-tempered review in which I attacked him for trivial faults in his unfledged verse. I met wise, prim, charming Aldanov; decrepit Kuprin, carefully carrying a bottle of *vin ordinaire* through rainy streets; Ayhenvald—a Russian version of Walter Pater—later killed by a trolleycar; Marina Tsvetaev, wife of a double agent, and poet of genius, who, in the late thirties, returned to Russia and perished there. But the author that interested me most was naturally Sirin. He belonged to my generation. Among the young writers produced in exile he was the loneliest and most arrogant one. Beginning with the appearance of his first novel in 1925 and throughout the next fifteen years, until he vanished as strangely as he had come, his work kept provoking an acute and rather morbid interest on the part of critics. Just as Marxist publicists of the eighties in old Russia would have denounced his lack of concern with the economic structure of society, so the mystagogues of *émigré* letters deplored his lack of religious insight and of moral preoccupation. Everything about him was bound to offend Russian conventions and especially that Russian sense of decorum which, for example, an American offends so dangerously today, when in the presence of Soviet military men of distinction he happens to lounge with both hands in his trouser pockets. Conversely, Sirin's admirers made much, perhaps too much, of his unusual style, brilliant precision, functional imagery and that sort of thing. Russian readers who had been raised on the sturdy straightforwardness of Russian realism and had called the bluff of decadent cheats, were impressed by the mirror-like angles of his clear but weirdly misleading sentences and by the fact that the real life of his books flowed in his figures of speech, which one critic has compared to "windows giving upon a contiguous world . . . a rolling corollary, the shadow of a train of thought." Across the dark sky of exile, Sirin passed, to use a simile of a more conservative nature, like a meteor, and disappeared, leaving nothing much else behind him than a vague sense of uneasiness.

From Chapter Fourteen

I

They are passing, posthaste, posthaste, the gliding years—to use a soul-rending Horatian inflection. The years are passing, my dear, and presently nobody will know what you and I know. Our child is growing; the roses of Paestum, of misty Paestum, are gone; mechanically minded idiots are tinkering and tampering with forces of nature that mild mathematicians, to their own secret surprise, appear to have foreshadowed; so perhaps it is time we examined ancient snapshots, cave drawings of trains and planes, strata of toys in the lumbered closet.

We shall go still further back, to a morning in May 1934, and plot with respect to this fixed point the graph of a section of Berlin. There I was walking home, at 5 A.M., from the maternity hospital near Bayerischer Platz, to which I had taken you a couple of hours earlier. Spring flowers adorned the portraits of Hindenburg and Hitler in the window of a shop that sold frames and colored photographs. Leftist groups of sparrows were holding loud morning sessions in lilacs and limes. A limpid dawn had completely unsheathed one side of the empty street. On the other side, the houses still looked blue with cold, and various long shadows were gradually being telescoped, in the matter-of-fact manner young day has when taking over from night in a well-groomed, well-watered city, where the tang of tarred pavements underlies the sappy smells of shade trees; but to me the optical part of the business seemed quite new, like some unusual way of laying the table, because I had never seen that particular street at daybreak before, although, on the other hand, I had often passed there, childless, on sunny evenings.

In the purity and vacuity of the less familiar hour, the shadows were on the wrong side of the street, investing it with a sense of not inelegant inversion, as when one sees reflected in the mirror of a barbershop the window toward which the melancholy barber, while stropping his razor, turns his gaze (as they all do at such times), and, framed in that reflected window, a stretch of sidewalk shunting a procession of unconcerned pedestrians in the wrong direction, into an abstract world that all at once stops being droll and loosens a torrent of terror.

Whenever I start thinking of my love for a person, I am in the habit of immediately drawing radii from my love—from my heart, from the tender nucleus of a personal matter—to monstrously remote points of the universe. Something impels me to measure the consciousness of my love against such unimaginable and incalculable things as the behavior of nebulae (whose very remoteness seems a form of insanity), the dreadful pitfalls of eternity, the unknowledgeable beyond the unknown, the helplessness, the cold, the sickening involutions and interpenetrations of space and time. It is a pernicious habit, but I can do nothing about it. It can be compared to the uncontrollable flick of an insomniac's tongue checking a jagged tooth in the night of his mouth and bruising itself in doing so but still persevering. I have known people who, upon accidentally touching something—a doorpost, a wall—had to go through a certain very rapid and systematic sequence of manual contacts with various surfaces in the room before returning to a balanced existence. It cannot be helped; I must know where I stand, where you and my son stand. When that slow-motion, silent explosion of love takes place in me, unfolding its melting fringes and overwhelming me with the sense of something much vaster, much more enduring and powerful than the accumulation of matter or energy in any imaginable cosmos, then my mind cannot but pinch itself to see if it is really awake. I have to make a rapid inventory of the universe, just as a man in a dream tries to condone the absurdity of his position by making sure he is dreaming. I have to have all space and all time participate in my emotion, in my mortal love, so that the edge of its mortality is taken off, thus helping me to fight the utter degradation, ridicule, and horror of having developed an infinity of sensation and thought within a finite existence.

Since, in my metaphysics, I am a confirmed non-unionist and have no use for organized tours through anthropomorphic paradises, I am left to my own, not negligible devices when I think of the best things in life; when, as now, I look back upon my almost couvade-like concern with our baby. You remember the discoveries we made (supposedly made by all parents):

the perfect shape of the miniature fingernails of the hand you silently showed me as it lay, stranded starfish-wise, on your palm; the epidermic texture of limb and cheek, to which attention was drawn in dimmed, faraway tones, as if the softness of touch could be rendered only by the softness of distance; that swimming, sloping, elusive something about the dark-bluish tint of the iris which seemed still to retain the shadows it had absorbed of ancient, fabulous forests where there were more birds than tigers and more fruit than thorns, and where, in some dappled depth, man's mind had been born; and, above all, an infant's first journey into the next dimension, the newly established nexus between eye and reachable object, which the career boys in biometrics or in the rat-maze racket think they can explain. It occurs to me that the closest reproduction of the mind's birth obtainable is the stab of wonder that accompanies the precise moment when, gazing at a tangle of twigs and leaves, one suddenly realizes that what had seemed a natural component of that tangle is a marvelously disguised insect or bird.

There is also keen pleasure (and, after all, what else should the pursuit of science produce?) in meeting the riddle of the initial blossoming of man's mind by postulating a voluptuous pause in the growth of the rest of nature, a lolling and loafing which allowed first of all the formation of *Homo poeticus*— without which *sapiens* could not have been evolved. "Struggle for life" indeed! The curse of battle and toil leads man back to the boar, to the grunting beast's crazy obsession with the search for food. You and I have frequently remarked upon that maniacal glint in a housewife's scheming eye as it roves over food in a grocery or about the morgue of a butcher's shop. Toilers of the world, disband! Old books are wrong. The world was made on a Sunday.

ELEVEN STORIES

Terra Incognita

❧❧❧❧❧

The sound of the waterfall grew more and more muffled, until it finally dissolved altogether, and we moved through the wildwood of a hitherto unexplored region. We walked, and had been walking, for a long time already—in front, Gregson and I; our eight native porters behind, one after the other; last of all, whining and protesting at every step, came Cook. I knew that Gregson had recruited him on the advice of a local hunter. Cook had insisted that he was ready to do anything to get out of Zonraki, where they pass half the year brewing their *"vongho"* and the other half drinking it. It remained unclear, however— or else I was already beginning to forget many things, as we walked on and on—exactly who this Cook was. (A runaway sailor, perhaps?)

Gregson strode on beside me, sinewy, lanky, with bare, bony knees. He held a long-handled green butterfly net like a banner. The porters, big, glossy-brown Badonians with thick manes of hair and cobalt arabesques between their eyes, whom we had also engaged in Zonraki, walked with a springy, even step. Behind them straggled Cook, bloated, red-haired, with a drooping underlip, hands in pockets and carrying nothing. I recalled vaguely that at the outset of the expedition he had chattered a lot and made obscure jokes, in that manner of his that was a mixture of insolence and servility, reminiscent of a Shakespearean clown; but soon his spirits fell and he grew glum and began to neglect his duties, which included interpreting, since Gregson's understanding of the Badonian dialect was still poor.

There was still something languorous and velvety about the heat. A stifling fragrance came from the inflorescences of *Vallieria mirifica,* mother-of-pearl in color and resembling clusters of soap bubbles, that arched across the narrow, dry stream bed along which we proceeded with rustling step. The branches of the porphyroferous trees intertwined with those of the black-leafed limia to form a tunnel, penetrated here and there by a ray of hazy light. Above, in the thick mass of vegetation, among brilliant pendulous racemes and strange dark tangles of some kind, hoary monkeys snapped and chattered, while a cometlike bird flashed like Bengal light, crying out in its small, shrill voice. I kept telling myself that my head was heavy from the long march, the heat, the medley of colors, and the forest din, but secretly I knew that I was ill, and surmised that it was the local fever. I had resolved, however, to conceal my condition from Gregson, and had assumed a cheerful, even merry air, when disaster struck.

"It's my fault," said Gregson. "I should never have got involved with him."

We were now alone. Cook and all eight of the natives, with tent, folding boat, supplies, and collections, had deserted us and vanished noiselessly while we busied ourselves in the thick bush, collecting fascinating insects. I think we tried to catch up with the fugitives: I do not recall clearly, but in any case, we failed. We had to decide whether to return to Zonraki or continue our projected itinerary, across as yet unknown country, toward the Gurano Hills. The unknown won out. We moved on. I was already shivering all over and deafened by quinine, but still went on collecting nameless plants, while Gregson, though fully realizing the danger of our situation, continued catching butterflies and Diptera as avidly as ever.

We had scarcely walked half a mile when suddenly Cook

overtook us. His shirt was torn—apparently by himself, deliberately—and he was panting and gasping. Without a word Gregson drew his revolver and prepared to shoot the scoundrel, but Cook threw himself at Gregson's feet and, shielding his head with both arms, began to swear that the natives had led him away by force and had wanted to eat him (which was a lie, for the Badonians are not cannibals). I suspect that he had easily incited them, stupid and timorous as they were, to abandon the dubious journey, but had not taken into account that he could not keep up with their powerful stride, and, having fallen hopelessly behind, had returned to us. Because of him invaluable collections were lost. He had to die. But Gregson put away the revolver and we moved on, with Cook wheezing and stumbling behind.

The woods were gradually thinning. I was tormented by strange hallucinations. I gazed at the weird tree trunks, around some of which were coiled thick, flesh-colored snakes; suddenly I thought I saw, between the trunks, as though through my fingers, the mirror of a half-open wardrobe with lazy reflections, but then I took hold of myself, looked more carefully, and found that it was only the deceptive glimmer of an acreana bush (a curly plant with large berries resembling plump prunes). After a while the trees parted altogether and the sky rose before us like a solid wall of blue. We were at the top of a steep incline. Below shimmered and steamed an enormous marsh, and far beyond was visible the trembling silhouette of a mauve-colored range of hills.

"I swear to God we must turn back," said Cook in a sobbing voice. "I swear to God we'll perish in these swamps—I've got seven daughters and a dog at home. Let's turn back—we know the way. . . ." He wrung his hands, and the sweat rolled from his fat, red-browed face. "Home, home," he kept repeating. "You've caught enough bugs. Let's go home."

Gregson and I began to descend the stony slope. At first Cook remained standing above, a small white figure against the monstrously green background of forest; but suddenly he threw up his hands, uttered a cry, and started to slither down after us.

The slope narrowed, forming a rocky crest that reached out like a long promontory into the marshes; they sparkled through the steamy haze. The noonday sky, now freed of its leafy veils, hung oppressively over us with its blinding darkness—yes, its blinding darkness, for there is no other way to describe it. I tried not to look up; but in this sky, at the very verge of my field of vision, there floated, always keeping up with me, whitish phantoms of plaster, stucco curlicues and rosettes, like those used to adorn European ceilings; however, I had only to look directly at them and they would vanish, instantly dropping away somewhere, and again the tropical sky would thunder in its even, dense blueness. We were still walking along the rocky promontory, but it kept tapering and betraying us. Around it grew golden marsh reeds, like a million bared swords gleaming in the sun. Here and there flashed elongated pools, and over them hung dark swarms of midges. A large swamp flower, related to the orchid, stretched toward me its drooping, downy lip, which seemed smeared as if with egg yolk. Gregson swung his net and sank to his hips in the brocaded ooze as a gigantic butterfly, with one flap of its satin wings, sailed away from him over the reeds, toward the shimmer of pale emanations, where the indistinct folds of a window curtain seemed to hang. "I must not," I said to myself, "I must not. . . ." I shifted my gaze and walked on beside Gregson, now over rock, now across hissing and lip-smacking soil. I felt chills, in spite of the greenhouse heat. I foresaw that in a moment I would collapse altogether, that the designs and convexities of delirium, showing through the sky and through the golden reeds, would gain complete control of my consciousness. At times Gregson and Cook seemed to grow transparent, and I thought I saw, through them, wallpaper with an endlessly repeated design of reeds. I took hold of myself, strained to keep my eyes open, and moved on. Cook by now was crawling on all fours, yelling, and snatching at

Gregson's legs, but the latter would shake him off and keep walking. I looked at Gregson, at his stubborn profile, and felt, to my horror, that I was forgetting who Gregson was, and why I was with him.

Meanwhile we kept sinking into the ooze more and more frequently, deeper and deeper; the insatiable mire would suck at us, and, wriggling, we would slip free. Cook kept falling down and crawling, covered with insect bites, all swollen and soaked, and, dear God, how he would squeal when disgusting bevies of minute, bright-green hydrotic snakes, attracted by our sweat, would take off in pursuit of us, tensing and uncoiling to sail two yards and then another two. I, however, was much more frightened by something else: Now and then, on my left (always, for some reason, on my left), listing among the repetitious reeds, what seemed a large armchair but was actually a strange, cumbersome gray amphibian, whose name Gregson refused to tell me, would rise out of the swamp.

"A break," said Gregson abruptly. "Let's take a break."

By a stroke of luck we managed to scramble onto an islet of rock, surrounded by the swamp vegetation. Gregson took off his knapsack and issued us some native patties, smelling of ipecacuanha, and a dozen acreana fruit. How thirsty I was, and how little help was the scanty, astringent juice of the acreana. . . .

"Look, how odd," Gregson said to me, not in English but in some other language, so that Cook would not understand. "We must get through to the hills, but look, how odd—could the hills have been a mirage?—they are no longer visible."

I raised myself up from my pillow and leaned my elbow on the resilient surface of the rock. . . . Yes, it was true that the hills were no longer visible; there was only the quivering vapor hanging over the marsh. Once again everything around me assumed an ambiguous transparency. I leaned back and said softly to Gregson, "You probably can't see, but something keeps trying to come through."

"What are you talking about?" asked Gregson.

I realized that what I was saying was nonsense and stopped. My head was spinning and there was a humming in my ears; Gregson, down on one knee, was rummaging through his knapsack, but there was no medicine there, and my supply was exhausted. Cook sat in silence, morosely picking at a rock. Through a tear in his shirtsleeve there showed a strange tattoo on his arm: a crystal drinking glass with a teaspoon, very well executed.

"Vallier is sick—haven't you got some tablets?" Gregson said to him. I did not hear the exact words, but I could guess the general sense of their talk, which would grow absurd and somehow spherical when I tried to listen more closely.

Cook turned slowly and the glassy tattoo slid off his skin to one side, remaining suspended in midair; then it floated off, floated off, and I pursued it with my frightened gaze, but as I turned away it lost itself in the vapor of the swamp, with a last faint glimmer.

"Serves you right," muttered Cook. "It's just too bad. The same will happen to you and me. Just too bad. . . ."

In the course of the last few minutes—that is, ever since we had stopped to rest on the rock islet—he seemed to have grown larger, had swelled, and there was now something mocking and dangerous about him. Gregson took off his sun helmet and, pulling out a dirty handkerchief, wiped his forehead, which was orange over the brows, and white above that. Then he put on his helmet again, leaned over to me, and said, "Pull yourself together, please" (or words to that effect). "We shall try to move on. The vapor is hiding the hills, but they are there. I am certain we have covered about half the swamp." (This is all very approximate.)

"Murderer," said Cook under his breath. The tattoo was now again on his forearm; not the entire glass, though, but one side of it—there was not quite enough room for the remainder, which quivered in space, casting reflections. "Murderer," Cook repeated with satisfaction, raising his inflamed eyes. "I told you we would get stuck here. Black dogs eat too much carrion. Mi, re, fa, sol."

"He's a clown," I softly informed Gregson, "a Shakespearean clown."

"Clow, clow, clow," Gregson answered, "clow, clow—clo, clo, clo . . . Do you hear," he went on, shouting in my ear. "You must get up. We have to move on."

The rock was as white and as soft as a bed. I raised myself a little, but immediately fell back on the pillow.

"We shall have to carry him," said Gregson's faraway voice. "Give me a hand."

"Fiddlesticks," replied Cook (or so it sounded to me). "I suggest we enjoy some fresh meat before he dries up. Fa, sol, mi, re."

"He's sick, he's sick, too," I cried to Gregson. "You're here with two lunatics. Go ahead alone. You'll make it . . . Go—"

"Fat chance we'll let him go," said Cook.

Meanwhile delirious visions, taking advantage of the general confusion, were quietly and firmly establishing themselves. The lines of a dim ceiling stretched and crossed in the sky. A large armchair rose, as if supported from below, out of the swamp. Glossy birds flew through the haze of the marsh and, as they settled, one turned into the wooden knob of a bedpost, another into a decanter. Gathering all my will power, I focused my gaze and drove off this dangerous trash. Above the reeds flew real birds with long flame-colored tails. The air buzzed with insects. Gregson was waving away a varicolored fly, and at the same time trying to determine its species. Finally he could contain himself no longer and caught it in his net. His motions underwent curious changes, as if someone were reshuffling them. I saw him in different poses simultaneously; he was divesting himself of himself, as if he were made of many glass Gregsons whose outlines did not coincide. Then he condensed again, and stood up firmly. He was shaking Cook by the shoulder.

"You are going to help me carry him," Gregson was saying

distinctly. "If you were not a traitor, we would not be in this mess."

Cook remained silent, but slowly flushed purple.

"See here, Cook, you'll regret this," said Gregson. "I'm telling you for the last time—"

At this point something occurred that had been ripening for a long time. Cook drove his head like a bull into Gregson's stomach. They both fell; Gregson had time to get his revolver out, but Cook managed to knock it out of his hand. Then they clutched each other and started rolling in their embrace, panting deafeningly. I looked at them, helpless. Cook's broad back would grow tense and the vertebrae would show through his shirt; but suddenly, instead of his back, a leg, also his, would appear, covered with red hairs and with a blue vein running up the shin, and Gregson was rolling on top of him. Gregson's helmet flew off and wobbled away, like half of an enormous cardboard egg. From somewhere in the labyrinth of their bodies Cook's fingers wriggled out, clenching a rusty but sharp knife; the knife entered Gregson's back as if it were clay, but Gregson only gave a grunt, and they both rolled over several times. When I next saw my friend's back, the handle and top half of the blade protruded, while his hands had locked around Cook's thick neck, which crunched as he squeezed, and Cook's legs were twitching. They made one last full revolution, and now only a quarter of the blade was visible—no, a fifth . . . no, now not even that much showed: it had entered completely. Gregson grew still after having piled on top of Cook, who had also become motionless.

I watched, and it seemed to me (fogged as my senses were by fever) that this was all a harmless game, that in a moment they would get up and, when they had caught their breath, would peacefully carry me off across the swamp toward the cool blue hills, to some shady place with babbling water. But suddenly, at this last stage of my mortal illness—for I knew that in a few minutes I would die—in these final minutes everything grew completely lucid; I realized that all that was taking place around me was not the trick of an inflamed imagination, not the veil of delirium, through which unwelcome glimpses of my supposedly real existence in a distant European metropolis (the wallpaper, the armchair, the glass of lemonade) were trying to show. I realized that the obtrusive room was fictitious, since everything beyond death is, at best, fictitious: an imitation of life hastily knocked together, the furnished rooms of nonexistence. I realized that reality was here, here beneath this wonderful, frightening tropical sky, among those gleaming sword-like reeds, in this vapor hanging over them, and the thick-lipped flowers clinging to the flat islet, where, beside me, lay two clinched corpses. And, having realized this, I found within the strength to crawl over to them and pull the knife from the back of Gregson, my leader, my dear friend. He was dead, quite dead, and all the little bottles in his pockets were broken and crushed. Cook, too, was dead, and his ink-black tongue protruded from his mouth. I pried open Gregson's fingers and turned his body over. His lips were half open and bloody; his face, which already seemed hardened, appeared badly shaven; the bluish whites of his eyes showed between the lids. For the last time, I saw all this distinctly, consciously, with the seal of authenticity on everything—their skinned knees, the bright flies circling over them, the females of those flies, already seeking a spot for oviposition. Fumbling with my enfeebled hands, I took a fat notebook out of my shirt pocket, but here I was overcome by weakness; I sat down and my head drooped. And yet I conquered this impatient fog of death and looked around. Blue air, heat, solitude . . . And how sorry I felt for Gregson, who would never return home! I even remembered his wife and old cook, his parrots, and many other things. Then I thought about our discoveries, our precious finds, the rare, still undescribed plants and creatures that now would never be named by us. I was alone. Hazier flashed the reeds, dimmer flamed the sky. My eyes followed an exquisite beetle that was crawling across a stone, but I had no strength left to catch it. Everything around me was fading, leaving bare the scenery of death—some realistic furniture and four walls. My last motion was to open the book, which was damp with my sweat, for I absolutely had to make a note of something; but, alas, it slipped out of my hand. I groped all along the blanket, but the book was no longer there.

Berlin, 1931
Translated by Dmitri Nabokov
and the author

Cloud, Castle, Lake

❧❧❧❧

One of my representatives—a modest, mild bachelor, very efficient—happened to win a pleasure trip at a charity ball given by Russian refugees. That was in 1936 or 1937. The Berlin summer was in full flood (it was the second week of damp and cold, so that it was a pity to look at everything which had turned green in vain, and only the sparrows kept cheerful); he did not care to go anywhere, but when he tried to sell his ticket at the office of the Bureau of Pleasantrips he was told that to do so he would have to have special permission from the Ministry of Transportation; when he tried them, it turned out that first he would have to draw up a complicated petition at a notary's on stamped paper; and besides, a so-called "certificate of non-absence from the city for the summertime" had to be obtained from the police.

So he sighed a little, and decided to go. He borrowed an aluminum flask from friends, repaired his soles, bought a belt and a fancy-style flannel shirt—one of those cowardly things which shrink in the first wash. Incidentally, it was too large for that likable little man, his hair always neatly trimmed, his eyes so intelligent and kind. I cannot remember his name at the moment. I think it was Vasili Ivanovich.

He slept badly the night before the departure. And why? Because he had to get up unusually early, and hence took along into his dreams the delicate face of the watch ticking on his night table; but mainly because that very night, for no reason at all, he began to imagine that this trip, thrust upon him by a feminine Fate in a low-cut gown, this trip which he had accepted so reluctantly, would bring him some wonderful, tremulous happiness. This happiness would have something in common with his childhood, and with the excitement aroused in him by Russian lyrical poetry, and with some evening sky line once seen in a dream, and with that lady, another man's wife, whom he had hopelessly loved for seven years—but it would be even fuller and more significant than all that. And besides, he felt that the really good life must be oriented toward something or someone.

The morning was dull, but steam-warm and close, with an inner sun, and it was quite pleasant to rattle in a streetcar to the distant railway station where the gathering place was: several people, alas, were taking part in the excursion. Who would they be, these drowsy beings, drowsy as seem all creatures still unknown to us? By Window No. 6, at 7 A.M., as was indicated in the directions appended to the ticket, he saw them (they were already waiting; he had managed to be late by about three minutes).

A lanky blond young man in Tyrolese garb stood out at once. He was burned the color of a cockscomb, had huge brick-red knees with golden hairs, and his nose looked lacquered. He was the leader furnished by the Bureau, and as soon as the newcomer had joined the group (which consisted of four women and as many men) he led it off toward a train lurking behind other trains, carrying his monstrous knapsack with terrifying ease, and firmly clanking with his hobnailed boots.

Everyone found a place in an empty car, unmistakably third-class, and Vasili Ivanovich, having sat down by himself and put a peppermint into his mouth, opened a little volume of Tyutchev, whom he had long intended to reread; but he was requested to put the book aside and join the group. An elderly bespectacled post-office clerk, with skull, chin, and upper lip a

bristly blue as if he had shaved off some extraordinarily luxuri-
ant and tough growth especially for this trip, immediately announced that he had been to Russia and knew some Russian—
for instance, *patzlui*—and, recalling philanderings in Tsaritsyn,
winked in such a manner that his fat wife sketched out in the
air the outline of a backhand box on the ear. The company was
getting noisy. Four employees of the same building firm were
tossing each other heavyweight jokes: a middle-aged man,
Schultz; a younger man, Schultz also, and two fidgety young
women with big mouths and big rumps. The red-headed, rather
burlesque widow in a sport skirt knew something too about
Russia (the Riga beaches). There was also a dark young man
by the name of Schramm, with lusterless eyes and a vague velvety vileness about his person and manners, who constantly
switched the conversation to this or that attractive aspect of
the excursion, and who gave the first signal for rapturous appreciation; he was, as it turned out later, a special stimulator
from the Bureau of Pleasantrips.

The locomotive, working rapidly with its elbows, hurried
through a pine forest, then—with relief—among fields. Only
dimly realizing as yet all the absurdity and horror of the situation, and perhaps attempting to persuade himself that everything was very nice, Vasili Ivanovich contrived to enjoy the
fleeting gifts of the road. And indeed, how enticing it all is,
what charm the world acquires when it is wound up and
moving like a merry-go-round! The sun crept toward a corner
of the window and suddenly spilled over the yellow bench. The
badly pressed shadow of the car sped madly along the grassy
bank, where flowers blended into colored streaks. A crossing:
a cyclist was waiting, one foot resting on the ground. Trees appeared in groups and singly, revolving coolly and blandly, displaying the latest fashions. The blue dampness of a ravine. A
memory of love, disguised as a meadow. Wispy clouds—grey-
hounds of heaven.

We both, Vasili Ivanovich and I, have always been impressed

by the anonymity of all the parts of a landscape, so dangerous for the soul, the impossibility of ever finding out where that path you see leads—and look, what a tempting thicket! It happened that on a distant slope or in a gap in the trees there would appear and, as it were, stop for an instant, like air retained in the lungs, a spot so enchanting—a lawn, a terrace—such perfect expression of tender well-meaning beauty—that it seemed that if one could stop the train and go thither, forever, to you, my love . . . But a thousand beech trunks were already madly leaping by, whirling in a sizzling sun pool, and again the chance for happiness was gone.

At the stations, Vasili Ivanovich would look at the configuration of some entirely insignificant objects—a smear on the platform, a cherry stone, a cigarette butt—and would say to himself that never, never would he remember these three little things here in that particular interrelation, this pattern, which he now could see with such deathless precision; or again, looking at a group of children waiting for a train, he would try with all his might to single out at least one remarkable destiny—in the form of a violin or a crown, a propeller or a lyre—and would gaze until the whole party of village schoolboys appeared as on an old photograph, now reproduced with a little white cross above the face of the last boy on the right: the hero's childhood.

But one could look out of the window only by snatches. All had been given sheet music with verses from the Bureau:

> Stop that worrying and moping,
> Take a knotted stick and rise,
> Come a-tramping in the open
> With the good, the hearty guys!
>
> Tramp your country's grass and stubble,
> With the good, the hearty guys,
> Kill the hermit and his trouble
> And to hell with doubts and sighs!

In a paradise of heather
Where the field mouse screams and dies,
Let us march and sweat together
With the steel-and-leather guys!

This was to be sung in chorus: Vasili Ivanovich, who not only could not sing but could not even pronounce German words clearly, took advantage of the drowning roar of mingling voices and merely opened his mouth while swaying slightly, as if he were really singing—but the leader, at a sign from the subtle Schramm, suddenly stopped the general singing and, squinting askance at Vasili Ivanovich, demanded that he sing solo. Vasili Ivanovich cleared his throat, timidly began, and after a minute of solitary torment all joined in; but he did not dare thereafter to drop out.

He had with him his favorite cucumber from the Russian store, a loaf of bread, and three eggs. When evening came, and the low crimson sun entered wholly the soiled seasick car, stunned by its own din, all were invited to hand over their provisions, in order to divide them evenly—this was particularly easy, as all except Vasili Ivanovich had the same things. The cucumber amused everybody, was pronounced inedible, and was thrown out of the window. In view of the insufficiency of his contribution, Vasili Ivanovich got a smaller portion of sausage.

He was made to play cards. They pulled him about, questioned him, verified whether he could show the route of the trip on a map—in a word, all busied themselves with him, at first good-naturedly, then with malevolence, which grew with the approach of night. Both girls were called Greta; the redheaded widow somehow resembled the rooster-leader; Schramm, Schultz, and the other Schultz, the post-office clerk and his wife, all gradually melted together, merged together, forming one collective, wobbly, many-handed being, from which one could not escape. It pressed upon him from all sides. But suddenly at some station all climbed out, and it was already dark, although in the west there still hung a very long, very pink cloud, and farther along the track, with a soul-piercing light, the star of a lamp trembled through the slow smoke of the engine, and crickets chirped in the dark, and from somewhere there came the odor of jasmine and hay, my love.

They spent the night in a tumble-down inn. A mature bed-bug is awful, but there is a certain grace in the motions of silky silverfish. The post-office clerk was separated from his wife, who was put with the widow; he was given to Vasili Ivano-vich for the night. The two beds took up the whole room. Quilt on top, chamber pot below. The clerk said that somehow he did not feel sleepy, and began to talk of his Russian adventures, rather more circumstantially than in the train. He was a great bully of a man, thorough and obstinate, clad in long cotton drawers, with mother-of-pearl claws on his dirty toes, and bear's fur between fat breasts. A moth dashed about the ceiling, hobnobbing with its shadow. "In Tsaritsyn," the clerk was saying, "there are now three schools, a German, a Czech, and a Chinese one. At any rate, that is what my brother-in-law says; he went there to build tractors."

Next day, from early morning to five o'clock in the afternoon, they raised dust along a highway, which undulated from hill to hill; then they took a green road through a dense fir wood. Vasili Ivanovich, as the least burdened, was given an enormous round loaf of bread to carry under his arm. How I hate you, our daily! But still his precious, experienced eyes noted what was necessary. Against the background of fir-tree gloom a dry needle was hanging vertically on an invisible thread.

Again they piled into a train, and again the small partition-less car was empty. The other Schultz began to teach Vasili Ivanovich how to play the mandolin. There was much laughter. When they got tired of that, they thought up a capital game, which was supervised by Schramm. It consisted of the follow-

ing: the women would lie down on the benches they chose, under which the men were already hidden, and when from under
one of the benches there would emerge a ruddy face with ears,
or a big outspread hand, with a skirt-lifting curve of the fingers
(which would provoke much squealing), then it would be revealed who was paired off with whom. Three times Vasili Ivanovich lay down in filthy darkness, and three times it turned
out that there was no one on the bench when he crawled out
from under. He was acknowledged the loser and was forced to
eat a cigarette butt.

They spent the night on straw mattresses in a barn, and early
in the morning set out again on foot. Firs, ravines, foamy
streams. From the heat, from the songs which one had constantly to bawl, Vasili Ivanovich became so exhausted that during the midday halt he fell asleep at once, and awoke only
when they began to slap at imaginary horseflies on him. But
after another hour of marching, that very happiness of which
he had once half dreamt was suddenly discovered.

It was a pure, blue lake, with an unusual expression of its
water. In the middle, a large cloud was reflected in its entirety.
On the other side, on a hill thickly covered with verdure (and
the darker the verdure, the more poetic it is), towered, arising
from dactyl to dactyl, an ancient black castle. Of course, there
are plenty of such views in Central Europe, but just this one—
in the inexpressible and unique harmoniousness of its three
principal parts, in its smile, in some mysterious innocence it
had, my love! my obedient one!—was something so unique, and
so familiar, and so long-promised, and it so *understood* the be-
holder that Vasili Ivanovich even pressed his hand to his heart,
as if to see whether his heart was there in order to give it away.

At some distance, Schramm, poking into the air with the
leader's alpenstock, was calling the attention of the excur-
sionists to something or other; they had settled themselves
around on the grass in poses seen in amateur snapshots, while
the leader sat on a stump, his behind to the lake, and was

having a snack. Quietly, concealing himself in his own shadow, Vasili Ivanovich followed the shore, and came to a kind of inn. A dog still quite young greeted him; it crept on its belly, its jaws laughing, its tail fervently beating the ground. Vasili Ivanovich accompanied the dog into the house, a piebald two-storied dwelling with a winking window beneath a convex tiled eyelid; and he found the owner, a tall old man vaguely resembling a Russian war veteran, who spoke German so poorly and with such a soft drawl that Vasili Ivanovich changed to his own tongue, but the man understood as in a dream and continued in the language of his environment, his family.

Upstairs was a room for travelers. "You know, I shall take it for the rest of my life," Vasili Ivanovich is reported to have said as soon as he had entered it. The room itself had nothing remarkable about it. On the contrary, it was a most ordinary room, with a red floor, daisies daubed on the white walls, and a small mirror half filled with the yellow infusion of the reflected flowers—but from the window one could clearly see the lake with its cloud and its castle, in a motionless and perfect correlation of happiness. Without reasoning, without considering, only entirely surrendering to an attraction the truth of which consisted in its own strength, a strength which he had never experienced before, Vasili Ivanovich in one radiant second realized that here in this little room with that view, beautiful to the verge of tears, life would at last be what he had always wished it to be. What exactly it would be like, what would take place here, that of course he did not know, but all around him were help, promise, and consolation—so that there could not be any doubt that he must live here. In a moment he figured out how he would manage it so as not to have to return to Berlin again, how to get the few possessions that he had—books, the blue suit, her photograph. How simple it was turning out! As my representative, he was earning enough for the modest life of a refugee Russian.

"My friends," he cried, having run down again to the

meadow by the shore, "my friends, good-by. I shall remain for good in that house over there. We can't travel together any longer. I shall go no farther. I am not going anywhere. Good-by!"

"How is that?" said the leader in a queer voice, after a short pause, during which the smile on the lips of Vasili Ivanovich slowly faded, while the people who had been sitting on the grass half rose and stared at him with stony eyes.

"But why?" he faltered. "It is here that . . ."

"Silence!" the post-office clerk suddenly bellowed with extraordinary force. "Come to your senses, you drunken swine!"

"Wait a moment, gentlemen," said the leader, and, having passed his tongue over his lips, he turned to Vasili Ivanovich.

"You probably have been drinking," he said quietly. "Or have gone out of your mind. You are taking a pleasure trip with us. Tomorrow, according to the appointed itinerary—look at your ticket—we are all returning to Berlin. There can be no question of anyone—in this case you—refusing to continue this communal journey. We were singing today a certain song —try and remember what it said. That's enough now! Come, children, we are going on."

"There will be beer at Ewald," said Schramm in a caressing voice. "Five hours by train. Hikes. A hunting lodge. Coal mines. Lots of interesting things."

"I shall complain," wailed Vasili Ivanovich. "Give me back my bag. I have the right to remain where I want. Oh, but this is nothing less than an invitation to a beheading"—he told me he cried when they seized him by the arms.

"If necessary we shall carry you," said the leader grimly, "but that is not likely to be pleasant. I am responsible for each of you, and shall bring back each of you, alive or dead."

Swept along a forest road as in a hideous fairy tale, squeezed, twisted, Vasili Ivanovich could not even turn around, and only felt how the radiance behind his back receded, fractured by trees, and then it was no longer there, and all around the dark firs fretted but could not interfere. As soon as everyone had got into the car and the train had pulled off, they began to beat him—they beat him a long time, and with a good deal of inventiveness: It occured to them, among other things, to use a corkscrew on his palms; then on his feet. The post-office clerk, who had been to Russia, fashioned a knout out of a stick and a belt, and began to use it with devilish dexterity. Atta boy! The other men relied more on their iron heels, whereas the women were satisfied to pinch and slap. All had a wonderful time.

After returning to Berlin, he called on me, was much changed, sat down quietly, putting his hands on his knees, told his story; kept on repeating that he must resign his position, begged me to let him go, insisted that he could not continue, that he had not the strength to belong to mankind any longer. Of course, I let him go.

Marienbad, 1937
Translated by Peter Pertzov
and the author

The Visit to the Museum

❧❧❧❧❧

Several years ago a friend of mine in Paris—a person with oddities, to put it mildly—learning that I was going to spend two or three days at Montisert, asked me to drop in at the local museum where there hung, he was told, a portrait of his grandfather by Leroy. Smiling and spreading out his hands, he related a rather vague story to which I confess I paid little attention, partly because I do not like other people's obtrusive affairs, but chiefly because I had always had doubts about my friend's capacity to remain this side of fantasy. It went more or less as follows: after the grandfather died in their St. Petersburg house back at the time of the Russo-Japanese War, the contents of his apartment in Paris were sold at auction. The portrait, after some obscure peregrinations, was acquired by the museum of Leroy's native town. My friend wished to know if the portrait was really there; if there, if it could be ransomed; and if it could, for what price. When I asked why he did not get in touch with the museum, he replied that he had written several times, but had never received an answer.

I made an inward resolution not to carry out the request—I could always tell him I had fallen ill or changed my itinerary. The very notion of seeing sights, whether they be museums or ancient buildings, is loathsome to me; besides, the good freak's commission seemed absolute nonsense. It so happened, however, that, while wandering about Montisert's empty streets in search of a stationery store, and cursing the spire of a long-necked cathedral, always the same one, that kept popping up at the end of every street, I was caught in a violent downpour which immediately went about accelerating the fall of the maple leaves, for the fair weather of a southern October was holding on by a mere thread. I dashed for cover and found myself on the steps of the museum.

It was a building of modest proportions, constructed of many-colored stones, with columns, a gilt inscription over the frescoes of the pediment, and a lion-legged stone bench on either side of the bronze door. One of its leaves stood open, and the interior seemed dark against the shimmer of the shower. I stood for a while on the steps, but, despite the overhanging roof, they were gradually growing speckled. I saw that the rain had set in for good, and so, having nothing better to do, I decided to go inside. No sooner had I trod on the smooth, resonant flagstones of the vestibule than the clatter of a moved stool came from a distant corner, and the custodian—a banal pensioner with an empty sleeve—rose to meet me, laying aside his newspaper and peering at me over his spectacles. I paid my franc and, trying not to look at some statues at the entrance (which were as traditional and as insignificant as the first number in a circus program), I entered the main hall.

Everything was as it should be: gray tints, the sleep of substance, matter dematerialized. There was the usual case of old, worn coins resting in the inclined velvet of their compartments. There was, on top of the case, a pair of owls, Eagle Owl and Long-eared, with their French names reading "Grand Duke" and "Middle Duke" if translated. Venerable minerals lay in their open graves of dusty papier-mâché; a photograph of an astonished gentleman with a pointed beard dominated an assortment of strange black lumps of various sizes. They bore a great resemblance to frozen frass, and I paused involuntarily over them, for I was quite at a loss to guess their nature, composition and function. The custodian had been following me with felted steps, always keeping a respectful distance; now, however, he came up, with one hand behind his back and the ghost of the other in his pocket, and gulping, if one judged by his Adam's apple.

"What are they?" I asked.

"Science has not yet determined," he replied, undoubtedly having learned the phrase by rote. "They were found," he continued in the same phony tone, "in 1895, by Louis Pradier, Municipal Councillor and Knight of the Legion of Honor," and his trembling finger indicated the photograph.

"Well and good," I said, "but who decided, and why, that they merited a place in the museum?"

"And now I call your attention to this skull!" the old man cried energetically, obviously changing the subject.

"Still, I would be interested to know what they are made of," I interrupted.

"Science . . ." he began anew, but stopped short and looked crossly at his fingers, which were soiled with dust from the glass.

I proceeded to examine a Chinese vase, probably brought back by a naval officer; a group of porous fossils; a pale worm in clouded alcohol; a red-and-green map of Montisert in the seventeenth century; and a trio of rusted tools bound by a funereal ribbon—a spade, a mattock and a pick. "To dig in the past," I thought absent-mindedly, but this time did not seek clarification from the custodian, who was following me noiselessly and meekly, weaving in and out among the display cases. Beyond the first hall there was another, apparently the last, and in its center a large sarcophagus stood like a dirty bathtub, while the walls were hung with paintings.

At once my eye was caught by the portrait of a man between two abominable landscapes (with cattle and "atmosphere"). I moved closer and, to my considerable amazement, found the very object whose existence had hitherto seemed to me but the figment of an unstable mind. The man, depicted in wretched oils, wore a frock coat, whiskers and a large pince-nez on a cord; he bore a likeness to Offenbach, but, in spite of the work's vile conventionality, I had the feeling one could make out in his features the horizon of a resemblance, as it were, to my friend. In one corner, meticulously traced in carmine against a black background, was the signature *Leroy* in a hand as commonplace as the work itself.

I felt a vinegarish breath near my shoulder, and turned to meet the custodian's kindly gaze. "Tell me," I asked, "supposing someone wished to buy one of these paintings, whom should he see?"

"The treasures of the museum are the pride of the city," replied the old man, "and pride is not for sale."

Fearing his eloquence, I hastily concurred, but nevertheless asked for the name of the museum's director. He tried to distract me with the story of the sarcophagus, but I insisted. Finally he gave me the name of one M. Godard and explained where I could find him.

Frankly, I enjoyed the thought that the portrait existed. It is fun to be present at the coming true of a dream, even if it is not one's own. I decided to settle the matter without delay. When I get in the spirit, no one can hold me back. I left the museum with a brisk, resonant step, and found that the rain had stopped, blueness had spread across the sky, a woman in besplattered stockings was spinning along on a silver-shining bicycle, and only over the surrounding hills did clouds still hang. Once again the cathedral began playing hide-and-seek with me, but I outwitted it. Barely escaping the onrushing tires of a furious red bus packed with singing youths, I crossed the asphalt thoroughfare and a minute later was ringing at the garden gate of M. Godard. He turned out to be a thin, middle-aged gentleman in high collar and dickey, with a pearl in the knot of his tie, and a face very much resembling a Russian wolfhound; as if that were not enough, he was licking his chops in a most doglike manner, while sticking a stamp on an envelope, when I entered his small but lavishly furnished room with its malachite inkstand on the desk and a strangely familiar Chinese vase on the mantel. A pair of fencing foils hung crossed over the mirror, which reflected the narrow gray back of his head. Here and there photographs of a warship pleasantly broke up the blue flora of the wallpaper.

"What can I do for you?" he asked, throwing the letter he had just sealed into the wastebasket. This act seemed unusual to me; however, I did not see fit to interfere. I explained in brief my reason for coming, even naming the substantial sum with which my friend was willing to part, though he had asked me not to mention it, but wait instead for the museum's terms.

"All this is delightful," said M. Godard. "The only thing is, you are mistaken—there is no such picture in our museum."

"What do you mean there is no such picture? I have just seen it! Portrait of a Russian nobleman, by Gustave Leroy."

"We do have one Leroy," said M. Godard when he had leafed through an oilcloth notebook and his black fingernail had stopped at the entry in question. "However, it is not a portrait but a rural landscape: The Return of the Herd."

I repeated that I had seen the picture with my own eyes five minutes before and that no power on earth could make me doubt its existence.

"Agreed," said M. Godard, "but I am not crazy either. I have been curator of our museum for almost twenty years now and know this catalog as well as I know the Lord's Prayer. It says here Return of the Herd and that means the herd is returning, and, unless perhaps your friend's grandfather is depicted as a shepherd, I cannot conceive of his portrait's existence in our museum."

"He is wearing a frock coat," I cried. "I swear he is wearing a frock coat!"

"And how did you like our museum in general?" M. Godard asked suspiciously. "Did you appreciate the sarcophagus?"

"Listen," I said (and I think there was already a tremor in

my voice), "do me a favor—let's go there this minute, and let's make an agreement that if the portrait is there, you will sell it."

"And if not?" inquired M. Godard.

"I shall pay you the sum anyway."

"All right," he said. "Here, take this red-and-blue pencil and using the red—the red, please—put it in writing for me."

In my excitement I carried out his demand. Upon glancing at my signature, he deplored the difficult pronunciation of Russian names. Then he appended his own signature and, quickly folding the sheet, thrust it into his waistcoat pocket.

"Let's go," he said freeing a cuff.

On the way he stepped into a shop and bought a bag of sticky looking caramels which he began offering me insistently; when I flatly refused, he tried to shake out a couple of them into my hand. I pulled my hand away. Several caramels fell on the sidewalk; he stopped to pick them up and then overtook me at a trot. When we drew near the museum we saw the red tourist bus (now empty) parked outside.

"Aha," said M. Godard, pleased. "I see we have many visitors today."

He doffed his hat and, holding it in front of him, walked decorously up the steps.

All was not well at the museum. From within issued rowdy cries, lewd laughter, and even what seemed like the sound of a scuffle. We entered the first hall; there the elderly custodian was restraining two sacrilegists who wore some kind of festive emblems in their lapels and were altogether very purple-faced and full of pep as they tried to extract the municipal councillor's merds from beneath the glass. The rest of the youths, members of some rural athletic organization, were making noisy fun, some of the worm in alcohol, others of the skull. One joker was in rapture over the pipes of the steam radiator, which he pretended was an exhibit; another was taking aim at an owl with his fist and forefinger. There were about thirty of them in all, and their motion and voices created a condition of crush and thick noise.

M. Godard clapped his hands and pointed at a sign read-ing "Visitors to the Museum must be decently attired." Then he pushed his way, with me following, into the second hall. The whole company immediately swarmed after us. I steered Godard to the portrait; he froze before it, chest inflated, and then stepped back a bit, as if admiring it, and his feminine heel trod on somebody's foot.

"Splendid picture," he exclaimed with genuine sincerity. "Well, let's not be petty about this. You were right, and there must be an error in the catalog."

As he spoke, his fingers, moving as it were on their own, tore up our agreement into little bits which fell like snowflakes into a massive spittoon.

"Who's the old ape?" asked an individual in a striped jersey, and, as my friend's grandfather was depicted holding a glowing cigar, another funster took out a cigarette and prepared to bor-row a light from the portrait.

"All right, let us settle on the price," I said, "and, in any case, let's get out of here."

"Make way, please!" shouted M. Godard, pushing aside the curious.

There was an exit, which I had not noticed previously, at the end of the hall and we thrust our way through to it.

"I can make no decision," M. Godard was shouting above the din. "Decisiveness is a good thing only when supported by law. I must first discuss the matter with the mayor, who has just died and has not yet been elected. I doubt that you will be able to purchase the portrait but nonetheless I would like to show you still other treasures of ours."

We found ourselves in a hall of considerable dimensions. Brown books, with a half-baked look and coarse, foxed pages, lay open under glass on a long table. Along the walls stood dummy soldiers in jack-boots with flared tops.

"Come, let's talk it over," I cried out in desperation, trying to direct M. Godard's evolutions to a plush-covered sofa in a corner. But in this I was prevented by the custodian. Flailing his one arm, he came running after us, pursued by a merry crowd of youths, one of whom had put on his head a copper helmet with a Rembrandtesque gleam.

"Take it off, take it off!" shouted M. Godard, and someone's shove made the helmet fly off the hooligan's head with a clatter.

"Let us move on," said M. Godard, tugging at my sleeve, and we passed into the section of Ancient Sculpture.

I lost my way for a moment among some enormous marble legs, and twice ran around a giant knee before I again caught sight of M. Godard, who was looking for me behind the white ankle of a neighboring giantess. Here a person in a bowler, who must have clambered up her, suddenly fell from a great height to the stone floor. One of his companions began helping him up, but they were both drunk, and, dismissing them with a wave of the hand, M. Godard rushed on to the next room, radiant with Oriental fabrics; there hounds raced across azure carpets, and a bow and quiver lay on a tiger skin.

Strangely, though, the expanse and motley only gave me a feeling of oppressiveness and imprecision, and, perhaps because new visitors kept dashing by or perhaps because I was impatient to leave the unnecessarily spreading museum and amid calm and freedom conclude my business negotiations with M. Godard, I began to experience a vague sense of alarm. Meanwhile we had transported ourselves into yet another hall, which must have been really enormous, judging by the fact that it housed the entire skeleton of a whale, resembling a frigate's frame; beyond were visible still other halls, with the oblique sheen of large paintings, full of storm clouds, among which floated the delicate idols of religious art in blue and pink vestments; and all this resolved itself in an abrupt turbulence of misty draperies, and chandeliers came aglitter and fish with translucent frills meandered through illuminated aquariums. Racing up a staircase, we saw, from the gallery above, a crowd of gray-haired people with umbrellas examining a gigantic mock-up of the universe.

At last, in a somber but magnificent room dedicated to the history of steam machines, I managed to halt my carefree guide for an instant.

"Enough!" I shouted. "I'm leaving. We'll talk tomorrow."

He had already vanished. I turned and saw, scarcely an inch from me, the lofty wheels of a sweaty locomotive. For a long time I tried to find the way back among models of railroad stations. How strangely glowed the violet signals in the gloom beyond the fan of wet tracks, and what spasms shook my poor heart! Suddenly everything changed again: in front of me stretched an infinitely long passage, containing numerous office cabinets and elusive, scurrying people. Taking a sharp turn, I found myself amid a thousand musical instruments; the walls, all mirror, reflected an enfilade of grand pianos, while in the center there was a pool with a bronze Orpheus atop a green rock. The aquatic theme did not end here as, racing back, I ended up in the Section of Fountains and Brooks, and it was difficult to walk along the winding, slimy edges of those waters.

Now and then, on one side or the other, stone stairs, with puddles on the steps, which gave me a strange sensation of fear, would descend into misty abysses, whence issued whistles, the rattle of dishes, the clatter of typewriters, the ring of hammers and many other sounds, as if, down there, were exposition halls of some kind or other, already closing or not yet completed. Then I found myself in darkness and kept bumping into unknown furniture until I finally saw a red light and walked out onto a platform that clanged under me—and suddenly, beyond it, there was a bright parlor, tastefully furnished in Empire style, but not a living soul, not a living soul. . . . By now I was indescribably terrified, but every time I turned and tried to retrace my steps along the passages, I found myself in hitherto unseen places—a greenhouse with hydrangeas and broken windowpanes with the darkness of artificial night showing through beyond; or a deserted laboratory with dusty alembics on its tables. Finally I ran into a room of some sort with coatracks monstrously loaded down with black coats and astrakhan furs; from beyond a door came a burst of applause, but when I flung the door open, there was no theater, but only a soft opacity and splendidly counterfeited fog with the perfectly convincing blotches of indistinct streetlights. More than convincing! I advanced, and immediately a joyous and unmistakable sensation of reality at last replaced all the unreal trash amid which I had just been dashing to and fro. The stone beneath my feet was real sidewalk, powdered with wonderfully fragrant, newly fallen snow in which the infrequent pedestrians had already left fresh black tracks. At first the quiet and the snowy coolness of the night, somehow strikingly familiar, gave me a pleasant feeling after my feverish wanderings. Trustfully, I started to conjecture just where I had come out, and why the snow, and what were those lights exaggeratedly but indistinctly beaming here and there in the brown darkness. I examined and, stooping, even touched a round spur stone on the curb, then glanced at the palm of my hand, full of wet granular cold, as if hoping to read an explanation there. I felt how lightly, how naïvely I was clothed, but the distinct realization that I had escaped from the museum's maze was still so strong that, for the first two or three minutes, I experienced neither surprise nor fear. Continuing my leisurely examination, I looked up at the house beside which I was standing and was immediately struck by the sight of iron steps and railings that descended into the snow on their way to the cellar. There was a twinge in my heart, and it was with a new, alarmed curiosity that I glanced at the pavement, at its white cover along which stretched black lines, at the brown sky across which there kept sweeping a mysterious light, and at the massive parapet some distance away. I sensed that there was a drop beyond it; something was creaking and gurgling down there. Further on, beyond the murky cavity, stretched a chain of fuzzy lights. Scuffling along the snow in my soaked shoes, I walked a few paces, all the time glancing at the dark house on my right; only in a single window did a lamp glow softly under its green-glass shade.

Here, a locked wooden gate. . . . There, what must be the shutters of a sleeping shop. . . . And by the light of a street-lamp whose shape had long been shouting to me its impossible message, I made out the ending of a sign— *". . . inka Sapog"* *(". . . oe Repair")*—but no, it was not the snow that had obliterated the "hard sign" at the end. "No, no, in a minute I shall wake up," I said aloud, and, trembling, my heart pounding, I turned, walked on, stopped again. From somewhere came the receding sound of hooves, the snow sat like a skullcap on a slightly leaning spur stone, and indistinctly showed white on the woodpile on the other side of the fence, and already I knew, irrevocably, where I was. Alas, it was not the Russia I remembered, but the factual Russia of today, forbidden to me, hopelessly slavish, and hopelessly my own native land. A semi-phantom in a light foreign suit, I stood on the impassive snow of an October night, somewhere on the Moyka or the Fontanka Canal, or perhaps on the Obvodny, and I had to do something, go somewhere, run, desperately protect my fragile, illegal life. Oh, how many times in my sleep I had experienced a similar sensation! Now, though, it was reality. Everything was real— the air that seemed to mingle with scattered snowflakes, the still unfrozen canal, the floating fish house, and that peculiar squareness of the darkened and the yellow windows. A man in a fur cap, with a briefcase under his arm, came toward me out of the fog, gave me a startled glance, and turned to look again when he had passed me. I waited for him to disappear and then, with a tremendous haste, began pulling out everything I had in my pockets, ripping up papers, throwing them into the snow and stamping them down. There were some documents, a letter from my sister in Paris, five hundred francs, a handkerchief, cigarettes; however, in order to shed all the integument of exile, I would have to tear off and destroy my clothes, my linen, my shoes, everything, and remain ideally naked; and, even though I was already shivering from my anguish and from the cold, I did what I could.

But enough. I shall not recount how I was arrested, nor tell

of my subsequent ordeals. Suffice it to say that it cost me incredible patience and effort to get back abroad, and that, ever
since, I have forsworn carrying out commissions entrusted one
by the insanity of others.

Paris, 1939
Translated by Dmitri Nabokov
and the author

Spring in Fialta

❦❦❦❦

Spring in Fialta is cloudy and dull. Everything is damp: the piebald trunks of the plane trees, the juniper shrubs, the railings, the gravel. Far away, in a watery vista between the jagged edges of pale bluish houses, which have tottered up from their knees to climb the slope (a cypress indicating the way), the blurred Mount St. George is more than ever remote from its likeness on the picture post cards which since 1910, say (those straw hats, those youthful cabmen), have been courting the tourist from the sorry-go-round of their prop, among amethyst-toothed lumps of rock and the mantelpiece dreams of sea shells. The air is windless and warm, with a faint tang of burning. The sea, its salt drowned in a solution of rain, is less glaucous than gray with waves too sluggish to break into foam.

It was on such a day in the early thirties that I found myself, all my senses wide open, on one of Fialta's steep little streets, taking in everything at once, that marine rococo on the stand, and the coral crucifixes in a shopwindow, and the dejected poster of a visiting circus, one corner of its drenched paper detached from the wall, and a yellow bit of unripe orange peel on the old, slate-blue sidewalk, which retained here and there a fading memory of ancient mosaic design. I am fond of Fialta; I am fond of it because I feel in the hollow of those violaceous syllables the sweet dark dampness of the most rumpled of small flowers, and because the altolike name of a lovely

Crimean town is echoed by its viola; and also because there is something in the very somnolence of its humid Lent that especially anoints one's soul. So I was happy to be there again, to trudge uphill in inverse direction to the rivulet of the gutter, hatless, my head wet, my skin already suffused with warmth although I wore only a light mackintosh over my shirt.

I had come on the Caparabella express, which, with that reckless gusto peculiar to trains in mountainous country, had done its thundering best to collect throughout the night as many tunnels as possible. A day or two, just as long as a breathing spell in the midst of a business trip would allow me, was all I expected to stay. I had left my wife and children at home, and that was an island of happiness always present in the clear north of my being, always floating beside me, and even through me, I dare say, but yet keeping on the outside of me most of the time.

A pantless infant of the male sex, with a taut mud-gray little belly, jerkily stepped down from a doorstep and waddled off, bowlegged, trying to carry three oranges at once, but continuously dropping the variable third, until he fell himself, and then a girl of twelve or so, with a string of heavy beads around her dusky neck and wearing a skirt as long as that of a gypsy, promptly took away the whole lot with her more nimble and more numerous hands. Nearby, on the wet terrace of a café, a waiter was wiping the slabs of tables; a melancholy brigand hawking local lollipops, elaborate-looking things with a lunar gloss, had placed a hopelessly full basket on the cracked balustrade, over which the two were conversing. Either the drizzle had stopped or Fialta had got so used to it that she herself did not know whether she was breathing moist air or warm rain. Thumb-filling his pipe from a rubber pouch as he walked, a plus-foured Englishman of the solid exportable sort came from under an arch and entered a pharmacy, where large pale sponges in a blue vase were dying a thirsty death behind their glass. What luscious elation I felt rippling through my veins, how

gratefully my whole being responded to the flutters and efflu-
via of that gray day saturated with a vernal essence which itself
it seemed slow in perceiving! My nerves were unusually receptive after a sleepless night; I assimilated everything: the whistling of a thrush in the almond trees beyond the chapel, the
peace of the crumbling houses, the pulse of the distant sea,
panting in the mist, all this together with the jealous green of
bottle glass bristling along the top of a wall and the fast colors
of a circus advertisement featuring a feathered Indian on a
rearing horse in the act of lassoing a boldly endemic zebra,
while some thoroughly fooled elephants sat brooding upon their
star-spangled thrones.

Presently the same Englishman overtook me. As I absorbed
him along with the rest, I happened to notice the sudden side-
roll of his big blue eye straining at its crimson canthus, and the
way he rapidly moistened his lips—because of the dryness of
those sponges, I thought; but then I followed the direction of
his glance, and saw Nina.

Every time I had met her during the fifteen years of our—
well, I fail to find the precise term for our kind of relationship
—she had not seemed to recognize me at once; and this time
too she remained quite still for a moment, on the opposite
sidewalk, half turning toward me in sympathetic incertitude
mixed with curiosity, only her yellow scarf already on the
move like those dogs that recognize you before their owners
do—and then she uttered a cry, her hands up, all her ten fingers
dancing, and in the middle of the street, with merely the frank
impulsiveness of an old friendship (just as she would rapidly
make the sign of the cross over me every time we parted), she
kissed me thrice with more mouth than meaning, and then
walked beside me, hanging on to me, adjusting her stride to
mine, hampered by her narrow brown skirt perfunctorily slit
down the side.

"Oh yes, Ferdie is here too," she replied and immediately in
her turn inquired nicely after Elena.

"Must be loafing somewhere around with Segur," she went on in reference to her husband. "And I have some shopping to do; we leave after lunch. Wait a moment, where are you leading me, Victor dear?"

Back into the past, back into the past, as I did every time I met her, repeating the whole accumulation of the plot from the very beginning up to the last increment—thus in Russian fairy tales the already told is bunched up again at every new turn of the story. This time we had met in warm and misty Fialta, and I could not have celebrated the occasion with greater art, could not have adorned with brighter vignettes the list of fate's former services, even if I had known that this was to be the last one; the last one, I maintain, for I cannot imagine any heavenly firm of brokers that might consent to arrange me a meeting with her beyond the grave.

My introductory scene with Nina had been laid in Russia quite a long time ago, around 1917 I should say, judging by certain left-wing theater rumblings backstage. It was at some birthday party at my aunt's on her country estate, near Luga, in the deepest folds of winter (how well I remember the first sign of nearing the place: a red barn in a white wilderness). I had just graduated from the Imperial Lyceum; Nina was already engaged: although she was of my age and of that of the century, she looked twenty at least, and this in spite or perhaps because of her neat slender build, whereas at thirty-two that very slightness of hers made her look younger. Her fiancé was a guardsman on leave from the front, a handsome heavy fellow, incredibly well-bred and stolid, who weighed every word on the scales of the most exact common sense and spoke in a velvety baritone, which grew even smoother when he addressed her; his decency and devotion probably got on her nerves; and he is now a successful if somewhat lonesome engineer in a most distant tropical country.

Windows light up and stretch their luminous lengths upon the dark billowy snow, making room for the reflection of the fan-shaped light above the front door between them. Each of the two side-pillars is fluffily fringed with white, which rather spoils the lines of what might have been a perfect ex libris for the book of our two lives. I cannot recall why we had all wandered out of the sonorous hall into the still darkness, peopled only with firs, snow-swollen to twice their size; did the watchmen invite us to look at a sullen red glow in the sky, portent of nearing arson? Possibly. Did we go to admire an equestrian statue of ice sculptured near the pond by the Swiss tutor of my cousins? Quite as likely. My memory revives only on the way back to the brightly symmetrical mansion toward which we tramped in a single file along a narrow furrow between snowbanks, with that crunch-crunch-crunch which is the only comment that a taciturn winter night makes upon humans. I walked last; three singing steps ahead of me walked a small bent shape; the firs gravely showed their burdened paws. I slipped and dropped the dead flashlight someone had forced upon me; it was devilishly hard to retrieve; and instantly attracted by my curses, with an eager, low laugh in anticipation of fun, Nina dimly veered toward me. I call her Nina, but I could hardly have known her name yet, hardly could we have had time, she and I, for any preliminary; "Who's that?" she asked with interest—and I was already kissing her neck, smooth and quite fiery hot from the long fox fur of her coat collar, which kept getting into my way until she clasped my shoulder, and with the candor so peculiar to her gently fitted her generous, dutiful lips to mine.

But suddenly parting us by its explosion of gaiety, the theme of a snowball fight started in the dark, and someone, fleeing, falling, crunching, laughing and panting, climbed a drift, tried to run, and uttered a horrible groan: deep snow had performed the amputation of an arctic. And soon after, we all dispersed to our respective homes, without my having talked with Nina, nor made any plans about the future, about those fifteen itinerant years that had already set out toward the dim horizon, loaded with the parts of our unassembled meetings; and as I watched her in the maze of gestures and shadows of gestures of which the rest of that evening consisted (probably parlor games—with Nina persistently in the other camp), I was astonished, I remember, not so much by her inattention to me after that warmth in the snow as by the innocent naturalness of that inattention, for I did not yet know that had I said a word it would have changed at once into a wonderful sunburst of kindness, a cheerful, compassionate attitude with all possible co-operation, as if woman's love were spring water containing salubrious salts which at the least notice she ever so willingly gave anyone to drink.

"Let me see, where did we last meet," I began (addressing the Fialta version of Nina) in order to bring to her small face with prominent cheekbones and dark-red lips a certain expression I knew; and sure enough, the shake of her head and the puckered brow seemed less to imply forgetfulness than to deplore the flatness of an old joke; or to be more exact, it was as if all those cities where fate had fixed our various rendezvous without ever attending them personally, all those platforms and stairs and three-walled rooms and dark back alleys, were trite settings remaining after some other lives all brought to a close long before and were so little related to the acting out of our own aimless destiny that it was almost bad taste to mention them.

I accompanied her into a shop under the arcades; there, in the twilight beyond a beaded curtain, she fingered some red leather purses stuffed with tissue paper, peering at the price tags, as if wishing to learn their museum names. She wanted, she said, exactly that shape but in fawn, and when after ten minutes of frantic rustling the old Dalmatian found such a freak by a miracle that has puzzled me ever since, Nina, who was about to pick some money out of my hand, changed her mind and went through the streaming beads without having bought anything.

Outside it was just as milky dull as before; the same smell of burning, stirring my Tartar memories, drifted from the bare windows of the pale houses; a small swarm of gnats was busy darning the air above a mimosa, which bloomed listlessly, her sleeves trailing to the very ground; two workmen in broad-brimmed hats were lunching on cheese and garlic, their backs against a circus billboard, which depicted a red hussar and an orange tiger of sorts; curious—in his effort to make the beast as ferocious as possible, the artist had gone so far that he had come back from the other side, for the tiger's face looked positively human.

"*Au fond,* I wanted a comb," said Nina with belated regret.

How familiar to me were her hesitations, second thoughts, third thoughts mirroring first ones, ephemeral worries between trains. She had always either just arrived or was about to leave, and of this I find it hard to think without feeling humiliated by the variety of intricate routes one feverishly follows in order to keep that final appointment which the most confirmed dawdler knows to be unavoidable. Had I to submit before judges of our earthly existence a specimen of her average pose, I would have perhaps placed her leaning upon a counter at Cook's, left calf crossing right shin, left toe tapping floor, sharp elbows and coin-spilling bag on the counter, while the employee, pencil in hand, pondered with her over the plan of an eternal sleeping car.

After the exodus from Russia, I saw her—and that was the second time—in Berlin at the house of some friends. I was about to get married; she had just broken with her fiancé. As I entered that room I caught sight of her at once and, having glanced at the other guests, I instinctively determined which of the men knew more about her than I. She was sitting in the corner of a couch, her feet pulled up, her small comfortable body folded in the form of a Z; an ash tray stood aslant on the couch near one of her heels; and, having squinted at me and listened to my name, she removed her stalklike cigarette holder from her lips and proceeded to utter slowly and joyfully, "Well, of all people—" and at once it became clear to everyone, beginning with her, that we had long been on intimate terms: unquestionably, she had forgotten all about the actual kiss, but somehow because of that trivial occurrence she found herself recollecting a vague stretch of warm, pleasant friendship, which in reality had never existed between us. Thus the whole cast of our relationship was fraudulently based upon an imaginary amity—which had nothing to do with her random good will. Our meeting proved quite insignificant in regard to the words we said, but already no barriers divided us; and when that night I happened to be seated beside her at supper, I shamelessly tested the extent of her secret patience.

Then she vanished again; and a year later my wife and I were seeing my brother off to Posen, and when the train had gone, and we were moving toward the exit along the other side of the platform, suddenly near a car of the Paris express I saw Nina, her face buried in the bouquet she held, in the midst of a group of people whom she had befriended without my knowledge and who stood in a circle gaping at her as idlers gape at a street row, a lost child, or the victim of an accident. Brightly she signaled to me with her flowers; I introduced her to Elena, and in that life-quickening atmosphere of a big railway station where everything is something trembling on the brink of something else, thus to be clutched and cherished, the exchange of a few words was enough to enable two totally dissimilar women to start calling each other by their pet names the very next time they met. That day, in the blue shade of the Paris car, Ferdinand was first mentioned: I learned with a ridiculous pang that she was about to marry him. Doors were beginning to slam; she quickly but piously kissed her friends, climbed into the vestibule, disappeared; and then I saw her through the glass settling herself in her compartment, having suddenly forgotten about us or passed into another world, and we all, our hands in our pockets, seemed to be spying upon an utterly unsuspecting life moving in that aquarium dimness, until she grew aware of us and drummed on the windowpane, then raised her eyes, fumbling at the frame as if hanging a picture, but nothing happened; some fellow passenger helped her, and she leaned out, audible and real, beaming with pleasure; one of us, keeping up with the stealthily gliding car, handed her a magazine and a Tauchnitz (she read English only when traveling); all was slipping away with beautiful smoothness, and I held a platform ticket crumpled beyond recognition, while a song of the last century (connected, it has been rumored, with some Parisian drama of love) kept ringing and ringing in my head, having emerged, God knows why, from the music box of memory, a sobbing ballad which often used to be sung by an old maiden aunt of mine, with a face as yellow as Russian church wax, but whom nature had given such a powerful, ecstatically full voice that it seemed to swallow her up in the glory of a fiery cloud as soon as she would begin:

> *On dit que tu te maries,*
> *tu sais que j'en vais mourir,*

and that melody, the pain, the offense, the link between hymen and death evoked by the rhythm, and the voice itself of the dead singer, which accompanied the recollection as the sole owner of the song, gave me no rest for several hours after Nina's departure and even later arose at increasing intervals like the last flat little waves sent to the beach by a passing ship, lapping ever more infrequently and dreamily, or like the bronze agony of a vibrating belfry after the bell ringer has already reseated himself in the cheerful circle of his family. And another year or two later, I was in Paris on business; and one morning on the landing of a hotel, where I had been looking up a film-actor fellow, there she was again, clad in a gray tailored suit, waiting for the elevator to take her down, a key dangling from her fingers. "Ferdinand has gone fencing," she said conversationally; her eyes rested on the lower part of my face as if she were lip reading, and after a moment of reflection (her amatory comprehension was matchless), she turned and rapidly swaying on slender ankles led me along the sea-blue carpeted passage. A chair at the door of her room supported a tray with the remains of breakfast—a honeystained knife, crumbs on the gray porcelain; but the room had already been done, and because of our sudden draft a wave of muslin embroidered with white dahlias got sucked in, with a shudder and knock, between the responsive halves of the French window, and only when the door had been locked did they let go that curtain with something like a blissful sigh; and a little later I stepped out on the diminutive cast-iron balcony beyond to inhale a combined smell of dry maple leaves and gasoline—the dregs of the hazy blue morning street; and as I did not yet realize the presence of that growing morbid pathos which was to embitter so my subsequent meetings with Nina, I was probably quite as collected and carefree as she was, when from the hotel I accompanied her to some office or other to trace a suitcase she had lost, and thence to the café where her husband was holding session with his court of the moment.

I will not mention the name (and what bits of it I happen to give here appear in decorous disguise) of that man, that Franco-Hungarian writer. . . . I would rather not dwell upon him at all, but I cannot help it—he is surging up from under my pen. Today one does not hear much about him; and this is good, for it proves that I was right in resisting his evil spell, right in experiencing a creepy chill down my spine whenever this or that new book of his touched my hand. The fame of his likes circulates briskly but soon grows heavy and stale; and as for history it will limit his life story to the dash between two dates. Lean and arrogant, with some poisonous pun ever ready to fork out and quiver at you, and with a strange look of expectancy in his dull brown veiled eyes, this false wag had, I daresay, an irresistible effect on small rodents. Having mastered the art of verbal invention to perfection, he particularly prided himself on being a weaver of words, a title he valued higher than that of a writer; personally, I never could understand what was the good of thinking up books, of penning things that had not really happened in some way or other; and I remember once saying to him as I braved the mockery of his encouraging nods that, were I a writer, I should allow only my heart to have imagination, and for the rest rely upon memory, that long-drawn sunset shadow of one's personal truth.

I had known his books before I knew him; a faint disgust was already replacing the aesthetic pleasure which I had suffered his first novel to give me. At the beginning of his career, it had been possible perhaps to distinguish some human landscape, some old garden, some dream-familiar disposition of trees through the stained glass of his prodigious prose . . . but with every new book the tints grew still more dense, the gules and purpure still more ominous; and today one can no longer see anything at all through that blazoned, ghastly rich glass, and it seems that were one to break it, nothing but a perfectly black void would face one's shivering soul. But how dangerous he was in his prime, what venom he squirted, with what whips he lashed when provoked! The tornado of his passing satire left a barren waste where felled oaks lay in a row, and the dust still twisted, and the unfortunate author of some adverse review, howling with pain, spun like a top in the dust.

At the time we met, his *"Passage à niveau"* was being acclaimed in Paris; he was, as they say, "surrounded," and Nina (whose adaptability was an amazing substitute for the culture she lacked) had already assumed if not the part of a muse at least that of a soul mate and subtle adviser, following Ferdinand's creative convolutions and loyally sharing his artistic tastes; for although it is wildly improbable that she had ever waded through a single volume of his, she had a magic knack of gleaning all the best passages from the shop talk of literary friends.

An orchestra of women was playing when we entered the

café; first I noted the ostrich thigh of a harp reflected in one of
the mirror-faced pillars, and then I saw the composite table
(small ones drawn together to form a long one) at which, with
his back to the plush wall, Ferdinand was presiding; and for a
moment his whole attitude, the position of his parted hands,
and the faces of his table companions all turned toward him reminded me in a grotesque, nightmarish way of something I
did not quite grasp, but when I did so in retrospect, the suggested comparison struck me as hardly less sacrilegious than
the nature of his art itself. He wore a white turtle-neck sweater
under a tweed coat; his glossy hair was combed back from the
temples, and above it cigarette smoke hung like a halo; his
bony, Pharaohlike face was motionless: the eyes alone roved
this way and that, full of dim satisfaction. Having forsaken the
two or three obvious haunts where naïve amateurs of Montpar-
nassian life would have expected to find him, he had started
patronizing this perfectly bourgeois establishment because of
his peculiar sense of humor, which made him derive ghoulish
fun from the pitiful *specialité de la maison*—this orchestra composed of half a dozen weary-looking, self-conscious ladies
interlacing mild harmonies on a crammed platform and not
knowing, as he put it, what to do with their motherly bosoms,
quite superfluous in the world of music. After each number he
would be convulsed by a fit of epileptic applause, which the
ladies had stopped acknowledging and which was already arousing, I thought, certain doubts in the minds of the proprietor of
the café and its fundamental customers, but which seemed
highly diverting to Ferdinand's friends. Among these I recall:
an artist with an impeccably bald though slightly chipped head,
which under various pretexts he constantly painted into his
eye-and-guitar canvases; a poet, whose special gag was the
ability to represent, if you asked him, Adam's Fall by means of
five matches; a humble businessman who financed surrealist
ventures (and paid for the *apéritifs*) if permitted to print in a
corner eulogistic allusions to the actress he kept; a pianist, pre-

sentable insofar as the face was concerned, but with a dreadful expression of the fingers; a jaunty but linguistically impotent Soviet writer fresh from Moscow, with an old pipe and a new wrist watch, who was completely and ridiculously unaware of the sort of company he was in; there were several other gentlemen present who have become confused in my memory, and doubtless two or three of the lot had been intimate with Nina. She was the only woman at the table; there she stooped, eagerly sucking at a straw, the level of her lemonade sinking with a kind of childish celerity, and only when the last drop had gurgled and squeaked, and she had pushed away the straw with her tongue, only then did I finally catch her eye, which I had been obstinately seeking, still not being able to cope with the fact that she had had time to forget what had occurred earlier in the morning—to forget it so thoroughly that upon meeting my glance, she replied with a blank questioning smile, and only after peering more closely did she remember suddenly what kind of answering smile I was expecting. Meanwhile, Ferdinand (the ladies having temporarily left the platform after pushing away their instruments like so many pieces of furniture) was juicily drawing his cronies' attention to the figure of and elderly luncher in a far corner of the café, who had, as some Frenchmen for some reason or other have, a little red ribbon or something on his coat lapel and whose gray beard combined with his mustache to form a cosy yellowish nest for his sloppily munching mouth. Somehow the trappings of old age always amused Ferdie.

I did not stay long in Paris, but that week proved sufficient to engender between him and me that fake chumminess the imposing of which he had such a talent for. Subsequently I even turned out to be of some use to him: my firm acquired the film rights of one of his more intelligible stories, and then he had a good time pestering me with telegrams. As the years passed, we found ourselves every now and then beaming at each other in some place, but I never felt at ease in his presence, and that day in Fialta, too, I experienced a familiar depression upon learning that he was on the prowl nearby; one thing, however, considerably cheered me up: the flop of his recent play.

And here he was coming toward us, garbed in an absolutely waterproof coat with belt and pocket flaps, a camera across his shoulder, double rubber soles to his shoes, sucking with an imperturbability that was meant to be funny a long stick of moonstone candy, that specialty of Fialta's. Beside him, walked the dapper, doll-like, rosy Segur, a lover of art and a perfect fool; I never could discover for what purpose Ferdinand needed him; and I still hear Nina exclaiming with a moaning tenderness that did not commit her to anything: "Oh, he is such a darling, Segur!" They approached; Ferdinand and I greeted each other lustily, trying to crowd into hand shake and back slap as much fervor as possible, knowing by experience that actually that was all but pretending it was only a preface; and it always happened like that: after every separation we met to the accompaniment of strings being excitedly tuned, in a bustle of geniality, in the hubbub of sentiments taking their seats; but the ushers would close the doors, and after that no one was admitted.

Segur complained to me about the weather, and at first I did not understand what he was talking about; even if the moist, gray, greenhouse essence of Fialta might be called "weather," it was just as much outside of anything that could serve us as a topic of conversation as was, for instance, Nina's slender elbow, which I was holding between finger and thumb, or a bit of tin foil someone had dropped, shining in the middle of the cobbled street in the distance.

We four moved on, vague purchases still looming ahead. "God, what an Indian!" Ferdinand suddenly exclaimed with fierce relish, violently nudging me and pointing at a poster. Further on, near a fountain, he gave his stick of candy to a native child, a swarthy girl with beads round her pretty neck; we stopped to wait for him: he crouched, saying something to her, addressing her sooty-black lowered eyelashes, and then he caught up with us, grinning and making one of those remarks with which he loved to spice his speech. Then his attention was drawn by an unfortunate object exhibited in a souvenir shop: a dreadful marble imitation of Mount St. George showing a black tunnel at its base, which turned out to be the mouth of an inkwell, and with a compartment for pens in the semblance of railroad tracks. Open-mouthed, quivering, all agog with sardonic triumph, he turned that dusty, cumbersome, and perfectly irresponsible thing in his hands, paid without bargaining, and with his mouth still open came out carrying the monster. Like some autocrat who surrounds himself with hunchbacks and dwarfs, he would become attached to this or that hideous object; this infatuation might last from five minutes to several days or even longer if the thing happened to be animate.

Nina wistfully alluded to lunch, and seizing the opportunity when Ferdinand and Segur stopped at a post office, I hastened to lead her away. I still wonder what exactly she meant to me, that small dark woman of the narrow shoulders and "lyrical limbs" (to quote the expression of a mincing *émigré* poet, one of the few men who had sighed platonically after her), and still less do I understand what was the purpose of fate in bringing us constantly together. I did not see her for quite a long while after my sojourn in Paris, and then one day when I came home from my office I found her having tea with my wife and examining on her silk-hosed hand, with her wedding ring gleaming through, the texture of some stockings bought cheap in Tauentzienstrasse. Once I was shown her photograph in a fashion magazine full of autumn leaves and gloves and windswept golf links. On a certain Christmas she sent me a picture post card with snow and stars. On a Riviera beach she almost escaped my notice behind her dark glasses and terra-cotta tan. Another day, having dropped in on an ill-timed errand at the house of some strangers where a party was in progress,

I saw her scarf and fur coat among alien scarecrows on a coat rack. In a bookshop she nodded to me from a page of one of her husband's stories, a page referring to an episodic servant girl, but smuggling in Nina in spite of the author's intention: "Her face," he wrote, "was rather nature's snapshot than a meticulous portrait, so that when . . . tried to imagine it, all he could visualize were fleeting glimpses of disconnected features: the downy outline of her pommettes in the sun, the amber-tinted brown darkness of quick eyes, lips shaped into a friendly smile which was always ready to change into an ardent kiss."

Again and again she hurriedly appeared in the margins of my life, without influencing in the least its basic text. One summer morning (Friday—because housemaids were thumping out carpets in the sun-dusted yard), my family was away in the country and I was lolling and smoking in bed when I heard the bell ring with tremendous violence—and there she was in the hall having burst in to leave (incidentally) a hairpin and (mainly) a trunk illuminated with hotel labels, which a fortnight later was retrieved for her by a nice Austrian boy, who (according to intangible but sure symptoms) belonged to the same very cosmopolitan association of which I was a member. Occasionally, in the middle of a conversation her name would be mentioned, and she would run down the steps of a chance sentence, without turning her head. While traveling in the Pyrénées, I spent a week at the château belonging to people with whom she and Ferdinand happened to be staying, and I shall never forget my first night there: how I waited, how certain I was that without my having to tell her she would steal to my room, how she did not come, and the din thousands of crickets made in the delirious depth of the rocky garden dripping with moonlight, the mad bubbling brooks, and my struggle between blissful southern fatigue after a long day of hunting on the screes and the wild thirst for her stealthy coming, low laugh, pink ankles above the swan's-down trimming of high-heeled slippers; but the night raved on, and she did not come, and when next day, in the course of a general ramble in the mountains, I told her of my waiting, she clasped her hands in dismay—and at once with a rapid glance estimated whether the backs of the gesticulating Ferd and his friend had sufficiently receded. I remember talking to her on the telephone across half of Europe (on her husband's business) and not recognizing at first her eager barking voice; and I remember once dreaming of her: I dreamt that my eldest girl had run in to tell me the doorman was sorely in trouble—and when I had gone down to him, I saw lying on a trunk, a roll of burlap under her head, pale-lipped and wrapped in a woolen kerchief, Nina fast asleep, as miserable refugees sleep in Godforsaken railway stations. And regardless of what happened to me or to her, in between, we never discussed anything, as we never thought of each other during the intervals in our destiny, so that when we met the pace of life altered at once, all its atoms were recombined, and we lived in another, lighter time-medium, which was measured not by the lengthy separations but by those few meetings of which a short, supposedly frivolous life was thus artificially formed. And with each new meeting I grew more and more apprehensive; no—I did not experience any inner emotional collapse, the shadow of tragedy did not haunt our revels, my married life remained unimpaired, while on the other hand her eclectic husband ignored her casual affairs although deriving some profit from them in the way of pleasant and useful connections. I grew apprehensive because something lovely, delicate, and unrepeatable was being wasted: something which I abused by snapping off poor bright bits in gross haste while neglecting the modest but true core which perhaps it kept offering me in a pitiful whisper. I was apprehensive because, in the long run, I was somehow accepting Nina's life, the lies, the futility, the gibberish of that life. Even in the absence of any sentimental discord, I felt myself bound to seek for a rational, if not moral, interpretation of my existence, and this meant choosing between the world in which I sat for my portrait, with my wife, my young daughters, the Doberman pinscher (idyllic garlands, a signet ring, a slender cane), between that happy, wise, and good world . . . and what? Was there any practical chance of life together with Nina, life I could barely imagine, for it would be penetrated, I knew, with a passionate, intolerable bitterness and every moment of it would be aware of a past, teeming with protean partners. No, the thing was absurd. And moreover was she not chained to her husband by something stronger than love—the staunch friendship between two convicts? Absurd! But then what should I have done with you, Nina, how should I have disposed of the store of sadness that had gradually accumulated as a result of our seemingly carefree, but really hopeless meetings?

Fialta consists of the old town and of the new one; here and there, past and present are interlaced, struggling either to disentangle themselves or to thrust each other out; each one has its own methods: the newcomer fights honestly—importing palm trees, setting up smart tourist agencies, painting with creamy lines the red smoothness of tennis courts; whereas the sneaky old-timer creeps out from behind a corner in the shape of some little street on crutches or the steps of stairs leading nowhere. On our way to the hotel, we passed a half-built white villa, full of litter within, on a wall of which again the same elephants, their monstrous baby knees wide apart, sat on huge, gaudy drums; in ethereal bundles the equestrienne (already with a penciled mustache) was resting on a broad-backed steed; and a tomato-nosed clown was walking a tightrope, balancing an umbrella ornamented with those recurrent stars—a vague symbolic recollection of the heavenly fatherland of circus performers. Here, in the Riviera part of Fialta, the wet gravel crunched in a more luxurious manner, and the lazy sighing of the sea was more audible. In the back yard of the hotel, a kitchen boy armed with a knife was pursuing a hen which was clucking madly as it raced for its life. A bootblack offered me his ancient throne with a toothless smile. Under the plane trees stood a motorcycle of German make, a mud-bespattered limousine, and a yellow long-bodied Icarus that looked like a giant scarab: ("That's ours—Segur's, I mean," said Nina, adding, "Why don't you come with us, Victor?" although she knew very well that I could not come); in the lacquer of its elytra a gouache of sky and branches was engulfed; in the metal of one of the bomb-shaped lamps we ourselves were momentarily reflected, lean filmland pedestrians passing along the convex surface; and then, after a few steps, I glanced back and foresaw, in an almost optical sense, as it were, what really happened an hour or so later: the three of them wearing motoring helmets, getting in, smiling and waving to me, transparent to me like ghosts, with the color of the world shining through them, and then they were moving, receding, diminishing (Nina's last ten-fingered farewell); but actually the automobile was still standing quite motionless, smooth and whole like an egg, and Nina under my outstretched arm was entering a laurel-flanked doorway, and as we sat down we could see through the window Ferdinand and Segur, who had come by another way, slowly approaching.

There was no one on the veranda where we lunched except the Englishman I had recently observed; in front of him, a long glass containing a bright crimson drink threw an oval reflection on the tablecloth. In his eyes, I noticed the same bloodshot desire, but now it was in no sense related to Nina; that avid look was not directed at her at all, but was fixed on the upper right-hand corner of the broad window near which he was sitting.

Having pulled the gloves off her small thin hands, Nina, for the last time in her life, was eating the shellfish of which she was so fond. Ferdinand also busied himself with food, and I took advantage of his hunger to begin a conversation which gave me the semblance of power over him: to be specific, I mentioned his recent failure. After a brief period of fashionable religious conversion, during which grace descended upon him and he undertook some rather ambiguous pilgrimages, which ended in a decidedly scandalous adventure, he had turned his dull eyes toward barbarous Moscow. Now, frankly speaking, I have always been irritated by the complacent conviction that a ripple of stream of consciousness, a few healthy obscenities, and a dash of communism in any old slop pail will alchemically and automatically produce ultramodern literature; and I will contend until I am shot that art as soon as it is brought into contact with politics inevitably sinks to the level of any ideological trash. In Ferdinand's case, it is true, all this was rather irrelevant: the muscles of his muse were exceptionally strong, to say nothing of the fact that he didn't care a damn for the plight of the underdog; but because of certain obscurely mischievous undercurrents of that sort, his art had become still more repulsive. Except for a few snobs none had understood the play; I had not seen it myself, but could well imagine that elaborate Kremlinesque night along the impossible spirals of which he spun various wheels of dismembered symbols; and now, not without pleasure, I asked him whether he had read a recent bit of criticism about himself.

"Criticism!" he exclaimed. "Fine criticism! Every slick jackanapes sees fit to read me a lecture. Ignorance of my work is their bliss. My books are touched gingerly, as one touches something that may go bang. Criticism! They are examined from every point of view except the essential one. It is as if a naturalist, in describing the equine genus, started to jaw about saddles or Mme. de V. (he named a well-known literary hostess, who indeed strongly resembled a grinning horse). I would like some of that pigeon's blood, too," he continued in the same loud, ripping voice, addressing the waiter, who understood his desire only after he had looked in the direction of the long-nailed finger which unceremoniously pointed at the Englishman's glass. For some reason or other, Segur mentioned Ruby Rose, the lady who painted flowers on her breast, and the conversation

took on a less insulting character. Meanwhile the big Englishman suddenly made up his mind, got up on a chair, stepped
from there on to the window sill, and stretched up till he reached
that coveted corner of the frame where rested a compact furry
moth, which he deftly slipped into a pillbox.

". . . rather like Wouwerman's white horse," said Ferdinand, in regard to something he was discussing with Segur.

"Tu es très hippique ce matin," remarked the latter.

Soon they both left to telephone. Ferdinand was particularly
fond of long-distance calls, and particularly good at endowing
them, no matter what the distance, with a friendly warmth when
it was necessary, as for instance now, to make sure of free lodgings.

From afar came the sounds of music—a trumpet, a zither.
Nina and I set out to wander again. The circus on its way to
Fialta had apparently sent out runners: an advertising pageant
was tramping by; but we did not catch its head, as it had turned
uphill into a side alley: the gilded back of some carriage was
receding, a man in a burnoose led a camel, a file of four mediocre Indians carried placards on poles, and behind them, by
special permission, a tourist's small son in a sailor suit sat rev-
erently on a tiny pony.

We wandered by a café where the tables were now almost dry
but still empty; the waiter was examining (I hope he adopted
it later) a horrible foundling, the absurd inkstand affair, stowed
by Ferdinand on the banisters in passing. At the next corner
we were attracted by an old stone stairway, and we climbed up,
and I kept looking at the sharp angle of Nina's step as she ascended, raising her skirt, its narrowness requiring the same gesture as formerly length had done; she diffused a familiar
warmth, and going up beside her, I recalled the last time we had
come together. It had been in a Paris house, with many people
around, and my dear friend Jules Darboux, wishing to do me a
refined aesthetic favor, had touched my sleeve and said, "I
want you to meet—" and led me to Nina, who sat in the corner

of a couch, her body folded Z-wise, with an ash tray at her heel, and she took a long turquoise cigarette holder from her lips and joyfully, slowly exclaimed, "Well, of all people——" and then all evening my heart felt like breaking, as I passed from group to group with a sticky glass in my fist, now and then looking at her from a distance (she did not look . . .), and listened to scraps of conversation, and overheard one man saying to another, "Funny, how they all smell alike, burnt leaf through whatever perfume they use, those angular dark-haired girls," and as it often happens, a trivial remark related to some unknown topic coiled and clung to one's own intimate recollection, a parasite of its sadness.

At the top of the steps, we found ourselves on a rough kind of terrace. From here one could see the delicate outline of the dove-colored Mount St. George with a cluster of bone-white flecks (some hamlet) on one of its slopes; the smoke of an indiscernible train undulated along its rounded base—and suddenly disappeared; still lower, above the jumble of roofs, one could perceive a solitary cypress, resembling the moist-twirled black tip of a water-color brush; to the right, one caught a glimpse of the sea, which was gray, with silver wrinkles. At our feet lay a rusty old key, and on the wall of the half-ruined house adjoining the terrace, the ends of some wire still remained hanging . . . I reflected that formerly there had been life here, a family had enjoyed the coolness at nightfall, clumsy children had colored pictures by the light of a lamp . . . We lingered there as if listening to something; Nina, who stood on higher ground, put a hand on my shoulder and smiled, and carefully, so as not to crumple her smile, kissed me. With an unbearable force, I relived (or so it now seems to me) all that had ever been between us beginning with a similar kiss; and I said (substituting for our cheap, formal "thou" that strangely full and expressive "you" to which the circumnavigator, enriched all around, returns), "Look here—what if I love you?" Nina glanced at me, I repeated those words, I wanted to add

. . . but something like a bat passed swiftly across her face, a quick, queer, almost ugly expression, and she, who would utter coarse words with perfect simplicity, became embarrassed; I also felt awkward . . . "Never mind, I was only joking," I hastened to say, lightly encircling her waist. From somewhere a firm bouquet of small, dark, unselfishly smelling violets appeared in her hands, and before she returned to her husband and car, we stood for a little while longer by the stone parapet, and our romance was even more hopeless than it had ever been. But the stone was as warm as flesh, and suddenly I understood something I had been seeing without understanding—why a piece of tin foil had sparkled so on the pavement, why the gleam of a glass had trembled on a tablecloth, why the sea was ashimmer: somehow, by imperceptible degrees, the white sky above Fialta had got saturated with sunshine, and now it was sunpervaded throughout, and this brimming white radiance grew broader and broader, all dissolved in it, all vanished, all passed, and I stood on the station platform of Mlech with a freshly bought newspaper, which told me that the yellow car I had seen under the plane trees had suffered a crash beyond Fialta, having run at full speed into the truck of a traveling circus entering the town, a crash from which Ferdinand and his friend, those invulnerable rogues, those salamanders of fate, those basilisks of good fortune, had escaped with local and temporary injury to their scales, while Nina, in spite of her longstanding, faithful imitation of them, had turned out after all to be mortal.

Paris, 1938
Translated by Peter Pertzov
and the author

"That in Aleppo Once..."

~~~~~~

Dear V.—Among other things, this is to tell you that at last I am here, in the country whither so many sunsets have led. One of the first persons I saw was our good old Gleb Alexandrovich Gekko gloomily crossing Columbus Avenue in quest of the *petit café du coin* which none of us three will ever visit again. He seemed to think that somehow or other you were betraying our national literature, and he gave me your address with a deprecatory shake of his gray head, as if you did not deserve the treat of hearing from me.

I have a story for you. Which reminds me—I mean putting it like this reminds me—of the days when we wrote our first udder-warm bubbling verse, and all things, a rose, a puddle, a lighted window, cried out to us: "I'm a rhyme!" Yes, this is a most useful universe. We play, we die: ig-rhyme, umi-rhyme. And the sonorous souls of Russian verbs lend a meaning to the wild gesticulation of trees or to some discarded newspaper sliding and pausing, and shuffling again, with abortive flaps and apterous jerks along an endless wind-swept embankment. But just now I am not a poet. I come to you like that gushing lady in Chekhov who was dying to be described.

I married, let me see, about a month after you left France and a few weeks before the gentle Germans roared into Paris. Although I can produce documentary proofs of matrimony, I am positive now that my wife never existed. You may know her name from some other source, but that does not matter: it is the name of an illusion. Therefore, I am able to speak of her with as much detachment as I would of a character in a story (one of your stories, to be precise).

It was love at first touch rather than at first sight, for I had met her several times before without experiencing any special emotions; but one night, as I was seeing her home, something quaint she had said made me stoop with a laugh and lightly kiss her on the hair—and of course we all know of that blinding blast which is caused by merely picking up a small doll from the floor of a carefully abandoned house: the soldier involved hears nothing; for him it is but an ecstatic soundless and boundless expansion of what had been during his life a pin point of light in the dark center of his being. And really, the reason we think of death in celestial terms is that the visible firmament, especially at night (above our blacked-out Paris with the gaunt arches of its Boulevard Exelmans and the ceaseless Alpine gurgle of desolate latrines), is the most adequate and ever-present symbol of that vast silent explosion.

But I cannot discern her. She remains as nebulous as my best poem—the one you made such gruesome fun of in the *Literaturnïe Zapiski*. When I want to imagine her, I have to cling mentally to a tiny brown birthmark on her downy forearm, as one concentrates upon a punctuation mark in an illegible sentence. Perhaps, had she used a greater amount of make-up or used it more constantly, I might have visualized her face today, or at least the delicate transverse furrows of dry, hot rouged lips; but I fail, I fail—although I still feel their elusive touch now and then in the blindman's buff of my senses, in that sobbing sort of dream when she and I clumsily clutch at each other through a heartbreaking mist and I cannot see the color of her eyes for the blank luster of brimming tears drowning their irises.

She was much younger than I—not as much younger as was Nathalie of the lovely bare shoulders and long earrings in relation to swarthy Pushkin; but still there was a sufficient margin for that kind of retrospective romanticism which finds pleasure in imitating the destiny of a unique genius (down to the jealousy, down to the filth, down to the stab of seeing her almond-shaped eyes turn to her blond Cassio behind her peacock-feathered fan) even if one cannot imitate his verse. She liked mine though, and would scarcely have yawned as the other was wont to do every time her husband's poem happened to exceed the length of a sonnet. If she has remained a phantom to me, I may have been one to her: I suppose she had been solely attracted by the obscurity of my poetry; then tore a hole through its veil and saw a stranger's unlovable face.

As you know, I had been for some time planning to follow the example of your fortunate flight. She described to me an uncle of hers who lived, she said, in New York: he had taught riding at a Southern college and had wound up by marrying a wealthy American woman; they had a little daughter born deaf. She said she had lost their address long ago, but a few days later it miraculously turned up, and we wrote a dramatic letter to which we never received any reply. This did not much matter, as I had already obtained a sound affidavit from Professor Lomchenko of Chicago; but little else had been done in the way of getting the necessary papers, when the invasion began, whereas I foresaw that if we stayed on in Paris some helpful compatriot of mine would sooner or later point out to the interested party sundry passages in one of my books where I argued that, with all her many black sins, Germany was still bound to remain forever and ever the laughing stock of the world.

So we started upon our disastrous honeymoon. Crushed and jolted amid the apocalyptic exodus, waiting for unscheduled trains that were bound for unknown destinations, walking through the stale stage setting of abstract towns, living in a permanent twilight of physical exhaustion, we fled; and the farther we fled, the clearer it became that what was driving us on was something more than a booted and buckled fool with his

assortment of variously propelled junk—something of which
he was a mere symbol, something monstrous and impalpable, a
timeless and faceless mass of immemorial horror that still keeps
coming at me from behind even here, in the green vacuum of
Central Park.

Oh, she bore it gamely enough—with a kind of dazed cheerfulness. Once, however, quite suddenly she started to sob in a
sympathetic railway carriage. "The dog," she said, "the dog we
left. I cannot forget the poor dog." The honesty of her
grief shocked me, as we had never had any dog. "I know," she
said, "but I tried to imagine we had actually bought that setter.
And just think, he would be now whining behind a locked
door." There had never been any talk of buying a setter.

I should also not like to forget a certain stretch of high-road
and the sight of a family of refugees (two women, a child)
whose old father, or grandfather, had died on the way. The sky
was a chaos of black and flesh-colored clouds with an ugly sunburst beyond a hooded hill, and the dead man was lying on his
back under a dusty plane tree. With a stick and their hands
the women had tried to dig a roadside grave, but the soil was
too hard; they had given it up and were sitting side by side,
among the anemic poppies, a little apart from the corpse and
its upturned beard. But the little boy was still scratching and
scraping and tugging until he tumbled a flat stone and forgot
the object of his solemn exertions as he crouched on his
haunches, his thin, eloquent neck showing all its vertebrae to
the headsman, and watched with surprise and delight thousands of minute brown ants seething, zigzagging, dispersing,
heading for places of safety in the Gard, and the Aude, and the
Drome, and the Var, and the Basses-Pyrénées—we two paused
only in Pau.

Spain proved too difficult and we decided to move on to Nice.
At a place called Faugères (a ten-minute stop) I squeezed out
of the train to buy some food. When a couple of minutes later I
came back, the train was gone, and the muddled old man re-

sponsible for the atrocious void that faced me (coal dust glittering in the heat between naked indifferent rails, and a lone piece
of orange peel) brutally told me that, anyway, I had had no
right to get out.

In a better world I could have had my wife located and told
what to do (I had both tickets and most of the money); as it
was, my nightmare struggle with the telephone proved futile,
so I dismissed the whole series of diminutive voices barking at
me from afar, sent two or three telegrams which are probably
on their way only now, and late in the evening took the next
local to Montpellier, farther than which her train would not
stumble. Not finding her there, I had to choose between two
alternatives: going on because she might have boarded the
Marseilles train which I had just missed, or going back because
she might have returned to Faugères. I forget now what tangle
of reasoning led me to Marseilles and Nice.

Beyond such routine action as forwarding false data to a few
unlikely places, the police did nothing to help: one man bellowed at me for being a nuisance; another sidetracked the question by doubting the authenticity of my marriage certificate
because it was stamped on what he contended to be the wrong
side; a third, a fat *commissaire* with liquid brown eyes confessed that he wrote poetry in his spare time. I looked up various acquaintances among the numerous Russians domiciled or
stranded in Nice. I heard those among them who chanced to
have Jewish blood talk of their doomed kinsmen crammed into
hell-bound trains; and my own plight, by contrast, acquired a
commonplace air of irreality while I sat in some crowded café
with the milky blue sea in front of me and a shell-hollow murmur behind telling and retelling the tale of massacre and misery,
and the gray paradise beyond the ocean, and the ways and
whims of harsh consuls.

A week after my arrival an indolent plain-clothes man
called upon me and took me down a crooked and smelly street
to a black-stained house with the word "hotel" almost erased by
dirt and time; there, he said, my wife had been found. The girl

he produced was an absolute stranger, of course; but my
friend Holmes kept on trying for some time to make her and me
confess we were married, while her taciturn and muscular bed-
fellow stood by and listened, his bare arms crossed on his
striped chest.

When at length I got rid of those people and had wandered
back to my neighborhood, I happened to pass by a compact
queue waiting at the entrance of a food store; and there, at the
very end, was my wife, straining on tiptoe to catch a glimpse of
what exactly was being sold. I think the first thing she said to
me was that she hoped it was oranges.

Her tale seemed a trifle hazy, but perfectly banal. She had
returned to Faugères and gone straight to the Commissariat instead of making inquiries at the station, where I had left a message for her. A party of refugees suggested that she join them;
she spent the night in a bicycle shop with no bicycles, on the
floor, together with three elderly women who lay, she said, like
three logs in a row. Next day she realized that she had not
enough money to reach Nice. Eventually she borrowed some
from one of the log-women. She got into the wrong train, however, and traveled to a town the name of which she could not
remember. She had arrived at Nice two days ago and had
found some friends at the Russian church. They had told
her I was somewhere around, looking for her, and would
surely turn up soon.

Some time later, as I sat on the edge of the only chair in m'
garret and held her by her slender young hips (she was com'
ing her soft hair and tossing her head back with every strok(.),
her dim smile changed all at once into an odd quiver and she
placed one hand on my shoulder, staring down at me as if I
were a reflection in a pool, which she had noticed for the first
time.

"I've been lying to you, dear," she said. "*Ya lgunia.* I stayed
for several nights in Montpellier with a brute of a man I met
on the train. I did not want it at all. He sold hair lotions."

The time, the place, the torture. Her fan, her gloves, her mask. I spent that night and many others getting it out of her bit by bit, but not getting it all. I was under the strange delusion that first I must find out every detail, reconstruct every minute, and only then decide whether I could bear it. But the limit of desired knowledge was unattainable, nor could I ever foretell the approximate point after which I might imagine myself satiated, because of course the denominator of every fraction of knowledge was potentially as infinite as the number of intervals between the fractions themselves.

Oh, the first time she had been too tired to mind, and the next had not minded because she was sure I had deserted her; and she apparently considered that such explanations ought to be a kind of consolation prize for me instead of the nonsense and agony they really were. It went on like that for eons, she breaking down every now and then, but soon rallying again, answering my unprintable questions in a breathless whisper or trying with a pitiful smile to wriggle into the semisecurity of irrelevant commentaries, and I crushing and crushing the mad molar till my jaw almost burst with pain, a flaming pain which seemed somehow preferable to the dull, humming ache of humble endurance.

And mark, in between the periods of this inquest, we were trying to get from reluctant authorities certain papers which in their turn would make it lawful to apply for a third kind which would serve as a steppingstone toward a permit enabling the holder to apply for yet other papers which might or might not give him the means of discovering how and why it had happened. For even if I could imagine the accursed recurrent scene, I failed to link up its sharp-angled grotesque shadows with the dim limbs of my wife as she shook and rattled and dissolved in my violent grasp.

So nothing remained but to torture each other, to wait for hours on end in the Prefecture, filling forms, conferring with friends who had already probed the innermost viscera of all visas, pleading with secretaries, and filling forms again, with the result that her lusty and versatile traveling salesman became blended in a ghastly mix-up with rat-whiskered snarling officials, rotting bundles of obsolete records, the reek of violet ink, bribes slipped under gangrenous blotting paper, fat flies tickling moist necks with their rapid cold padded feet, new-laid clumsy concave photographs of your six subhuman doubles, the tragic eyes and patient politeness of petitioners born in Slutzk, Starodub, or Bobruisk, the funnels and pulleys of the Holy Inquisition, the awful smile of the bald man with the glasses, who had been told that his passport could not be found.

I confess that one evening, after a particularly abominable day, I sank down on a stone bench weeping and cursing a mock world where millions of lives were being juggled by the clammy hands of consuls and *commissaires*. I noticed she was crying too, and then I told her that nothing would really have mattered the way it mattered now, had she not gone and done what she did.

"You will think me crazy," she said with a vehemence that, for a second, almost made a real person of her, "but I didn't— I swear that I didn't. Perhaps I live several lives at once. Perhaps I wanted to test you. Perhaps this bench is a dream and we are in Saratov or on some star."

It would be tedious to niggle the different stages through which I passed before accepting finally the first version of her delay. I did not talk to her and was a good deal alone. She would glimmer and fade, and reappear with some trifle she thought I would appreciate—a handful of cherries, three precious cigarettes or the like—treating me with the unruffled mute sweetness of a nurse that trips from and to a gruff convalescent. I ceased visiting most of our mutual friends because they had lost all interest in my passport affairs and seemed to have turned vaguely inimical. I composed several poems. I drank all the wine I could get. I clasped her one day to my groaning breast, and we went for a week to Caboule and lay on the round pink

pebbles of the narrow beach. Strange to say, the happier our
new relations seemed, the stronger I felt an undercurrent of
poignant sadness, but I kept telling myself that this was an
intrinsic feature of all true bliss.

In the meantime, something had shifted in the moving pattern of our fates and at last I emerged from a dark and hot
office with a couple of plump *visas de sortie* cupped in my trembling hands. Into these the U.S.A. serum was duly injected,
and I dashed to Marseilles and managed to get tickets for the
very next boat. I returned and tramped up the stairs. I saw a
rose in a glass on the table—the sugar pink of its obvious
beauty, the parasitic air bubbles clinging to its stem. Her two
spare dresses were gone, her comb was gone, her checkered
coat was gone, and so was the mauve hairband with a mauve
bow that had been her hat. There was no note pinned to the
pillow, nothing at all in the room to enlighten me, for of course
the rose was merely what French rhymsters call *une cheville*.

I went to the Veretennikovs, who could tell me nothing; to
the Hellmans, who refused to say anything; and to the Elagins,
who were not sure whether to tell me or not. Finally the old
lady—and you know what Anna Vladimirovna is like at crucial
moments—asked for her rubber-tipped cane, heavily but energetically dislodged her bulk from her favorite armchair, and
took me into the garden. There she informed me that, being
twice my age, she had the right to say I was a bully and a cad.

You must imagine the scene: the tiny graveled garden with
its blue Arabian Nights jar and solitary cypress; the cracked
terrace where the old lady's father had dozed with a rug on his
knees when he retired from his Novgorod governorship to spend
a few last evenings in Nice; the pale-green sky; a whiff of vanilla
in the deepening dusk; the crickets emitting their metallic trill
pitched at two octaves above middle C; and Anna Vladimirovna, the folds of her cheeks jerkily dangling as she flung at
me a motherly but quite undeserved insult.

During several preceding weeks, my dear V., every time she

had visited by herself the three or four families we both knew, my ghostly wife had filled the eager ears of all those kind people with an extraordinary story. To wit: that she had madly fallen in love with a young Frenchman who could give her a turreted home and a crested name; that she had implored me for a divorce and I had refused; that in fact I had said I would rather shoot her and myself than sail to New York alone; that she had said her father in a similar case had acted like a gentleman; that I had answered I did not give a hoot for her *cocu de père*.

There were loads of other preposterous details of the kind— but they all hung together in such a remarkable fashion that no wonder the old lady made me swear I would not seek to pursue the lovers with a cocked pistol. They had gone, she said, to a château in Lozère. I inquired whether she had ever set eyes upon the man. No, but she had been shown his picture. As I was about to leave, Anna Vladimirovna, who had slightly relaxed and had even given me her five fingers to kiss, suddenly flared up again, struck the gravel with her cane, and said in her deep strong voice: "But one thing I shall never forgive you —her dog, that poor beast which you hanged with your own hands before leaving Paris."

Whether the gentleman of leisure had changed into a traveling salesman, or whether the metamorphosis had been reversed, or whether again he was neither the one nor the other, but the nondescript Russian who had courted her before our marriage—all this was absolutely inessential. She had gone. That was the end. I should have been a fool had I begun the nightmare business of searching and waiting for her all over again.

On the fourth morning of a long and dismal sea voyage, I met on the deck a solemn but pleasant old doctor with whom I had played chess in Paris. He asked me whether my wife was very much incommoded by the rough seas. I answered that I had sailed alone; whereupon he looked taken aback and then said he had seen her a couple of days before going on board, namely in Marseilles, walking, rather aimlessly he thought, along the embankment. She said that I would presently join her with bag and tickets.

This is, I gather, the point of the whole story—although if you write it, you had better not make him a doctor, as that kind of thing has been overdone. It was at that moment that I suddenly knew for certain that she had never existed at all. I shall tell you another thing. When I arrived I hastened to satisfy a certain morbid curiosity: I went to the address she had given me once; it proved to be an anonymous gap between two office buildings; I looked for her uncle's name in the directory; it was not there; I made some inquiries, and Gekko, who knows everything, informed me that the man and his horsey wife existed all right, but had moved to San Francisco after their deaf little girl had died.

Viewing the past graphically, I see our mangled romance engulfed in a deep valley of mist between the crags of two matter-of-fact mountains: life had been real before, life will be real from now on, I hope. Not tomorrow, though. Perhaps after tomorrow. You, happy mortal, with your lovely family (how is Ines? how are the twins?) and your diversified work (how are the lichens?), can hardly be expected to puzzle out my misfortune in terms of human communion, but you may clarify things for me through the prism of your art.

Yet the pity of it. Curse your art, I am hideously unhappy. She keeps on walking to and fro where the brown nets are spread to dry on the hot stone slabs and the dappled light of the water plays on the side of a moored fishing boat. Somewhere, somehow, I have made some fatal mistake. There are tiny pale bits of broken fish scales glistening here and there in the brown meshes. It may all end in *Aleppo* if I am not careful. Spare me, V.: you would load your dice with an unbearable implication if you took that for a title.

Boston, 1943

The Assistant Producer

~~~~~~

Meaning? Well, because sometimes life is merely that—an Assistant Producer. Tonight we shall go to the movies. Back to the Thirties, and down the Twenties, and round the corner to the old Europe Picture Palace. She was a celebrated singer. Not opera, not even *Cavalleria Rusticana*, not anything like that. "La Slavska"—that is what the French called her. Style: one-tenth *tzigane*, one-seventh Russian peasant girl (she had been that herself originally), and five-ninths popular—and by popular I mean a hodgepodge of artificial folklore, military melodrama, and official patriotism. The fraction left unfilled seems sufficient to represent the physical splendor of her prodigious voice.

Coming from what was, geographically at least, the very heart of Russia, it eventually reached the big cities, Moscow, St. Petersburg, and the Tsar's milieu where that sort of style was greatly appreciated. In Feodor Chaliapin's dressing room there hung a photograph of her: Russian headgear with pearls, hand propping cheek, dazzling teeth between fleshy lips, and a great clumsy scrawl right across: "For you, Fedyusha." Stars of snow, each revealing, before the edges melted, its complex symmetry, would gently come to rest on the shoulders and sleeves and mustaches and caps—all waiting in a queue for the box office to open. Up to her very death she treasured above all—or pretended to do so—a fancy medal and a huge brooch that had been given her by the Tsarina. They came from the firm of jewelers which used to do such profitable business by presenting the Imperial couple on every festive occasion with this or that emblem (each year increasing in worth) of massive Tsardom: some great lump of amethyst with a ruby-studded bronze troika stranded on top like Noah's Ark on Mount Ararat, or a sphere of crystal the size of a watermelon surmounted by a gold eagle with square diamond eyes very much like those of Rasputin (many years later some of the less symbolic ones were exhibited at a World's Fair by the Soviets as samples of their own thriving Art).

Had things gone on as they were seeming to go, she might have been still singing tonight in a central-heated Hall of Nobility or at Tsarskoye, and I should be turning off her broadcast voice in some remote corner of steppe-mother Siberia. But destiny took the wrong turning; and when the Revolution happened, followed by the War of the Reds and the Whites, her wily peasant soul chose the more practical party.

Ghostly multitudes of ghostly Cossacks on ghost-horseback are seen charging through the fading name of the assistant producer. Then dapper General Golubkov is disclosed idly scanning the battlefield through a pair of opera glasses. When movies and we were young, we used to be shown what the sights divulged neatly framed in two connected circles. Not now. What we do see next is General Golubkov, all indolence suddenly gone, leaping into the saddle, looming sky-high for an instant on his rearing steed and then rocketing into a crazy attack.

But the unexpected is the infra-red in the spectrum of Art: instead of the conditional *ra-ta-ta* reflex of machine gunnery, a woman's voice is heard singing afar. Nearer, still nearer, and finally all-pervading. A gorgeous contralto voice expanding into whatever the musical director found in his files in the way of Russian lilt. Who is this leading the infra-Reds? A woman. The singing spirit of that particular, especially well-trained battalion. Marching in front, trampling the alfalfa and pouring out her Volga-Volga song. Dapper and daring *djighit* Golubkov (now we know what he had descried), although wounded in several spots, manages to snatch her up on the gallop, and, lusciously struggling, she is borne away.

Strangely enough, that vile script was enacted in reality. I myself have known at least two reliable witnesses of the event; and the sentries of history have let it pass unchallenged. Very soon we find her maddening the officers' mess with her dark buxom beauty and wild, wild songs. She was a Belle Dame with a good deal of Merci, and there was a punch about her that Louise von Lenz or the Green Lady lacked. She it was who sweetened the general retreat of the Whites, which began shortly after her magic appearance at General Golubkov's camp. We get a gloomy glimpse of ravens, or crows, or whatever birds proved available, wheeling in the dusk and slowly descending upon a plain littered with bodies somewhere in Ventura County. A White soldier's dead hand is still clutching a medallion with his mother's face. A Red soldier near by has on his shattered breast a letter from home with the same old woman blinking through the dissolving lines.

And then, in traditional contrast, pat comes a mighty burst of music and song with a rhythmic clapping of hands and stamping of booted feet and we see General Golubkov's staff in full revelry—a lithe Georgian dancing with a dagger, the self-conscious samovar reflecting distorted faces, the Slavska throwing her head back with a throaty laugh, and the fat man of the corps, horribly drunk, braided collar undone, greasy lips pursed for a bestial kiss, leaning across the table (close-up of an overturned glass) to hug—nothingness, for wiry and perfectly sober General Golubkov has deftly removed her and now, as they both stand facing the gang, says in a cold, clear voice: "Gentlemen, I want to present you my bride"—and in the stunned silence that follows, a stray bullet from outside chances to shatter the dawn-blue windowpane, after which a roar of applause greets the glamorous couple.

There is little doubt that her capture had not been wholly a fortuitous occurrence. Indeterminism is banned from the studio. It is even less doubtful that when the great exodus began and they, as many others, meandered via Sirkedji to Motz-strasse and Rue Vaugirard, the General and his wife already formed one team, one song, one cipher. Quite naturally he be-came an efficient member of the W.W. (White Warriors Union), traveling about, organizing military courses for Rus-sian boys, arranging relief concerts, unearthing barracks for the destitute, settling local disputes, and doing all this in a most unobtrusive manner. I suppose it was useful in some ways, that W.W. Unfortunately for its spiritual welfare, it was quite in-capable of cutting itself off from monarchist groups abroad and did not feel, as the *émigré* intelligentsia felt, the dreadful vul-garity, the Ur-Hitlerism of those ludicrous but vicious organiza-tions. When well-meaning Americans ask me whether I know charming Colonel So-and-so or grand old Count de Kickoffsky, I have not the heart to tell them the dismal truth.

But there was also another type of person connected with the W.W. I am thinking of those adventurous souls who helped the cause by crossing the frontier through some snow-muffled fir forest, to potter about their native land in the vari-ous disguises worked out, oddly enough, by the social revolu-tionaries of yore, and quietly bring back to the little café in Paris called "Esh-Bubliki," or to the little *Kneipe* in Berlin that had no special name, the kind of useful trifles which spies are sup-posed to bring back to their employers. Some of those men had become abstrusely entangled with the spying departments of other nations and would give an amusing jump if you came from behind and tapped them on the shoulder. A few went a-scouting for the fun of the thing. One or two perhaps really believed that in some mystical way they were preparing the resurrection of a sacred, if somewhat musty, past.

2

We are now going to witness a most weirdly monotonous series of events. The first president of the W.W. to die was the leader of the whole White movement and by far the best man of the lot; and certain dark symptoms attending his sudden illness suggested a poisoner's shadow. The next president, a huge, strong fellow with a voice of thunder and a head like a cannon ball, was kidnapped by persons unknown; and there are reasons to believe that he died from an overdose of chloroform. The third president—but my reel is going too fast. Actually it took seven years to remove the first two—not because this sort of thing cannot be done more briskly, but because there were particular circumstances that necessitated some very precise timing, so as to co-ordinate one's steady ascent with the spacing of sudden vacancies. Let us explain.

Golubkov was not only a very versatile spy (a triple agent to be exact); he was also an exceedingly ambitious little fellow. Why the vision of presiding over an organization that was but a sunset behind a cemetery happened to be so dear to him is a conundrum only for those who have no hobbies or passions. He wanted it very badly—that is all. What is less intelligible is the faith he had in being able to safeguard his puny existence in the crush between the formidable parties whose dangerous money and dangerous help he received. I want all your attention now, for it would be a pity to miss the subtleties of the situation.

The Soviets could not be much disturbed by the highly improbable prospect of a phantom White Army ever being able to resume war operations against their consolidated bulk; but they could be very much irritated by the fact that scraps of information about forts and factories, gathered by elusive W.W. meddlers, were automatically falling into grateful German hands. The Germans were little interested in the recondite color variations of *émigré* politics, but what did annoy them was the blunt patriotism of a W.W. president every now and then obstructing on ethical grounds the smooth flow of friendly collaboration.

Thus, General Golubkov was a godsend. The Soviets firmly expected that under his rule all W.W. spies would be well known to them—and shrewdly supplied with false information for eager German consumption. The Germans were equally sure that through him they would be guaranteed a good cropping of their own absolutely trustworthy agents distributed among the usual W.W. ones. Neither side had any illusions concerning Golubkov's loyalty, but each assumed that it would turn to its own profit the fluctuations of double-crossing. The dreams of simple Russian folk, hard-working families in remote parts of the Russian diaspora, plying their humble but honest trades, as they would in Saratov or Tver, bearing fragile children and naïvely believing that the W.W. was a kind of King Arthur's Round Table that stood for all that had been, and would be, sweet and decent and strong in fairy tale Russia— these dreams may well strike the film pruners as an excrescence upon the main theme.

When the W.W. was founded, General Golubkov's candidacy (purely theoretical, of course, for nobody expected the leader to die) was very far down the list—not because his legendary gallantry was insufficiently appreciated by his fellow officers, but because he happened to be the youngest general in the army. Toward the time of the next president's election Golubkov had already disclosed such tremendous capacities as an organizer that he felt he could safely cross out quite a few intermediate names in the list, incidentally sparing the lives of their bearers. After the second general had been removed, many of the W.W. members were convinced that General Fedchenko, the next candidate, would surrender in favor of the younger and more efficient man the rights that his age, reputation, and academic distinction entitled him to enjoy.

The old gentleman, however, though doubtful of the enjoyment, thought it cowardly to avoid a job that had cost two men their lives. So Golubkov set his teeth and started to dig again.

Physically he lacked attraction. There was nothing of your popular Russian general about him, nothing of that good, burly, popeyed, thick-necked sort. He was lean, frail, with sharp features, a clipped mustache, and the kind of haircut that is called by Russians "hedgehog": short, wiry, upright, and compact. There was a thin silver bracelet round his hairy wrist, and he offered you neat homemade Russian cigarettes or English prune-flavored "Kapstens," as he pronounced it, snugly arranged in an old roomy cigarette case of black leather that had accompanied him through the presumable smoke of numberless battles. He was extremely polite and extremely inconspicuous.

Whenever the Slavska "received," which she would do at the homes of her various Maecenases (a Baltic baron of sorts, a Dr. Bachrach whose first wife had been a famous Carmen, or a Russian merchant of the old school who, in inflation-mad Berlin, was having a wonderful time buying up blocks of houses for ten pounds sterling apiece), her silent husband would unobtrusively thread his way among the visitors, bringing you a sausage-and-cucumber sandwich or a tiny frosty-pale glass of vodka; and while the Slavska sang (on those informal occasions she used to sing seated with her fist at her cheek and her elbow cupped in the palm of her other hand) he would stand apart, leaning against something, or would tiptoe toward a distant ash tray which he would gently place on the fat arm of your chair.

I consider that, artistically, he overstressed his effacement, unwittingly introducing a hired-lackey note—which now seems singularly appropriate; but he of course was trying to base his existence upon the principle of contrast and would get a marvelous thrill from exactly knowing by certain sweet signs—a bent head, a rolling eye—that So-and-so at the far end of the room was drawing a newcomer's attention to the fascinating fact that such a dim, modest man was the hero of incredible exploits in a legendary war (taking towns singlehanded and that sort of thing).

3

German film companies, which kept sprouting like poisonous mushrooms in those days (just before the child of light learned to talk), found cheap labor in hiring those among the Russian *émigrés* whose only hope and profession was their past—that is, a set of totally unreal people—to represent "real" audiences in pictures. The dovetailing of one phantasm into another produced upon a sensitive person the impression of living in a Hall of Mirrors, or rather a prison of mirrors, and not even knowing which was the glass and which was yourself.

Indeed, when I recall the halls where the Slavska sang, both in Berlin and in Paris, and the type of people one saw there, I feel as if I were technicoloring and sonorizing some very ancient motion picture where life had been a gray vibration and funerals a scamper, and where only the sea had been tinted (a sickly blue), while some hand machine imitated off stage the hiss of the asynchronous surf. A certain shady character, the terror of relief organizations, a bald-headed man with mad eyes, slowly floats across my field of vision with his legs bent in a sitting position, like an elderly fetus, and then miraculously fits into a back-row seat. Our friend the Count is also here, complete with high collar and dingy spats. A venerable but worldly priest, with his cross gently heaving on his ample chest, sits in the front row and looks straight ahead.

The items of these Right Wing festivals that the Slavska's name evokes in my mind were of the same unreal nature as was her audience. A variety artist with a fake Slav name, one of those guitar virtuosos that come as a cheap first in music hall

programs, would be most welcome here; and the flashy orna-
ments on his glass-paneled instrument, and his sky-blue silk
pants, would go well with the rest of the show. Then some
bearded old rascal in a shabby cutaway coat, former member
of the Holy Russ First, would take the chair and vividly describe what the Israel-sons and the Phreemasons (two secret
Semitic tribes) were doing to the Russian people.

And now, ladies and gentlemen, we have the great pleasure
and honor— There she would stand against a dreadful background of palms and national flags, and moisten her rich painted
lips with her pale tongue, and leisurely clasp her kid-gloved
hands on her corseted stomach, while her constant accom-
panist, marble-faced Joseph Levinsky, who had followed her,
in the shadow of her song, to the Tsar's private concert hall
and to Comrade Lunacharsky's salon, and to nondescript places
in Constantinople, produced his brief introductory series of
stepping-stone notes.

Sometimes, if the house was of the right sort, she would sing
the national anthem before launching upon her limited but ever
welcome repertoire. Inevitably there would be that lugubri-
ous "Old Road to Kaluga" (with a thunderstruck pine tree at
the forty-ninth verst), and the one that begins, in the German
translation printed beneath the Russian text, *"Du bist im Schnee
begraben, mein Russland,"* and the ancient folklore ballad
(written by a private person in the eighties) about the robber
chieftain and his lovely Persian Princess, whom he threw into
the Volga when his crew accused him of going soft.

Her artistic taste was nowhere, her technique haphazard, her
general style atrocious; but the kind of people for whom music
and sentiment are one, or who like songs to be mediums for the
spirits of circumstances under which they had been first appre-
hended in an individual past, gratefully found in the tremendous sonorities of her voice both a nostalgic solace and a patriotic kick. She was considered especially effective when a strain
of wild recklessness rang through her song. Had this abandon

been less blatantly shammed it might still have saved her from utter vulgarity. The small, hard thing that was her soul stuck out of her song, and the most her temperament could attain was but an eddy, not a free torrent. When nowadays in some Russian household the Gramophone is put on, and I hear her canned contralto, it is with something of a shudder that I recall the meretricious imitation she gave of reaching her vocal climax, the anatomy of her mouth fully displayed in a last passionate cry, her blue-black hair beautifully waved, her crossed hands pressed to the beribboned medal on her bosom as she acknowledged the orgy of applause, her broad dusky body rigid even when she bowed, crammed as it was into strong silver satin which made her look like a matron of snow or a mermaid of honor.

4

You will see her next (if the censor does not find what follows offensive to piety) kneeling in the honey-colored haze of a crowded Russian church, lustily sobbing side by side with the wife or widow (she knew exactly which) of the general whose kidnapping had been so nicely arranged by her husband and so deftly performed by those big, efficient, anonymous men that the boss had sent down to Paris.

You will see her also on another day, two or three years later, while she is singing in a certain *appartement,* Rue George Sand, surrounded by admiring friends—and look, her eyes narrow slightly, her singing smile fades, as her husband, who had been detained by the final details of the business in hand, now quietly slips in and with a soft gesture rebukes a grizzled colonel's attempt to offer him his own seat; and through the unconscious flow of a song delivered for the ten-thousandth time she peers at him (she is slightly nearsighted like Anna Karenin) trying to discern some definite sign, and then, as she drowns

and his painted boats sail away, and the last telltale circular ripple on the Volga River, Samara County, dissolves into dull
eternity (for this is the very last song that she will ever sing),
her husband comes up to her and says in a voice that no clapping of human hands can muffle: "Masha, the tree will be
felled tomorrow!"

That bit about the tree was the only dramatic treat that
Golubkov allowed himself during his dove-gray career. We
shall condone the outburst if we remember that this was the
ultimate General blocking his way and that next day's event
would automatically bring on his own election. There had been
lately some mild jesting among their friends (Russian humor
being a wee bird satisfied with a crumb) about the amusing little
quarrel that those two big children were having, she petulantly
demanding the removal of the huge old poplar that darkened
her studio window at their suburban summer house, and he
contending that the sturdy old fellow was her greenest admirer
(sidesplitting, this) and so ought to be spared. Note too the
good-natured roguishness of the fat lady in the ermine cape as
she taunts the gallant General for giving in so soon, and the
Slavska's radiant smile and outstretched jelly-cold arms.

Next day, late in the afternoon, General Golubkov escorted
his wife to her dressmaker, sat there for a while reading the
Paris-Soir, and then was sent back to fetch one of the dresses
she wanted loosened and had forgotten to bring. At suitable
intervals she gave a passable imitation of telephoning home
and volubly directing his search. The dressmaker, an Armenian
lady, and a seamstress, little Princess Tumanov, were much
entertained in the adjacent room by the variety of her rustic
oaths (which helped her not to dry up in a part that her
imagination alone could not improvise). This threadbare alibi
was not intended for the patching up of past tenses in case
anything went wrong—for nothing could go wrong; it was
merely meant to provide a man whom none would ever dream
of suspecting with a routine account of his movements when

people would want to know who had seen General Fedchenko last. After enough imaginary wardrobes had been ransacked Golubkov was seen to return with the dress (which long ago, of course, had been placed in the car). He went on reading his paper while his wife kept trying things on.

5

The thirty-five minutes or so during which he was gone proved quite a comfortable margin. About the time she started fooling with that dead telephone, he had already picked up the General at an unfrequented corner and was driving him to an imaginary appointment the circumstances of which had been so framed in advance as to make its secrecy natural and its attendance a duty. A few minutes later he pulled up and they both got out. "This is not the right street," said General Fedchenko. "No," said General Golubkov, "but it is a convenient one to park my car on. I should not like to leave it right in front of the café. We shall take a short cut through that lane. It is only two minutes' walk." "Good, let us walk," said the old man and cleared his throat.

In that particular quarter of Paris the streets are called after various philosophers, and the lane they were following had been named by some well-read city father Rue Pierre Labime. It gently steered you past a dark church and some scaffolding into a vague region of shuttered private houses standing somewhat aloof within their own grounds behind iron railings on which moribund maple leaves would pause in their flight between bare branch and wet pavement. Along the left side of that lane there was a long wall with crossword puzzles of brick showing here and there through its rough grayness; and in that wall there was at one spot a little green door.

As they approached it, General Golubkov produced his battle-scarred cigarette case and presently stopped to light up. General Fedchenko, a courteous non-smoker, stopped too.

There was a gusty wind ruffling the dusk, and the first match went out. "I still think—" said General Fedchenko in reference to some petty business they had been discussing lately, "I still think," he said (to say something as he stood near that little green door), "that if Father Fedor insists on paying for all those lodgings out of his own funds, the least we can do is to supply the fuel." The second match went out too. The back of a passer-by hazily receding in the distance at last disappeared. General Golubkov cursed the wind at the top of his voice, and as this was the all-clear signal the green door opened and three pairs of hands with incredible speed and skill whisked the old man out of sight. The door slammed. General Golubkov lighted his cigarette and briskly walked back the way he had come.

The old man was never seen again. The quiet foreigners who had rented a certain quiet house for one quiet month had been innocent Dutchmen or Danes. It was but an optical trick. There is no green door, but only a gray one, which no human strength can burst open. I have vainly searched through admirable encyclopedias: there is no philosopher called Pierre Labime.

But I have seen the toad in her eyes. We have a saying in Russian: *vsevo dvoe i est; smert' da sovest'*—which may be rendered thus: "There are only two things that really exist— one's death and one's conscience." The lovely thing about humanity is that at times one may be unaware of doing right, but one is always aware of doing wrong. A very horrible criminal, whose wife had been even a worse one, once told me in the days when I was a priest that what had troubled him all through was the inner shame of being stopped by a still deeper shame from discussing with her the puzzle: whether perhaps in her heart of hearts she despised him or whether she secretly wondered if perhaps in his heart of hearts he despised her. And that is why I know perfectly well the kind of face General Golubkov and his wife had when the two were at last alone.

6

Not for very long, however. About 10 P.M. General L., the W.W. Secretary, was informed by General R. that Mrs. Fedchenko was extremely worried by her husband's unaccountable absence. Only then did General L. remember that about lunchtime the President had told him in a rather casual way (but that was the old gentleman's manner) that he had some business in town in the late afternoon and that if he was not back by 8 P.M. would General L. please read a note left in the middle drawer of the President's desk. The two generals now rushed to the office, stopped short, rushed back for the keys General L. had forgotten, rushed again, and finally found the note. It read: "An odd feeling obsesses me of which later I may be ashamed. I have an appointment at 5:30 P.M. in a café 45 Rue Descartes. I am to meet an informer from the other side. I suspect a trap. The whole thing has been arranged by General Golubkov, who is taking me there in his car."

We shall skip what General L. said and what General R. replied—but apparently they were slow thinkers and proceeded to lose some more time in a muddled telephone talk with an indignant café owner. It was almost midnight when the Slavska, clad in a flowery dressing gown and trying to look very sleepy, let them in. She was unwilling to disturb her husband, who, she said, was already asleep. She wanted to know what it was all about and had perhaps something happened to General Fedchenko. "He has vanished," said honest General L. The Slavska said, "Akh!" and crashed in a dead swoon, almost wrecking the parlor in the process. The stage had not lost quite so much as most of her admirers thought.

Somehow or other the two generals managed not to impart to General Golubkov anything about the little note, so that when he accompanied them to the W.W. headquarters he was under the impression that they really wanted to discuss with him whether to ring up the police at once or first go for advice to eighty-eight-year-old Admiral Gromoboyev, who for some obscure reason was considered the Solomon of the W.W.

"What does this mean?" said General L. handing the fatal note to Golubkov. "Peruse it, please."

Golubkov perused—and knew at once that all was lost. We shall not bend over the abyss of his feelings. He handed the note back with a shrug of his thin shoulders.

"If this has been really written by the General," he said, "and I must admit it looks very similar to his hand, then all I can say is that somebody has been impersonating me. However, I have grounds to believe that Admiral Gromoboyev will be able to exonerate me. I suggest we go there at once."

"Yes," said General L., "we had better go now, although it is very late."

General Golubkov swished himself into his raincoat and went out first. General R. helped General L. to retrieve his muffler. It had half slipped down from one of those vestibule chairs which are doomed to accommodate things, not people. General L. sighed and put on his old felt hat, using both hands for this gentle action. He moved to the door. "One moment, General," said General R. in a low voice. "I want to ask you something. As one officer to another, are you absolutely sure that . . . well, that General Golubkov is speaking the truth?"

"That's what we shall find out," answered General L., who was one of those people who believe that so long as a sentence is a sentence it is bound to mean something.

They delicately touched each other's elbows in the doorway. Finally the slightly older man accepted the privilege and made a jaunty exit. Then they both paused on the landing, for the staircase struck them as being very still. "General!" cried General L. in a downward direction. Then they looked at each other. Then hurriedly, clumsily, they stomped down the ugly steps, and emerged, and stopped under a black drizzle, and looked this way and that, and then at each other again.

She was arrested early on the following morning. Never once during the inquest did she depart from her attitude of grief-stricken innocence. The French police displayed a queer listlessness in dealing with possible clews, as if it assumed that the disappearance of Russian generals was a kind of curious local custom, an Oriental phenomenon, a dissolving process which perhaps ought not to occur but which could not be prevented. One had, however, the impression that the *Sûreté* knew more about the workings of that vanishing trick than diplomatic wisdom found fit to discuss. Newspapers abroad treated the whole matter in a good-natured but bantering and slightly bored manner. On the whole, "L'affaire Slavska" did not make good headlines—Russian *émigrés* were decidedly out of focus. By an amusing coincidence both a German press agency and a Soviet one laconically stated that a pair of White Russian generals in Paris had absconded with the White Army funds.

7

The trial was strangely inconclusive and muddled, witnesses did not shine, and the final conviction of the Slavska on a charge of kidnapping was debatable on legal grounds. Irrelevant trifles kept obscuring the main issue. The wrong people remembered the right things and vice versa. There was a bill signed by a certain Gaston Coulot, farmer, *"pour un arbre abattu."* General L. and General R. had a dreadful time at the hands of a sadistic barrister. A Parisian *clochard,* one of those colorful ripe-nosed unshaven beings (an easy part, that) who keep all their earthly belongings in their voluminous pockets and wrap their feet in layers of bursting newspapers when the last sock is gone and are seen comfortably seated, with widespread legs and a bottle of wine against the crumbling wall of some building that has never been completed, gave a lurid account of having observed from a certain vantage point an old man being roughly handled. Two Russian women, one of whom had been treated some time before for acute hysteria, said they saw on the day of the crime General Golubkov and General Fedchenko driving in the former's car. A Russian violinist while sitting in the diner of a German train—but it is useless to retell all those lame rumors.

We get a few last glimpses of the Slavska in prison. Meekly knitting in a corner. Writing to Mrs. Fedchenko tear-stained letters in which she said that they were sisters now, because both their husbands had been captured by the Bolsheviks. Begging to be allowed the use of a lipstick. Sobbing and praying in the arms of a pale young Russian nun who had come to tell her of a vision she had had which disclosed the innocence of General Golubkov. Clamoring for the New Testament which the police were keeping—keeping mainly from the experts who had so nicely begun deciphering certain notes scribbled in the margin of St. John's Gospel. Some time after the outbreak of World War Two, she developed an obscure internal trouble and when, one summer morning, three German officers arrived at the prison hospital and desired to see her, at once, they were told she was dead—which possibly was the truth.

Boston, 1943

Signs and Symbols

❧❧❧

I

For the fourth time in as many years they were confronted with
the problem of what birthday present to bring a young man
who was incurably deranged in his mind. He had no desires.
Man-made objects were to him either hives of evil, vibrant with
a malignant activity that he alone could perceive, or gross comforts for which no use could be found in his abstract world.
After eliminating a number of articles that might offend him
or frighten him (anything in the gadget line for instance was
taboo), his parents chose a dainty and innocent trifle: a basket
with ten different fruit jellies in ten little jars.

At the time of his birth they had been married already for
a long time; a score of years had elapsed, and now they were
quite old. Her drab gray hair was done anyhow. She wore
cheap black dresses. Unlike other women of her age (such as
Mrs. Sol, their next-door neighbor, whose face was all pink
and mauve with paint and whose hat was a cluster of brookside
flowers), she presented a naked white countenance to the fault-
finding light of spring days. Her husband, who in the old country had been a fairly successful businessman, was now wholly
dependent on his brother Isaac, a real American of almost forty
years standing. They seldom saw him and had nicknamed him
"the Prince."

That Friday everything went wrong. The underground train
lost its life current between two stations, and for a quarter of an

hour one could hear nothing but the dutiful beating of one's heart and the rustling of newspapers. The bus they had to take next kept them waiting for ages; and when it did come, it was crammed with garrulous high-school children. It was raining hard as they walked up the brown path leading to the sanitarium. There they waited again; and instead of their boy shuffling into the room as he usually did (his poor face blotched with acne, ill-shaven, sullen, and confused), a nurse they knew, and did not care for, appeared at last and brightly explained that he had again attempted to take his life. He was all right, she said, but a visit might disturb him. The place was so miserably understaffed, and things got mislaid or mixed up so easily, that they decided not to leave their present in the office but to bring it to him next time they came.

She waited for her husband to open his umbrella and then took his arm. He kept clearing his throat in a special resonant way he had when he was upset. They reached the bus-stop shelter on the other side of the street and he closed his umbrella. A few feet away, under a swaying and dripping tree, a tiny half-dead unfledged bird was helplessly twitching in a puddle.

During the long ride to the subway station, she and her husband did not exchange a word; and every time she glanced at his old hands (swollen veins, brown-spotted skin), clasped and twitching upon the handle of his umbrella, she felt the mounting pressure of tears. As she looked around trying to hook her mind onto something, it gave her a kind of soft shock, a mixture of compassion and wonder, to notice that one of the passengers, a girl with dark hair and grubby red toenails, was weeping on the shoulder of an older woman. Whom did that woman resemble? She resembled Rebecca Borisovna, whose daughter had married one of the Soloveichiks—in Minsk, years ago.

The last time he had tried to do it, his method had been, in the doctor's words, a masterpiece of inventiveness; he would

have succeeded, had not an envious fellow patient thought he
was learning to fly—and stopped him. What he really wanted
to do was to tear a hole in his world and escape.

The system of his delusions had been the subject of an
elaborate paper in a scientific monthly, but long before that
she and her husband had puzzled it out for themselves. "Refer-
ential mania," Herman Brink had called it. In these very rare
cases the patient imagines that everything happening around
him is a veiled reference to his personality and existence. He
excludes real people from the conspiracy—because he considers himself to be so much more intelligent than other men. Phenomenal nature shadows him wherever he goes. Clouds in the
staring sky transmit to one another, by means of slow signs,
incredibly detailed information regarding him. His inmost
thoughts are discussed at nightfall, in manual alphabet, by
darkly gesticulating trees. Pebbles or stains or sun flecks form
patterns representing in some awful way messages which he
must intercept. Everything is a cipher and of everything he is
the theme. Some of the spies are detached observers, such as
glass surfaces and still pools; others, such as coats in store windows, are prejudiced witnesses, lynchers at heart; others again
(running water, storms) are hysterical to the point of insanity,
have a distorted opinion of him and grotesquely misinterpret
his actions. He must be always on his guard and devote every
minute and module of life to the decoding of the undulation of
things. The very air he exhales is indexed and filed away. If
only the interest he provokes were limited to his immediate surroundings—but alas it is not! With distance the torrents of wild
scandal increase in volume and volubility. The silhouettes of
his blood corpuscles, magnified a million times, flit over vast
plains; and still farther, great mountains of unbearable solidity
and height sum up in terms of granite and groaning firs the ultimate truth of his being.

2

When they emerged from the thunder and foul air of the subway, the last dregs of the day were mixed with the street lights. She wanted to buy some fish for supper, so she handed him the basket of jelly jars, telling him to go home. He walked up to the third landing and then remembered he had given her his keys earlier in the day.

In silence he sat down on the steps and in silence rose when some ten minutes later she came, heavily trudging upstairs, wanly smiling, shaking her head in deprecation of her silliness. They entered their two-room flat and he at once went to the mirror. Straining the corners of his mouth apart by means of his thumbs, with a horrible masklike grimace, he removed his new hopelessly uncomfortable dental plate and severed the long tusks of saliva connecting him to it. He read his Russian-language newspaper while she laid the table. Still reading, he ate the pale victuals that needed no teeth. She knew his moods and was also silent.

When he had gone to bed, she remained in the living room with her pack of soiled cards and her old albums. Across the narrow yard where the rain tinkled in the dark against some battered ash cans, windows were blandly alight and in one of them a black-trousered man with his bare elbows raised could be seen lying supine on an untidy bed. She pulled the blind down and examined the photographs. As a baby he looked more surprised than most babies. From a fold in the album, a German maid they had had in Leipzig and her fat-faced fiancé fell out. Minsk, the Revolution, Leipzig, Berlin, Leipzig, a slanting house front badly out of focus. Four years old, in a park: moodily, shyly, with puckered forehead, looking away from an eager squirrel as he would from any other stranger. Aunt Rosa, a fussy, angular, wild-eyed old lady, who had lived in a tremulous world of bad news, bankruptcies, train accidents, cancerous growths—until the Germans put her to death, together with all the people she had worried about. Age six— that was when he drew wonderful birds with human hands and feet, and suffered from insomnia like a grown-up man. His cousin, now a famous chess player. He again, aged about eight, already difficult to understand, afraid of the wallpaper in the passage, afraid of a certain picture in a book which merely showed an idyllic landscape with rocks on a hillside and an old cart wheel hanging from the branch of a leafless tree. Aged ten: the year they left Europe. The shame, the pity, the humiliating difficulties, the ugly, vicious, backward children he was with in that special school. And then came a time in his life, coinciding with a long convalescence after pneumonia, when those little phobias of his which his parents had stubbornly regarded as the eccentricities of a prodigiously gifted child hardened as it were into a dense tangle of logically interacting illusions, making him totally inaccessible to normal minds.

This, and much more, she accepted—for after all living did mean accepting the loss of one joy after another, not even joys in her case—mere possibilities of improvement. She thought of the endless waves of pain that for some reason or other she and her husband had to endure; of the invisible giants hurting her boy in some unimaginable fashion; of the incalculable amount of tenderness contained in the world; of the fate of this tenderness, which is either crushed, or wasted, or transformed into madness; of neglected children humming to themselves in unswept corners; of beautiful weeds that cannot hide from the farmer and helplessly have to watch the shadow of his simian stoop leave mangled flowers in its wake, as the monstrous darkness approaches.

3

It was past midnight when from the living room she heard her husband moan; and presently he staggered in, wearing over his nightgown the old overcoat with astrakhan collar which he much preferred to the nice blue bathrobe he had.

"I can't sleep," he cried.

"Why," she asked, "why can't you sleep? You were so tired."

"I can't sleep because I am dying," he said and lay down on the couch.

"Is it your stomach? Do you want me to call Dr. Solov?"

"No doctors, no doctors," he moaned. "To the devil with doctors! We must get him out of there quick. Otherwise we'll be responsible. Responsible!" he repeated and hurled himself into a sitting position, both feet on the floor, thumping his forehead with his clenched fist.

"All right," she said quietly, "we shall bring him home tomorrow morning."

"I would like some tea," said her husband and retired to the bathroom.

Bending with difficulty, she retrieved some playing cards and a photograph or two that had slipped from the couch to the floor: knave of hearts, nine of spades, ace of spades, Elsa and her bestial beau.

He returned in high spirits, saying in a loud voice: "I have it all figured out. We will give him the bedroom. Each of us will spend part of the night near him and the other part on this couch. By turns. We will have the doctor see him at least twice a week. It does not matter what the Prince says. He won't have to say much anyway because it will come out cheaper."

The telephone rang. It was an unusual hour for their telephone to ring. His left slipper had come off and he groped for it with his heel and toe as he stood in the middle of the room, and childishly, toothlessly, gaped at his wife. Having more English than he did, it was she who attended to calls.

"Can I speak to Charlie," said a girl's dull little voice.

"What number you want? No. That is not the right number."

The receiver was gently cradled. Her hand went to her old tired heart.

"It frightened me," she said.

He smiled a quick smile and immediately resumed his excited monologue. They would fetch him as soon as it was day. Knives would have to be kept in a locked drawer. Even at his worst he presented no danger to other people.

The telephone rang a second time. The same toneless anxious young voice asked for Charlie.

"You have the incorrect number. I will tell you what you are doing: you are turning the letter O instead of the zero."

They sat down to their unexpected festive midnight tea. The birthday present stood on the table. He sipped noisily; his face was flushed; every now and then he imparted a circular motion to his raised glass so as to make the sugar dissolve more thoroughly. The vein on the side of his bald head where there was a large birthmark stood out conspicuously and, although he had shaved that morning, a silvery bristle showed on his chin. While she poured him another glass of tea, he put on his spectacles and re-examined with pleasure the luminous yellow, green, red little jars. His clumsy moist lips spelled out their eloquent labels: apricot, grape, beech plum, quince. He had got to crab apple, when the telephone rang again.

Boston, 1948

First Love

~~~~~~~

I

In the early years of this century, a travel agency on Nevski Avenue displayed a three-foot-long model of an oak-brown international sleeping car. In delicate verisimilitude it completely outranked the painted tin of my clockwork trains. Unfortunately it was not for sale. One could make out the blue upholstery inside, the embossed leather lining of the compartment walls, their polished panels, inset mirrors, tulip-shaped reading lamps, and other maddening details. Spacious windows alternated with narrower ones, single or geminate, and some of these were of frosted glass. In a few of the compartments, the beds had been made.

The then great and glamorous Nord Express (it was never the same after World War One when its elegant brown became a nouveau-riche blue), consisting solely of such international cars and running but twice a week, connected St. Petersburg with Paris. I would have said: directly with Paris, had passengers not been obliged to change from one train to a superficially similar one at the Russo-German frontier (Verzhbolovo-Eydtkuhnen), where the ample and lazy Russian sixty-and-a-half-inch gauge was replaced by the fifty-six-and-a-half-inch standard of Europe and coal succeeded birch logs.

In the far end of my mind I can unravel, I think, at least five such journeys to Paris, with the Riviera or Biarritz as their ul-

timate destination. In 1909, the year I now single out, our
party consisted of eleven people and one dachshund. Wearing gloves and a traveling cap, my father sat reading a book in
the compartment he shared with our tutor. My brother and I
were separated from them by a washroom. My mother and
her maid, Natasha, occupied a compartment adjacent to ours.
Next came my two small sisters, their English governess, Miss
Lavington, and a Russian nurse. The odd one of our party,
my father's valet, Osip (whom, a decade later, the pedantic
Bolsheviks were to shoot, because he appropriated our bicycles
instead of turning them over to the nation), had a stranger for
companion.

Historically and artistically, the year had started with a political cartoon in *Punch:* goddess England bending over goddess
Italy, on whose head one of Messina's bricks has landed—
probably, the worst picture *any* earthquake has ever inspired.
In April of that year, Peary had reached the North Pole. In
May, Shalyapin had sung in Paris. In June, bothered by rumors
of new and better Zeppelins, the United States War Department had told reporters of plans for an aerial Navy. In July,
Blériot had flown from Calais to Dover (with a little additional
loop when he lost his bearings). It was late August now. The
firs and marshes of Northwestern Russia sped by, and on the
following day gave way to German pine-woods and heather.

At a collapsible table, my mother and I played a card game
called *durachki*. Although it was still broad daylight, our cards,
a glass, and on a different plane the locks of a suitcase were reflected in the window. Through forest and field, and in sudden
ravines, and among scuttling cottages, those discarnate gam-
blers kept steadily playing on for steadily sparkling stakes. It
was a long, very long game: on this gray winter morning, in
the looking glass of my bright hotel room, I see shining the
same, the very same, locks of that now seventy-year-old valise,
a highish, heavyish *nécessaire de voyage* of pigskin, with "H.N."
elaborately interwoven in thick silver under a similar coronet,

which had been bought in 1897 for my mother's wedding trip to Florence. In 1917 it transported from St. Petersburg to the Crimea and then to London a handful of jewels. Around 1930, it lost to a pawnbroker its expensive receptacles of crystal and silver leaving empty the cunningly contrived leathern holders on the inside of the lid. But that loss has been amply recouped during the thirty years it then traveled with me—from Prague to Paris, from St. Nazaire to New York and through the mirrors of more than two hundred motel rooms and rented houses, in forty-six states. The fact that of our Russian heritage the hardiest survivor proved to be a traveling bag is both logical and emblematic.

"Ne budet-li, tï ved' usta! [Haven't you had enough, aren't you tired]?" my mother would ask, and then would be lost in thought as she slowly shuffled the cards. The door of the compartment was open and I could see the corridor window, where the wires—six thin black wires—were doing their best to slant up, to ascend skywards, despite the lightning blows dealt them by one telegraph pole after another; but just as all six, in a triumphant swoop of pathetic elation, were about to reach the top of the window, a particularly vicious blow would bring them down, as low as they had ever been, and they would have to start all over again.

When, on such journeys as these, the train changed its pace to a dignified amble and all but grazed housefronts and shop signs, as we passed through some big German town, I used to feel a twofold excitement, which terminal stations could not provide. I saw a city, with its toylike trams, linden trees, and brick walls enter the compartment, hobnob with the mirrors, and fill to the brim the windows on the corridor side. This informal contact between train and city was one part of the thrill. The other was putting myself in the place of some passer-by who, I imagined, was moved as I would be moved myself to see the long, romantic, auburn cars, with their intervestibular connecting curtains as black as bat wings and their metal lettering copper-bright in the low sun, unhurriedly negotiate an iron bridge across an everyday thoroughfare and then turn, with all windows suddenly ablaze, around a last block of houses.

There were drawbacks to those optical amalgamations. The wide-windowed dining car, a vista of chaste bottles of mineral water, miter-folded napkins, and dummy chocolate bars (whose wrappers—Cailler, Kohler, and so forth—enclosed nothing but wood), would be perceived at first as a cool haven beyond a consecution of reeling blue corridors; but as the meal progressed toward its fatal last course, and more and more dreadfully one equilibrist with a full tray would back against our table to let another equilibrist pass with another full tray, I would keep catching the car in the act of being recklessly sheathed, lurching waiters and all, in the landscape, while the landscape itself went through a complex system of motion, the day-time moon stubbornly keeping abreast of one's plate, the distant meadows opening fanwise, the near trees sweeping up on invisible swings toward the track, a parallel rail line all at once committing suicide by anastomosis, a bank of nictitating grass rising, rising, rising, until the little witness of mixed velocities was made to disgorge his portion of *omelette aux confitures de fraises*.

It was at night, however, that the *Compagnie Internationale des Wagons-Lits et des Grands Express Européens* lived up to the magic of its name. From my bed under my brother's bunk (Was he asleep? Was he there at all?), in the semidarkness of our compartment, I watched things, and parts of things, and shadows, and sections of shadows cautiously moving about and getting nowhere. The woodwork gently creaked and crackled. Near the door that led to the toilet, a dim garment on a peg and, higher up, the tassel of the blue, bivalved night light swung rhythmically. It was hard to correlate those halting approaches, that hooded stealth, with the headlong rush of the outside night, which I knew *was* rushing by, spark-streaked, illegible.

I would put myself to sleep by the simple act of identifying myself with the engine driver. A sense of drowsy well-being

invaded my veins as soon as I had everything nicely arranged—
the carefree passengers in their rooms enjoying the ride I was
giving them, smoking, exchanging knowing smiles, nodding,
dozing; the waiters and cooks and train guards (whom I had
to place somewhere) carousing in the diner; and myself, gog-
gled and begrimed, peering out of the engine cab at the tapering track, at the ruby or emerald point in the black distance.
And then, in my sleep, I would see something totally different
—a glass marble rolling under a grand piano or a toy engine
lying on its side with its wheels still working gamely.

A change in the speed of the train sometimes interrupted the
current of my sleep. Slow lights were stalking by; each, in passing, investigated the same chink, and then a luminous compass
measured the shadows. Presently, the train stopped with a
long-drawn Westinghousian sigh. Something (my brother's
spectacles, as it proved next day) fell from above. It was marvelously exciting to move to the foot of one's bed, with part of
the bedclothes following, in order to undo cautiously the catch
of the window shade, which could be made to slide only halfway up, impeded as it was by the edge of the upper berth.

Like moons around Jupiter, pale moths revolved about a
lone lamp. A dismembered newspaper stirred on a bench.
Somewhere on the train one could hear muffled voices, somebody's comfortable cough. There was nothing particularly interesting in the portion of station platform before me, and still
I could not tear myself away from it until it departed of its own
accord.

Next morning, wet fields with misshapen willows along the
radius of a ditch or a row of poplars afar, traversed by a horizontal band of milky-white mist, told one that the train was
spinning through Belgium. It reached Paris at 4 P.M., and even
if the stay was only an overnight one, I had always time to purchase something—say, a little brass *Tour Eiffel,* rather roughly
coated with silver paint—before we boarded, at noon on the
following day, the Sud-Express, which, on its way to Madrid,

dropped us around 10 P.M. at the La Négresse station of Biarritz, a few miles from the Spanish frontier.

2

Biarritz still retained its quiddity in those days. Dusty blackberry bushes and weedy *terrains à vendre* bordered the road that led to our villa. The Carlton was still being built. Some thirty-six years had to elapse before Brigadier General Samuel McCroskey would occupy the royal suite of the Hôtel du Palais, which stands on the site of a former palace, where, in the sixties, that incredibly agile medium, Daniel Home, is said to have been caught stroking with his bare foot (in imitation of a ghost hand) the kind, trustful face of Empress Eugénie. On the promenade near the Casino, an elderly flower girl, with carbon eyebrows and a painted smile, nimbly slipped the plump torus of a carnation into the buttonhole of an intercepted stroller whose left jowl accentuated its royal fold as he glanced down sideways at the coy insertion of the flower.

The rich-hued Oak Eggars questing amid the brush were quite unlike ours (which did not breed on oak, anyway), and here the Speckled Woods haunted not woods, but hedges and had tawny, not pale-yellowish, spots. Cleopatra, a tropical-looking, lemon-and-orange Brimstone, languorously flopping about in gardens, had been a sensation in 1907 and was still a pleasure to net.

Along the back line of the *plage,* various seaside chairs and stools supported the parents of straw-hatted children who were playing in front on the sand. I could be seen on my knees trying to set a found comb aflame by means of a magnifying glass. Men sported white trousers that to the eye of today would look as if they had comically shrunk in the washing; ladies wore, that particular season, light coats with silk-faced lapels, hats with big crowns and wide brims, dense embroidered white veils, frill-fronted blouses, frills at their wrists, frills on their parasols. The breeze salted one's lips. At a tremendous pace a stray Clouded Yellow came dashing across the palpitating *plage*.

Additional movement and sound were provided by venders hawking *cacahuètes,* sugared violets, pistachio ice cream of a heavenly green, cachou pellets, and huge convex pieces of dry, gritty, waferlike stuff that came from a red barrel. With a distinctness that no later superpositions have dimmed, I see that waffleman stomp along through deep mealy sand, with the heavy cask on his bent back. When called, he would sling it off his shoulder by a twist of its strap, bang it down on the sand in a Tower of Pisa position, wipe his face with his sleeve, and proceed to manipulate a kind of arrow-and-dial arrangement with numbers on the lid of the cask. The arrow rasped and whirred around. Luck was supposed to fix the size of a sou's worth of wafer. The bigger the piece, the more I was sorry for him.

The process of bathing took place on another part of the beach. Professional bathers, burly Basques in black bathing suits, were there to help ladies and children enjoy the terrors of the surf. Such a *baigneur* would place the *client* with his back to the incoming wave and hold him by the hand as the rising, rotating mass of foamy, green water violently descended from behind, knocking one off one's feet with one mighty wallop. After a dozen of these tumbles, the *baigneur,* glistening like a seal, would lead his panting, shivering, moistly snuffling charge landward, to the flat foreshore, where an unforgettable old woman with gray hairs on her chin promptly chose a bathing robe from several hanging on a clothesline. In the security of a little cabin, one would be helped by yet another attendant to peel off one's soggy, sand-heavy bathing suit. It would plop onto the boards, and, still shivering, one would step out of it and trample on its bluish, diffuse stripes. The cabin smelled of pine. The attendant, a hunchback with beaming wrinkles, brought a basin of steaming-hot water, in which one immersed one's feet. From him I learned, and have preserved ever since in a glass cell of my memory, that "butterfly" in the Basque language is *misericoletea*—or at least it sounded so (among the seven words I have found in dictionaries the closest approach is *micheletea*).

3

On the browner and wetter part of the *plage,* that part which at low tide yielded the best mud for castles, I found myself digging, one day, side by side with a little French girl called Colette.

She would be ten in November, I had been ten in April. Attention was drawn to a jagged bit of violet mussel shell upon which she had stepped with the bare sole of her narrow long-toed foot. No, I was not English. Her greenish eyes seemed flecked with the overflow of the freckles that covered her sharp-featured face. She wore what might now be termed a playsuit, consisting of a blue jersey with rolled-up sleeves and blue knitted shorts. I had taken her at first for a boy and then had been puzzled by the bracelet on her thin wrist and the cork-screw brown curls dangling from under her sailor cap.

She spoke in birdlike bursts of rapid twitter, mixing governess English and Parisian French. Two years before, on the same *plage,* I had been much attached to Zina, the lovely, sun-tanned, bad-tempered little daughter of a Serbian naturopath—she had, I remember (absurdly, for she and I were only eight at the time), a *grain de beauté* on her apricot skin just below the heart, and there was a horrible collection of chamber pots, full and half-full, and one with surface bubbles, on the floor of the hall in her family's boardinghouse lodgings which I visited early one morning to be given by her, as she was being dressed, a dead hummingbird moth found by the cat. But when I met Colette, I knew at once that this was the real thing. Colette seemed to me so much stranger than all my other chance playmates at Biarritz! I somehow acquired the feeling that she was less happy than I, less loved. A bruise on her delicate, downy forearm gave rise to awful conjectures. "He pinches as bad as my mummy," she said, speaking of a crab. I evolved various schemes to save her from her parents, who were *"des bourgeois de Paris"* as I heard somebody tell my mother with a slight shrug. I interpreted the disdain in my own fashion, as I knew that those people had come all the way from Paris in their blue-and-yellow limousine (a fashionable adventure in those days) but had drably sent Colette with her dog and governess by an ordinary coach-train. The dog was a female fox terrier with bells on her collar and a most waggly behind. From sheer exuberance, she would lap up salt water out of Colette's toy pail. I remembered the sail, the sunset, and the lighthouse pictured on that pail, but I cannot recall the dog's name, and this bothers me.

During the two months of our stay at Biarritz, my passion for Colette all but surpassed my passion for Cleopatra. Since my parents were not keen to meet hers, I saw her only on the beach; but I thought of her constantly. If I noticed she had been crying, I felt a surge of helpless anguish that brought tears to my own eyes. I could not destroy the mosquitoes that had left their bites on her frail neck, but I could, and did, have a successful fist-fight with a red-haired boy who had been rude to her. She used to give me warm handfuls of hard candy. One day, as we were bending together over a starfish, and Colette's ringlets were tickling my ear, she suddenly turned toward me and kissed me on the cheek. So great was my emotion that all I could think of saying was, "You little monkey."

I had a gold coin that I assumed would pay for our elopement. Where did I want to take her? Spain? America? The mountains above Pau? *"Là-bas, là-bas, dans la montagne,"* as I had heard Carmen sing at the opera. One strange night, I lay awake, listening to the recurrent thud of the ocean and planning our flight. The ocean seemed to rise and grope in the darkness and then heavily fall on its face.

Of our actual getaway, I have little to report. My memory retains a glimpse of her obediently putting on rope-soled canvas shoes, on the lee side of a flapping tent, while I stuffed a folding butterfly net into a brown-paper bag. The next glimpse is of our evading pursuit by entering a pitch-dark *cinéma* near the Casino (which, of course, was absolutely out of bounds). There we sat, holding hands across the dog, which now and then gently jingled in Colette's lap, and were shown a jerky, drizzly, but highly exciting bullfight at St. Sebástian. My final glimpse is of myself being led along the promenade by Linderovski. His long legs move with a kind of ominous briskness and I can see the muscles of his grimly set jaw working under the tight skin. My bespectacled brother, aged nine, whom he happens to hold with his other hand, keeps trotting out forward to peer at me with awed curiosity, like a little owl.

Among the trivial souvenirs acquired at Biarritz before leaving, my favorite was not the small bull of black stone and not the sonorous sea shell but something which now seems almost symbolic—a meerschaum penholder with a tiny peephole of crystal in its ornamental part. One held it quite close to one's eye, screwing up the other, and when one had got rid of the shimmer of one's own lashes, a miraculous photographic view of the bay and of the line of cliffs ending in a lighthouse could be seen inside.

And now a delightful thing happens. The process of re-creating that penholder and the microcosm in its eyelet stimulates my memory to a last effort. I try again to recall the name of Colette's dog—and, triumphantly, along those remote beaches, over the glossy evening sands of the past, where each footprint slowly fills up with sunset water, here it comes, here it comes, echoing and vibrating: Floss, Floss, Floss!

Colette was back in Paris by the time we stopped there for a day before continuing our homeward journey; and there, in a fawn park under a cold blue sky, I saw her (by arrangement between our mentors, I believe) for the last time. She carried a hoop and a short stick to drive it with, and everything about her was extremely proper and stylish in an autumnal, Parisian, *tenue-de-ville-pour-fillettes* way. She took from her governess and slipped into my brother's hand a farewell present, a box of sugar-coated almonds, meant, I knew, solely for me; and instantly she was off, tap-tapping her glinting hoop through light and shade, around and around a fountain choked with dead leaves, near which I stood. The leaves mingle in my memory with the leather of her shoes and gloves, and there was, I remember, some detail in her attire (perhaps a ribbon on her Scottish cap, or the pattern of her stockings) that reminded me then of the rainbow spiral in a glass marble. I still seem to be holding that wisp of iridescence, not knowing exactly where to fit it, while she runs with her hoop ever faster around me and finally dissolves among the slender shadows cast on the graveled path by the interlaced arches of its low looped fence.

Boston, 1948—Montreux, 1965

Scenes from the Life of a Double Monster

~~~~~~

Some years ago Dr. Fricke asked Lloyd and me a question that I shall try to answer now. With a dreamy smile of scientific delectation he stroked the fleshy cartilaginous band uniting us— *omphalopagus diaphragmo-xiphodidymus,* as Pancoast has dubbed a similar case—and wondered if we could recall the very first time either of us, or both, realized the peculiarity of our condition and destiny. All Lloyd could remember was the way our Grandfather Ibrahim (or Ahim, or Ahem—irksome lumps of dead sounds to the ear of today!) would touch what the doctor was touching and call it a bridge of gold. I said nothing.

Our childhood was spent atop a fertile hill above the Black Sea on our grandfather's farm near Karaz. His youngest daughter, rose of the East, gray Ahem's pearl (if so, the old scoundrel might have taken better care of her), had been raped in a roadside orchard by our anonymous sire and had died soon after giving birth to us—of sheer horror and grief, I imagine. One set of rumors mentioned a Hungarian peddler; another favored a German collector of birds or some member of his expedition —his taxidermist, most likely. Dusky, heavily necklaced aunts, whose voluminous clothes smelled of rose oil and mutton, attended with ghoulish zest to the wants of our monstrous infancy.

Soon neighboring hamlets learned the astounding news and

began delegating to our farm various inquisitive strangers. On feast days you could see them laboring up the slopes of our hill, like pilgrims in bright-colored pictures. There was a shepherd seven feet tall, and a small bald man with glasses, and soldiers, and the lengthening shadows of cypresses. Children came too, at all times, and were shooed away by our jealous nurses; but almost daily some black-eyed, cropped-haired youngster in dark-patched, faded-blue pants would manage to worm his way through the dogwood, the honeysuckle, the twisted Judas trees, into the cobbled court with its old rheumy fountain where little Lloyd and Floyd (we had other names then, full of corvine aspirates—but no matter) sat quietly munching dried apricots under a whitewashed wall. Then, suddenly, the aitch would see an eye, the Roman two a one, the scissors a knife.

There can be, of course, no comparison between this impact of knowledge, disturbing as it may have been, and the emotional shock my mother received (by the way, what clean bliss there is in this deliberate use of the possessive singular!). She must have been aware that she was being delivered of twins; but when she learned, as no doubt she did, that the twins were conjoined ones—what did she experience then? With the kind of unrestrained, ignorant, passionately communicative folks that surrounded us, the highly vocal household just beyond the limits of her tumbled bed must, surely, have told her at once that something had gone dreadfully wrong; and one can be certain that her sisters, in the frenzy of their fright and compassion, showed her the double baby. I am not saying that a mother cannot love such a double thing—and forget in this love the dark dews of its unhallowed origin; I only think that the mixture of revulsion, pity, and a mother's love was too much for her. Both components of the double series before her staring eyes were healthy, handsome little components, with a silky fair fuzz on their violet-pink skulls, and well-formed rubbery arms and legs that moved like the many limbs of some wonderful sea animal. Each was eminently normal, but together they formed a monster. Indeed, it is strange to think that the presence of a mere band of tissue, a flap of flesh not much longer than a lamb's liver, should be able to transform joy, pride, tenderness, adoration, gratitude to God into horror and despair.

In our own case, everything was far simpler. Adults were much too different from us in all respects to afford any analogy, but our first coeval visitor was to me a mild revelation. While Lloyd placidly contemplated the awe-struck child of seven or eight who was peering at us from under a humped and likewise peering fig tree, I remember appreciating in full the essential difference between the newcomer and me. He cast a short blue shadow on the ground, and so did I; but in addition to that sketchy, and flat, and unstable companion which he and I owed to the sun and which vanished in dull weather I possessed yet another shadow, a palpable reflection of my corporal self, that I always had by me, at my left side, whereas my visitor had somehow managed to lose his, or had unhooked it and left it at home. Linked Lloyd and Floyd were complete and normal; he was neither.

But perhaps, in order to elucidate these matters as thoroughly as they deserve, I should say something of still earlier recollections. Unless adult emotions stain past ones, I think I can vouch for the memory of a faint disgust. By virtue of our anterior duplexity, we lay originally front to front, joined at our common navel, and my face in those first years of our existence was constantly brushed by my twin's hard nose and wet lips. A tendency to throw our heads back and avert our faces as much as possible was a natural reaction to those bothersome contacts. The great flexibility of our band of union allowed us to assume reciprocally a more or less lateral position, and as we learned to walk we waddled about in this side-by-side attitude, which must have seemed more strained than it really was, making us look, I suppose, like a pair of drunken dwarfs supporting each other. For a long time we kept reverting in sleep to our fetal position; but whenever the discomfort it engendered woke us up, we would again jerk our faces away, in regardant revulsion, with a double wail.

I insist that at three or four our bodies obscurely disliked their clumsy conjunction, while our minds did not question its normalcy. Then, before we could have become mentally aware of its drawbacks, physical intuition discovered means of tempering them, and thereafter we hardly gave them a thought. All our movements became a judicious compromise between the common and the particular. The pattern of acts prompted by this or that mutual urge formed a kind of gray, evenly woven, generalized background against which the discrete impulse, his or mine, followed a brighter and sharper course; but (guided as it were by the warp of the background pattern) it never went athwart the common weave or the other twin's whim.

I am speaking at present solely of our childhood, when nature could not yet afford to have us undermine our hard-won vitality by any conflict between us. In later years I have had occasion to regret that we did not perish or had not been surgically separated, before we left that initial stage at which an ever-present rhythm, like some kind of remote tom-tom beating in the jungle of our nervous system, was alone responsible for the regulation of our movements. When, for example, one of us was about to stoop to possess himself of a pretty daisy and the other, at exactly the same moment, was on the point of stretching up to pluck a ripe fig, individual success depended upon whose movement happened to conform to the current ictus of our common and continuous rhythm, whereupon, with a very brief, chorealike shiver, the interrupted gesture of one twin would be swallowed and dissolved in the enriched ripple of the other's completed action. I say "enriched" because the ghost of the unpicked flower somehow seemed to be also there, pulsating between the fingers that closed upon the fruit.

There might be a period of weeks and even months when the guiding beat was much more often on Lloyd's side than on mine, and then a period might follow when I would be on top of the wave; but I cannot recall any time in our childhood when frustration or success in these matters provoked in either of us resentment or pride.

Somewhere within me, however, there must have been some sensitive cell wondering at the curious fact of a force that would suddenly sweep me away from the object of a casual desire and drag me to other, uncoveted things that were thrust into the sphere of my will instead of being consciously reached for and enveloped by its tentacles. So, as I watched this or that chance child which was watching Lloyd and me, I remember pondering a twofold problem: first, whether, perhaps, a single bodily state had more advantages than ours possessed; and second, whether *all* other children were single. It occurs to me now that quite often problems puzzling me were twofold: possibly a trickle of Lloyd's cerebration penetrated my mind and one of the two linked problems was his.

When greedy Grandfather Ahem decided to show us to visitors for money, among the flocks that came there was always some eager rascal who wanted to hear us talk to each other. As happens with primitive minds, he demanded that his ears corroborate what his eyes saw. Our folks bullied us into gratifying such desires and could not understand what was so distressful about them. We could have pleaded shyness; but the truth was that we never really *spoke* to each other, even when we were alone, for the brief broken grunts of infrequent expostulation that we sometimes exchanged (when, for instance, one had just cut his foot and had had it bandaged and the other wanted to go paddling in the brook) could hardly pass for a dialogue. The communication of simple essential sensations we performed wordlessly: shed leaves riding the stream of our shared blood. Thin thoughts also managed to slip through and travel between us. Richer ones each kept to himself, but even then there occurred odd phenomena. This is why I suspect that despite his calmer nature, Lloyd was struggling with the same new realities that were puzzling me. He forgot much when he grew up. I have forgotten nothing.

Not only did our public expect us to talk, it also wanted us to play together. Dolts! They derived quite a kick from having us match wits at checkers or *muzla*. I suppose had we happened to be opposite-sex twins they would have made us commit incest in their presence. But since mutual games were no more customary with us than conversation, we suffered subtle torments when obliged to go through the cramped motions of bandying a ball somewhere between our breastbones or making believe to wrest a stick from each other. We drew wild applause by running around the yard with our arms around each other's shoulders. We could jump and whirl.

A salesman of patent medicine, a bald little fellow in a dirty-white Russian blouse, who knew some Turkish and English, taught us sentences in these languages; and then we had to demonstrate our ability to a fascinated audience. Their ardent faces still pursue me in my nightmares, for they come whenever my dream producer needs supers. I see again the gigantic bronze-faced shepherd in multicolored rags, the soldiers from Karaz, the one-eyed hunchbacked Armenian tailor (a monster in his own right), the giggling girls, the sighing old women, the children, the young people in Western clothes—burning eyes, white teeth, black gaping mouths; and, of course, Grandfather Ahem, with his nose of yellow ivory and his beard of gray wool, directing the proceedings or counting the soiled paper money and wetting his big thumb. The linguist, he of the embroidered blouse and bald head, courted one of my aunts but kept watching Ahem enviously through his steel-rimmed spectacles.

By the age of nine, I knew quite clearly that Lloyd and I presented the rarest of freaks. This knowledge provoked in me neither any special elation nor any special shame; but once a hysterical cook, a mustached woman, who had taken a great liking to us and pitied our plight, declared with an atrocious oath that she would, then and there, slice us free by means of a shiny knife that she suddenly flourished (she was at once overpowered by our grandfather and one of our newly acquired uncles); and after that incident I would often dally with an indolent daydream, fancying myself somehow separated from poor Lloyd, who somehow retained his monsterhood.

I did not care for that knife business, and anyway the manner of separation remained very vague; but I distinctly imagined the sudden melting away of my shackles and the feeling of lightness and nakedness that would ensue. I imagined myself climbing over the fence—a fence with bleached skulls of farm animals that crowned its pickets—and descending toward the beach. I saw myself leaping from boulder to boulder and diving into the twinkling sea, and scrambling back onto the shore and scampering about with other naked children. I dreamed of this at night—saw myself fleeing from my grandfather and carrying away with me a toy, or a kitten, or a little crab pressed to my left side. I saw myself meeting poor Lloyd, who appeared to me in my dream hobbling along, hopelessly joined to a hobbling twin while I was free to dance around them and slap them on their humble backs.

I wonder if Lloyd had similar visions. It has been suggested by doctors that we sometimes pooled our minds when we dreamed. One gray-blue morning he picked up a twig and drew a ship with three masts in the dust. I had just seen myself drawing that ship in the dust of a dream I had dreamed the preceding night.

An ample black shepherd's cloak covered our shoulders, and, as we squatted on the ground, all but our heads and Lloyd's hand was concealed within its falling folds. The sun had just risen and the sharp March air was like layer upon layer of semitransparent ice through which the crooked Judas trees in rough bloom made blurry spots of purplish pink. The long low white house behind us, full of fat women and their foul-smelling husbands, was fast asleep. We did not say anything; we did not even look at each other; but, throwing his twigs away, Lloyd put his right arm around my shoulder, as he always did when he wished both of us to walk fast; and with the edge of our common raiment trailing among dead weeds, while pebbles kept running from under our feet, we made our way toward the alley of cypresses that led down to the shore.

It was our first attempt to visit the sea that we could see from our hilltop softly glistening afar and leisurely, silently breaking on glossy rocks. I need not strain my memory at this point to place our stumbling flight at a definite turn in our destiny. A few weeks before, on our twelfth birthday, Grandfather Ibrahim had started to toy with the idea of sending us in the company of our newest uncle on a six-month tour through the country. They kept haggling about the terms, and had quarreled and even fought, Ahem getting the upper hand.

We feared our grandfather and loathed Uncle Novus. Presumably, after a dull forlorn fashion (knowing nothing of life, but being dimly aware that Uncle Novus was endeavoring to cheat Grandfather) we felt we should try to do something in order to prevent a showman from trundling us around in a moving prison, like apes or eagles; or perhaps we were prompted merely by the thought that this was our last chance to enjoy by ourselves our small freedom and do what we were absolutely forbidden to do: go beyond a certain picket fence, open a certain gate.

We had no trouble in opening that rickety gate, but did not manage to swing it back into its former position. A dirty-white lamb, with amber eyes and a carmine mark painted upon its hard flat forehead, followed us for a while before getting lost in the oak scrub. A little lower but still far above the valley, we had to cross the road that circled around the hill and connected our farm with the highway running along the shore. The thudding of hoofs and the rasping of wheels came descending upon us; and we dropped, cloak and all, behind a bush. When the rumble subsided, we crossed the road and continued along a weedy slope. The silvery sea gradually concealed itself behind cypresses and remnants of old stone walls. Our black cloak began to feel hot and heavy but still we persevered under its protection, being afraid that otherwise some passer-by might notice our infirmity.

We emerged upon the highway, a few feet from the audible sea—and there, waiting for us under a cypress, was a carriage we knew, a cartlike affair on high wheels, with Uncle Novus in the act of getting down from the box. Crafty, dark, ambitious, unprincipled little man! A few minutes before, he had caught sight of us from one of the galleries of our grandfather's house and had not been able to resist the temptation of taking advantage of an escapade which miraculously allowed him to seize us without any struggle or outcry. Swearing at the two timorous horses, he roughly helped us into the cart. He pushed our heads down and threatened to hurt us if we attempted to peep from under our cloak. Lloyd's arm was still around my shoulder, but a jerk of the cart shook it off. Now the wheels were crunching and rolling. It was some time before we realized that our driver was not taking us home.

Twenty years have passed since that gray spring morning, but it is much better preserved in my mind than many a later event. Again and again I run it before my eyes like a strip of cinematic film, as I have seen great jugglers do when reviewing their acts. So I review all the stages and circumstances and incidental details of our abortive flight—the initial shiver, the gate, the lamb, the slippery slope under our clumsy feet. To the thrushes we flushed we must have presented an extraordinary sight, with that black cloak around us and our two shorn heads on thin necks sticking out of it. The heads turned this way and that, warily, as at last the shore-line highway was reached. If at that moment some adventurous stranger had stepped onto the shore from his boat in the bay, he would have surely experienced a thrill of ancient enchantment to find himself confronted by a gentle mythological monster in a landscape of cypresses and white stones. He would have worshiped it, he would have shed sweet tears. But, alas, there was nobody to greet us there save that worried crook, our nervous kidnaper, a small doll-faced man wearing cheap spectacles, one glass of which was doctored with a bit of tape.

Ithaca, 1950

Lance

⮿⮿⮿⮿⮿

I
_____

The name of the planet, presuming it has already received one, is immaterial. At its most favorable opposition, it may very well be separated from the earth by only as many miles as there are years between last Friday and the rise of the Himalayas—a million times the reader's average age. In the telescopic field of one's fancy, through the prism of one's tears, any particularities it presents should be no more striking than those of existing planets. A rosy globe, marbled with dusky blotches, it is one of the countless objects diligently revolving in the infinite and gratuitous awfulness of fluid space.

My planet's *maria* (which are not seas) and its *lacus* (which are not lakes) have also, let us suppose, received names; some less jejune, perhaps, than those of garden roses; others, more pointless than the surnames of their observers (for, to take actual cases, that an astronomer should have been called Lampland is as marvelous as that an entomologist should have been called Krautwurm); but most of them of so antique a style as to vie in sonorous and corrupt enchantment with place names pertaining to romances of chivalry.

Just as our Pinedales, down here, have often little to offer beyond a shoe factory on one side of the tracks and the rusty inferno of an automobile dump on the other, so those seductive Arcadias and Icarias and Zephyrias on planetary maps may quite likely turn out to be dead deserts lacking even the milkweed that graces our dumps. Selenographers will confirm this, but then, their lenses serve them better than ours do. In the present instance, the greater the magnification, the more the mottling of the planet's surface looks as if it were seen by a submerged swimmer peering up through semitranslucent water. And if certain connected markings resemble in a shadowy way the line-and-hole pattern of a Chinese-checkers board, let us consider them geometrical hallucinations.

I not only debar a too definite planet from any role in my story—from the role every dot and full stop should play in my story (which I see as a kind of celestial chart)—I also refuse to have anything to do with those technical prophecies that scientists are reported to make to reporters. Not for me is the rocket racket. Not for me are the artificial little satellites that the earth is promised; landing star-strips for spaceships ("spacers")—one, two, three, four, and then thousands of strong castles in the air each complete with cookhouse and keep, set up by terrestrial nations in a frenzy of competitive confusion, phony gravitation, and savagely flapping flags.

Another thing I have not the slightest use for is the special-equipment business—the airtight suit, the oxygen apparatus—suchlike contraptions. Like old Mr. Boke, of whom we shall hear in a minute, I am eminently qualified to dismiss these practical matters (which anyway are doomed to seem absurdly impractical to future spaceshipmen, such as old Boke's only son), since the emotions that gadgets provoke in me range from dull distrust to morbid trepidation. Only by a heroic effort can I make myself unscrew a bulb that has died an inexplicable death and screw in another, which will light up in my face with the hideous instancy of a dragon's egg hatching in one's bare hand.

Finally, I utterly spurn and reject so-called "science fiction." I have looked into it, and found it as boring as the mystery-story magazines—the same sort of dismally pedestrian writing with oodles of dialogue and loads of commutational humor. The clichés are, of course, disguised; essentially, they are the same throughout all cheap reading matter, whether it spans the universe or the living room. They are like those "assorted" cookies that differ from one another only in shape and shade, whereby their shrewd makers ensnare the salivating consumer in a mad Pavlovian world where, at no extra cost, variations in simple visual values influence and gradually replace flavor, which thus goes the way of talent and truth.

So the good guy grins, and the villain sneers, and a noble heart sports a slangy speech. Star tsars, directors of Galactic Unions, are practically replicas of those peppy, red-haired executives in earthy earth jobs, that illustrate with their little crinkles the human interest stories of the well-thumbed slicks in beauty parlors. Invaders of Denebola and Spica, Virgo's finest, bear names beginning with Mac; cold scientists are usually found under Steins; some of them share with the super-galactic gals such abstract labels as Biola or Vala. Inhabitants of foreign planets, "intelligent" beings, humanoid or of various mythic makes, have one remarkable trait in common: their intimate structure is never depicted. In a supreme concession to biped propriety, not only do centaurs wear loincloths; they wear them about their forelegs.

This seems to complete the elimination—unless anybody wants to discuss the question of time? Here again, in order to focalize young Emery L. Boke, that more or less remote descendant of mine who is to be a member of the first interplanetary expedition (which, after all, is the one humble postulate of my tale), I gladly leave the replacement by a pretentious "2" or "3" of the honest "1" in our "1900" to the capable paws of *Starzan* and other comics and atomics. Let it be 2145 A.D. or 200 A.A., it does not matter. I have no desire to barge into vested interests of any kind. This is strictly an amateur performance, with quite casual stage properties and a minimum of scenery, and the quilled remains of a dead porcupine in a corner of the old barn. We are here among friends, the Browns and the

Bensons, the Whites and the Wilsons, and when somebody goes out for a smoke, he hears the crickets, and a distant farm dog (who waits, between barks, to listen to what we cannot hear). The summer night sky is a mess of stars. Emery Lancelot Boke, at twenty-one, knows immeasurably more about them than I, who am fifty and terrified.

2

Lance is tall and lean, with thick tendons and greenish veins on his sun-tanned forearms and a scar on his brow. When doing nothing—when sitting ill at ease as he sits now, leaning forward from the edge of a low armchair, his shoulders hunched up, his elbows propped on his big knees—he has a way of slowly clasping and unclasping his handsome hands, a gesture I borrow for him from one of his ancestors. An air of gravity, of uncomfortable concentration (all thought is uncomfortable, and young thought especially so), is his usual expression; at the moment, however, it is a manner of mask, concealing his furious desire to get rid of a long-drawn tension. As a rule, he does not smile often, and besides "smile" is too smooth a word for the abrupt, bright contortion that now suddenly illumes his mouth and eyes as the shoulders hunch higher, the moving hands stop in a clasped position and he lightly stamps the toe of one foot. His parents are in the room, and also a chance visitor, a fool and a bore, who is not aware of what is happening—for this is an awkward moment in a gloomy house on the eve of a fabulous departure.

An hour goes by. At last the visitor picks up his top hat from the carpet and leaves. Lance remains alone with his parents, which only serves to increase the tension. Mr. Boke I see plainly enough. But I cannot visualize Mrs. Boke with any degree of clarity, no matter how deep I sink into my difficult trance. I know that her cheerfulness—small talk, quick beat of eyelashes—is something she keeps up not so much for the sake of her son as for that of her husband, and his aging heart, and old Boke realizes this only too well and, on top of his own monstrous anguish, he has to cope with her feigned levity, which disturbs him more than would an utter and unconditional collapse. I am somewhat disappointed that I cannot make out her features. All I manage to glimpse is an effect of melting light on one side of her misty hair, and in this, I suspect, I am insidiously influenced by the standard artistry of modern photography and I feel how much easier writing must have been in former days when one's imagination was not hemmed in by innumerable visual aids, and a frontiersman looking at his first giant cactus or his first high snows was not necessarily reminded of a tire company's pictorial advertisement.

In the case of Mr. Boke, I find myself operating with the features of an old professor of history, a brilliant medievalist, whose white whiskers, pink pate, and black suit are famous on a certain sunny campus in the deep South, but whose sole asset in connection with this story (apart from a slight resemblance to a long-dead great-uncle of mine) is that his appearance is out of date. Now if one is perfectly honest with oneself, there is nothing extraordinary in the tendency to give to the manners and clothes of a distant day (which happens to be placed in the future) an old-fashioned tinge, a badly pressed, badly groomed, dusty something, since the terms "out of date," "not of our age," and so on are in the long run the only ones in which we are able to imagine and express a strangeness no amount of research can foresee. The future is but the obsolete in reverse.

In that shabby room, in the tawny lamplight, Lance talks of some last things. He has recently brought from a desolate spot in the Andes, where he has been climbing some as yet unnamed peak, a couple of adolescent chinchillas—cinder-gray, phenomenally furry, rabbit-sized rodents (*Hystricomorpha*), with long whiskers, round rumps, and petallike ears. He keeps them indoors in a wire-screened pen and gives them peanuts, puffed rice, raisins to eat, and, as a special treat, a violet or an aster. He hopes they will breed in the fall. He now repeats to his mother a few emphatic instructions—to keep his pets' food crisp and their pen dry, and never forget their daily dust bath (fine sand mixed with powdered chalk) in which they roll and kick most lustily. While this is being discussed, Mr. Boke lights and relights a pipe and finally puts it away. Every now and then, with a false air of benevolent absent-mindedness, the old man launches upon a series of sounds and motions that deceive nobody; he clears his throat and, with his hands behind his back, drifts towards a window; or he begins to produce a tight-lipped tuneless humming; and seemingly driven by that small nasal motor, he wanders out of the parlor. But no sooner has he left the stage than he throws off, with a dreadful shiver, the elaborate structure of his gentle, bumbling impersonation act. In a bedroom or bathroom, he stops as if to take, in abject solitude, a deep spasmodic draught from some secret flask, and presently staggers out again, drunk with grief.

The stage has not changed when he quietly returns to it, buttoning his coat and resuming that little hum. It is now a matter of minutes. Lance inspects the pen before he goes, and leaves Chin and Chilla sitting on their haunches, each holding a flower. The only other thing that I know about these last moments is that any such talk as "Sure you haven't forgotten the silk shirt that came from the wash?" or "You remember where you put those new slippers?" is excluded. Whatever Lance takes with him is already collected at the mysterious and unmentionable and absolutely awful place of his zero-hour departure; he needs nothing of what we need; and he steps out of the house, empty-handed and hatless, with the casual lightness of one walking to the newsstand—or to a glorious scaffold.

3

Terrestrial space loves concealment. The most it yields to the eye is a panoramic view. The horizon closes upon the receding traveler like a trap door in slow motion. For those who remain, any town a day's journey from here is invisible, whereas you can easily see such transcendencies as, say, a lunar amphitheater and the shadow cast by its circular ridge. The conjurer who displays the firmament has rolled up his sleeves and performs in full view of the little spectators. Planets may dip out of sight (just as objects are obliterated by the blurry curve of one's own cheekbone); but they are back when the earth turns its head. The nakedness of the night is appalling. Lance has left; the fragility of his young limbs grows in direct ratio to the distance he covers. From their balcony, the old Bokes look at the infinitely perilous night sky and wildly envy the lot of fishermen's wives.

If Boke's sources are accurate, the name "Lanceloz del Lac" occurs for the first time in Verse 3676 of the twelfth-century "Roman de la Charrete." Lance, Lancelin, Lancelotik—diminutives murmured at the brimming, salty, moist stars. Young knights in their teens learning to harp, hawk, and hunt; the Forest Dangerous and the Dolorous Tower; Aldebaran, Betelgeuze—the thunder of Saracenic war cries. Marvelous deeds of arms, marvelous warriors, sparkling within the awful constellations above the Bokes' balcony: Sir Percard the Black Knight, and Sir Perimones the Red Knight, and Sir Pertolepe the Green Knight, and Sir Persant the Indigo Knight, and that bluff old party Sir Grummore Grummursum, muttering northern oaths under his breath. The field glass is not much good, the chart is all crumpled and damp, and: "You do not hold the flashlight properly"—this to Mrs. Boke.

Draw a deep breath. Look again.

Lancelot is gone; the hope of seeing him in life is about equal to the hope of seeing him in eternity. Lancelot is banished from the country of L'Eau Grise (as we might call the Great Lakes) and now rides up in the dust of the night sky almost as fast as our local universe (with the balcony and the pitch-black, optically spotted garden) speeds toward King Arthur's Harp, where Vega burns and beckons—one of the few objects that can be identified by the aid of this goddam diagram. The sidereal haze makes the Bokes dizzy—gray incense, insanity, infinity-sickness. But they cannot tear themselves away from the nightmare of space, cannot go back to the lighted bedroom, a corner of which shows in the glass door. And presently *the* planet rises, like a tiny bonfire.

There, to the right, is the Bridge of the Sword leading to the Otherworld (*"dont nus estranges ne retorne"*). Lancelot crawls over it in great pain, in ineffable anguish. "Thou shalt not pass a pass that is called the Pass Perilous." But another enchanter commands: "You shall. You shall even acquire a sense of humor that will tide you over the trying spots." The brave old Bokes think they can distinguish Lance scaling, on crampons, the verglased rock of the sky or silently breaking trail through the soft snows of nebulae. Boötes, somewhere between Camp X and XI, is a great glacier all rubble and icefall. We try to make out the serpentine route of ascent; seem to distinguish the light leanness of Lance among the several roped silhouettes. Gone! Was it he or Denny (a young biologist, Lance's best friend)? Waiting in the dark valley at the foot of the vertical sky, we recall (Mrs. Boke more clearly than her husband) those special names for crevasses and Gothic structures of ice that Lance used to mouth with such professional gusto in his alpine boyhood (he is several light-years older by now); the séracs and the schrunds; the avalanche and its thud; French echoes and Germanic magic hobnailnobbing up there as they do in medieval romances.

Ah, there he is again! Crossing through a notch between two stars; then, very slowly, attempting a traverse on a cliff face so sheer, and with such delicate holds that the mere evocation of those groping fingertips and scraping boots fills one with acrophobic nausea. And through streaming tears the old Bokes see Lance now marooned on a shelf of stone and now climbing again and now, dreadfully safe, with his ice ax and pack, on a peak above peaks, his eager profile rimmed with light.

Or is he already on his way down? I assume that no news comes from the explorers and that the Bokes prolong their pathetic vigils. As they wait for their son to return, his every avenue of descent seems to run into the precipice of their despair. But perhaps he has swung over those high-angled wet slabs that fall away vertically into the abyss, has mastered the overhang, and is now blissfully glissading down steep celestial snows?

As, however, the Bokes' doorbell does not ring at the logical culmination of an imagined series of footfalls (no matter how patiently we space them as they come nearer and nearer in our mind), we have to thrust him back and have him start his ascent all over again, and then put him even further back, so that he is still at headquarters (where the tents are, and the open latrines, and the begging, black-footed children) long after we had pictured him bending under the tulip tree to walk up the lawn to the door and the doorbell. As if tired by the many appearances he has made in his parents' minds, Lance now plows wearily through mud puddles, then up a hillside, in the haggard landscape of a distant war, slipping and scrambling up the dead grass of the slope. There is some routine rock work ahead, and then the summit. The ridge is won. Our losses are heavy. How is one notified? By wire? By registered letter? And who is the executioner—a special messenger or the regular plodding, florid-nosed postman, always a little high (he has troubles of his own)? Sign here. Big thumb. Small cross. Weak pencil. Its dull-violet wood. Return it. The illegible signature of teetering disaster.

But nothing comes. A month passes. Chin and Chilla are in fine shape and seem very fond of each other—sleep together in the nest box, cuddled up in a fluffy ball. After many tries, Lance had discovered a sound with definite chinchillan appeal, produced by pursing the lips and emitting in rapid succession several soft, moist "surpths," as if taking sips from a straw when most of one's drink is finished and only its dregs are drained.

But his parents cannot produce it—the pitch is wrong or something. And there is such an intolerable silence in Lance's room, with its battered books, and the spotty white shelves, and the old shoes, and the relatively new tennis racket in its preposterously secure press, and a penny on the closet floor—and all this begins to undergo a prismatic dissolution, but then you tighten the screw and everything is again in focus. And presently the Bokes return to their balcony. Has he reached his goal—and if so, does he see us?

4

The classical ex-mortal leans on his elbow from a flowered ledge to contemplate this earth, this toy, this teetotum gyrating on slow display in its model firmament, every feature so gay and clear—the painted oceans, and the praying woman of the Baltic, and a still of the elegant Americas caught in their trapeze act, and Australia like a baby Africa lying on its side. There may be people among my coevals who half expect their spirits to look down from Heaven with a shudder and a sigh at their native planet and see it girdled with latitudes, stayed with meridians, and marked, perhaps, with the fat, black, diabolically curving arrows of global wars; or, more pleasantly, spread out before their gaze like one of those picture maps of vacational Eldorados, with a reservation Indian beating a drum here, a girl clad in shorts there, conical conifers climbing the cones of mountains, and anglers all over the place.

Actually, I suppose, my young descendant on his first night out, in the imagined silence of an inimaginable world, would have to view the surface features of our globe through the depth of its atmosphere; this would mean dust, scattered reflections, haze, and all kinds of optical pitfalls, so that continents, if they appeared at all through the varying clouds, would slip by in queer disguises, with inexplicable gleams of color and unrecognizable outlines.

But all this is a minor point. The main problem is: Will the mind of the explorer survive the shock? One tries to perceive the nature of that shock as plainly as mental safety permits. And if the mere act of imagining the matter is fraught with hideous risks, how, then, will the real pang be endured and overcome?

First of all, Lance will have to deal with the atavistic moment. Myths have become so firmly entrenched in the radiant sky that common sense is apt to shirk the task of getting at the uncommon sense behind them. Immortality must have a star to stand on if it wishes to branch and blossom and support thousands of blue-plumed angel birds all singing as sweetly as little eunuchs. Deep in the human mind, the concept of dying is synonymous with that of leaving the earth. To escape its gravity means to transcend the grave, and a man upon finding himself on another planet has really no way of proving to himself that he is not dead—that the naïve old myth has not come true.

I am not concerned with the moron, the ordinary hairless ape, who takes everything in his stride; his only childhood memory is of a mule that bit him; his only consciousness of the future a vision of board and bed. What I am thinking of is the man of imagination and science, whose courage is infinite because his curiosity surpasses his courage. Nothing will keep him back. He is the ancient *curieux,* but of a hardier build, with a ruddier heart. When it comes to exploring a celestial body, his is the satisfaction of a passionate desire to feel with his own fingers, to stroke, and inspect, and smile at, and inhale, and stroke again—with that same smile of nameless, moaning, melting pleasure—the never-before-touched matter of which the celestial object is made. Any true scientist (not, of course, the fraudulent mediocrity, whose only treasure is the ignorance he hides like a bone) should be capable of experiencing that sensuous pleasure of direct and divine knowledge. He may be twenty and he may be eighty-five but without that tingle there is no science. And of that stuff Lance is made.

Straining my fancy to the utmost, I see him surmounting the

panic that the ape might not experience at all. No doubt Lance may have landed in an orange-colored dust cloud somewhere in the middle of the Tharsis desert (if it is a desert) or near some purple pool—Phoenicis or Oti (if these are lakes after all). But on the other hand . . . You see, as things go in such matters, something is sure to be solved at once, terribly and irrevocably, while other things come up one by one and are puzzled out gradually. When I was a boy . . .

When I was a boy of seven or eight, I used to dream a vaguely recurrent dream set in a certain environment, which I have never been able to recognize and identify in any rational manner, though I have seen many strange lands. I am inclined to make it serve now, in order to patch up a gaping hole, a raw wound in my story. There was nothing spectacular about that environment, nothing monstrous or even odd: just a bit of non-committal stability represented by a bit of level ground and filmed over with a bit of neutral nebulosity; in other words, the indifferent back of a view rather than its face. —The nuisance of that dream was that for some reason I could not walk *around* the view to meet it on equal terms. There lurked in the mist a mass of something—mineral matter or the like—oppressively and quite meaninglessly shaped, and, in the course of my dream, I kept filling some kind of receptacle (translated as "pail") with smaller shapes (translated as "pebbles"), and my nose was bleeding but I was too impatient and excited to do anything about it. And every time I had that dream, suddenly somebody would start screaming behind me, and I awoke screaming too, thus prolonging the initial anonymous shriek, with its initial note of rising exultation, but with no meaning attached to it any more—if there *had* been a meaning. Speaking of Lance, I would like to submit that something on the lines of my dream— But the funny thing is that as I reread what I have set down, its background, the factual memory vanishes— has vanished altogether by now—and I have no means of proving to myself that there is any personal experience behind its description. What I wanted to say was that perhaps Lance and his companions, when they reached their planet, felt something akin to my dream—which is no longer mine.

5

And they were back! A horseman, clappity-clap, gallops up the cobbled street to the Bokes' house through the driving rain and shouts out the tremendous news as he stops short at the gate, near the dripping liriodendron, while the Bokes come tearing out of the house like two hystricomorphic rodents. They are back! The pilots, and the astrophysicists, and one of the naturalists, are back (the other, Denny, is dead and has been left in Heaven, the old myth scoring a curious point there).

On the sixth floor of a provincial hospital, carefully hidden from newspapermen, Mr. and Mrs. Boke are told that their boy is in a little waiting room, second to the right, ready to receive them; there is something, a kind of hushed deference, about the tone of this information, as if it referred to a fairy tale king. They will enter quietly; a nurse, a Mrs. Coover, will be there all the time. Oh, he's all right, they are told—can go home next week, as a matter of fact. However, they should not stay more than a couple of minutes, and no questions, please—just chat about something or other. *You* know. And then say you will be coming again tomorrow or day after tomorrow.

Lance, gray-robed, crop-haired, tan gone, changed, unchanged, changed, thin, nostrils stopped with absorbent cotton, sits on the edge of a couch, his hands clasped, a little embarrassed. Gets up wavily, with a beaming grimace, and sits down again. Mrs. Coover, the nurse, has blue eyes and no chin.

A ripe silence. Then Lance: "It was wonderful. Perfectly wonderful. I am going back in November."

Pause.

"I think," says Mr. Boke, "that Chilla is with child."

Quick smile, little bow of pleased acknowledgment. Then, in a narrative voice: *"Je vais dire ça en français. Nous venions d'arriver——"*

"Show them the President's letter," says Mrs. Coover.

"We had just got there," Lance continues, "and Denny was still alive, and the first thing he and I saw——"

In a sudden flutter, Nurse Coover interrupts: "No, Lance, no. No, Madam, please. No contacts, doctor's orders, *please*."

Warm temple, cold ear.

Mr. and Mrs. Boke are ushered out. They walk swiftly—although there is no hurry, no hurry whatever, down the corridor, along its shoddy, olive-and-ocher wall, the lower olive separated from the upper ocher by a continuous brown line leading to the venerable elevators. Going up (glimpse of patriarch in wheel-chair). Going back in November (Lancelin). Going down (the old Bokes). There are, in that elevator, two smiling women and, the object of their bright sympathy, a girl with a baby, besides the gray-haired, bent, sullen elevator man, who stands with his back to everybody.

Ithaca, 1952

The Vane Sisters

I

I might never have heard of Cynthia's death, had I not run, that night, into D., whom I had also lost track of for the last four years or so; and I might never have run into D., had I not got involved in a series of trivial investigations.

The day, a compunctious Sunday after a week of blizzards, had been part jewel, part mud. In the midst of my usual afternoon stroll through the small hilly town attached to the girls' college where I taught French literature, I had stopped to watch a family of brilliant icicles drip-dripping from the eaves of a frame house. So clear-cut were their pointed shadows on the white boards behind them that I was sure the shadows of the falling drops should be visible too. But they were not. The roof jutted too far out, perhaps, or the angle of vision was faulty, or, again, I did not chance to be watching the right icicle when the right drop fell. There was a rhythm, an alternation in the dropping that I found as teasing as a coin trick. It led me to inspect the corners of several house blocks, and this brought me to Kelly Road, and right to the house where D. used to live when he was instructor here. And as I looked up at the eaves of the adjacent garage with its full display of transparent stalactites backed by their blue silhouettes, I was rewarded at last, upon choosing one, by the sight of what might be described as the dot of an exclamation mark leaving its ordinary position to glide down very fast—a jot faster than the thaw-drop it raced.

This twinned twinkle was delightful but not completely satisfying; or rather it only sharpened my appetite for other tidbits of light and shade, and I walked on in a state of raw awareness that seemed to transform the whole of my being into one big eyeball rolling in the world's socket.

Through peacocked lashes I saw the dazzling diamond reflection of the low sun on the round back of a parked automobile. To all kinds of things a vivid pictorial sense had been restored by the sponge of the thaw. Water in overlapping festoons flowed down one sloping street and turned gracefully into another. With ever so slight a note of meretricious appeal, narrow passages between buildings revealed treasures of brick and purple. I remarked for the first time the humble fluting—last echoes of grooves on the shafts of columns—ornamenting a garbage can, and I also saw the rippling upon its lid—circles diverging from a fantastically ancient center. Erect, dark-headed shapes of dead snow (left by the blades of a bulldozer last Friday) were lined up like rudimentary penguins along the curbs, above the brilliant vibration of live gutters.

I walked up, and I walked down, and I walked straight into a delicately dying sky, and finally the sequence of observed and observant things brought me, at my usual eating time, to a street so distant from my usual eating place that I decided to try a restaurant which stood on the fringe of the town. Night had fallen without sound or ceremony when I came out again. The lean ghost, the elongated umbra cast by a parking meter upon some damp snow, had a strange ruddy tinge; this I made out to be due to the tawny red light of the restaurant sign above the sidewalk; and it was then—as I sauntered there, wondering rather wearily if in the course of my return tramp I might be lucky enough to find the same in neon blue it was then that a car crunched to a standstill near me and D. got out of it with an exclamation of feigned pleasure.

He was passing, on his way from Albany to Boston, through the town he had dwelt in before, and more than once in my life have I felt that stab of vicarious emotion followed by a rush of personal irritation against travelers who seem to feel nothing at all upon revisiting spots that ought to harass them at every step with wailing and writhing memories. He ushered me back into the bar that I had just left, and after the usual exchange of buoyant platitudes came the inevitable vacuum which he filled with the random words: "Say, I never thought there was anything wrong with Cynthia Vane's heart. My lawyer tells me she died last week."

2

He was still young, still brash, still shifty, still married to the gentle, exquisitely pretty woman who had never learned or suspected anything about his disastrous affair with Cynthia's hysterical young sister, who in her turn had known nothing of the interview I had had with Cynthia when she suddenly summoned me to Boston to make me swear I would talk to D. and get him "kicked out" if he did not stop seeing Sybil at once—or did not divorce his wife (whom incidentally she visualized through the prism of Sybil's wild talk as a termagant and a fright). I had cornered him immediately. He had said there was nothing to worry about—had made up his mind, anyway, to give up his college job and move with his wife to Albany where he would work in his father's firm; and the whole matter, which had threatened to become one of those hopelessly entangled situations that drag on for years, with peripheral sets of well-meaning friends endlessly discussing it in universal secrecy—and even founding, among themselves, new intimacies upon its alien woes—came to an abrupt end.

I remember sitting next day at my raised desk in the large classroom where a mid-year examination in French Lit was being held on the eve of Sybil's suicide. She came in on high heels, with a suitcase, dumped it in a corner where several other bags were stacked, with a single shrug slipped her fur coat off her thin shoulders, folded it on her bag, and with two or three other girls stopped before my desk to ask when would I mail them their grades. It would táke me a week, beginning from tomorrow, I said, to read the stuff. I also remember wondering whether D. had already informed her of his decision—and I felt acutely unhappy about my dutiful little student as during one hundred and fifty minutes my gaze kept reverting to her, so childishly slight in close-fitting gray, and kept observing that carefully waved dark hair, that small, small-flowered hat with a little hyaline veil as worn that season and under it her small face broken into a cubist pattern by scars due to a skin disease, pathetically masked by a sun-lamp tan that hardened her features, whose charm was further impaired by her having painted everything that could be painted, so that the pale gums of her teeth between cherry-red chapped lips and the diluted black ink of her eyes under darkened lids were the only visible openings into her beauty.

Next day, having arranged the ugly copybooks alphabetically, I plunged into their chaos of scripts and came prematurely to Valevsky and Vane, whose books I had somehow misplaced. The first was dressed up for the occasion in a semblance of legibility, but Sybil's work displayed her usual combination of several demon hands. She had begun in very pale, very hard pencil which had conspicuously embossed the blank verso, but had produced little of permanent value on the upper-side of the page. Happily the tip soon broke, and Sybil continued in another, darker lead, gradually lapsing into the blurred thickness of what looked almost like charcoal, to which, by sucking the blunt point, she had contributed some traces of lipstick. Her work, although even poorer than I had expected, bore all the signs of a kind of desperate conscientiousness, with underscores, transposes, unnecessary footnotes, as if she were intent upon rounding up things in the most respectable manner possible. Then she had borrowed Mary Valevsky's fountain pen

and added: *"Cette examain est finie ainsi que ma vie. Adieu,
jeunes filles!* Please, *Monsieur le Professeur,* contact *ma soeur*
and tell her that Death was not better than D minus, but definitely better than Life minus D."

I lost no time in ringing up Cynthia who told me it was all
over—had been all over since eight in the morning—and asked
me to bring her the note, and when I did, beamed through her
tears with proud admiration for the whimsical use ("Just like
her!") Sybil had made of an examination in French literature. In
no time she "fixed" two highballs, while never parting with
Sybil's notebook—by now splashed with soda water and tears—
and went on studying the death message, whereupon I was
impelled to point out to her the grammatical mistakes in it and
to explain the way "girl" is translated in American colleges lest
students innocently bandy around the French equivalent of
"wench," or worse. These rather tasteless trivialities pleased
Cynthia hugely as she rose, with gasps, above the heaving surface of her grief. And then, holding that limp notebook as if it
were a kind of passport to a casual Elysium (where pencil points
do not snap and a dreamy young beauty with an impeccable
complexion winds a lock of her hair on a dreamy forefinger, as
she meditates over some celestial test), Cynthia led me upstairs, to a chilly little bedroom just to show me, as if I were
the police or a sympathetic Irish neighbor, two empty pill bottles and the tumbled bed from which a tender, inessential body,
that D. must have known down to its last velvet detail, had been
already removed.

3

It was four or five months after her sister's death that I began
seeing Cynthia fairly often. By the time I had come to New
York for some vocational research in the Public Library she
had also moved to that city where for some odd reason (in

vague connection, I presume, with artistic motives) she had taken what people, immune to gooseflesh, term a "cold water" flat, down in the scale of the city's transverse streets. What attracted me were neither her ways, which I thought repulsively vivacious, nor her looks, which other men thought striking. She had wide-spaced eyes very much like her sister's, of a frank, frightened blue with dark points in a radial arrangement. The interval between her thick black eyebrows was always shiny, and shiny too were the fleshy volutes of her nostrils. The coarse texture of her epiderm looked almost masculine, and, in the stark lamplight of her studio, you could see the pores of her thirty-two-year-old face fairly gaping at you like something in an aquarium. She used cosmetics with as much zest as her little sister had, but with an additional slovenliness that would result in her big front teeth getting some of the rouge. She was handsomely dark, wore a not too tasteless mixture of fairly smart heterogeneous things, and had a so-called good figure; but all of her was curiously frowsy, after a way I obscurely associated with left-wing enthusiasms in politics and "advanced" banalities in art, although, actually, she cared for neither. Her coily hair-do, on a part-and-bun basis, might have looked feral and bizarre had it not been thoroughly domesticated by its own soft unkemptness at the vulnerable nape. Her fingernails were gaudily painted, but badly bitten and not clean. Her lovers were a silent young photographer with a sudden laugh and two older men, brothers, who owned a small printing establishment across the street. I wondered at their tastes whenever I glimpsed, with a secret shudder, the higgledy-piggledy striation of black hairs that showed all along her pale shins through the nylon of her stockings with the scientific distinctness of a preparation flattened under glass; or when I felt, at her every movement, the dullish, stalish, not particularly conspicuous but all-pervading and depressing emanation that her seldom bathed flesh spread from under weary perfumes and creams.

Her father had gambled away the greater part of a comfortable fortune, and her mother's first husband had been of Slav origin, but otherwise Cynthia Vane belonged to a good, respectable family. For aught we know, it may have gone back to kings and soothsayers in the mists of ultimate islands. Transferred to a newer world, to a landscape of doomed, splendid deciduous trees, her ancestry presented, in one of its first phases, a white churchful of farmers against a black thunderhead, and then an imposing array of townsmen engaged in mercantile pursuits, as well as a number of learned men, such as Dr. Jonathan Vane, the gaunt bore (1780-1839), who perished in the conflagration of the steamer "Lexington" to become later an habitué of Cynthia's tilting table. I have always wished to stand genealogy on its head, and here I have an opportunity to do so, for it is the last scion, Cynthia, and Cynthia alone, who will remain of any importance in the Vane dynasty. I am alluding of course to her artistic gift, to her delightful, gay, but not very popular paintings which the friends of her friends bought at long intervals and I dearly should like to know where they went after her death, those honest and poetical pictures that illumined her living room—the wonderfully detailed images of metallic things, and my favorite "Seen Through a Windshield"—a windshield partly covered with rime, with a brilliant trickle (from an imaginary car roof) across its transparent part and, through it all, the sapphire flame of the sky and a green and white fir tree.

4

Cynthia had a feeling that her dead sister was not altogether pleased with her—had discovered by now that she and I had conspired to break her romance; and so, in order to disarm her shade, Cynthia reverted to a rather primitive type of sacrificial offering (tinged, however, with something of Sybil's humor), and began to send to D.'s business address, at deliberately unfixed dates, such trifles as snapshots of Sybil's tomb in a poor light; cuttings of her own hair which was indistinguishable from Sybil's; a New England sectional map with an inked-in cross, midway between two chaste towns, to mark the spot where D. and Sybil had stopped on October the twenty-third, in broad daylight, at a lenient motel, in a pink and brown forest; and, twice, a stuffed skunk.

Being as a conversationalist more voluble than explicit, she never could describe in full the theory of intervenient auras that she had somehow evolved. Fundamentally there was nothing particularly new about her private creed since it presupposed a fairly conventional hereafter, a silent solarium of immortal souls (spliced with mortal antecedents) whose main recreation consisted of periodical hoverings over the dear quick. The interesting point was a curious practical twist that Cynthia gave to her tame metaphysics. She was sure that her existence was influenced by all sorts of dead friends each of whom took turns in directing her fate much as if she were a stray kitten which a schoolgirl in passing gathers up, and presses to her cheek, and carefully puts down again, near some suburban hedge—to be stroked presently by another transient hand or carried off to a world of doors by some hospitable lady.

For a few hours, or for several days in a row, and sometimes recurrently, in an irregular series, for months or years, anything that happened to Cynthia, after a given person had died, would be, she said, in the manner and mood of that person. The event might be extraordinary, changing the course of one's life; or it might be a string of minute incidents just sufficiently clear to stand out in relief against one's usual day and then shading off into still vaguer trivia as the aura gradually faded. The influence might be good or bad; the main thing was that its source could be identified. It was like walking through a person's soul, she said. I tried to argue that she might not always be able to determine the exact source since not everybody has a recognizable soul; that there are anonymous letters and Christmas presents which anybody might send; that, in fact, what Cynthia called "a usual day" might be itself a weak solution of mixed auras or simply the routine shift of a humdrum guardian angel. And what about God? Did or did not people who would resent any omnipotent dictator on earth look forward to one in heaven? And wars? What a dreadful idea—dead soldiers still fighting with living ones, or phantom armies trying to get at each other through the lives of crippled old men.

But Cynthia was above generalities as she was beyond logic. "Ah, that's Paul," she would say when the soup spitefully boiled over, or: "I guess good Betty Brown is dead"—when she won a beautiful and very welcome vacuum cleaner in a charity lottery. And, with Jamesian meanderings that exasperated my French mind, she would go back to a time when Betty and Paul had not yet departed, and tell me of the showers of well-meant, but odd and quite unacceptable bounties—beginning with an old purse that contained a check for three dollars which she picked up in the street and, of course, returned (to the aforesaid Betty Brown—this is where she first comes in —a decrepit colored woman hardly able to walk), and ending with an insulting proposal from an old beau of hers (this is where Paul comes in) to paint "straight" pictures of his house and family for a reasonable remuneration—all of which followed upon the demise of a certain Mrs. Page, a kindly but petty old party who had pestered her with bits of matter-of-fact advice since Cynthia had been a child.

Sybil's personality, she said, had a rainbow edge as if a little out of focus. She said that had I known Sybil better I would have at once understood how Sybil-like was the aura of minor events which, in spells, had suffused her, Cynthia's, existence after Sybil's suicide. Ever since they had lost their mother they had intended to give up their Boston home and move to New York, where Cynthia's paintings, they thought, would have a chance to be more widely admired; but the old home had clung to them with all its plush tentacles. Dead Sybil, however, had proceeded to separate the house from its view—a thing that affects fatally the sense of home. Right across the narrow street a building project had come into loud, ugly scaffolded life. A pair of familiar poplars died that spring, turning to blond skeletons. Workmen came and broke up the warm-colored lovely old sidewalk that had a special violet sheen on wet April days and had echoed so memorably to the morning footsteps of museum-bound Mr. Lever, who upon retiring from business at sixty had devoted a full quarter of a century exclusively to the study of snails.

Speaking of old men, one should add that sometimes these posthumous auspices and interventions were in the nature of parody. Cynthia had been on friendly terms with an eccentric librarian called Porlock who in the last years of his dusty life had been engaged in examining old books for miraculous misprints such as the substitution of "l" for the second "h" in the word "hither." Contrary to Cynthia, he cared nothing for the thrill of obscure predictions; all he sought was the freak itself, the chance that mimics choice, the flaw that looks like a flower; and Cynthia, a much more perverse amateur of mis-shapen or illicitly connected words, puns, logogriphs, and so on, had helped the poor crank to pursue a quest that in the light of the example she cited struck me as statistically insane. Anyway, she said, on the third day after his death she was reading a magazine and had just come across a quotation from an imperishable poem (that she, with other gullible readers, believed to have been really composed in a dream) when it dawned upon her that "Alph" was a prophetic sequence of the initial letters of Anna Livia Plurabelle (another sacred river running through, or rather around, yet another fake dream), while the additional "h" modestly stood, as a private signpost, for the word that had so hypnotized Mr. Porlock. And I wish I could recollect that novel or short story (by some contemporary writer, I believe) in which, unknown to its author, the first letters of the words in its last paragraph formed, as deciphered by Cynthia, a message from his dead mother.

5

I am sorry to say that not content with these ingenious fancies Cynthia showed a ridiculous fondness for spiritualism. I refused to accompany her to sittings in which paid mediums took part: I knew too much about that from other sources. I did consent, however, to attend little farces rigged up by Cynthia and her two poker-faced gentlemen-friends of the printing shop. They were podgy, polite, and rather eerie old fellows, but I satisfied myself that they possessed considerable wit and culture. We sat down at a light little table, and crackling tremors started almost as soon as we laid our fingertips upon it. I was treated to an assortment of ghosts who rapped out their reports most readily though refusing to elucidate anything that I did not quite catch. Oscar Wilde came in and in rapid garbled French, with the usual anglicisms, obscurely accused Cynthia's dead parents of what appeared in my jottings as *"plagiatisme."* A brisk spirit contributed the unsolicited information that he, John Moore, and his brother Bill had been coal miners in Colorado and had perished in an avalanche at "Crested Beauty" in January 1883. Frederic Myers, an old hand at the game, hammered out a piece of verse (oddly resembling Cynthia's own fugitive productions) which in part reads in my notes:

> *What is this—a conjurer's rabbit,*
> *Or a flawy but genuine gleam—*
> *Which can check the perilous habit*
> *And dispel the dolorous dream?*

Finally, with a great crash and all kinds of shudderings and jiglike movements on the part of the table, Leo Tolstoy visited our little group and, when asked to identify himself by specific traits of terrene habitation, launched upon a complex description of what seemed to be some Russian type of architectural woodwork ("figures on boards—man, horse, cock, man, horse, cock"), all of which was difficult to take down, hard to understand, and impossible to verify.

I attended two or three other sittings which were even sillier but I must confess that I preferred the childish entertainment they afforded and the cider we drank (Podgy and Pudgy were teetotallers) to Cynthia's awful house parties.

She gave them at the Wheelers' nice flat next door—the sort of arrangement dear to her centrifugal nature, but then, of course, her own living room always looked like a dirty old palette. Following a barbaric, unhygienic, and adulterous custom, the guests' coats, still warm on the inside, were carried by quiet, baldish Bob Wheeler into the sanctity of a tidy bedroom and heaped on the conjugal bed. It was also he who poured out the drinks, which were passed around by the young photographer while Cynthia and Mrs. Wheeler took care of the canapés.

A late arrival had the impression of lots of loud people unnecessarily grouped within a smoke-blue space between two mirrors gorged with reflections. Because, I suppose, Cynthia wished to be the youngest in the room, the women she used to invite, married or single, were, at the best, in their precarious forties; some of them would bring from their homes, in dark taxis, intact vestiges of good looks, which, however, they lost as the party progressed. It has always amazed me—the capacity sociable week-end revelers have of finding almost at once, by a purely empiric but very precise method, a common denominator of drunkenness, to which everybody loyally sticks before descending, all together, to the next level. The rich friendliness of the matrons was marked by tomboyish overtones, while the fixed inward look of amiably tight men was like a sacrilegious parody of pregnancy. Although some of the guests were connected in one way or another with the arts, there was no inspired talk, no wreathed, elbow-propped heads, and of course no flute girls. From some vantage point where she had been sitting in a stranded mermaid pose on the pale carpet with one or two younger fellows, Cynthia, her face varnished with a film of beaming sweat, would creep up on her knees, a proffered plate of nuts in one hand, and crisply tap with the other the athletic leg of Cochran or Corcoran, an art dealer, ensconced, on a pearl-gray sofa, between two flushed, happily disintegrating ladies.

At a further stage there would come spurts of more riotous gaiety. Corcoran or Coransky would grab Cynthia or some other wandering woman by the shoulder and lead her into a corner to confront her with a grinning imbroglio of private jokes and rumors, whereupon, with a laugh and a toss of her head, she would break away. And still later there would be flurries of intersexual chumminess, jocular reconciliations, a bare fleshy arm flung around another woman's husband (he standing very upright in the midst of a swaying room), or a sudden rush of flirtatious anger, of clumsy pursuit—and the quiet half smile of Bob Wheeler picking up glasses that grew like mushrooms in the shade of chairs.

After one last party of that sort, I wrote Cynthia a perfectly harmless and, on the whole, well-meant note, in which I poked a little Latin fun at some of her guests. I also apologized for not having touched her whisky, saying that as a Frenchman I preferred the grape to the grain. A few days later I met her on the steps of the Public Library, in the broken sun, under a weak cloudburst, opening her amber umbrella, struggling with a couple of armpitted books (of which I relieved her for a moment), "Footfalls on the Boundary of Another World," by Robert Dale Owen, and something on "Spiritualism and Christianity"; when, suddenly, with no provocation on my part, she blazed out at me with vulgar vehemence, using poisonous words, saying—through pear-shaped drops of sparse rain—that I was a prig and a snob; that I only saw the gestures and disguises of people; that Corcoran had rescued from drowning, in two different oceans, two men—by an irrelevant coincidence both called Corcoran; that romping and screeching Joan Winter had a little girl doomed to grow completely blind in a few months; and that the woman in green with the freckled chest whom I had snubbed in some way or other had written a national best-seller in 1932. Strange Cynthia! I had been told she could be thunderously rude to people whom she liked and respected; one had, however, to draw the line somewhere and since I had by then sufficiently studied her interesting auras and other odds and ids, I decided to stop seeing her altogether.

6

The night D. informed me of Cynthia's death I returned after eleven to the two-storied house I shared, in horizontal section, with an emeritus professor's widow. Upon reaching the porch I looked with the apprehension of solitude at the two kinds of darkness in the two rows of windows: the darkness of absence and the darkness of sleep.

I could do something about the first but could not duplicate the second. My bed gave me no sense of safety; its springs only made my nerves bounce. I plunged into Shakespeare's sonnets—and found myself idiotically checking the first letters of the lines to see what sacramental words they might form. I got FATE (LXX), ATOM (CXX) and, twice, TAFT (LXXXVIII, CXXXI). Every now and then I would glance around to see how the objects in my room were behaving. It was strange to think that if bombs began to fall I would feel little more than a gambler's excitement (and a great deal of earthy relief) whereas my heart would burst if a certain suspiciously tense-looking little bottle on yonder shelf moved a fraction of an inch to one side. The silence, too, was suspiciously compact as if deliberately forming a black back-drop for the nerve flash caused by any small sound of unknown origin. All traffic was dead. In vain did I pray for the groan of a truck up Perkins Street. The woman above who used to drive me crazy by the booming thuds occasioned by what seemed monstrous feet of stone (actually, in diurnal life, she was a small dumpy creature resembling a mummified guinea pig) would have earned my blessings had she now trudged to her bathroom. I put out my light and cleared my throat several times so as to be responsible for at least *that* sound. I thumbed a mental ride with a very remote automobile but it dropped me before I had a chance to doze off. Presently a crackle (due, I hoped, to a discarded and crushed sheet of paper opening like a mean, stubborn night flower)—started and stopped in the waste-paper basket, and my bed-table responded with a little click. It would have been just like Cynthia to put on right then a cheap poltergeist show.

I decided to fight Cynthia. I reviewed in thought the modern era of raps and apparitions, beginning with the knockings of 1848, at the hamlet of Hydesville, N.Y., and ending with grotesque phenomena at Cambridge, Mass.; I evoked the anklebones and other anatomical castanets of the Fox sisters (as described by the sages of the University of Buffalo); the mysteriously uniform type of delicate adolescent in bleak Epworth or Tedworth, radiating the same disturbances as in old Peru; solemn Victorian orgies with roses falling and accordions floating to the strains of sacred music; professional imposters regurgitating moist cheesecloth; Mr. Duncan, a lady medium's dignified husband, who, when asked if he would submit to a search, excused himself on the ground of soiled underwear; old Alfred Russel Wallace, the naïve naturalist, refusing to believe that the white form with bare feet and unperforated earlobes before him, at a private pandemonium in Boston, could be prim Miss Cook whom he had just seen asleep, in her curtained corner, all dressed in black, wearing laced-up boots and earrings; two other investigators, small, puny, but reasonably intelligent and active men, closely clinging with arms and legs about Eusapia, a large, plump elderly female reeking of garlic, who still managed to fool them; and the sceptical and embarrassed magician, instructed by charming Margery's "control" not to get lost in the bathrobe's lining but to follow up the left stocking until he reached the bare thigh—upon the warm skin of which he felt a "teleplastic" mass that appeared to the touch uncommonly like cold, uncooked liver.

7

I was appealing to flesh, and the corruption of flesh, to refute and defeat the possible persistence of discarnate life. Alas, these conjurations only enhanced my fear of Cynthia's phantom. Atavistic peace came with dawn, and when I slipped into sleep, the sun through the tawny window shades penetrated a dream that somehow was full of Cynthia.

This was disappointing. Secure in the fortress of daylight, I said to myself that I had expected more. She, a painter of glass-bright minutiæ—and now so vague! I lay in bed, thinking my dream over and listening to the sparrows outside: Who knows, if recorded and then run backward, those bird sounds might not become human speech, voiced words, just as the latter become a twitter when reversed? I set myself to re-read my dream—backward, diagonally, up, down—trying hard to unravel something Cynthia-like in it, something strange and suggestive that must be there.

I could isolate, consciously, little. Everything seemed blurred, yellow-clouded, yielding nothing tangible. Her inept acrostics, maudlin evasions, theopathies—every recollection formed ripples of mysterious meaning. Everything seemed yellowly blurred, illusive, lost.

Ithaca, 1951

ESSAYS AND
CRITICISM

On a Book Entitled Lolita

After doing my impersonation of suave John Ray, the character in *Lolita* who pens the Foreword, any comments coming straight from me may strike one—may strike me, in fact—as an impersonation of Vladimir Nabokov talking about his own book. A few points, however, have to be discussed; and the autobiographic device may induce mimic and model to blend.

Teachers of Literature are apt to think up such problems as "What is the author's purpose?" or, still worse, "What is the guy trying to say?" Now, I happen to be the kind of author who in starting to work on a book has no other purpose than to get rid of that book and who, when asked to explain its origin and growth, has to rely on such ancient terms as Interreaction of Inspiration and Combination—which, I admit, sounds like a conjurer explaining one trick by performing another.

The first little throb of *Lolita* went through me late in 1939 or early in 1940, in Paris, at a time when I was laid up with a severe attack of intercostal neuralgia. As far as I can recall, the initial shiver of inspiration was somehow prompted by a newspaper story about an ape in the Jardin des Plantes who, after months of coaxing by a scientist, produced the first drawing ever charcoaled by an animal: this sketch showed the bars of the poor creature's cage. The impulse I record had no textual connection with the ensuing train of thought, which resulted, however, in a prototype of my present novel, a short story some thirty pages long. I wrote it in Russian, the language in which I had been writing novels since 1924 (the best of these are not translated into English, and all are prohibited for political reasons in Russia). The man was a Central European, the anonymous nymphet was French, and the loci were Paris and Provence. I had him marry the little girl's sick mother who soon died, and after a thwarted attempt to take advantage of the orphan in a hotel room, Arthur (for that was his name) threw himself under the wheels of a truck. I read the story one blue-papered wartime night to a group of friends—Mark Aldanov, two social revolutionaries, and a woman doctor; but I was not pleased with the thing and destroyed it sometime after moving to America in 1940.

Around 1949, in Ithaca, upstate New York, the throbbing, which had never quite ceased, began to plague me again. Combination joined inspiration with fresh zest and involved me in a new treatment of the theme, this time in English—the language of my first governess in St. Petersburg, circa 1903, a Miss Rachel Home. The nymphet, now with a dash of Irish blood, was really much the same lass, and the basic marrying-her-mother idea also subsisted; but otherwise the thing was new and had grown in secret the claws and wings of a novel.

The book developed slowly, with many interruptions and asides. It had taken me some forty years to invent Russia and Western Europe, and now I was faced by the task of inventing America. The obtaining of such local ingredients as would allow me to inject a modicum of average "reality" (one of the few words which mean nothing without quotes) into the brew of individual fancy, proved at fifty a much more difficult process than it had been in the Europe of my youth when receptiveness and retention were at their automatic best. Other books intervened. Once or twice I was on the point of burning the unfinished draft and had carried my Juanita Dark as far as the shadow of the leaning incinerator on the innocent lawn, when I was stopped by the thought that the ghost of the destroyed book would haunt my files for the rest of my life.

Every summer my wife and I go butterfly hunting. The specimens are deposited at scientific institutions, such as the Museum of Comparative Zoology at Harvard or the Cornell University collection. The locality labels pinned under these butterflies will be a boon to some twenty-first-century scholar with a taste for recondite biography. It was at such of our headquarters as Telluride, Colorado; Afton, Wyoming; Portal, Arizona; and Ashland, Oregon, that *Lolita* was energetically resumed in the evenings or on cloudy days. I finished copying the thing out in longhand in the spring of 1954, and at once began casting around for a publisher.

At first, on the advice of a wary old friend, I was meek enough to stipulate that the book be brought out anonymously. I doubt that I shall ever regret that soon afterwards, realizing how likely a mask was to betray my own cause, I decided to sign *Lolita*. The four American publishers, W, X, Y, Z, who in turn were offered the typescript and had their readers glance at it, were shocked by *Lolita* to a degree that even my wary old friend F.P. had not expected.

While it is true that in ancient Europe, and well into the eighteenth century (obvious examples come from France), deliberate lewdness was not inconsistent with flashes of comedy, or vigorous satire, or even the verve of a fine poet in a wanton mood, it is also true that in modern times the term "pornography" connotes mediocrity, commercialism, and certain strict rules of narration. Obscenity must be mated with banality because every kind of aesthetic enjoyment has to be entirely replaced by simple sexual stimulation which demands the traditional word for direct action upon the patient. Old rigid rules must be followed by the pornographer in order to have his patient feel the same security of satisfaction as, for example, fans of detective stories feel—stories where, if you do not watch out, the real murderer may turn out to be, to the fan's disgust, artistic originality (who for instance would want a detective story without a single dialogue in it?). Thus, in pornographic novels, action has to be limited to the copulation of clichés. Style, structure, imagery should never distract the reader from his tepid lust. The novel must consist of an alternation of sexual scenes. The passages in between must be reduced to sutures of sense, logical bridges of the simplest design, brief expositions and explanations, which the reader will probably skip but must know they exist in order not to feel cheated (a mentality stemming from the routine of "true" fairy tales in childhood). Moreover, the sexual scenes in the book must follow a crescendo line, with new variations, new combinations, new sexes, and a steady increase in the number of participants (in a Sade play they call the gardener in), and therefore the end of the book must be more replete with lewd lore than the first chapters.

Certain techniques in the beginning of *Lolita* (Humbert's Journal, for example) misled some of my first readers into assuming that this was going to be a lewd book. They expected the rising succession of erotic scenes; when these stopped, the readers stopped, too, and felt bored and let down. This, I suspect, is one of the reasons why not all the four firms read the typescript to the end. Whether they found it pornographic or not did not interest me. Their refusal to buy the book was based not on my treatment of the theme but on the theme itself, for there are at least three themes which are utterly taboo as far as most American publishers are concerned. The two others are: a Negro-White marriage which is a complete and glorious success resulting in lots of children and grandchildren; and the total atheist who lives a happy and useful life, and dies in his sleep at the age of 106.

Some of the reactions were very amusing: one reader suggested that his firm might consider publication if I turned my Lolita into a twelve-year-old lad and had him seduced by Humbert, a farmer, in a barn, amidst gaunt and arid surroundings, all this set forth in short, strong, "realistic" sentences ("He acts crazy. We all act crazy, I guess. I guess God acts crazy." Etc.). Although everybody should know that I detest symbols and allegories (which is due partly to my old feud with Freudian voodooism and partly to my loathing of generalizations devised by literary mythists and sociologists), an otherwise intelligent reader who flipped through the first part described *Lolita* as "Old Europe debauching young America," while another flipper saw in it "Young America debauching old Europe." Publisher X, whose advisers got so bored with Humbert that they never got beyond page 188, had the naïveté to write me that Part Two was too long. Publisher Y, on the other hand, regretted there were no good people in the book. Publisher Z said if he printed *Lolita,* he and I would go to jail.

No writer in a free country should be expected to bother about the exact demarcation between the sensuous and the sensual; this is preposterous; I can only admire but cannot emulate the accuracy of judgment of those who pose the fair young mammals photographed in magazines where the general neckline is just low enough to provoke a past master's chuckle and just high enough not to make a postmaster frown. I presume there exist readers who find titillating the display of mural words in those hopelessly banal and enormous novels which are typed out by the thumbs of tense mediocrities and called "powerful" and "stark" by the reviewing hack. There are gentle souls who would pronounce *Lolita* meaningless because it does not teach them anything. I am neither a reader nor a writer of didactic fiction, and, despite John Ray's assertion, *Lolita* has no moral in tow. For me a work of fiction exists only insofar as it affords me what I shall bluntly call aesthetic bliss, that is a sense of being somehow, somewhere, connected with other states of being where art (curiosity, tenderness, kindness, ecstasy) is the norm. There are not many such books. All the rest is either topical trash or what some call the Literature of Ideas, which very often is topical trash coming in huge blocks of plaster that are carefully transmitted from age to age until somebody comes along with a hammer and takes a good crack at Balzac, at Gorki, at Mann.

Another charge which some readers have made is that

Lolita is anti-American. This is something that pains me considerably more than the idiotic accusation of immorality. Considerations of depth and perspective (a suburban lawn, a mountain meadow) led me to build a number of North American sets. I needed a certain exhilarating milieu. Nothing is more exhilarating than philistine vulgarity. But in regard to philistine vulgarity there is no intrinsic difference between Palearctic manners and Nearctic manners. Any proletarian from Chicago can be as bourgeois (in the Flaubertian sense) as a duke. I chose American motels instead of Swiss hotels or English inns only because I am trying to be an American writer and claim only the same rights that other American writers enjoy. On the other hand, my creature Humbert is a foreigner and an anarchist, and there are many things, besides nymphets, in which I disagree with him. And all my Russian readers know that my old worlds—Russian, British, German, French—are just as fantastic and personal as my new one is.

Lest the little statement I am making here seem an airing of grudges, I must hasten to add that besides the lambs who read the typescript of *Lolita* or its Olympia Press edition in a spirit of "Why did he have to write it?" or "Why should I read about maniacs?" there have been a number of wise, sensitive, and staunch people who understood my book much better than I can explain its mechanism here.

Every serious writer, I dare say, is aware of this or that published book of his as of a constant comforting presence. Its pilot light is steadily burning somewhere in the basement and a mere touch applied to one's private thermostat instantly results in a quiet little explosion of familiar warmth. This presence, this glow of the book in an ever accessible remoteness is a most companionable feeling, and the better the book has conformed to its prefigured contour and color the ampler and smoother it glows. But even so, there are certain points, byroads, favorite hollows that one evokes more eagerly and enjoys more tenderly than the rest of one's book. I have not reread *Lolita* since I

went through the proofs in the winter of 1954 but I find it to
be a delightful presence now that it quietly hangs about the
house like a summer day which one knows to be bright behind
the haze. And when I thus think of *Lolita,* I seem always to
pick out for special delectation such images as Mrs. Taxovich,
or that class list of Ramsdale School, or Charlotte saying
"waterproof," or Lolita in slow motion advancing toward
Humbert's gifts, or the pictures decorating the stylized garret of
Gaston Godin, or the Kasbeam barber (who cost me a month
of work), or Lolita playing tennis, or the hospital at Elphin-
stone, or pale, pregnant, beloved, irretrievable Dolly Schiller
dying in Gray Star (the capital town of the book), or the
tinkling sounds of the valley town coming up the mountain
trail (on which I caught the first known female of *Lycaeides
sublivens* Nabokov). These are the nerves of the novel. These
are the secret points, the subliminal co-ordinates by means of
which the book is plotted—although I realize very clearly that
these and other scenes will be skimmed over or not noticed, or
never even reached, by those who begin reading the book under the impression that it is something on the lines of *Memoirs
of a Woman of Pleasure* or *Les Amours de Milord Grosvit.*
That my novel does contain various allusions to the physiologi-
cal urges of a pervert is quite true. But after all we are not children, not illiterate juvenile delinquents, not English public
school boys who after a night of homosexual romps have to endure the paradox of reading the Ancients in expurgated versions.

It is childish to study a work of fiction in order to gain information about a country or about a social class or about the
author. And yet one of my very few intimate friends, after
reading *Lolita,* was sincerely worried that I (I!) should be
living "among such depressing people"—when the only discomfort I really experienced was to live in my workshop among
discarded limbs and unfinished torsos.

After Olympia Press, in Paris, published the book, an American critic suggested that *Lolita* was the record of my love affair with the romantic novel. The substitution "English language" for "romantic novel" would make this elegant formula more correct. But here I feel my voice rising to a much too strident pitch. None of my American friends have read my Russian books and thus every appraisal on the strength of my English ones is bound to be out of focus. My private tragedy, which cannot, and indeed should not, be anybody's concern, is that I had to abandon my natural idiom, my untrammeled, rich, and infinitely docile Russian tongue for a second-rate brand of English, devoid of any of those apparatuses—the baffling mirror, the black velvet backdrop, the implied associations and traditions—which the native illusionist, frac-tails flying, can magically use to transcend the heritage in his own way.

November 12, 1956

Introduction to Bend Sinister

Bend Sinister was the first novel I wrote in America, and that was half a dozen years after she and I had adopted each other. The greater part of the book was composed in the winter and spring of 1945-1946, at a particularly cloudless and vigorous period of life. My health was excellent. My daily consumption of cigarettes had reached the four-package mark. I slept at least four or five hours, the rest of the night walking pencil in hand about the dingy little flat in Craigie Circle, Cambridge, Massachusetts, where I lodged under an old lady with feet of stone and above a young woman with hypersensitive hearing. Every day including Sundays, I would spend up to ten hours studying the structure of certain butterflies in the laboratorial paradise of the Harvard Museum of Comparative Zoology; but three times a week I stayed there only till noon and then tore myself away from microscope and camera lucida to travel to Wellesley (by tram and bus, or subway and railway), where I taught college girls Russian grammar and literature.

The book was finished on a warm rainy night, more or less as described at the end of Chapter Eighteen. A kind friend, Edmund Wilson, read the typescript and recommended the book to Allen Tate, who had Holt publish it in 1947. I was deeply immersed in other labors but nonetheless managed to discern the dull thud it made. Praises, as far as I can recall, rang out only in two weeklies—*Time* and *The New Yorker,* I think.

The term "bend sinister" means a heraldic bar or band drawn from the left side (and popularly, but incorrectly, supposed to denote bastardy). This choice of title was an attempt to suggest an outline broken by refraction, a distortion in the mirror of being, a wrong turn taken by life, a sinistral and sinister world. The title's drawback is that a solemn reader looking for "general ideas" or "human interest" (which is much the same thing) in a novel may be led to look for them in this one.

There exist few things more tedious than a discussion of general ideas inflicted by author or reader upon a work of fiction. The purpose of this foreword is not to show that *Bend Sinister* belongs or does not belong to "serious literature" (which is a euphemism for the hollow profundity and the ever-welcome commonplace). I have never been interested in what is called the literature of social comment (in journalistic and commercial parlance: "great books"). I am not "sincere," I am not "provocative," I am not "satirical." I am neither a didacticist nor an allegorizer. Politics and economics, atomic bombs, primitive and abstract art forms, the entire Orient, symptoms of "thaw" in Soviet Russia, the Future of Mankind, and so on, leave me supremely indifferent. As in the case of my *Invitation to a Beheading*—with which this book has obvious affinities —automatic comparisons between *Bend Sinister* and Kafka's creations or Orwell's clichés would go merely to prove that the automaton could not have read either the great German writer or the mediocre English one.

Similarly, the influence of my epoch on my present book is as negligible as the influence of my books, or at least of this book, on my epoch. There can be distinguished, no doubt, certain reflections in the glass directly caused by the idiotic and despicable regimes that we all know and that have brushed against me in the course of my life: worlds of tyranny and torture, of Fascists and Bolshevists, of Philistine thinkers and jack-booted baboons. No doubt, too, without those infamous models before me I could not have interlarded this fantasy with bits of

Lenin's speeches, and a chunk of the Soviet constitution, and gobs of Nazi pseudo-efficiency.

While the system of holding people in hostage is as old as the oldest war, a fresher note is introduced when a tyrannic state is at war with its own subjects and may hold any citizen in hostage with no law to restrain it. An even more recent improvement is the subtle use of what I shall term "the lever of love" —the diabolical method (applied so successfully by the Soviets) of tying a rebel to his wretched country by his own twisted heartstrings. It is noteworthy, however, that in *Bend Sinister* Paduk's still young police state—where a certain dull-wittedness is a national trait of the people (augmenting thereby the possibilities of muddling and bungling so typical, thank God, of all tyrannies)—lags behind actual regimes in successfully working this lever of love, for which at first it rather haphazardly gropes, losing time on the needless persecution of Krug's friends, and only by chance realizing (in Chapter Fifteen) that by grabbing his little child one would force him to do whatever one wished.

The story in *Bend Sinister* is not really about life and death in a grotesque police state. My characters are not "types," not carriers of this or that "idea." Paduk, the abject dictator and Krug's former schoolmate (regularly tormented by the boys, regularly caressed by the school janitor); Doctor Alexander, the government's agent; the ineffable Hustav; icy Crystalsen and hapless Kolokololiteïshchikov; the three Bachofen sisters; the farcical policeman Mac; the brutal and imbecile soldiers—all of them are only absurd mirages, illusions oppressive to Krug during his brief spell of being, but harmlessly fading away when I dismiss the cast.

The main theme of *Bend Sinister,* then, is the beating of Krug's loving heart, the torture an intense tenderness is subjected to—and it is for the sake of the pages about David and his father that the book was written and should be read. Two other themes accompany the main one: the theme of dim-brained brutality which thwarts its own purpose by destroying the right child and keeping the wrong one; and the theme of Krug's blessed madness when he suddenly perceives the simple reality of things and knows but cannot express in the words of his world that he and his son and his wife and everybody else are merely my whims and megrims.

Is there any judgment on my part carried out, any sentence pronounced, any satisfaction given to the moral sense? If imbeciles and brutes can punish other brutes and imbeciles, and if crime still retains an objective meaning in the meaningless world of Paduk (all of which is doubtful), we may affirm that crime *is* punished at the end of the book when the uniformed waxworks are really hurt, and the dummies are at last in quite dreadful pain, and pretty Mariette gently bleeds, staked and torn by the lust of forty soldiers.

The plot starts to breed in the bright broth of a rain puddle. The puddle is observed by Krug from a window of the hospital where his wife is dying. The oblong pool, shaped like a cell that is about to divide, reappears subthematically throughout the novel, as an ink blot in Chapter Four, an inkstain in Chapter Five, spilled milk in Chapter Eleven, the infusoria-like image of ciliated thought in Chapter Twelve, the footprint of a phosphorescent islander in Chapter Eighteen, and the imprint a soul leaves in the intimate texture of space in the closing paragraph. The puddle thus kindled and rekindled in Krug's mind remains linked up with the image of his wife not only because he had contemplated the inset sunset from her death-bedside, but also because this little puddle vaguely evokes in him my link with him: a rent in his world leading to another world of tenderness, brightness and beauty.

And a companion image even more eloquently speaking of Olga is the vision of her divesting herself of herself, of her jewels, of the necklace and tiara of earthly life, in front of a brilliant mirror. It is this picture that appears six times in the course of a dream, among the liquid, dream-refracted memories of Krug's boyhood (Chapter Five).

Paronomasia is a kind of verbal plague, a contagious sickness in the world of words; no wonder they are monstrously and ineptly distorted in Padukgrad, where everybody is merely an anagram of everybody else. The book teems with stylistic distortions, such as puns crossed with anagrams (in Chapter Two, the Russian circumference, *krug,* turns into a Teutonic cucumber, *gurk,* with an additional allusion to Krug's reversing his journey across the bridge); suggestive neologisms (the *amorandola*—a local guitar); parodies of narrative clichés ("who had overheard the last words" and "who seemed to be the leader of the group," Chapter Two); spoonerisms ("silence" and "science" playing leapfrog in Chapter Seventeen); and of course the hybridization of tongues.

The language of the country, as spoken in Padukgrad and Omigod, as well as in the Kur valley, the Sakra mountains and the region of Lake Malheur, is a mongrel blend of Slavic and Germanic with a strong strain of ancient Kuranian running through it (and especially prominent in ejaculations of woe); but colloquial Russian and German are also used by representatives of all groups, from the vulgar Ekwilist soldier to the discriminating intellectual. Ember, for instance, in Chapter Seven, gives his friend a sample of three first lines of Hamlet's soliloquy (Act III, Scene I) translated into the vernacular (with a pseudo-scholarly interpretation of the first phrase taken to refer to the contemplated killing of Claudius, i.e., "is the murder to be or not to be?"). He follows this up with a Russian version of part of the Queen's speech in Act IV, Scene VII (also not without a built-in scholium) and a splendid Russian rendering of the prose passage in Act III, Scene II, beginning, "Would not this, Sir, and a forest of feathers. . . ." Problems of translation, fluid transitions from one tongue to another, semantic transparencies yielding layers of receding or welling sense are as characteristic of Sinisterbad as are the monetary problems of more habitual tyrannies.

In this crazy-mirror of terror and art a pseudo-quotation made up of obscure Shakespeareanisms (Chapter Three) somehow produces, despite its lack of literal meaning, the blurred diminutive image of the acrobatic performance that so gloriously supplies the bravura ending for the next chapter. A chance selection of iambic incidents culled from the prose of *Moby Dick* appears in the guise of "a famous American poem" (Chapter Twelve). If the "admiral" and his "fleet" in a trite official speech (Chapter Four) are at first mis-heard by the widower as "animal" and its "feet," this is because the chance reference, coming just before, to a man losing his wife dims and distorts the next sentence. When in Chapter Three Ember recalls four best-selling novels, the alert commuter cannot fail to notice that the titles of three of them form, roughly, the lavatorial injunction not to Flush the Toilet when the Train Passes through Towns and Villages, while the fourth alludes to Werfel's trashy *Song of Bernadette,* half altar bread and half bonbon. Similarly, at the beginning of Chapter Six, where some other popular romances of the day are mentioned, a slight shift in the spectrum of meaning replaces the title *Gone with the Wind* (filched from Dowson's *Cynara*) with that of *Flung Roses* (filched from the same poem), and a fusion between two cheap novels (by Remarque and Sholokhov) produces the neat *All Quiet on the Don.*

Stéphane Mallarmé has left three or four immortal bagatelles, and among these is *L'Après-Midi d'un Faune* (first drafted in 1865). Krug is haunted by a passage from this voluptuous eclogue where the faun accuses the nymph of disengaging herself from his embrace *"sans pitié du sanglot dont j'étais encore ivre"* ("spurning the spasm with which I still was drunk"). Fractured parts of this line re-echo through the book, cropping up for instance in the *malarma ne donje* of Dr. Azureus' wail of rue (Chapter Four) and in the *donje te zankoriv* of apologetic Krug when he interrupts the kiss of the university student and his little Carmen (foreshadowing Mariette) in the same chapter. Death, too, is a ruthless interruption; the widower's heavy sensuality seeks a pathetic outlet in Mariette, but as he avidly clasps the haunches of the chance nymph he is about to enjoy, a deafening din at the door breaks the throbbing rhythm forever.

It may be asked if it is really worth an author's while to devise and distribute these delicate markers whose very nature requires that they be not too conspicuous. Who will bother to notice that Pankrat Tzikutin, the shabby old pogromystic (Chapter Thirteen) is Socrates Hemlocker; that "the child is bold" in the allusion to immigration (Chapter Eighteen) is a stock phrase used to test a would-be American citizen's reading ability; that Linda did not steal the porcelain owlet after all (beginning of Chapter Ten); that the urchins in the yard (Chapter Seven) have been drawn by Saul Steinberg; that the "other rivermaid's father" (Chapter Seven) is James Joyce who wrote *Winnipeg Lake* (ibid.); and that the last word of the book is *not* a misprint (as assumed in the past by at least one proofreader)? Most people will not even mind having missed all this; well-wishers will bring their own symbols and mobiles, and portable radios, to my little party; ironists will point out the fatal fatuity of my explications in this foreword and advise me to have footnotes next time (footnotes always seem comic to a certain type of mind). In the long run, however, it is only the author's private satisfaction that counts. I reread my books rarely, and then only for the utilitarian purpose of controlling a translation or checking a new edition; but when I do go through them again, what pleases me most is the wayside murmur of this or that hidden theme.

Thus, in the second paragraph of Chapter Five comes the first intimation that "someone is in the know"—a mysterious intruder who takes advantage of Krug's dream to convey his own peculiar code message. The intruder is not the Viennese Quack (all my books should be stamped Freudians, Keep Out), but an anthropomorphic deity impersonated by me. In the last chapter of the book this deity experiences a pang of pity for his creature and hastens to take over. Krug, in a sudden moonburst of madness, understands that he is in good hands: nothing on earth really matters, there is nothing to fear, and death is but a question of style, a mere literary device, a musical resolution. And as Olga's rosy soul, emblemized already in an earlier chapter (Nine), bombinates in the damp dark at the bright window of my room, comfortably Krug returns unto the bosom of his maker.

Montreux, September 9, 1963

Foreword[1] to Mihail Lermontov's
A Hero of Our Time

~~~~~

1

In 1841, a few months before his death (in a pistol duel with a fellow officer at the foot of Mount Mashuk in the Caucasus), Mihail Lermontov (1814-1841) composed a prophetic poem:

> In noon's heat, in a dale of Dagestan,
> With lead inside my breast, stirless I lay;
> The deep wound still smoked on; my blood
> Kept trickling drop by drop away.

> On the dale's sand alone I lay. The cliffs
> Crowded around in ledges steep,
> And the sun scorched their tawny tops
> And scorched me—but I slept death's sleep.

> And in a dream I saw an evening feast
> That in my native land with bright lights shone;
> Among young women crowned with flowers,
> A merry talk concerning me went on.

> But in the merry talk not joining,
> One of them sat there lost in thought,
> And in a melancholy dream
> Her young soul was immersed—God knows by what.

> And of a dale in Dagestan she dreamt;
> In that dale lay the corpse of one she knew;
> Within his breast a smoking wound showed black,
> And blood ran in a stream that colder grew.

[1] Written by Vladimir Nabokov for the English-language edition of Lermontov's novel, of which he was cotranslator with his son, Dmitri Nabokov.

This remarkable composition (which, in the original, is in iambic pentameter throughout, with alternate feminine and masculine rhymes) might be entitled "The Triple Dream."

There is an initial dreamer (Lermontov, or more exactly, his poetical impersonator) who dreams that he lies dying in a valley of Eastern Caucasus. This is Dream One, dreamt by Dreamer One.

The fatally wounded man (Dreamer Two) dreams in his turn of a young woman sitting at a feast in St. Petersburg or Moscow. This is Dream Two within Dream One.

The young woman sitting at the feast sees in her mind Dreamer Two (who dies in the course of the poem) in the surroundings of remote Dagestan. This is Dream Three within Dream Two within Dream One—which describes a spiral by bringing us back to the first stanza.

The whorls of these five strophes have a certain structural affinity with the interlacings of the five stories that make up Lermontov's novel, *A Hero of Our Time* (*Geroy Nashego Vremeni*).

In the first two stories, "Bela" and "Maksim Maksimich," Lermontov or, more exactly, his fictional impersonator, an inquisitive traveler, relates a journey he made along the Military Georgian Road (*Voenno-gruzinskaya doroga*) in the Caucasus around 1837. This is Narrator One.

On the way north from Tiflis he meets an old campaigner, Maksim Maksimich. They travel together for a while and Maksim Maksimich tells Narrator One about a certain Grigoriy Pechorin who, five years before, in the Chechnya Region, north of Dagestan, kidnapped a Circassian girl. Maksim Maksimich is Narrator Two, and the story is "Bela."

At a second meeting on the road (in "Maksim Maksimich"), Narrator One and Narrator Two come across Pechorin in the flesh. Henceforth, Pechorin, whose journal Narrator One publishes, becomes Narrator Three, for it is from his journal that the remaining three stories are posthumously drawn.

It will be marked by the good reader that the structural trick consists in bringing Pechorin gradually nearer and nearer until he takes over; but by the time he takes over he is dead. In the first story, Pechorin is twice removed from the reader since his personality is described through Maksim Maksimich, whose words are transmitted to us by Narrator One. In the second story the personality of Narrator Two no longer stands between Pechorin and Narrator One, who, at last, sees the hero for himself. Maksim Maksimich is, in fact, pathetically eager to produce the real Pechorin on top of the subject of his yarn. And, finally, in the last three stories, both Narrator One and Narrator Two step aside, and the reader meets Pechorin, Narrator Three, face to face.

This involute structure is responsible for blurring somewhat the time sequence of the novel. The five stories grow, revolve, reveal, and mask their contours, turn away and reappear in a new attitude or light like five mountain peaks attending a traveler along the meanders of a Caucasian canyon road. The traveler is Lermontov, not Pechorin. The five tales are placed in the novel according to the order in which the events become known to Narrator One; but their chronological sequence is different, going something like this:

1. Around 1830 an officer, Grigoriy Pechorin (Narrator Three), on his way from St. Petersburg to the Caucasus, whither he is being sent on some military errand to a detachment on active duty, happens to be stranded at the village of Taman (a port facing the NE coast of the Crimea). An adventure he has there forms the subject of "Taman," the third story in the book.

2. After some time spent on active duty in skirmishes with the mountain tribes, Pechorin, on May 10, 1832, arrives for a rest at a Caucasian spa, Pyatigorsk. At Pyatigorsk and at Kislovodsk, a neighboring resort, he participates in a series of dramatic events that lead to his killing a fellow officer in a duel on June 17. These events are related by him in the fourth story, "Princess Mary."

3. On June 19, the military authorities have Pechorin dis-

patched to a fort in the Chechnya Region, Northeast Caucasus, where he arrives only in autumn (after an unexplained delay). There he meets the junior captain Maksim Maksimich. This is related to Narrator One by Narrator Two in the first story, "Bela."

4. In December of the same year (1832) Pechorin leaves the fort for a fortnight, which he spends in a Cossack settlement north of the Terek River, and there has the adventure described by him in the fifth (last) story, "The Fatalist."

5. In the spring of 1833, he kidnaps a Circassian girl who is assassinated by a bandit four and a half months later. In December 1833, Pechorin leaves for Georgia and some time later goes home to St. Petersburg. This is related in "Bela."

6. Some four years later, in the autumn of 1837, Narrator One and Narrator Two, on their way north, stop at the town of Vladikavkaz and there run into Pechorin who, in the meantime, has returned to the Caucasus, and is now on his way south, to Persia. This is related by Narrator One in "Maksim Maksimich," the second story in the book.

7. In 1838 or 1839, on his way back from Persia, Pechorin dies under circumstances possibly related to a prediction made to him that he would die in consequence of an unfortunate marriage. Narrator One now publishes the dead man's journal, obtained from Narrator Two. Pechorin's death is mentioned by Narrator One in his editorial Foreword (1841) to Pechorin's Journal containing "Taman," "Princess Mary," and "The Fatalist."

Thus the order of the five stories, in relation to Pechorin, is: "Taman," "Princess Mary," "The Fatalist," "Bela," and "Maksim Maksimich."

It is unlikely that Lermontov foresaw the plot of "Princess Mary" while he was writing "Bela." The details of Pechorin's arrival at the Kamennïy Brod Fort, as given in "Bela" by Maksim Maksimich, do not quite tally with the details given by Pechorin himself in "Princess Mary."

The inconsistencies in the five stories are numerous and glaring, but the narrative surges on with such speed and force; such manly and romantic beauty pervades it; and the general purpose of Lermontov breathes such fierce integrity, that the reader does not stop to wonder why the mermaid in "Taman" assumed that Pechorin could not swim, or why the Captain of Dragoons thought that Pechorin's seconds would not want to supervise the loading of the pistols. The plight of Pechorin, who is forced, after all, to face Grushnitski's pistol, would be rather ridiculous, had we not understood that our hero relied not on chance but on fate. This is made quite clear in the last and best story, "The Fatalist," where the crucial passage also turns on a pistol being or not being loaded, and where a kind of duel by proxy is fought between Pechorin and Vulich, with Fate, instead of the smirking dragoon, supervising the lethal arrangements.

A special feature of the structure of our book is the monstrous but perfectly organic part that eavesdropping plays in it. Now Eavesdropping is only one form of a more general device which can be classified under the heading of Coincidence, to which belongs, for instance, the Coincidental Meeting—another variety. It is pretty clear that when a novelist desires to combine the traditional tale of romantic adventure (amorous intrigue, jealousy, revenge, etc.) with a narrative in the first person, and has no desire to invent new techniques, he is somewhat limited in the choice of devices.

The eighteenth-century epistolary form of novel (with the heroine writing to her girl friend, and the hero writing to his old schoolmate, followed by at least ten other combinations) was so stale by Lermontov's time that he could hardly have used it; and since, on the other hand, our author was more eager to have his story move than to vary, elaborate and conceal the methods of its propulsion, he employed the convenient device of having his Maksim Maksimich and Pechorin overhear, spy upon, and witness any such scene as was needed for the elucidation or the promotion of the plot. Indeed, the author's use of this device is so consistent throughout the book that it ceases to strike the reader as a marvelous vagary of chance and becomes, as it were, the barely noticeable routine of fate.

In "Bela," there are three cases of eavesdropping: from behind a fence, Narrator Two overhears a boy trying to coax a robber into selling him a horse; and later on, the same Narrator overhears, first from under a window, and then from behind a door, two crucial conversations between Pechorin and Bela.

In "Taman," from behind a jutting rock, Narrator Three overhears a conversation between a girl and a blind lad, which informs everybody concerned, including the reader, of the smuggling business; and the same eavesdropper, from another point of vantage, a cliff above the shore, overhears the final conversation between the smugglers.

In "Princess Mary," Narrator Three eavesdrops as many as eight times, in consequence of which he is always in the know. From behind the corner of a covered walk, he sees Mary retrieving the mug dropped by disabled Grushnitski; from behind a tall shrub, he overhears a sentimental dialogue between the two; from behind a stout lady, he overhears the talk that leads to an attempt, on the part of the dragoon, to have Mary insulted by a pre-Dostoevskian drunk; from an unspecified distance, he stealthily watches Mary yawning at Grushnitski's jokes; from the midst of a ballroom crowd, he catches her ironic retorts to Grushnitski's romantic entreaties; from outside "an improperly closed shutter," he sees and hears the dragoon plotting with Grushnitski to fake a duel with him, Pechorin; through a window curtain which is "not completely drawn," he observes Mary pensively sitting on her bed; in a restaurant, from behind a door that leads to the corner room, where Grushnitski and his friends are assembled, Pechorin hears himself accused of visiting Mary at night; and finally, and most conveniently, Dr. Werner, Pechorin's second, overhears a conversation between the dragoon and Grushnitski, which leads Werner and Pechorin to conclude that only one pistol will be loaded. This accumulation of knowledge on the part of the hero causes the reader to await, with frantic interest, the inevitable scene when Pechorin will crush Grushnitski with the disclosure of this knowledge.

2

This is the first English translation of Lermontov's novel. The book has been paraphrased into English several times, but never translated before. The experienced hack may find it quite easy to turn Lermontov's Russian into slick English clichés by means of judicious omission, amplification, and levigation; and he will tone down everything that might seem unfamiliar to the meek and imbecile reader visualized by his publisher. But the honest translator is faced with a different task.

In the first place, we must dismiss, once and for all the conventional notion that a translation "should read smoothly," and "should not sound like a translation" (to quote the would-be compliments, addressed to vague versions, by genteel reviewers who never have and never will read the original texts). In point of fact, any translation that does *not* sound like a translation is bound to be inexact upon inspection; while, on the other hand, the only virtue of a good translation is faithfulness and completeness. Whether it reads smoothly or not, depends on the model, not on the mimic.

In attempting to translate Lermontov, I have gladly sacrificed to the requirements of exactness a number of important things—good taste, neat diction, and even grammar (when some characteristic solecism occurs in the Russian text). The English reader should be aware that Lermontov's prose style in Russian is inelegant; it is dry and drab; it is the tool of an energetic, incredibly gifted, bitterly honest, but definitely inexperienced young man. His Russian is, at times, almost as crude as Stendhal's French; his similes and metaphors are utterly com-

monplace; his hackneyed epithets are only redeemed by occasionally being incorrectly used. Repetition of words in descriptive sentences irritates the purist. And all this, the translator should faithfully render, no matter how much he may be
tempted to fill out the lapse and delete the redundancy.

When Lermontov started to write, Russian prose had already
evolved that predilection for certain terms that became typical
of the Russian novel. Every translator becomes aware, in the
course of his task, that, apart from idiomatic locutions, the
"From" language has a certain number of constantly iterated
words which, though readily translatable, occur in the "Into"
language far less frequently and less colloquially. Through long
use, these words have become mere pegs or signs, the meeting
places of mental associations, the reunions of related notions.
They are tokens of sense, rather than particularizations of
sense. Of the hundred or so peg words familiar to any student of
Russian literature, the following may be listed as being especial
favorites with Lermontov:

zadúmat'sya	To become pensive; to lapse into thought; to be lost in thought.
podoytí	To approach; to go up to.
prinyát' vid	To assume an air (serious, gay, etc.). Fr. *prendre un air*.
molchát'	To be silent. Fr. *se taire*.
mel'kát'	To flick; to flicker; to dart; to be glimpsed.
neiz'yasnímïy	Ineffable (a Gallicism).
gíbkiy	Supple; flexible. Too often said of human bodies.
mráchnïy	Gloomy.
prístal'no	Intently; fixedly; steadily; steadfastly (said of looking, gazing, peering, etc.).
nevól'no	Involuntarily. Fr. *malgré soi*.
on nevól'no zadúmalsya	He could not help growing thoughtful.

vdrug	Suddenly.
uzhé	Already; by now.

It is the translator's duty to have, as far as possible, these words reoccur in English as often, and as irritatingly, as they do in the Russian text; I say, as far as possible, because in some cases the word has two or more shades of meaning depending on the context. "A slight pause," or "a moment of silence," for instance, may render the recurrent *minuta molchan'ya* better than "a minute of silence" would.

Another thing that has to be kept in mind is that in one language great care is taken by novelists to tabulate certain facial expressions, gestures, or motions that writers in another language will take for granted and mention seldom, or not at all. The nineteenth-century Russian writer's indifference to exact shades of visual color leads to an acceptance of rather droll epithets condoned by literary usage (a surprising thing in the case of Lermontov, who was not only a painter in the literal sense, but saw colors and was able to name them); thus in the course of *A Hero* the faces of various people turn purple, red, rosy, orange, yellow, green and blue. A romantic epithet of Gallic origin that occurs four times in the course of the novel is *tusklaya blednost', paleur mate,* dull (or lusterless) pallor. In "Taman," the delinquent girl's face is covered with "a dull pallor betraying inner agitation." In "Princess Mary," this phenomenon occurs three times: a dull pallor is spread over Mary's face when she accuses Pechorin of disrespect; a dull pallor is spread over Pechorin's face revealing "the traces of painful insomnia"; and just before the duel, a dull pallor is spread over Grushnitski's cheeks as his conscience struggles with his pride.

Besides such code sentences as "her lips grew pale," "he flushed," "her hand trembled slightly," and so forth, emotions are signaled by certain abrupt and violent gestures. In "Bela," Pechorin hits the table with his fist to punctuate with a bang his words "she won't belong to anybody but me." Two pages further, it is his forehead he strikes with his fist (a gesture deemed Oriental by some commentators) upon realizing he has bungled the seduction and driven Bela to tears. In his turn, Grushnitski strikes the table with his fist when convinced by Pechorin's remarks that Mary is merely a flirt. And the Captain of Dragoons does the same when demanding attention. There is also a great deal of the "seizing his arm," "taking him by the arm," and "pulling by the sleeve" business throughout the novel.

"Stamping on the ground" is another emotional signal much in favor with Lermontov, and, in Russian literature of the time, this was new. Maksim Maksimich, in "Bela," stamps his foot in self-accusation. Grushnitski, in "Princess Mary," stamps his in petulance, and the Captain of Dragoons stamps his in disgust.

3

It is unnecessary to discuss here Pechorin's character. The good reader will easily understand it by studying the book; but so much nonsense has been written about Pechorin, by those who adopt a sociological approach to literature, that a few warning words must be said.

We should not take, as seriously as most Russian commentators, Lermontov's statement in his Introduction (a stylized bit of make-believe in its own right) that Pechorin's portrait is "composed of all the vices of our generation." Actually, the bored and bizarre hero is a product of several generations, some of them non-Russian; he is the fictional descendant of a number of fictional self-analysts, beginning with Saint-Preux (the lover of Julie d'Etange in Rousseau's *Julie ou la nouvelle Héloïse,* 1761) and Werther (the admirer of Charlotte S—— in Goethe's *Die Leiden des jungen Werthers,* 1774, known to Russians mainly in French versions such as that by Sévelinges, 1804), going through Chateaubriand's *René* (1802), Constant's *Adolphe* (1815), and the heroes of Byron's long poems (especially *The Giaour*, 1813, and *The Corsair*, 1814, known to Russians in Pichot's French prose versions, from 1820 on), and ending with Pushkin's *Eugene Onegin* (1825-1832) and with various more ephemeral products of the French novelists of the first half of the century (Nodier, Balzac, etc.). Pechorin's association with a given time and a given place tends to lend a new flavor to the transplanted fruit, but it is doubtful whether much is added to an appreciation of this flavor by generalizing about the exacerbation of thought produced in independent minds by the tyranny of Nicholas I's reign (1825-1856).

The point to be marked in a study of *A Hero of Our Time* is that, though of tremendous and at times somewhat morbid interest to the sociologist, the "time" is of less interest to the student of literature than the "hero." In the latter, young Lermontov managed to create a fictional person whose romantic dash and cynicism, tigerlike suppleness and eagle eye, hot blood and cool head, tenderness and taciturnity, elegance and brutality, delicacy of perception and harsh passion to dominate, ruthlessness and awareness of it, are of lasting appeal to readers of all countries and centuries—especially to young readers; for it would seem that the veneration elderly critics have for *A Hero* is rather a glorified recollection of youthful readings in the summer twilight, and of ardent self-identification, than the direct result of a mature consciousness of art.

Of the other characters in the book there is, likewise, little to say. The most endearing one is obviously the old Captain Maksim Maksimich, stolid, gruff, naïvely poetical, matter-of-fact, simple-hearted, and completely neurotic. His hysterical behavior at the abortive meeting with his old friend Pechorin is one of the passages most dear to human-interest readers. Of the several villains in the book, Kazbich and his florid speech (as rendered by Maksim Maksimich) are an obvious product of literary orientalia, while the American reader may be excused for substituting the Indians of Fenimore Cooper for

Lermontov's Circassians. In the worst story of the book, "Taman" (deemed by some Russian critics the greatest, for reasons incomprehensible to me), Yanko is saved from utter banality when we notice that the connection between him and the blind lad is a pleasing echo of the scene between hero and hero-worshiper in "Maksim Maksimich."

Another kind of interplay occurs in "Princess Mary." If Pechorin is a romantic shadow of Lermontov, Grushnitski, as Russian critics have already noted, is a grotesque shadow of Pechorin, and the lowest level of imitation is supplied by Pechorin's valet. Grushnitski's evil genius, the Captain of Dragoons, is little more than a stock character of comedy, and the continuous references to the hugger-mugger he indulges in are rather painful. No less painful is the skipping and singing of the wild girl in "Taman." Lermontov was singularly inept in his descriptions of women. Mary is the generalized young thing of novelettes, with no attempt at individualization except perhaps her "velvety" eyes, which however are forgotten in the course of the story. Vera is a mere phantom, with a phantom birthmark on her cheek; Bela, an Oriental beauty on the lid of a box of Turkish delight.

What, then, makes the everlasting charm of this book? Why is it so interesting to read and reread? Certainly not for its style —although, curiously enough, Russian schoolteachers used to see in it the perfection of Russian prose. This is a ridiculous opinion, voiced (according to a memoirist) by Chehov, and can only be held if and when a moral quality or a social virtue is confused with literary art, or when an ascetic critic regards the rich and ornate with such suspicion that, in contrast, the awkward and frequently commonplace style of Lermontov seems delightfully chaste and simple. But genuine art is neither chaste nor simple, and it is sufficient to glance at the prodigiously elaborate and magically artistic style of Tolstoy (who, by some, is considered to be a literary descendant of Lermontov) to realize the depressing flaws of Lermontov's prose.

But if we regard him as a storyteller, and if we remember that Russian prose was still in her teens, and the man still in his middle twenties when he wrote, then we do marvel indeed at the superb energy of the tale and at the remarkable rhythm into which the paragraphs, rather than the sentences, fall. It is the agglomeration of otherwise insignificant words that come to life. When we start to break the sentence or the verse line into its quantitative elements, the banalities we perceive are often shocking, the shortcomings not seldom comic; but, in the long run, it is the compound effect that counts, and this final effect can be traced down in Lermontov to the beautiful timing of all the parts and particles of the novel. Its author was careful to dissociate himself from his hero; but, for the emotional type of reader, much of the novel's poignancy and fascination resides in the fact that Lermontov's own tragic fate is somehow superimposed upon that of Pechorin, just as the Dagestan dream acquires an additional strain of pathos when the reader realizes that the poet's dream came true.

From Nikolai Gogol

❧ *The Government Specter* ❧

I

The history of the production of Gogol's comedy *The Government Inspector* on the Russian stage and of the extraordinary stir it created has of course little to do with Gogol, the subject of these notes, but still a few words about those alien matters may be not unnecessary. As it was inevitable that simple minds would see in the play a social satire violently volleyed at the idyllic system of official corruption in Russia, one wonders what hopes the author or anybody else could have had of seeing the play performed. The censors' committee was as blatantly a collection of cringing noodles or pompous asses as all such organizations are, and the mere fact of a writer's daring to portray officers of the state otherwise than as abstract figures and symbols of superhuman virtue was a crime that sent shivers down the censors' fat backs. That *The Government Inspector* happened to be the greatest play ever written in Russian (and never surpassed since) was naturally a matter infinitely remote from the committee's mind.

But a miracle happened; a kind of miracle singularly in keeping with the physics of Gogol's upside-down world. The Supreme Censor, the One above all, Whose God-like level of being was so lofty as to be hardly mentionable by thick human tongues, the radiant, totalitarian Tsar Himself, in a fit of most unexpected glee commanded the play to be passed and staged.

It is difficult to conjecture what pleased Nicholas I in *The*

Government Inspector. The man who a few years before had red-penciled the manuscript of Pushkin's *Boris Godunov* with inane remarks suggesting the turning of that tragedy into a novel on the lines of Walter Scott, and generally was as immune to authentic literature as all rulers are (not excepting Frederic the Great or Napoleon) can hardly be suspected of having seen anything better in Gogol's play than slapstick entertainment. On the other hand a satirical farce (if we imagine for a moment such a delusion in regard to *The Government Inspector*) seems unlikely to have attracted the Tsar's priggish and humorless mind. Given that the man had brains—at least the brains of a politician—it would rather detract from their quantity to suppose that he so much enjoyed the prospect of having his vassals thoroughly shaken up as to be blind to the dangers of having the man in the street join in the imperial mirth. In fact he is reported to have remarked after the first performance: "Everybody has got his due, I most of all"; and if this report is true (which it probably is not) it would seem that the evolutionary link between criticism of corruption under a certain government and criticism of the government itself must have been apparent to the Tsar's mind. We are left to assume that the permission to have the play staged was due to a sudden whim on the Tsar's part, just as the appearance of such a writer as Gogol was a most unexpected impulse on the part of whatever spirit may be held responsible for the development of Russian literature in the beginning of the Nineteenth Century. In signing this permission a despotic ruler was, curiously enough, injecting a most dangerous germ into the blood of Russian writers; dangerous to the idea of monarchy, dangerous to official iniquity, and dangerous—which danger is the most important of the three—to the art of literature; for Gogol's play was misinterpreted by the civic-minded as a social protest and engendered in the fifties and sixties a seething mass of literature denouncing corruption and other social defects and an orgy of literary criticism denying the title of writer to anyone who did not devote his novel or short story to the castigation of district police-officers and moujik-thrashing squires. And ten years later the Tsar had completely forgotten the play and had not the vaguest idea who Gogol was and what he had written.

The first performance of *The Government Inspector* was a vile affair in regard to acting and setting, and Gogol was most bitter in his criticism of the abominable wigs and clownish clothes and gross over-acting that the theater inflicted upon his play. This started the tradition of staging *The Government Inspector* as a burlesque; later to this was added a background suggestive of a *comédie de mœurs;* so that the Twentieth Century inherited a strange concoction of extravagant Gogolian speech and dingy matter-of-fact setting—a state of affairs only solved now and then by the personality of some actor of genius. Strange, it was in the years when the written word was dead in Russia, as it has been now for a quarter of a century, that the Russian producer Meyerhold, in spite of all his distortions and additions, offered a stage version of *The Government Inspector* which conveyed something of the real Gogol.

Only once have I seen the play performed in a foreign language (in English) and it is not a memory I care to evoke. As to the translation of the book, there is little to choose between the Seltzer and Constance Garnett versions. Though totally lacking verbal talent, Garnett has made hers with a certain degree of care and it is thus less irritating than some of the monstrous versions of *The Overcoat* and *Dead Souls*. In a way it may be compared to Guizot's tame translation of *Hamlet*. Of course, nothing has remained of Gogol's style. The English is dry and flat, and always unbearably demure. None but an Irishman should ever try tackling Gogol. Here are some typical instances of inadequate translation (and these may be multiplied): Gogol in his remarks about the two squires, Bobchinsky and Dobchinsky, briefly describes them as both having plump little bellies (or, as he says in another place, "they simply must have protruding tummies—pointed little ones like pregnant

women have") which conveys the idea of small and otherwise
thin and puny men—and this is most essential for producing
the correct impression that Dobchinsky and Bobchinsky must
convey. But Constance Garnett translates this as "both rather
corpulent," murdering Gogol. I sometimes think that these old
English "translations" are remarkably similar to the so-called
Thousand Pieces Execution which was popular at one time
in China. The idea was to cut out from the patient's body one
tiny square bit the size of a cough lozenge, say, every five minutes or so until bit by bit (all of them selected with discrimina-
tion so as to have the patient live to the nine-hundred-ninety-
ninth piece) his whole body was delicately removed.

There are also a number of downright mistakes in that translation such as "clear soup" instead of "oatmeal soup" (which
the Charity Commissioner ought to have been giving the sick at
the hospital) or—and this is rather funny—a reference to one
of the five or six books that the Judge had ever read in his life
as "The Book of John the Mason," which sounds like something biblical, when the text really refers to a book of adventures concerning John Mason (or attributed to him), an
English diplomatist of the Sixteenth Century and Fellow of All
Souls who was employed on the Continent in collecting information for the Tudor sovereigns.

2
———

The plot of *The Government Inspector* is as unimportant
as the plots of all Gogol books. Moreover, in the case of the
play, the scheme is the common property of all playwriters:
the squeezing of the last drop out of some amusing quid pro
quo. It would appear that Pushkin suggested it to Gogol when
he told him that while staying at an inn in Nizhni-Novgorod
he was mistaken for an important official from the capital; but
on the other hand, Gogol, with his head stuffed with old plays

ever since his days of amateur theatricals at school (old plays translated into indifferent Russian from three or four languages), might have easily dispensed with Pushkin's prompting. It is strange, the morbid inclination we have to derive satisfaction from the fact (generally false and always irrelevant) that a work of art is traceable to a "true story." Is it because we begin to respect ourselves more when we learn that the writer, just like ourselves, was not clever enough to make up a story himself? Or is something added to the poor strength of our imagination when we know that a tangible fact is at the base of the "fiction" we mysteriously despise? Or taken all in all, have we here that adoration of the truth which makes little children ask the storyteller, "Did it really happen?" and prevented old Tolstoy in his hyperethical stage from trespassing upon the rights of the deity and creating, as God creates, perfectly imaginary people? However that may be, some forty years after that first night a certain political *émigré* was desirous of having Karl Marx (whose *Capital* he was translating in London) know Chernyshevsky, who was a famous radical and conspirator banished to Siberia in the sixties (and one of those critics who vigorously proclaimed the coming of the "Gogolian" era in Russian literature, meaning by this euphemism, which would have horrified Gogol, the duty on the part of novelists to work solely for the improvement of social and political conditions). The political *émigré* returned secretly to Russia and traveled to the remote Yakoutsk region in the disguise of a Member of the Geographical Society (a nice point, this) in order to kidnap the Siberian prisoner; and his plan was thwarted owing to the fact that more and more people all along his meandering itinerary mistook him for a Government Inspector traveling incognito—exactly as had happened in Gogol's play. This vulgar imitation of artistic fiction on the part of life is somehow more pleasing than the opposite thing.

The epigraph to the play is a Russian proverb which says, "Do not chafe at the looking glass if your mug is awry." Gogol,

of course, never drew portraits—he used looking glasses and
as a writer lived in his own looking glass world. Whether the
reader's face was a fright or a beauty did not matter a jot, for
not only was the mirror of Gogol's own making and with a special refraction of its own, but also the reader to whom the proverb was addressed belonged to the same Gogolian world of
goose-like, pig-like, pie-like, nothing-on-earth-like facial phenomena. Even in his worst writings Gogol was always good at
creating his reader, which is the privilege of great writers. Thus
we have a circle, a closed family-circle, one might say. It does
not open into the world. Treating the play as a social satire (the
public view) or as a moral one (Gogol's belated amendment)
meant missing the point completely. The characters of *The Government Inspector* whether subject or not to imitation by flesh
and blood, were true only in the sense that they were true creatures of Gogol's fancy. Most conscientiously, Russia, that land
of eager pupils, started at once living up to these fancies—but
that was her business, not Gogol's. In the Russia of Gogol's day
bribery flourished as beautifully as it did, and does, anywhere
on the Continent—and, on the other hand, there doubtless
existed far more disgusting scoundrels in any Russian town of
Gogol's time than the good-natured rogues of *The Government
Inspector.* I have a lasting grudge against those who like their
fiction to be educational or uplifting, or national, or as healthy
as maple syrup and olive oil, so that is why I keep harping on
this rather futile side of *The Government Inspector* question.

3

The play begins with a blinding flash of lightning and ends in
a thunderclap. In fact it is wholly placed in the tense gap between the flash and the crash. There is no so-called "exposition." Thunderbolts do not lose time explaining meteorological
conditions. The whole world is one ozone-blue shiver and we

are in the middle of it. The only stage tradition of his time that
Gogol retained was the soliloquy, but then people do talk to
themselves aloud during the nervous hush before a storm while
waiting for the bang to come. The characters are nightmare
people in one of those dreams when you think you have waked
up while all you have done is to enter the most dreadful (most
dreadful in its sham reality) region of dreams. Gogol has a peculiar manner of letting "secondary" dream characters pop out
at every turn of the play (or novel, or story), to flaunt for a
second their life-like existence (as that Colonel P. who passed
by in *Shponka's Dream* or many a creature in *Dead Souls*).
In *The Government Inspector* this manner is apparent from the
start in the weird private letter which the Town-Mayor
Skvoznik-Dmukhanovsky reads aloud to his subordinates—
School Inspector Khlopov, Judge Lyapkin-Tyapkin (Mr. Slap-
Dash), Charity Commissioner Zemlyanika (Mr. Strawberry—
an overripe brown strawberry wounded by the lip of a frog),
and so forth. Note the nightmare names so different from, say,
the sleek "Hollywood Russian" pseudonyms Vronsky, Oblon-
sky, Bolkonsky etc. used by Tolstoy. (The names Gogol invents are really nicknames which we surprise in the very act of
turning into family names—and a metamorphosis is a thing always exciting to watch.) After reading the important part of
the letter referring to the impending arrival of a governmental
inspector from Petersburg the Mayor automatically continues
to read aloud and his mumbling engenders remarkable secondary beings that struggle to get into the front row.

". . . my sister Anna Kyrillovna and her husband have
come to stay with us; Ivan Kyrillovich [apparently a brother,
judging by the patronymic] has grown very fat and keeps
playing the violin."

The beauty of the thing is that these secondary characters
will not appear on the stage later on. We all know those casual
allusions at the beginning of Act I to Aunt So-and-so or to
the Stranger met on the train. We all know that the "by the way"

which introduces these people really means that the Stranger
with the Australian accent or the Uncle with the comical hobby
would have never been mentioned if they were not to breeze in
a moment later. Indeed the "by the way" is generally a sure indi-
cation, the masonic sign of conventional literature, that the person alluded to will turn out to be the main character of the play.
We all know that trite trick, that coy spirit haunting first acts in
Scribia as well as on Broadway. A famous playwright has said
(probably in a testy reply to a bore wishing to know the secrets
of the craft) that if in the first act a shot gun hangs on the wall,
it must go off in the last act. But Gogol's guns hang in midair
and do not go off—in fact the charm of his allusions is exactly
that nothing whatever comes of them.

In giving his instructions to his subordinates in view of preparing and repairing things for the arrival of the Government
Inspector, the Mayor refers to the Judge's clerk.

". . . a knowing fellow, I daresay, but he has such a smell
coming from him—as if he had just emerged from a vodka dis-
tillery. . . . I meant to mention it to you [to the Judge] long
ago but something or other kept putting it out of my head.
Remedies may be found if, as he says, it is his natural odor:
you might suggest to him a diet of onions or garlic, or something
of that kind. In a case like this Christian Ivanovich [the silent
District Doctor of German extraction] might help by supplying
this or that drug."

To which the Judge retorts:

"No, it is a thing impossible to dislodge: he tells me that his
wet nurse dropped him when he was a baby and that there has
been a slight smell of vodka hanging about him ever since."

"Well [says the Mayor] I just wanted to draw your attention
to it, that is all." And he turns to another official.

We shall never hear about that unfortunate clerk again, but
there he is, alive, a whimsical, smelly creature of that "injured"
kind over which Gogol smacked his lips.

Other secondary beings have no time to come out in full at-

tire, so impatient are they to jump into the play between two
sentences. The Mayor is now drawing the attention of the
School Inspector to his assistants:

"One of them, for instance, the one with the fat face . . .
can't think of his name . . . well, every time he begins his
class, he simply must make a grimace, like this [shows how]
and then he starts to massage his chin from under his cravat. Of
course if he makes faces only at the boys, it does not much matter—it may be even necessary in his department for all I know
of those things; but consider what might happen if he did it in
front of a visitor—that would be really dreadful: His Excellency
the Government Inspector or anybody else might think it was
meant for him. Goodness only knows what consequences that
might have."

"What on earth am I to do with him, pray? [replies the
School Inspector]. I have spoken to him several times already.
Only the other day when our Marshal of Nobility was about to
enter the classroom he went into such facial contortions as I
have never yet seen. He did not mean anything, bless his kind
heart, but *I* got a wigging: suggesting revolutionary ideas to
youth, that's what they said."

Immediately afterwards another homunculus appears [rather
like the little firm heads of witch doctors bursting out of the
body of an African explorer in a famous short story]. The
Mayor refers to the history teacher:

"He is a scholar, no doubt, and has acquired loads of learning, but there—he lectures with such vehemence that he loses
all self-control. I happened to hear him once: so long as he was
talking about the Assyrians and the Babylonians it was—well,
one could stand it; but when he got to Alexander the Great,
then—no, I simply can't describe his state. Lord, I thought the
house was on fire! He dashed out of his desk and banged a chair
against the floor with all his might! Alexander the Great was
a hero, we all know that, but is this a reason to break chairs? It
is wasting Government property."

"Ah yes, he is vehement [admits the School Inspector with a sigh] I have mentioned it to him several times. He answers: whether you like it or not, I can't help forfeiting my own life in the cause of learning."

The Postmaster, to whom the Mayor talks next, asking him to unseal and read the letters that pass through his office (which the good man had been doing for his own pleasure for years), is instrumental in letting out another homunculus.

"It's a great pity [he says to the Mayor] that you don't read those letters yourself: they contain some admirable passages. The other day for instance a lieutenant was writing to a friend and describing a ball he had been to—in a most waggish style. . . . Oh, very, very nice: 'My life, dear friend,' he wrote, 'floats in empyrean bliss: lots of young ladies, band playing, banner galloping . . .'—all of it written with great, great feeling."

Two quarrelsome country squires are mentioned next by the Judge, Cheptovich and Varkhovinsky, neighbors, who have taken proceedings against each other which will probably last all their lives (while the Judge merrily courses hares on the lands of both). Then as Dobchinsky and Bobchinsky make their dramatic appearance with the news that they have discovered the Government Inspector living incognito at the local inn, Gogol parodies his own fantastic meandering way (with gushes of seemingly irrelevant details) of telling a story: all the personal friends of Bobchinsky come bobbing up as the latter launches upon the report of his and Dobchinsky's sensational discovery: "So I ran to see Korobkin [Mr. Box] and not finding Korobkin at home [Jack-in-the-box had left it], I called on Rastakovsky [Mr. Blankety-Blank], and not finding Rastakovsky at home . . . [of all the homunculi only these two will appear as visitors at the end of the last act by special request of the stage management]." At the inn where Bobchinsky and Dobchinsky see the person whom they wrongly suspect to be the Government Inspector they interview the inn-keeper Vlass

—and here—among the gasps and splutters of Bobchinsky's feverish speech (trying to tell it all before his double, Dobchinsky, can interrupt him) we obtain this lovely detailed information concerning Vlass (for in Gogol's world the more a person hurries the more he loiters on the way):

". . . and so Dobchinsky beckoned with his finger and called the inn-keeper—you know, the inn-keeper Vlass—his wife has borne him a child three weeks ago—such a smart little beggar—will keep an inn just like his father does. . . ."

Note how the newborn Anonymous Vlassovich manages to grow up and live a whole life in the space of a second. Bobchinsky's panting speech seems to provoke an intense fermentation in the backstage world where those homunculi breed.

There are some more to come. The room where Khlestakov —the sham Government Inspector—dwells is identified by the fact that some officers who had also chanced to pass through that town some time before had a fight there over cards. One of the Mayor's men, the policeman Prokhorov, is alluded to in the following way.

The Mayor, in blustering haste to the policeman Svistunov: "Where are the others? . . . Dear me, I had ordered Prokhorov to be here, too. Where is Prokhorov?"

The Policeman: "Prokhorov is at the police station, but he cannot be put to any good use."

The Mayor: "How's that?"

The Policeman: "Well, just as I say: he was brought in this morning in a carriage dead drunk. Two buckets of water have been poured over him already, but he has not come round yet."

"But how on earth did you let him get into such a state?" the Mayor asks a moment later, and the Police Officer (incidentally called Ukhovyortov—a name which contains the idea of "viciously hitting people on the ear" all in one word) replies: "The Lord knows. There was a brawl in the suburb yesterday—he went there to settle matters and came back drunk."

After this orgy of secondary characters surging at the close of the first act there is a certain lull in the second which introduces Khlestakov. True, a gambling infantry captain, who was great at piling up tricks, appears to the echoes of cheerful card-slapping as Khlestakov recalls the money he lost to him in the town of Pensa; but otherwise the active, ardent Khlestakov theme is too vigorous in this act (with the Mayor visiting him at the inn) to suffer any intruders. They come creeping back in the third act: Zemlyanika's daughter, we learn, wears a blue frock—and so she floats by in between the speeches, a pink and blue provincial maiden.

When upon his arrival at the Mayor's house Khlestakov, in the most famous scene of the Russian stage, starts showing off for the benefit of the ladies, the secondary characters that come tumbling out of his speech (for at last they had been set rolling by Khlestakov's natural garrulousness and the Mayor's wine) are of another race, so to speak, than those we have already met. They are of a lighter, almost transparent texture in keeping with Khlestakov's own iridescent temperament—phantoms in the guise of civil servants, gleeful imps coming to the assistance of the versatile devil ventriloquizing through Khlestakov. Dobchinsky's children, Vanya, Lisanka, or the inn-keeper's boy existed somewhere or other, but these do not exist at all, as such. The allusions have become delusions. But because of the crescendo of lies on Khlestakov's part the driving force of these metaphysical creatures is more felt in its reaction upon the course of the play than were the idyllic gambols of the little people in the background of Act I.

"Ah, Petersburg!" exclaims Khlestakov. "That is what I call life! Perhaps you think I am just a copying clerk? [which he was]. No, Sir, the head of my section is right chummy with me. Has a way, you know, of slapping me on the shoulder and saying: 'Come and have dinner with me, old chap.' I only look in at the office for a couple of minutes, just to tell them: 'Do this, do that.' And then the copying clerk, old rat, goes with his pen

—trrk, trrk, scraping and scribbling away. [In long drawn accents] It was even suggested that I be made a Collegiate Assessor. [Again trippingly] But thought I to myself, what's the use? And there is the office boy [these are bearded men in Russia] running up the stairs after me with a brush—'Allow me, Sir,' he says, 'I'll just give a bit of shining to your shoes.' " Much later we learn that the office "boy's" name was Mikhey, and that he drank like a fish.

Further on, when, according to Khlestakov, soldiers rushed out of the guardhouse as he passed and gave the grand salute: "Their officer whom I knew very well said to me afterwards: 'Well, well, old boy, I am damned if we did not take you for the Commander-in-Chief!' "

When he starts talking of his Bohemian and literary connections, there even appears a goblin impersonating Pushkin: "I hobnob with Pushkin. Many a time have I said to him: 'Well, old Push, how are things going?'—'As usual, my dear fellow,' he says, 'very much as usual.' Quite a character!"

Then other bigwigs come jostling and buzzing and tumbling over each other as Khlestakov rushes on in an ecstasy of invention: Cabinet Ministers, Ambassadors, Counts, Princes, Generals, the Tsar's Advisors, a shadow of the Tsar himself, and "Messengers, messengers, messengers, thirty-five thousand messengers," spermatozoids of the brain—and then suddenly in a drunken hiccup they all fade; but not before a real allusion (at least real in the same sense as the little people of Act I were "real"), the ghost of needy clerk Khlestakov's slatternly cook Mavroosha peeps out for a dreadful instant through a chink of Khlestakov's speech in the midst of all those golden ghosts and dream ambassadors—to help him out of his skimpy overcoat (that carrick, to be exact, which later on Gogol was to immortalize as the attribute of a transcendental "chinovnik").

In the next act, when one by one the nervous officials present their respects to Khlestakov, who borrows money from each (they think that they are bribing him) we learn the names of Zemlyanika's children—Nicholas, Ivan, Elizabeth, Mary and Perepetuya: it was probably gentle Perepetuya who wore the pale blue frock. Of Dobchinsky's three children, two have been mentioned already by the Mayor's wife as being her god-children. They and the eldest boy are uncommonly like the Judge, who visits Mrs. Dobchinsky every time her poor little husband is away. The eldest boy was born before Dobchinsky married that wayward lady. Dobchinsky says to Khlestakov: "I make bold to ask your assistance in regard to a most delicate circumstance. . . . My eldest son, Sir, was born before I was married. . . . Oh, it is only a manner of speaking. I engendered him exactly as though in lawful wedlock, and made it perfectly right afterwards by sealing the bonds, Sir, of legitimate matrimony, Sir. Well, now I want him to be, in a manner of speaking, altogether my legitimate son, Sir, and to be called the same as I: Dobchinsky, Sir." (The French "sauf votre respect," though much too long, would perhaps better render the meaning of the humble little hiss—an abbreviation of "Soodar" —"Sir," which Dobchinsky adds to this or that word at the fall of his sentences.)

"I would not have troubled you," he goes on, "but I feel sorry for him, seeing his many gifts. The little fellow, you see, is something quite special—promises a lot: he can recite verses and such like things by heart, and whenever he happens to come across a penknife he makes a wee little carriage—as clever as a conjurer, Sir."

One more character appears in the background of the act: it is when Khlestakov decides to write about those weird provincial officials to his friend Tryapichkin (Mr. Ragman) who is a sordid little journalist with mercenary and pamphleteering inclinations, a rascal with a knack of making laughing stocks of those he chooses to chastise in his cheap but vicious articles. For one instant he winks and leers over Khlestakov's shoulder. He is the last to appear—no, not quite the last, for the ultimate phantom will be the gigantic shadow of the real Government Inspector.

This secondary world, bursting as it were through the background of the play, is Gogol's true kingdom. It is remarkable that these sisters and husbands and children, eccentric school-teachers, vodka-bewitched clerks and policemen, country squires quarreling for fifty years over the position of a fence, romantic officers who cheat at cards, wax sentimental over provincial balls and take a ghost for the Commander-in-Chief, these copying clerks and fantastic messengers—all these creatures whose lively motion constitutes the very material of the play, not only do not interfere with what theatrical managers call "action" but apparently assist the play to be eminently play-able.

4

Not only live creatures swarm in that irrational background but numerous objects are made to play a part as important as that of the characters: the hatbox which the Mayor places upon his head instead of his hat when stamping out in official splen-dor and absent-minded haste to meet a threatening phantom, is a Gogolian symbol of the sham world where hats are heads, hatboxes hats, and braided collars the backbones of men. The hurried note which the Mayor sends from the inn to his wife telling her of the exalted guest whom she must get ready to re-ceive gets mixed up with Khlestakov's hotel bill, owing to the Mayor having used the first scrap of paper that came to hand: "I hasten to tell you, my dearest, that I was in a most sorry plight at first; but thanks to my trusting in the mercy of God 2 salted cucumbers extra and ½ a portion of caviare, 1 rouble 25 kopeks." This confusion is again a piece of sound logic within Gogol's world, where the name of a fish is an outburst of divine music to the ears of gourmets, and cucumbers are metaphysical beings at least as potent as a provincial town mayor's private deity. These cucumbers breed in Khlestakov's eloquent description of his ideal of noble living: "On the table for instance there is a watermelon [which is but a sublimated cucumber]—not an ordinary watermelon but one that costs 700 roubles." The watery soup "with feathers or something floating in it" [instead of golden eyelets of shimmering fat] which Khlestakov has to be content with at the inn is transformed in the speech referring to his life in the capital into a *potage* that comes in a pan "straight from Paris by steamer"—the smoke of that imaginary steamer being as it were the heavenly exhalation of that imaginary soup. When Khlestakov is being made comfortable in his carriage the Mayor has a blue Persian rug brought from the store room (which is crammed with the compulsory offerings of his bearded subjects—the town merchants); Khlestakov's valet adds to this a padding of hay—and the rug is transformed into a magic carpet on which Khlestakov makes his volatile exit backstage to the silvery sound of the horse-bells and to the coachman's lyrical admonition to his magical steeds: "Hey you, my winged ones!" ("Hey vy, zalyotnye!" which literally means, "the ones that fly far"): Russian coachmen are apt to invent fond names for their horses—and Gogol, it may be assumed (for the benefit of those who like to know the personal experiences of writers) was to acquire a good deal of viatic lore during the endless peregrinations of his later years; and this gust of poetry, in which Khlestakov—the dreamy infantile swindler—fades out seems to blow open the gates for Gogol's own departure from the Russia he had invented towards distant hazy climes where numberless German watering towns, Italian ruins, Parisian restaurants and Palestine's shrines were to get mixed up in much the same way as Providence and a couple of cucumbers did in the distracted Mayor's letter.

5

It is amusing to recall that this dream play, this "Government Specter," was treated as a skit on actual conditions in Russia. It is still more amusing to think that Gogol in his first dismal effort to check those dangerous revolutionary allusions to his play pointed out that there was at least one positive character in it: Laughter. The truth is that the play is not a "comedy" at all, just as Shakespeare's dream-plays *Hamlet* or *Lear* cannot be called "tragedies." A bad play is more apt to be good comedy or good tragedy than the incredibly complicated creations of such men as Shakespeare or Gogol. In this sense Molière's stuff (for what it is worth) is "comedy" i.e. something as readily assimilated as a hot dog at a football game, something of one dimension and absolutely devoid of the huge, seething, prodigiously poetic background that makes true drama. And in the same sense O'Neill's *Mourning Becomes Electra* (for what *that* is worth) is, I suppose, a "tragedy."

Gogol's play is poetry in action, and by poetry I mean the mysteries of the irrational as perceived through rational words. True poetry of that kind provokes—not laughter and not tears —but a radiant smile of perfect satisfaction, a purr of beatitude —and a writer may well be proud of himself if he can make his readers, or more exactly some of his readers, smile and purr that way.

Khlestakov's very name is a stroke of genius, for it conveys to the Russian reader an effect of lightness and rashness, a prattling tongue, the swish of a slim walking cane, the slapping sound of playing cards, the braggadocio of a nincompoop and the dashing ways of a lady-killer (minus the capacity for completing this or any other action). He flutters through the play as indifferent to a full comprehension of the stir he creates, as he is eager to grab the benefits that luck is offering him. He is a gentle soul, a dreamer in his own way, and a certain sham charm hangs about him, the grace of a petit-maître that affords the ladies a refined pleasure as being in contrast with the boorish ways of the burly town worthies. He is utterly and deliciously vulgar, and the ladies are vulgar, and the worthies are vulgar—in fact the whole play is (somewhat like *Madame Bovary*) composed by blending in a special way different aspects of vulgarity so that the prodigious artistic merit of the final result is due (as with all masterpieces) not to *what* is said but to *how* it is said—to the dazzling combinations of drab parts. As in the scaling of insects the wonderful color effect may be due not to the pigment of the scales but to their position and refractive power, so Gogol's genius deals not in the intrinsic qualities of computable chemical matter (the "real life" of literary critics) but in the mimetic capacities of the physical phenomena produced by almost intangible particles of re-created life. I have employed the term "vulgarity" for lack of a more precise one; so Pushkin in *Eugene Onegin* inserted the English word "vulgar" with apologies for not finding in the Russian language its exact counterpart.

6

The charges directed against *The Government Inspector* by resentful people who saw in it an insidious attack against Russian officialdom had a disastrous effect upon Gogol. It may be said to have been the starting point of the persecution mania that in various forms afflicted him to the very end of his life. The position was rather curious: fame, in its most sensational form, had come to him; the Court was applauding his play with almost vicious glee; the stuffed shirts of high officialdom were losing their stuffing as they moved uneasily in their orchestra seats; disreputable critics were discharging stale venom; such critics whose opinion was worth something were lauding Gogol to the stars for what they thought was a great satire; the popular playwright Kukolnik shrugged his shoulders and said the play was nothing but a silly farce; young people repeated with gusto its best jokes and discovered Khlestakovs and Skvosnik-Dmu-khanovskys among their acquaintances. Another man would have reveled in this atmosphere of praise and scandal. Pushkin would have merely shown his gleaming Negro teeth in a good-natured laugh—and turned to the unfinished manuscript of his current masterpiece. Gogol did what he had done after the *Kuechelgarten* fiasco: he fled, or rather slithered, to foreign lands.

He did something else, too. In fact he did the worst thing that a writer could do under the circumstances: he started explaining in print such points of his play as his critics had either missed or directed against him. Gogol, being Gogol and living in a looking-glass world, had a knack of thoroughly planning his works *after* he had written and published them. This system he applied to *The Government Inspector*. He appended a kind of epilogue to it in which he explained that the real Government Inspector who looms at the end of the last act is the Conscience of Man. And that the other characters are the Passions in our Souls. In other words one was supposed to believe that these Passions were symbolized by grotesque and corrupt provincial officials and that the higher Conscience was symbolized by the Government. This explanation has the same depressing effect as his later considerations of related subjects have—unless we can believe that he was pulling his reader's leg—or his own. Viewed as a plain statement we have here the incredible fact of a writer totally misunderstanding and distorting the sense of his own work. He did the same to *Dead Souls,* as will be seen.

He was a strange sick creature—and I am not sure that his explanation of *The Government Inspector* is not the kind of deceit that is practiced by madmen. It is difficult to accept the notion that what distressed him so dreadfully about the reception of his play was his failure to be recognized as a prophet, a teacher, a lover of mankind (giving mankind a warming for its own good). There is not a speck of didacticism in the play and it is inconceivable that the author could be unaware of this; but as I say, he was given to dreaming things into his books long after they had been written. On the other hand the kind of lesson which critics—quite wrongly—discerned in the play was a social and almost revolutionary one which was highly distasteful to Gogol. He may have been apprehensive of the Court suddenly changing its august and fickle mind owing to the too violent praise in radical circles and to the too violent blame in reactionary ones—and thus cutting short the performances and profits (and a future pension maybe). He may have seen his literary career in Russia hampered for years to come by vigilant censors. He may too have been shocked and hurt by the fact that people whom he respected as good Christians (though the "good Christian" theme in its full form was to appear somewhat later) and good officials (which was to become synonymous with the first) were grieved and revolted by what they termed a "coarse and trivial farce." But what seems to have tormented him above all was the knowledge of being talked about by thousands of people and not being able to hear, let alone control, the talk. The buzz that reached him was ominous and monstrous because it was a buzz. The pats he received on his back seemed to him to imply ironic sneers directed at people whom he respected, so that these sneers were also directed at himself. The interest that perfect strangers showed in regard to him seemed alive with dark stratagems and incalculable dangers (beautiful word, stratagem—a treasure in a cave). I shall have occasion to speak in quite a different book of a lunatic who constantly felt that all the parts of the landscape and movements of inanimate objects were a complex code of allusion to his own being, so that the whole universe seemed to him to be conversing about him by means of signs. Something of that sinister and almost cosmic dumb-show can be inferred from the morbid view Gogol took of his sudden celebrity. He fancied a hostile Russia creeping and whispering all around him and trying to destroy him both by blaming and praising his play. In June 1836 he left for Western Europe.

It is said that on the eve of his departure Pushkin, whom he was never to see again, visited him and spent all night rummaging together with him among his manuscripts and reading the beginning of *Dead Souls,* a first draft of which had already been made by Gogol about that time. The picture is pleasing—too pleasing perhaps to be true. For some reason or other (possibly from a morbid dislike of any responsibility) Gogol in after years was most anxious to have people believe that all he had written before 1837, that is, before Pushkin's death, had been directly due to the latter's suggestion and influence. As Gogol's art was as far removed from that of Pushkin as could be and as moreover Pushkin had other problems to tackle than guiding the pen of a literary acquaintance, the information so readily supplied by Gogol himself is hardly worth serious consideration. The lone candle lighting up the midnight scene may go out without any qualms on our part. What is far more likely is that Gogol stole abroad without bidding farewell to any of his friends. We know from a letter of his that he did not even say good-bye to Zhukovsky with whom he was on much more intimate terms than with Pushkin.

From the Commentary to
Eugene Onegin

❧❧❧❧❧

❧ *On Romanticism* ❧

XXIII

Thus did he write, "obscurely" and "limply"
(what we call romanticism—
though no romanticism here in the least
4 do I see; but what's that to us?),

—TRANSLATED BY VLADIMIR NABOKOV

2/romanticism:

As happens in zoological nomenclature when a string of obsolete, synonymous, or misapplied names keeps following the correct designation of a creature throughout the years, and not only cannot be shaken off, or ignored, or obliterated within brackets, but actually grows on with time, so in literary history the vague terms "classicism," "sentimentalism," "romanticism," "realism," and the like straggle on and on, from textbook to textbook. There are teachers and students with square minds who are by nature meant to undergo the fascination of categories. For them, "schools" and "movements" are everything; by painting a group symbol on the brow of mediocrity, they condone their own incomprehension of true genius.

I cannot think of any masterpiece the appreciation of which would be enhanced in any degree or manner by the knowledge that it belonged to this or that school; and, conversely, I could name any number of third-rate works that are kept artificially alive for centuries through their being assigned by the school-man to this or that "movement" in the past.

These concepts are harmful chiefly because they distract the student from direct contact with, and direct delight in, the quiddity of individual artistic achievement (which, after all, alone matters and alone survives); but, moreover, each of them is subject to such a variety of interpretation as to become meaningless in its own field, that of the classification of knowledge. Since, however, these terms exist and keep banging against every cobble over which their tagged victims keep trying to escape the gross identification, we are forced to reckon with them. For the needs of the present comments, I am prepared to accept the following practical definitions:

"Classical" in regard to a literary work of our era suggests the imitation of ancient models, in traditional matter and manner. Russians use the term "pseudoclassical" for anachronistic imitations in which the Roman or Greek wears a powdered wig.

"Sentimental" implies little beyond the shedding of conventional tears over the misadventure of conventional virtue in verse or prose.

A "realistic" work of fiction is one wherein the author is ready to name or describe without fear of traditional restriction any physical or moral detail pertaining to the world he perceives. (In this sense *EO* is neither sentimental nor realistic, while containing elements of both; it parodies the classical and leans toward the romantic.)

The fourth term in this series, "romanticism," requires a closer discussion of its main varieties as known in Pushkin's time. We can distinguish at least eleven forms or phases of the thing:

(1) The primitive, popular sense: Johnson's *Dictionary* defines a "romance" as "a military fable of the middle ages." But the "military fable" has an Arcadian sequel, and in the seventeenth century, in England, "romantic" is definitely suggestive of the delightful lives of shepherds and retired knights living on honey and cheese. Both the "military" and "pastoral"

parts fall under our first definition of "romantic" as characterizing the flights of fancy in popular literature during a period of time between the fall of Rome and the revival of letters.

(2) "The addition of strangeness to beauty" (Walter Pater, *Appreciations*: "Postscript"). An intensive preoccupation with the passionate and the fantastic. The retired knight is a necromancer; the moon rises over Arcadia in a new part of the ruined sky. As early as 1665-1666, Pepys describes a site (Windsor Castle) as "the most romantique castle that is in the world." In 1799, Campbell notes that " 'Tis distance lends enchantment to the view."

(3) The Highland subspecies and the eerie note. To paraphrase Beattie, *The Minstrel* (1772), "The grotesque and ghostly appearance of a landscape, especially by the light of the moon, diffuses an habitual gloom over the fancy and gives it that romantic cast that disposes to invention and that melancholy which inclines one to the fear of unseen things."

(4) The romanesque: a "romanesque" person feels as "romantic" such landscapes, lakescapes, and seascapes as recall either direct emotion (love, friendship, old ambitions and longings) or the description of similar places in popular novels and poems of the sentimental or fantastic kind. "Il [Fonsalbe] a rendu à mes déserts quelque chose de leur beauté heureuse, et du *romantisme* de leur sites *alpestres*" (Senancour, *Oberman,* Letter LXXXVII).

(5) The German subspecies (a hybrid, with a strong strain of sentimentalism). Reveries, visions, apparitions, tombstones, moonshine. The pictorial grading into the metaphysical. Lofty sentiments couched in a flaccid and nebulous idiom. The expression in poetry of the soul's endless approach to a dimly perceived perfection.

(6) The textbook synthetic conception of c. 1810: a combination of "melancholy" as the essence of Northern (Germanic, "Ossianic") poetry and of Renaissance vividness and vigor (e.g., Shakespeare). Romantic as implying "modern and

284 ESSAYS AND CRITICISM

picturesque" and as opposed to "classical" (the latter standing
for "antique and sculpturesque"): this seems to be the end
product of cogitations on the matter by the well-meaning but
hardly readable cofounder (with his brother, Friedrich, the
philosopher, 1772-1829) of the romantic school of German
literature, August Wilhelm von Schlegel (1767-1845), tutor of
Mme de Staël's children (c. 1805-1815); he assisted her in her
work *De l'Allemagne*; was ennobled and invested with many
decorations, and delivered his lectures on dramatic art and
literature in Vienna, 1808.*

(7) A romantic epic is one in which the tragic and the comic,
the lofty and the lowly, the sacred and the profane, the metaphysical generalization and the physical detail, and so forth are
pleasingly mingled (cf. the program of *EO* as set down in the
Prefatory Piece).

(8) "Romantic" as applied to a style abounding in vivid
specific details (local color, exotic landscapes, national peculiarities, realistic popular traits, new shades of perception, emotion, and meaning, etc.) as opposed, in such writings as those
by Chateaubriand or Victor Hugo, to the generalized mist of
sentimentalism; e.g., the waters of Lamartine (it will be noticed
that, on the other hand, the mist plus the melancholy is somehow also "romantic," although directly opposed to the specific
brightness and this is why the same Lamartine figures among
the romantics).

(9) A new style in poetry, free of classic rigidity and conven-
tionalism, permitting enjambments, mobile caesuras, and other
liberties.

(10) Literary genres not known to the ancients.

(11) "Modern" as opposed to "ancient" in any literary form.

There is a good deal of overlapping in these concepts, and
no wonder some muddle existed in Pushkin's mind as to what

* His *Über dramatische Kunst und Literatur* (1809-1811) was translated
into French (*Cours de littérature dramatique,* Paris, 1814, 3 vols.) by
Albertine Adrienne Necker de Saussure, Mme de Staël's cousin; and this
translation Pushkin had carefully read.

should be termed "romantic" in the strict sense, a question that interested him and his fellow writers more acutely than it does us.

In a note entitled "On Poetry Classical and Romantic" (1825), our poet accuses French critics of confusing the issue by referring to romanticism all such poetry as is characterized either by "the stamp of dreaminess and Germanic ideology" or is founded upon "the prejudices and traditions of the common people." He maintains that the distinction between classicism and romanticism can be drawn only in terms of form and not of subject matter. His definition of romantic poetry reads: "All such genres of poetical composition as were not known to the ancients or have since changed in form." According to our poet, western European poetry in the Dark Ages was at best an elegant bauble, a troubadour's triolet. Two circumstances, however, had a vigorous influence on its eventual course: the invasion of the Moors, "who inspired it with frenzy and tenderness, a leaning toward the marvelous and rich Oriental eloquence," and the Crusades, which imbued it "with piety and naïveté, a new code of heroism, and the loose morals of camp life." This was, according to Pushkin, the origin of romanticism.

In the same note, and elsewhere, Pushkin is hard on French "pseudoclassicism" as personified by Boileau: "It originated belowstairs and never went further than the salon. . . . It dressed the maudlin conceits of medieval romanticism in the severe garb of classicism." In a postscriptum, however, to this 1825 note he praises La Fontaine's *Contes* and Voltaire's *Pucelle* as masterpieces of pure romantic poetry. We should not forget that "pure French classicists," such as Corneille, Racine, and Molière, were among Pushkin's favorite writers.

In another MS note (1830), Pushkin continues:

> The French critics have their own notions of romanticism. They either assign to it all works bearing the stamp of melancholy and reverie or apply the term to neologisms and bad grammar.

Thus André Chénier, a poet permeated with the spirit of an-
tiquity, a poet whose very defects are owing to his desire to
give the French language the forms of Greek versification [this
is a singular error on Pushkin's part], becomes a romanticist
for them.

❧ *The Art of the Duel* ❧

XXIX

The pistols have already gleamed.
The mallet clanks against the ramrod.
Into the polyhedral barrel go the balls,
4 and the first time the cock has clicked.
Now powder in a grayish streamlet
is poured into the pan. The jagged,
securely screwed-in flint
8 is raised anew. Behind a near stump
perturbed Guillot places himself.
The two foes shed their cloaks.
Thirty-two steps Zaretski
12 with eminent exactness has paced off,
has placed his friends apart at the utmost points,
and each takes his pistol.

XXX

"Now march toward each other." Coolly,
not aiming yet, the two foes
with firm tread, slowly, evenly
4 traversed four paces,
four mortal stairs.
His pistol Eugene then,

      not ceasing to advance,
  8 gently the first began to raise.
      Now they have stepped five paces more,
      and Lenski, closing his left eye,
      started to level also—but right then
 12 Onegin fired. . . . Struck have
      the appointed hours: the poet
      in silence drops his pistol.

—TRANSLATED BY VLADIMIR NABOKOV

XXIX-XXX

The hostile meeting described here is the classical duel *à volonté* of the French code, partly derived from the Irish and English pistol duel, for which the basic code duello was adopted in Tipperary about 1775. According to this Clonmel Code and to an additional rule adopted in Galway, firing was regulated by signal, or word of command, or at pleasure, and in the last case, either party might advance "even to touch muzzle." In the favorite Continental variation, however, a stretch of ground at mid-distance could not be trespassed upon, and this was called the *barrière* (a term stemming from the oldest form of any pistol duel, the French one, which was fought on horseback, with the combatants divided by posts placed some ten yards asunder to represent the nearest range from which they were permitted to fire). The affair was conducted as follows.

The adjustment of the preliminary ceremonies would comprise not only the actual "calling out" or, in English parlance of the time, "calling upon," with the dispatch of a written challenge or "message," technically termed "cartel of defiance" (Six: IX), but also a conference between the seconds; we shall note that the latter formality is omitted in the present case, nor are the conditions of combat set down in writing by the witnesses, as formal usage would demand. It is not necessary to assume that suicide notes, at least, have been deposited, with a view to exempt the survivor from prosecution; officially, duels were forbidden, which did not affect, however, their frequency; the participants remained unpunished when no death followed, but even in case of a fatal result influence in high places helped to mitigate, or eliminate altogether, such penalties as imprisonment or banishment.

The parties repair to the selected spot. The seconds mark the ground at a certain number of paces (yards); for instance, in the present case, thirty-two yards are measured off, and the combatants, after a given signal, are allowed to reduce the distance by walking toward each other (otherwise, twelve paces or less would do). The limits of this progression are fixed by a number of paces being told off between the extreme marks, leaving a space of, say, twelve paces in the center of the ground: this is *la barrière,* the boundary, a kind of no man's land beyond the inner limits of which neither man can advance; its boundaries would be generally marked by the coats, carricks, or pelisses doffed by the combatants.

The pistols are loaded or "charged" by the seconds, and the duel begins. The principals take their positions at the extreme points of the ground, facing each other and keeping the muzzles of their pistols pointing down. At a given signal (*Marchez! Skhodites'!,* meaning "March toward each other"), they advance upon each other and may fire whenever they think proper. Onegin starts gently leveling his pistol when both have advanced four paces; they walk another five, and Lenski is killed on the first fire. If Onegin, while taking aim, had discharged his pistol without effect, or if it had snapped, or even if a severe hit had not utterly disabled Lenski, the latter might have made him come up to the *barrière* limit and at twelve paces taken a long cool aim at him. This was one of the reasons why serious duelists preferred to have the other fellow fire first. If after the exchange the adversaries still felt bloodthirsty, they might have the pistols reloaded (or use a fresh brace) and begin all over again. This type of duel, with variations (for example, the *barrière* idea seems to have been less clearly defined in the Irish and English duels), was popular in France, Russia, Great Britain, and the Southern states of America from the end of the eighteenth century to about 1840 and was still fought in Latin and Slav countries in our time. The reader should not imagine, when reading this chapter, anything resembling the "back-to-back-march-face-about-fire" affair popularized in modern times by movies and cartoons. This was a variant invented in France in the 1830's and popular with Parisian journalists later on.

The description of the Lenski-Onegin duel is, on our poet's part, a personal recollection in regard to various details, and, in regard to its issue, a personal prediction.

Pushkin had been out at least three times before his fatal meeting with d'Anthès. His first, with Rïleev, occurred presumably between May 6 and 9, 1820, in the district of Tsarskoe Selo (see my n. to Four: XIX: 5). In his next affair (1822, first week of January, 9 A.M., at a mile and a half from Kishinev), with Colonel Starov, commander of the Chasseur Regiment, for adversary, accurate aim was impaired by a raging snowstorm; the boundary was set at sixteen paces for the first exchange and narrowed to twelve for the second. In the spring of the same year, in a vineyard near Kishinev, he fought with another military man named Zubov. In these three duels no blood was shed; very few details are known about them, but it would seem that in the first and third Pushkin discharged his pistol into the air.

In his fourth and last encounter, with Baron Georges Charles d'Anthès, also known as Baron Georges de Heeckeren, on January 27, at 4:30 P.M., near St. Petersburg (on the north side of the Neva, some 1500 feet north of the Black River, in a pine grove a little way off the Kolomyaki road), the parties took their ground at a distance of twenty paces, and Pushkin was mortally wounded at the first fire. Here are the conditions of the duel.

1. Les deux adversaires seront placés à vingt pas de distance, à cinq pas chacun des deux barrières qui seront distantes de dix pas entre elles.

2. Armés chacun d'un pistolet, à un signal donné, ils pourront en s'avançant l'un sur l'autre, sans cependant dans aucun cas dépasser la barrière, faire usage de leurs armes.

3. Il reste convenu en outre qu'un coup de feu parti, il ne sera plus permis à chacun des deux adversaires de changer de place pour que celui des deux qui aura tiré le premier essuie dans tous les cas le feu de son adversaire à la même distance.

4. Les deux parties ayant tiré, s'il n'y a point de résultat on recommencerait l'affaire . . . en remettant les adversaires à la même distance de vingt pas. . . .

The six clauses, of which I quote four, were signed on January 27, 1837, at 2:30 P.M., in St. Petersburg. Two hours later Pushkin received a wound in the lower abdomen and died of traumatic peritonitis at 2:45 P.M., January 29.

The circumstances that led to Pushkin's tragic death can be briefly summarized as follows.

In 1833 the Dutch minister, Baron Jacob Theodore van Heeckeren (Jacques Thierry Borchard Anne van Heeckeren-Beverwaert, 1791-1884), who after a leave of absence was returning to his post in St. Petersburg, at an inn befriended a young Alsatian gentleman going the same way. This was Georges Charles d'Anthès (1812-1895), a native of Colmar and onetime student at Saint-Cyr. According to Louis Metman, the official (and not always reliable) biographer of the family, the d'Anthès had originated on Gottland Island and had been established since the seventeenth century in Alsace, where a Jean Henri Anthès, *manufacteur d'armes blanches,* was ennobled in 1731. The father of Georges d'Anthès had been baronized by Napoleon I. Our hero's military studies in France had been interrupted by the July Revolution, which ended the reign of Charles X (1824-1830) and hoisted Louis Philippe upon the throne. D'Anthès remained faithful to Charles and went to seek his fortune at the court of Tsar Nicholas I, who liked legitimists.

Georges d'Anthès and his protector arrived by steamer on October 8, 1833. Pushkin, who happened to be keeping a journal at the time, jotted down on January 26, 1834, almost exactly three years before his fatal duel, that a foreigner, Baron d'Anthès, had been received into the Chevalier Guards. He met d'Anthès in St. Petersburg at the end of July 1834. Natalia Pushkin and the two children, Maria and Aleksandr, were spending the summer on her mother's estate in the province of Kaluga, after a miscarriage she had suffered in March of that year. She returned to St. Petersburg in the autumn and bore a third child (Grigoriy) in May 1835, and a fourth (Natalia) a year later. There is no proof that her relations with d'Anthès, who fell in love with her at the close of 1834, ever went further than flirtatious conversations and snatched kisses; this was bad enough, but it is also true that her husband had affairs with other women, among whom was her sister Alexandra. Her other (elder) sister, Ekaterina, was madly enamored of d'Anthès.

In the summer of 1836, the Pushkins rented a villa in the suburbs, near the Black River (I have read somewhere that the name Black River, known as early as 1710, came from its peculiar dusky tint, owing to the fact that the dense alder shrubs growing along its banks and dipping their roots in the water produced a dark, tawny suffusion of alnein in it), and both Natalia and Ekaterina saw a good deal of d'Anthès. July passed in an atmosphere full of billets-doux, *petits jeux,* rides, and picnics, and somehow, in the course of that month, Ekaterina Goncharov became pregnant (a circumstance carefully camouflaged in the annals of the Heeckeren-d'Anthès family, but conclusively proved by Grossman in *Krasnaya niva,* XXIV, 1929). It is certain that by the early fall of 1836 rumors were circulating about a possible marriage between her and d'Anthès (by now Baron de Heeckeren—his father having officially ceded him in April of that year to the Dutch minister). It is also certain that d'Anthès' courtship of Natalia Pushkin, a source of passionate interest to the *grand monde,* went on just as before.

Vienna society a few years earlier had found great fun in conferring on people various absurd certificates. A coterie of effeminate young men decided to renew the fad in St. Petersburg. A member of this giggling clique, Prince Pyotr Dolgoruki (nicknamed in society *le bancal,* "bowlegs"), cooked up an anonymous letter that Pushkin and his friends received by the (recently inaugurated) city mail on November 4, 1836:

> Les Grands-Croix, Commandeurs et Chevaliers du Sérénissime Ordre des *Cocus,* réunis en grand Chapitre sous la présidence du vénérable grand-Maître de l'Ordre, S. E. D. L. Narychkine, *ont nommé à l'unanimité Mr. Alexandre Pouchkine coadjuteur du grand Maître de l'Ordre des Cocus et historiographe de l'Ordre.*
>
> *Le sécrétaire pérpétuel:* Cte *J. Borch*

I have preserved the orthography. The secretary is Count Joseph Borch: him and his wife, Lyubov, the *monde* dubbed a model couple because "she lived with the coachman, and he with the postilion." The venerable Grand Master is His Excellency Dmitri Lvovich Narïshkin, whose wife, Maria, had been the mistress of Tsar Alexander I for many years. It is surmised that this "certificate" should be construed in the sense that Pushkin had been cocufied by the Tsar. This was not so. Although the potentate had had his eye on Natalia Pushkin even before she married, she is thought to have become his mistress for a brief spell only after our poet's death.

That the hand is a Russian's is clear from the very attempts to disguise it (for example, by forming the French *u* as a Russian *i,* which in block-letter script is the mirror image of *N*); but Pushkin, for some reason never explained, decided it had been written by Heeckeren. Soviet graphologists proved (in 1927) that it was Dolgoruki's work; his subsequent forgeries lend strong psychological support to his authorship. He belonged to the Heeckeren set, but it was Heeckeren and d'Anthès whom Pushkin immediately saw as the main villains. On November 7 he called out Lieutenant d'Anthès; a hectic period of *pourparlers* ensued, with Pushkin's friend Zhukovski doing his best to patch up matters. On November 17 Pushkin took back his challenge on the grounds that d'Anthès had proposed to Ekaterina Goncharov—which it was high time he did, since she was now five months with child. He married her on January 10, 1837. On January 24 Pushkin had a mysterious interview with the Tsar. During the fortnight following his wedding d'Anthès continued to pay court to Natalia Pushkin on every possible occasion.

On January 26 Pushkin sent an insulting letter to the Dutch minister, accusing him of being "the pimp of his bastard." This last epithet was a perfectly gratuitous insult since Heeckeren was a confirmed homosexual, a fact well known to our poet. For reasons of protocol, Heeckeren abstained from challenging Pushkin, and it was d'Anthès who immediately called him out.

Pushkin's second was his old schoolmate, Lieutenant Colonel Konstantin Danzas, and that of d'Anthès was Viscount Laurent d'Archiac, a secretary of the French embassy. The duel took place on Wednesday, January 27. Both sleighs arrived in the vicinity of the so-called Commandant's Villa about 4 P.M., with dusk already dulling the frosty air. While the two seconds and d'Anthès were engaged in trampling out a twenty-yard-long path in the snow, Pushkin, enveloped in a bearskin pelisse, sat waiting on a snowdrift. The seconds marked the ten-yard boundary with their shed carricks, and the duel began. Pushkin at once walked up his five paces to the boundary. D'Anthès made four paces and fired. Pushkin fell on Danzas' military carrick, but after a pause of a few seconds raised himself on one arm and declared he had enough strength to fire. His pistol had stuck barrel down in the snow; another was given him, and Pushkin took slow careful aim at his adversary, whom he had ordered to come up to the boundary. The shock of the ball, which hit d'Anthès in the forearm, bowled him over, and Pushkin, thinking he had killed him, exclaimed, "Bravo!" and threw his pistol up into the air. He was carried to the livery coupé that had conveyed the passionately anxious Dutch minister to the vicinity of the ground (Heeckeren then quietly transferred himself to one of the hack sleighs).

D'Anthès later had a distinguished career in France. In *Les Châtiments,* bk. IV, no. VI, a fine diatribe of thirty resounding Alexandrines "Ecrit le 17 Juillet 1851, en descendant de la tribune," Victor Hugo qualified the members of Napoleon III's senate, including d'Anthès, as follows (ll. 1-2, 7):

> Ces hommes qui mourront, foule abjecte et grossière,
> Sont de la boue avant d'être de la poussière.
>
> Ils mordent les talons de qui marche en avant.

It is extremely curious to discover—as I have from a work by Baron Ludovic de Vaux, *Les Tireurs de pistolet* (Paris, 1883), pp. 149-50—that the son of Georges and Catherine Heeckeren d'Anthès, Louis Joseph Maurice Charles Georges (1843-1902), was one of the most celebrated duelists of his day. "Baron Georges de Heeckeren . . . grand, gros et fort, yeux clairs et barbe blonde," while heading in the sixties a counterguerrilla action in Mexico, "se prit de querelle," at a hotel in Monterey, "avec un Américain qui mettait les pieds sur la table avant le dessert" and fought a duel with him "à l'américaine au revolver et lui brisa le bras. . . . Rentré en France il eut un duel à l'épée avec Albert Roge. . . . Tout le monde se rappelle son duel avec le Prince Dolgorouki dans lequel il fracassa l'épaule de son adversaire après avoir subi son feu à dix pas. . . . C'est un charmant viveur . . . qui compte beaucoup d'amis à Paris et qui le mérite bien."

From Eugene Onegin

❧❦❧

I

"My uncle has most honest principles:
when taken ill in earnest,
he has made one respect him
4 and nothing better could invent.
To others his example is a lesson;
but, good God, what a bore
to sit by a sick man both day and night,
8 without moving a step away!
What base perfidiousness
the half-alive one to amuse,
adjust for him the pillows,
12 sadly present the medicine,
sigh—and think inwardly
when *will* the devil take you?"

II

Thus a young scapegrace thought,
with posters flying in the dust,
by the most lofty will of Zeus
4 the heir of all his relatives.
Friends of Lyudmila and Ruslan!
The hero of my novel,

without preambles, forthwith,
8 I'd like to have you meet:
Onegin, a good pal of mine,
was born upon the Neva's banks,
where maybe you were born,
12 or used to shine, my reader!
There formerly I too promenaded—
but harmful is the North to me.

III

Having served excellently, nobly,
his father lived by means of debts;
gave three balls yearly
4 and squandered everything at last.
Fate guarded Eugene:
at first, Madame looked after him;
later, Monsieur replaced her.
8 The child was boisterous but nice.
Monsieur l'Abbé, a poor wretch of a Frenchman,
not to wear out the infant,
would teach him everything in play,
12 bothered him not with stern moralization,
scolded him slightly for his pranks,
and to the Letniy Sad took him for walks.

IV

Then, when tumultuous youth's
season for Eugene came,
season of hopes and tender melancholy,
4 Monsieur was ousted from the place.
Now my Onegin is at large:

hair cut after the latest fashion,
dressed like a London Dandy—
8 and finally he saw the World.
In French impeccably
he could express himself and write,
danced the mazurka lightly,
12 and bowed unconstrainedly—
what would you more? The World decided
he was clever and very nice.

V

All of us had a bit of schooling
in something and somehow:
hence education, God be praised,
4 is in our midst not hard to flaunt.
Onegin was, in the opinion of many
(judges resolute and stern),
a learned fellow but a pedant.
8 He had the happy talent,
without constraint, in conversation
slightly to touch on everything,
keep silent, with an expert's learned air,
12 during a grave discussion,
and provoke the smiles of ladies
with the fire of unexpected epigrams.

VI

Latin has gone at present out of fashion;
still, to tell you the truth,
he had enough knowledge of Latin
4 to make out epigraphs,

descant on Juvenal,
put at the bottom of a letter *vale*,
and he remembered, though not without fault,
8 two lines from the *Aeneid*.
He had no urge to rummage
in the chronological dust
of the earth's historiography,
12 but anecdotes of days gone by,
from Romulus to our days,
he did keep in his memory.

VII
___

Lacking the lofty passion not to spare
life for the sake of sounds,
an iamb from a trochee—
4 no matter how we strove—he could not tell apart;
dispraised Homer, Theocritus,
but read, in compensation, Adam Smith,
and was a deep economist:
8 that is, he could assess the way
a state grows rich,
and what it lives upon, and why
it needs not gold
12 when it has got the simple product.
His father could not understand him,
and mortgaged his lands.

VIII
___

All Eugene knew besides
I have no leisure to recount;
but where he was a veritable genius,

4 what he more firmly knew than all the arts,
   what since his prime had been to him
   toil, anguish, joy,
   what occupied the livelong day
8 his fretting indolence—
   was the art of soft passion
   which Naso sang,
   wherefore a sufferer he ended
12 his brilliant and tumultuous span
   in Moldavia, in the wild depth of steppes,
   far from his Italy.

     —TRANSLATED BY VLADIMIR NABOKOV, 1967

Reply to My Critics

In regard to my novels my position is different. I cannot imagine myself writing a letter-to-the-editor in reply to an unfavorable review, let alone devoting almost a whole day to composing a magazine article of explanation, retaliation, and protest. I have waited at least thirty years to take notice—casual and amused notice—of some scurvy abuse I met with in my "V. Sirin" disguise but that pertains to bibliography. My inventions, my circles, my special islands are infinitely safe from exasperated readers. Nor have I ever yielded to the wild desire to thank a benevolent critic—or at least to express somehow my tender awareness of this or that friendly writer's sympathy and understanding, which in some extraordinary way seem always to coincide with talent and originality, an interesting, though not quite inexplicable phenomenon.

If, however, adverse criticism happens to be directed not at those acts of fancy, but at such a matter-of-fact work of reference as my annotated translation of *Eugene Onegin* (hereafter referred to as *EO*), other considerations take over. Unlike my novels, *EO* possesses an ethical side, moral and human elements. It reflects the compiler's honesty or dishonesty, skill or sloppiness. If told I am a bad poet, I smile; but if told I am a poor scholar, I reach for my heaviest dictionary.

I do not think I have received all the reviews that appeared after *EO* was published; I fail to locate a few that I was sure I

had in my chaotic study; but judging by the numerous ones
that did reach me, one might conclude that trying to translate an
author literally represents an approach entirely devised by me;
that it had never been heard of before; and that there was something offensive and even sinister about such a method and
undertaking. Promoters and producers of what Anthony Burgess calls "arty translations," carefully rhymed, pleasantly modulated versions containing, say, eighteen per cent of sense plus
thirty-two of nonsense and fifty of neutral padding, are I think
more prudent than they realize. While ostensibly tempted by
impossible dreams, they are subliminally impelled by a kind of
self-preservation. The "arty translation" protects them by concealing and camouflaging ignorance or incomplete information
or the fuzzy edge of limited knowledge. Stark literalism, on
the other hand, would expose their fragile frame to unknown and
incalculable perils.

It is quite natural, then, that the solidly unionized professional paraphrast experiences a surge of dull hatred and fear,
and in some cases real panic, when confronted with the possibility that a shift in fashion, or the influence of an adventurous
publishing house, may suddenly remove from his head the
cryptic rose-bush he carries or the maculated shield erected between him and the specter of inexorable knowledge. As a result
the canned music of rhymed versions is enthusiastically advertised, and accepted, and the sacrifice of textual precision
applauded as something rather heroic, whereas only suspicion
and bloodhounds await the gaunt, graceless literalist groping
around in despair for the obscure word that would satisfy im-
passioned fidelity and accumulating in the process a wealth of
information which only makes the advocates of pretty camou-
flage tremble or sneer.

These observations, although suggested by specific facts,
should not be construed in a strictly *pro-domo-sua* sense. My
EO falls short of the ideal crib. It is still not close enough and
not ugly enough. In future editions I plan to defowlerize it still

more drastically. I think I shall turn it entirely into utilitarian prose, with a still bumpier brand of English, rebarbative barricades of square brackets and tattered banners of reprobate words, in order to eliminate the last vestiges of bourgeois poesy and concession to rhythm. This is something to look forward to. For the moment, all I wish is merely to put on record my utter disgust with the general attitude, amoral and philistine, towards literalism.

It is indeed wonderful how indifferent critics are to the amount of unwillful deceit going on in the translation trade. I recall once opening a copy of Bely's *Petersburg* in English, and lighting upon a monumental howler in a famous passage about a blue coupé which had been hopelessly discolored by the translator's understanding *kubovïy* (which means "blue") as "cubic"! This has remained a model and a symbol. But who cares and why bother? Mr. Rosen in *The Saturday Review* (28 November 1964) ends his remarks on rhymed versions of *Eugene Onegin* with the expression of a rapturous hope: "It only remains for a talented poet like Robert Lowell to take advantage [of these versions] to produce a poem in English that really sings and soars." But this is an infernal vision to me who can distinguish in the most elaborate imitation the simple schoolboy howler from the extraneous imagery within which it is so pitifully imbedded. Again—what does it matter? "It is part of the act," as Mr. Edmund Wilson would say. The incredible errors in the translations from the Russian which are being published nowadays with frenetic frequency, are dismissed as trivial blemishes that only a pedant would note.

Even Professor Muchnic, who in a recent issue of the *New York Review of Books* delicately takes Mr. Guy Daniels apart as if he were an unfamiliar and possibly defective type of coffee machine, neglects to point out that in both versions of Lermontov's poem which she quotes—Daniels' effort and Baring's very minor (*pace* Mirski) poem—the same grotesque imp blows a strident trumpet. For we have here an admirable

example of one of those idiomatic freaks that for reasons of mental balance foreigners should not even try to rationalize. Lermontov's Russian goes: *Sosedka est' u nih odna . . . Kak vspomnish', kak davno rasstalis'!* And the literal sense is:
"They have a certain neighbor [*fem.*] . . . Oh, to think how
long ago we parted!" The form *vspomnish'* looks like the second person singular of "remember," but in this intonational
arrangement it should be the first person in literal translation
since it is addressed by the speaker to himself. Now, both ver-
sionists being ignorant of idiomatic Russian did not hesitate to
use the second person (though actually the result gives a painfully didactic twist to the sentence, which should have made
the translator think twice). Baring's version (which Professor
Muchnic, I am sorry to say, calls "a wonderfully precise reproduction of the sense, the idiom") runs: "We had a neighbor
. . . and *you remember* I and she. . . ." While the more
humble Daniels translates: "There was a girl as *you'll recall*. . . ." I have underlined the shared boner. The point is
not that one version is better than the other (frankly there is
not much to choose between the two); the point is that unwittingly *both* use the same wrong person as if all paraphrasts were
interconnected omphalically by an ectoplasmic band.

Despite the fierce attitude towards literalism, I still find a
little surprising the intensity of human passions that my rather
dry, rather dull work provokes. Hack reviewers rush to the defense of the orthodox Soviet publicists whom I "chastise" and
of whom they have never heard before. A more or less displaced
Russian in New York maintains that my commentary is nothing but a collection of obscure trifles and that besides he remembers having heard it all many years ago in Gorki from his
high-school teacher, A. A. Artamonov.

The word "mollitude," which I use a few times, has been
now so often denounced that it threatens to become almost a
household word, like "nymphet." One of my most furious and
inarticulate attackers seems to be an intimate friend of Belinski

(born 1811), as well as of all the paraphrasts I "persecute."
The fury is, I suppose, pardonable and noble, but there would
be no sense in my reacting to it. I shall also ignore some of the
slapstick—such as a little item in *The New Republic* (3 April
1965) which begins, "Inspector Nabokov has revisited the
scene of the crime in *L'affaire Oneguine*" and is prompted by a
sordid little grudge of which the editor, presumably, had no
knowledge. A reviewer writing in the *Novïy Zhurnal* (No. 77),
Mr. Moris Fridberg—whom I am afraid I shall be accused of
having invented—employs a particularly hilarious brand of bad
Russian (*kak izvestno dlya lyubogo studenta,* as known "for"
every student) to introduce the interesting idea that textual
fidelity is unnecessary because "in itself the subject-matter of
[Pushkin's] work is not very important." He goes on to complain that I do not say a word about such Pushkinists as Modza-
levski, Tomashevski, Bondi, Shchyogolev and Gofman—a
statement that proves he has not only not read my commentary,
but has not even consulted the Index; and on top of that he confuses me with Professor Arndt whose preliminary remarks
about his "writing not for experts but students" Mr. Fridberg
ascribes to me. A still more luckless gentleman (in the
Los Angeles Times) is so incensed by the pride and prejudice
of my commentary that he virtually chokes on his wrath and
after enticingly entitling his article "Nabokov Fails as a Translator" has to break it off abruptly without having made one
single reference to the translation itself. Among the more serious articles there is a long one in the *New York Times Book
Review,* 28 June 1964, by Mr. Ernest Simmons, who obligingly
corrects what he takes to be a misprint in One: XXV: 5;
"Chadaev," he says, should be "Chaadaev"; but from my
note to that passage he should have seen that "Chadaev" is
one of the three forms of that name, and also happens to be
Pushkin's own spelling in that particular line, which otherwise
would not have scanned.

For obvious reasons I cannot discuss all the sympathetic reviews. I shall only refer to some of them in order to acknowledge certain helpful suggestions and corrections. I am grateful to John Bayley (*The Observer,* 29 November 1964) for drawing my attention to what he calls—much too kindly, alas—"the only slip" in my commentary: *"Auf allen Gipfeln"* (in the reference to Goethe's poem) should be corrected to *"Ueber allen Gipfeln."* (I can add at least one other: My note to Two: XXXV: 8 contains a silly blunder and should be violently deleted.) Anthony Burgess in *Encounter* has suddenly and conclusively abolished my sentimental fondness for FitzGerald by showing how he falsified the "witty metaphysical tent-maker's" actual metaphors in *"Awake! for morning in the bowl of Night. . . ."* John Wain, in *The Listener* (29 April 1965), by a sheer feat of style has made me at once sorry for one of my "victims" and weak with laughter: "This [the discussion of prosody], by the way, is the section in which Arthur Hugh Clough gets described as a poetaster; the effect is like that of seeing an innocent bystander suddenly buried by a fall of snow from a roof. . . ." J. Thomas Shaw, in *The Russian Review* (April 1965), observes that I should have promoted Pushkin after his graduation to the tenth civil rank ("collegiate secretary") instead of leaving him stranded on the fourteenth rung of the ladder; but I cannot find in my copy the misprinted Derzhavin date which he also cites; and I strongly object to his listing James Joyce, whom I revere, among those writers whom I condemn "in contemptuous asides" (apparently Mr. Shaw has dreadfully misunderstood what I say about Joyce's characters falling asleep by applying it to Joyce's readers). Finally, the anonymous reviewer in the *Times Literary Supplement* (28 January 1965) is perfectly right when he says that in my notes I do not discuss Pushkin's art in sufficient detail; he makes a number of attractive suggestions which, together with those of two other reviewers and several correspondents, would make a fifth volume, or at least a very handsome *Festschrift.* The same reviewer is much too lenient when he remarks that "a careful scrutiny of every line has failed to reveal a single careless error in translation." There are at least two: in Four: XLIII: 2, the word "but" should be deleted, and in Five: XI: 3, "lawn" should be "plain."

The longest, most ambitious, most captious, and, alas, most reckless, article is Mr. Edmund Wilson's in the *New York Review of Books* (15 July 1965), and this I now select for a special examination.

A number of earnest simpletons consider Mr. Wilson to be an authority in my field ("he misses few of Nabokov's lapses," as one hasty well-wisher puts it in a letter to the *NYR*, on 26 August), and no doubt such delusions should not be tolerated; still, I am not sure that the necessity to defend my work from blunt jabs and incompetent blame would have been a sufficient incentive for me to discuss that article, had I not been moved to do so by the unusual, unbelievable, and highly entertaining opportunity that I am unexpectedly given by Mr. Wilson himself of refuting practically every item of criticism in his enormous piece. The mistakes and misstatements in it form an uninterrupted series so complete as to seem artistic in reverse, making one wonder if, perhaps, it had not been woven that way on purpose to be turned into something pertinent and coherent when reflected in a looking glass. I am unaware of any other such instance in the history of literature. It is a polemicist's dream come true, and one must be a poor sportsman to disdain what it offers.

As Mr. Wilson points out with such disarming good humor at the beginning of his piece, he and I are old friends. I fully reciprocate "the warm affection sometimes chilled by exasperation" that he says he feels for me. When I first came to America a quarter of a century ago, he wrote to me, and called on me, and was most kind to me in various matters, not necessarily pertaining to his profession. I have always been grateful to him for the tact he showed in not reviewing any of my novels while constantly saying flattering things about me in the so-called literary circles where I seldom revolve. We have had many exhilarating talks, have exchanged many frank letters. A patient confidant of his long and hopeless infatuation with the Russian language and literature, I have invariably done my best to explain to him his monstrous mistakes of pronunciation, grammar, and interpretation. As late as 1957, at one of our last meetings, in Ithaca, upstate New York, where I lived at the time, we both realized with amused dismay that, despite my frequent comments on Russian prosody, he still could not scan Russian verse. Upon being challenged to read *Evgeniy Onegin* aloud, he started to perform with great gusto, garbling every second word, and turning Pushkin's iambic line into a kind of spastic anapaest with a lot of jaw-twisting haws and rather endearing little barks that utterly jumbled the rhythm and soon had us both in stitches.

In the present case, I greatly regret that Mr. Wilson did not consult me about his perplexities, as he used to in the past. Here are some of the ghastly blunders that might have been so easily avoided.

"Why," asks Mr. Wilson, "should Nabokov call the word *netu* an old-fashioned and dialect form of *net*. It is in constant colloquial use and what I find one usually gets for an answer when one asks for some book in the Soviet bookstore in New York." Mr. Wilson has mistaken the common colloquial *netu* which means "there is not," "we do not have it," etc., for the obsolete *netu* which he has never heard and which as I explain in my note to Three: III: 12, is a form of *net* in the sense of "not so" (the opposite of "yes").

"The character called *yo*," Mr. Wilson continues, "is pronounced . . . more like 'yaw' than like the 'yo' in 'yonder.' " Mr. Wilson should not try to teach me how to pronounce this, or any other, Russian vowel. My "yo" is the standard rendering of the sound. The "yaw" sound he suggests is grotesque and quite wrong. I can hear Mr. Wilson—whose accent in Russian I know so well—asking that bookseller of his for *"Myawrtvïe Dushï"* ("Dead Souls"). No wonder he did not get it.

"Vse," according to Mr. Wilson (explaining two varieties of

the Russian for "all"), "is applied to people, and *vsyo* to
things." This is a meaningless pronouncement. *Vse* is merely
the plural of *ves'* (masculine), *vsya* (feminine), and *vsyo*
(neuter).

Mr. Wilson is puzzled by my assertion that the adjective *zloy*
is the only one-syllable adjective in Russian. "How about the
one-syllable predicative adjectives?" he asks. The answer is
simple: I am not talking of predicative adjectives. Why drag
them in? Such forms as *mudr* ("is wise"), *glup* ("is stupid"),
ploh ("is very sick indeed") are not adjectives at all, but adverb-
ish mongrels which may differ in sense from the related adjectives.

In discussing the word *pochuya* Mr. Wilson confuses it with
chuya ("sensing") (see my letter about this word in the *New
Statesman,* 23 April 1965) and says that had Pushkin used
pochuyav, only then should I have been entitled to put "having
sensed." "Where," queries Mr. Wilson, "is our scrupulous lit-
eralness?" Right here. My friend is unaware that despite the
different endings, *pochuyav* and *pochuya* happen to be inter-
changeable, both being "past gerunds," and both meaning exactly the same thing.

All this is rather extraordinary. Every time Mr. Wilson starts
examining a Russian phrase he makes some ludicrous slip. His
didactic purpose is defeated by such errors, as it is also by the
strange tone of his article. Its mixture of pompous aplomb and
peevish ignorance is hardly conducive to a sensible discussion
of Pushkin's language and mine—or indeed any language, for,
as we shall presently see, Mr. Wilson's use of English is also
singularly imprecise and misleading.

First of all it is simply not true to say, as he does, that in my
review of Professor Arndt's translation (*NYR,* 30 August
1964) "Nabokov dwelt especially on what he regarded as Professor Arndt's Germanisms and other infelicities of phrasing,
without apparently being aware of how vulnerable he himself
was." I dwelled especially on Arndt's mistranslations. What Mr.

Wilson regards as my infelicities may be more repellent to him for psychological reasons than "anything in Arndt," but they belong to another class of error than Arndt's or any other paraphrast's casual blunders, and what is more Mr. Wilson knows it. I dare him to deny that he deliberately confuses the issue by applying the term "niggling attack" to an indignant examination of the insults dealt out to Pushkin's masterpiece in yet another arty translation. Mr. Wilson affirms that "the only characteristic Nabokov trait" in my translation (aside from an innate "sado-masochistic" urge "to torture both the reader and himself," as Mr. Wilson puts it in a clumsy attempt to stick a particularly thick and rusty pin into my effigy) is my "addiction to rare and unfamiliar words." It does not occur to him that I may have rare and unfamiliar things to convey; that is his loss. He goes on, however, to say that in view of my declared intention to provide students with a trot such words are "entirely inappropriate" here, since it would be more to the point for the student to look up the Russian word than the English one. I shall stop only one moment to consider Mr. Wilson's pathetic assumption that a student can read Pushkin, or any other Russian poet, by "looking up" every word (after all, the result of this simple method is far too apparent in Mr. Wilson's own mistranslations and misconceptions), or that a reliable and complete *Russko-angliyskiy slovar'* not only exists (it does not) but is more easily available to the student than, say, the second unabridged edition (1960) of Webster's, which I really must urge Mr. Wilson to acquire. Even if that miraculous *slovar'* did exist, there would still be the difficulty of choosing, without my help, the right shade between two near synonyms and avoiding, without my guidance, the trap-falls of idiomatic phrases no longer in use.

Edmund Wilson sees himself (not quite candidly, I am afraid, and certainly quite erroneously) as a commonsensical, artless, average reader with a natural vocabulary of, say, six hundred basic words. No doubt such an imaginary reader may be sometimes puzzled and upset by the tricky terms I find necessary to use here and there—very much here and there. But how many such innocents will tackle *EO* anyway? And what does Mr. Wilson mean by implying I should not use words that in the process of lexicographic evolution begin to occur only at the level of a "fairly comprehensive dictionary"? When does a dictionary cease being an abridged one and start growing "fairly" and then "extremely" comprehensive? Is the sequence: vest-pocket, coat-pocket, great coat-pocket, my three book shelves, Mr. Wilson's rich library? And should the translator simply omit any reference to an idea or an object if the only right word—a word he happens to know as a teacher or a naturalist, or an inventor of words—is discoverable in the revised edition of a standard dictionary but not in its earlier edition or *vice versa?* Disturbing possibilities! Nightmarish doubts! And how does the harassed translator know that somewhere on the library ladder he has just stopped short of Wilson's Fairly Comprehensive and may safely use "polyhedral" but not "lingonberry"? (Incidentally, the percentage of what Mr. Wilson calls "dictionary words" in my translation is really so absurdly small that I have difficulty in finding examples.)

Mr. Wilson can hardly be unaware that once a writer chooses to youthen or resurrect a word, it lives again, sobs again, stumbles all over the cemetery in doublet and trunk hose, and will keep annoying stodgy grave-diggers as long as that writer's book endures. In several instances, English archaisms have been used in my *EO* not merely to match Russian antiquated words but to revive a nuance of meaning present in the ordinary Russian term but lost in the English one. Such terms are not meant to be idiomatic. The phrases I decide upon aspire towards literality, not readability. They are steps in the ice, pitons in the sheer rock of fidelity. Some are mere signal words whose only purpose is to suggest or indicate that a certain pet term of Pushkin's has recurred at that point. Others have been chosen for their Gallic touch implicit in this or that Russian attempt to imitate a French turn of phrase. All have pedigrees of agony and rejection and reinstatement, and should be treated as convalescents and ancient orphans, and not hooted at as impostors by a critic who says he admires some of my books. I do not care if a word is "archaic" or "dialect" or "slang"; I am an eclectic democrat in this matter, and whatever suits me, goes. My method may be wrong but it is a method, and a genuine critic's job should have been to examine the method itself instead of crossly fishing out of my pond some of the oddities with which I had deliberately stocked it.

Let me now turn to what Mr. Wilson calls my "infelicities" and "aberrations" and explain to him why I use the words he does not like or does not know.

In referring to Onegin's not being attracted by the picture of family life Pushkin in Four: XIII: 5 uses the phrase *semeystvennoy kartinoy*. The modern term is *semeynoy kartinoy* and had Pushkin chosen it, I might have put "family picture." But I had to indicate the presence of Pushkin's rarer word and used therefore the rarer "familistic" as a signal word.

In order to indicate the archaic note in *vospomnya* (used by Pushkin on One: XLVII: 6-7 instead of *vspomnya,* or *vspomniv,* or *vspominaya*) as well as to suggest the deep sonorous diction of both lines (*vospomnya prezhnih let romanï, vospomnya,* etc.), I had to find something more reverberating and evocative than "recalling intrigues of past years," etc., and whether Mr. Wilson (or Mr. N. for that matter) likes it or not, nothing more suitable than "rememorating" for *vospomnya* can be turned up.

Mr. Wilson also dislikes "curvate," a perfectly plain and technically appropriate word which I have used to render *krivïe* because I felt that "curved" or "crooked" did not quite do justice to Onegin's regularly bent manicure scissors.

Similarly, not a passing whim but the considerations of prolonged thought led me to render Four: IX: 5 *privïchkoy zhizni izbalovan* as "spoiled by a habitude of life." I needed the Gallic touch and found it preferable in allusive indefinitude—Pushkin's line is elegantly ambiguous—to "habit of life" or "life's habit." "Habitude" is the right and good word here. It is not labeled "dialect" or "obsolete" in Webster's great dictionary.

Another perfectly acceptable word is "rummer," which I befriended because of its kinship with *ryumka,* and because I wished to find for the *ryumki* of Five: XXIX: 4 a more generalized wineglass than the champagne flutes of XXXII: 8-9, which are also *ryumki.* If Mr. Wilson consults my notes, he will see that on second thought I demoted the non-obsolete but rather oversized cups of XXIX to jiggers of vodka tossed down before the first course.

I cannot understand why Mr. Wilson is puzzled by "dit" (Five: VIII: 13) which I chose instead of "ditty" to parallel "kit" instead of "kitty" in the next line, and which will now, I hope, enter or re-enter the language. Possibly, the masculine rhyme I needed here may have led me a little astray from the servile path of literalism (Pushkin has simply *pesnya*— "song"). But it is not incomprehensible; after all, anybody who knows what, say, "titty" means ("in nail-making the part that ejects the half-finished nail") can readily understand what "tit" means ("the part that ejects the finished nail").

Next on Mr. Wilson's list of inappropriate words is "gloam." It is a poetic word, and Keats has used it. It renders perfectly the *mgla* of the gathering evening shadows in Four: XLVII: 8, as well as the soft darkness of trees in Three: XVI: 11. It is better than "murk," a dialect word that Mr. Wilson uses for *mgla,* with my sanction, in another passage—the description of a wintry dawn.

In the same passage which both I and Mr. Wilson have translated, my "shippon" is as familiar to anyone who knows the English countryside as Mr. Wilson's "byre" should be to a New England farmer. Both "shippon" and "byre" are unknown to pocket-dictionary readers; both are listed in the three-centimeter-thick Penguin (1965). But I prefer "shippon" for *hlev* because I see its shape as clearly as that of the Russian cow-house it resembles, but see only a Vermont barn when I try to visualize "byre."

Then there is "scrab": "he scrabs the poor thing up," *bednyazhku tsaptsarap* (One: XIV: 8). This *tsaptsarap*—a "verbal interjection" presupposing (as Pushkin notes when employing it in another poem) the existence of the artificial verb *tsaptsarapat'*, jocular and onomatopoeic—combines *tsapat'* ("to snatch") with *tsarapat'* ("to scratch"). I rendered Pushkin's uncommon word by the uncommon "scrab up," which combines "grab" and "scratch," and am proud of it. It is in fact a wonderful find.

I shall not analyze the phrase "in his lunes" that Mr. Wilson for good measure has included among my "aberrations." It occurs not in my translation, which he is discussing, but in the flow of my ordinary comfortable descriptive prose which we can discuss another time.

We now come to one of the chief offenders: "mollitude." For Pushkin's Gallic *nega* I needed an English counterpart of *mollesse* as commonly used in such phrases as *il perdit ses jeunes années dans la mollesse et la volupté* or *son cœur nage dans la mollesse*. It is incorrect to say, as Mr. Wilson does, that readers can never have encountered "mollitude." Readers of Browning have. In this connection Mr. Wilson wonders how I would have translated *chistïh neg* in one of Pushkin's last elegies —would I have said "pure mollitudes"? It so happens that I translated that little poem thirty years ago, and when Mr. Wilson locates my version (in the Introduction to one of my novels) he will note that the genitive plural of *nega* is a jot different in sense from the singular.

In Mr. Wilson's collection of *bêtes noires* my favorite is "sapajou." He wonders why I render *dostoyno starïh obez'yan* as "worthy of old sapajous" and not as "worthy of old monkeys." True, *obez'yana* means any kind of monkey but it so happens that neither "monkey" nor "ape" is good enough in the context.

"Sapajou" (which technically is applied to two genera of neotropical monkeys) has in French a colloquial sense of "ruffian," "lecher," "ridiculous chap." Now, in lines 1-2 and 9-11 of Four: VII ("the less we love a woman, the easier 'tis to be liked by her . . . but that grand game is worthy of old sapajous of our forefathers' vaunted times") Pushkin echoes a moralistic passage in his own letter written in French from Kishinev to his young brother in Moscow in the autumn of 1822, that is seven months before beginning *Eugene Onegin* and two years before reaching Canto Four. The passage, well known to readers of Pushkin, goes: *Moins on aime une femme et plus on est sûr de l'avoir . . . mais cette jouissance est digne d'un vieux sapajou du dix-huitième siècle.* Not only could I not resist the temptation of retranslating the *obez'yan* of the canto into the Anglo-French "sapajous" of the letter, but I was also looking forward to somebody's pouncing on that word and allowing me to retaliate with that wonderfully satisfying reference. Mr. Wilson obliged—and here it is.

"There are also actual errors of English," continues Mr. Wilson, and gives three examples: "dwelled," which I prefer to "dwelt"; "about me," which in Two: XXXIX: 14, is used to render *obo mne* instead of the better "of me"; and the word "loaden," which Mr. Wilson "had never heard before." But "dwelled" is marked in my dictionary only "less usual"—not "incorrect"; "remind about" is not quite impossible (*e.g.,* "remind me about it tomorrow"); as to "loaden," which Mr. Wilson suggests replacing by "loadened," *his* English wobbles, not mine, since "loaden" *is* the correct past particle and participial adjective of "load."

In the course of his strange defense of Arndt's version—in which according to Mr. Wilson I had been assiduously tracking down Germanisms—he asserts that "it is not difficult to find Russianisms in Nabokov" and turns up *one,* or the shadow of one ("left us" should be "has left us" in a passage that I cannot trace). Surely there must be more than one such slip in a work fifteen hundred pages long devoted by a Russian to a Russian poem; however, the two other Russianisms Mr. Wilson lists are the figments of his own ignorance:

In translating *slushat' shum morskoy* (Eight: IV: 11) I chose the archaic and poetic transitive turn "to listen the sound of the sea" because the relevant passage has in Pushkin a stylized archaic tone. Mr. Wilson may not care for this turn—I do not much care for it either—but it is silly of him to assume that I lapsed into a naïve Russianism not being really aware that, as he tells me, "in English you have to listen *to* something." First, it is Mr. Wilson who is not aware of the fact that there exists an analogous construction in Russian *prislushivat'sya k zvuku,* "to listen closely to the sound"—which, of course, makes nonsense of the exclusive Russianism imagined by him, and secondly, had he happened to leaf through a certain canto of *Don Juan,* written in the year Pushkin was beginning his poem, or a certain *Ode to Memory,* written when Pushkin's poem was being finished, my learned friend would have concluded that Byron ("Listening debates not very wise or witty") and Tennyson ("Listening the lordly music") must have had quite as much Russian blood as Pushkin and I.

In the mazurka of Canto Five one of the dancers "leads Tatiana with Olga" (*podvyol Tat'yanu s Ol'goy*) towards Onegin. This has little to do with the idiomatic *mï s ney* (which is lexically "we with her," but may mean "she and I") that Mr. Wilson mentions. Actually, in order to cram both girls into the first three feet of Five: XLIV: 3, Pushkin allowed himself a minor solecism. The construction *podvyol Tat'yanu i Ol'gu* would have been better Russian (just as "Tatiana and Olga" would have been better English), but it would not have scanned. Now Mr. Wilson should note carefully that this unfortunate *Tat'yanu s Ol'goy* has an additional repercussion: it clashes unpleasantly with the next line where the associative form is compulsory: *Onegin s Ol'goyu poshyol,* "Onegin goes with Olga."

Throughout my translation I remain a thousand times more faithful to Pushkin's Russian than to Wilson's English and therefore in these passages I did not hesitate to reproduce both the solecism and the ensuing clash.

"The handling of French is peculiar," grimly observes Mr. Wilson, and adduces three instances:

"The name of Rousseau's heroine is," he affirms, "given on one page as Julie and on the next as Julia." This is an absurd cavil since she is named Julie, all the thirteen times she is mentioned in the course of the four-page note referring to her (the note to Three: IX: 7), as well as numerous times elsewhere (see Index); but maybe Mr. Wilson has confused her with Augustus' or Byron's girl (see Index again).

The second "peculiar" example refers to the word *monde* in the world-of-fashion sense copiously described in my note to One: V: 8 (*le monde, le beau monde, le grand monde*). According to Mr. Wilson it should always appear with its *"le"* in the translation of the poem. This is an inept practice, of course (advocated mainly by those who, like Mr. Wilson, are insecure and self-conscious in their use of *le* and *la*), and would have resulted in saying *"le* noisy *monde"* instead of "the noisy *monde"* (Eight: XXXIV: 12). English writers of the eighteenth and nineteenth centuries wrote "the *monde,"* not *"le monde."* I am sure that if Mr. Wilson consults the OED, which I do not have here, he will find examples from Walpole, Byron, Thackeray and others. What was good enough for them is good enough for Pushkin and me.

Finally, in this peculiar group of peculiar French there is the word *sauvage,* which according to Mr. Wilson should not have appeared in my rendering of Two: XXV: 5, *dika, pechal'na, molchaliva,* "*sauvage,* sad, silent"; but apart from the fact that it has no exact English equivalent, I chose this signal word to warn readers that Pushkin was using *dika* not simply in the sense of "wild" or "unsociable" but in a Gallic sense as a translation of *"sauvage."* Incidentally, it often occurs in English novels of the time along with *monde* and *ennui.*

"As for the classics," says Mr. Wilson, "Zoilus should be Zoïlus and Eol, Aeolus." But the diacritical sign is quite superfluous in the first case (see, for instance, Webster) and "Eol" is a poetical abbreviation constantly cropping up in English poetry. Moreover, Mr. Wilson can find the full form in my Index. I am unable to prevent my own Zoilus from imitating a bright and saucy schoolboy, but really he should not tell me how to spell the plural of "automaton" which has two endings, both correct. And what business does he have to rebuke me for preferring Theocritus to Virgil and to insinuate that I have read neither?

There is also the strange case of "stuss." "What does N. mean," queries Mr. Wilson, "when he speaks of Pushkin's addiction to stuss? This is not an English word and if he means the Hebrew word for nonsense which has been absorbed into German, it ought to be italicized and capitalized. But even on this assumption it hardly makes sense." This is Mr. Wilson's nonsense, not mine. "Stuss" is the English name of a card game which I discuss at length in my notes on Pushkin's addiction to gambling. Mr. Wilson should really consult *some* of my notes (and Webster's dictionary).

Then there is Mr. Nabokov's style. My style may be all Mr. Wilson says, clumsy, banal, etc. But in regard to the examples he gives it is not *unnecessarily* clumsy, banal, etc. If in translating *toska lyubvi Tat'yanu gonit* (Three: XVI: 1), "the ache of love chases Tatiana" (not "the ache of loss," as Mr. Wilson nonsensically misquotes), I put "chases" instead of the "pursues" that Mr. Wilson has the temerity to propose, I do so not only because "pursues" is in Russian not *gonit* but *presleduet,* but also because, as Mr. Wilson has not noticed, it would be a misleading repetition of the "pursue" used in the preceding stanza (*tebya presleduyut mechtï,* "daydreams pursue you"), and my method is to repeat a term at close range only when Pushkin repeats it.

When the nurse says to Tatiana *nu delo, delo, ne gnevaysya, dusha moya,* and I render it by "this now makes sense, do not be cross with me, my soul," Mr. Wilson in a tone of voice remindful of some seventeenth-century French pedant discoursing on high and low style, declares that "make sense" and "my soul" do not go together, as if he knew which terms in the nurse's Russian go together or do not!

As I have already said, many of the recurring words I use (ache, pal, mollitude, and so on) are what I call "signal words," *i.e.,* terms meant, among other things, to indicate the recurrence of the corresponding Russian word. Style, indeed! It is correct information I wish to give and not samples of "correct style." I translate *ochen' milo postupil . . . nash priyatel'* in the beginning of Four: XVIII (which is also the beginning of the least artistic section in Four: XVIII-XXII) by "very nicely did our pal act," and this Mr. Wilson finds "vulgarly phrased"; but Mr. Wilson stomps in where I barely dare to tread because he is quite unaware that the corresponding Russian phrase is also trite and trivial. There simply exists no other way of rendering that genteel *ochen' milo* (Pushkin is imitating here a simpering reader), and if I chose here and elsewhere the signal word "pal" to render the colloquial turn of *priyatel'*, it is because there exists no other way of expressing it. "Pal" retains the unpleasant flippancy of *priyatel'* as used here, besides reproducing its first and last letters. *Priyatel' Vil'son* would be, for instance, a flippant and nasty phrase, out of place in a serious polemical text. Or does Mr. Wilson really think that the passage in question is better rendered by Professor Arndt? ("My reader, can you help bestowing praise on Eugene for the fine part he played with stricken Tanya?")

Mr. Wilson's last example in the series pertaining to "bad style" has to do with the end of Seven: XXXII. When rendering the elegiac terms in which Tatiana takes leave of her country home, I had to take into account their resemblance to the diction of Pushkin's youthful elegy addressed to a beloved country place (Farewell, ye faithful coppices, etc.), and also to that of Lenski's last poem. It was a question of adjustment and alignment. This is why I have Tatiana say in a stilted and old-fashioned idiom, "Farewell, pacific sites, farewell, secluded (note the old-fashioned pronunciation of the corresponding *uedinen-nïy*) refuge! Shall I see you?" "Such passages," says Mr. Wilson, "sound like the products of those computers which are supposed to translate Russian into English." But since those computers are fed only the basic Russian Mr. Wilson has mastered, and are directed by anthropologists and progressive linguists, the results would be *his* comic versions, and not my clumsy but literal translation.

Probably the most rollicking part of Mr. Wilson's animadversions is the one in which he offers his own mistranslation as the perfection I should have tried to emulate.

My rendering of *gusey kriklivïh karavan tyanulsya k yugu* (Four: XLI: 11 and beginning of 12) is "the caravan of clamorous geese was tending southward" but, as I note in my commentary, *kriklivïh* is lexically "screamy" and the idiomatic *tyanulsya* conveys a very special blend of meaning, with the sense of "progressing in a given direction" predominating over the simple "stretching" obtainable from pocket-dictionaries (see also note to Seven: IV: 14). Mr. Wilson thinks that in his own version of the coming of winter in Four, part of which I quote in my Commentary with charitably italicized errors, he is "almost literally accurate and a good deal more poetically vivid than Nabokov." The "almost" is very lenient since "loud-tongued geese" is much too lyrical and "stretching" fails to bring out the main element of the contextual *tyanulsya*.

A still funnier sight is Mr. Wilson trying to show me how to translate properly *ego loshadka, sneg pochuya, pletyotsya rïs'yu kak nibud'* (Five: II: 3-4) which in my literal rendering is "his naggy, having sensed the snow, shambles at something like a trot." Mr. Wilson's own effort, which goes "his poor (?) horse sniffing (?) the snow, attempting (?) a trot, plods (?) through it (?)," besides being a medley of gross mistranslations, is an example of careless English. If, however, we resist the unfair temptation of imagining Mr. Wilson's horse plodding through my trot and have it plod through Mr. Wilson's snow, we obtain the inept picture of an unfortunate beast of burden laboriously working its way through that snow, whereas in reality Pushkin celebrates relief, not exertions. The peasant is not "rejoicing" or "feeling festive," as paraphrasts have it (not knowing Pushkin's use of *torzhestvovat'* here and elsewhere), but celebrating the coming of winter, since the snow under the sleigh facilitates the little nag's progress and is especially welcome after a long snowless autumn of muddy ruts and reluctant cart wheels.

Although Mr. Wilson finds my Commentary overdone, he cannot help suggesting three additions. In a ludicrous display of pseudo-scholarship he insinuates that I "seem to think" (I do not, and never did) that the application by the French of the word "goddams" to the English (which I do not even discuss) begins in the eighteenth century. He would like me to say that it goes back to the fifteenth century. Why should I? Because he looked it up?

He also would have liked me to mention in connection with the "pensive vampire" (Three: XII: 8) of Polidori's novelette (1819) another variety of vampire which Pushkin alluded to in a poem of 1834 suggested by Mérimée's well-known pastiche. But *that* vampire is the much coarser *vurdalak,* a lowly graveyard ghoul having nothing to do with the romantic allusion in Canto Three (1824); besides he appeared ten years later (and three years after Pushkin had finished *Eugene Onegin*)—quite outside the period limiting my interest in vampires.

The most sophisticated suggestion, however, volunteered by Mr. Wilson, concerns the evolution of the adjective *krasnïy* which "means both red and beautiful." May this not be influenced "by the custom in Old Russia, described in Hakluyt's *Voyages,* of the peasant women's painting large red spots on their cheeks in order to beautify themselves?" This is a preposterous gloss, somehow reminding one of Freud's explaining a patient's passion for young women by the fact that the poor fellow in his self-abusing boyhood used to admire Mt. Jungfrau from the window of a water closet.

I shall not say much about the paragraph that Mr. Wilson devotes to my notes on prosody. It is simply not worth while. He has skimmed my "tedious and interminable appendix" and has not understood what he managed to glean. From our conversations and correspondence in former years I well know that, like Onegin, he is incapable of comprehending the mechanism of verse—either Russian or English. This being so, he should have refrained from "criticizing" my essay on the subject. With one poke of his stubby pencil he reintroduces the wretched old muddle I take such pains to clear up and fussily puts back the "secondary accents" and "spondees" where I show they do not belong. He makes no attempt to assimilate my terminology, he obstinately ignores the similarities and distinctions I discuss, and indeed I cannot believe he has read more than a few lines of the thing.

My "most serious failure," according to Mr. Wilson, "is one of interpretation." Had he read my commentary with more attention he would have seen that I do not believe in *any* kind of "interpretation" so that his or my "interpretation" can be neither a failure nor a success. In other words, I do not believe in the old-fashioned, naïve, and musty method of human-interest criticism championed by Mr. Wilson that consists of removing the characters from an author's imaginary world to the imaginary, but generally far less plausible, world of the critic who then proceeds to examine these displaced characters as if they were "real people." In my commentary I have given examples and made some innocent fun of such criticism (steering clear, however, from any allusion to Mr. Wilson's extraordinary misconceptions in *The Triple Thinkers*).

I have also demonstrated the factual effect of Pushkin's characterizations as related to the structure of the poem. There are certain inconsistencies in his treatment of his hero which are especially evident, and in a way especially attractive, in the beginning of Canto Six. In a note to Six: XXVIII: 7, I stress the uncanny, dreamlike quality of Onegin's behavior just before and during the duel. It is purely a question of architectonics —not of personal interpretation. My facts are objective and irrefutable. I remain with Pushkin in Pushkin's world. I am not concerned with Onegin's being gentle or cruel, energetic or indolent, kind or unkind ("you are simply very kind-hearted," says a woman to him quoted in his diary; he is "*zloy,* unkind," says Mr. Wilson); I am concerned only with Pushkin's overlooking, in the interest of the plot, that Onegin, who according to Pushkin is a punctilious *homme du monde* and an experienced duellist, would hardly choose a servant for second or shoot to kill in the kind of humdrum affair where vanity is amply satisfied by sustaining one's adversary's fire without returning it.

The actual cause of the encounter is however quite plausible in Pushkin: upon finding himself at a huge vulgar feast (Five: XXXI) so unlike the informal party promised him by Lenski (Four: XLIX), Onegin is quite right to be furious with his deceitful or scatterbrained young friend, just as Lenski is quite justified in calling him out for flirting with Olga. Onegin accepts the challenge instead of laughing it off as he would have done if Lenski had chosen a less pedantic second. Pushkin stresses the fact that Onegin "sincerely loves the youth" but that *amour propre* is sometimes stronger than friendship. That is all. One should stick to that and not try to think up "deep" variations which are not even new; for what Mr. Wilson inflicts upon me, in teaching me how to understand Onegin, is the old solemn nonsense of Onegin's hating and envying Lenski for being capable of idealism, devoted love, ecstatic German romanticism and the like "when he himself is so sterile and empty." Actually, it is just as easy, and just as irrelevant (yet more fashionable—Mr. Wilson is behind the times), to argue that

Reply to My Critics

Onegin, not Lenski, is the true idealist, that he loathes Lenski because he perceives in him the future fat swinish squire Lenski is doomed to become, and so he raises slowly his pistol and . . . but Lenski in malignant cold blood is also raising his pistol, and God knows who would have killed whom had not the author followed wisely the old rule of sparing one's more interesting character while the novel is still developing. If anybody takes "a mean advantage," as Mr. Wilson absurdly puts it (none of the principals can derive any special "advantage" in a *duel à volonté*), it is not Onegin, but Pushkin.

So much for my "most serious failure."

All that now remains to be examined is Mr. Wilson's concern for reputations—Pushkin's reputation as a linguist and the reputations of Sainte-Beuve and others as writers.

With an intensity of feeling that he shares with Russian monolinguists who have debated the subject, Mr. Wilson scolds me for underrating Pushkin's knowledge of English and "quite disregarding the evidence." I supply the evidence, not Mr. Wilson, not Sidorov, and not even Pushkin's own father (a cocky old party who maintained that his son used to speak fluent Spanish, let alone English). Had Mr. Wilson carefully consulted my notes to One: XXXVIII: 9, he would have convinced himself that I prove with absolute certainty that neither in 1821, nor 1833, nor 1836, was Pushkin able to understand simple English phrases. My demonstration remains unassailable, and it is this evidence that Mr. Wilson disregards while referring me to stale generalities or to an idiotic anecdote about the Raevski girls' teaching Pushkin English in a Crimean bower. Mr. Wilson knows nothing about the question. He is not even aware that Pushkin got the style of his "Byronic" tales from Pichot and Zhukovski, or that Pushkin's copying out extracts from foreign writers means nothing. Mr. Wilson, too, may have copied extracts, and we see the results. He complains I do not want to admit that Pushkin's competence in language was considerable, but I can only reply that Mr. Wilson's notion of such competence and my notion of it are completely dissimilar. I realize, of course, that my friend has a vested interest in the matter, but I can assure him that Pushkin spoke excellent eighteenth-century French, but had only a gentleman's smattering of other foreign languages.

Finally—Mr. Wilson is horrified by my "instinct to take digs at great reputations." Well, it cannot be helped; Mr. Wilson must accept my instinct, and wait for the next crash. I refuse to be guided and controlled by a communion of established views and academic traditions, as he wants me to be. What right has he to prevent me from finding mediocre and over-rated people like Balzac, Dostoevsky, Sainte-Beuve, or Stendhal, that pet of all those who like their French plain? How much has Mr. Wilson enjoyed Mme de Staël's novels? Has he ever studied Balzac's absurdities and Stendhal's *clichés?* Has he examined the melodramatic muddle and phony mysticism of Dostoevski? Can he really venerate that arch-vulgarian, Sainte-Beuve? And why should I be forbidden to consider that Chaykovski's hideous and insulting libretto is not saved by a music whose cloying banalities have pursued me ever since I was a curly-haired boy in a velvet box? If I am allowed to display my very special and very subjective admiration for Pushkin, Browning, Krïlov, Chateaubriand, Griboedov, Senancour, Küchelbecker, Keats, Hodasevich, to name only a few of those I praise in my notes, I should be also allowed to bolster and circumscribe that praise by pointing out to the reader my favorite bogeys and shams in the hall of false fame.

In his rejoinder to my letter of 26 August 1965, in the *NYR*, Mr. Wilson says that on rereading his article he felt it sounded "more damaging" than he had meant it to be. His article, entirely consisting, as I have shown, of quibbles and blunders, can be damaging only to his own reputation—and that is the last look I shall ever take at the dismal scene.

—VLADIMIR NABOKOV
February 1966

A NOVEL
AND
THREE EXCERPTS

From Despair

~~~~~~

❦ *Chapter Nine* ❦

To tell the truth, I feel rather weary. I keep on writing from noon to dawn, producing a chapter per day—or more. What a great powerful thing art is! In my situation, I ought to be flustering, scurrying, doubling back. . . . There is of course no immediate danger, and I dare say such danger there will never be, but, nevertheless, it is a singular reaction, this sitting still and writing, writing, writing, or ruminating at length, which is much the same, really. And the further I write, the clearer it becomes that I will not leave matters so but hang on till my main object is attained, when I will most certainly take the risk of having my work published—not much of a risk, either, for as soon as my manuscript is sent out I shall fade away, the world being large enough to afford a place of concealment to a quiet man with a beard.

It was not spontaneously that I decided to forward my work to the penetrating novelist, whom, I think, I have mentioned already, even addressing him personally through the medium of my story.

I may be mistaken, as I have long ago abandoned reading over what I write—no time left for that, let alone its nauseating effect upon me.

I had first toyed with the idea of sending the thing straight to some editor—German, French, or American—but it is written in Russian and not all is translatable, and—well, to be frank, I am rather particular about my literary coloratura and firmly believe that the loss of a single shade or inflection would hopelessly mar the whole. I have also thought of sending it to the U.S.S.R., but I lack the necessary addresses, nor do I know how it is done and whether my manuscript would be read, for I employ, by force of habit, the Old-Regime spelling, and to re-write it would be quite beyond my powers. Did I say "rewrite"? Well, I hardly know if I shall stand the strain of writing it at all.

Having at last made up my mind to give my manuscript to one who is sure to like it and do his best to have it published, I am fully aware of the fact that my chosen one (you, my first reader) is an *émigré* novelist, whose books cannot possibly ap-pear in the U.S.S.R. Maybe, however, an exception will be made for this book, considering that it was not you who actually wrote it. Oh, how I cherish the hope that in spite of your *émigré* signature (the diaphanous spuriousness of which will deceive nobody) my book may find a market in the U.S.S.R.! As I am far from being an enemy of the Soviet rule, I am sure to have unwittingly expressed certain notions in my book, which correspond perfectly to the dialectical demands of the current moment. It even seems to me sometimes that my basic theme, the resemblance between two persons, has a profound al-legorical meaning. This remarkable physical likeness probably appealed to me (subconsciously!) as the promise of that ideal sameness which is to unite people in the classless society of the future; and by striving to make use of an isolated case, I was, though still blind to social truths, fulfilling, nevertheless, a cer-tain social function. And then there is something else; the fact of my not being wholly successful when putting that resem-blance of ours to practical use can be explained away by purely social-economic causes, that is to say, by the fact that Felix and I belonged to different, sharply defined classes, the fusion of which none can hope to achieve single-handed, especially now-adays, when the conflict of classes has reached a stage where compromise is out of the question. True, my mother was of

low birth and my father's father herded geese in his youth,
which explains where, exactly, a man of my stamp and habits
could have got that strong, though still incompletely expressed
leaning towards Genuine Consciousness. In fancy, I visualize a
new world, where all men will resemble one another as Hermann and Felix did; a world of Helixes and Fermanns; a
world where the worker fallen dead at the feet of his machine
will be at once replaced by his perfect double smiling the serene
smile of perfect socialism. Therefore I do think that Soviet
youths of today should derive considerable benefit from a
study of my book under the supervision of an experienced
Marxist who would help them to follow through its pages the
rudimentary wriggles of the social message it contains. Aye, let
other nations, too, translate it into their respective languages,
so that American readers may satisfy their craving for gory
glamour; the French discern mirages of sodomy in my partiality
for a vagabond; and Germans relish the skittish side of a semi-
Slavonic soul. Read, read it, as many as possible, ladies and
gentlemen! I welcome you all as my readers.

Not an easy book to write, though. It is now especially, just
as I am getting to the part which treats, so to speak, of decisive
action, it is now that the arduousness of my task appears to me
in full; here I am, as you see, twisting and turning and being
garrulous about matters which rightly belong to the preface of
a book and are misplaced in what the reader may deem its most
essential chapter. But I have tried to explain already that, however shrewd and wary the approaches may seem, it is not my
rational part which is writing, but solely my memory, that devious memory of mine. For, you see, *then,* i.e. at the precise
hour at which the hands of my story have stopped, I had
stopped too; was dallying, as I am dallying now; was engaged
in a similar kind of tangled reasoning having nothing to do with
my business, the appointed hour of which was steadily nearing.
I had started in the morning though my meeting with Felix was
fixed for five o'clock in the afternoon, but I had been unable to

stay at home, so that now I was wondering how to dispose of all that dull-white mass of time separating me from my appointment. I sat at my ease, even somnolently, as I steered with one finger and slowly drove through Berlin, down quiet, cold, whispering streets; and so it went on and on, until I noticed that I had left Berlin behind. The colors of the day were reduced to a mere two: black (the pattern of the bare trees, the asphalt) and whitish (the sky, the patches of snow). It continued, my sleepy transportation. For some time there dangled before my eyes one of those large, ugly rags that a truck trundling something long and poky is required to hang on the protruding hind end; then it disappeared, having presumably taken a turning. Still I did not move on any quicker. A taxicab dashed out of a side street in front of me, put on the brakes with a screech, and owing to the road being rather slippery, went into a grotesque spin. I calmly sailed past, as if drifting downstream. Farther, a woman in deep mourning was crossing obliquely, practically with her back to me; I neither sounded my horn, nor changed my quiet smooth motion, but glided past within a couple of inches from the edge of her veil; she did not even notice me—a noiseless ghost. Every kind of vehicle overtook me; for quite a while a crawling tramcar kept abreast of me; and out of the corner of my eye I could see the passengers, stupidly sitting face to face. Once or twice I struck a badly cobbled stretch; and hens were already appearing; short wings expanded and long necks stretched out, this fowl or that would come running across the road. A little later I found myself driving along an endless highway, past stubbled fields with snow lying here and there; and in a perfectly deserted locality my car seemed to sink into a slumber, as if turning from blue to dove-gray—slowing down gradually and coming to a stop, and I leaned my head on the wheel in a fit of elusive musing. What could my thoughts be about? About nothing or nothings; it was all very involved and I was almost asleep, and in a half swoon I kept deliberating with myself about some nonsense, kept remembering some discussion I had had with somebody once on some station platform as to whether one ever sees the sun in one's dreams, and presently the feeling grew upon me that there was a great number of people around, all speaking together, and then falling silent and giving one another dim errands and dispersing without a sound. After some time I moved on, and at noon, dragging through some village, I decided to halt, since even at such a drowsy pace I was bound to reach Koenigsdorf in an hour or so, and that was still too early. So I dawdled in a dark and dismal beer house, where I sat quite alone in a back room of sorts, at a big table, and there was an old photograph on the wall—a group of men in frock coats, with curled-up moustachios, and some in the front row had bent one knee with a carefree expression and two at the sides had even stretched themselves seal fashion, and this called to my mind similar groups of Russian students. I had a lot of lemon water there and resumed my journey in the same sleepy mood, quite indecently sleepy, in fact. Next, I remember stopping at some bridge: an old woman in blue woolen trousers and with a bag behind her shoulders was busy repairing some mishap to her bicycle. Without getting out of my car I gave her several pieces of advice, all quite unbidden and useless; and after that I was silent, and propping my cheek with my fist, remained gaping at her for a long time: there she was fussing and fussing, but at last my eyelids twitched and lo, there was no woman there: she had wobbled away long ago. I pursued my course, trying, as I did, to multiply in my head one uncouth number by another just as awkward. I did not know what they signified and whence they had floated up, but since they had come I considered it fit to bait them, and so they grappled and dissolved. All of a sudden it struck me that I was driving at a crazy speed; that the car was lapping up the road, like a conjurer swallowing yards of ribbon; but I glanced at the speedometer-needle: it was trembling at fifty kilometers; and there passed by, in slow succession, pines, pines, pines. Then, too, I remember meeting two small pale-faced schoolboys with their books held together by a strap; and I talked to them. They both had unpleasant birdlike features, making me think of young crows. They seemed to be a little afraid of me, and when I drove off, kept staring after me, black mouths wide open, one taller, the other shorter. And then, with a start, I noticed that I had reached Koenigsdorf and, looking at my watch, saw that it was almost five. When passing the red station-building, I reflected that perchance Felix was late and had not yet come down those steps I saw beyond that gaudy chocolate-stand, and that there were no means whatever of deducing from the exterior air of that squat brick edifice whether he had already passed there or not. However that might be, the train by which he had been ordered to come to Koenigsdorf arrived at 2:55, so that if Felix had not missed it—

Oh, my reader! He had been told to get off at Koenigsdorf and march north following the highway as far as the tenth kilometer marked by a yellow post; and now I was tearing along that road: unforgettable moments! Not a soul about. During winter the bus ran there but twice a day—morning and noon; on the entire ten kilometers' stretch all that I met was a cart drawn by a bay horse. At last, in the distance, like a yellow finger, the familiar post stood up, grew bigger, attained its natural size; it wore a skullcap of snow. I pulled up and looked about me. Nobody. The yellow post was very yellow indeed. To my right, beyond the field, the wood was painted a flat gray on the backdrop of the pale sky. Nobody. I got out of my car and with a bang that was louder than any shot, slammed the door after me. And all at once I noticed that, from behind the interlaced twigs of a bush growing in the ditch, there stood looking at me, as pink as a waxwork and with a jaunty little mustache, and, really, quite gay—

Placing one foot on the footboard of the car and like an enraged tenor slashing my hand with the glove I had taken off, I glared steadily at Felix. Grinning uncertainly, he came out of the ditch.

"You scoundrel," I uttered through my teeth with extraordinary operatic force, "you scoundrel and double-crosser," I

repeated, now giving my voice full scope and slashing myself
with the glove still more furiously (all was rumble and thunder
in the orchestra between my vocal outbursts). "How did you
dare blab, you cur? How did you dare, how did you dare ask
others for advice, boast that you had had your way and that at
such a date and at such a place— Oh, you deserve to be shot!"
—(growing din, clangor, and then again my voice)—"Much
have you gained, idiot! The game's up, you've blundered
badly, not a groat will you see, baboon!" (crash of cymbals in
the orchestra).

Thus I swore at him, with cold avidity observing the while
his expression. He was utterly taken aback; and honestly of-
fended. Pressing one hand to his breast, he kept shaking his
head. That fragment of opera came to an end, and the broadcast speaker resumed in his usual voice:

"Let it pass—I've been scolding you like that, as a pure formality, to be on the safe side. . . . My dear fellow, you do
look funny, it's a regular makeup!"

By my special order, he had let his mustache grow; even
waxed it, I think. Apart from that, on his own account, he had
allowed his face a couple of curled cutlets. I found that pretentious growth highly entertaining.

"You have, of course, come by the way I told you?" I inquired, smiling.

"Yes," he replied, "I followed your orders. As for bragging
—well, you know yourself, I'm a lonely man and no good at
chatting with people."

"I know, and join you in your sighs. Tell me, did you meet
anyone on this road?"

"When I saw a cart or something, I hid in the ditch, as you
told me to do."

"Splendid. Your features anyhow are sufficiently concealed.
Well, no good loafing about here. Get into the car. Oh, leave
that alone—you'll take off your bag afterwards. Get in quick,
we must drive off."

"Where to?" he queried.

334 A NOVEL AND THREE EXCERPTS

"Into that wood."

"There?" he asked and pointed with his stick.

"Yes, right there. Will you or won't you get in, damn you?"

He surveyed the car contentedly. Without hurry he climbed in and sat down beside me.

I turned the steering wheel, with the car slowly moving. Ick. And once again: ick. (We left the road for the field.) Under the tires thin snow and dead grass crackled. The car bounced on humps of ground, we bounced too. He spoke the while:

"I'll manage this car without any trouble (bump). Lord, what a ride I'll take (bump). Never fear (bump-bump) I won't do it any harm!"

"Yes, the car will be yours. For a short space of time (bump) yours. Now, keep awake, my fellow, look about you. There's nobody on the road, is there?"

He glanced back and then shook his head. We drove, or better say crept, up a gentle and fairly smooth slope into the forest. There, among the foremost pines, we stopped and got out. No more with the longing of ogling indigence, but with an owner's quiet satisfaction, Felix continued to admire the glossy blue Icarus. A dreamy look then came into his eyes. Quite likely (please, note that I am asserting nothing, merely saying: "quite likely") quite likely then, his thoughts flowed as follows: "What if I slip away in this natty two-seater? I get the cash in advance, so that's all right. I'll let him believe I'm going to do what he wants, and roll away instead, far away. He just can't inform the police, so he'll have to keep quiet. And me, in my own car—"

I interrupted the course of those pleasant thoughts.

"Well, Felix, the great moment has come. You're to change your clothes and remain in the car all alone in this wood. In half an hour's time it will begin to grow dark; no risk of anyone intruding upon you. You'll spend the night here—you'll have my overcoat on—just feel how nice and thick it is—ah, I thought so; besides, the car is quite warm inside, you'll sleep perfectly; then, as soon as day begins to break— But we'll discuss that afterwards; let me first give you the necessary appearance, or we'll never have done before dark. To start with, you must have a shave."

"A shave?" Felix repeated after me, with silly surprise. "How's that? I've got no razor with me, and I really don't know what one can find in a wood to shave with, barring stones."

"Why stones? Such a blockhead as you ought to be shaven with an axe. But I have thought of everything. I've brought the instrument, and I'll do it myself."

"Well, that's mighty funny," he chuckled. "Wonder what'll come of it. Now, mind you don't cut my throat with that razor of yours."

"Don't be afraid, you fool, it's a safety one. So, please. . . . Yes, sit down somewhere. Here, on the footboard, if you like."

He sat down after having shaken off his knapsack. I produced my parcel and placed the shaving articles on the footboard. Had to hurry: the day looked pinched and wan, the air grew duller and duller. And what a hush. . . . It seemed, that silence, inherent, inseparable from those motionless boughs, those straight trunks, those lusterless patches of snow here and there on the ground.

I took off my overcoat so as to operate with more freedom. Felix was curiously examining the bright teeth of the safety razor and its silvery grip. Then he examined the shaving brush; put it to his cheek to test its softness; it was, indeed, delightfully fluffy: I had paid seventeen marks fifty for it. He was quite fascinated, too, by the tube of expensive shaving cream.

"Come, let's begin," I said. "Shaving and waving. Sit a little sideways, please, otherwise I can't get at you properly."

I took a handful of snow, squeezed out a curling worm of soap into it, beat it up with the brush and applied the icy lather to his whiskers and mustache. He made faces, leered; a frill of lather had invaded one nostril: he wrinkled his nose, because it tickled.

"Head back," I said, "farther still."

Rather awkwardly resting my knee on the footboard, I started scraping his whiskers off; the hairs crackled, and there was something disgusting in the way they got mixed up with the foam; I cut him slightly, and that stained it with blood. When I attacked his mustache, he puckered up his eyes, but bravely made no sound, although it must have been anything but pleasant: I was working hastily, his bristles were tough, the razor pulled.

"Got a handkerchief?" I asked.

He drew some rag out of his pocket. I used it to wipe away from his face, very carefully, blood, snow and lather. His cheeks shone now—brand new. He was gloriously shaven; in one place only, near the ear, there showed a red scratch running into a little ruby which was about to turn black. He passed his palm over the shaven parts.

"Wait a bit," I said, "that's not all. Your eyebrows need improving: they're somewhat thicker than mine."

I produced scissors and neatly clipped off a few hairs.

"That's capital now. As to your hair, I'll brush it when you've changed your shirt."

"Going to give me yours?" he asked, and deliberately felt the silk of my shirt collar.

"Hullo, your fingernails are not exactly clean!" I exclaimed blithely.

Many a time had I done Lydia's hands—I was good at it, so that now I had not much difficulty in putting those ten rude nails in order, and while doing so I kept comparing our hands: his were larger and darker; but never mind, I thought, they'll pale by and by. As I never wore any wedding ring, all I had to add to his hand was my wrist watch. He moved his fingers, turning his wrist this way and that, very pleased.

"Now, quick. Let's change. Take off everything, my friend, to the last stitch."

"Ugh," grunted Felix, "it'll be cold."

"Never mind. Takes one minute only. Please hurry up."

He removed his old brown coat, pulled off his dark, shaggy sweater over his head. The shirt underneath was a muddy green with a tie of the same material. Then he took off his formless shoes, peeled off his socks (darned by a masculine hand) and hiccuped ecstatically as his bare toe touched the wintry soil. Your common man loves to go barefoot: in summer, on gay grass, the very first thing he does is take off his shoes and socks; but in winter, too, it is no mean pleasure—recalling as it does one's childhood, perhaps, or something like that.

I stood aloof, undoing my cravat, and kept looking at Felix attentively.

"Go on, go on," I cried, noticing that he had slowed down a bit.

It was not without a bashful little squirm that he let his trousers slip down from his white hairless thighs. Lastly he took off his shirt. In the cold wood there stood in front of me a naked man.

Incredibly fast, with the flick and dash of a Fregoli, I undressed, tossed over to him my outer envelope of shirt and drawers, deftly, while he was laboriously putting that on, plucked out of the suit I had shed several things—money, cigarette-case, brooch, gun—and stuffed them into the pockets of the tightish trousers which I had drawn on with the swiftness of a variety virtuoso. Although his sweater proved to be warm enough, I kept my muffler, and as I had lost weight lately, his coat fitted me almost to perfection. Should I offer him a cigarette? No, that would be in bad taste.

Felix meanwhile had attired himself in my shirt and drawers; his feet were still bare, I gave him socks and garters, but noticed all at once that his toes needed some trimming too. . . . He placed his foot on the footboard of the car and we got in a bit of hasty pedicuring. They snapped loud and flew far, those ugly black parings, and in recent dreams I have often seen them speckling the ground much too conspicuously. I am afraid he had time to catch a chill, poor soul, standing there in his shirt.

Then he washed his feet with snow, as some bathless rake in Maupassant does, and pulled on the socks, without noticing the hole in one heel.

"Hurry up, hurry up," I kept repeating. "It'll be dark presently, and I must be going. See. I'm already dressed. God, what big shoes! And where is that cap of yours? Ah, here it is, thanks."

He belted the trousers. With the provident help of the shoehorn he squeezed his feet into my black buckskin shoes. I helped him to cope with the spats and the lilac necktie. Finally, gingerly taking his comb, I smoothed his greasy hair well back from brow and temples.

He was ready now. There he stood before me, my double, in my quiet dark-gray suit. Surveyed himself with a foolish smile. Investigated pockets. Was pleased with the lighter. Replaced the odds and ends, but opened the wallet. It was empty.

"You promised me money in advance," said Felix coaxingly.

"That's right," I replied withdrawing my hand from my pocket and disclosing a fistful of notes. "Here it is. I'll count out your share and give it you in a minute. What about those shoes, do they hurt?"

"They do," said Felix. "They hurt dreadfully. But I'll hold out somehow. I'll take them off for the night, I expect. And where must I go with that car tomorrow?"

"Presently, presently. . . . I'll make it all clear. Look, the place ought to be tidied up. . . . You've scattered your rags. . . . What have you got in that bag?"

"I'm like a snail, I carry my house on my back," said Felix. "Are you taking the bag with you? I've got half a sausage in it. Like to have some?"

"Later. Pack in all those things, will you? That shoehorn too. And the scissors. Good. Now put on my overcoat and let us verify for the last time whether you can pass for me."

"You won't forget the money?" he inquired.

"I keep on telling you I won't. Don't be an ass. We are on

the point of settling it. The cash is here, in my pocket—in your former pocket, to be correct. Now, buck up, please."

He got into my handsome camel-hair overcoat and (with special care) put on my elegant hat. Then came the last touch: yellow gloves.

"Good. Just take a few steps. Let's see how it all fits you."

He came toward me, now thrusting his hands into his pockets, now drawing them out again.

When he got quite near, he squared his shoulders, pretending to swagger, aping a fop.

"Is that all, is that all," I kept saying aloud. "Wait, let me have a thorough— Yes, seems to be all. . . . Now turn, I'd like a back view—"

He turned, and I shot him between the shoulders.

I remember various things: that puff of smoke, hanging in midair, then displaying a transparent fold and vanishing slowly; the way Felix fell; for he did not fall at once; first he terminated a movement still related to life, and that was a full turn almost; he intended, I think, swinging before me in jest, as before a mirror; so that, inertly bringing that poor piece of foolery to an end, he (already pierced) came to face me, slowly spread his hands as if asking: "What's the meaning of this?"—and getting no reply, slowly collapsed backward. Yes, I remember all that; I remember, too, the shuffling sound he made on the snow, when he began to stiffen and jerk, as if his new clothes were uncomfortable; soon he was still, and then the rotation of the earth made itself felt, and only his hat moved quietly, separating from his crown and falling back, mouth opened, as if it were saying "good-bye" for its owner (or again, bringing to one's mind the stale sentence: "all present bared their heads"). Yes, I remember all that, but there is one thing memory misses: the report of my shot. True, there remained in my ears a persistent singing. It clung to me and crept over me, and trembled upon my lips. Through that veil of sound, I went up to the body and, with avidity, looked.

There are mysterious moments and that was one of them. Like an author reading his work over a thousand times, probing and testing every syllable, and finally unable to say of this brindle of words whether it is good or not, so it happened with me, so it happened— But there is the maker's secret certainty; which never can err. At that moment when all the required features were fixed and frozen, our likeness was such that really I could not say who had been killed, I or he. And while I looked, it grew dark in the vibrating wood, and with that face before me slowly dissolving, vibrating fainter and fainter, it seemed as if I were looking at my image in a stagnant pool.

Being afraid to besmirch myself I did not handle the body; did not ascertain whether it was indeed quite, quite dead; I knew instinctively that it was so, that my bullet had slid with perfect exactitude along the short, air-dividing furrow which both will and eye had grooved. Must hurry, must hurry, cried old Mister Murry, as he thrust his arms through his pants. Let us not imitate him. Swiftly, sharply, I looked about me. Felix had put everything, except the pistol, into the bag himself; yet I had self-possession enough to make sure he had not dropped anything; and I even went so far as to brush the footboard where I had been cutting his nails and to unbury his comb which I had trampled into the ground but now decided to discard later. Next I accomplished something planned a long time ago: I had turned the car and stopped it on a bit of timbered ground slightly sloping down, roadward; I now rolled my little Icarus a few yards forward so as to make it visible in the morning from the highway, thus leading to the discovery of my corpse.

Night came sweeping down rapidly. The drumming in my ears had all but died away. I plunged into the wood, repassing as I did so, not far from the body; but I did not stop any more— only picked up the bag, and, unflinchingly, at a smart pace, as if indeed I had not those stone-heavy shoes on my feet, I went round the lake, never leaving the forest, on and on, in the ghostly gloaming, among ghostly snow. . . . But how beautifully I knew the right direction, how accurately, how vividly I had visualized it all, when, in summer, I used to study the paths leading to Eichenberg!

I reached the station in time. Ten minutes later, with the serviceableness of an apparition, there arrived the train I wanted. I spent half the night in a clattering, swaying third-class carriage, on a hard bench, and next to me were two elderly men, playing cards, and the cards they used were extraordinary: large, red and green, with acorns and beehives. After midnight I had to change; a couple of hours later I was already moving westwards; then, in the morning, I changed anew, this time into a fast train. Only then, in the solitude of the lavatory, did I examine the contents of the knapsack. Besides the things crammed into it lately (blood-stained handkerchief included), I found a few shirts, a piece of sausage, two large apples, a leathern sole, five marks in a lady's purse, a passport; and my letters to Felix. The apples and sausage I ate there and then, in the W.C.; but I put the letters into my pocket and examined the passport with the liveliest interest. It was in good order. He had been to Mons and Metz. Oddly enough, his pictured face did not resemble mine closely; it could, of course, easily pass for my photo—still, that made an odd impression upon me, and I remember thinking that here was the real cause of his being so little aware of our likeness: he saw himself in a glass, that is to say, from right to left, not sunway as in reality. Human fat-headedness, carelessness, slackness of senses, all this was revealed by the fact that even the official definitions in the brief list of personal features did not quite correspond with the epithets in my own passport (left at home). A trifle to be sure, but a characteristic one. And under "profession," he, that numbskull, who had played the fiddle, surely, in the way lackadaisical footmen in Russia used to twang guitars on summer evenings, was called a "musician," which at once turned me into a musician too. Later in the day, at a small border town,

I purchased a suitcase, an overcoat, and so forth, upon which both bag and gun were discarded—no, I will not say what I did with them: be silent, Rhenish waters! And presently, a very unshaven gentleman in a cheap black overcoat was on the safer side of the frontier and heading south.

Translated by Dmitri Nabokov
and the author

From Invitation to a Beheading

~~~

✍ *Chapter Eight* ✍

(There are some who sharpen a pencil toward themselves, as if they were peeling a potato, and there are others who slice away from themselves, as though whittling a stick . . . Rodion was of the latter number. He had an old penknife with several blades and a corkscrew. The corkscrew slept on the outside.)

"Today is the eighth day" (wrote Cincinnatus with the pencil, which had lost more than a third of its length) "and not only am I still alive, that is, the sphere of my own self still limits and eclipses my being, but, like any other mortal, I do not know my mortal hour and can apply to myself a formula that holds for everyone: the probability of a future decreases in inverse proportion to its theoretical remoteness. Of course in my case discretion requires that I think in terms of very small numbers —but that is all right, that is all right—I am alive. I had a strange sensation last night—and it was not the first time—: I am taking off layer after layer, until at last . . . I do not know how to describe it, but I know this: through the process of gradual divestment I reach the final, indivisible, firm, radiant point, and this point says: I am! like a pearl ring embedded in a shark's gory fat—O my eternal, my eternal . . . and this point is enough for me—actually nothing more is necessary. Perhaps as a citizen of the next century, a guest who has arrived ahead of time (the hostess is not yet up), perhaps sim-

ply a carnival freak in a gaping, hopelessly festive world, I have
lived an agonizing life, and I would like to describe that agony
to you—but I am obsessed by the fear that there will not be
time enough. As far back as I can remember myself—and I remember myself with lawless lucidity, I have been my own accomplice, who knows too much, and therefore is dangerous. I
issue from such burning blackness, I spin like a top, with such
propelling force, such tongues of flame, that to this day I occasionally feel (sometimes during sleep, sometimes while im-
mersing myself in very hot water) that primordial palpitation
of mine, that first branding contact, the mainspring of my "I."
How I wriggled out, slippery, naked! Yes, from a realm forbidden and inaccessible to others, yes. I know something, yes
. . . but even now, when it is all over anyway, even now—I
am afraid that I may corrupt someone? Or will nothing come
of what I am trying to tell, its only vestiges being the corpses
of strangled words, like hanged men . . . evening silhouettes
of gammas and gerunds, gallow crows—I think I should prefer
the rope, since I know authoritatively and irrevocably that it
shall be the ax; a little time gained, time, which is now so precious to me that I value every respite, every postponement
. . . I mean time allotted to thinking; the furlough I allow my
thoughts for a free journey from fact to fantasy and return
. . . I mean much more besides, but lack of writing skill, haste,
excitement, weakness . . . I know something. I know something. But expression of it comes so hard! No, I cannot . . . I
would like to give up—yet I have the feeling of boiling and rising, a tickling, which may drive you mad if you do not express
it somehow. Oh no, I do not gloat over my own person, I do not
get all hot wrestling with my soul in a darkened room; I have
no desires, save the desire to express myself—in defiance of all
the world's muteness. How frightened I am. How sick with
fright. But no one shall take me away from myself. I am frightened—and now I am losing some thread, which I held so pal-
pably only a moment ago. Where is it? It has slipped out of my

grasp! I am trembling over the paper, chewing the pencil through to the lead, hunching over to conceal myself from the door through which a piercing eye stings me in the nape, and it seems I am right on the verge of crumpling everything and tearing it up. I am here through an error—not in this prison, specifically—but in this whole terrible, striped world; a world which seems not a bad example of amateur craftsmanship, but is in reality calamity, horror, madness, error—and look, the curio slays the tourist, the gigantic carved bear brings its wooden mallet down upon me. And yet, ever since early childhood, I have had dreams . . . In my dreams the world was ennobled, spiritualized; people whom in the waking state I feared so much appeared there in a shimmering refraction, just as if they were imbued with and enveloped by that vibration of light which in sultry weather inspires the very outlines of objects with life; their voices, their step, the expressions of their eyes and even of their clothes—acquired an exciting significance; to put it more simply, in my dreams the world would come alive, becoming so captivatingly majestic, free and ethereal, that afterwards it would be oppressive to breathe the dust of this painted life. But then I have long since grown accustomed to the thought that what we call dreams is semi-reality, the promise of reality, a foreglimpse and a whiff of it; that is, they contain, in a very vague, diluted state, more genuine reality than our vaunted waking life which, in its turn, is semi-sleep, an evil drowsiness into which penetrate in grotesque disguise the sounds and sights of the real world, flowing beyond the periphery of the mind—as when you hear during sleep a dreadful insidious tale because a branch is scraping on the pane, or see yourself sinking into snow because your blanket is sliding off. But how I fear awakening! How I fear that second, or rather split second, already cut short then, when, with a lumberjack's grunt— But what is there to fear? Will it not be for me simply the shadow of an ax, and shall I not hear the downward vigorous grunt with the ear of a different world? Still I am afraid! One cannot write it off so easily. Neither is it good that my thoughts keep getting sucked into the cavity of the future—I want to think about something else, clarify other things . . . but I write obscurely and limply, like Pushkin's lyrical duelist. Soon, I think, I shall evolve a third eye on the back of my neck, between my brittle vertebrae: a mad eye, wide open, with a dilating pupil and pink venation on the glossy ball. Keep away! Even stronger, more hoarsely: hands off! I can foresee it all! And how often do my ears ring with the sob I am destined to emit and the terrible gurgling cough, uttered by the beheaded tyro. But all of this is not the point, and my discourse on dreams and waking is also not the point . . . Wait! There, I feel once again that I shall really express myself, shall bring the words to bay. Alas, no one taught me this kind of chase, and the ancient inborn art of writing is long since forgotten—forgotten are the days when it needed no schooling, but ignited and blazed like a forest fire—today it seems just as incredible as the music that once used to be extracted from a monstrous pianoforte, music that would nimbly ripple or suddenly hack the world into great, gleaming blocks—I myself picture all this so clearly, but you are not I, and therein lies the irreparable calamity. Not knowing how to write, but sensing with my criminal intuition how words are combined, what one must do for a commonplace word to come alive and to share its neighbor's sheen, heat, shadow, while reflecting itself in its neighbor and renewing the neighboring word in the process, so that the whole line is live iridescence; while I sense the nature of this kind of word propinquity, I am nevertheless unable to achieve it, yet that is what is indispensable to me for my task, a task of not now and not here. Not here! The horrible 'here,' the dark dungeon, in which a relentlessly howling heart is encarcerated, this 'here' holds and constricts me. But what gleams shine through at night, and what— It exists, my dream world, it must exist, since, surely there must be an original of the clumsy copy. Dreamy, round, and blue, it turns slowly to-

ward me. It is as if you are lying supine, with eyes closed, on
an overcast day, and suddenly the gloom stirs under your eyelids, and slowly becomes first a langorous smile, then a warm
feeling of contentment, and you know that the sun has come
out from behind the clouds. With just such a feeling my world
begins: the misty air gradually clears, and it is suffused with
such radiant, tremulous kindness, and my soul expands so
freely in its native realm.—But then what, then what? Yes,
that is the line beyond which I lose control . . . Brought up
into the air, the word bursts, as burst those spherical fishes
that breathe and blaze only in the compressed murk of the
depths when brought up in the net. However I am making one
last effort—and I think I have caught my prey . . . but it is
only a fleeting apparition of my prey! *There, tam, là-bas,* the
gaze of men glows with inimitable understanding; *there* the
freaks that are tortured here walk unmolested; *there* time takes
shape according to one's pleasure, like a figured rug whose folds
can be gathered in such a way that two designs will meet—and
the rug is once again smoothed out, and you live on, or else
superimpose the next image on the last, endlessly, endlessly,
with the leisurely concentration of a woman selecting a belt
to go with her dress—now she glides in my direction, rhythmically butting the velvet with her knees, comprehending everything and comprehensible to me . . . *There, there* are the
originals of those gardens where we used to roam and hide
in this world; *there* everything strikes one by its bewitching
evidence, by the simplicity of perfect good; *there* everything
pleases one's soul, everything is filled with the kind of fun that
children know; *there* shines the mirror that now and then
sends a chance reflection here . . . And what I say is not it,
not quite it, and I am getting mixed up, getting nowhere, talking nonsense, and the more I move about and search in the
water where I grope on the sandy bottom for a glimmer I have
glimpsed, the muddier the water grows, and the less likely it
becomes that I shall grasp it. No, I have as yet said nothing, or,

rather, said only bookish words . . . and in the end the logical thing would be to give up and I would give up if I were laboring for a reader existing today, but as there is in the world
not a single human who can speak my language; or, more simply, not a single human who can speak; or, even more simply,
not a single human; I must think only of myself, of that force
which urges me to express myself. I am cold, weakened, afraid,
the back of my head blinks and cringes, and once again gazes
with insane intensity, but, in spite of everything, I am chained
to this table like a cup to a drinking fountain, and will not rise
till I have said what I want. I repeat (gathering new momentum in the rhythm of repetitive incantations), I repeat: there
is something I know, there is something I know, there is something. . . . When still a child, living still in a canary-yellow,
large, cold house where they were preparing me and hundreds
of other children for secure nonexistence as adult dummies,
into which all my coevals turned without effort or pain; already
then, in those accursed days, amid rag books and brightly
painted school materials and soul-chilling drafts, I knew without knowing, I knew without wonder, I knew as one knows
oneself, I knew what it is impossible to know—and, I would
say, I knew it even more clearly than I do now. For life has
worn me down: continual uneasiness, concealment of my
knowledge, pretense, fear, a painful straining of all my nerves
—not to let down, not to ring out . . . and even to this day I
still feel an ache in that part of my memory where the very
beginning of this effort is recorded, that is, the occasion when I
first understood that things which to me had seemed natural
were actually forbidden, impossible, that any thought of them
was criminal. Well do I remember that day! I must have just
learned how to make letters, since I remember myself wearing on my fifth finger the little copper ring that was given to
children who already knew how to copy the model words from
the flower beds in the school garden, where petunias, phlox
and marigold spelled out lengthy adages. I was sitting with my

feet up on the low window sill and looking down as my school-mates, dressed in the same kind of long pink smocks as I, held hands and circled around a beribboned pole. Why was I left out? In punishment? No. Rather, the reluctance of the other children to have me in their game and the mortal embarrass-ment, shame and dejection I myself felt when I joined them made me prefer that white nook of the sill, sharply marked off by the shadow of the half-open casement. I could hear the ex-clamations required by the game and the strident commands of the red-haired 'pedagoguette'; I could see her curls and her spectacles, and with the squeamish horror that never left me I watched her give the smallest children shoves to make them whirl faster. And that teacher, and the striped pole, and the white clouds, now and then letting through the gliding sun, which would suddenly spill out passionate light, searching for something, were all repeated in the flaming glass of the open window . . . In short, I felt such fear and sadness that I tried to submerge within myself, to slow down and slip out of the senseless life that was carrying me onward. Just then, at the end of the stone gallery where I was sitting, appeared the senior educator—I do not recall his name—a fat, sweaty, shaggy-chested man, who was on his way to the bathing place. While still at a distance he shouted to me, his voice amplified by the acoustics, to go into the garden; he approached quickly and flourished his towel. In my sadness, in my abstraction, uncon-sciously and innocently, instead of descending into the garden by the stairs (the gallery was on the third floor), not thinking what I was doing, but really acting obediently, even submis-sively, I stepped straight from the window sill onto the elastic air and—feeling nothing more than a half-sensation of bare-footedness (even though I had shoes on)—slowly and quite naturally strode forward, still absently sucking and examining the finger in which I had caught a splinter that morning . . . Suddenly, however, an extraordinary, deafening silence brought me out of my reverie, and I saw below me, like pale daisies, the upturned faces of the stupefied children, and the pedagoguette, who seemed to be falling backward; I saw also the globes of the trimmed shrubs, and the falling towel that had not yet reached the lawn; I saw myself, a pink-smocked boy, standing transfixed in midair; turning around, I saw, but three aerial paces from me, the window I had just left, and, his hairy arm extended in malevolent amazement, the—"

(Here, unfortunately, the light in the cell went out—Rodion always turned it off exactly at ten.)

Translated by Dmitri Nabokov
and the author

From The Gift

~~~~~

Yasha and I had entered Berlin University at almost exactly the same time, but I did not know him although we must have passed each other many times. Diversity of subjects—he took philosophy, I studied infusoria—diminished the possibility of our association. If I were to return now into that past, enriched in but one respect—awareness of the present day—and retrace exactly all my interlooping steps, then I would certainly notice his face, now so familiar to me through snapshots. It is a funny thing, when you imagine yourself returning into the past with the contraband of the present, how weird it would be to encounter there, in unexpected places, the prototypes of today's acquaintances, so young and fresh, who in a kind of lucid lunacy do not recognize you; thus a woman, for instance, whom one loves since yesterday, appears as a young girl, standing practically next to one in a crowded train, while the chance passerby who fifteen years ago asked you the way in the street now works in the same office as you. Among this throng of the past only a dozen or so faces would acquire this anachronistic importance: low cards transfigured by the radiance of the trump. And then how confidently one could . . . But alas, even when you do happen, in a dream, to make such a return journey, then, at the border of the past your present intellect is completely invalidated, and amid the surroundings of a classroom hastily assembled by the nightmare's clumsy property man, you again

351

do not know your lesson—with all the forgotten shades of those school throes of old.

At the university Yasha made close friends with two fellow students, Rudolf Baumann, a German, and Olya G., a compatriot—the Russian-language papers did not print her name in full. She was a girl of his age and set, even, I think, from the same town as he. Their families, however, were not acquainted. Only once did I have a chance to see her, at a literary soirée about two years after Yasha's death—I remember her remarkably broad and clear forehead, her aquamarine eyes and her large red mouth with black fuzz over the upper lip and a plump mole at the wick; she stood with her arms folded across her soft bosom, at once arousing in me all the proper literary associations, such as the dust of a fair summer evening and the threshold of a highway tavern, and a bored girl's observant gaze. As for Rudolf, I never saw him myself and can conclude only from the words of others that he had pale blond hair brushed back, was swift in his movements and handsome—in a hard, sinewy way, remindful of a gundog. Thus I use a different method to study each of the three individuals, which affects both their substance and their coloration, until, at the last minute, the rays of a sun that is my own and yet is incomprehensible to me, strikes them and equalizes them in the same burst of light.

Yasha kept a diary and in those notes he neatly defined the mutual relationship between him, Rudolf and Olya as "a triangle inscribed in a circle." The circle represented the normal, simple, "Euclidian" (as he put it) friendship that united all three, so that if it alone had existed their union would have remained happy, carefree and unbroken. But the triangle inscribed within it was a different system of relationships, complex, agonizing and slow in forming, which had an existence of its own, quite independent of its common enclosure of uniform friendship. This was the banal triangle of tragedy, formed within an idyllic circle, and the mere presence of such a suspi-

ciously neat structure, to say nothing of the fashionable counter-
point of its development, would never have permitted me to
make it into a short story or novel.

"I am fiercely in love with the soul of Rudolf," wrote Yasha
in his agitated, neoromantic style. "I love its harmonious proportions, its health, the joy it has in living. I am fiercely in love
with this naked, suntanned, lithe soul, which has an answer to
everything and proceeds through life as a self-confident woman
does across a ballroom floor. I can imagine only in the most
complex, abstract manner, next to which Kant and Hegel are
child's play, the fierce ecstasy I would experience if only . . .
If only what? What can I do with his soul? This is what kills
me—this yearning for some most mysterious tool (thus Al-
brecht Koch yearned for "golden logic" in the world of madmen). My blood throbs, my hands grow icy like a schoolgirl's
when I remain alone with him, and he knows this and I become repulsive to him and he does not conceal his disgust. I
am fiercely in love with his soul—and this is just as fruitless as
falling in love with the moon."

Rudolf's squeamishness is understandable, but if one looks
at the matter more closely, one suspects that Yasha's passion
was perhaps not so abnormal after all, that his excitement was
after all very much akin to that of many a Russian youth in the
middle of last century, trembling with happiness when, raising
his silky eyelashes, his pale-browed teacher, a future leader,
a future martyr, would turn to him; and I would have refused
to see in Yasha's case an incorrigible deviation had Rudolf
been to the least degree a teacher, a martyr, or a leader; and
not what he really was, a so-called "Bursch," a German "regular guy," notwithstanding a certain propensity for obscure
poetry, lame music, lopsided art—which did not affect in him
that fundamental soundness by which Yasha was captivated, or
thought he was.

The son of a respectable fool of a professor and a civil servant's daughter, he had grown up in wonderful bourgeois sur-

roundings, between a cathedral-like sideboard and the backs of dormant books. He was good-natured although not good; sociable, and yet a little skittish; impulsive, and at the same time calculating. He fell in love with Olya conclusively after a bicycle ride with her and Yasha in the Black Forest, a tour which, as he later testified at the inquest, "was an eye-opener for all three of us"; he fell in love with her on the lowest level, primitively and impatiently, but from her he received a sharp rebuff, made all the stronger by the fact that Olya, an indolent, grasping, morosely freakish girl, had in her turn (in those same fir woods, by the same round, black lake) "realized she had fallen for" Yasha, who was just as oppressed by this as Rudolf was by Yasha's ardor, and as she herself was by the ardor of Rudolf, so that the geometric relationship of their inscribed feelings was complete, reminding one of the traditional and somewhat mysterious interconnections in the *dramatis personae* of eighteenth-century French playwrights where X is the *amante* of Y ("the one in love with Y") and Y is the *amant* of Z ("the one in love with Z").

By winter, the second winter of their friendship, they had become clearly aware of the situation; the winter was spent in studying its hopelessness. On the surface everything seemed to be fine: Yasha read incessantly; Rudolf played hockey, masterfully speeding the puck across the ice; Olya studied the history of art (which, in the context of the epoch, sounds—as does the tone of the entire drama in question—like an unbearably typical, and therefore false, note); within, however, a hidden agonizing torment was growing, which became formidably destructive the moment that these unfortunate young people began to find some pleasure in their threefold torture.

For a long time they abided by a tacit agreement (each knowing, shamelessly and hopelessly, everything about the others) never to mention their feelings when the three of them were together; but whenever one of them was absent, the other two would inevitably set to discussing his passion and his suffering. For some reason they celebrated New Year's Eve in the restaurant of one of the Berlin railroad stations—perhaps because at railroad stations the armament of time is particulary impressive—and then they went slouching through the varicolored slush of grim festive streets, and Rudolf ironically proposed a toast to the exposure of their friendship—and since that time, at first discreetly, but soon with all the rapture of frankness, they would jointly discuss their feelings with all three present. It was then that the triangle began to erode its circumference.

The elder Chernyshevskis, as well as Rudolf's parents and Olya's mother (a sculptress, obese, black-eyed, and still handsome, with a low voice, who had buried two husbands and used to wear long necklaces that looked like bronze chains), not only did not sense that something doomful was growing, but would have confidently replied (should an aimless questioner have turned up among the angels already converging, already swarming and fussing professionally around the cradle where lay a dark little newborn revolver) that everything was all right, that everybody was happy. Afterwards, though, when everything had happened, their cheated memories made every effort to find in the routine past course of identically tinted days, traces and evidence of what was to come—and, surprisingly, they would find them. Thus Mme. G., paying a call of condolence on Mme. Chernyshevski, fully believed what she was saying when she insisted she had had presentiments of the tragedy for a long time—since the very day when she had come into the half-dark drawing room where, in motionless poses on a couch, in the various sorrowful inclinations of allegories on tombstone bas-reliefs, Olya and her two friends were sitting in silence; this was but a fleeting momentary harmony of shadows, but Mme. G. professed to have noticed that moment, or, more likely, she had set it aside in order to return to it a few months later.

By spring the revolver had grown. It belonged to Rudolf,

but for a long time passed inconspicuously from one to the
other, like a warm ring sliding on a string in a parlor game, or
a playing card with Black Mary. Strange as it may seem, the
idea of disappearing, all three together, in order that—already
in a different world—an ideal and flawless circle might be restored, was being developed most actively by Olya, although
now it is hard to determine who first proposed it and when.
The role of poet in this enterprise was taken by Yasha—his position seemed the most hopeless since, after all, it was the most
abstract; there are, however, sorrows that one does not cure by
death, since they can be treated much more simply by life and
its changing yearnings: a material bullet is powerless against
them, while on the other hand, it copes perfectly well with
the coarser passions of hearts like Rudolf's and Olya's.

A solution had now been found and discussions of it
became especially fascinating. In mid-April, at the flat the
Chernyshevskis then had, something happened that apparently
served as the final impulse for the *dénouement*. Yasha's parents
had peacefully left for the cinema across the street. Rudolf unexpectedly got drunk and let himself go, Yasha dragged him
away from Olya and all this happened in the bathroom, and
presently Rudolf, in tears, was picking up the money that had
somehow fallen out of his trouser pockets, and what oppression
all three felt, what shame, and how tempting was the relief offered by the finale scheduled for the next day.

After dinner on Thursday the eighteenth, which was also the
eighteenth anniversary of the death of Olya's father, they
equipped themselves with the revolver, which had become by
now quite burly and independent, and in light, flimsy weather
(with a damp west wind and the violet rust of pansies in every
garden) set off on streetcar fifty-seven for the Grunewald where
they planned to find a lonely spot and shoot themselves one
after the other. They stood on the rear platform of the tram,
all three wearing raincoats, with pale puffy faces—and Yasha's
big-peaked cap, which he had not worn for about four

years and had for some reason put on today, gave him an
oddly plebeian look; Rudolf was hatless and the wind ruffled his blond hair, thrown back from the temples; Olya stood
leaning against the rear railing, gripping the black stang with
a white, firm hand that had a prominent ring on its index finger
—and gazed with narrowed eyes at the streets flicking by, and
all the time kept stepping by mistake on the treadle of the
gentle little bell in the floor (intended for the huge, stonelike
foot of the motorman when the rear of the car became
the front). This group was noticed from inside the car, through
the door, by Yuliy Filippovich Posner, former tutor of a cousin
of Yasha's. Leaning out quickly—he was an alert, self-confident person—he beckoned to Yasha, who, recognizing him,
went inside.

"Good thing I ran across you," said Posner, and after he had
explained in detail that he was going with his five-year-old
daughter (sitting separately by a window with her rubber-soft
nose pressed against the glass) to visit his wife in a maternity
ward, he produced his wallet and from the wallet his calling
card, and then, taking advantage of an accidental stop made
by the car (the trolley had come off the wire on a curve),
crossed out his old address with a fountain pen and wrote the
new one above it. "Here," he said, "give this to your cousin as
soon as he comes back from Basel and remind him, please, that
he still has several of my books which I need, which I need very
much."

The tramcar was speeding along the Hohenzollerndamm and
on its rear platform Olya and Rudolf continued to stand just as
sternly as before in the wind, but a certain mysterious change
had occurred: by the act of leaving them alone, although only
for a minute (Posner and his daughter got off very soon),
Yasha had, as it were, broken the alliance and had initiated
his separation from them, so that when he rejoined them on
the platform he was, though as much unaware of it as they were,
already on his own and the invisible crack, in keeping with the

law governing all cracks, continued irresistibly to creep and widen.

In the solitude of the spring forest where the wet, dun birches, particularly the smaller ones, stood around blankly with all their attention turned inside themselves; not far from the dove-gray lake (on whose vast shore there was not a soul except for a little man who was tossing a stick into the water at the request of his dog) they easily found a convenient lonely spot and right away got down to business; to be more exact, Yasha got down to business: he had that honesty of spirit that imparts to the most reckless act an almost everyday simplicity. He said he would shoot himself first by right of seniority (he was a year older than Rudolf and a month older than Olya) and this simple remark rendered unnecessary the stroke of drawn lots, which, in its coarse blindness, would probably have fallen on him anyway; and throwing off his raincoat and without bidding his friends farewell (which was only natural in view of their identical destination), silently, with clumsy haste, he walked down the slippery, pine-covered slope into a ravine heavily overgrown with scrub oak and bramble bushes, which, despite April's limpidity, completely concealed him from the others.

These two stood for a long time waiting for the shot. They had no cigarettes with them, but Rudolf was clever enough to feel in the pocket of Yasha's raincoat where he found an unopened pack. The sky had grown overcast, the pines were rustling cautiously and it seemed from below that their blind branches were groping for something. High above and fabulously fast, their long necks extended, two wild ducks flew past, one slightly behind the other. Afterwards Yasha's mother used to show the visiting card, DIPL. ING. JULIUS POSNER, on the reverse of which Yasha had written in pencil, *Mummy, Daddy, I am still alive, I am very scared, forgive me.* Finally Rudolf could stand it no longer and climbed down to see what was the matter with him. Yasha was sitting on a log among last year's still unanswered leaves, but he did not turn; he only said: "I'll be ready in a minute." There was something tense about his back, as if he were controlling an acute pain. Rudolf rejoined Olya, but no sooner had he reached her than both of them heard the dull pop of the shot, while in Yasha's room life went on for a few more hours as if nothing had happened—the cast-off banana skin on a plate, the volume of Annenski's poems *The Cypress Chest* and that of Khodasevich's *The Heavy Lyre* on the chair by the bed, the ping-pong bat on the couch; he was killed outright; to revive him, however, Rudolf and Olya dragged him through the bushes to the reeds and there desperately sprinkled him and rubbed him, so that he was all smudged with earth, blood and silt when the police later found the body. Then the two began calling for help, but nobody came: architect Ferdinand Stockschmeisser had long since left with his wet setter.

They returned to the place where they had waited for the shot and here dusk begins to fall on the story. The one clear thing is that Rudolf, whether because a certain terrestrial vacancy had opened for him or because he was simply a coward, lost all desire to shoot himself, and Olya, even if she had persisted in her intention, could do nothing since he had immediately hidden the revolver. In the woods, where it had grown cold and dark, with a blind drizzle crepitating around, they remained for a long time until a stupidly late hour. Rumor has it that it was then that they became lovers, but this would be really too flat. At about midnight, at the corner of a street poetically named Lilac Lane, a police sergeant listened skeptically to their horrible, voluble tale. There is a kind of hysterical state that assumes the semblance of childish swaggering.

If Mme. Chernyshevski had met Olya immediately after the event then perhaps some kind of sentimental sense would have come of it for them both. Unfortunately the meeting occurred only several months later, because, in the first place, Olya went away, and in the second, Mme. Chernyshevski's grief did not immediately take on that industrious, and even enraptured, form that Fyodor found when he came on the scene. Olya was in a certain sense unlucky: it so happened that Olya had come back for her step-brother's engagement party and the house was full of guests; and when Mme. Chernyshevski arrived without warning, beneath a heavy mourning veil, with a choice selection from her sorrowful archives (photographs, letters) in her handbag, all prepared for the rapture of shared tears, she was met by a morosely polite, morosely impatient young woman in a semitransparent dress, with blood-red lips and a fat white-powdered nose, and one could hear from the little side room where she took her guest the wailing of a phonograph, and of course no communion of souls came of it. "All I did was to take a long look at her," recounted Mme. Chernyshevski—after which she carefully snipped off, on many little snapshots, both Olya and Rudolf; the latter, however, had visited her at once and had rolled at her feet and pounded his head on the soft corner of the divan, and then had walked off with his wonderful bouncy stride down the Kurfürstendamm, which glistened after a spring shower.

Yasha's death had its most painful effect on his father. He had to spend the whole summer in a sanatorium and he never really recovered: the partition dividing the room temperature of reason from the infinitely ugly, cold, ghostly world into which Yasha had passed suddenly crumbled, and to restore it was impossible, so that the gap had to be draped in makeshift fashion and one tried not to look at the stirring folds. Ever since that day the other world began to seep into his life; but there was no way of resolving this constant intercourse with Yasha's spirit and he finally told his wife about it, in the vain hope that he might thus render harmless a phantom that secrecy had nurtured: the secrecy must have grown back, for soon he again had to seek the tedious, essentially mortal, glass-and-rubber help of doctors. Thus he lived only half in our world, at which he grasped the more greedily and desperately, and when one

listened to his sprightly speech and looked at his regular features, it was difficult to imagine the unearthly experiences of
this healthy-looking, plump little man, with his bald spot and
the thin hair on either side, but then all the more strange was
the convulsion that suddenly disfigured him; also the fact that
sometimes for weeks on end he wore a gray cloth glove on his
right hand (he suffered from eczema) hinted eerily at a
mystery, as if, repelled by life's unclean touch, or burned by
another life, he was reserving his bare handclasp for inhuman,
hardly imaginable meetings. Meanwhile nothing stopped with
Yasha's death and many interesting things were happening: in
Russia one observed the spread of abortions and the revival of
summer houses; in England there were strikes of some kind or
other; Lenin met a sloppy end; Duse, Puccini and Anatole
France died; Mallory and Irvine perished near the summit of
Everest; and old Prince Dolgorukiy, in shoes of plaited leather
thong, secretly visited Russia to see again the buckwheat in
bloom.

> *Translated by Dmitri Nabokov*
> *and the author*

Pnin

❧❧❧❧

❧ Chapter One ❧

I

_____

The elderly passenger sitting on the north-window side of
that inexorably moving railway coach, next to an empty seat
and facing two empty ones, was none other than Professor Timofey Pnin. Ideally bald, sun-tanned, and clean-shaven, he began
rather impressively with that great brown dome of his, tortoise-
shell glasses (masking an infantile absence of eyebrows), apish
upper lip, thick neck, and strong-man torso in a tightish tweed
coat, but ended, somewhat disappointingly, in a pair of spindly
legs (now flanneled and crossed) and frail-looking, almost
feminine feet.

His sloppy socks were of scarlet wool with lilac lozenges; his
conservative black oxfords had cost him about as much as all
the rest of his clothing (flamboyant goon tie included). Prior
to the nineteen-forties, during the staid European era of his life,
he had always worn long underwear, its terminals tucked into
the tops of neat silk socks, which were clocked, soberly colored,
and held up on his cotton-clad calves by garters. In those days,
to reveal a glimpse of that white underwear by pulling up a
trouser leg too high would have seemed to Pnin as indecent as
showing himself to ladies minus collar and tie; for even when
decayed Mme. Roux, the concierge of the squalid apartment
house in the Sixteenth Arrondissement of Paris—where Pnin,
after escaping from Leninized Russia and completing his college education in Prague, had spent fifteen years—happened to

come up for the rent while he was without his *faux col,* prim Pnin would cover his front stud with a chaste hand. All this underwent a change in the heady atmosphere of the New World. Nowadays, at fifty-two, he was crazy about sun-bathing, wore sport shirts and slacks, and when crossing his legs would carefully, deliberately, brazenly display a tremendous stretch of bare shin. Thus he might have appeared to a fellow passenger; but except for a soldier asleep at one end and two women absorbed in a baby at the other, Pnin had the coach to himself.

Now a secret must be imparted. Professor Pnin was on the wrong train. He was unaware of it, and so was the conductor, already threading his way through the train to Pnin's coach. As a matter of fact, Pnin at the moment felt very well satisfied with himself. When inviting him to deliver a Friday-evening lecture at Cremona—some two hundred versts west of Waindell, Pnin's academic perch since 1945—the vice-president of the Cremona Women's Club, a Miss Judith Clyde, had advised our friend that the most convenient train left Waindell at 1:52 P.M., reaching Cremona at 4:17; but Pnin—who, like so many Russians, was inordinately fond of everything in the line of timetables, maps, catalogues, collected them, helped himself freely to them with the bracing pleasure of getting something for nothing, and took especial pride in puzzling out schedules for himself—had discovered, after some study, an inconspicuous reference mark against a still more convenient train (Lv. Waindell 2:19 P.M., Ar. Cremona 4:32 P.M.); the mark indicated that Fridays, and Fridays only, the two-nineteen stopped at Cremona on its way to a distant and much larger city, graced likewise with a mellow Italian name. Unfortunately for Pnin, his timetable was five years old and in part obsolete.

He taught Russian at Waindell College, a somewhat provincial institution characterized by an artificial lake in the middle of a landscaped campus, by ivied galleries connecting the various halls, by murals displaying recognizable members of the faculty in the act of passing on the torch of knowledge from

Aristotle, Shakespeare, and Pasteur to a lot of monstrously built farm boys and farm girls, and by a huge, active, buoyantly thriving German Department which its Head, Dr. Hagen, smugly called (pronouncing every syllable very distinctly) "a university within a university."

In the Fall Semester of that particular year (1950), the enrollment in the Russian Language courses consisted of one student, plump and earnest Betty Bliss, in the Transitional Group, one, a mere name (Ivan Dub, who never materialized) in the Advanced, and three in the flourishing Elementary: Josephine Malkin, whose grandparents had been born in Minsk; Charles McBeth, whose prodigious memory had already disposed of ten languages and was prepared to entomb ten more; and languid Eileen Lane, whom somebody had told that by the time one had mastered the Russian alphabet one could practically read "Anna Karamazov" in the original. As a teacher, Pnin was far from being able to compete with those stupendous Russian ladies, scattered all over academic America, who, without having had any formal training at all, manage somehow, by dint of intuition, loquacity, and a kind of maternal bounce, to infuse a magic knowledge of their difficult and beautiful tongue into a group of innocent-eyed students in an atmosphere of Mother Volga songs, red caviar, and tea; nor did Pnin, as a teacher, ever presume to approach the lofty halls of modern scientific linguistics, that ascetic fraternity of phonemes, that temple wherein earnest young people are taught not the language itself, but the method of teaching others to teach that method; which method, like a waterfall splashing from rock to rock, ceases to be a medium of rational navigation but perhaps in some fabulous future may become instrumental in evolving esoteric dialects—Basic Basque and so forth—spoken only by certain elaborate machines. No doubt Pnin's approach to his work was amateurish and lighthearted, depending as it did on exercises in a grammar brought out by the Head of a Slavic Department in a far greater college than Waindell—a venerable fraud whose Russian was a joke but who would generously lend his dignified name to the products of anonymous drudgery. Pnin, despite his many shortcomings, had about him a disarming, old-fashioned charm which Dr. Hagen, his staunch protector, insisted before morose trustees was a delicate imported article worth paying for in domestic cash. Whereas the degree in sociology and political economy that Pnin had obtained with some pomp at the University of Prague around 1925 had become by midcentury a doctorate in desuetude, he was not altogether miscast as a teacher of Russian. He was beloved not for any essential ability but for those unforgettable digressions of his, when he would remove his glasses to beam at the past while massaging the lenses of the present. Nostalgic excursions in broken English. Autobiographical tidbits. How Pnin came to the *Soedinyonnïe Shtatï* (the United States). "Examination on ship before landing. Very well! 'Nothing to declare?' 'Nothing.' Very well! Then political questions. He asks: 'Are you anarchist?' I answer"—time out on the part of the narrator for a spell of cozy mute mirth—" 'First what do we understand under "Anarchism"? Anarchism practical, metaphysical, theoretical, mystical, abstractical, individual, social? When I was young,' I say, 'all this had for me signification.' So we had a very interesting discussion, in consequence of which I passed two whole weeks on Ellis Island"—abdomen beginning to heave; heaving; narrator convulsed.

But there were still better sessions in the way of humor. With an air of coy secrecy, benevolent Pnin, preparing the children for the marvelous treat he had once had himself, and already revealing, in an uncontrollable smile, an incomplete but formidable set of tawny teeth, would open a dilapidated Russian book at the elegant leatherette marker he had carefully placed there; he would open the book, whereupon as often as not a look of the utmost dismay would alter his plastic features; agape, feverishly, he would flip right and left through the volume, and minutes might pass before he found the right page—

or satisfied himself that he had marked it correctly after all. Usually the passage of his choice would come from some old and naïve comedy of merchant-class habitus rigged up by Ostrovski almost a century ago, or from an equally ancient but even more dated piece of trivial Leskovian jollity dependent on verbal contortions. He delivered these stale goods with the rotund gusto of the classical Alexandrinka (a theater in Petersburg), rather than with the crisp simplicity of the Moscow Artists; but since to appreciate whatever fun those passages still retained one had to have not only a sound knowledge of the vernacular but also a good deal of literary insight, and since his poor little class had neither, the performer would be alone in enjoying the associative subtleties of his text. The heaving we have already noted in another connection would become here a veritable earthquake. Directing his memory, with all the lights on and all the masks of the mind a-miming, toward the days of his fervid and receptive youth (in a brilliant cosmos that seemed all the fresher for having been abolished by one blow of history), Pnin would get drunk on his private wines as he produced sample after sample of what his listeners politely surmised was Russian humor. Presently the fun would become too much for him; pear-shaped tears would trickle down his tanned cheeks. Not only his shocking teeth but also an astonishing amount of pink upper-gum tissue would suddenly pop out, as if a jack-in-the-box had been sprung, and his hand would fly to his mouth, while his big shoulders shook and rolled. And although the speech he smothered behind his dancing hand was now doubly unintelligible to the class, his complete surrender to his own merriment would prove irresistible. By the time he was helpless with it he would have his students in stitches, with abrupt barks of clockwork hilarity coming from Charles and a dazzling flow of unsuspected lovely laughter transfiguring Josephine, who was not pretty, while Eileen, who was, dissolved in a jelly of unbecoming giggles.

All of which does not alter the fact that Pnin was on the wrong train.

How should we diagnose his sad case? Pnin, it should be particularly stressed, was anything but the type of that good-natured German platitude of last century, *der zerstreute Professor*. On the contrary, he was perhaps too wary, too persistently on the lookout for diabolical pitfalls, too painfully on the alert lest his erratic surroundings (unpredictable America) inveigle him into some bit of preposterous oversight. It was the world that was absent-minded and it was Pnin whose business it was to set it straight. His life was a constant war with insensate objects that fell apart, or attacked him, or refused to function, or viciously got themselves lost as soon as they entered the sphere of his existence. He was inept with his hands to a rare degree; but because he could manufacture in a twinkle a one-note mouth organ out of a pea pod, make a flat pebble skip ten times on the surface of a pond, shadowgraph with his knuckles a rabbit (complete with blinking eye), and perform a number of other tame tricks that Russians have up their sleeves, he believed himself endowed with considerable manual and mechanical skill. On gadgets he doted with a kind of dazed, superstitious delight. Electric devices enchanted him. Plastics swept him off his feet. He had a deep admiration for the zipper. But the devoutly plugged-in clock would make nonsense of his mornings after a storm in the middle of the night had paralyzed the local power station. The frame of his spectacles would snap in mid-bridge, leaving him with two identical pieces, which he would vaguely attempt to unite, in the hope, perhaps, of some organic marvel of restoration coming to the rescue. The zipper a gentleman depends on most would come loose in his puzzled hand at some nightmare moment of haste and despair.

And he still did not know that he was on the wrong train.

A special danger area in Pnin's case was the English language. Except for such not very helpful odds and ends as "the rest is silence," "nevermore," "weekend," "who's who," and a few ordinary words like "eat," "street," "fountain pen," "gangster," "Charleston," "marginal utility," he had had no Eng-

lish at all at the time he left France for the States. Stubbornly
he sat down to the task of learning the language of Fenimore
Cooper, Edgar Poe, Edison, and thirty-one Presidents. In 1941,
at the end of one year of study, he was proficient enough to use
glibly terms like "wishful thinking" and "okey-dokey." By
1942 he was able to interrupt his narration with the phrase, "To
make a long story short." By the time Truman entered his second term, Pnin could handle practically any topic; but otherwise progress seemed to have stopped despite all his efforts,
and by 1950 his English was still full of flaws. That autumn he
supplemented his Russian courses by delivering a weekly lecture in a so-called symposium ("Wingless Europe: A Survey of
Contemporary Continental Culture") directed by Dr. Hagen.
All our friend's lectures, including sundry ones he gave out of
town, were edited by one of the younger members of the German Department. The procedure was somewhat complicated.
Professor Pnin laboriously translated his own Russian verbal
flow, teeming with idiomatic proverbs, into patchy English.
This was revised by young Miller. Then Dr. Hagen's secretary, a Miss Eisenbohr, typed it out. Then Pnin deleted the passages he could not understand. Then he read it to his weekly
audience. He was utterly helpless without the prepared text,
nor could he use the ancient system of dissimulating his infirmity by moving his eyes up and down—snapping up an eye-
ful of words, reeling them off to his audience, and drawing out
the end of the sentence while diving for the next. Pnin's worried eye would be bound to lose its bearings. Therefore he
preferred reading his lectures, his gaze glued to his text, in a
slow, monotonous baritone that seemed to climb one of those
interminable flights of stairs used by people who dread elevators.

The conductor, a gray-headed fatherly person with steel
spectacles placed rather low on his simple, functional nose and
a bit of soiled adhesive tape on his thumb, had now only three
coaches to deal with before reaching the last one, where Pnin
rode.

Pnin in the meantime had yielded to the satisfaction of a special Pninian craving. He was in a Pninian quandary. Among other articles indispensable for a Pninian overnight stay in a strange town, such as shoe trees, apples, dictionaries, and so on, his Gladstone bag contained a relatively new black suit he planned to wear that night for the lecture ("Are the Russian People Communist?") before the Cremona ladies. It also contained next Monday's symposium lecture ("Don Quixote and Faust"), which he intended to study the next day, on his way back to Waindell, and a paper by the graduate student, Betty Bliss ("Dostoevski and Gestalt Psychology"), that he had to read for Dr. Hagen, who was her main director of cerebration. The quandary was as follows: If he kept the Cremona manuscript—a sheaf of typewriter-size pages, carefully folded down the center—on his person, in the security of his body warmth, the chances were, theoretically, that he would forget to transfer it from the coat he was wearing to the one he would wear. On the other hand, if he placed the lecture in the pocket of the suit in the bag *now,* he would, he knew, be tortured by the possibility of his luggage being stolen. On the third hand (these mental states sprout additional forelimbs all the time), he carried in the inside pocket of his present coat a precious wallet with two ten-dollar bills, the newspaper clipping of a letter he had written, with my help, to the *New York Times* in 1945 anent the Yalta conference, and his certificate of naturalization; and it was physically possible to pull out the wallet, if needed, in such a way as fatally to dislodge the folded lecture. During the twenty minutes he had been on the train, our friend had already opened his bag twice to play with his various papers. When the conductor reached the car, diligent Pnin was perusing with difficulty Betty's last effort, which began, "When we consider the mental climate wherein we all live, we cannot notice . . ."

The conductor entered; did not awake the soldier; promised the women he would let them know when they would be about to arrive; and presently was shaking his head over Pnin's ticket. The Cremona stop had been abolished two years before.

"Important lecture!" cried Pnin. "What to do? It is a *catastrof!*"

Gravely, comfortably, the gray-headed conductor sank into the opposite seat and consulted in silence a tattered book full of dog-eared insertions. In a few minutes, namely at 3:08, Pnin would have to get off at Whitchurch; this would enable him to catch the four-o'clock bus that would deposit him, around six, at Cremona.

"I was thinking I gained twelve minutes, and now I have lost nearly two whole hours," said Pnin bitterly. Upon which, clearing his throat and ignoring the consolation offered by the kind gray-head ("You'll make it."), he took off his reading glasses, collected his stone-heavy bag, and repaired to the vestibule of the car so as to wait there for the confused greenery skimming by to be cancelled and replaced by the definite station he had in mind.

2

Whitchurch materialized as scheduled. A hot, torpid expanse of cement and sun lay beyond the geometrical solids of various clean-cut shadows. The local weather was unbelievably summery for October. Alert, Pnin entered a waiting room of sorts, with a needless stove in the middle, and looked around. In a solitary recess, one could make out the upper part of a perspiring young man who was filling out forms on the broad wooden counter before him.

"Information, please," said Pnin. "Where stops four-o'clock bus to Cremona?"

"Right across the street," briskly answered the employee without looking up.

"And where possible to leave baggage?"

"That bag? I'll take care of it."

And with the national informality that always nonplused Pnin, the young man shoved the bag into a corner of his nook.

"Quittance?" queried Pnin, Englishing the Russian for "receipt" (*kvitantsiya*).

"What's that?"

"Number?" tried Pnin.

"You don't need a number," said the fellow, and resumed his writing.

Pnin left the station, satisfied himself about the bus stop, and entered a coffee shop. He consumed a ham sandwich, ordered another, and consumed that too. At exactly five minutes to four, having paid for the food but not for an excellent toothpick which he carefully selected from a neat little cup in the shape of a pine cone near the cash register, Pnin walked back to the station for his bag.

A different man was now in charge. The first had been called home to drive his wife in all haste to the maternity hospital. He would be back in a few minutes.

"But I must obtain my valise!" cried Pnin.

The substitute was sorry but could not do a thing.

"It is there!" cried Pnin, leaning over and pointing.

This was unfortunate. He was still in the act of pointing when he realized that he was claiming the wrong bag. His index finger wavered. That hesitation was fatal.

"My bus to Cremona!" cried Pnin.

"There is another at eight," said the man.

What was our poor friend to do? Horrible situation! He glanced streetward. The bus had just come. The engagement meant an extra fifty dollars. His hand flew to his right side. *It* was there, *slava Bogu* (thank God)! Very well! He would not wear his black suit—*vot i vsyo* (that's all). He would retrieve it on his way back. He had lost, dumped, shed many more valuable things in his day. Energetically, almost lightheartedly, Pnin boarded the bus.

He had endured this new stage of his journey only a few city blocks when an awful suspicion crossed his mind. Ever since he had been separated from his bag, the tip of his left forefinger had been alternating with the proximal edge of his right elbow in checking a precious presence in his inside coat pocket. All of a sudden he brutally yanked it out. It was Betty's paper.

Emitting what he thought were international exclamations of anxiety and entreaty, Pnin lurched out of his seat. Reeling, he reached the exit. With one hand the driver grimly milked out a handful of coins from his little machine, refunded him the price of the ticket, and stopped the bus. Poor Pnin landed in the middle of a strange town.

He was less strong than his powerfully puffed-out chest might imply, and the wave of hopeless fatigue that suddenly submerged his topheavy body, detaching him, as it were, from reality, was a sensation not utterly unknown to him. He found himself in a damp, green, purplish park, of the formal and funereal type, with the stress laid on somber rhododendrons, glossy laurels, sprayed shade trees and closely clipped lawns; and hardly had he turned into an alley of chestnut and oak, which the bus driver had curtly told him led back to the railway station, than that eerie feeling, that tingle of unreality overpowered him completely. Was it something he had eaten? That pickle with the ham? Was it a mysterious disease that none of his doctors had yet detected? My friend wondered, and I wonder, too.

I do not know if it has ever been noted before that one of the main characteristics of life is discreteness. Unless a film of flesh envelops us, we die. Man exists only insofar as he is separated from his surroundings. The cranium is a space-traveler's helmet. Stay inside or you perish. Death is divestment, death is communion. It may be wonderful to mix with the landscape, but to do so is the end of the tender ego. The sensation poor Pnin experienced was something very like that divestment, that communion. He felt porous and pregnable. He was sweating. He was terrified. A stone bench among the laurels saved him from collapsing on the sidewalk. Was his seizure a heart attack? I doubt it. For the nonce I am his physician, and let me repeat, I doubt it. My patient was one of those singular and unfortunate people who regard their heart ("a hollow, muscular organ," according to the gruesome definition in *Webster's New Collegiate Dictionary*, which Pnin's orphaned bag contained) with a queasy dread, a nervous repulsion, a sick hate, as if it were some strong slimy untouchable monster that one had to be parasitized with, alas. Occasionally, when puzzled by his tumbling and tottering pulse, doctors examined him more thoroughly, the cardiograph outlined fabulous mountain ranges and indicated a dozen fatal diseases that excluded one another. He was afraid of touching his own wrist. He never attempted to sleep on his left side, even in those dismal hours of the night when the insomniac longs for a third side after trying the two he has.

And now, in the park of Whitchurch, Pnin felt what he had felt already on August 10, 1942, and February 15 (his birthday), 1937, and May 18, 1929, and July 4, 1920—that the repulsive automaton he lodged had developed a consciousness of its own and not only was grossly alive but was causing him pain and panic. He pressed his poor bald head against the stone back of the bench and recalled all the past occasions of similar discomfort and despair. Could it be pneumonia this time? He had been chilled to the bone a couple of days before in one of those hearty American drafts that a host treats his guests to after the second round of drinks on a windy night. And suddenly Pnin (was he dying?) found himself sliding back into his own childhood. This sensation had the sharpness of retrospective detail that is said to be the dramatic privilege of drowning individuals, especially in the former Russian Navy— a phenomenon of suffocation that a veteran psychoanalyst, whose name escapes me, has explained as being the subconsciously evoked shock of one's baptism which causes an explosion of intervening recollections between the first immersion and the last. It all happened in a flash but there is no way of rendering it in less than so many consecutive words.

Pnin came from a respectable, fairly well-to-do, St. Petersburg family. His father, Dr. Pavel Pnin, an eye specialist of considerable repute, had once had the honor of treating Leo Tolstoy for a case of conjunctivitis. Timofey's mother, a frail, nervous little person with a waspy waist and bobbed hair, was the daughter of the once famous revolutionary Umov (rhymes with "zoom off") and of a German lady from Riga. Through his half swoon, he saw his mother's approaching eyes. It was a Sunday in midwinter. He was eleven. He had been preparing lessons for his Monday classes at the First Gymnasium when a strange chill pervaded his body. His mother took his temperature, looked at her child with a kind of stupefaction, and immediately called her husband's best friend, the pediatrician Belochkin. He was a small, beetle-browed man, with a short beard and cropped hair. Easing the skirts of his frock coat, he sat down on the edge of Timofey's bed. A race was run between the doctor's fat golden watch and Timofey's pulse (an easy winner). Then Timofey's torso was bared, and to it Belochkin pressed the icy nudity of his ear and the sandpapery side of his head. Like the flat sole of some monopode, the ear ambulated all over Timofey's back and chest, gluing itself to this or that patch of skin and stomping on to the next. No sooner had the doctor left than Timofey's mother and a robust servant girl with safety pins between her teeth encased the distressed little patient in a strait-jacket-like compress. It consisted of a layer of soaked linen, a thicker layer of absorbent cotton, and another of tight flannel, with a sticky diabolical oilcloth— the hue of urine and fever—coming between the clammy pang of the linen next to his skin and the excruciating squeak of the cotton around which the outer layer of flannel was wound. A poor cocooned pupa, Timosha (Tim) lay under a mass of additional blankets; they were of no avail against the branching chill that crept up his ribs from both sides of his frozen spine. He could not close his eyes because his eyelids stung so. Vision was but oval pain with oblique stabs of light; familiar shapes became the breeding places of evil delusions. Near his bed was a four-section screen of polished wood, with pyrographic designs representing a bridle path felted with fallen leaves, a lily pond, an old man hunched up on a bench, and a squirrel holding a reddish object in its front paws. Timosha, a methodical child, had often wondered what that object could be (a nut? a pine cone?), and now that he had nothing else to do, he set himself to solve this dreary riddle, but the fever that hummed in his head drowned every effort in pain and panic. Still more oppressive was his tussle with the wallpaper. He had always been able to see that in the vertical plane a combination made up of three different clusters of purple flowers and seven different oak leaves was repeated a number of times with soothing exactitude; but now he was bothered by the undismissable fact that he could not find what system of inclusion and circumscription governed the horizontal recurrence of the pattern; that such a recurrence existed was proved by his being able to pick out here and there, all along the wall from bed to wardrobe and from stove to door, the reappearance of this or that element of the series, but when he tried traveling right or left from any chosen set of three inflorescences and seven leaves, he forthwith lost himself in a meaningless tangle of rhododendron and oak. It stood to reason that if the evil designer—the destroyer of minds, the friend of fever—had concealed the key of the pattern with such monstrous care, that key must be as precious as life itself and, when found, would regain for Timofey Pnin his everyday health, his everyday world; and this lucid—alas, too lucid—thought forced him to persevere in the struggle.

A sense of being late for some appointment as odiously exact as school, dinner, or bedtime added the discomfort of awkward haste to the difficulties of a quest that was grading into delirium. The foliage and the flowers, with none of the intricacies of their warp disturbed, appeared to detach themselves in one undulating body from their pale-blue background which, in its turn, lost its papery flatness and dilated in depth till the specta-tor's heart almost burst in response to the expansion. He could still make out through the autonomous garlands certain parts of the nursery more tenacious of life than the rest, such as the lacquered screen, the gleam of a tumbler, the brass knobs of his bedstead, but these interfered even less with the oak leaves and rich blossoms than would the reflection of an inside object in a windowpane with the outside scenery perceived through the same glass. And although the witness and victim of these phantasms was tucked up in bed, he was, in accordance with the twofold nature of his surroundings, simultaneously seated on a bench in a green and purple park. During one melting mo-ment, he had the sensation of holding at last the key he had sought; but, coming from very far, a rustling wind, its soft volume increasing as it ruffled the rhododendrons—now blos-somless, blind—confused whatever rational pattern Timofey Pnin's surroundings had once had. He was alive and that was sufficient. The back of the bench against which he still sprawled felt as real as his clothes, or his wallet, or the date of the Great Moscow Fire—1812.

A gray squirrel sitting on comfortable haunches on the ground before him was sampling a peach stone. The wind paused, and presently stirred the foliage again.

The seizure had left him a little frightened and shaky, but he argued that had it been a real heart attack, he would have surely felt a good deal more unsettled and concerned, and this round-about piece of reasoning completely dispelled his fear. It was now four-twenty. He blew his nose and trudged to the station.

The initial employee was back. "Here's your bag," he said cheerfully. "Sorry you missed the Cremona bus."

"At least"—and what dignified irony our unfortunate friend tried to inject into that "at least"—"I hope everything is good with your wife?"

"She'll be all right. Have to wait till tomorrow, I guess."

"And now," said Pnin, "where is located the public telephone?"

The man pointed with his pencil as far out and sideways as he could without leaving his lair. Pnin, bag in hand, started to go, but he was called back. The pencil was now directed streetward.

"Say, see those two guys loading that truck? They're going to Cremona right now. Just tell them Bob Horn sent you. They'll take you."

3

Some people—and I am one of them—hate happy ends. We feel cheated. Harm is the norm. Doom should not jam. The avalanche stopping in its tracks a few feet above the cowering village behaves not only unnaturally but unethically. Had I been reading about this mild old man, instead of writing about him, I would have preferred him to discover, upon his arrival to Cremona, that his lecture was not this Friday but the next. Actually, however, he not only arrived safely but was in time for dinner—a fruit cocktail, to begin with, mint jelly with the anonymous meat course, chocolate syrup with the vanilla ice cream. And soon afterwards, surfeited with sweets, wearing his black suit, and juggling three papers, all of which he had stuffed into his coat so as to have the one he wanted among the rest (thus thwarting mischance by mathematical necessity), he sat on a chair near the lectern, while, at the lectern, Judith Clyde, an ageless blonde in aqua rayon, with large, flat cheeks stained a beautiful candy pink and two bright eyes basking in blue lunacy behind a rimless pince-nez, presented the speaker:

"Tonight," she said, "the speaker of the evening—— This, by the way, is our third Friday night; last time, as you all remember, we all enjoyed hearing what Professor Moore had to say about agriculture in China. Tonight we have here, I am proud

to say, the Russian-born, and citizen of this country, Professor
—now comes a difficult one, I am afraid—Professor Pun-neen.
I hope I have it right. He hardly needs any introduction, of
course, and we are all happy to have him. We have a long evening before us, a long and rewarding evening, and I am sure you
would all like to have time to ask him questions afterwards. Incidentally, I am told his father was Dostoevski's family doctor,
and he has traveled quite a bit on both sides of the Iron Curtain. Therefore I will not take up your precious time any longer
and will only add a few words about our next Friday lecture in
this program. I am sure you will all be delighted to know that
there is a grand surprise in store for all of us. Our next lecturer
is the distinguished poet and prose writer, Miss Linda Lacefield. We all know she has written poetry, prose, and some short
stories. Miss Lacefield was born in New York. Her ancestors on
both sides fought on both sides in the Revolutionary War. She
wrote her first poem before graduation. Many of her poems—
three of them, at least—have been published in *Response, A
Hundred Love Lyrics by American Women*. In 1922 she received the cash prize offered by——"

But Pnin was not listening. A faint ripple stemming from his
recent seizure was holding his fascinated attention. It lasted
only a few heartbeats, with an additional systole here and there
—last, harmless echoes—and was resolved in demure reality
as his distinguished hostess invited him to the lectern; but
while it lasted, how limpid the vision was! In the middle of the
front row of seats he saw one of his Baltic aunts, wearing the
pearls and the lace and the blond wig she had worn at all the
performances given by the great ham actor Khodotov, whom
she had adored from afar before drifting into insanity. Next
to her, shyly smiling, sleek dark head inclined, gentle brown
gaze shining up at Pnin from under velvet eyebrows, sat a dead
sweetheart of his, fanning herself with a program. Murdered,
forgotten, unrevenged, incorrupt, immortal, many old friends
were scattered throughout the dim hall among more recent

people, such as Miss Clyde, who had modestly regained a front seat. Vanya Bednyashkin, shot by the Reds in 1919 in Odessa because his father had been a Liberal, was gaily signaling to his former schoolmate from the back of the hall. And in an inconspicuous situation Dr. Pavel Pnin and his anxious wife, both a little blurred but on the whole wonderfully recovered from their obscure dissolution, looked at their son with the same life-consuming passion and pride that they had looked at him with that night in 1912 when, at a school festival, commemorating Napoleon's defeat, he had recited (a bespectacled lad all alone on the stage) a poem by Pushkin.

The brief vision was gone. Old Miss Herring, retired Professor of History, author of *Russia Awakes* (1922), was bending across one or two intermediate members of the audience to compliment Miss Clyde on her speech, while from behind that lady another twinkling old party was thrusting into her field of vision a pair of withered, soundlessly clapping hands.

〜 *Chapter Two* 〜

I
_____

The famous Waindell College bells were in the midst of their morning chimes.

Laurence G. Clements, a Waindell scholar, whose only popular course was the Philosophy of Gesture, and his wife Joan, Pendelton '30, had recently parted with their daughter, her father's best student: Isabel had married in her junior year a Waindell graduate with an engineering job in a remote Western State.

The bells were musical in the silvery sun. Framed in the picture window, the little town of Waindell—white paint, black pattern of twigs—was projected, as if by a child, in primitive perspective devoid of aerial depth, into the slate-gray hills; everything was prettily frosted with rime; the shiny parts of parked cars shone; Miss Dingwall's old Scotch terrier, a cylindrical small boar of sorts, had started upon his rounds up Warren Street and down Spelman Avenue and back again; but no amount of neighborliness, landscaping, and change ringing could soften the season; in a fortnight, after a ruminant pause, the academic year would enter its most winterly phase, the Spring Term, and the Clementses felt dejected, apprehensive, and lonely in their nice old drafty house that now seemed to hang about them like the flabby skin and flapping clothes of some fool who had gone and lost a third of his weight. Isabel was so young after all, and so vague, and they really knew nothing about her in-laws beyond that wedding selection of marchpane faces in a hired hall with the vaporous bride so helpless without her glasses.

The bells, under the enthusiastic direction of Dr. Robert Trebler, active member of the Music Department, were still going strong in the angelic sky, and over a frugal breakfast of oranges and lemons Laurence, blondish, baldish, and unwholesomely fat, was criticizing the head of the French Department, one of the people Joan had invited to meet Professor Entwistle of Goldwin University at their house that evening. "Why on earth," he fumed, "did you have to ask that fellow Blorenge, a mummy, a bore, one of the stucco pillars of education?"

"I *like* Ann Blorenge," said Joan, stressing her affirmation and affection with nods. "A vulgar old cat!" cried Laurence. "A pathetic old cat," murmured Joan—and it was then that Dr. Trebler stopped and the hallway telephone took over.

Technically speaking, the narrator's art of integrating telephone conversations still lags far behind that of rendering dialogues conducted from room to room, or from window to window across some narrow blue alley in an ancient town with water so precious, and the misery of donkeys, and rugs for sale, and minarets, and foreigners and melons, and the vibrant morning echoes. When Joan, in her brisk long-limbed way, got to the compelling instrument before it gave up, and said hullo (eyebrows up, eyes roaming), a hollow quiet greeted her; all she could hear was the informal sound of a steady breathing; presently the breather's voice said, with a cozy foreign accent: "One moment, excuse me"—this was quite casual, and he continued to breathe and perhaps hem and hum or even sigh a little to the accompaniment of a crepitation that evoked the turning over of small pages.

"Hullo!" she repeated.

"You are," suggested the voice warily, "Mrs. Fire?"

"No," said Joan, and hung up. "And besides," she went on, swinging back into the kitchen and addressing her husband who was sampling the bacon she had prepared for herself, "you cannot deny that Jack Cockerell considers Blorenge to be a first-rate administrator."

"What was that telephone call?"

"Somebody wanting Mrs. Feuer or Fayer. Look here, if you deliberately neglect everything George——" [Dr. O. G. Helm, their family doctor]

"Joan," said Laurence, who felt much better after that opalescent rasher, "Joan, my dear, you are aware, aren't you, that you told Margaret Thayer yesterday you wanted a roomer?"

"Oh, gosh," said Joan—and obligingly the telephone rang again.

"It is evident," said the same voice, comfortably resuming the conversation, "that I employed by mistake the name of the informer. I am connected with Mrs. Clement?"

"Yes, this is Mrs. Clements," said Joan.

"Here speaks Professor——" There followed a preposterous little explosion. "I conduct the classes in Russian. Mrs. Fire, who is now working at the library part time——"

"Yes—Mrs. Thayer, I know. Well, do you want to see that room?"

He did. Could he come to inspect it in approximately half

an hour? Yes, she would be in. Untenderly she cradled the receiver.

"What was it this time?" asked her husband, looking back, pudgy freckled hand on banister, on his way upstairs to the security of his study.

"A cracked ping-pong ball. Russian."

"Professor Pnin, by God!" cried Laurence. " 'I know him well: he is the brooch——' Well, I flatly refuse to have that freak in my house."

He trudged up, truculently. She called after him:

"Lore, did you finish writing that article last night?"

"Almost." He had turned the corner of the stairs—she heard his hand squeaking on the banisters, then striking them. "I will today. First I have that damned EOS examination to prepare."

This stood for the Evolution of Sense, his greatest course (with an enrollment of twelve, none even remotely apostolic) which had opened and would close with the phrase destined to be overquoted one day: The evolution of sense is, in a sense, the evolution of nonsense.

2
———

Half an hour later, Joan glanced over the moribund cactuses in the sun-porch window and saw a raincoated, hatless man, with a head like a polished globe of copper, optimistically ringing at the front door of her neighbor's beautiful brick house. The old Scotty stood beside him in much the same candid attitude as he. Miss Dingwall came out with a mop, let the slowpoke, dignified dog in, and directed Pnin to the Clements' clapboard residence.

Timofey Pnin settled down in the living room, crossed his legs *po amerikanski* (the American way), and entered into some unnecessary detail. It was a curriculum vitae in a nutshell—a coconut shell. Born in St. Petersburg in 1898. Both parents died of typhus in 1917. Left for Kiev in 1918. Was with the White Army five months, first as a "field telephonist," then at the Military Information Office. Escaped from Red-invaded Crimea to Constantinople in 1919. Completed university education——

"Say, I was there as a child exactly the same year," said pleased Joan. "My father went to Turkey on a government mission and took us along. We might have met! I remember the word for water. And there was a rose garden——"

"Water in Turkish is 'su,' " said Pnin, a linguist by necessity, and went on with his fascinating past: Completed university education in Prague. Was connected with various scientific institutions. Then—— "Well, to make a long story very short: habitated in Paris from 1925, abandoned France at beginning of Hitler war. Is now here. Is American citizen. Is teaching Russian and such like subjects at Vandal College. From Hagen, Head of German Department, obtainable all references. Or from the College Home for Single Instructors."

Hadn't he been comfortable there?

"Too many people," said Pnin. "Inquisitive people. Whereas special privacy is now to me absolutely necessary." He coughed into his fist with an unexpected cavernous sound (which somehow reminded Joan of a professional Don Cossack she had once met) and then took the plunge: "I must warn: will have all my teeth pulled out. It is a repulsive operation."

"Well, come upstairs," said Joan brightly.

Pnin peered into Isabel's pink-walled, white-flounced room. It had suddenly begun to snow, though the sky was pure platinum, and the slow scintillant downcome got reflected in the silent looking glass. Methodically Pnin inspected Hoecker's "Girl with a Cat" above the bed, and Hunt's "The Belated Kid" above the bookshelf. Then he held his hand at a little distance from the window.

"Is temperature uniform?"

Joan dashed to the radiator.

"Piping hot," she reported.

"I am asking—are there currents of air?"

"Oh yes, you will have plenty of air. And here is the bathroom—small, but all yours."

"No *douche?*" inquired Pnin, looking up. "Maybe it is better so. My friend, Professor Chateau of Columbia, once broke his leg in two places. Now I must think. What price are you prepared to demand? I ask it, because I will not give more than a dollar per day—not including, of course, nootrition."

"All right," said Joan with that pleasant, quick laugh of hers.

The same afternoon, one of Pnin's students, Charles McBeth ("A madman, I think, judging by his compositions," Pnin used to say), zestfully brought over Pnin's luggage in a pathologically purplish car with no fenders on the left side, and after an early dinner at The Egg and We, a recently inaugurated and not very successful little restaurant which Pnin frequented from sheer sympathy with failure, our friend applied himself to the pleasant task of Pninizing his new quarters. Isabel's adolescence had gone with her, or, if not, had been eradicated by her mother, but traces of the girl's childhood somehow had been allowed to remain, and before finding the most advantageous situations for his elaborate sun lamp, huge Russian-alphabet typewriter in a broken coffin fixed with Scotch tape, five pairs of handsome, curiously small shoes with ten shoe trees rooted in them, a coffee grinding-and-boiling contraption which was not quite as good as the one that had exploded last year, a couple of alarm clocks running the same race every night, and seventy-four library books, mainly old Russian periodicals solidly bound by WCL, Pnin delicately exiled to a chair on the landing half a dozen forlorn volumes, such as *Birds at Home, Happy Days in Holland,* and *My First Dictionary* ("With more than 600 illustrations depicting zoos, the human body, farms, fires—all scientifically chosen"), and also a lone wooden bead with a hole through the center.

Joan, who used the word "pathetic" perhaps a little too often, declared she would ask that pathetic savant for a drink with their guests, to which her husband replied he was also a pathetic savant and would go to a movie if she carried out her threat. However, when Joan went up to Pnin with her offer he declined the invitation, saying, rather simply, he had resolved not to use alcohol any more. Three couples and Entwistle arrived around nine, and by ten the little party was in full swing, when suddenly Joan, while talking to pretty Gwen Cockerell, noticed Pnin, in a green sweater, standing in the doorway that led to the foot of the stairs and holding aloft, for her to see, a tumbler. She sped toward him—and simultaneously her husband almost collided with her as he trotted across the room to stop, choke, abolish Jack Cockerell, head of the English Department, who, with his back to Pnin, was entertaining Mrs. Hagen and Mrs. Blorenge with his famous act—he being one of the greatest, if not the greatest, mimics of Pnin on the campus. His model, in the meantime, was saying to Joan: "This is not a clean glass in the bathroom, and there exist other troubles. It blows from the floor, and it blows from the walls——" But Dr. Hagen, a pleasant, rectangular old man, had noticed Pnin, too, and was greeting him joyfully, and the next moment Pnin, his tumbler replaced by a highball, was being introduced to Professor Entwistle.

"*Zdrastvuyte kak pozhivaete horosho spasibo,*" Entwistle rattled off in excellent imitation of Russian speech—and indeed he rather resembled a genial Tsarist colonel in mufti. "One night in Paris," he went on, his eyes twinkling, "at the *Ougolok* cabaret, this demonstration convinced a group of Russian revelers that I was a compatriot of theirs—posing as an American, don't you know."

"In two-three years," said Pnin, missing one bus but boarding the next, "I will also be taken for an American," and everybody roared except Professor Blorenge.

"We'll get you an electric heater," Joan told Pnin confidentially, as she offered him some olives.

"What make heater?" asked Pnin suspiciously.

"That remains to be seen. Any other complaints?"

"Yes—sonic disturbance," said Pnin. "I hear every, every sound from downstairs, but now it is not the place to discuss it, I think."

3

The guests started to leave. Pnin trudged upstairs, a clean glass in his hand. Entwistle and his host were the last to come out on the porch. Wet snow drifted in the black night.

"It's such a pity," said Professor Entwistle, "that we cannot tempt you to come to Goldwin for good. We have Schwarz and old Crates, who are among your greatest admirers. We have a real lake. We have everything. We even have a Professor Pnin on our staff."

"I know, I know," said Clements, "but these offers I keep getting are coming too late. I plan to retire soon, and till then I prefer to remain in the musty but familiar hole. How did you like"—he lowered his voice—"Monsieur Blorenge?"

"Oh, he struck me as a capital fellow. In some ways, however, I must say he reminded me of that probably legendary figure, the Chairman of French, who thought Chateaubriand was a famous *chef*."

"Careful," said Clements. "That story was first told about Blorenge, and is true."

4

Next morning heroic Pnin marched to town, walking a cane in the European manner (up-down, up-down) and letting his gaze dwell upon various objects in a philosophical effort to imagine what it would be to see them again after the ordeal and then recall what it had been to perceive them through the prism of its expectation. Two hours later he was trudging back, leaning on his cane and not looking at anything. A warm flow of pain was gradually replacing the ice and wood of the anesthetic in his thawing, still half-dead, abominably martyred mouth. After that, during a few days he was in mourning for an intimate part of himself. It surprised him to realize how fond he had been of his teeth. His tongue, a fat sleek seal, used to flop and slide so happily among the familiar rocks, checking the contours of a battered but still secure kingdom, plunging from cave to cove, climbing this jag, nuzzling that notch, finding a shred of sweet seaweed in the same old cleft; but now not a landmark remained, and all there existed was a great dark wound, a terra incognita of gums which dread and disgust forbade one to investigate. And when the plates were thrust in, it was like a poor fossil skull being fitted with the grinning jaws of a perfect stranger.

There were, as per plan, no lectures, nor did he attend the examinations given for him by Miller. Ten days passed—and suddenly he began to enjoy the new gadget. It was a revelation, it was a sunrise, it was a firm mouthful of efficient, alabastrine, humane America. At night he kept his treasure in a special glass of special fluid where it smiled to itself, pink and pearly, as perfect as some lovely representative of deep-sea flora. The great work on Old Russia, a wonderful dream mixture of folklore, poetry, social history, and *petite histoire,* which for the last ten years or so he had been fondly planning, now seemed accessible at last, with headaches gone, and this new amphitheater of translucid plastics implying, as it were, a stage and a performance. When the Spring Term began his class could not help noticing the sea change, as he sat coquettishly tapping with the rubber end of a pencil upon those even, too even, incisors and canines while some student translated some sentence in old and ruddy Professor Oliver Bradstreet Mann's *Elementary Russian* (actually written from beginning to end by two frail drudges, John and Olga Krotki, both dead today), such as "The boy is playing with his nurse and his uncle."

And one evening he waylaid Laurence Clements, who was in the act of scuttling up to his study, and with incoherent exclamations of triumph started to demonstrate the beauty of the thing, the ease with which it could be taken out and put in again, and urged surprised but not unfriendly Laurence to have all his teeth out first thing tomorrow.

"You will be a reformed man like I," cried Pnin.

It should be said for both Laurence and Joan that rather soon they began to appreciate Pnin at his unique Pninian worth, and this despite the fact that he was more of a poltergeist than a lodger. He did something fatal to his new heater and gloomily said never mind, it would soon be spring now. He had an irritating way of standing on the landing and assiduously brushing his clothes there, the brush clinking against the buttons, for at least five minutes every blessed morning. He had a passionate intrigue with Joan's washing machine. Although forbidden to come near it, he would be caught trespassing again and again. Casting aside all decorum and caution, he would feed it anything that happened to be at hand, his handkerchief, kitchen towels, a heap of shorts and shirts smuggled down from his room, just for the joy of watching through that porthole what looked like an endless tumble of dolphins with the staggers. One Sunday, after checking the solitude, he could not resist, out of sheer scientific curiosity, giving the mighty machine a pair of rubber-soled canvas shoes stained with clay and chlorophyll to play with; the shoes tramped away with a dreadful arhythmic sound, like an army going over a bridge, and came back without their soles, and Joan appeared from her little sitting room behind the pantry and said in sadness, "Again, Timofey?" But she forgave him, and liked to sit with him at the kitchen table, both cracking nuts or drinking tea. Desdemona, the old colored charwoman, who came on Fridays and with whom at one time God had gossiped daily (" 'Desdemona,' the Lord would say to me, 'that man George is no good.' "), happened to glimpse Pnin basking in the unearthly lilac light of his sun lamp, wearing nothing but shorts, dark glasses, and a dazzling Greek Catholic cross on his broad chest, and insisted thereafter that he was a saint. Laurence, on going up to his study one day, a secret and sacred lair cunningly carved out of the attic, was incensed to find the mellow lights on and fat-naped Pnin braced on his thin legs serenely browsing in a corner: "Excuse me, I only am grazing," as the gentle intruder (whose English was growing richer at a surprising pace) remarked, glancing over the higher of his two shoulders; but somehow that very afternoon a chance reference to a rare author, a passing allusion tacitly recognized in the middle distance of an idea, an adventurous sail descried on the horizon, led insensibly to a tender mental concord between the two men, both of whom were really at ease only in their warm world of natural scholarship. There are human solids and there are human surds, and Clements and Pnin belonged to the latter variety. Thenceforth they would often devise, as they met and stopped on thresholds, on landings, on two different levels of staircase steps (exchanging altitudes and turning to each other anew), or as they walked in opposite directions up and down a room which at the moment existed for them only as an *espace meublé,* to use a Pninian term. It soon transpired that Timofey was a veritable encyclopedia of Russian shrugs and shakes, had tabulated them, and could add something to Laurence's files on the philosophical interpretation of pictorial and non-pictorial, national and environmental gestures. It was very pleasant to see the two men discuss a legend or a religion, Timofey blossoming out in amphoric motion, Laurence chopping away with one hand. Laurence even made a film of what Timofey considered to be the essentials of Russian "carpalistics," with Pnin in a polo shirt, a Gioconda smile on his lips, demonstrating the movements underlying such Russian verbs—used in reference to hands—as *mahnut', vsplesnut', razvesti:* the one-hand downward loose shake of weary relinquishment; the two-hand dramatic splash of amazed distress; and the "disjunctive" motion—

hands traveling apart to signify helpless passivity. And in con-clusion, very slowly, Pnin showed how, in the international "shaking the finger" gesture, a half turn, as delicate as the switch of the wrist in fencing, metamorphosed the Russian solemn symbol of pointing up, "the Judge in Heaven sees you!" into a German air picture of the stick—"something is coming to you!" "However," added objective Pnin, "Russian metaphysical police can break physical bones also very well."

With apologies for his "negligent toilet," Pnin showed the film to a group of students—and Betty Bliss, a graduate work-ing in Comparative Literature, where Pnin was assisting Dr. Hagen, announced that Timofey Pavlovich looked exactly like Buddha in an Oriental moving picture she had seen in the Asiatic Department. This Betty Bliss, a plump maternal girl of some twenty-nine summers, was a soft thorn in Pnin's aging flesh. Ten years before she had had a handsome heel for a lover, who had jilted her for a little tramp, and later she had had a dragging, hopelessly complicated, Chekhovian rather than Dostoevskian affair with a cripple who was now married to his nurse, a cheap cutie. Poor Pnin hesitated. In principle, marriage was not excluded. In his new dental glory, he went so far one seminar session, after the rest had gone, as to hold her hand on his palm and pat it while they were sitting together and dis-cussing Turgenev's poem in prose: "How fair, how fresh were the roses." She could hardly finish reading, her bosom bursting with sighs, the held hand aquiver. "Turgenev," said Pnin, put-ting the hand back on the table, "was made by the ugly, but adored by him, singer Pauline Viardot to play the idiot in charades and *tableaux vivants,* and Madam Pushkin said: 'You annoy me with your verses, Pushkin'—and in old age—to think only!—the wife of colossus, colossus Tolstoy liked much better than him a stoopid moozishan with a red noz!"

Pnin had nothing against Miss Bliss. In trying to visualize a serene senility, he saw her with passable clarity bringing him his lap robe or refilling his fountain pen. He liked her all right—but his heart belonged to another woman.

The cat, as Pnin would say, cannot be hid in a bag. In order to explain my poor friend's abject excitement, one evening in the middle of the term—when he received a certain telegram and then paced his room for at least forty minutes—it should be stated that Pnin had not always been single. The Clementses were playing Chinese checkers among the reflections of a comfortable fire when Pnin came clattering downstairs, slipped, and almost fell at their feet like a supplicant in some ancient city full of injustice, but retrieved his balance—only to crash into the poker and tongs.

"I have come," he said, panting, "to inform, or more correctly ask you, if I can have a female visitor Saturday—in the day, of course. She is my former wife, now Dr. Liza Wind—maybe you have heard in psychiatric circles."

5

There are some beloved women whose eyes, by a chance blend of brilliancy and shape, affect us not directly, not at the moment of shy perception, but in a delayed and cumulative burst of light when the heartless person is absent, and the magic agony abides, and its lenses and lamps are installed in the dark. Whatever eyes Liza Pnin, now Wind, had, they seemed to reveal their essence, their precious-stone water, only when you evoked them in thought, and then a blank, blind, moist aquamarine blaze shivered and stared as if a spatter of sun and sea had got between your own eyelids. Actually her eyes were of a light transparent blue with contrasting black lashes and bright pink canthus, and they slightly stretched up templeward, where a set of feline little lines fanned out from each. She had a sweep of dark brown hair above a lustrous forehead, and a snow-and-rose complexion, and she used a very light red lipstick, and save for a certain thickness of ankle and wrist, there was hardly a flaw to her full-blown, animated, elemental, not particularly well-groomed beauty.

Pnin, then a rising young scholar and she, a more limpid mermaid than now but practically the same person, had met around 1925, in Paris. He wore a sparse auburn beard (today only white bristles would sprout if he did not shave—poor Pnin, poor albino porcupine!), and this divided monastic growth, topped by a fat glossy nose and innocent eyes, nicely epitomized the physique of old-fashioned intellectual Russia. A small job at the Aksakov Institute, rue Vert-Vert, combined with another at Saul Bagrov's Russian bookshop, rue Gresset, supplied him with a livelihood. Liza Bogolepov, a medical student just turned twenty, and perfectly charming in her black silk jumper and tailor-made skirt, was already working at the Meudon sanatorium directed by that remarkable and formidable old lady, Dr. Rosetta Stone, one of the most destructive psychiatrists of the day; and, moreover, Liza wrote verse—mainly in halting anapaest; indeed, Pnin saw her for the first time at one of those literary soirées where young *émigré* poets, who had left Russia in their pale, unpampered pubescence, chanted nostalgic elegies dedicated to a country that could be little more to them than a sad stylized toy, a bauble found in the attic, a crystal globe which you shake to make a soft luminous snowstorm inside over a minuscule fir tree and a log cabin of papier-mâché. Pnin wrote her a tremendous love letter—now safe in a private collection—and she read it with tears of self-pity while recovering from a pharmacopoeial attempt at suicide because of a rather silly affair with a littérateur who is now—— But no matter. Five analysts, intimate friends of hers, all said: "Pnin—and a baby at once."

Marriage hardly changed their manner of life except that she moved into Pnin's dingy apartment. He went on with his Slavic studies, she with her psychodramatics and her lyrical ovipositing, laying all over the place like an Easter rabbit, and in those green and mauve poems—about the child she wanted to bear, and the lovers she wanted to have, and St. Petersburg (courtesy Anna Akhmatov)—every intonation, every image, every simile had been used before by other rhyming rabbits. One of her admirers, a banker, and straightforward patron of the arts, selected among the Parisian Russians an influential literary critic, Zhorzhik Uranski, and for a champagne dinner at the *Ougolok* had the old boy devote his next *feuilleton* in one of the Russian-language newspapers to an appreciation of Liza's muse, on whose chestnut curls Zhorzhik calmly placed Anna Akhmatov's coronet, whereupon Liza burst into happy tears —for all the world like little Miss Michigan or the Oregon Rose Queen. Pnin, who was not in the know, carried about a folded clipping of that shameless rave in his honest pocketbook, naïvely reading out passages to this or that amused friend until it got quite frayed and smudgy. Nor was he in the know concerning graver matters, and in fact was actually pasting the remnants of the review in an album when, on a December day in 1938, Liza telephoned from Meudon, saying that she was going to Montpellier with a man who understood her "organic ego," a Dr. Eric Wind, and would never see Timofey again. An unknown French woman with red hair called for Liza's things and said, well, you cellar rat, there is no more any poor lass to *taper dessus*—and a month or two later there dribbled in from Dr. Wind a German letter of sympathy and apology assuring *lieber Herr Pnin* that he, Dr. Wind, was eager to marry "the woman who has come out of your life into mine." Pnin of course would have given her a divorce as readily as he would his life, with the wet stems cut and a bit of fern, and all of it wrapped up as crisply as at the earth-smelling florist's when the rain makes gray and green mirrors of Easter day; but it transpired that in South America Dr. Wind had a wife with a tortuous mind and a phony passport, who did not wish to be bothered until certain plans of her own took shape. Meanwhile the New World had started to beckon Pnin too: from New York a great friend of his, Professor Konstantin Chateau, offered him every assistance for a migratory voyage. Pnin informed Dr. Wind of his plans and sent Liza the last issue of an *émigré* magazine where she was mentioned on page 202. He was halfway through the dreary hell that had been devised by European bureaucrats (to the vast amusement of the Soviets) for holders of that miserable thing, the Nansen Passport (a kind of parolee's card issued to Russian *émigrés*), when one damp April day in 1940 there was a vigorous ring at his door and Liza tramped in, puffing and carrying before her like a chest of drawers a seven-month pregnancy, and announced, as she tore off her hat and kicked off her shoes, that it had all been a mistake, and from now on she was again Pnin's faithful and lawful wife, ready to follow him wherever he went—even beyond the ocean if need be. Those days were probably the happiest in Pnin's life—it was a permanent glow of weighty, painful felicity—and the vernalization of the visas, and the preparations, and the medical examination, with a deaf-and-dumb doctor applying a dummy stethoscope to Pnin's jammed heart through all his clothes, and the kind Russian lady (a relative of mine) who was so helpful at the American Consulate, and the journey to Bordeaux, and the beautiful clean ship—everything had a rich fairy-tale tinge to it. He was not only ready to adopt the child when it came but was passionately eager to do so, and she listened with a satisfied, somewhat cowish expression to the pedagogical plans he unfolded, for he actually seemed to forehear the babe's vagitus, and its first word in the near future. She had always been fond of sugar-coated almonds, but now she consumed fabulous quantities of them (two pounds between Paris and Bordeaux), and ascetic Pnin contemplated her greed with shakes and shrugs of delighted awe, and something about the smooth silkiness of those *dragées* remained in his mind, forever mingled with the memory of her taut skin, her complexion, her flawless teeth.

It was a little disappointing that as soon as she came aboard she gave one glance at the swelling sea, said: *"Nu, eto izvinite* (Nothing doing)," and promptly retired into the womb of the ship, within which, for most of the crossing, she kept lying on her back in the cabin she shared with the loquacious wives of the three laconic Poles—a wrestler, a gardener, and a barber—

whom Pnin got as cabin mates. On the third evening of the voyage, having remained in the lounge long after Liza had gone to sleep, he cheerfully accepted a game of chess proposed by the former editor of a Frankfurt newspaper, a melancholy baggy-eyed patriarch in a turtle-neck sweater and plus fours. Neither was a good player; both were addicted to spectacular but quite unsound sacrifices of pieces; each was overanxious to win; and the proceedings were furthermore enlivened by Pnin's fantastic brand of German (*"Wenn Sie so, dann ich so, und Pferd fliegt"*). Presently another passenger came up, said *entschuldigen Sie,* could he watch their game? And sat down beside them. He had reddish hair cropped close and long pale eyelashes resembling fish moths, and he wore a shabby double-breasted coat, and soon he was clucking under his breath and shaking his head every time the patriarch, after much dignified meditation, lurched forward to make a wild move. Finally this helpful spectator, obviously an expert, could not resist pushing back a pawn his compatriot had just moved, and pointing with a vibrating index to a rook instead—which the old Frankfurter incontinently drove into the armpit of Pnin's defense. Our man lost, of course, and was about to leave the lounge when the expert overtook him, saying *entschuldigen Sie,* could he talk for a moment to Herr Pnin? ("You see, I know your name," he remarked parenthetically, lifting his useful index)—and suggested a couple of beers at the bar. Pnin accepted, and when the tankards were placed before them the polite stranger continued thus: "In life, as in chess, it is always better to analyze one's motives and intentions. The day we came on board I was like a playful child. Next morning, however, I began already to fear that an astute husband—this is not a compliment, but a hypothesis in retrospection—would sooner or later study the passenger list. Today my conscience has tried me and found me guilty. I can endure the deception no longer. Your health. This is not at all our German nectar but it is better than Coca-Cola. My name is Dr. Eric Wind; alas, it is not unknown to you."

Pnin, in silence, his face working, one palm still on the wet bar, had started to slither clumsily off his uncomfortable mush-room seat, but Wind put five long sensitive fingers on his sleeve.

"*Lasse mich, lasse mich,*" wailed Pnin, trying to beat off the limp fawning hand.

"Please!" said Dr. Wind. "Be just. The prisoner has always the last word; it is his right. Even the Nazis admit it. And first of all—I want you to allow me to pay at least one half of the lady's passage."

"*Ach nein, nein, nein,*" said Pnin. "Let us finish this night-mare conversation (*diese koschmarische Sprache*)."

"As you like," said Dr. Wind, and proceeded to impress upon pinned Pnin the following points: That it had all been Liza's idea—"simplifying matters, you know, for the sake of our child" (the "our" sounded tripersonal); that Liza should be treated as a very sick woman (pregnancy being really the sub-limation of a death wish); that he (Dr. Wind) would marry her in America—"where I am also going," Dr. Wind added for clarity; and that he (Dr. Wind) should at least be permitted to pay for the beer. From then on to the end of the voyage that had turned from green and silver to a uniform gray, Pnin busied himself overtly with his English-language manuals, and al-though immutably meek with Liza, tried to see her as little as he could without awakening her suspicions. Every now and then Dr. Wind would appear from nowhere and make from afar signs of recognition and reassurance. And at last, when the great statue arose from the morning haze where, ready to be ignited by the sun, pale, spellbound buildings stood like those mysterious rectangles of unequal height that you see in bar graph representations of compared percentages (natural re-sources, the frequency of mirages in different deserts), Dr. Wind resolutely walked up to the Pnins and identified him-self—"because all three of us must enter the land of liberty with pure hearts." And after a bathetic sojourn on Ellis Island, Timofey and Liza parted.

There were complications—but at last Wind married her.

In the course of the first five years in America, Pnin glimpsed her on several occasions in New York; he and the Winds were naturalized on the same day; then, after his removal to Waindell in 1945, half a dozen years passed without any meetings or correspondence. He heard of her, however, from time to time. Recently (in December 1951) his friend Chateau had sent him an issue of a journal of psychiatry with an article written by Dr. Albina Dunkelberg, Dr. Eric Wind, and Dr. Liza Wind on "Group Psychotherapy Applied to Marriage Counseling." Pnin used to be always embarrassed by Liza's *"psihooslinïe"* ("psychoasinine") interests, and even now, when he ought to have been indifferent, he felt a twinge of revulsion and pity. Eric and she were working under the great Bernard Maywood, a genial giant of a man—referred to as "The Boss" by over-adaptive Eric—at a Research Bureau attached to a Planned Parenthood Center. Encouraged by his and his wife's protector, Eric evolved the ingenious idea (possibly not his own) of side-tracking some of the more plastic and stupid clients of the Center into a psychotherapeutic trap—a "tension-releasing" circle on the lines of a quilting bee, where young married women in groups of eight relaxed in a comfortable room amid an atmosphere of cheerful first-name informality, with doctors at a table facing the group, and a secretary unobtrusively taking notes, and traumatic episodes floating out of everybody's childhood like corpses. At these sessions, the ladies were made to discuss among themselves with absolute frankness their problems of marital maladjustment, which entailed, of course, comparing notes on their mates, who later were interviewed, too, in a special "husband group," likewise very informal, with a great passing around of cigars and anatomic charts. Pnin skipped the actual reports and case histories—and there is no need to go here into those hilarious details. Suffice it to say that already at the third session of the female group, after this or that lady had gone home and seen the light and come back to describe the newly discovered sensation to her still blocked but rapt sisters, a ringing note of revivalism pleasingly colored the proceedings ("Well, girls, when George last night——") And this was not all. Dr. Eric Wind hoped to work out a technique that would allow bringing all those husbands and wives together in a joint group. Incidentally it was deadening to hear him and Liza smacking their lips over the word "group." In a long letter to distressed Pnin, Professor Chateau affirmed that Dr. Wind even called Siamese twins "a group." And indeed progressive, idealistic Wind dreamed of a happy world consisting of Siamese centuplets, anatomically conjoined communities, whole nations built around a communicating liver. "It is nothing but a kind of microcosmos of communism—all that psychiatry," rumbled Pnin, in his answer to Chateau. "Why not leave their private sorrows to people? Is sorrow not, one asks, the only thing in the world people really possess?"

6

"Look," said Joan Saturday morning to her husband, "I have decided to tell Timofey they will have the house to themselves today from two to five. We must give those pathetic creatures every possible chance. There are things I can do in town, and you will be dropped at the library."

"It so happens," answered Laurence, "that I have not the least intention to be dropped or otherwise moved anywhere today. Besides, it is highly improbable they will need eight rooms for their reunion."

Pnin put on his new brown suit (paid for by the Cremona lecture) and, after a hurried lunch at The Egg and We, walked through the snow-patched park to the Waindell bus station, arriving there almost an hour too early. He did not bother to puzzle out why exactly Liza had felt the urgent need to see him on her way back from visiting St. Bartholomew's, the preparatory school near Boston that her son would go to next fall: all he knew was that a flood of happiness foamed and rose behind the invisible barrier that was to burst open any moment now. He met five buses, and in each of them clearly made out Liza waving to him through a window as she and the other passengers started to file out, and then one bus after another was drained and she had not turned up. Suddenly he heard her sonorous voice (*"Timofey, zdrastvuy!"*) behind him, and, wheeling around, saw her emerge from the only Greyhound he had decided would not bring her. What change could our friend discern in her? What change could there be, good God! There she was. She always felt hot and buoyant, no matter the cold, and now her sealskin coat was wide open on her frilled blouse as she hugged Pnin's head and he felt the grapefruit fragrance of her neck, and kept muttering: *"Nu nu, vot i horosho, nu vot"*— mere verbal heart props—and she cried out: "Oh, he has splendid new teeth!" He helped her into a taxi, her bright diaphanous scarf caught on something, and Pnin slipped on the pavement, and the taximan said "Easy," and took her bag from him, and everything had happened before, in this exact sequence.

It was, she told him as they drove up Park Street, a school in the English tradition. No, she did not want to eat anything, she had had a big lunch at Albany. It was a "very fancy" school —she said this in English—the boys played a kind of indoor tennis with their hands, between walls, and there would be in his form a —— (she produced with false nonchalance a well-known American name which meant nothing to Pnin because it was not that of a poet or a president). "By the way," interrupted Pnin, ducking and pointing, "you can just see a corner of the campus from here." All this was due ("Yes, I see, *vizhu, vizhu, kampus kak kampus:* The usual kind of thing"), all this, including a scholarship, was due to the influence of Dr. Maywood ("You know, Timofey, some day you should write him a word, just a little sign of courtesy"). The Principal, a clergyman, had shown her the trophies Bernard had won there as a boy. Eric of course had wanted Victor to go to a public school but had been overruled. The Reverend Hopper's wife was the niece of an English Earl.

"Here we are. This is my *palazzo*," said jocose Pnin, who had not been able to concentrate on her rapid speech.

They entered—and he suddenly felt that this day which he had been looking forward to with such fierce longing was passing much too quickly—was going, going, would be gone in a few minutes. Perhaps, he thought, if she said right away what she wanted of him the day might slow down and be really enjoyed.

"What a gruesome place, *kakoy zhutkiy dom*," she said, sitting on the chair near the telephone and taking off her galoshes—such familiar movements! "Look at that aquarelle with the minarets. They must be terrible people."

"No," said Pnin, "they are my friends."

"My dear Timofey," she said, as he escorted her upstairs, "you have had some pretty awful friends in your time."

"And here is my room," said Pnin.

"I think I'll lie on your virgin bed, Timofey. And I'll recite you some verses in a minute. That hellish headache of mine is seeping back again. I felt so splendid all day."

"I have some aspirin."

"Uhn-uhn," she said, and this acquired negative stood out strangely against her native speech.

He turned away as she started to take off her shoes, and the sound they made toppling to the floor reminded him of very old days.

She lay back, black-skirted, white-bloused, brown-haired, with one pink hand over her eyes.

"How is everything with you?" asked Pnin (have her say what she wants of me, quick!) as he sank into the white rocker near the radiator.

"Our work is very interesting," she said, still shielding her eyes, "but I must tell you I don't love Eric any more. Our relations have disintegrated. Incidentally Eric dislikes his child.

He says he is the land father and you, Timofey, are the water father."

Pnin started to laugh: he rolled with laughter, the rather juvenile rocker fairly cracking under him. His eyes were like stars and quite wet.

She looked at him curiously for an instant from under her plump hand—and went on:

"Eric is one hard emotional block in his attitude toward Victor. I don't know how many times the boy must have killed him in his dreams. And, with Eric, verbalization—I have long noticed—confuses problems instead of clarifying them. He is a very difficult person. What is your salary, Timofey?"

He told her.

"Well," she said, "it is not grand. But I suppose you can even lay something aside—it is more than enough for your needs, for your microscopic needs, Timofey."

Her abdomen tightly girdled under the black skirt jumped up two or three times with mute, cozy, good-natured reminiscential irony—and Pnin blew his nose, shaking his head the while, in voluptuous, rapturous mirth.

"Listen to my latest poem," she said, her hands now along her sides as she lay perfectly straight on her back, and she sang out rhythmically, in long-drawn, deep-voiced tones:

> *"Ya nadela tyomnoe plat'e,*
> *I monashenki ya skromney;*
> *Iz slonovoy kosti raspyat'e*
> *Nad holodnoy postel'yu moey.*
>
> *No ogni nebïvalïh orgiy*
> *Prozhigayut moyo zabïtyo*
> *I shepchu ya imya Georgiy—*
> *Zolotoe imya tvoyo!*
>
> *(I have put on a dark dress*
> *And am more modest than a nun;*

An ivory crucifix
Is over my cold bed.

But the lights of fabulous orgies
Burn through my oblivion,
And I whisper the name George—
Your golden name!)"

"He is a very interesting man," she went on, without any interval. "Practically English, in fact. He flew a bomber in the war and now he is with a firm of brokers who have no sympathy with him and do not understand him. He comes from an ancient family. His father was a dreamer, had a floating casino, you know, and all that, but was ruined by some Jewish gangsters in Florida and voluntarily went to prison for another man; it is a family of heroes."

She paused. The silence in the little room was punctuated rather than broken by the throbbing and tinkling in those whitewashed organ pipes.

"I made Eric a complete report," Liza continued with a sigh. "And now he keeps assuring me he can cure me if I co-operate. Unfortunately I am also co-operating with George."

She pronounced George as in Russian—both *g*'s hard, both *e*'s longish.

"Well, *c'est la vie,* as Eric so originally says. How can you sleep with that string of cobweb hanging from the ceiling?" She looked at her wrist watch. "Goodness, I must catch the bus at four-thirty. You must call a taxi in a minute. I have something to say to you of the utmost importance."

Here it was coming at last—so late.

She wanted Timofey to lay aside every month a little money for the boy—because she could not ask Bernard Maywood now—and she might die—and Eric did not care what happened —and somebody ought to send the lad a small sum now and then, as if coming from his mother—pocket money, you know —he would be among rich boys. She would write Timofey giving him an address and some more details. Yes—she never doubted that Timofey was a darling (*"Nu kakoy zhe ti dushka"*). And now where was the bathroom? And would he please telephone for the taxi?

"Incidentally," she said, as he was helping her into her coat and as usual searching with a frown for the fugitive armhole while she pawed and groped, "you know, Timofey, this brown suit of yours is a mistake: a gentleman does not wear brown."

He saw her off, and walked back through the park. To hold her, to keep her—just as she was—with her cruelty, with her vulgarity, with her blinding blue eyes, with her miserable poetry, with her fat feet, with her impure, dry, sordid, infantile soul. All of a sudden he thought: If people are reunited in Heaven (I don't believe it, but suppose), then how shall I stop it from creeping upon me, over me, that shriveled, helpless, lame thing, her soul? But this is the earth, and I am, curiously enough, alive, and there is something in me and in life——

He seemed to be quite unexpectedly (for human despair seldom leads to great truths) on the verge of a simple solution of the universe but was interrupted by an urgent request. A squirrel under a tree had seen Pnin on the path. In one sinuous tendril-like movement, the intelligent animal climbed up to the brim of a drinking fountain and, as Pnin approached, thrust its oval face toward him with a rather coarse spluttering sound, its cheeks puffed out. Pnin understood and after some fumbling he found what had to be pressed for the necessary results. Eying him with contempt, the thirsty rodent forthwith began to sample the stocky sparkling pillar of water, and went on drinking for a considerable time. "She has fever, perhaps," thought Pnin, weeping quietly and freely, and all the time politely pressing the contraption down while trying not to meet the unpleasant eye fixed upon him. Its thirst quenched, the squirrel departed without the least sign of gratitude.

The water father continued upon his way, came to the end of

the path, then turned into a side street where there was a small bar of log-cabin design with garnet glass in its casement windows.

7

When Joan with a bagful of provisions, two magazines, and three parcels, came home at a quarter past five, she found in the porch mailbox a special-delivery air-mail letter from her daughter. More than three weeks had elapsed since Isabel had briefly written her parents to say that, after a honeymoon in Arizona, she had safely reached her husband's home town. Juggling with her packages, Joan tore the envelope open. It was an ecstatically happy letter, and she gulped it down, everything swimming a little in the radiance of her relief. On the outside of the front door she felt, then saw with brief surprise, Pnin's keys, like a bit of his fondest viscera, dangling with their leathern case from the lock; she used them to open the door, and as soon as she had entered she heard, coming from the pantry, a loud anarchistic knocking—cupboards being opened and shut one after the other.

She put her bag and parcels down on the sideboard in the kitchen and asked in the direction of the pantry: "What are you looking for, Timofey?"

He came out of there, darkly flushed, wild-eyed, and she was shocked to see that his face was a mess of unwiped tears.

"I search, John, for the viscous and sawdust," he said tragically.

"I am afraid there is no soda," she answered with her lucid Anglo-Saxon restraint. "But there is plenty of whisky in the dining-room cabinet. However, I suggest we both have some nice hot tea instead."

He made the Russian "relinquishing" gesture.

"No, I don't want anything at all," he said, and sat down at the kitchen table with an awful sigh.

She sat down next to him and opened one of the magazines she had bought.

"We are going to look at some pictures, Timofey."

"I do not want, John. You know I do not understand what is advertisement and what is not advertisement."

"You just relax, Timofey, and I'll do the explaining. Oh, look—I like this one. Oh, this is very clever. We have here a combination of two ideas—the Desert Island and the Girl in the Puff. Now, look, Timofey—please"—he reluctantly put on his reading glasses—"this is a desert island with a lone palm, and this is a bit of broken raft, and this is a shipwrecked mariner, and this is the ship's cat he saved, and this here, on that rock——"

"Impossible," said Pnin. "So small island, moreover with palm, cannot exist in such big sea."

"Well, it exists here."

"Impossible isolation," said Pnin.

"Yes, but—— Really, you are not playing fair, Timofey. You know perfectly well you agree with Lore that the world of the mind is based on a compromise with logic."

"I have reservations," said Pnin. "First of all, logic herself——"

"All right, I'm afraid we are wandering away from our little joke. Now, you look at the picture. So this is the mariner, and this is the pussy, and this is a rather wistful mermaid hanging around, and now look at the puffs right above the sailor and the pussy."

"Atomic bomb explosion," said Pnin sadly.

"No, not at all. It is something much funnier. You see, these round puffs are supposed to be the projections of their thoughts. And now at last we are getting to the amusing part. The sailor imagines the mermaid as having a pair of legs, and the cat imagines her as all fish."

"Lermontov," said Pnin, lifting two fingers, "has expressed everything about mermaids in only two poems. I cannot understand American humor even when I am happy, and I must say——" He removed his glasses with trembling hands, elbowed the magazine aside, and, resting his head on his arm, broke into muffled sobs.

She heard the front door open and close, and a moment later Laurence peeped into the kitchen with facetious furtiveness. Joan's right hand waved him away; her left directed him to the rainbow-rimmed envelope on top of the parcels. The private smile she flashed was a summary of Isabel's letter; he grabbed it and, no more in jest, tiptoed out again.

Pnin's unnecessarily robust shoulders continued to shake. She closed the magazine and for a minute studied its cover: toy-bright school tots, Isabel and the Hagen child, shade trees still off duty, a white spire, the Waindell bells.

"Doesn't she want to come back?" asked Joan softly.

Pnin, his head on his arm, started to beat the table with his loosely clenched fist.

"I haf nofing," wailed Pnin between loud, damp sniffs, "I haf nofing left, nofing, nofing!"

❧ Chapter Three ❧

I

During the eight years Pnin had taught at Waindell College he had changed his lodgings—for one reason or another, mainly sonic—about every semester. The accumulation of consecutive rooms in his memory now resembled those displays of grouped elbow chairs on show, and beds, and lamps, and inglenooks which, ignoring all space-time distinctions, commingle in the soft light of a furniture store beyond which it snows, and the dusk deepens, and nobody really loves anybody. The rooms of his Waindell period looked especially trim in comparison with

one he had had in uptown New York, midway between Tsen-
tral Park and Reeverside, on a block memorable for the waste-
paper along the curb, the bright pat of dog dirt somebody had
already slipped upon, and a tireless boy pitching a ball against
the steps of the high brown porch; and even that room became
positively dapper in Pnin's mind (where a small ball still re-
bounded) when compared with the old, now dust-blurred lodgings of his Central European, Nansen-passport period.

With age, however, Pnin had become choosy. Pretty fixtures
no longer sufficed. Waindell was a quiet townlet, and Waindellville, in a notch of the hills, was yet quieter; but nothing was
quiet enough for Pnin. There had been, at the start of his life
here, that studio in the thoughtfully furnished College Home
for Single Instructors, a very nice place despite certain gregari-
ous drawbacks ("Ping-pong, Pnin?" "I don't any more play
at games of infants"), until workmen came and started to drill
holes in the street—Brainpan Street, Pningrad—and patch
them up again, and this went on and on, in fits of shivering
black zigzags and stunned pauses, for weeks, and it did not
seem likely they would ever find again the precious tool they
had entombed by mistake. There had been (to pick out here
and there only special offenders) that room in the eminently
hermetic-looking Dukc's Lodge, Waindellville: a delightful
kabinet, above which, however, every evening, among crashing
bathroom cascades and banging doors, two monstrous statues
on primitive legs of stone would grimly tramp—shapes hard to
reconcile with the slender build of his actual upstairs neighbors,
who turned out to be the Starrs, of the Fine Arts Department
("I am Christopher, and this is Louise"), an angelically gentle
couple keenly interested in Dostoevski and Shostakovich.
There had been—in yet another rooming house—a still cozier
bedroom-study, with nobody butting in for a free lesson in Russian; but as soon as the formidable Waindell winter began to
penetrate the coziness by means of sharp little drafts, coming
not only from the window but even from the closet and the

base plugs, the room had developed something like a streak of madness or mystic delusion—namely, a tenacious murmur of music, more or less classical, oddly located in Pnin's silver-washed radiator. He tried to muffle it up with a blanket, as if it were a caged songbird, but the song persisted until Mrs. Thayer's old mother was removed to the hospital where she died, upon which the radiator switched to Canadian French.

He tried habitats of another type: rooms for rent in private houses which, although differing from each other in many respects (not all, for instance, were clapboard ones; a few were stucco, or at least partly stucco), had one generic characteristic in common: in their parlor or stair-landing bookcases Hendrik Willem van Loon and Dr. Cronin were inevitably present; they might be separated by a flock of magazines, or by some glazed and buxom historical romance, or even by Mrs. Garnett impersonating somebody (and in such houses there would be sure to hang somewhere a Toulouse-Lautrec poster), but you found the pair without fail, exchanging looks of tender recognition, like two old friends at a crowded party.

2

He had returned for a spell to the College Home, but so had the pavement drillers, and there had cropped up other nuisances besides. At present Pnin was still renting the pink-walled, white-flounced second-floor bedroom in the Clements' house, and this was the first house he really liked and the first room he had occupied for more than a year. By now he had weeded out all trace of its former occupant; or so he thought, for he did not notice, and probably never would, a funny face scrawled on the wall just behind the headboard of the bed and some half-erased height-level marks penciled on the doorjamb, beginning from a four-foot altitude in 1940.

For more than a week now, Pnin had had the run of the

house: Joan Clements had left by plane for a Western state to visit her married daughter, and a couple of days later, at the very beginning of his spring course in philosophy, Professor Clements, summoned by a telegram, had flown West too.

Our friend had a leisurely breakfast, pleasantly based on the milk that had not been discontinued, and at half-past nine prepared for his usual walk to the campus.

It warmed my heart, the Russian-intelligentski way he had of getting into his overcoat: his inclined head would demonstrate its ideal baldness, and his large, Duchess of Wonderland chin would firmly press against the crossed ends of his green muffler to hold it in place on his chest while, with a jerk of his broad shoulders, he contrived to get into both armholes at once; another heave and the coat was on.

He picked up his *portfel'* (briefcase), checked its contents, and walked out.

He was still at a newspaper's throw from his porch when he remembered a book the college library had urgently requested him to return, for the use of another reader. For a moment he struggled with himself; he still needed the volume; but kindly Pnin sympathized too much with the passionate clamor of another (unknown) scholar not to go back for the stout and heavy tome: It was Volume 18—mainly devoted to Tolstoyana—of *Sovetskiy Zolotoy Fond Literaturï* (Soviet Gold Fund of Literature), *Moskva-Leningrad, 1940.*

3

The organs concerned in the production of English speech sounds are the larynx, the velum, the lips, the tongue (that punchinello in the troupe), and, last but not least, the lower jaw; mainly upon its overenergetic and somewhat ruminant motion did Pnin rely when translating in class passages in the Russian grammar or some poem by Pushkin. If his Russian was music, his English was murder. He had enormous difficulty ("dzeefee-cooltsee" in Pninian English) with depalatization, never managing to remove the extra Russian moisture from *t*'s and *d*'s before the vowels he so quaintly softened. His explosive "hat" ("I never go in a hat even in winter") differed from the common American pronunciation of "hot" (typical of Waindell townspeople, for example) only by its briefer duration, and thus sounded very much like the German verb *hat* (has). Long *o*'s with him inevitably became short ones: his "no" sounded positively Italian, and this was accentuated by his trick of triplicating the simple negative ("May I give you a lift, Mr. Pnin?" "No-no-no, I have only two paces from here"). He did not possess (nor was he aware of this lack) any long *oo*: all he could muster when called upon to utter "noon" was the lax vowel of the German *"nun."* ("I have no classes in after*nun* on Tuesday. Today is Tuesday.")

Tuesday—true; but what day of the month, we wonder. Pnin's birthday for instance fell on February 3, by the Julian calendar into which he had been born in St. Petersburg in 1898. He never celebrated it nowadays, partly because, after his departure from Russia, it sidled by in a Gregorian disguise (thirteen—no, twelve days late), and partly because during the academic year he existed mainly on a motuweth frisas basis.

On the chalk-clouded blackboard, which he wittily called the grayboard, he now wrote a date. In the crook of his arm he still felt the bulk of *Zol. Fond Lit.* The date he wrote had nothing to do with the day this was in Waindell:

December 26, 1829

He carefully drilled in a big white full stop, and added underneath:

3:03 P.M. St. Petersburg

Dutifully this was taken down by Frank Backman, Rose Balsamo, Frank Carroll, Irving D. Herz, beautiful, intelligent Marilyn Hohn, John Mead, Jr., Peter Volkov, and Allan Bradbury Walsh.

Pnin, rippling with mute mirth, sat down again at his desk: he had a tale to tell. That line in the absurd Russian grammar, *"Brozhu li ya vdol' ulits shumnïh* (Whether I wander along noisy streets)," was really the opening of a famous poem. Although Pnin was supposed in this Elementary Russian class to stick to language exercises (*"Mama, telefon! Brozhu li ya vdol' ulits shumnïh. Ot Vladivostoka do Vashingtona 5000 mil'."*), he took every opportunity to guide his students on literary and historical tours.

In a set of eight tetrametric quatrains Pushkin described the morbid habit he always had—wherever he was, whatever he was doing—of dwelling on thoughts of death and of closely inspecting every passing day as he strove to find in its cryptogram a certain "future anniversary": the day and month that would appear, somewhere, sometime upon his tombstone.

" 'And where will fate send me,' imperfective future, 'death,' " declaimed inspired Pnin, throwing his head back and translating with brave literality, " 'in fight, in travel, or in waves? Or will the neighboring dale'—*dolina,* same word, 'valley' we would now say—'accept my refrigerated ashes,' *poussière,* 'cold dust' perhaps more correct. 'And though it is indifferent to the insensible body . . .' "

Pnin went on to the end and then, dramatically pointing with the piece of chalk he still held, remarked how carefully Pushkin had noted the day and even the minute of writing down that poem.

"But," exclaimed Pnin in triumph, "he died on a quite, quite different day! He died——" The chair back against which Pnin was vigorously leaning emitted an ominous crack, and the class resolved a pardonable tension in loud young laughter.

(Sometime, somewhere—Petersburg? Prague?—one of the two musical clowns pulled out the piano stool from under the other, who remained, however, playing on, in a seated, though seatless, position, with his rhapsody unimpaired. Where? Circus Busch, Berlin!)

4

Pnin did not bother to leave the classroom between his dismissed Elementary and the Advanced that was trickling in. The office where *Zol. Fond Lit.* now lay, partly enveloped in Pnin's green muffler, on the filing case, was on another floor, at the end of a resonant passage and next to the faculty lavatory. Till 1950 (this was 1953—how time flies!) he had shared an office in the German Department with Miller, one of the younger instructors, and then was given for his exclusive use Office R, which formerly had been a lumber room but had now been completely renovated. During the spring he had lovingly Pninized it. It had come with two ignoble chairs, a cork bulletin board, a can of floor wax forgotten by the janitor, and a humble pedestal desk of indeterminable wood. He wangled from the Administration a small steel file with an entrancing locking device. Young Miller, under Pnin's direction, embraced and brought over Pnin's part of a sectional bookcase. From old Mrs. McCrystal, in whose white frame house he had spent a mediocre winter (1949-50), Pnin purchased for three dollars a faded, once Turkish rug. With the help of the janitor he screwed onto the side of the desk a pencil sharpener—that highly satisfying, highly philosophical implement that goes ticonderoga-ticonderoga, feeding on the yellow finish and sweet wood, and ends up in a kind of soundlessly spinning ethereal void as we all must. He had other, even more ambitious plans, such as an armchair and a tall lamp. When, after a summer spent teaching in Washington, Pnin returned to his office, an obese dog lay asleep on his rug, and his furniture had been moved to a darker part of the office, so as to make room for a magnificent stainless-steel desk and a swivel chair to match, in which sat writing and smiling to himself the newly imported Austrian scholar, Dr. Bodo von Falternfels; and thenceforth, so far as Pnin was concerned, Office R had gone to seed.

5

———————

At noon, as usual, Pnin washed his hands and head.

He picked up in Office R his overcoat, muffler, book, and briefcase. Dr. Falternfels was writing and smiling; his sandwich was half unwrapped; his dog was dead. Pnin walked down the gloomy stairs and through the Museum of Sculpture. Humanities Hall, where, however, Ornithology and Anthropology also lurked, was connected with another brick building, Frieze Hall, which housed the dining rooms and the Faculty Club, by means of a rather rococo openwork gallery: it went up a slope, then turned sharply and wandered down toward a routine smell of potato chips and the sadness of balanced meals. In summer its trellis was alive with quivering flowers; but now through its nakedness an icy wind blew, and someone had placed a found red mitten upon the spout of the dead fountain that stood where one branch of the gallery led to the President's House.

President Poore, a tall, slow, elderly man wearing dark glasses, had started to lose his sight a couple of years before and was now almost totally blind. With solar regularity, however, he would be led every day by his niece and secretary to Frieze Hall; he came, a figure of antique dignity, moving in his private darkness to an invisible luncheon, and although everybody had long grown accustomed to his tragic entrance, there was invariably the shadow of a hush while he was being steered to his carved chair and while he groped for the edge of the table; and it was strange to see, directly behind him on the wall, his stylized likeness in a mauve double-breasted suit and mahogany shoes, gazing with radiant magenta eyes at the scrolls handed him by Richard Wagner, Dostoevski, and Confucius, a group that Oleg Komarov, of the Fine Arts Department, had painted a decade ago into Lang's celebrated mural of 1938, which carried all around the dining room a pageant of historical figures and Waindell faculty members.

Pnin, who wanted to ask his compatriot something, sat down beside him. This Komarov, a Cossack's son, was a very short man with a crew cut and a death's-head's nostrils. He and Serafima, his large, cheerful, Moscow-born wife, who wore a Tibetan charm on a long silver chain that hung down to her ample, soft belly, would throw Russki parties every now and then, with Russki hors d'oeuvres and guitar music and more or less phony folk songs—occasions at which shy graduate students would be taught vodka-drinking rites and other stale Russianisms; and after such feasts, upon meeting gruff Pnin, Serafima and Oleg (she raising her eyes to heaven, he covering his with one hand) would murmur in awed self-gratitude: *"Gospodi, skol'ko mï im dayom!* (My, what a lot we give them!)" —"them" being the benighted American people. Only another Russian could understand the reactionary and Sovietophile blend presented by the pseudo-colorful Komarovs, for whom an ideal Russia consisted of the Red Army, an anointed monarch, collective farms, anthroposophy, the Russian Church and the Hydro-Electric Dam. Pnin and Oleg Komarov were usually in a subdued state of war, but meetings were inevitable, and such of their American colleagues as deemed the Komarovs "grand people" and mimicked droll Pnin were sure the painter and Pnin were excellent friends.

It would be hard to say, without applying some very special tests, which of them, Pnin or Komarov, spoke the worse English; probably Pnin; but for reasons of age, general education, and a slightly longer stage of American citizenship, he found it possible to correct Komarov's frequent English interpolations, and Komarov resented this even more than he did Pnin's *antikvarnïy liberalizm.*

"Look here, Komarov (*Poslushayte, Komarov*"—a rather discourteous manner of address)—said Pnin. "I cannot understand who else here might want this book; certainly none of my students; and if it is you, I cannot understand why you should want it anyway."

"I don't," answered Komarov, glancing at the volume. "Not interested," he added in English.

Pnin moved his lips and lower jaw mutely once or twice, wanted to say something, did not, and went on with his salad.

6

This being Tuesday, he could walk over to his favorite haunt immediately after lunch and stay there till dinner time. No gallery connected Waindell College Library with any other buildings, but it was intimately and securely connected with Pnin's heart. He walked past the great bronze figure of the first president of the college, Alpheus Frieze, in sports cap and knickerbockers, holding by its horns the bronze bicycle he was eternally about to mount, judging by the position of his left foot, forever glued to the left pedal. There was snow on the saddle and snow in the absurd basket that recent pranksters had attached to the handle bars. *"Huligani,"* fumed Pnin, shaking his head—and slipped slightly on a flag of the path that meandered down a turfy slope among the leafless elms. Besides the big book under his right arm, he carried in his left hand his briefcase, and old, Central European-looking, black *portfel'*, and this he swung rhythmically by its leathern grip as he marched to his books, to his scriptorium in the stacks, to his paradise of Russian lore.

An elliptic flock of pigeons, in circular volitation, soaring gray, flapping white, and then gray again, wheeled across the limpid, pale sky, above the College Library. A train whistled afar as mournfully as in the steppes. A skimpy squirrel dashed over a patch of sunlit snow, where a tree trunk's shadow, olive-green on the turf, became grayish blue for a stretch, while the tree itself, with a brisk, scrabbly sound, ascended, naked, into the sky, where the pigeons swept by for a third and last time. The squirrel, invisible now in a crotch, chattered, scolding the delinquents who would pot him out of his tree. Pnin, on the dirty black ice of the flagged path, slipped again, threw up one arm in an abrupt convulsion, regained his balance, and, with a solitary smile, stooped to pick up *Zol. Fond Lit.*, which lay wide open to a snapshot of a Russian pasture with Lyov Tolstoy trudging across it toward the camera and some long-maned horses behind him, their innocent heads turned toward the photographer too.

V boyu li, v stranstvii, v volnah? In fight, in travel, or in waves? Or on the Waindell campus? Gently champing his dentures, which retained a sticky layer of cottage cheese, Pnin went up the slippery library steps.

Like so many aging college people, Pnin had long ceased to notice the existence of students on the campus, in the corridors, in the library—anywhere, in brief, save in functional class-room concentrations. In the beginning, he had been much upset by the sight of some of them, their poor young heads on their forearms, fast asleep among the ruins of knowledge; but now, except for a girl's comely nape here and there, he saw nobody in the Reading Room.

Mrs. Thayer was at the circulation desk. Her mother and Mrs. Clements' mother had been first cousins.

"How are you today, Professor Pnin?"

"I am very well, Mrs. Fire."

"Laurence and Joan aren't back yet, are they?"

"No. I have brought this book back because I received this card——"

"I wonder if poor Isabel will really get divorced."

"I have not heard. Mrs. Fire, permit me to ask——"

"I suppose we'll have to find you another room, if they bring her back with them."

"Mrs. Fire, permit me to ask something or other. This card which I received yesterday—could you maybe tell me who is the other reader?"

"Let me check."

She checked. The other reader proved to be Timofey Pnin; Volume 18 had been requested by him the Friday before. It was also true that this Volume 18 was already charged to this Pnin, who had had it since Christmas and now stood with his hands upon it, like an ancestral picture of a magistrate.

"It can't be!" cried Pnin. "I requested on Friday Volume 19, year 1947, not 18, year 1940."

"But look—you wrote Volume 18. Anyway, 19 is still being processed. Are you keeping this?"

"Eighteen, 19," muttered Pnin. "There is not great difference! I put the year correctly, *that* is important! Yes, I still need 18—and send to me a more effishant card when 19 available."

Growling a little, he took the unwieldy, abashed book to his favorite alcove and laid it down there, wrapped in his muffler.

They can't read, these women. The year was plainly inscribed.

As usual he marched to the Periodicals Room and there glanced at the news in the latest (Saturday, February 12—and this was Tuesday, O Careless Reader!) issue of the Russian-language daily published, since 1918, by an *émigré* group in Chicago. As usual, he carefully scanned the advertisements. Dr. Popov, photographed in his new white smock, promised elderly people new vigor and joy. A music corporation listed Russian phonograph records for sale, such as "Broken Life, a Waltz" and "The Song of a Front-Line Chauffeur." A somewhat Gogolian mortician praised his hearses de luxe, which were also available for picnics. Another Gogolian person, in Miami, offered "a two-room apartment for non-drinkers (*dlya trezvïh*), among fruit trees and flowers," while in Hammond a room was wistfully being let "in a small quiet family"—and for no special reason the reader suddenly saw, with passionate and ridiculous lucidity, his parents, Dr. Pavel Pnin and Valeria Pnin, he with a medical journal, she with a political review, sitting in two armchairs, facing each other in a small, cheerfully lighted drawing room on Galernaya Street, St. Petersburg, forty years ago.

He also perused the current item in a tremendously long and tedious controversy between three *émigré* factions. It had started by Faction A's accusing Faction B of inertia and illustrating it by the proverb, "He wishes to climb the fir tree but is afraid to scrape his shins." This had provoked an acid Letter to the Editor from "An Old Optimist," entitled "Fir Trees and Inertia" and beginning: "There is an old American saying 'He who lives in a glass house should not try to kill two birds with one stone.' " In the present issue, there was a two-thousand-word *feuilleton* contributed by a representative of Faction C and headed "On Fir Trees, Glass Houses, and Optimism," and Pnin read this with great interest and sympathy.

He then returned to his carrell for his own research.

He contemplated writing a *Petite Histoire* of Russian culture, in which a choice of Russian Curiosities, Customs, Literary Anecdotes, and so forth would be presented in such a way as to reflect in miniature *la Grande Histoire*—Major Concatenations of Events. He was still at the blissful stage of collecting his material; and many good young people considered it a treat and an honor to see Pnin pull out a catalogue drawer from the comprehensive bosom of a card cabinet and take it, like a big nut, to a secluded corner and there make a quiet mental meal of it, now moving his lips in soundless comment, critical, satisfied, perplexed, and now lifting his rudimentary eyebrows and forgetting them there, left high upon his spacious brow where they remained long after all trace of displeasure or doubt had gone. He was lucky to be at Waindell. Sometime in the nineties the eminent bibliophile and Slavist John Thurston Todd (his bearded bust presided over the drinking fountain), had visited hospitable Russia, and after his death the books he had amassed there quietly chuted into a remote stack. Wearing rubber gloves so as to avoid being stung by the *amerikanski* electricity in the metal of the shelving, Pnin would go to those books and gloat over them: obscure magazines of the Roaring Sixties in marbled boards; century-old historical monographs, their somnolent pages foxed with fungus spots; Russian classics in horrible and pathetic cameo bindings, whose molded profiles of poets reminded dewy-eyed Timofey of his boyhood, when he could idly palpate on the book cover Pushkin's slightly chafed side whisker or Zhukovski's smudgy nose.

Today from Kostromskoy's voluminous work (Moscow, 1855) on Russian myths—a rare book, not to be removed from the library—Pnin, with a not unhappy sigh, started to copy out a passage referring to the old pagan games that were still practiced at the time, throughout the woodlands of the Upper Volga, in the margins of Christian ritual. During a festive week in May—the so-called Green Week which graded into Whitsuntide—peasant maidens would make wreaths of buttercups and frog orchises; then, singing snatches of ancient love chants, they hung these garlands on riverside willows; and on Whitsunday the wreaths were shaken down into the river, where, unwinding, they floated like so many serpents while the maidens floated and chanted among them.

A curious verbal association struck Pnin at this point; he could not catch it by its mermaid tail but made a note on his index card and plunged back into Kostromskoy.

When Pnin raised his eyes again, it was dinnertime.

Doffing his spectacles, he rubbed with the knuckles of the hand that held them his naked and tired eyes and, still in thought, fixed his mild gaze on the window above, where, gradually, through his dissolving meditation, there appeared the violet-blue air of dusk, silver-tooled by the reflection of the fluorescent lights of the ceiling, and, among spidery black twigs, a mirrored row of bright book spines.

Before leaving the library, he decided to look up the correct pronunciation of "interested," and discovered that Webster, or at least the battered 1930 edition lying on a table in the Browsing Room, did not place the stress accent on the third syllable, as he did. He sought a list of errata at the back, failed to find one, and, upon closing the elephantine lexicon, realized with a pang that he had immured somewhere in it the index card with notes that he had been holding all this time. Must now search and search through 2500 thin pages, some torn! On hearing his interjection, suave Mr. Case, a lank, pink-faced librarian with sleek white hair and a bow tie, strolled up, took up the colossus by both ends, inverted it, and gave it a slight shake, whereupon it shed a pocket comb, a Christmas card, Pnin's notes, and a gauzy wraith of tissue paper, which descended with infinite listlessness to Pnin's feet and was replaced by Mr. Case on the Great Seals of the United States and Territories.

Pnin pocketed his index card and, while doing so, recalled without any prompting what he had not been able to recall a while ago:

. . . plila i pela, pela i plila . . .
. . . she floated and she sang, she sang and floated . . .

Of course! Ophelia's death! *Hamlet!* In good old Andrey Kroneberg's Russian translation, 1844—the joy of Pnin's youth, and of his father's and grandfather's young days! And here, as in the Kostromskoy passage, there is, we recollect, also a willow and also wreaths. But where to check properly? Alas, *"Gamlet" Vil'yama Shekspira* had not been acquired by Mr. Todd, was not represented in Waindell College Library, and whenever you were reduced to look up something in the English version, you never found this or that beautiful, noble, sonorous line that you remembered all your life from Kroneberg's text in Vengerov's splendid edition. Sad!

It was getting quite dark on the sad campus. Above the distant, still sadder hills there lingered, under a cloud bank, a depth of tortoise-shell sky. The heart-rending lights of Waindellville, throbbing in a fold of those dusky hills, were putting on their usual magic, though actually, as Pnin well knew, the place, when you got there, was merely a row of brick houses, a service station, a skating rink, a supermarket. As he walked to the little tavern in Library Lane for a large portion of Virginia ham and a good bottle of beer, Pnin suddenly felt very tired. Not only had the *Zol. Fond* tome become even heavier after its unnecessary visit to the library, but something that Pnin had half heard in the course of the day, and had been reluctant to follow up, now bothered and oppressed him, as does, in retrospection, a blunder we have made, a piece of rudeness we have allowed ourselves, or a threat we have chosen to ignore.

7

Over an unhurried second bottle, Pnin debated with himself his next move or, rather, mediated in a debate between weary-brained Pnin, who had not been sleeping well lately, and an insatiable Pnin, who wished to continue reading at home, as always, till the 2 A.M. freight train moaned its way up the valley. It was decided at last that he would go to bed immediately after attending the program presented by intense Christopher and Louise Starr every second Tuesday at New Hall, rather high-brow music and unusual movie offerings which President Poore, in answer to some absurd criticism last year, had termed "probably the most inspiring and inspired venture in the entire academic community."

ZFL was now asleep in Pnin's lap. To his left sat two Hindu students. At his right there was Professor Hagen's daughter, a hoydenish Drama major. Komarov, thank goodness, was too far behind for his scarcely interesting remarks to carry.

The first part of the program, three ancient movie shorts,

bored our friend: that cane, that bowler, that white face, those black, arched eyebrows, those twitchy nostrils meant nothing to him. Whether the incomparable comedian danced in the sun with chapleted nymphs near a waiting cactus, or was a prehistoric man (the supple cane now a supple club), or was glared at by burly Mack Swain at a hectic night club, old-fashioned, humorless Pnin remained indifferent. "Clown," he snorted to himself. "Even Glupishkin and Max Linder used to be more comical."

The second part of the program consisted of an impressive Soviet documentary film, made in the late forties. It was supposed to contain not a jot of propaganda, to be all sheer art, merrymaking, and the euphoria of proud toil. Handsome, unkempt girls marched in an immemorial Spring Festival with banners bearing snatches of old Russian ballads such as *"Ruki proch ot Korei,"* *"Bas les mains devant la Corée,"* *"La paz vencera a la guerra,"* *"Der Friede besiegt den Krieg."* A flying ambulance was shown crossing a snowy range in Tajikistan. Kirghiz actors visited a sanatorium for coal miners among palm trees and staged there a spontaneous performance. In a mountain pasture somewhere in legendary Ossetia, a herdsman reported by portable radio to the local Republic's Ministry of Agriculture on the birth of a lamb. The Moscow Metro shimmered, with its columns and statues, and six would-be travelers seated on three marble benches. A factory worker's family spent a quiet evening at home, all dressed up, in a parlor choked with ornamental plants, under a great silk lampshade. Eight thousand soccer fans watched a match between Torpedo and Dynamo. Eight thousand citizens at Moscow's Electrical Equipment Plant unanimously nominated Stalin candidate from the Stalin Election District of Moscow. The latest Zim passenger model started out with the factory worker's family and a few other people for a picnic in the country. And then——

"I must not, I must not, oh it is idiotical," said Pnin to himself as he felt—unaccountably, ridiculously, humiliatingly—his tear glands discharge their hot, infantine, uncontrollable fluid.

In a haze of sunshine—sunshine projecting in vaporous shafts between the white boles of birches, drenching the pendulous foliage, trembling in eyelets upon the bark, dripping onto the long grass, shining and smoking among the ghosts of racemose bird cherries in scumbled bloom—a Russian wildwood enveloped the rambler. It was traversed by an old forest road with two soft furrows and a continuous traffic of mushrooms and daisies. The rambler still followed in mind that road as he trudged back to his anachronistic lodgings; was again the youth who had walked through those woods with a fat book under his arm; the road emerged into the romantic, free, beloved radiance of a great field unmowed by time (the horses galloping away and tossing their silvery manes among the tall flowers), as drowsiness overcame Pnin, who was now fairly snug in bed with two alarm clocks alongside, one set at 7:30, the other at 8, clicking and clucking on his night table.

Komarov, in a sky-blue shirt, bent over the guitar he was tuning. A birthday party was in progress, and calm Stalin cast with a thud his ballot in the election of governmental pallbearers. In fight, in travel . . . waves or Waindell. . . . "Wonderful!" said Dr. Bodo von Falternfels, raising his head from his writing.

Pnin had all but lapsed into velvety oblivion when some frightful accident happened outside: groaning and clutching at its brow, a statue was making an extravagant fuss over a broken bronze wheel—and then Pnin was awake, and a caravan of lights and of shadowy humps progressed across the window shade. A car door slammed, a car drove off, a key unlocked the brittle, transparent house, three vibrant voices spoke; the house, and the chink under Pnin's door, lit up with a shiver. It was a fever, it was an infection. In fear and helplessness, toothless, nightshirted Pnin heard a suitcase one-leggedly but briskly stomping upstairs, and a pair of young feet tripping up steps so familiar to them, and one could already make out the sound of eager breathing. . . . In fact, the automatic revival of happy homecomings from dismal summer camps would have actually had Isabel kick open—Pnin's—door, had not her mother's warning yelp stopped her in time.

❧ *Chapter Four* ❧

I

The King, his father, wearing a very white sports shirt open at the throat and a very black blazer, sat at a spacious desk whose highly polished surface twinned his upper half in reverse, making of him a kind of court card. Ancestral portraits darkened the walls of the vast paneled room. Otherwise, it was not unlike the headmaster's study at St. Bart's School, on the Atlantic Seaboard, some three thousand miles west of the imagined Palace. A copious spring shower kept lashing at the french windows, beyond which young greenery, all eyes, shivered and streamed. Nothing but this sheet of rain seemed to separate and protect the Palace from the revolution that for several days had been rocking the city. . . . Actually, Victor's father was a cranky refugee doctor, whom the lad had never much liked and had not seen now for almost two years.

The King, his more plausible father, had decided not to abdicate. No newspapers were coming out. The Orient Express was stranded, with all its transient passengers, at a suburban station, on the platform of which, reflected in puddles, picturesque peasants stood and gaped at the curtained windows of the long, mysterious cars. The Palace, and its terraced gardens, and the city below the palatial hill, and the main city square, where decapitations and folk dances had already started, despite the weather—all this was at the heart of a cross whose arms terminated in Trieste, Graz, Budapest, and

Zagreb, as designated in *Rand McNally's Ready Reference Atlas of the World*. And at the heart of that heart sat the King, pale and calm, and on the whole closely resembling his son as that under-former imagined he would look at forty himself. Pale and calm, a cup of coffee in his hand, his back to the emerald-and-gray window, the King sat listening to a masked messenger, a corpulent old nobleman in a wet cloak, who had managed to make his way through the rebellion and the rain from the besieged Council Hall to the isolated Palace.

"Abdication! One third of the alphabet!" coldly quipped the King, with the trace of an accent. "The answer is no. I prefer the unknown quantity of exile."

Saying this, the King, a widower, glanced at the desk photograph of a beautiful dead woman, at those great blue eyes, that carmine mouth (it was a colored photo, not fit for a king, but no matter). The lilacs, in sudden premature bloom, wildly beat, like shut-out maskers, at the dripping panes. The old messenger bowed and walked backward through the wilderness of the study, wondering secretly whether it would not be wiser for him to leave history alone and make a dash for Vienna where he had some property. . . . Of course, Victor's mother was not really dead; she had left his everyday father, Dr. Eric Wind (now in South America), and was about to be married in Buffalo to a man named Church.

Victor indulged night after night in these mild fancies, trying to induce sleep in his cold cubicle which was exposed to every noise in the restless dorm. Generally he did not reach that crucial flight episode when the King alone—*solus rex* (as chess problem makers term royal solitude)—paced a beach on the Bohemian Sea, at Tempest Point, where Percival Blake, a cheerful American adventurer, had promised to meet him with a powerful motorboat. Indeed, the very act of postponing that thrilling and soothing episode, the very protraction of its lure, coming as it did on top of the repetitive fancy, formed the main mechanism of its soporific effect.

An Italian film made in Berlin for American consumption, with a wild-eyed youngster in rumpled shorts, pursued through slums and ruins and a brothel or two by a multiple agent; a version of *The Scarlet Pimpernel*, recently staged at St. Martha's, the nearest girls' school; an anonymous Kafkaesque story in a *ci devant* avant-garde magazine read aloud in class by Mr. Pennant, a melancholy Englishman with a past; and, not least, the residue of various family allusions of long standing to the flight of Russian intellectuals from Lenin's regime thirty-five years ago—these were the obvious sources of Victor's fantasies; they may have been, at one time, intensely affecting; by now they had become frankly utilitarian, as a simple and pleasant drug.

2

He was now fourteen but looked two or three years older—not because of his lanky height, close on six feet, but because of a casual ease of demeanor, an expression of amiable aloofness about his plain but clean-cut features, and a complete lack of clumsiness or constraint which, far from precluding modesty and reserve, lent a sunny something to his shyness and a detached blandness to his quiet ways. Under his left eye a brown mole almost the size of a cent punctuated the pallor of his cheek. I do not think he loved anybody.

In his attitude toward his mother, passionate childhood affection had long since been replaced by tender condescension, and all he permitted himself was an inward sigh of amused submission to fate when, in her fluent and flashy New York English, with brash metallic nasalities and soft lapses into furry Russianisms, she regaled strangers in his presence with stories that he had heard countless times and that were either overembroidered or untrue. It was more trying when among such strangers Dr. Eric Wind, a completely humorless pedant who believed that his English (acquired in a German high school) was impeccably pure, would mouth a stale facetious phrase, saying "the pond" for the ocean, with the confidential and arch air of one who makes his audience the precious gift of a fruity colloquialism. Both parents, in their capacity of psychotherapists, did their best to impersonate Laius and Jocasta, but the boy proved to be a very mediocre little Oedipus. In order not to complicate the modish triangle of Freudian romance (father, mother, child), Liza's first husband had never been mentioned. Only when the Wind marriage started to disintegrate, about the time that Victor was enrolled at St. Bart's, Liza informed him that she had been Mrs. Pnin before she left Europe. She told him that this former husband of hers had migrated to America too—that in fact he would soon see Victor; and since everything Liza alluded to (opening wide her radiant black-lashed blue eyes) invariably took on a veneer of mystery and glamour, the figure of the great Timofey Pnin, scholar and gentleman, teaching a practically dead language at the famous Waindell College some three hundred miles northwest of St. Bart's, acquired in Victor's hospitable mind a curious charm, a family resemblance to those Bulgarian kings or Mediterranean princes who used to be world-famous experts in butterflies or sea shells. He therefore experienced pleasure when Professor Pnin entered into a staid and decorous correspondence with him; a first letter, couched in beautiful French but very indifferently typed, was followed by a picture postcard representing the Gray Squirrel. The card belonged to an educational series depicting Our Mammals and Birds; Pnin had acquired the whole series specially for the purpose of this correspondence. Victor was glad to learn that "squirrel" came from a Greek word which meant "shadow-tail." Pnin invited Victor to visit him during the next vacation and informed the boy that he would meet him at the Waindell bus station. "To be recognized," he wrote, in English, "I will appear in dark spectacles and hold a black briefcase with my monogram in silver."

3

Both Eric and Liza Wind were morbidly concerned with heredity, and instead of delighting in Victor's artistic genius, they used to worry gloomily about its genetic cause. Art and science had been represented rather vividly in the ancestral past. Should one trace Victor's passion for pigments back to Hans Andersen (no relation to the bedside Dane), who had been a stained-glass artist in Lübeck before losing his mind (and believing himself to be a cathedral) soon after his beloved daughter married a gray-haired Hamburg jeweler, author of a monograph on sapphires and Eric's maternal grandfather? Or was Victor's almost pathological precision of pencil and pen a by-product of Bogolepov's science? For Victor's mother's great-grandfather, the seventh son of a country pope, had been no other than that singular genius, Feofilakt Bogolepov, whose only rival for the title of greatest Russian mathematician was Nikolay Lobachevski. One wonders.

Genius is non-conformity. At two, Victor did not make little spiral scribbles to express buttons or portholes, as a million tots do, why not you? Lovingly he made his circles perfectly round and perfectly closed. A three-year-old child, when asked to copy a square, shapes one recognizable corner and then is content to render the rest of the outline as wavy or circular; but Victor at three not only copied the researcher's (Dr. Liza Wind's) far from ideal square with contemptuous accuracy but added a smaller one beside the copy. He never went through that initial stage of graphic activity when infants draw *Kopffüsslers* (tadpole people), or humpty dumpties with L-like legs, and arms ending in rake prongs; in fact, he avoided the human form altogether and when pressed by Papa (Dr. Eric Wind) to draw Mama (Dr. Liza Wind), responded with a lovely undulation, which he said was her shadow on the new refrigerator. At four, he evolved an individual stipple. At five, he began to draw objects in perspective—a side wall nicely foreshortened, a tree dwarfed by distance, one object half masking another. And at six, Victor already distinguished what so many adults never learn to see—the colors of shadows, the difference in tint between the shadow of an orange and that of a plum or of an avocado pear.

To the Winds, Victor was a problem child insofar as he refused to be one. From the Wind point of view, every male child had an ardent desire to castrate his father and a nostalgic urge to re-enter his mother's body. But Victor did not reveal any behavior disorder, did not pick his nose, did not suck his thumb, was not even a nail biter. Dr. Wind, with the object of eliminating what he, a radiophile, termed "the static of personal relationship," had his impregnable child tested psychometrically at the Institute by a couple of outsiders, young Dr. Stern and his smiling wife (I am Louis and this is Christina). But the results were either monstrous or nil: the seven-year-old subject scored on the so-called Godunov Drawing-of-an-Animal Test a sensational mental age of seventeen, but on being given a Fairview Adult Test promptly sank to the mentality of a two-year-old. How much care, skill, inventiveness have gone to devise those marvelous techniques! What a shame that certain patients refuse to co-operate! There is, for instance, the Kent-Rosanoff Absolutely Free Association Test, in which little Joe or Jane is asked to respond to a Stimulus Word, such as table, duck, music, sickness, thickness, low, deep, long, happiness, fruit, mother, mushroom. There is the charming Bièvre Interest-Attitude Game (a blessing on rainy afternoons), in which little Sam or Ruby is asked to put a little mark in front of the things about which he or she feels sort of fearful, such as dying, falling, dreaming, cyclones, funerals, father, night, operation, bedroom, bathroom, converge, and so forth; there is the Augusta Angst Abstract Test in which the little one (*das Kleine*) is made to express a list of terms ("groaning," "pleasure," "darkness") by means of unlifted lines. And there is, of course, the Doll Play, in which Patrick or Patricia is given two identical rubber dolls and a cute little bit of clay which Pat must fix on one of them before he or she starts playing, and oh the lovely doll house, with so many rooms and lots of quaint miniature objects, including a chamber pot no bigger than a cupule, and a medicine chest, and a poker, and a double bed, and even a pair of teeny-weeny rubber gloves in the kitchen, and you may be as mean as you like and do anything you want to Papa doll if you think he is beating Mama doll when they put out the lights in the bedroom. But bad Victor would not play with Lou and Tina, ignored the dolls, struck out all the listed words (which was against the rules), and made drawings that had no subhuman significance whatever.

Nothing of the slightest interest to therapists could Victor be made to discover in those beautiful, *beautiful* Rorschach ink blots, wherein children see, or should see, all kinds of things, seascapes, escapes, capes, the worms of imbecility, neurotic tree trunks, erotic galoshes, umbrellas, and dumbbells. Nor did any of Victor's casual sketches represent the so-called mandala—a term supposedly meaning (in Sanskrit) a magic ring, and applied by Dr. Jung and others to any doodle in the shape of a more or less fourfold spreading structure, such as a halved mangosteen, or a cross, or the wheel on which egos are broken like Morphos, or more exactly, the molecule of carbon, with its four valences—that main chemical component of the brain, automatically magnified and reflected on paper.

The Sterns reported that "unfortunately the psychic value of Victor's Mind Pictures and Word Associations is completely obscured by the boy's artistic inclinations." And thenceforth the Winds' little patient, who had trouble in going to sleep and lacked appetite, was allowed to read in bed till after midnight and evade oatmeal in the morning.

4
———

In planning her boy's education, Liza had been torn between two libidos: to endow him with the latest benefits of

Modern Child Psychotherapy, and to find, among American frames of religious reference, the nearest approach to the melodious and wholesome amenities of the Greek Catholic Church, that mild communion whose demands on one's conscience are so small in comparison with the comforts it offers.

Little Victor at first went to a progressive kindergarten in New Jersey, and then, upon the advice of some Russian friends, attended a day school there. The school was directed by an Episcopal clergyman who proved to be a wise and gifted educator, sympathetic to superior children, no matter how bizarre or rowdy they might be; Victor was certainly a little peculiar, but on the other hand very quiet. At twelve, he went to St. Bartholomew's.

Physically, St. Bart's was a great mass of self-conscious red brick, erected in 1869 on the outskirts of Cranton, Masachusetts. Its main building formed three sides of a large quadrangle, the fourth being a cloistered passage. Its gabled gatehouse was glossily coated on one side with American ivy and tipped somewhat top-heavily with a Celtic cross of stone. The ivy rippled in the wind like the back skin of a horse. The hue of red brick is fondly supposed to grow richer with time; that of good old St. Bart's had only grown dirty. Under the cross and immediately over the sonorous-looking but really echoless arc of the entrance was carved a dagger of sorts, an attempt to represent the butcher's knife so reproachfully held (in the Vienna Missal) by St. Bartholomew, one of the Apostles—the one, namely, who had been flayed alive and exposed to the flies in the summer of 65 A.D. or thereabouts, in Albanopolis, now Derbent, southeastern Russia. His coffin, when cast by a furious king into the Caspian Sea, had blandly sailed all the way to Lipari Island off the coast of Sicily—probably a legend, seeing that the Caspian had been strictly an inland affair ever since the Pleistocene. Beneath this heraldic weapon—which rather resembled a carrot pointing upward—an inscription in burnished church text read: *"Sursum."* Two gentle English shepherd dogs belonging to one of the masters and greatly attached to each other could generally be found drowsing in their private Arcadia on a lawn before the gate.

Liza on her first visit to the school had greatly admired everything about it from the fives courts and the chapel to the plaster casts in the corridors and the photographs of cathedrals in the classrooms. The three lower forms were assigned to dormitories with windowed alcoves; there was a master's room at the end. Visitors could not help admiring the fine gymnasium. Very evocative, too, were the oaken seats and hammer-beamed roof of the chapel, a Romanesque structure that had been donated half a century ago by Julius Schonberg, wool manufacturer, brother of the world-famous Egyptologist Samuel Schonberg who perished in the Messina earthquake. There were twenty-five masters and the headmaster, the Reverend Archibald Hopper, who on warm days wore elegant clerical gray and performed his duties in radiant ignorance of the intrigue that was on the point of dislodging him.

5

Although Victor's eye was his supreme organ, it was rather by smells and sounds that the neutral notion of St. Bart's impressed itself on his consciousness. There was the musty, dull reek of old varnished wood in the dorms, and the night sounds in the alcoves—loud gastric explosions and a special squeaking of bed springs, accentuated for effect—and the bell in the hallway, in the hollow of one's headache, at 6:45 A.M. There was the odor of idolatry and incense coming from the burner that hung on chains and on shadows of chains from the ribbed ceiling of the chapel; and there was the Reverend Hopper's mellow voice, nicely blending vulgarity with refinement; and Hymn 166, "Sun of My Soul," which new boys were required to learn by heart; and there was, in the locker room, the immemorial sweat of the hamper on wheels, which held a communal supply of athletic supporters—a beastly gray tangle, from which one had to untwist a strap for oneself to put on at the start of the sport period—and how harsh and sad the clusters of cries from each of the four playing fields!

With an intelligence quotient of about a hundred and eighty and an average grade of ninety, Victor easily ranked first in a class of thirty-six and was, in fact, one of the three best scholars in the school. He had little respect for most of his teachers; but he revered Lake, a tremendously obese man with shaggy eyebrows and hairy hands and an attitude of somber embarrassment in the presence of athletic, rosy-cheeked lads (Victor was neither). Lake was enthroned, Buddhalike, in a curiously neat studio that looked more like a reception room in an art gallery than a workshop. Nothing adorned its pale gray walls except two identically framed pictures: a copy of Gertrude Käsebier's photographic masterpiece "Mother and Child" (1897), with the wistful, angelic infant looking up and away (at what?); and a similarly toned reproduction of the head of Christ from Rembrandt's "The Pilgrims of Emmaus," with the same, though slightly less celestial, expression of eyes and mouth.

He had been born in Ohio, had studied in Paris and Rome, had taught in Ecuador and Japan. He was a recognized art expert, and it puzzled people why, during the past ten winters, Lake chose to bury himself at St. Bart's. While endowed with the morose temper of genius, he lacked originality and was aware of that lack; his own paintings always seemed beautifully clever imitations, although one could never quite tell whose manner he mimicked. His profound knowledge of innumerable techniques, his indifference to "schools" and "trends," his detestation of quacks, his conviction that there was no difference whatever between a genteel aquarelle of yesterday and, say, conventional neo-plasticism or banal non-objectivism of today, and that nothing but individual talent mattered—these views made of him an unusual teacher. St. Bart's was not particularly pleased either with Lake's methods or with their results, but kept him on because it was fashionable to have at least one distinguished freak on the staff. Among the many exhilarating things Lake taught was that the order of the solar spectrum is not a closed circle but a spiral of tints from cadmium red and oranges through a strontian yellow and a pale paradisal green to cobalt blues and violets, at which point the sequence does not grade into red again but passes into another spiral, which starts with a kind of lavender gray and goes on to Cinderella shades transcending human perception. He taught that there is no such thing as the Ashcan School or the Cache Cache School or the Cancan School. That the work of art created with string, stamps, a Leftist newspaper, and the droppings of doves is based on a series of dreary platitudes. That there is nothing more banal and more bourgeois than paranoia. That Dali is really Norman Rockwell's twin brother kidnaped by gypsies in babyhood. That Van Gogh is second-rate and Picasso supreme, despite his commercial foibles; and that if Degas could immortalize a *calèche*, why could not Victor Wind do the same to a motor car?

One way to do it might be by making the scenery penetrate the automobile. A polished black sedan was a good subject, especially if parked at the intersection of a tree-bordered street and one of those heavyish spring skies whose bloated gray clouds and amoeba-shaped blotches of blue seem more physical than the reticent elms and evasive pavement. Now break the body of the car into separate curves and panels; then put it together in terms of reflections. These will be different for each part: the top will display inverted trees with blurred branches growing like roots into a washily photographed sky, with a whalelike building swimming by—an architectural afterthought; one side of the hood will be coated with a band of rich celestial cobalt; a most delicate pattern of black twigs will be mirrored in the outside surface of the rear window; and a remarkable desert view, a distended horizon, with a remote house here and a lone tree there, will stretch along the bumper. This mimetic and integrative process Lake called the necessary "naturalization" of man-made things. In the streets of Cranton, Victor would find a suitable specimen of car and loiter around it. Suddenly the sun, half masked but dazzling, would join him. For the sort of theft Victor was contemplating there could be no better accomplice. In the chrome plating, in the glass of a sun-rimmed headlamp, he would see a view of the street and himself comparable to the miscrocosmic version of a room (with a dorsal view of diminutive people) in that very special and very magical small convex mirror that, half a millennium ago, Van Eyck and Petrus Christus and Memling used to paint into their detailed interiors, behind the sour merchant or the domestic Madonna.

To the latest issue of the school magazine Victor had contributed a poem about painters, over the *nom de guerre* Moinet, and under the motto "Bad reds should all be avoided; even if carefully manufactured, they are still bad" (quoted from an old book on the technique of painting but smacking of a political aphorism). The poem began:

> Leonardo! Strange diseases
> strike at madders mixed with lead:
> nun-pale now are Mona Lisa's
> lips that you had made so red.

He dreamed of mellowing his pigments as the Old Masters had done—with honey, fig juice, poppy oil, and the slime of pink snails. He loved water colors and he loved oils, but was wary of the too fragile pastel and the too coarse distemper. He studied his mediums with the care and patience of an insatiable child—one of those painter's apprentices (it is now Lake who is dreaming!), lads with bobbed hair and bright eyes who would spend years grinding colors in the workshop of some great Italian skiagrapher, in a world of amber and paradisal glazes. At eight, he had once told his mother that he wanted to paint air. At nine, he had known the sensuous delight of a graded wash. What did it matter to him that gentle chiaroscuro, off-spring of veiled values and translucent undertones, had long since died behind the prison bars of abstract art, in the poor-house of hideous primitivism? He placed various objects in turn—an apple, a pencil, a chess pawn, a comb—behind a glass of water and peered through it at each studiously: the red apple became a clear-cut red band bounded by a straight horizon, half a glass of Red Sea, Arabia Felix. The short pencil, if held obliquely, curved like a stylized snake, but if held verti-cally became monstrously fat—almost pyramidal. The black pawn, if moved to and fro, divided into a couple of black ants. The comb, stood on end, resulted in the glass's seeming to fill with beautifully striped liquid, a zebra cocktail.

6

On the eve of the day on which Victor had planned to arrive, Pnin entered a sport shop in Waindell's Main Street and asked for a football. The request was unseasonable but he was offered one.

"No, no," said Pnin, "I do not wish an egg or, for example, a torpedo. I want a simple football ball. Round!"

And with wrists and palms he outlined a portable world. It was the same gesture he used in class when speaking of the "harmonical wholeness" of Pushkin.

The salesman lifted a finger and silently fetched a soccer ball.

"Yes, this I will buy," said Pnin with dignified satisfaction.

Carrying his purchase, wrapped in brown paper and Scotch-taped, he entered a bookstore and asked for *Martin Eden*.

"Eden, Eden, Eden," the tall dark lady in charge repeated rapidly, rubbing her forehead. "Let me see, you don't mean a book on the British statesman? Or do you?"

"I mean," said Pnin, "a celebrated work by the celebrated American writer Jack London."

"London, London, London," said the woman, holding her temples.

Pipe in hand, her husband, a Mr. Tweed, who wrote topical poetry, came to the rescue. After some search he brought from the dusty depths of his not very prosperous store an old edition of *The Son of the Wolf*.

"I'm afraid," he said, "that's all we have by this author."

"Strange!" said Pnin. "The vicissitudes of celebrity! In Russia, I remember, everybody—little children, full-grown people, doctors, advocates—everybody read and reread him. This is not his best book but O.K., O.K., I will take it."

On coming home to the house where he roomed that year, Professor Pnin laid out the ball and the book on the desk of the guest room upstairs. Cocking his head, he surveyed these gifts. The ball did not look nice in its shapeless wrappings; he disrobed it. Now it showed its handsome leather. The room was tidy and cozy. A schoolboy should like that picture of a snowball knocking off a professor's top hat. The bed had just been made by the cleaning woman; old Bill Sheppard, the landlord, had come up from the first floor and had gravely screwed a new bulb into the desk lamp. A warm humid wind pressed through the open window, and one could hear the noise of an exuberant creek that ran below. It was going to rain. Pnin closed the window.

In his own room, on the same floor, he found a note. A laconic wire from Victor had been transmitted by phone: it said that he would be exactly twenty-four hours late.

7

———

Victor and five other boys were being held over one precious day of Easter vacation for smoking cigars in the attic. Victor, who had a queasy stomach and no dearth of olfactory phobias (all of which had been lovingly concealed from the Winds), had not actually participated in the smoking, beyond a couple of wry puffs; several times he had dutifully followed to the forbidden attic two of his best friends—adventurous, boisterous boys, Tony Brade, Jr., and Lance Boke. You penetrated there through the trunk room and then up an iron ladder, which emerged upon a catwalk right under the roof. Here the fascinating, strangely brittle skeleton of the building became both visible and tangible, with all its beams and boards, maze of partitions, sliced shadows, flimsy laths through which the foot collapsed to a crepitation of plaster dislodged from unseen ceilings beneath. The labyrinth ended in a small platform hooded within a recess at the very peak of the gable, among a motley mess of old comic books and recent cigar ashes. The ashes were discovered; the boys confessed. Tony Brade, the grandson of a famous St. Bart's headmaster, was given permission to leave, for family reasons; a fond cousin wished to see him before sailing for Europe. Wisely, Tony begged to be detained with the rest.

The headmaster in Victor's time was, as I have already said, the Reverend Mr. Hopper, a dark-haired, fresh-faced pleasant nonentity, greatly admired by Bostonian matrons. As Victor and his fellow culprits were at dinner with the entire Hopper family, various crystalline hints were dropped here and there, especially by sweet-voiced Mrs. Hopper, an Englishwoman whose aunt had married an earl; the Reverend might relent and the six boys be taken that last evening to a movie in town instead of being sent early to bed. And after dinner, with a kindly wink, she bade them accompany the Reverend, who briskly walked hallward.

Old-fashioned trustees might find it proper to condone the floggings that Hopper had inflicted on special offenders once or twice in the course of his brief and undistinguished career; but what no boy could stomach was the little mean smirk which crooked the headmaster's red lips as he paused on his way to the hall to pick up a neatly folded square of cloth—his cassock and surplice; the station wagon was at the door, and "putting the clinch on the punishment," as the boys expressed it, the false clergyman treated them to a guest performance at Rudbern, twelve miles away, in a cold brick church, before a meager congregation.

8

Theoretically, the simplest way to reach Waindell from Cranton was to get by taxi to Framingham, catch a fast train to Albany, and then a local for a shorter stretch in a northwestern direction; actually, the simplest way was also the most unpractical one. Whether there was some old solemn feud between those railways, or whether both had united to grant a sporting chance to other means of conveyance, the fact remained that no matter how you juggled with timetables, a three-hour wait at Albany between trains was the briefest you could hope to achieve.

There was a bus leaving Albany at 11 A.M. and arriving at Waindell at around 3 P.M. but that meant taking the 6:31 A.M train from Framingham; Victor felt he could not get up in time; he took, instead, a slightly later and considerably slower train that allowed him to catch at Albany the last bus to Waindell, which deposited him there at half past eight in the evening.

It rained all the way. It was raining when he arrived at the Waindell terminal. Because of a streak of dreaminess and a gentle abstraction in his nature, Victor in any queue was always at its very end. He had long since grown used to this handicap, as one grows used to weak sight or a limp. Stooping a little because of his height, he followed without impatience the passengers that filed out through the bus onto the shining asphalt: two lumpy old ladies in semitransparent raincoats, like potatoes in cellophane; a small boy of seven or eight with a crew cut and a frail, hollowed nape; a many-angled, diffident, elderly cripple, who declined all assistance and came out in parts; three rosy-kneed Waindell coeds in shorts; the small boy's exhausted mother; a number of other passengers; and then— Victor, with a grip in his hand and two magazines under his arm.

In an archway of the bus station a totally bald man with a brownish complexion, wearing dark glasses and carrying a black briefcase, was bending in amiable interrogatory welcome over the thin-necked little boy, who, however, kept shaking his head and pointing to his mother, who was waiting for her luggage to emerge from the Greyhound's belly. Shyly and gaily Victor interrupted the *quid pro quo*. The brown-domed gentleman took off his glasses and, unbending himself, looked up, up, up at tall, tall, tall Victor, at his blue eyes and reddish-brown hair. Pnin's well-developed zygomatic muscles raised and rounded his tanned cheeks; his forehead, his nose, and even his large beautiful ears took part in the smile. All in all, it was an extremely satisfactory meeting.

Pnin suggested leaving the luggage and walking one block— if Victor was not afraid of the rain (it was pouring hard, and the asphalt glistened in the darkness, tarnlike, under large, noisy trees). It would be, Pnin conjectured, a treat for the boy to have a late meal in a diner.

"You arrived well? You had no disagreeable adventures?"

"None, sir."

"You are very hungry?"

"No, sir. Not particularly."

"My name is Timofey," said Pnin, as they made themselves comfortable at a window table in the shabby old diner. "Second syllable pronounced as 'muff,' ahksent on last syllable, 'ey' as in 'prey' but a little more protracted. 'Timofey Pavlovich Pnin,' which means 'Timothy the son of Paul.' The pahtronymic has the ahksent on the first syllable and the rest is sloored —Timofey Pahlch. I have a long time debated with myself—let us wipe these knives and these forks—and have concluded that you must call me simply Mr. Tim or, even shorter, Tim, as do some of my extremely sympathetic colleagues. It is—what do you want to eat? Veal cutlet? O.K., I will also eat veal cutlet— it is naturally a concession to America, my new country, wonderful America which sometimes surprises me but always provokes respect. In the beginning I was greatly embarrassed——"

In the beginning Pnin was greatly embarrassed by the ease with which first names were bandied about in America: after a single party, with an iceberg in a drop of whisky to start and with a lot of whisky in a little tap water to finish, you were supposed to call a gray-templed stranger "Jim," while he called you "Tim" for ever and ever. If you forgot and called him next morning Professor Everett (his real name to you) it was (for him) a horrible insult. In reviewing his Russian friends throughout Europe and the United States, Timofey Pahlch could easily count at least sixty dear people whom he had intimately known since, say, 1920, and whom he never called anything but Vadim Vadimich, Ivan Hristoforovich, or Samuil Izrailevich, as the case might be, and who called him by his name and patronymic with the same effusive sympathy, over a strong warm handshake, whenever they met: "Ah, Timofey Pahlch! *Nu kak?* (Well how?) *A vï, baten'ka, zdorovo postareli* (Well, well, old boy, you certainly don't look any younger)!"

Pnin talked. His talk did not amaze Victor, who had heard many Russians speak English, and he was not bothered by the fact that Pnin pronounced the word "family" as if the first syllable were the French for "woman."

"I speak in French with much more facility than in English," said Pnin, "but you—*vous comprenez le français? Bien? Assez bien? Un peu?*"

"*Très un peu,*" said Victor.

"Regrettable, but nothing to be done. I will now speak to you about sport. The first description of box in Russian literature we find in a poem by Mihail Lermontov, born 1814, killed

1841—easy to remember. The first description of tennis, on the other hand, is found in *Anna Karenin,* Tolstoy's novel, and is related to year 1875. In youth one day, in the Russian countryside, latitude of Labrador, a racket was given to me to play with the family of the Orientalist Gotovtsev, perhaps you have heard. It was, I recollect, a splendid summer day and we played, played, played until all the twelve balls were lost. You also will recollect the past with interest when old.

"Another game," continued Pnin, lavishly sugaring his coffee, "was naturally *kroket*. I was a champion of *kroket*. However, the favorite national recreation was so-called *gorodki*, which means 'little towns.' One remembers a place in the garden and the wonderful atmosphere of youth: I was strong, wore an embroidered Russian shirt, nobody plays now such healthy games."

He finished his cutlet and proceeded with the subject:

"One drew," said Pnin, "a big square on the ground, one placed there, like columns, cylindrical pieces of wood, you know, and then from some distance one threw at them a thick stick, very hard, like a boomerang, with a wide, wide development of the arm—excuse me—fortunately it is sugar, not salt."

"I still hear," said Pnin, picking up the sprinkler and shaking his head a little at the surprising persistence of memory, "I still hear the *trakh!,* the crack when one hit the wooden pieces and they jumped in the air. Will you not finish the meat? You do not like it?"

"It's awfully good," said Victor, "but I am not very hungry."

"Oh, you must eat more, much more if you want to be a footballist."

"I'm afraid I don't care much for football. In fact, I hate football. I'm not very good at any game, really."

"You are not a lover of football?" said Pnin, and a look of dismay crept over his large expressive face. He pursed his lips. He opened them—but said nothing. In silence he ate his vanilla ice cream, which contained no vanilla and was not made of cream.

"We will now take your luggage and a taxi," said Pnin.

As soon as they reached the Sheppard house, Pnin ushered Victor into the parlor and rapidly introduced him to his landlord, old Bill Sheppard, formerly superintendent of the college grounds (who was totally deaf and wore a white button in one ear), and to his brother, Bob Sheppard, who had recently come from Buffalo to live with Bill after the latter's wife died. Leaving Victor with them for a minute, Pnin hastily stomped upstairs. The house was a vulnerable construction, and objects in the rooms downstairs reacted with various vibrations to the vigorous footsteps on the upper landing and to the sudden rasp of a window sash in the guest room.

"Now that picture there," deaf Mr. Sheppard was saying, pointing with a didactic finger at a large muddy water color on the wall, "represents the farm where my brother and I used to spend summers fifty years ago. It was painted by my mother's schoolmate, Grace Wells: her son, Charlie Wells, owns that hotel in Waindellville—I am sure Dr. Neen has met him—a very very fine man. My late wife was an artist too. I shall show you some works of hers in a moment. Well, that tree there, behind that barn—you can just make it out——"

A terrible clatter and crash came from the stairs: Pnin, on his way down, had lost his footing.

"In the spring of 1905," said Mr. Sheppard, wagging his index at the picture, "under that cottonwood tree——"

He noticed that his brother and Victor had hurried out of the room to the foot of the stairs. Poor Pnin had come down the last steps on his back. He lay supine for a moment, his eyes moving to and fro. He was helped to his feet. No bones were broken.

Pnin smiled and said: "It is like the splendid story of Tolstoy —you must read one day, Victor—about Ivan Ilyich Golovin who fell and got in consequence kidney of the cancer. Victor will now come upstairs with me."

Victor followed, with grip. There was a reproduction of Van Gogh's "La Berceuse" on the landing and Victor, in passing, acknowledged it with a nod of ironic recognition. The guest room was full of the noise of the rain falling on fragrant branches in the framed blackness of the open window. On the desk lay a wrapped-up book and a ten-dollar bill. Victor beamed and bowed to his gruff but kindly host. "Unwrap," said Pnin.

With courteous eagerness, Victor obeyed. Then he sat down on the edge of the bed and, his auburn hair coming down in glossy lanks over his right temple, his striped tie dangling out of the front of his gray jacket, his bulky gray-flanneled knees parted, zestfully opened the book. He intended to praise it— first, because it was a gift, and second, because he believed it to be a translation from Pnin's mother tongue. He remembered there had been at the Psychotherapeutic Institute a Dr. Yakov London from Russia. Rather unfortunately, Victor lit upon a passage about Zarinska, the Yukon Indian Chief's daughter, and lightheartedly mistook her for a Russian maiden. "Her great black eyes were fixed upon her tribesmen in fear and in defiance. So extreme the tension, she had forgotten to breathe . . ."

"I think I'm going to like this," said polite Victor. "Last summer I read *Crime and*——" A young yawn distended his staunchly smiling mouth. With sympathy, with approval, with heartache Pnin looked at Liza yawning after one of those long happy parties at the Arbenins' or the Polyanskis' in Paris, fifteen, twenty, twenty-five years ago.

"No more reading today," said Pnin. "I know that it is a very exciting book but you will read and read tomorrow. I wish you good night. The bathroom is across the landing."

He shook hands with Victor and marched to his own room.

9

It still rained. All the lights in the Sheppard house were out. The brook in the gully behind the garden, a trembling trickle most of the time, was tonight a loud torrent that tumbled over itself in its avid truckling to gravity, as it carried through corridors of beech and spruce last year's leaves, and some leafless twigs, and a brand-new, unwanted soccer ball that had recently rolled into the water from the sloping lawn after Pnin disposed of it by defenestration. He had fallen asleep at last, despite the discomfort in his back, and in the course of one of those dreams that still haunt Russian fugitives, even when a third of a century has elapsed since their escape from the Bolsheviks, Pnin saw himself fantastically cloaked, fleeing through great pools of ink under a cloud-barred moon from a chimerical palace, and then pacing a desolate strand with his dead friend Ilya Isidorovich Polyanski as they waited for some mysterious deliverance to arrive in a throbbing boat from beyond the hopeless sea. The Sheppard brothers were both awake in their adjacent beds, on their Beautyrest mattresses; the younger listened in the dark to the rain and wondered if after all they should sell the house with its audible roof and wet garden; the elder lay thinking of silence, of a green damp churchyard, of an old farm, of a poplar that years ago lightning had struck, killing John Head, a dim, distant relation. Victor had, for once, fallen asleep as soon as he put his head under his pillow—a recently evolved method about which Dr. Eric Wind (sitting on a bench, near a fountain, in Quito, Ecuador) would never learn. Around half past one the Sheppards started to snore, the deaf one doing it with a rattle at the end of each exhalation and many volumes louder than the other, a modest and melancholy wheezer. On the sandy beach where Pnin was still pacing (his worried friend had gone home for a map), there appeared before him a set of approaching footprints, and he awoke with a gasp. His back hurt. It was now past four. The rain had stopped.

Pnin sighed a Russian "okh-okh-okh" sigh, and sought a more comfortable position. Old Bill Sheppard trudged to the downstairs bathroom, brought down the house, then trudged back.

Presently all were asleep again. It was a pity nobody saw the display in the empty street, where the auroral breeze wrinkled a large luminous puddle, making of the telephone wires reflected in it illegible lines of black zigzags.

⮿ *Chapter Five* ⮿

I

From the top platform of an old, seldom used lookout tower—a "prospect tower" as it was formerly termed—that stood on a wooded hill eight hundred feet high, called Mount Ettrick, in one of the fairest of New England's fair states, the adventurous summer tourist (Miranda or Mary, Tom or Jim, whose penciled names were almost obliterated on the balustrade) might observe a vast sea of greenery, composed mainly of maple, beech, tacamahac, and pine. Some five miles west, a slender white church steeple marked the spot where nestled the small town of Onkwedo, once famous for its springs. Three miles north, in a riverside clearing at the foot of a grassy knoll, one could distinguish the gables of an ornate house (variously known as Cook's, Cook's Place, Cook's Castle, or The Pines—its initial appellation). Along the south side of Mount Ettrick, a state highway continued east after passing through Onkwedo. Numerous dirt roads and foot trails crisscrossed the timbered plain within the triangle of land limited by the somewhat tortuous hypotenuse of a rural paved road that weaved northeast from Onkwedo to The Pines, the long cathetus of the state highway just mentioned, and the short cathetus of a river spanned by a steel bridge near Mount Ettrick and a wooden one near Cook's.

On a dull warm day in the summer of 1954, Mary or Almira, or, for that matter, Wolfgang von Goethe, whose name had been carved in the balustrade by some old-fashioned wag, might have noticed an automobile that had turned off the highway just before reaching the bridge and was now nosing and poking this way and that in a maze of doubtful roads. It moved warily and unsteadily, and whenever it changed its mind, it would slow down and raise dust behind like a back-kicking dog. At times it might seem, to a less sympathetic soul than our imagined observer, that this pale blue, egg-shaped two-door sedan, of uncertain age and in mediocre condition, was manned by an idiot. Actually its driver was Professor Timofey Pnin, of Waindell College.

Pnin had started taking lessons at the Waindell Driving School early in the year, but "true understanding," as he put it, had come to him only when, a couple of months later, he had been laid up with a sore back and had done nothing but study with deep enjoyment the forty-page *Driver's Manual*, issued by the State Governor in collaboration with another expert, and the article on "Automobile" in the *Encyclopedia Americana*, with illustrations of Transmissions, and Carburetors, and Brakes, and a Member of the Glidden Tour, *circa* 1905, stuck in the mud of a country road among depressing surroundings. Then and only then was the dual nature of his initial inklings transcended at last as he lay on his sickbed, wiggling his toes and shifting phantom gears. During actual lessons with a harsh instructor who cramped his style, issued unnecessary directives in yelps of technical slang, tried to wrestle the wheel from him at corners, and kept irritating a calm, intelligent pupil with expressions of vulgar detraction, Pnin had been totally unable to combine perceptually the car he was driving in his mind and the car he was driving on the road. Now the two fused at last. If he failed the first time he took his driver's-license test, it was mainly because he started an argument with the examiner in an ill-timed effort to prove that nothing could be more humiliating to a rational creature than being required to encourage the development of a base conditional reflex by stopping at a red light when there was not an earthly soul around, heeled or wheeled. He was more circumspect the next time, and passed. An irresistible senior, enrolled in his Russian Language course, Marilyn Holm, sold him for a hundred dollars her humble old car: she was getting married to the owner of a far grander machine. The trip from Waindell to Onkwedo, with an overnight stop at a tourist home, had been slow and difficult but uneventful. Just before entering Onkwedo, he had pulled up at a gas station and had got out for a breath of country air. An inscrutable white sky hung over a clover field, and from a pile of firewood near a shack came a rooster's cry, jagged and gaudy—a vocal coxcomb. Some chance intonation on the part of this slightly hoarse bird, combined with the warm wind pressing itself against Pnin in search of attention, recognition, anything, briefly reminded him of a dim dead day when he, a Petrograd University freshman, had arrived at the small station of a Baltic summer resort, and the sounds, and the smells, and the sadness——

"Kind of muggy," said the hairy-armed attendant, as he started to wipe the windshield.

Pnin took a letter out of his wallet, unfolded the tiny mimeographed-sketch map attached to it, and asked the attendant how far was the church at which one was supposed to turn left to reach Cook's Place. It was really striking how the man resembled Pnin's colleague at Waindell College, Dr. Hagen —one of those random likenesses as pointless as a bad pun.

"Well, there is a better way to get there," said the false Hagen. "The trucks have messed up that road, and besides you won't like the way it winds. Now you just drive on. Drive through the town. Five miles out of Onkwedo, just after you have passed the trail to Mount Ettrick on your left, and just before reaching the bridge, take the first left turn. It's a good gravel road."

He stepped briskly around the hood and lunged with his rag at the windshield from the other side.

"You turn north and go on bearing north at each crossing—there are quite a few logging trails in those woods but you just bear north and you'll get to Cook's in twelve minutes flat. You can't miss it."

Pnin had now been in that maze of forest roads for about an hour and had come to the conclusion that "bear north," and in fact the word "north" itself, meant nothing to him. He also could not explain what had compelled him, a rational being, to listen to a chance busybody instead of firmly following the pedantically precise instructions that his friend, Alexandr Petrovich Kukolnikov (known locally as Al Cook) had sent him when inviting him to spend the summer at his large and hospitable country house. Our luckless car operator had by now lost himself too thoroughly to be able to go back to the highway, and since he had little experience in maneuvering on rutty narrow roads, with ditches and even ravines gaping on either side, his various indecisions and gropings took those bizarre visual forms that an observer on the lookout tower might have followed with a compassionate eye; but there was no living creature in that forlorn and listless upper region except for an ant who had his own troubles, having, after hours of inept perseverance, somehow reached the upper platform and the balustrade (his *autostrada*) and was getting all bothered and baffled much in the same way as that preposterous toy car progressing below. The wind had subsided. Under the pale sky the sea of tree tops seemed to harbor no life. Presently, however, a gun shot popped, and a twig leaped into the sky. The dense upper boughs in that part of the otherwise stirless forest started to move in a receding sequence of shakes or jumps, with a swinging lilt from tree to tree, after which all was still again. Another minute passed, and then everything happened at once: the ant found an upright beam leading to the roof of the tower and started to ascend it with renewed zest; the sun appeared; and Pnin at the height of hopelessness, found himself on a paved road with a rusty but still glistening sign directing wayfarers "To The Pines."

2

Al Cook was a son of Piotr Kukolnikov, wealthy Moscow merchant of Old-Believers antecedents, self-made man, Maecenas and philanthropist—the famous Kukolnikov who under the last Tsar had been twice imprisoned in a fairly comfortable fortress for giving financial assistance to Social-Revolutionary groups (terrorists, mainly), and under Lenin had been put to death as an "Imperialistic spy" after almost a week of medieval tortures in a Soviet jail. His family reached America via Harbin, around 1925, and young Cook by dint of quiet perseverance, practical acumen, and some scientific training, rose to a high and secure position in a great chemical concern. A kindly, very reserved man of stocky build, with a large immobile face that was tied up in the middle by a neat little pince-nez, he looked what he was—a Business Executive, a Mason, a Golfer, a prosperous and cautious man. He spoke beautifully correct, neutral English, with only the softest shadow of a Slavic accent, and was a delightful host, of the silent variety, with a twinkling eye, and a highball in each hand; and only when some very old and beloved Russian friend was his midnight guest would Alexandr Petrovich suddenly start to discuss God, Lermontov, Liberty, and divulge a hereditary streak of rash idealism that would have greatly confused a Marxist eavesdropper.

He married Susan Marshall, the attractive, voluble, blond daughter of Charles G. Marshall, the inventor, and because one could not imagine Alexandr and Susan otherwise than raising a huge healthy family, it came as a shock to me and other well-wishers to learn that as the result of an operation Susan would remain childless all her life. They were still young, loved each other with a sort of old-world simplicity and integrity very soothing to observe, and instead of populating their country place with children and grandchildren, they collected, every even-year summer, elderly Russians (Cook's fathers or uncles,

as it were); on odd-year summers they would have *amerikantsï*
(Americans), Alexandr's business acquaintances or Susan's relatives and friends.

This was the first time Pnin was coming to The Pines but I
had been there before. *Émigré* Russians—liberals and intellectuals who had left Russia around 1920—could be found swarming all over the place. You would find them in every patch of
speckled shade, sitting on rustic benches and discussing *émigré*
writers—Bunin, Aldanov, Sirin; lying suspended in hammocks,
with the Sunday issue of a Russian-language newspaper over
their faces in traditional defense against flies; sipping tea with
jam on the veranda; walking in the woods and wondering about
the edibility of local toadstools.

Samuil Lvovich Shpolyanski, a large majestically calm old
gentleman, and small, excitable, stuttering Count Fyodor
Nikitich Poroshin, both of whom, around 1920, had been
members of one of those heroic Regional Governments that were
formed in the Russian provinces by democratic groups to with-
stand Bolshevik dictatorship, would pace the avenue of pines
and discuss the tactics to be adopted at the next joint meeting of the Free Russia Committee (which they had founded in
New York) with another, younger, anti-Communist organization. From a pavilion half smothered by locust trees came fragments of a heated exchange between Professor Bolotov, who
taught the History of Philosophy, and Professor Chateau, who
taught the Philosophy of History: "Reality is Duration," one
voice, Bolotov's, would boom. "It is not!" the other would
cry. "A soap bubble is as real as a fossil tooth!"

Pnin and Chateau, both born in the late nineties of the nineteenth century, were comparative youngsters. Most of the other
men had seen sixty and had trudged on. On the other hand, a
few of the ladies, such as Countess Poroshin and Madam Bolotov, were still in their late forties and, thanks to the hygienic
atmosphere of the New World, had not only preserved, but improved, their good looks. Some parents brought their offspring

with them—healthy, tall, indolent, difficult American children of college age, with no sense of nature, and no Russian, and no interest whatsoever in the niceties of their parents' backgrounds and pasts. They seemed to live at The Pines on a physical and mental plane entirely different from that of their parents: now and then passing from their own level to ours through a kind of interdimensional shimmer; responding curtly to a well-meaning Russian joke or anxious piece of advice, and then fading away again; keeping always aloof (so that one felt one had engendered a brood of elves), and preferring any Onkwedo store product, any sort of canned goods to the marvelous Russian foods provided by the Kukolnikov household at loud, long dinners on the screened porch. With great distress Poroshin would say of his children (Igor and Olga, college sophomores), "My twins are exasperating. When I see them at home during breakfast or dinner and try to tell them most interesting, most exciting things —for instance, about local elective self-government in the Russian Far North in the seventeenth century or, say, something about the history of the first medical schools in Russia—there is, by the way, an excellent monograph by Chistovich on the subject, published in 1883—they simply wander off and turn on the radio in their rooms." Both young people were around the summer Pnin was invited to The Pines. But they stayed invisible; they would have been hideously bored in this out-of-the-way place, had not Olga's admirer, a college boy whose surname nobody seemed to know, arrived from Boston for the weekend in a spectacular car, and had not Igor found a congenial companion in Nina, the Bolotov girl, a handsome slattern with Egyptian eyes and brown limbs, who went to a dancing school in New York.

The household was looked after by Praskovia, a sturdy, sixty-year-old woman of the people with the vivacity of one a score of years younger. It was an exhilarating sight to watch her as she stood on the back porch surveying the chickens, knuckles on hips, dressed in baggy homemade shorts and a matronly blouse with rhinestones. She had nursed Alexandr and his brother when both were children in Harbin and now she was helped in her household duties by her husband, a gloomy and stolid old Cossack whose main passions in life were amateur bookbinding—a self-taught and almost pathological process that he was impelled to inflict upon any old catalogue or pulp magazine that came his way; the making of fruit liqueurs; and the killing of small forest animals.

Of that season's guests, Pnin knew well Professor Chateau, a friend of his youth, with whom he had attended the University of Prague in the early twenties, and he was also well acquainted with the Bolotovs, whom he had last seen in 1949 when he welcomed them with a speech at a formal dinner given them by the Association of Russian Émigré Scholars at the Barbizon-Plaza, upon the occasion of Bolotov's arrival from France. Personally, I never cared much for Bolotov and his philosophical works, which so oddly combine the obscure and the trite; the man's achievement is perhaps a mountain—but a mountain of platitudes; I have always liked, however, Varvara, the seedy philosopher's exuberant buxom wife. When she first visited The Pines, in 1951, she had never seen the New England countryside before. Its birches and bilberries deceived her into placing mentally Lake Onkwedo, not on the parallel of, say, Lake Ohrida in the Balkans, where it belonged, but on that of Lake Onega in northern Russia, where she had spent her first fifteen summers, before fleeing from the Bolsheviks to western Europe, with her aunt Lidia Vinogradov, the well-known feminist and social worker. Consequently the sight of a hummingbird in probing flight, or a catalpa in ample bloom, produced upon Varvara the effect of some unnatural or exotic vision. More fabulous than pictures in a bestiary were to her the tremendous porcupines that came to gnaw at the delicious, gamy old wood of the house, or the elegant, eerie little skunks that sampled the cat's milk in the backyard. She was nonplused and enchanted by the number of plants and

creatures she could not identify, mistook Yellow Warblers for
stray canaries, and on the occasion of Susan's birthday was
known to have brought, with pride and panting enthusiasm, for
the ornamentation of the dinner table, a profusion of beautiful
poison-ivy leaves, hugged to her pink, freckled breast.

3

The Bolotovs and Madam Shpolyanski, a little lean woman in
slacks, were the first people to see Pnin as he cautiously turned
into a sandy avenue, bordered with wild lupines, and, sitting
very straight, stiffly clutching the steering wheel as if he were
a farmer more used to his tractor than to his car, entered, at
ten miles an hour and in first gear, the grove of old, disheveled,
curiously authentic-looking pines that separated the paved
road from Cook's Castle.

Varvara buoyantly rose from the seat of the pavilion—where
she and Roza Shpolyanski had just discovered Bolotov reading
a battered book and smoking a forbidden cigarette. She greeted
Pnin with a clapping of hands, while her husband showed as
much geniality as he was capable of by slowly waving the
book he had closed on his thumb to mark the place. Pnin killed
the motor and sat beaming at his friends. The collar of his
green sport shirt was undone; his partly unzipped windbreaker
seemed too tight for his impressive torso; his bronzed bald
head, with the puckered brow and conspicuous vermicular
vein on the temple, bent low as he wrestled with the door handle
and finally dived out of the car.

"*Avtomobil', kostyum—nu pryamo amerikanets* (a veritable
American), *pryamo Ayzenhauer!*" said Varvara, and introduced
Pnin to Roza Abramovna Shpolyanski

"We had some mutual friends forty years ago," remarked
that lady, peering at Pnin with curiosity.

"Oh, let us not mention such astronomical figures," said

Bolotov, approaching and replacing with a grass blade the thumb he had been using as a bookmarker. "You know," he continued, shaking Pnin's hand, "I am rereading *Anna Karenin* for the seventh time and I derive as much rapture as I did, not forty, but sixty, years ago, when I was a lad of seven. And, every time, one discovers new things—for instance I notice now that Lyov Nikolaich does not know on what day his novel starts: it seems to be Friday because that is the day the clockman comes to wind up the clocks in the Oblonski house, but it is also Thursday as mentioned in the conversation at the skating rink between Lyovin and Kitty's mother."

"What on earth does it matter," cried Varvara. "Who on earth wants to know the exact day?"

"I can tell you the exact day," said Pnin, blinking in the broken sunlight and inhaling the remembered tang of northern pines. "The action of the novel starts in the beginning of 1872, namely on Friday, February the twenty-third by the New Style. In his morning paper Oblonski reads that Beust is rumored to have proceeded to Wiesbaden. This is of course Count Friedrich Ferdinand von Beust, who had just been appointed Austrian Ambassador to the Court of St. James's. After presenting his credentials, Beust had gone to the Continent for a rather protracted Christmas vacation—had spent there two months with his family, and was now returning to London, where, according to his own memoirs in two volumes, preparations were under way for the thanksgiving service to be held in St. Paul's on February the twenty-seventh for the recovering from typhoid fever of the Prince of Wales. However (*odnako*), it really is hot here (*i zharko zhe u vas*)! I think I shall now present myself before the most luminous orbs (*presvetlie ochi,* jocular) of Alexandr Petrovich and then go for a dip (*okupnutsya,* also jocular) in the river he so vividly describes in his letter."

"Alexandr Petrovich is away till Monday, on business or pleasure," said Varvara Bolotov, "but I think you will find Susanna Karlovna sun-bathing on her favorite lawn behind the house. Shout before you approach too near."

4
_____

Cook's Castle was a three-story brick-and-timber mansion
built around 1860 and partly rebuilt half a century later, when
Susan's father purchased it from the Dudley-Greene family in
order to make of it a select resort hotel for the richer patrons
of the curative Onkwedo Springs. It was an elaborate and ugly
building in a mongrel style, with the Gothic bristling through
remnants of French and Florentine, and when originally designed might have belonged to the variety which Samuel Sloan,
an architect of the time, classified as An Irregular Northern
Villa "well adapted to the highest requirements of social life"
and called "Northern" because of "the aspiring tendency of its
roof and towers." The piquancy of these pinnacles and the
merry, somewhat even inebriated air the mansion had of having
been composed of several smaller Northern Villas, hoisted into
midair and knocked together anyhow, with parts of unas-
similated roofs, half-hearted gables, cornices, rustic quoins,
and other projections sticking out on all sides, had, alas, but
briefly attracted tourists. By 1920, the Onkwedo waters had
mysteriously lost whatever magic they had contained, and after
her father's death Susan had vainly tried to sell The Pines,
since they had another more comfortable house in the residential quarter of the industrial city where her husband worked.
However, now that they had got accustomed to use the Castle
for entertaining their numerous friends, Susan was glad that
the meek beloved monster had found no purchaser.

Within, the diversity was as great as without. Four spacious
rooms opened from the large hall that retained something of its
hostelic stage in the generous dimensions of the grate. The
hand rail of the stairs, and at least one of its spindles, dated
from 1720, having been transferred to the house, while it
was being built, from a far older one, whose very site was no
longer exactly known. Very ancient, too, were the beautiful

sideboard panels of game and fish in the dining room. In the half a dozen rooms of which each of the upper floors consisted, and in the two wings in the rear, one could discover, among disparate pieces of furniture, some charming satinwood bureau, some romantic rosewood sofa, but also all kinds of bulky and miserable articles, broken chairs, dusty marble-topped tables, morose *étagères* with bits of dark-looking glass in the back as mournful as the eyes of old apes. The chamber Pnin got was a pleasant southeast one on the upper floor: it had remnants of gilt paper on the walls, an army cot, a plain washstand, and all kinds of shelves, brackets, and scrollwork moldings. Pnin shook open the casement, smiled at the smiling forest, again remembered a distant first day in the country, and presently walked down, clad in a new navy-blue bathrobe and wearing on his bare feet a pair of ordinary rubber overshoes, a sensible precaution if one intends to walk through damp and, perhaps, snake-infested grass. On the garden terrace he found Chateau.

Konstantin Ivanich Chateau, a subtle and charming scholar of pure Russian lineage despite his surname (derived, I am told, from that of a Russianized Frenchman who adopted orphaned Ivan), taught at a large New York university and had not seen his very dear Pnin for at least five years. They embraced with a warm rumble of joy. I confess to have been myself, at one time, under the spell of angelic Konstantin Ivanich— namely, when we used to meet every day in the winter of 1935 or 1936 for a morning stroll under the laurels and nettle trees of Grasse, southern France, where he then shared a villa with several other Russian expatriates. His soft voice, the gentlemanly St. Petersburgan burr of his *r*'s, his mild, melancholy caribou eyes, the auburn goatee he continuously twiddled, with a shredding motion of his long, frail fingers—everything about Chateau (to use a literary formula as old-fashioned as he) produced a rare sense of well-being in his friends. Pnin and he talked for a while, comparing notes. As not unusual with firm-principled exiles, every time they met after a separation they not only endeavored to catch up with a personal past, but also to sum up by means of a few rapid passwords—allusions, intonations impossible to render in a foreign language—the course of recent Russian history, thirty-five years of hopeless injustice following a century of struggling justice and glimmering hope. Next, they switched to the usual shop talk of European teachers abroad, sighing and shaking heads over the "typical American college student" who does not know geography, is immune to noise, and thinks education is but a means to get eventually a remunerative job. Then they inquired about each other's work in progress, and both were extremely modest and reticent about their respective researches. Finally, as they walked along a meadow path, brushing against the goldenrod, toward the wood where a rocky river ran, they spoke of their healths: Chateau, who looked so jaunty, with one hand in the pocket of his white flannel trousers and his lustring coat rather rakishly opened on a flannel waistcoat, cheerfully said that in the near future he would have to undergo an exploratory operation of the abdomen, and Pnin said, laughing, that every time *he* was X-rayed, doctors vainly tried to puzzle out what they termed "a shadow behind the heart."

"Good title for a bad novel," remarked Chateau.

As they were passing a grassy knoll just before entering the wood, a pink-faced venerable man in a seersucker suit, with a shock of white hair and a tumefied purple nose resembling a huge raspberry, came striding toward them down the sloping field, a look of disgust contorting his features.

"I have to go back for my hat," he cried dramatically as he drew near.

"Are you acquainted?" murmured Chateau, fluttering his hands introductively. "Timofey Pavlich Pnin, Ivan Ilyich Gramineev."

"*Moyo pochtenie* (My respects)," said both men, bowing to each other over a powerful handshake.

"I thought," resumed Gramineev, a circumstantial narrator,

"that the day would continue as overcast as it had begun. By stupidity (*po gluposti*) I came out with an unprotected head. Now the sun is roasting my brains. I have to interrupt my work."

He gestured toward the top of the knoll. There his easel stood in delicate silhouette against the blue sky. From that crest he had been painting a view of the valley beyond, complete with quaint old barn, gnarled apple tree, and kine.

"I can offer you my panama," said kind Chateau, but Pnin had already produced from his bathrobe pocket a large red handkerchief: he expertly twisted each of its corners into a knot.

"Admirable. . . . Most grateful," said Gramineev, adjusting this headgear.

"One moment," said Pnin. "You must tuck in the knots."

This done, Gramineev started walking up the field toward his easel. He was a well-known, frankly academic painter, whose soulful oils—"Mother Volga," "Three Old Friends (lad, nag, dog), "April Glade," and so forth—still graced a museum in Moscow.

"Somebody told me," said Chateau, as he and Pnin continued to progress riverward, "that Liza's boy has an extraordinary talent for painting. Is that correct?"

"Yes," answered Pnin. "All the more vexing (*tem bolee obidno*) that his mother, who I think is about to marry a third time, took Victor suddenly to California for the rest of the summer, whereas if he had accompanied me here, as had been planned, he would have had the splendid opportunity of being coached by Gramineev."

"You exaggerate the splendor," softly rejoined Chateau.

They reached the bubbling and glistening stream. A concave ledge between higher and lower diminutive cascades formed a natural swimming pool under the alders and pines. Chateau, a non-bather, made himself comfortable on a boulder. Throughout the academic year Pnin had regularly exposed his body to the radiation of a sun lamp; hence, when he stripped down to his bathing trunks, he glowed in the dappled sunlight of the riverside grove with a rich mahogany tint. He removed his cross and his rubbers.

"Look, how pretty," said observant Chateau.

A score of small butterflies, all of one kind, were settled on a damp patch of sand, their wings erect and closed, showing their pale undersides with dark dots and tiny orange-rimmed peacock spots along the hind-wing margins; one of Pnin's shed rubbers disturbed some of them and, revealing the celestial hue of their upper surface, they fluttered around like blue snowflakes before settling again.

"Pity Vladimir Vladimirovich is not here," remarked Chateau. "He would have told us all about these enchanting insects."

"I have always had the impression that his entomology was merely a pose."

"Oh no," said Chateau. "You will lose it some day," he added, pointing to the Greek Catholic cross on a golden chainlet that Pnin had removed from his neck and hung on a twig. Its glint perplexed a cruising dragonfly.

"Perhaps I would not mind losing it," said Pnin. "As you well know, I wear it merely from sentimental reasons. And the sentiment is becoming burdensome. After all, there is too much of the physical about this attempt to keep a particle of one's childhood in contact with one's breastbone."

"You are not the first to reduce faith to a sense of touch," said Chateau, who was a practicing Greek Catholic and deplored his friend's agnostic attitude.

A horsefly applied itself, blind fool, to Pnin's bald head, and was stunned by a smack of his meaty palm.

From a smaller boulder than the one upon which Chateau was perched, Pnin gingerly stepped down into the brown and blue water. He noticed he still had his wrist watch—removed it and left it inside one of his rubbers. Slowly swinging

his tanned shoulders, Pnin waded forth, the loopy shadows of
leaves shivering and slipping down his broad back. He stopped
and breaking the glitter and shade around him, moistened his
inclined head, rubbed his nape with wet hands, soused in turn
each armpit, and then, joining both palms, glided into the
water, his dignified breast stroke sending off ripples on either
side. Around the natural basin, Pnin swam in state. He swam
with a rhythmical splutter—half gurgle, half puff. Rhythmically
he opened his legs and widened them out at the knees while
flexing and straightening out his arms like a giant frog. After
two minutes of this, he waded out and sat on the boulder to
dry. Then he put on his cross, his wrist watch, his rubbers, and
his bathrobe.

5

Dinner was served on the screened porch. As he sat down
next to Bolotov and began to stir the sour cream in his red
botvinia (chilled beet soup), wherein pink ice cubes tinkled,
Pnin automatically resumed an earlier conversation.

"You will notice," he said, "that there is a significant difference between Lyovin's spiritual time and Vronski's physical
one. In mid-book, Lyovin and Kitty lag behind Vronski and
Anna by a whole year. When, on a Sunday evening in May
1876, Anna throws herself under that freight train, she has
existed more than four years since the beginning of the novel,
but in the case of the Lyovins, during the same period, 1872
to 1876, hardly three years have elapsed. It is the best example
of relativity in literature that is known to me."

After dinner, a game of croquet was suggested. These people favored the time-honored but technically illegal setting of
hoops, where two of the ten are crossed at the center of the
ground to form the so-called Cage or Mousetrap. It became
immediately clear that Pnin, who teamed with Madam Bolotov

against Shpolyanski and Countess Poroshin, was by far the best player of the lot. As soon as the pegs were driven in and the game started, the man was transfigured. From his habitual, slow, ponderous, rather rigid self, he changed into a terrifically mobile, scampering, mute, sly-visaged hunchback. It seemed to be always his turn to play. Holding his mallet very low and daintily swinging it between his parted spindly legs (he had created a minor sensation by changing into Bermuda shorts expressly for the game), Pnin foreshadowed every stroke with nimble aim-taking oscillations of the mallet head, then gave the ball an accurate tap, and forthwith, still hunched, and with the ball still rolling, walked rapidly to the spot where he had planned for it to stop. With geometrical gusto, he ran it through hoops, evoking cries of admiration from the onlookers. Even Igor Poroshin, who was passing by like a shadow with two cans of beer he was carrying to some private banquet, stopped for a second and shook his head appreciatively before vanishing in the shrubbery. Plaints and protests, however, would mingle with the applause when Pnin, with brutal indifference, croqueted, or rather rocketed, an adversary's ball. Placing in contact with it his own ball, and firmly putting his curiously small foot upon the latter, he would bang at his ball so as to drive the other up the country by the shock of the stroke. When appealed to, Susan said it was completely against the rules, but Madam Shpolyanski insisted it was perfectly acceptable and said that when she was a child her English governess used to call it a Hong Kong.

After Pnin had tolled the stake and all was over, and Varvara accompanied Susan to get the evening tea ready, Pnin quietly retired to a bench under the pines. A certain extremely unpleasant and frightening cardiac sensation, which he had experienced several times throughout his adult life, had come upon him again. It was not pain or palpitation, but rather an awful feeling of sinking and melting into one's physical surroundings—sunset, red boles of trees, sand, still air. Meanwhile Roza Shpolyanski, noticing Pnin sitting alone, and taking advantage of this, walked over to him (*"sidite, sidite!"* don't get up) and sat down next to him on the bench.

"In 1916 or 1917," she said, "you may have had occasion to hear my maiden name—Geller—from some great friends of yours."

"No, I don't recollect," said Pnin.

"It is of no importance, anyway. I don't think we ever met. But you knew well my cousins, Grisha and Mira Belochkin. They constantly spoke of you. He is living in Sweden, I think— and, of course, you have heard of his poor sister's terrible end. . . ."

"Indeed, I have," said Pnin.

"Her husband," said Madam Shpolyanski, "was a most charming man. Samuil Lvovich and I knew him and his first wife, Svetlana Chertok, the pianist, very intimately. He was interned by the Nazis separately from Mira, and died in the same concentration camp as did my elder brother Misha. You did not know Misha, did you? He was also in love with Mira once upon a time."

"*Tshay gotoff* (tea's ready)," called Susan from the porch in her funny functional Russian. "Timofey, Rozochka! *Tshay!*"

Pnin told Madam Shpolyanski he would follow her in a minute, and after she had gone he continued to sit in the first dusk of the arbor, his hands clasped on the croquet mallet he still held.

Two kerosene lamps cozily illuminated the porch of the country house. Dr. Pavel Antonovich Pnin, Timofey's father, an eye specialist, and Dr. Yakov Grigorievich Belochkin, Mira's father, a pediatrician, could not be torn away from their chess game in a corner of the veranda, so Madam Belochkin had the maid serve them there—on a special small Japanese table, near the one they were playing at—their glasses of tea in silver holders, the curd and whey with black bread, the Garden Strawberries, *zemlyanika*, and the other cultivated species, *klubnika* (Hautbois or Green Strawberries), and the radiant golden jams, and the various biscuits, wafers, pretzels, zwiebacks—instead of calling the two engrossed doctors to the main table at the other end of the porch, where sat the rest of the family and guests, some clear, some grading into a luminous mist. Dr. Belochkin's blind hand took a pretzel; Dr. Pnin's seeing hand took a rook. Dr. Belochkin munched and stared at the hole in his ranks; Dr. Pnin dipped an abstract zwieback into the hole of his tea.

The country house that the Belochkins rented that summer was in the same Baltic resort near which the widow of General N—— let a summer cottage to the Pnins on the confines of her vast estate, marshy and rugged, with dark woods hemming in a desolate manor. Timofey Pnin was again the clumsy, shy, obstinate, eighteen-year-old boy, waiting in the dark for Mira— and despite the fact that logical thought put electric bulbs into the kerosene lamps and reshuffled the people, turning them into aging *émigrés* and securely, hopelessly, forever wire-netting the lighted porch, my poor Pnin, with hallucinatory sharpness, imagined Mira slipping out of there into the garden and coming toward him among tall tobacco flowers whose dull white mingled in the dark with that of her frock. This feeling coincided somehow with the sense of diffusion and dilation within his chest. Gently he laid his mallet aside and, to dissipate the anguish, started walking away from the house, through the silent pine grove. From a car which was parked near the garden tool house and which contained presumably at least two of his fellow guests' children, there issued a steady trickle of radio music.

"Jazz, jazz, they always must have their jazz, those youngsters," muttered Pnin to himself, and turned into the path that led to the forest and river. He remembered the fads of his and Mira's youth, the amateur theatricals, the gypsy ballads, the passion she had for photography. Where were they now, those artistic snapshots she used to take—pets, clouds, flowers, an April glade with shadows of birches on wet-sugar snow, soldiers

posturing on the roof of a boxcar, a sunset skyline, a hand holding a book? He remembered the last day they had met, on the
Neva embankment in Petrograd, and the tears, and the stars,
and the warm rose-red silk lining of her karakul muff. The Civil
War of 1918–22 separated them: history broke their engagement. Timofey wandered southward, to join briefly the ranks
of Denikin's army, while Mira's family escaped from the Bolsheviks to Sweden and then settled down in Germany, where
eventually she married a fur dealer of Russian extraction. Sometime in the early thirties, Pnin, by then married too, accompanied his wife to Berlin, where she wished to attend a congress of
psychotherapists, and one night, at a Russian restaurant on
the Kurfürstendamm, he saw Mira again. They exchanged a
few words, she smiled at him in the remembered fashion, from
under her dark brows, with that bashful slyness of hers; and the
contour of her prominent cheekbones, and the elongated eyes,
and the slenderness of arm and ankle were unchanged, were
immortal, and then she joined her husband who was getting
his overcoat at the cloakroom, and that was all—but the pang
of tenderness remained, akin to the vibrating outline of verses
you know you know but cannot recall.

What chatty Madam Shpolyanski mentioned had conjured
up Mira's image with unusual force. This was disturbing. Only
in the detachment of an incurable complaint, in the sanity of
near death, could one cope with this for a moment. In order to
exist rationally, Pnin had taught himself, during the last ten
years, never to remember Mira Belochkin—not because, in
itself, the evocation of a youthful love affair, banal and brief,
threatened his peace of mind (alas, recollections of his marriage to Liza were imperious enough to crowd out any former
romance), but because, if one were quite sincere with oneself,
no conscience, and hence no consciousness, could be expected
to subsist in a world where such things as Mira's death were
possible. One had to forget—because one could not live with
the thought that this graceful, fragile, tender young woman with

those eyes, that smile, those gardens and snows in the background, had been brought in a cattle car to an extermination camp and killed by an injection of phenol into the heart, into the gentle heart one had heard beating under one's lips in the dusk of the past. And since the exact form of her death had not been recorded, Mira kept dying a great number of deaths in one's mind, and undergoing a great number of resurrections, only to die again and again, led away by a trained nurse, inoculated with filth, tetanus bacilli, broken glass, gassed in a sham shower bath with prussic acid, burned alive in a pit on a gasoline-soaked pile of beechwood. According to the investigator Pnin had happened to talk to in Washington, the only certain thing was that being too weak to work (though still smiling, still able to help other Jewish women), she was selected to die and was cremated only a few days after her arrival in Buchenwald, in the beautifully wooded Grosser Ettersberg, as the region is resoundingly called. It is an hour's stroll from Weimar, where walked Goethe, Herder, Schiller, Wieland, the inimitable Kotzebue and others. "*Aber warum*—but why—" Dr. Hagen, the gentlest of souls alive, would wail, "why had one to put that horrid camp so near!" for indeed, it was near—only five miles from the cultural heart of Germany—"that nation of universities," as the President of Waindell College, renowned for his use of the *mot juste,* had so elegantly phrased it when reviewing the European situation in a recent Commencement speech, along with the compliment he paid another torture house, "Russia—the country of Tolstoy, Stanislavski, Raskolnikov, and other great and good men."

Pnin slowly walked under the solemn pines. The sky was dying. He did not believe in an autocratic God. He did believe, dimly, in a democracy of ghosts. The souls of the dead, perhaps, formed committees, and these, in continuous session, attended to the destinies of the quick.

The mosquitoes were getting bothersome. Time for tea. Time for a game of chess with Chateau. That strange spasm was over, one could breathe again. On the distant crest of the knoll, at the exact spot where Gramineev's easel had stood a few hours before, two dark figures in profile were silhouetted against the ember-red sky. They stood there closely, facing each other. One could not make out from the road whether it was the Poroshin girl and her beau, or Nina Bolotov and young Poroshin, or merely an emblematic couple placed with easy art on the last page of Pnin's fading day.

❧ Chapter Six ❧

1

The 1954 Fall Term had begun. Again the marble neck of a homely Venus in the vestibule of Humanities Hall received the vermilion imprint, in applied lipstick, of a mimicked kiss. Again the *Waindell Recorder* discussed the Parking Problem. Again in the margins of library books earnest freshmen inscribed such helpful glosses as "Description of nature," or "Irony"; and in a pretty edition of Mallarmé's poems an especially able scholiast had already underlined in violet ink the difficult word *oiseaux* and scrawled above it "birds." Again autumn gales plastered dead leaves against one side of the latticed gallery leading from Humanities to Frieze Hall. Again, on serene afternoons, huge, amber-brown Monarch butterflies flapped over asphalt and lawn as they lazily drifted south, their incompletely retracted black legs hanging rather low beneath their polka-dotted bodies.

And still the College creaked on. Hard-working graduates, with pregnant wives, still wrote dissertations on Dostoevski and Simone de Beauvoir. Literary departments still labored under the impression that Stendhal, Galsworthy, Dreiser, and Mann were great writers. Word plastics like "conflict" and "pattern"

were still in vogue. As usual, sterile instructors successfully
endeavored to "produce" by reviewing the books of more fertile colleagues, and, as usual, a crop of lucky faculty members
were enjoying or about to enjoy various awards received earlier in the year. Thus, an amusing little grant was affording the
versatile Starr couple—baby-faced Christopher Starr and his
child-wife Louise, of the Fine Arts Department—the unique
opportunity of recording postwar folk songs in East Germany,
into which these amazing young people had somehow obtained
permission to penetrate. Tristram W. Thomas ("Tom" to his
friends), Professor of Anthropology, had obtained ten thousand
dollars from the Mandeville Foundation for a study of the eating habits of Cuban fishermen and palm climbers. Another
charitable institution had come to the assistance of Dr. Bodo
von Falternfels, to enable him to complete "a bibliography concerned with such published and manuscript material as has been
devoted in recent years to a critical appraisal of the influence of
Nietzsche's disciples on Modern Thought." And, last but not
least, the bestowal of a particularly generous grant was allowing
the renowned Waindell psychiatrist, Dr. Rudolph Aura, to
apply to ten thousand elementary school pupils the so-called
Fingerbowl Test, in which the child is asked to dip his index
in cups of colored fluids whereupon the proportion between
length of digit and wetted part is measured and plotted in all
kinds of fascinating graphs.

The Fall Term had begun, and Dr. Hagen was faced with a
complicated situation. During the summer, he had been infor-
mally approached by an old friend about whether he might consider accepting next year a delightfully lucrative professor-
ship at Seaboard, a far more important university than Waindell. This part of the problem was comparatively easy to solve.
On the other hand, there remained the chilling fact that the
department he had so lovingly built, with which Blorenge's
French Department, although far richer in funds, could not
vie in cultural impact, would be relinquished into the claws of

treacherous Falternfels, whom he, Hagen, had obtained from Austria and who had turned against him—had actually managed to appropriate by underhand methods the direction of *Europa Nova,* an influential quarterly Hagen had founded in 1945. Hagen's proposed departure—of which, as yet, he had divulged nothing to his colleagues—would have a still more heart-rending consequence: Assistant Professor Pnin must be left in the lurch. There had never been any regular Russian Department at Waindell and my poor friend's academic existence had always depended on his being employed by the eclectic German Department in a kind of Comparative Literature extension of one of its branches. Out of pure spite, Bodo was sure to lop off that limb, and Pnin, who had no life tenure at Waindell, would be forced to leave—unless some other literature-and-language Department agreed to adopt him. The only departments that seemed flexible enough to do so were those of English and French. But Jack Cockerell, Chairman of English, disapproved of everything Hagen did, considered Pnin a joke, and was, in fact, unofficially but hopefully haggling for the services of a prominent Anglo-Russian writer who, if necessary, could teach all the courses that Pnin must keep in order to survive. As a last resort, Hagen turned to Blorenge.

2

Two interesting characteristics distinguished Leonard Blorenge, Chairman of French Literature and Language; he disliked Literature and he had no French. This did not prevent him from traveling tremendous distances to attend Modern Language conventions, at which he would flaunt his ineptitude as if it were some majestic whim, and parry with great thrusts of healthy lodge humor any attempt to inveigle him into the subtleties of the parley-voo. A highly esteemed money-getter, he had recently induced a rich old man, whom three great uni-

versities had courted in vain, to promote with a fantastic endow-
ment a riot of research conducted by graduates under the direction of Dr. Slavski, a Canadian, toward the erection on a hill
near Waindell, of a "French Village," two streets and a square,
to be copied from those of the ancient little burg of Vandel in
the Dordogne. Despite the grandiose element always present in
his administrative illuminations, Blorenge personally was a
man of ascetic tastes. He had happened to go to school with
Sam Poore, Waindell's President, and for many years, regularly,
even after the latter had lost his sight, the two would go fishing
together on a bleak, wind-raked lake, at the end of a gravel road
lined with fireweed, seventy miles north of Waindell, in the kind
of dreary brush country—scrub oak and nursery pine—that,
in terms of nature, is the counterpart of a slum. His wife, a
sweet woman of simple antecedents, referred to him at her
club as "Professor Blorenge." He gave a course entitled "Great
Frenchmen," which he had had his secretary copy out from
a set of *The Hastings Historical and Philosophical Magazine*
for 1882-94, discovered by him in an attic and not represented
in the College Library.

3

Pnin had just rented a small house, and had invited the Ha-
gens and the Clementses, and the Thayers, and Betty Bliss to a
housewarming party. On the morning of that day, good Dr.
Hagen made a desperate visit to Blorenge's office and revealed
to him, and to him alone, the whole situation. When he told
Blorenge that Falternfels was a strong anti-Pninist, Blorenge
drily rejoined that so was he; in fact, after meeting Pnin socially, he "definitely felt" (it is truly a wonder how prone these
practical people are to feel rather than to think) that Pnin was
not fit even to loiter in the vicinity of an American college.
Staunch Hagen said that for several terms Pnin had been ad-

mirably dealing with the Romantic Movement and might surely handle Chateaubriand and Victor Hugo under the auspices of the French Department.

"Dr. Slavski takes care of that crowd," said Blorenge. "In fact, I sometimes think we overdo literature. Look, this week Miss Mopsuestia begins the Existentialists, your man Bodo does Romain Rolland, I lecture on General Boulanger and De Béranger. No, we have definitely enough of the stuff."

Hagen, playing his last card, suggested Pnin could teach a French language course: like many Russians, our friend had had a French governess as a child, and after the Revolution he lived in Paris for more than fifteen years.

"You mean," asked Blorenge sternly, "he can *speak* French?"

Hagen, who was well aware of Blorenge's special requirements, hesitated.

"Out with it, Herman! Yes or no?"

"I am sure he could adapt himself."

"He does speak it, eh?"

"Well, yes."

"In that case," said Blorenge, "we can't use him in First-Year French. It would be unfair to our Mr. Smith, who gives the elementary course this term and, naturally, is required to be only one lesson ahead of his students. Now it so happens that Mr. Hashimoto needs an assistant for his overflowing group in Intermediate French. Does your man *read* French as well as speak it?"

"I repeat, he can adapt himself," hedged Hagen.

"I know what adaptation means," said Blorenge, frowning. "In 1950, when Hash was away, I engaged that Swiss skiing instructor and he smuggled in mimeo copies of some old French anthology. It took us almost a year to bring the class back to its initial level. Now, if what's-his-name does not read French——"

"I'm afraid he does," said Hagen with a sigh.

"Then we can't use him at all. As you know, we believe only in speech records and other mechanical devices. No books are allowed."

"There still remains Advanced French," murmured Hagen.

"Carolina Slavski and I take care of that," answered Blorenge.

4

For Pnin, who was totally unaware of his protector's woes, the new Fall Term began particularly well: he had never had so few students to bother about, or so much time for his own research. This research had long entered the charmed stage when the quest overrides the goal, and a new organism is formed, the parasite so to speak of the ripening fruit. Pnin averted his mental gaze from the end of his work, which was so clearly in sight that one could make out the rocket of an asterisk, the flare of a "sic!" This line of land was to be shunned as the doom of everything that determined the rapture of endless approximation. Index cards were gradually loading a shoe box with their compact weight. The collation of two legends; a precious detail in manners or dress; a reference checked and found to be falsified by incompetence, carelessness, or fraud; the spine thrill of a felicitous guess; and all the innumerable triumphs of *bezkorïstnïy* (disinterested, devoted) scholarship—this had corrupted Pnin, this had made of him a happy, footnote-drugged maniac who disturbs the book mites in a dull volume, a foot thick, to find in it a reference to an even duller one. And on another, more human, plane there was the little brick house that he had rented on Todd Road, at the corner of Cliff Avenue.

It had lodged the family of the late Martin Sheppard, an uncle of Pnin's previous landlord in Creek Street and for many years the caretaker of the Todd property, which the town of

Waindell had now acquired for the purpose of turning its rambling mansion into a modern nursing home. Ivy and spruce muffled its locked gate, whose top Pnin could see on the far side of Cliff Avenue from a north window of his new home. This avenue was the crossbar of a T, in the left crotch of which he dwelt. Opposite the front of his house, immediately across Todd Road (the upright of the T) old elms screened the sandy shoulder of its patched-up asphalt from a cornfield east of it, while along its west side a regiment of young fir trees, identical upstarts, walked, campusward, behind a fence, for almost the whole distance to the next residence—the Varsity Football Coach's magnified cigar box, which stood half a mile south from Pnin's house.

The sense of living in a discrete building all by himself was to Pnin something singularly delightful and amazingly satisfying to a weary old want of his innermost self, battered and stunned by thirty-five years of homelessness. One of the sweetest things about the place was the silence—angelic, rural, and perfectly secure, thus in blissful contrast to the persistent cacophonies that had surrounded him from six sides in the rented rooms of his former habitations. And the tiny house was so spacious! With grateful surprise, Pnin thought that there had been no Russian revolution, no exodus, no expatriation in France, no naturalization in America, everything—at the best, at the best, Timofey!—would have been much the same: a professor-ship in Kharkov or Kazan, a suburban house such as this, old books within, late blooms without. It was—to be more pre-cise—a two-story house of cherry-red brick, with white shutters and a shingle roof. The green plat on which it stood had a frontage of about fifty arshins and was limited at the back by a vertical stretch of mossy cliff with tawny shrubs on its crest. A rudimentary driveway along the south side of the house led to a small whitewashed garage for the poor man's car Pnin owned. A curious basketlike net, somewhat like a glorified billiard pocket —lacking, however, a bottom—was suspended for some rea-

son above the garage door, upon the white of which it cast a
shadow as distinct as its own weave but larger and in a bluer
tone. Pheasants visited the weedy ground between the garage
and the cliff. Lilacs—those Russian garden graces, to whose
springtime splendor, all honey and hum, my poor Pnin greatly
looked forward—crowded in sapless ranks along one wall of the
house. And a tall deciduous tree, which Pnin, a birch-lime-wil-
low-aspen-poplar-oak man, was unable to identify, cast its large,
heart-shaped, rust-colored leaves and Indian-summer shadows
upon the wooden steps of the open porch.

A cranky-looking oil furnace in the basement did its best to
send up its weak warm breath through registers in the floors.
The kitchen looked healthy and gay, and Pnin had a great
time with all kinds of cookware, kettles and pans, toasters and
skillets, all of which came with the house. The living room was
scantily and dingily furnished, but had a rather attractive bay
harboring a huge old globe, where Russia was painted a pale
blue, with a discolored or scrubbled patch all over Poland. In
a very small dining room, where Pnin contemplated arranging
a buffet supper for his guests, a pair of crystal candlesticks
with pendants was responsible in the early mornings for iridescent reflections, which glowed charmingly on the sideboard and
reminded my sentimental friend of the stained-glass casements
that colored the sunlight orange and green and violet on the
verandas of Russian country houses. A china closet, every
time he passed by it, went into a rumbling act that also was
somehow familiar from dim back rooms of the past. The second floor consisted of two bedrooms, both of which had been
the abode of many small children, with incidental adults. The
floors were chafed by tin toys. From the wall of the chamber
Pnin decided to sleep in he had untacked a pennant-shaped red
cardboard with the enigmatic word "Cardinals" daubed on it
in white; but a tiny rocker for a three-year-old Pnin, painted
pink, was allowed to remain in its corner. A disabled sewing
machine occupied a passageway leading to the bathroom, where

the usual short tub, made for dwarfs by a nation of giants, took as long to fill as the tanks and basins of the arithmetic in Russian school books.

He was now ready to give that party. The living room had a sofa that could seat three, there were two wing-back chairs, an overstuffed easy chair, a chair with a rush seat, one hassock, and two footstools. All of a sudden he experienced an odd feeling of dissatisfaction as he checked the little list of his guests. It had body but it lacked bouquet. Of course, he was tremendously fond of the Clementses (real people—not like most of the campus dummies), with whom he had had such exhilarating talks in the days when he was their roomer; of course, he felt very grateful to Herman Hagen for many a good turn, such as that raise Hagen had recently arranged; of course, Mrs. Hagen was, in Waindell parlance, "a lovely person"; of course, Mrs. Thayer was always so helpful at the library, and her husband had such a soothing capacity for showing how silent a man could be if he strictly avoided comments on the weather. But there was nothing extraordinary, nothing original, about this combination of people, and old Pnin recalled those birthday parties in his boyhood—the half a dozen children invited who were somehow always the same, and the pinching shoes, and the aching temples, and the kind of heavy, unhappy, constraining dullness that would settle on him after all the games had been played and a rowdy cousin had started putting nice new toys to vulgar and stupid uses; and he also recalled the lone buzz in his ears when, in the course of a protracted hide-and-seek routine, after an hour of uncomfortable concealment, he emerged from a dark and stuffy wardrobe in the maid's chamber, only to find that all his playmates had already gone home.

While visiting a famous grocery between Waindellville and Isola, he ran into Betty Bliss, asked her, and she said she still remembered Turgenev's prose poem about roses, with its refrain "*Kak horoshi, kak svezhi* (How fair, how fresh)," and would certainly be delighted to come. He asked the celebrated mathematician, Professor Idelson, and his wife, the sculptress, and they said they would come with joy but later telephoned to say they were tremendously sorry—they had overlooked a previous engagement. He asked young Miller, by now an Associate Professor, and Charlotte, his pretty, freckled wife, but it turned out she was on the point of having a baby. He asked old Carrol, the Frieze Hall head janitor, with his son Frank, who had been my friend's only talented student and had written a brilliant doctor's thesis for him on the relationship between Russian, English, and German iambics; but Frank was in the Army, and old Carrol confessed that "the missus and I do not mix much with the profs." He rang up the residence of President Poore, whom he had once talked to (about improving the curriculum) at a lawn function, until it started to rain, and asked him to come, but President Poore's niece answered that her uncle nowadays "never visits with anybody except a few personal friends." He was about to give up the notion of enlivening his list, when a perfectly new and really admirable idea occurred to him.

5

Pnin and I had long since accepted the disturbing but seldom discussed fact that on any given college staff one could find not only a person who was uncommonly like one's dentist or the local postmaster, but also a person who had a twin within the same professional group. I know, indeed, of a case of triplets at a comparatively small college where, according to its sharp-eyed president, Frank Reade, the radix of the troika was, absurdly enough, myself; and I recall the late Olga Krotki once telling me that among the fifty or so faculty members of a war-time Intensive Language School, at which the poor, one-lunged lady had to teach Lethean and Fenugreek, there were as many

as six Pnins, besides the genuine and, to me, unique article.
It should not be deemed surprising, therefore, that even Pnin,
not a very observant man in everyday life, could not help becoming aware (sometime during his ninth year at Waindell)
that a lanky, bespectacled old fellow with scholarly strands of
steel-gray hair falling over the right side of his small but cor-
rugated brow, and with a deep furrow descending from each
side of his sharp nose to each corner of his long upper lip—a
person whom Pnin knew as Professor Thomas Wynn, Head of
the Ornithology Department, having once talked to him at some
party about gay golden orioles, melancholy cuckoos, and other
Russian countryside birds—was not always Professor Wynn. At
times he graded, as it were, into somebody else, whom Pnin
did not know by name but whom he classified, with a bright
foreigner's fondness for puns, as "Twynn" (or, in Pninian,
"Tvin"). My friend and compatriot soon realized that he could
never be sure whether the owlish, rapidly stalking gentleman,
whose path he would cross every other day at different points
of progress, between office and classroom, between classroom
and stairs, between drinking fountain and lavatory, was really
his chance acquaintance, the ornithologist, whom he felt bound
to greet in passing, or the Wynn-like stranger, who acknowledged that somber salute with exactly the same degree of automatic politeness as any chance acquaintance would. The moment of meeting would be very brief, since both Pnin and Wynn
(or Twynn) walked fast; and sometimes Pnin, in order to avoid
the exchange of urbane barks, would feign reading a letter on
the run, or would manage to dodge his rapidly advancing colleague and tormentor by swerving into a stairway and then continuing along a lower-floor corridor; but no sooner had he begun to rejoice in the smartness of the device than upon using
it one day he almost collided with Tvin (or Vin) pounding
along the subjacent passage. When the new Fall Term (Pnin's
tenth) began, the nuisance was aggravated by the fact
that Pnin's class hours had been changed, thus abolishing cer-

tain trends on which he had been learning to rely in his efforts
to elude Wynn and Wynn's simulator. It seemed he would have
to endure it always. For recalling certain other duplications in
the past—disconcerting likenesses he alone had seen—bothered Pnin told himself it would be useless to ask anybody's
assistance in unraveling the T. Wynns.

On the day of his party, as he was finishing a late lunch in
Frieze Hall, Wynn, or his double, neither of whom had ever
appeared there before, suddenly sat down beside him and said:

"I have long wanted to ask you something—you teach Russian, don't you? Last summer I was reading a magazine article on birds——"

("Vin! This is Vin!" said Pnin to himself, and forthwith
perceived a decisive course of action.)

"—well, the author of that article—I don't remember his
name, I think it was a Russian one—mentioned that in the Skoff
region, I hope I pronounce it right, a local cake is baked in the
form of a bird. Basically, of course, the symbol is phallic, but I
was wondering if you knew of such a custom?"

It was then that the brilliant idea flashed in Pnin's mind.

"Sir, I am at your service," he said with a note of exultation
quivering in his throat—for he now saw his way to pin down
definitely the personality of at least the initial Wynn who liked
birds. "Yes, sir. I know all about those *zhavoronki,* those
alouettes, those—we must consult a dictionary for the English
name. So I take the opportunity to extend a cordial invitation
to you to visit me this evening. Half past eight, postmeridian.
A little house-heating soirée, nothing more. Bring also your
spouse—or perhaps you are a Bachelor of Hearts?"

(Oh, punster Pnin!)

His interlocutor said he was not married. He would love to
come. What was the address?

"It is nine hundred ninety nine, Todd Rodd, very simple!
At the very very end of the rodd, where it unites with Cleef
Ahvnue. A leetle breek house and a beeg blahk cleef."

6
_____

That afternoon Pnin could hardly wait to start culinary operations. He began them soon after five and only interrupted them to don, for the reception of his guests, a sybaritic smoking jacket of blue silk, with tasseled belt and satin lapels, won at an *émigré* charity bazaar in Paris twenty years ago—how the time flies! This jacket he wore with a pair of old tuxedo trousers, likewise of European origin. Peering at himself in the cracked mirror of the medicine chest, he put on his heavy tortoise-shell reading glasses, from under the saddle of which his Russian potato nose smoothly bulged. He bared his synthetic teeth. He inspected his cheeks and chin to see if his morning shave still held. It did. With finger and thumb he grasped a long nostril hair, plucked it out after a second hard tug, and sneezed lustily, an "Ah!" of well-being rounding out the explosion.

At half past seven Betty arrived to help with final arrangements. Betty now taught English and History at Isola High School. She had not changed since the days when she was a buxom graduate student. Her pink-rimmed myopic gray eyes peered at you with the same ingenuous sympathy. She wore the same Gretchen-like coil of thick hair around her head. There was the same scar on her soft throat. But an engagement ring with a diminutive diamond had appeared on her plump hand, and this she displayed with coy pride to Pnin, who vaguely experienced a twinge of sadness. He reflected that there was a time he might have courted her—would have done so, in fact, had she not had a servant maid's mind, which had remained unaltered too. She could still relate a long story on a "she said-I said-she said" basis. Nothing on earth could make her disbelieve in the wisdom and wit of her favorite woman's magazine. She still had the curious trick—shared by two or three other small-town young women within Pnin's limited ken

—of giving you a delayed little tap on the sleeve in acknowledgment of, rather than in retaliation for, any remark reminding
her of some minor lapse: you would say, "Betty, you forgot to
return that book," or "I thought, Betty, you said you would
never marry," and before she actually answered, there it
would come, that demure gesture, retracted at the very moment
her stubby fingers came into contact with your wrist.

"He is a biochemist and is now in Pittsburgh," said Betty as
she helped Pnin to arrange buttered slices of French bread
around a pot of glossy-gray fresh caviar and to rinse three
large bunches of grapes. There was also a large plate of cold
cuts, real German pumpernickel, and a dish of very special
vinaigrette, where shrimps hobnobbed with pickles and peas,
and some miniature sausages in tomato sauce, and hot *pirozhki*
(mushroom tarts, meat tarts, cabbage tarts), and four kinds of
nuts, and various interesting Oriental sweets. Drinks were to be
represented by whisky (Betty's contribution), *ryabinovka* (a
rowanberry liqueur), brandy-and-grenadine cocktails, and of
course Pnin's Punch, a heady mixture of chilled Chateau
Yquem, grapefruit juice, and maraschino, which the solemn
host had already started to stir in a large bowl of brilliant aquamarine glass with a decorative design of swirled ribbing and lily
pads.

"My, what a lovely thing!" cried Betty.

Pnin eyed the bowl with pleased. surprise as if seeing it for
the first time. It was, he said, a present from Victor. Yes, how
was he, how did he like St. Bart's? He liked it so-so. He had
passed the beginning of the summer in California with his
mother, then had worked two months at a Yosemite hotel. A
what? A hotel in the Californian mountains. Well, he had returned to his school and had suddenly sent this.

By some tender coincidence the bowl had come on the very
day Pnin had counted the chairs and started to plan this party.
It had come enclosed in a box within another box inside a third
one, and wrapped up in an extravagant mass of excelsior and

paper that had spread all over the kitchen like a carnival storm. The bowl that emerged was one of those gifts whose first impact produces in the recipient's mind a colored image, a blazoned blur, reflecting with such emblematic force the sweet nature of the donor that the tangible attributes of the thing are dissolved, as it were, in this pure inner blaze, but suddenly and forever leap into brilliant being when praised by an outsider to whom the true glory of the object is unknown.

7

A musical tinkle reverberated through the small house, and the Clementses entered with a bottle of French champagne and a cluster of dahlias.

Dark-blue-eyed, long-lashed, bob-haired Joan wore an old black silk dress that was smarter than anything other faculty wives could devise, and it was always a pleasure to watch good old bald Tim Pnin bend slightly to touch with his lips the light hand that Joan, alone of all the Waindell ladies, knew how to raise to exactly the right level for a Russian gentleman to kiss. Laurence, fatter than ever, dressed in nice gray flannels, sank into the easy chair and immediately grabbed the first book at hand, which happened to be an English-Russian and Russian-English pocket dictionary. Holding his glasses in one hand, he looked away, trying to recall something he had always wished to check but now could not remember, and his attitude accentuated his striking resemblance, somewhat *en jeune,* to Jan van Eyck's ample-jowled, fluff-haloed Canon van der Paele, seized by a fit of abstraction in the presence of the puzzled Virgin to whom a super, rigged up as St. George, is directing the good Canon's attention. Everything was there—the knotty temple, the sad, musing gaze, the folds and furrows of facial flesh, the thin lips, and even the wart on the left cheek.

Hardly had the Clementses settled down than Betty let in

the man interested in bird-shaped cakes. Pnin was about to say "Professor Vin" but Joan—rather unfortunately, perhaps—interrupted the introduction with "Oh, we know Thomas! Who does not know Tom?" Tim Pnin returned to the kitchen, and Betty handed around some Bulgarian cigarettes.

"I thought, Thomas," remarked Clements, crossing his fat legs, "you were out in Havana interviewing palm-climbing fishermen?"

"Well, I'll be on my way after midyears," said Professor Thomas. "Of course, most of the actual field work has been done already by others."

"Still, it was nice to get that grant, wasn't it?"

"In our branch," replied Thomas with perfect composure, "we have to undertake many difficult journeys. In fact, I may push on to the Windward Islands. If," he added with a hollow laugh, "Senator McCarthy does not crack down on foreign travel."

"He received a grant of ten thousand dollars," said Joan to Betty, whose face dropped a curtsy as she made that special grimace consisting of a slow half-bow and tensing of chin and lower lip that automatically conveys, on the part of Bettys, a respectful, congratulatory, and slightly awed recognition of such grand things as dining with one's boss, being in *Who's Who,* or meeting a duchess.

The Thayers, who came in a new station wagon, presented their host with an elegant box of mints. Dr. Hagen, who came on foot, triumphantly held aloft a bottle of vodka.

"Good evening, good evening, good evening," said hearty Hagen.

"Dr. Hagen," said Thomas as he shook hands with him. "I hope the Senator did not see you walking about with that stuff."

The good Doctor had perceptibly aged since last year but was as sturdy and square-shaped as ever with his well-padded shoulders, square chin, square nostrils, leonine glabella, and rectangular brush of grizzled hair that had something topiary about it. He wore a black suit over a white nylon shirt, and a black tie with a red thunderbolt streaking down it. Mrs. Hagen had been prevented from coming, at the very last moment, by a dreadful migraine, alas.

Pnin served the cocktails "or better to say flamingo tails— specially for ornithologists," as he slyly quipped.

"Thank you!" chanted Mrs. Thayer, as she received her glass, raising her linear eyebrows, on that bright note of genteel inquiry which is meant to combine the notions of surprise, unworthiness, and pleasure. An attractive, prim, pink-faced lady of forty or so, with pearly dentures and wavy goldenized hair, she was the provincial cousin of the smart, relaxed Joan Clements, who had been all over the world, even in Turkey and Egypt, and was married to the most original and least liked scholar on the Waindell campus. A good word should be also put in at this point for Margaret Thayer's husband, Roy, a mournful and mute member of the Department of English, which, except for its ebullient chairman, Cockerell, was an aerie of hypochondriacs. Outwardly, Roy was an obvious figure. If you drew a pair of old brown loafers, two beige elbow patches, a black pipe, and two baggy eyes under heavy eyebrows, the rest was easy to fill out. Somewhere in the middle distance hung an obscure liver ailment, and somewhere in the background there was Eighteenth-Century Poetry, Roy's particular field, an overgrazed pasture, with the trickle of a brook and a clump of initialed trees; a barbed-wire arrangement on either side of this field separated it from Professor Stowe's domain, the preceding century, where the lambs were whiter, the turf softer, the rill purlier, and from Dr. Shapiro's early nineteenth century, with glen mists, sea fogs, and imported grapes. Roy Thayer avoided talking of his subject, avoided, in fact, talking of any subject, had squandered a decade of gray life on an erudite work dealing with a forgotten group of unnecessary poetasters, and kept a detailed diary, in cryptogrammed verse, which he hoped posterity would someday decipher and, in sober back-

cast, proclaim the greatest literary achievement of our time—
and for all I know, Roy Thayer, you might be right.

When everybody was comfortably lapping and lauding the
cocktails, Professor Pnin sat down on the wheezy hassock near
his newest friend and said:

"I have to report, sir, on the skylark, *zhavoronok* in Russian,
about which you made me the honor to interrogate me.
Take this with you to your home. I have here tapped on the
typewriting machine a condensed account with bibliography.
I think we will now transport ourselves to the other room where
a supper *à la fourchette* is, I think, awaiting us."

8

———————

Presently, guests with full plates drifted back into the parlor.
The punch was brought in.

"Gracious, Timofey, where on earth did you get that perfectly divine bowl!" exclaimed Joan.

"Victor presented it to me."

"But where did he *get* it?"

"Antiquaire store in Cranton, I think."

"Gosh, it must have cost a fortune."

"One dollar? Ten dollars? Less maybe?"

"Ten dollars—nonsense! Two hundred, I should say. *Look*
at it! Look at this writhing pattern. You know, you should
show it to the Cockerells. They know everything about old
glass. In fact, they have a Lake Dunmore pitcher that looks
like a poor relation of this."

Margaret Thayer admired it in her turn, and said that when
she was a child, she imagined Cinderella's glass shoes to be
exactly of that greenish blue tint; whereupon Professor Pnin
remarked that, *primo,* he would like everybody to say if contents were as good as container, and, *secundo,* that Cendril-
lon's shoes were not made of glass but of Russian squirrel fur—

vair, in French. It was, he said, an obvious case of the survival
of the fittest among words, *verre* being more evocative than
vair which, he submitted, came not from *varius,* variegated,
but from *veveritsa,* Slavic for a certain beautiful, pale, winter-
squirrel fur, having a bluish, or better say *sizïly,* columbine,
shade—from *columba,* Latin for "pigeon," as somebody here
well knows—so you see, Mrs. Fire, you were, in general, correct."

"The contents are fine," said Laurence Clements.

"This beverage is certainly delicious," said Margaret
Thayer.

("I always thought 'columbine' was some sort of flower,"
said Thomas to Betty, who lightly acquiesced.)

The respective ages of several children were then passed in
review. Victor would be fifteen soon. Eileen, the granddaughter
of Mrs. Thayer's eldest sister, was five. Isabel was twenty-three
and greatly enjoying a secretarial job in New York. Dr. Hagen's
daughter was twenty-four, and about to return from Europe,
where she had spent a wonderful summer touring Bavaria and
Switzerland with a very gracious old lady, Dorianna Karen,
famous movie star of the twenties.

The telephone rang. Somebody wanted to talk to Mrs. Sheppard. With a precision quite unusual for him in such matters,
unpredictable Pnin not only rattled off the woman's new address and telephone number, but also supplied those of her
eldest son.

9

By ten o'clock, Pnin's Punch and Betty's Scotch were causing
some of the guests to talk louder than they thought they did.
A carmine flush had spread over one side of Mrs. Thayer's
neck, under the little blue star of her left earring, and, sitting
very straight, she regaled her host with an account of the feud

between two of her co-workers at the library. It was a simple office story, but her changes of tone from Miss Shrill to Mr. Basso, and the consciousness of the soirée going on so nicely, made Pnin bend his head and guffaw ecstatically behind his hand. Roy Thayer was weakly twinkling to himself as he looked into his punch, down his gray porous nose, and politely listened to Joan Clements who, when she was a little high as she was now, had a fetching way of rapidly blinking, or even completely closing her black-lashed blue eyes, and of interrupting her sentences, to punctuate a clause or gather new momentum, by deep hawing pants: "But don't you think—haw—that what he is trying to do—haw—practically in all his novels—haw—is—haw—to express the fantastic recurrence of certain situations?" Betty remained her controlled little self, and expertly looked after the refreshments. In the bay end of the room, Clements kept morosely revolving the slow globe as Hagen, carefully avoiding the traditional intonations he would have used in more congenial surroundings, told him and grinning Thomas the latest story about Mrs. Idelson, communicated by Mrs. Blorenge to Mrs. Hagen. Pnin came up with a plate of nougat.

"This is not quite for your chaste ears, Timofey," said Hagen to Pnin, who always confessed he never could see the point of any "scabrous anecdote." "However——"

Clements moved away to rejoin the ladies. Hagen began to retell the story, and Thomas began to re-grin. Pnin waved a hand at the raconteur in a Russian disgusted "oh-go-on-with-you" gesture and said:

"I have heard quite the same anecdote thirty-five years ago in Odessa, and even then I could not understand what is comical in it."

10

At a still later stage of the party, certain rearrangements had again taken place. In a corner of the davenport, bored Clements was flipping through an album of *Flemish Masterpieces* that Victor had been given by his mother and had left with Pnin. Joan sat on a footstool, at her husband's knee, a plate of grapes in the lap of her wide skirt, wondering when would it be time to go without hurting Timofey's feelings. The others were listening to Hagen discussing modern education:

"You may laugh," he said, casting a sharp glance at Clements —who shook his head, denying the charge, and then passed the album to Joan, pointing out something in it that had suddenly provoked his glee.

"You may laugh, but I affirm that the only way to escape from the morass—just a drop, Timofey: that will do—is to lock up the student in a soundproof cell and eliminate the lecture room."

"Yes, that's it," said Joan to her husband under her breath, handing the album back to him.

"I am glad you agree, Joan," continued Hagen. "However, I have been called an *enfant terrible* for expounding this theory, and perhaps you will not go on agreeing so easily when you hear me out. Phonograph records on every possible subject will be at the isolated student's disposal . . ."

"But the personality of the lecturer," said Margaret Thayer. "Surely that counts for something."

"It does not!" shouted Hagen. "That is the tragedy! Who, for example, wants *him*"—he pointed to radiant Pnin—"who wants his personality? Nobody! They will reject Timofey's wonderful personality without a quaver. The world wants a machine, not a Timofey."

"One could have Timofey televised," said Clements.

"Oh, I would love that," said Joan, beaming at her host, and Betty nodded vigorously. Pnin bowed deeply to them with an "I-am-disarmed" spreading of both hands.

"And what do *you* think of my controversial plan?" asked Hagen of Thomas.

"I can tell you what Tom thinks," said Clements, still contemplating the same picture in the book that lay open on his knees. "Tom thinks that the best method of teaching anything is to rely on discussion in class, which means letting twenty young blockheads and two cocky neurotics discuss for fifty minutes something that neither their teacher nor they know. Now, for the last three months," he went on without any logical transition, "I have been looking for this picture, and here it is. The publisher of my new book on the Philosophy of Gesture wants a portrait of me, and Joan and I knew we had seen somewhere a stunning likeness by an Old Master but could not even recall his period. Well, here it is, here it is. The only retouching needed would be the addition of a sport shirt and the deletion of this warrior's hand."

"I must really protest," began Thomas.

Clements passed the open book to Margaret Thayer, and she burst out laughing.

"I must protest, Laurence," said Tom. "A relaxed discussion in an atmosphere of broad generalizations is a more realistic approach to education than the old-fashioned formal lecture."

"Sure, sure," said Clements.

Joan scrambled up to her feet and covered her glass with her narrow palm when Pnin offered to replenish it. Mrs. Thayer looked at her wrist watch, and then at her husband. A soft yawn distended Laurence's mouth. Betty asked Thomas if he knew a man called Fogelman, an expert in bats, who lived in Santa Clara, Cuba. Hagen asked for a glass of water or beer. Whom does he remind me of? thought Pnin suddenly. Eric Wind? Why? They are quite different physically.

11

The setting of the final scene was the hallway. Hagen could not find the cane he had come with (it had fallen behind a trunk in the closet).

"And *I* think I left my purse where I was sitting," said Mrs. Thayer, pushing her pensive husband ever so slightly toward the living room.

Pnin and Clements, in last-minute discourse, stood on either side of the living-room doorway, like two well-fed caryatids, and drew in their abdomens to let the silent Thayer pass. In the middle of the room Professor Thomas and Miss Bliss—he with his hands behind his back and rising up every now and then on his toes, she holding a tray—were standing and talking of Cuba, where a cousin of Betty's fiancé had lived for quite a while, Betty understood. Thayer blundered from chair to chair, and found himself with a white bag, not knowing really where he picked it up, his mind being occupied by the adumbrations of lines he was to write down later in the night:

We sat and drank, each with a separate past locked up in him, and fate's alarm clocks set at unrelated futures— when, at last, a wrist was cocked, and eyes of consorts met . . .

Meanwhile Pnin asked Joan Clements and Margaret Thayer if they would care to see how he had embellished the upstairs rooms. The idea enchanted them. He led the way. His so-called *kabinet* now looked very cozy, its scratched floor snugly covered with the more or less Pakistan rug which he had once acquired for his office and had recently removed in drastic silence from under the feet of the surprised Falternfels. A tartan lap robe, under which Pnin had crossed the ocean from Europe in 1940, and some endemic cushions disguised the unremovable bed. The pink shelves, which he had found supporting several generations of children's books—from *Tom the Bootblack, or the Road to Success* by Horatio Alger, Jr., 1889, through *Rolf in the Woods* by Ernest Thompson Seton, 1911, to a 1928 edition of *Compton's Pictured Encyclopedia* in ten volumes with foggy little photographs—were now loaded with three hundred sixty-five items from the Waindell College Library.

"And to think I have stamped all these," sighed Mrs. Thayer, rolling her eyes in mock dismay.

"Some stamped Mrs. Miller," said Pnin, a stickler for historical truth.

What struck the visitors most in the bedroom was a large folding screen that cut off the fourposter bed from insidious drafts, and the view from the row of small windows: a dark rock wall rising abruptly some fifty feet away, with a stretch of pale starry sky above the black growth of its crest. On the back lawn, across the reflection of a window, Laurence strolled into the shadows.

"At last you are really comfortable," said Joan.

"And you know what I will say to you," replied Pnin in a confidential undertone vibrating with triumph. "Tomorrow morning, under the curtain of mysteree, I will see a gentleman who is wanting to help me to buy this house!"

They came down again. Roy handed his wife Betty's bag. Herman found his cane. Margaret's bag was sought. Laurence reappeared.

"Good-by, good-by, Professor Vin!" sang out Pnin, his cheeks ruddy and round in the lamplight of the porch.

(Still in the hallway, Betty and Margaret Thayer admired proud Dr. Hagen's walking stick, recently sent him from Germany, a gnarled cudgel, with a donkey's head for knob. The head could move one ear. The cane had belonged to Dr. Hagen's Bavarian grandfather, a country clergyman. The mechanism of the other ear had broken down in 1914, according to a note the pastor had left. Hagen carried it, he said, in defense against a certain Alsatian in Greenlawn Lane. American dogs were not used to pedestrians. He always preferred walking to driving. The ear could not be repaired. At least, in Waindell.)

"Now I wonder why he called me that," said T. W. Thomas, Professor of Anthropology, to Laurence and Joan Clements as they walked through blue darkness toward four cars parked under the elms on the other side of the road.

"Our friend," answered Clements, "employs a nomenclature all his own. His verbal vagaries add a new thrill to life. His mispronunciations are mythopeic. His slips of the tongue are oracular. He calls my wife John."

"Still I find it a little disturbing," said Thomas.

"He probably mistook you for somebody else," said Clements. "And for all I know you *may* be somebody else."

Before they had crossed the street they were overtaken by Dr. Hagen. Professor Thomas, still looking puzzled, took his leave.

"Well," said Hagen.

It was a fair fall night, velvet below, steel above.

Joan asked:

"You're sure you don't want us to give you a lift?"

"It's a ten-minute walk. And a walk is a must on such a wonderful night."

The three of them stood for a moment gazing at the stars.

"And all these are worlds," said Hagen.

"Or else," said Clements with a yawn, "a frightful mess. I suspect it is really a fluorescent corpse, and we are inside it."

From the lighted porch came Pnin's rich laughter as he finished recounting to the Thayers and Betty Bliss how he, too, had once retrieved the wrong reticule.

"Come, my fluorescent corpse, let's be moving," said Joan. "It was so nice to see you, Herman. Give my love to Irmgard. What a delightful party. I have never seen Timofey so happy."

"Yes, thank you," answered Hagen absent-mindedly.

"You should have seen his face," said Joan, "when he told us he was going to talk to a real-estate man tomorrow about buying that dream house."

"He did? You're sure he said that?" Hagen asked sharply.

"Quite sure," said Joan. "And if anybody needs a house, it is certainly Timofey."

"Well, good night," said Hagen. "Glad you could come. Good night."

He waited for them to reach their car, hesitated, and then

marched back to the lighted porch, where, standing as on a stage, Pnin was shaking hands a second or third time with the Thayers and Betty.

("I would never," said Joan, as she backed the car and worked on the wheel, "but *never* have allowed my child to go abroad with that old Lesbian." "Careful," said Laurence, "he may be drunk but he is not out of earshot.")

"I shall not forgive you," said Betty to her merry host, "for not letting me do the dishes."

"I'll help him," said Hagen, ascending the porch steps and thumping upon them with his cane. "You, children, run along now."

There was a final round of handshakes, and the Thayers and Betty left.

12
———————

"First," said Hagen, as he and Pnin re-entered the living room, "I guess I'll have a last cup of wine with you."

"Perfect. Perfect!" cried Pnin. "Let us finish my *cruchon*." They made themselves comfortable, and Dr. Hagen said:

"You are a wonderful host, Timofey. This is a very delightful moment. My grandfather used to say that a glass of good wine should be always sipped and savored as if it were the last one before the execution. I wonder what you put into this punch. I also wonder if, as our charming Joan affirms, you are really contemplating buying this house?"

"Not contemplating—peeping a little at possibilities," replied Pnin with a gurgling laugh.

"I question the wisdom of it," continued Hagen, nursing his goblet.

"Naturally, I am expecting that I will get tenure at last," said Pnin rather slyly. "I am now Assistant Professor nine years. Years run. Soon I will be Assistant Emeritus. Hagen, why are you silent?"

"You place me in a very embarrassing position, Timofey. I hoped you would not raise this particular question."

"I do not raise the question. I say that I only expect—oh, not next year, but example given, at hundredth anniversary of Liberation of Serfs—Waindell will make me Associate."

"Well, you see, my dear friend, I must tell you a sad secret. It is not official yet, and you must promise not to mention it to anyone."

"I swear," said Pnin, raising his hand.

"You cannot but know," continued Hagen, "with what loving care I built our great department. I, too, am no longer young. You say, Timofey, you have been here for nine years. But I have been giving my all for *twenty-nine* years to this university! My modest all. As my friend, Dr. Kraft, wrote me the other day: you, Herman Hagen, have done alone more for Germany in America than all our missions have done in Germany for America. And what happens now? I have nursed this Falternfels, this dragon, in my bosom, and he has now worked himself into a key position. I spare you the details of the intrigue!"

"Yes," said Pnin with a sigh, "intrigue is horrible, horrible. But, on the other side, honest work will always prove its advantage. You and I will give next year some splendid new courses which I have planned long ago. On Tyranny. On the Boot. On Nicholas the First. On all the precursors of modern atrocity. Hagen, when we speak of injustice, we forget Armenian massacres, tortures which Tibet invented, colonists in Africa. . . . The history of man is the history of pain!"

Hagen bent over to his friend and patted him on his knobby knee.

"You are a wonderful romantic, Timofey, and under happier circumstances . . . However, I can tell you that in the Spring Term we *are* going to do something unusual. We are going to stage a Dramatic Program—scenes from Kotzebue to Hauptmann. I see it as a sort of apotheosis. . . . But let us not anticipate. I, too, am a romantic, Timofey, and therefore cannot work with people like Bodo, as our trustees wish me to do. Kraft is retiring at Seaboard, and it has been offered to me that I replace him, beginning next fall."

"I congratulate you," said Pnin warmly.

"Thanks, my friend. It is certainly a very fine and prominent position. I shall apply to a wider field of scholarship and administration the invaluable experience I have gained here. Of course, since I know Bodo will not continue you in the German Department, my first move was to suggest you come with me, but they tell me they have enough Slavists at Seaboard without you. So I spoke to Blorenge, but the French Department here is also full up. This is unfortunate, because Waindell feels that it would be too much of a financial burden to pay you for two or three Russian courses that have ceased to attract students. Political trends in America, as we all know, discourage interest in things Russian. On the other hand, you'll be glad to know that the English Department is inviting one of your most brilliant compatriots, a really fascinating lecturer—I have heard him once; I think he's an old friend of yours."

Pnin cleared his throat and asked:

"It signifies that they are firing me?"

"Now, don't take it too hard, Timofey. I'm sure your old friend——"

"Who is old friend?" queried Pnin, slitting his eyes.

Hagen named the fascinating lecturer.

Leaning forward, his elbows propped on his knees, clasping and unclasping his hands, Pnin said:

"Yes, I know him thirty years or more. We are friends, but there is one thing perfectly certain. I will never work under him."

"Well, I guess you should sleep on it. Perhaps some solution may be found. Anyway, we'll have ample opportunity to discuss these matters. We shall just go on teaching, you and I, as if nothing had happened, *nicht wahr?* We must be brave, Timofey!"

"So they have fired me," said Pnin, clasping his hands and nodding his head.

"Yes, we are in the same boat, in the same boat," said jovial Hagen, and he stood up. It was getting very late.

"I go now," said Hagen, who, though a lesser addict of the present tense than Pnin, also held it in favor. "It has been a wonderful party, and I would never have allowed myself to spoil the merriment if our mutual friend had not informed me of your optimistic intentions. Good night. Oh, by the way . . . Naturally, you will get your salary for the Fall Term in full, and then we shall see how much we can obtain for you in the Spring Term, especially if you will agree to take off some stupid office work from my poor old shoulders, and also if you will participate vitally in the Dramatic Program in New Hall. I think you should actually play in it, under my daughter's direction; it would distract you from sad thoughts. Now go to bed at once, and put yourself to sleep with a good mystery story."

On the porch he pumped Pnin's unresponsive hand with enough vigor for two. Then he flourished his cane and merrily marched down the wooden steps.

The screen door banged behind him.

"Der arme Kerl," muttered kindhearted Hagen to himself as he walked homeward. "At least, I have sweetened the pill."

13

From the sideboard and dining-room table Pnin removed to the kitchen sink the used china and silverware. He put away what food remained into the bright Arctic light of the refrigerator. The ham and tongue had all gone, and so had the little sausages; but the vinaigrette had not been a success, and enough caviar and meat tarts were left over for a meal or two tomorrow. "Boom-boom-boom," said the china closet as he passed by. He surveyed the living room and started to tidy it up. A last drop of Pnin's Punch glistened in its beautiful bowl. Joan had crooked a lipstick-stained cigarette butt in her saucer; Betty had left no trace and had taken all the glasses back to the kitchen. Mrs. Thayer had forgotten a booklet of pretty multicolored matches on her plate, next to a bit of nougat. Mr. Thayer had twisted into all kinds of weird shapes half a dozen paper napkins; Hagen had quenched a messy cigar in an uneaten bunchlet of grapes.

In the kitchen, Pnin prepared to wash up the dishes. He removed his silk coat, his tie, and his dentures. To protect his shirt front and tuxedo trousers, he donned a soubrette's dappled apron. He scraped various tidbits off the plates into a brown paper bag, to be given eventually to a mangy little white dog, with pink patches on its back, that visited him sometimes in the afternoon—there was no reason a human's misfortune should interfere with a canine's pleasure.

He prepared a bubble bath in the sink for the crockery, glass, and silverware, and with infinite care lowered the aquamarine bowl into the tepid foam. Its resonant flint glass emitted a sound full of muffled mellowness as it settled down to soak. He rinsed the amber goblets and the silverware under the tap, and submerged them in the same foam. Then he fished out the knives, forks, and spoons, rinsed them, and began to wipe them. He worked very slowly, with a certain vagueness of manner that might have been taken for a mist of abstraction in a less methodical man. He gathered the wiped spoons into a posy, placed them in a pitcher which he had washed but not dried, and then took them out one by one and wiped them all over again. He groped under the bubbles, around the goblets, and under the melodious bowl, for any piece of forgotten silver—and retrieved a nutcracker. Fastidious Pnin rinsed it, and was wiping it, when the leggy thing somehow slipped out of the towel and fell like a man from a roof. He almost caught it—his fingertips actually came into contact with it in midair, but this only helped to propel it into the treasure-concealing foam of the sink, where an excruciating crack of broken glass followed upon the plunge.

Pnin hurled the towel into a corner and, turning away, stood for a moment staring at the blackness beyond the threshold of the open back door. A quiet, lacy-winged little green insect circled in the glare of a strong naked lamp above Pnin's glossy bald head. He looked very old, with his toothless mouth half open and a film of tears dimming his blank, unblinking eyes. Then, with a moan of anguished anticipation, he went back to the sink and, bracing himself, dipped his hand deep into the foam. A jagger of glass stung him. Gently he removed a broken goblet. The beautiful bowl was intact. He took a fresh dish towel and went on with his household work.

When everything was clean and dry, and the bowl stood aloof and serene on the safest shelf of a cupboard, and the little bright house was securely locked up in the large dark night, Pnin sat down at the kitchen table and, taking a sheet of yellow scrap paper from its drawer, unclipped his fountain pen and started to compose the draft of a letter:

"Dear Hagen," he wrote in his clear firm hand, "permit me to recaputilate (crossed out) recapitulate the conversation we had tonight. It, I must confess, somewhat astonished me. If I had the honor to correctly understand you, you said——"

❧ *Chapter Seven* ❧

I

My first recollection of Timofey Pnin is connected with a speck of coal dust that entered my left eye on a spring Sunday in 1911.

It was one of those rough, gusty, and lustrous mornings in St. Petersburg, when the last transparent piece of Ladoga ice has been carried away to the gulf by the Neva, and her indigo weaves heave and lap the granite of the embankment, and the tugboats and huge barges, moored along the quay, creak and scrape rhythmically, and the mahogany and brass of anchored steam yachts shine in the skittish sun. I had been trying out a beautiful new English bicycle given me for my twelfth birthday, and, as I rode home to our rosy-stone house in the Morskaya, over parquet-smooth wooden pavements, the consciousness of having gravely disobeyed my tutor was less bothersome than the granule of smarting pain in the far north of my eyeball. Home remedies, such as the application of wads of cotton wool soaked in cool tea and the *tri-k-nosu* (rub-noseward) device, only made matters worse; and when I awoke next morning, the object lurking under my upper eyelid felt like a solid polygon that became more deeply embedded at every watery wink. In the afternoon I was taken to a leading ophthalmologist, Dr. Pavel Pnin.

One of those silly incidents that remain forever in a child's receptive mind marked the space of time my tutor and I spent in Dr. Pnin's sundust-and-plush waiting room, where the blue dab of a window in miniature was reflected in the glass dome of an ormolu clock on the mantelpiece, and two flies kept describing slow quadrangles around the lifeless chandelier. A lady, wearing a plumed hat, and her dark-spectacled husband were sitting in connubial silence on the davenport; then a cavalry officer entered and sat near the window reading a newspaper; then the husband repaired to Dr. Pnin's study; and then I noticed an odd expression on my tutor's face.

With my good eye I followed his stare. The officer was leaning toward the lady. In rapid French he berated her for something she had done or not done the day before. She gave him her gloved hand to kiss. He glued himself to its eyelet—and forthwith left, cured of whatever had ailed him.

In softness of features, body bulk, leanness of leg, apish shape of ear and upper lip, Dr. Pavel Pnin looked very like Timofey, as the latter was to look three or four decades later. In the father, however, a fringe of straw-colored hair relieved a wax-like calvity; he wore a black-rimmed pince-nez on a black ribbon like the late Dr. Chekhov; he spoke in a gentle stutter, very unlike his son's later voice. And what a divine relief it was when, with a tiny instrument resembling an elf's drumstick, the tender doctor removed from my eyeball the offending black atom! I wonder where that speck is now? The dull, mad fact is that it *does* exist somewhere.

Perhaps because on my visits to schoolmates I had seen other middle-class apartments, I unconsciously retained a picture of the Pnin flat that probably corresponds to reality. I can report therefore that as likely as not it consisted of two rows of rooms divided by a long corridor; on one side was the waiting room, the doctor's office, presumably a dining room and a drawing room further on; and on the other side were two or three bedrooms, a schoolroom, a bathroom, a maid's room, and a kitchen. I was about to leave with a phial of eye lotion, and my tutor was taking the opportunity to ask Dr. Pnin if eyestrain might cause gastric trouble, when the front door opened and shut. Dr. Pnin nimbly walked into the passage, voiced a query, received a quiet answer, and returned with his son Timofey, a thirteen-year-old *gimnazist* (classical school pupil) in his *gimnazicheskiy* uniform—black blouse, black pants, shiny black belt (I attended a more liberal school where we wore what we liked).

Do I really remember his crew cut, his puffy pale face, his red ears? Yes, distinctly. I even remember the way he imperceptibly removed his shoulder from under the proud paternal hand, while the proud paternal voice was saying: "This boy has just got a Five Plus (A+) in the Algebra examination." From the end of the corridor there came a steady smell of hashed-cabbage pie, and through the open door of the schoolroom I could see a map of Russia on the wall, books on a shelf, a stuffed squirrel, and a toy monoplane with linen wings and a rubber motor. I had a similar one but twice as big, bought in Biarritz. After one had wound up the propeller for some time, the rubber would change its manner of twist and develop fascinating thick whorls which predicted the end of its tether.

2

Five years later, after spending the beginning of the summer on our estate near St. Petersburg, my mother, my young brother, and I happened to visit a dreary old aunt at her curiously desolate country seat not far from a famous resort on the Baltic coast. One afternoon, as in concentrated ecstasy I was spreading, underside up, an exceptionally rare aberration of the Paphia Fritillary, in which the silver stripes ornamenting the lower surface of its hindwings had fused into an even expanse of metallic gloss, a footman came up with the information that the old lady requested my presence. In the reception hall I found her talking to two self-conscious youths in university student uniforms. One, with the blond fuzz, was Timofey Pnin, the other, with the russet down, was Grigoriy Belochkin. They had come to ask my grandaunt the permission to use an empty barn on the confines of her property for the staging of a play. This was a Russian translation of Arthur Schnitzler's three-act *Liebelei*. Ancharov, a provincial semiprofessional actor, with a reputation consisting mainly of faded newspaper clippings, was helping to rig up the thing. Would I participate? But at sixteen I was as arrogant as I was shy, and declined to play the anonymous gentleman in Act One. The interview ended in mutual embarrassment, not alleviated by Pnin or Belochkin overturning a glass of pear *kvas,* and I went back to my butterfly. A fortnight later I was somehow or other compelled to attend the performance. The barn was full of *dachniki* (vacationists) and disabled soldiers from a nearby hospital. I came with my brother, and next to me sat the steward of my aunt's estate, Robert Karlovich Horn, a cheerful plump person from Riga with bloodshot, porcelain-blue eyes, who kept applauding heartily at the wrong moments. I remember the odor of decorative fir branches, and the eyes of peasant children glistening through the chinks in the walls. The front seats were so close to the stage that when the betrayed husband produced a packet of love letters written to his wife by Fritz Lobheimer, dragoon and college student, and flung them into Fritz's face, you could see perfectly well that they were old postcards with the stamp corners cut off. I am perfectly sure that the small role of this irate Gentleman was taken by Timofey Pnin (though, of course, he might also have appeared as somebody else in the following acts); but a buff overcoat, bushy mustachios, and a dark wig with a median parting disguised him so thoroughly that the minuscule interest I took in his existence might not have warranted any conscious assurance on my part. Fritz, the young lover doomed to die in a duel, not only has that mysterious affair backstage with the Lady in Black Velvet, the Gentleman's wife, but toys with the heart of Christine, a naïve Viennese maiden. Fritz was played by stocky, forty year old Ancharov, who wore a warm-taupe make-up, thumped his chest with the sound of rug beating, and by his impromptu contributions to the role he had not deigned to learn almost paralyzed Fritz's pal, Theodor Kaiser (Grigoriy Belochkin). A moneyed old maid in real life, whom Ancharov humored, was miscast as Christine Weiring, the violinist's daughter. The role of the little milliner, Theodor's amoretta, Mizi Schlager, was charmingly acted by a pretty, slender-necked, velvet-eyed girl, Belochkin's sister, who got the greatest ovation of the night.

3

It is improbable that during the years of Revolution and Civil War which followed I had occasion to recall Dr. Pnin and his son. If I have reconstructed in some detail the precedent impressions, it is merely to fix what flashed through my mind when, on an April night in the early twenties, at a Paris café, I found myself shaking hands with auburn-bearded, infantine-eyed Timofey Pnin, erudite young author of several admirable papers on Russian culture. It was the custom among *émigré* writers and artists to gather at the Three Fountains after the recitals or lectures that were so popular among Russian expatriates; and it was on such an occasion that, still hoarse from my reading, I tried not only to remind Pnin of former meetings, but also to amuse him and other people around us with the unusual lucidity and strength of my memory. However, he denied everything. He said he vaguely recalled my grandaunt but had never met me. He said that his marks in algebra had always been poor and that, anyway, his father never displayed him to patients; he said that in *Zabava* (*Liebelei*) he had only acted the part of Christine's father. He repeated that we had never seen each other before. Our little discussion was nothing more than good-natured banter, and everybody laughed; and noticing how reluctant he was to recognize his own past, I switched to another, less personal, topic.

Presently I grew aware that a striking-looking young girl in a black silk sweater, with a golden band around her brown hair, had become my chief listener. She stood before me, right elbow resting on left palm, right hand holding cigarette between finger and thumb as a gypsy would, cigarette sending up its smoke; bright blue eyes half closed because of the smoke. She was Liza Bogolepov, a medical student who also wrote poetry. She asked me if she could send me for appraisal a batch of her poems. A little later at the same party, I noticed her sitting next to a repulsively hairy young composer, Ivan Nagoy; they were drinking *auf Bruderschaft,* which is performed by intertwining arms with one's co-drinker, and some chairs away Dr. Barakan, a talented neurologist and Liza's latest lover, was watching her with quiet despair in his dark almond-shaped eyes.

A few days later she sent me those poems; a fair sample of her production is the kind of stuff that *émigré* rhymsterettes

wrote after Akhmatova: lackadaisical little lyrics that tiptoed in
more or less anapaestic tetrameter and sat down rather heavily
with a wistful sigh:

> *Samotsvétov króme ochéy*
> *Net u menyá nikakíh,*
> *No est' róza eshchó nezhnéy*
> *Rózovïh gúb moíh.*
> *I yúnosha tíhiy skazál:*
> *"Vashe sérdtse vsegó nezhnéy . . ."*
> *I yá opustíla glazá . . .*

I have marked the stress accents, and transliterated the Russian with the usual understanding that *u* is pronounced like a
short "oo," *i* like a short "ee," and *zh* like a French "j." Such
incomplete rhymes as *skazal-glaza* were considered very elegant. Note also the erotic undercurrents and *cour d'amour* implications. A prose translation would go: "No jewels, save
my eyes, do I own, but I have a rose which is even softer than
my rosy lips. And a quiet youth said: 'There is nothing softer
than your heart.' And I lowered my gaze. . . ."

I wrote back telling Liza that her poems were bad and she
ought to stop composing. Sometime later I saw her in another
café, sitting at a long table, abloom and ablaze among a dozen
young Russian poets. She kept her sapphire glance on me with
a mocking and mysterious persistence. We talked. I suggested
she let me see those poems again in some quieter place. She
did. I told her they struck me as being even worse than they
had seemed at the first reading. She lived in the cheapest room
of a decadent little hotel with no bath and a pair of twittering
young Englishmen for neighbors.

Poor Liza! She had of course her artistic moments when she
would stop, entranced, on a May night in a squalid street to admire—nay, to adore—the motley remains of an old poster on
a wet black wall in the light of a street lamp, and the translucent green of linden leaves where they drooped next to the
lamp, but she was one of those women who combine healthy

good looks with hysterical sloppiness; lyrical outbursts with a very practical and very commonplace mind; a vile temper with sentimentality; and languorous surrender with a robust capacity for sending people on wild-goose errands. In the result of emotions and in the course of events, the narration of which would be of no public interest whatsoever, Liza swallowed a handful of sleeping pills. As she tumbled into unconsciousness she knocked over an open bottle of the deep-red ink which she used to write down her verses, and that bright trickle coming from under her door was noticed by Chris and Lew just in time to have her saved.

I had not seen her for a fortnight after that contretemps when, on the eve of my leaving for Switzerland and Germany, she waylaid me in the little garden at the end of my street, looking svelté and strange in a charming new dress as dove-gray as Paris, and wearing a really enchanting new hat with a blue bird's wing, and handed me a folded paper. "I want a last piece of advice from you," said Liza in what the French call a "white" voice. "This is an offer of marriage that I have received. I shall wait till midnight. If I don't hear from you, I shall accept it." She hailed a taxi and was gone.

The letter has by chance remained among my papers. Here it is:

"I am afraid you will be pained by my confession, my dear Lise" (the writer, though using Russian, called her throughout by this French form of her name, in order, I presume, to avoid both the too familiar 'Liza' and the too formal 'Elizaveta Innokentievna'). "It is always painful for a sensitive (*chutkiy*) person to see another in an awkward position. And I am definitely in an awkward position.

"You, Lise, are surrounded by poets, scientists, artists, dandies. The celebrated painter who made your portrait last year is now, it is said, drinking himself to death (*govoryat, spilsya*) in the wilds of Massachusetts. Rumor proclaims many other things. And here I am, daring to write to you.

"I am not handsome, I am not interesting, I am not talented. I am not even rich. But, Lise, I offer you everything I have, to the last blood corpuscle, to the last tear, everything. And, believe me, this is more than any genius can offer you because a genius needs to keep so much in store, and thus cannot offer you the whole of himself as I do. I may not achieve happiness, but I know I shall do everything to make you happy. I want you to write poems. I want you to go on with your psychotherapeutic research—in which I do not understand much, while questioning the validity of what I can understand. Incidentally, I am sending you under separate cover a pamphlet published in Prague by my friend Professor Chateau, which brilliantly refutes your Dr. Halp's theory of birth being an act of suicide on the part of the infant. I have permitted myself to correct an obvious misprint on page 48 of Chateau's excellent paper. I await your" (probably "decision," the bottom of the page with the signature had been cut off by Liza).

4

When half a dozen years later I revisited Paris, I learned that Timofey Pnin had married Liza Bogolepov soon after my departure. She sent me a published collection of her poems *Suhie Gubï* (Dry Lips) with the inscription in dark-red ink: "To a Stranger from a Stranger" (*neznakomtsu ot neznakomki*). I saw Pnin and her at an evening tea in the apartment of a famous *émigré,* a social revolutionary, one of those informal gatherings where old-fashioned terrorists, heroic nuns, gifted hedonists, liberals, adventurous young poets, elderly novelists and artists, publishers and publicists, free-minded philosophers and scholars would represent a kind of special knighthood, the active and significant nucleus of an exiled society which during the third of a century it flourished remained practically unknown to American intellectuals, for whom the notion of Rus-

sian emigration was made to mean by astute communist propaganda a vague and perfectly fictitious mass of so-called Trotski-
ites (whatever these are), ruined reactionaries, reformed or disguised Cheka men, titled ladies, professional priests, restaurant
keepers, and White Russian military groups, all of them of no
cultural importance whatever.

Taking advantage of Pnin's being engaged in a political discussion with Kerenski at the other end of the table, Liza informed me—with her usual crude candor—that she had "told
Timofey everything"; that he was "a saint" and had "pardoned"
me. Fortunately, she did not often accompany him to later re-
ceptions where I had the pleasure of sitting next to him, or
opposite him, in the company of dear friends, on our small lone
planet, above the black and diamond city, with the lamplight
on this or that Socratic cranium and a slice of lemon revolving
in the glass of stirred tea. One night, as Dr. Barakan, Pnin, and
I were sitting at the Bolotovs, I happened to be talking to the
neurologist about a cousin of his, Ludmila, now Lady D——,
whom I had known in Yalta, Athens, and London, when suddenly Pnin cried to Dr. Barakan across the table: "Now, don't
believe a word he says, Georgiy Aramovich. He makes up everything. He once invented that we were schoolmates in Russia
and cribbed at examinations. He is a dreadful inventor (*on
uzhasnïy vïdumshchik*)." Barakan and I were so astounded by
this outburst that we just sat and looked at each other in silence.

5

In the rememoration of old relationships, later impressions
often tend to be dimmer than earlier ones. I recall talking to
Liza and her new husband, Dr. Eric Wind, in between two acts
of a Russian play in New York sometime in the early forties.
He said he had a "really tender feeling for Herr Professor Pnin"
and gave me some bizarre details of their voyage together from

Europe in the beginning of World War II. I ran into Pnin several times during those years at various social and academic functions in New York; but the only vivid recollection I have is of our ride together on a west-side bus, on a very festive and very wet night in 1952. We had come from our respective colleges to participate in a literary and artistic program before a large *émigré* audience in downtown New York on the occasion of the hundredth anniversary of a great writer's death. Pnin had been teaching at Waindell since the mid-forties and never had I seen him look healthier, more prosperous, and more self-assertive. He and I turned out to be, as he quipped, *vos'midesyatniki* (men of the Eighties), that is, we both happened to have lodgings for the night in the West Eighties; and as we hung from adjacent straps in the crowded and spasmodic vehicle, my good friend managed to combine a vigorous ducking and twisting of the head (in his continuous attempts to check and re-check the numbers of cross streets) with a magnificent account of all he had not had sufficient time to say at the celebration on Homer's and Gogol's use of the Rambling Comparison.

6

When I decided to accept a professorship at Waindell, I stipulated that I could invite whomever I wanted for teaching in the special Russian Division I planned to inaugurate. With this confirmed, I wrote to Timofey Pnin offering him in the most cordial terms I could muster to assist me in any way and to any extent he desired. His answer surprised me and hurt me. Curtly he wrote that he was through with teaching and would not even bother to wait till the end of the Spring Term. Then he turned to other subjects. Victor (about whom I had politely inquired) was in Rome with his mother; she had divorced her third husband and married an Italian art dealer. Pnin concluded his letter by saying that to his great regret he would be leaving

Waindell two or three days before the public lecture that I was to give there Tuesday, February the fifteenth. He did not specify his destination.

The Greyhound that brought me to Waindell on Monday the fourteenth arrived after nightfall. I was met by the Cockerells, who treated me to a late supper at their house, where I discovered I was to spend the night, instead of sleeping at a hotel as I had hoped. Gwen Cockerell turned out to be a very pretty woman in her late thirties, with a kitten's profile and graceful limbs. Her husband, whom I had once met in New Haven and remembered as a rather limp, moon-faced, neutrally blond Englishman, had acquired an unmistakable resemblance to the man he had now been mimicking for almost ten years. I was tired and not overanxious to be entertained throughout the supper with a floor show, but I must admit that Jack Cockerell impersonated Pnin to perfection. He went on for at least two hours, showing me everything—Pnin teaching, Pnin eating, Pnin ogling a coed, Pnin narrating the epic of the electric fan which he had imprudently set going on a glass shelf right above the bathtub into which its own vibration had almost caused it to fall; Pnin trying to convince Professor Wynn, the ornithologist who hardly knew him, that they were old pals, Tim and Tom—and Wynn leaping to the conclusion that this was somebody impersonating Professor Pnin. It was all built of course around the Pninian gesture and the Pninian wild English, but Cockerell also managed to imitate such things as the subtle degree of difference between the silence of Pnin and the silence of Thayer, as they sat motionlessly ruminating in adjacent chairs at the Faculty Club. We got Pnin in the Stacks, and Pnin on the Campus Lake. We heard Pnin criticize the various rooms he had successively rented. We listened to Pnin's account of his learning to drive a car, and of his dealing with his first puncture on the way back from "the chicken farm of some Privy Counselor of the Tsar," where Cockerell supposed Pnin spent the summers. We arrived at last to Pnin's declaration one day that he had been "shot" by which, according to the impersonator, the poor fellow meant "fired"—(a mistake I doubt my friend could have made). Brilliant Cockerell also told of the strange feud between Pnin and his compatriot Komarov—the mediocre muralist who had kept adding fresco portraits of faculty members in the college dining hall to those already depicted there by the great Lang. Although Komarov belonged to another political faction than Pnin, the patriotic artist had seen in Pnin's dismissal an anti-Russian gesture and had started to delete a sulky Napoleon that stood between young, plumpish (now gaunt) Blorenge and young, mustached (now shaven) Hagen, in order to paint in Pnin; and there was the scene between Pnin and President Poore at lunch—an enraged, spluttering Pnin losing all control over what English he had, pointing a shaking forefinger at the preliminary outlines of a ghostly muzhik on the wall, and shouting that he would sue the college if his face appeared above that blouse; and there was his audience, imperturbable Poore, trapped in the dark of his total blindness, waiting for Pnin to peter out and then asking at large: "Is that foreign gentleman on our staff?" Oh, the impersonation was deliciously funny, and although Gwen Cockerell must have heard the program many times before, she laughed so loud that their old dog Sobakevich, a brown cocker with a tearstained face, began to fidget and sniff at me. The performance, I repeat, was magnificent, but it was too long. By midnight the fun began to thin; the smile I was keeping afloat began to develop, I felt, symptoms of labial cramp. Finally the whole thing grew to be such a bore that I fell wondering if by some poetical vengeance this Pnin business had not become with Cockerell the kind of fatal obsession which substitutes its own victim for that of the initial ridicule.

We had been having a good deal of Scotch, and sometime after midnight Cockerell made one of those sudden decisions that seem so bright and gay at a certain stage of intoxication. He said he was sure foxy old Pnin had not really left yesterday, but was lying low. So why not telephone and find out? He made the call, and although there was no answer to the series of compelling notes which simulate the far sound of actual ringing in an imaginary hallway, it stood to reason that this perfectly healthy telephone would have been probably disconnected, had Pnin really vacated the house. I was foolishly eager to say something friendly to my good Timofey Pahlich, and so after a little while I attempted to reach him too. Suddenly there was a click, a sonic vista, the response of a heavy breathing, and then a poorly disguised voice said: "He is not at home, he has gone, he has quite gone"—after which the speaker hung up; but none save my old friend, not even his best imitator, could rhyme so emphatically "at" with the German *"hat,"* "home" with the French *"homme,"* and "gone" with the head of "Goneril." Cockerell then proposed driving over to 999 Todd Road and serenading its burrowed tenant, but here Mrs. Cockerell intervened; and after an evening that somehow left me with the mental counterpart of a bad taste in the mouth, we all went to bed.

7

I spent a poor night in a charming, airy, prettily furnished room where neither window nor door closed properly, and where an omnibus edition of Sherlock Holmes which had pursued me for years supported a bedside lamp, so weak and wan that the set of galleys I had brought with me to correct could not sweeten insomnia. The thunder of trucks rocked the house every two minutes or so; I kept dozing off and sitting up with a gasp, and through the parody of a window shade some light from the street reached the mirror and dazzled me into thinking I was facing a firing squad.

I am so constituted that I absolutely must gulp down the juice of three oranges before confronting the rigors of day. So at seven-thirty I took a quick shower, and five minutes later was out of the house in the company of the long-eared and dejected Sobakevich.

The air was keen, the sky clear and burnished. Southward the empty road could be seen ascending a gray-blue hill among patches of snow. A tall leafless poplar, as brown as a broom, rose on my right, and its long morning shadow crossing to the opposite side of the street reached there a crenulated, cream-colored house which, according to Cockerell, had been thought by my predecessor to be the Turkish Consulate on account of crowds of fez wearers he had seen entering. I turned left, north-ward, and walked a couple of blocks downhill to a restaurant that I had noted on the eve; but the place had not opened yet, and I turned back. Hardly had I taken a couple of steps when a great truck carrying beer rumbled up the street, immediately followed by a small pale blue sedan with the white head of a dog looking out, after which came another great truck, exactly similar to the first. The humble sedan was crammed with bun-dles and suitcases; its driver was Pnin. I emitted a roar of greet-ing, but he did not see me, and my only hope was that I might walk uphill fast enough to catch him while the red light one block ahead kept him at bay.

I hurried past the rear truck, and had another glimpse of my old friend, in tense profile, wearing a cap with ear flaps and a storm coat; but next moment the light turned green, the little white dog leaning out yapped at Sobakevich, and everything surged forward—truck one, Pnin, truck two. From where I stood I watched them recede in the frame of the roadway, be-tween the Moorish house and the Lombardy poplar. Then the little sedan boldly swung past the front truck and, free at last, spurted up the shining road, which one could make out nar-rowing to a thread of gold in the soft mist where hill after hill made beauty of distance, and where there was simply no saying what miracle might happen.

Cockerell, brown-robed and sandaled, let in the cocker and

led me kitchenward, to a British breakfast of depressing kidney and fish.

"And now," he said, "I am going to tell you the story of Pnin rising to address the Cremona Women's Club and discovering he had brought the wrong lecture."

POEMS

Crash!
And if darkness could sound, it would sound like this giant
waking up in the torture house, trying to die
and not dying, and trying
not to cry and immediately crying
that he will, that he will, that he will do his best
to adjust his dark soul to the pressing request
of the only true frost,
and he pants and he gasps and he rasps and he wheezes:
ice is the solid form when the water freezes;
a volatile liquid (see "Refrigerating")
is permitted to pass into evaporating
coils, where it boils,
which somehow seems wrong,
and I wonder how long
it will rumble and shudder and crackle and pound;
Scudder, the Alpinist, slipped and was found
half a century later preserved in blue ice
with his bride and two guides and a dead edelweiss;
a German has proved that the snowflakes we see
are the germ cells of stars and the sea life to be;
hold
the line, hold the line, lest its tale be untold;
let it amble along through the thumping pain
and horror of dichlordisomethingmethane,
a trembling white heart with the frost froth upon it,
Nova Zembla, poor thing, with that B in her bonnet,
stunned bees in the bonnets of cars on hot roads,
Keep it Kold, says a poster in passing, and lo,
loads,

of bright fruit, and a ham, and some chocolate cream,
and three bottles of milk, all contained in the gleam
of that wide-open white
god, the pride and delight
of starry-eyed couples in dream kitchenettes,
and it groans and it drones and it toils and it sweats—
Shackleton, pemmican, penguin, Poe's Pym—
collapsing at last in the criminal
night.

June 6, 1942

A LITERARY DINNER

Come here, said my hostess, her face making room
for one of those pink introductory smiles
that link, like a valley of fruit trees in bloom,
the slopes of two names.
I want you, she murmured, to eat Dr. James.

I was hungry. The Doctor looked good. He had read
the great book of the week and had liked it, he said,
because it was powerful. So I was brought
a generous helping. His mauve-bosomed wife
kept showing me, very politely, I thought,
the tenderest bits with the point of her knife.
I ate—and in Egypt the sunsets were swell;
The Russians were doing remarkably well;
Had I met a Prince Poprinsky, whom he had known
in Caparabella, or was it Mentone?
They had traveled extensively, he and his wife;
her hobby was People, his hobby was Life.
All was good and well cooked, but the tastiest part
was his nut-flavored, crisp cerebellum. The heart
resembled a shiny brown date,
and I stowed all the studs on the edge of my plate.

April 11, 1942

A DISCOVERY

I found it in a legendary land
all rocks and lavender and tufted grass,
where it was settled on some sodden sand
hard by the torrent of a mountain pass.

The features it combines mark it as new
to science: shape and shade—the special tinge,
akin to moonlight, tempering its blue,
the dingy underside, the checquered fringe.

My needles have teased out its sculptured sex;
corroded tissues could no longer hide
that priceless mote now dimpling the convex
and limpid teardrop on a lighted slide.

Smoothly a screw is turned; out of the mist
two ambered hooks symmetrically slope,
or scales like battledores of amethyst
cross the charmed circle of the microscope.

I found it and I named it, being versed
in taxonomic Latin; thus became
godfather to an insect and its first
describer—and I want no other fame.

Wide open on its pin (though fast asleep),
and safe from creeping relatives and rust,
in the secluded stronghold where we keep
type specimens it will transcend its dust.

Dark pictures, thrones, the stones that pilgrims kiss,
poems that take a thousand years to die
but ape the immortality of this
red label on a little butterfly.

May 15, 1943

AN EVENING OF RUSSIAN POETRY

". . . seems to be the best train. Miss Ethel Winter of the Department of English will meet you at the station and . . ." FROM A LETTER ADDRESSED TO THE VISITING SPEAKER.

The subject chosen for tonight's discussion
is everywhere, though often incomplete:
when their basaltic banks become too steep,
most rivers use a kind of rapid Russian,
and so do children talking in their sleep.
My little helper at the magic lantern,
insert that slide and let the colored beam
project my name or any such like phantom
in Slavic characters upon the screen.
The other way, the other way. I thank you.

On mellow hills the Greek, as you remember,
fashioned his alphabet from cranes in flight;
his arrows crossed the sunset, then the night.
Our simple skyline and a taste for timber,
the influence of hives and conifers,
reshaped the arrows and the borrowed birds.
Yes, Sylvia?

"Why do you speak of words
when all we want is knowledge nicely browned?"

Because all hangs together—shape and sound,
heather and honey, vessel and content.
Not only rainbows—every line is bent,
and skulls and seeds and all good worlds are round,

like Russian verse, like our colossal vowels:
those painted eggs, those glossy pitcher flowers
that swallow whole a golden bumblebee,
those shells that hold a thimble and the sea.
Next question.

> *"Is your prosody like ours?"*

Well, Emmy, our pentameter may seem
to foreign ears as if it could not rouse
the limp iambus from its pyrrhic dream.
But close your eyes and listen to the line.
The melody unwinds; the middle word
is marvelously long and serpentine:
you hear one beat, but you have also heard
the shadow of another, then the third
touches the gong, and then the fourth one sighs.

It makes a very fascinating noise;
it opens slowly, like a grayish rose
in pedagogic films of long ago.

The rhyme is the line's birthday, as you know,
and there are certain customary twins
in Russian as in other tongues. For instance,
love automatically rhymes with blood,
nature with liberty, sadness with distance,
humane with everlasting, prince with mud,
moon with a multitude of words, but sun
and song and wind and life and death with none.

Beyond the seas where I have lost a scepter,
I hear the neighing of my dappled nouns,
soft participles coming down the steps,
treading on leaves, trailing their rustling gowns,

and liquid verbs in *ahla* and in *ili,*
Aonian grottoes, nights in the Altai,
black pools of sound with "l"s for water lilies.
The empty glass I touched is tinkling still,
but now 'tis covered by a hand and dies.

"Trees? Animals? Your favorite precious stone?"

The birch tree, Cynthia, the fir tree, Joan.
Like a small caterpillar on its thread,
my heart keeps dangling from a leaf long dead
but hanging still, and still I see the slender
white birch that stands on tiptoe in the wind,
and firs beginning where the garden ends,
the evening ember glowing through their cinders.

Among the animals that haunt our verse,
that bird of bards, regale of night, comes first:
scores of locutions mimicking its throat
render its every whistling, bubbling, bursting,
flutelike or cuckoolike or ghostlike note.
But lapidary epithets are few;
we do not deal in universal rubies.
The angle and the glitter are subdued;
our riches lie concealed. We never liked
the jeweler's window in the rainy night.

My back is Argus-eyed. I live in danger.
False shadows turn to track me as I pass
and, wearing beards, disguised as secret agents,
creep in to blot the freshly written page
and read the blotter in the looking glass.
And in the dark, under my bedroom window,
until, with a chill whir and shiver, day
presses its starter, warily they linger

or silently approach the door and ring
the bell of memory and run away.

Let me allude, before the spell is broken,
to Pushkin, rocking in his coach on long
and lonely roads: he dozed, then he awoke,
undid the collar of his traveling cloak,
and yawned, and listened to the driver's song.
Amorphous sallow bushes called *rakeety*,
enormous clouds above an endless plain,
songline and skyline endlessly repeated,
the smell of grass and leather in the rain.
And then the sob, the syncope (Nekrasov!),
the panting syllables that climb and climb,
obsessively repetitive and rasping,
dearer to some than any other rhyme.
And lovers meeting in a tangled garden,
dreaming of mankind, of untrammeled life,
mingling their longings in the moonlit garden,
where trees and hearts are larger than in life.
This passion for expansion you may follow
throughout our poetry. We want the mole
to be a lynx or turn into a swallow
by some sublime mutation of the soul.
But to unneeded symbols consecrated,
escorted by a vaguely infantile
path for bare feet, our roads were always fated
to lead into the silence of exile.

Had I more time tonight I would unfold
the whole amazing story—*neighuklúzhe,
nevynossímo*—but I have to go.

What did I say under my breath? I spoke
to a blind songbird hidden in a hat,

safe from my thumbs and from the eggs I broke
into the gibus brimming with their yolk.

And now I must remind you in conclusion,
that I am followed everywhere and that
space is collapsible, although the bounty
of memory is often incomplete:
once in a dusty place in Mora County
(half town, half desert, dump mound and mesquite)
and once in West Virginia (a muddy
red road between an orchard and a veil
of tepid rain) it came, that sudden shudder,
a Russian something that I could inhale
but could not see. Some rapid words were uttered—
and then the child slept on, the door was shut.

The conjurer collects his poor belongings—
the colored handkerchief, the magic rope,
the double-bottomed rhymes, the cage, the song.
You tell him of the passes you detected.
The mystery remains intact. The check
comes forward in its smiling envelope.

"How would you say 'delightful talk' in Russian?"
"How would you say 'good night'?"

   Oh, that would be:
Bezónnitza, tvoy vzor oonýl i stráshen;
lubóv moyá, otstóopnika prostée.
 (Insomnia, your stare is dull and ashen,
 my love, forgive me this apostasy.)

       March 3, 1945

RESTORATION

To think that any fool may tear
by chance the web of when and where.
O window in the dark! To think
that every brain is on the brink
of nameless bliss no brain can bear,

Unless there be no great surprise—
as when you learn to levitate
and, hardly trying, realize
—alone, in a bright room—that weight
is but your shadow, and you rise.

My little daughter wakes in tears:
She fancies that her bed is drawn
into a dimness which appears
to be the deep of all her fears
but which, in point of fact, is dawn.

I know a poet who can strip
a William Tell or Golden Pip
in one uninterrupted peel
miraculously to reveal,
revolving on his fingertip,

a snowball. So I would unrobe
turn inside out, pry open, probe
all matter, everything you see,
the skyline and its saddest tree,
the whole inexplicable globe,

to find the true, the ardent core
as doctors of old pictures do
when, rubbing out a distant door
or sooty curtain, they restore
the jewel of a bluish view.

March 9, 1952

LINES WRITTEN IN OREGON

Esmeralda! Now we rest
Here, in the bewitched and blest
Mountain forests of the West.

Here the very air is stranger.
Damzel, anchoret, and ranger
Share the woodland's dream and danger.

And to think I deemed you dead!
(In a dungeon, it was said;
Tortured, strangled); but instead—

Blue birds from the bluest fable,
Bear and hare in coats of sable,
Peacock moth on picnic table.

Huddled roadsigns softly speak
Of Lake Merlin, Castle Creek,
And (obliterated) Peak.

Do you recognize that clover?
Dandelions, *l'or du pauvre?*
(Europe, nonetheless, is over).

Up the turf, along the burn,
Latin lilies climb and turn
Into Gothic fir and fern.

Cornfields have befouled the prairies
But these canyons laugh! And there is
Still the forest with its fairies.

And I rest where I awoke
In the sea shade—*l'ombre glauque*—
Of a legendary oak;

Where the woods get ever dimmer,
Where the Phantom Orchids glimmer—
Esmeralda, *immer, immer*.

August 29, 1953

ODE TO A MODEL

I have followed you, model,
in magazine ads through all seasons,
from dead leaf on the sod
to red leaf on the breeze,

from your lily-white armpit
to the tip of your butterfly eyelash,
charming and pitiful,
silly and stylish.

Or in kneesocks and tartan
standing there like some fabulous symbol,
parted feet pointing outward
—pedal form of akimbo.

On a lawn, in a parody
of Spring and its cherry-tree,
near a vase and a parapet,
virgin practicing archery.

Ballerina, black-masked,
near a parapet of alabaster.
"Can one—somebody asked—
rhyme 'star' and 'disaster'?"

Can one picture a blackbird
as the negative of a small firebird?
Can a record, run backward,
turn "repaid" into "diaper"?

Can one marry a model?
Kill your past, make you real, raise a family,
by removing you bodily
from back numbers of Sham?

October 8, 1955

ON TRANSLATING *Eugene Onegin*

〜〜〜〜

1

What is translation? On a platter
A poet's pale and glaring head,
A parrot's screech, a monkey's chatter,
And profanation of the dead.
The parasites you were so hard on
Are pardoned if I have your pardon,
O, Pushkin, for my stratagem:
I traveled down your secret stem,
And reached the root, and fed upon it;
Then, in a language newly learned,
I grew another stalk and turned
Your stanza, patterned on a sonnet,
Into my honest roadside prose—
All thorn, but cousin to your rose.

2

Reflected words can only shiver
Like elongated lights that twist
In the black mirror of a river
Between the city and the mist.
Elusive Pushkin! Persevering,
I still pick up Tatiana's earring,

Still travel with your sullen rake.
I find another man's mistake,
I analyze alliterations
That grace your feasts and haunt the great
Fourth stanza of your Canto Eight.
This is my task—a poet's patience
And scholiastic passion blent:
Dove-droppings on your monument.

1955-1967

RAIN

∿∿∿

How mobile is the bed on these
nights of gesticulating trees
   when the rain clatters fast,
the tin-toy rain with dapper hoof
trotting upon an endless roof,
   traveling into the past.

Upon old roads the steeds of rain
slip and slow down and speed again
   through many a tangled year;
but they can never reach the last
dip at the bottom of the past
   because the sun is there.

April 21, 1956

THE BALLAD OF LONGWOOD GLEN

That Sunday morning, at half past ten,
Two cars crossed the creek and entered the glen.

In the first was Art Longwood, a local florist,
With his children and wife (now Mrs. Deforest).

In the one that followed, a ranger saw
Art's father, stepfather and father-in-law.

The three old men walked off to the cove.
Through tinkling weeds Art slowly drove.

Fair was the morning, with bright clouds afar.
Children and comics emerged from the car.

Silent Art, who could stare at a thing all day,
Watched a bug climb a stalk and fly away.

Pauline had asthma, Paul used a crutch.
They were cute little rascals but could not run much.

"I wish," said his mother to crippled Paul,
"Some man would teach you to pitch that ball."

Silent Art took the ball and tossed it high.
It stuck in a tree that was passing by.

And the grave green pilgrim turned and stopped.
The children waited, but no ball dropped.

"I never climbed trees in my timid prime,"
Thought Art; and forthwith started to climb.

Now and then his elbow or knee could be seen
In a jigsaw puzzle of blue and green.

Up and up Art Longwood swarmed and shinned,
And the leaves said *yes* to the questioning wind.

What tiaras of gardens! What torrents of light!
How accessible ether! How easy flight!

His family circled the tree all day.
Pauline concluded: "Dad climbed away."

None saw the delirious celestial crowds
Greet the hero from earth in the snow of the clouds.

Mrs. Longwood was getting a little concerned.
He never came down. He never returned.

She found some change at the foot of the tree.
The children grew bored. Paul was stung by a bee.

The old men walked over and stood looking up,
Each holding five cards and a paper cup.

Cars on the highway stopped, backed, and then
Up a rutted road waddled into the glen.

And the tree was suddenly full of noise,
Conventioners, fishermen, freckled boys.

Anacondas and pumas were mentioned by some,
And all kinds of humans continued to come:

Tree surgeons, detectives, the fire brigade.
An ambulance parked in the dancing shade.

A drunken rogue with a rope and a gun
Arrived on the scene to see justice done.

Explorers, dendrologists—all were there;
And a strange pale girl with gypsy hair.

And from Cape Fear to Cape Flattery
Every paper had: Man Lost in Tree.

And the sky-bound oak (where owls had perched
And the moon dripped gold) was felled and searched.

They discovered some inchworms, a red-cheeked gall,
And an ancient nest with a new-laid ball.

They varnished the stump, put up railings and signs.
Restrooms nestled in roses and vines.

Mrs. Longwood, retouched, when the children died,
Became a photographer's dreamy bride.

And now the Deforests, with *four* old men,
Like regular tourists visit the glen;

Munch their lunches, look up and down,
Wash their hands, and drive back to town.

July 6, 1957